BROTHER AGAINST BROTHER

As the lawmen spread out along the street, Brad Kincaid and Grace Sixkiller rode into town from the opposite direction. They were here seeking refuge, for the secret of their cabin in the Osage Nation was a secret no longer. And despite Grace Sixkiller's agonized plea, Brad had no intention of surrendering. Not to anyone, least of all his brother.

The young outlaw and his wife were approaching the livery stable when he spotted the marshals. His reaction was one of sheer reflex, without thought or regard for the consequences. Calmly, all in a motion, he reined his horse to a standstill and jerked a pistol. His hand blurred, then came level, frozen there a mere instant before the six-gun barked a cottony wad of smoke.

Owen never knew if the shot was meant for him. He saw Brad fire, the bullet tore by so close he could hear it fry the air, but he couldn't move. He could only stand there, paralyzed, watching in mute horror at what came next.

The marshals behind him, and those across the street, shouldered their rifles in unison. The first sharp crack blended into a rolling tattoo, and Brad was flung from his horse as if struck by lightning . . .

"Matt Braun has a genius for taking real characters out of the Old West and giving them flesh-and-blood immediacy."

—Dee Brown, author of *Bury My Heart at Wounded Knee*

The Kincaids

MATT BRAUN

St. Martin's Paperbacks

Quotations from *Collected Poems*, Harper & Row, Copyright 1922, 1950, Edna St. Vincent Millay and Norma Millay Ellis.

This is a work of fiction. All of the characters, organizations, and events portrayed in this novel are either products of the author's imagination or are used fictitiously.

THE KINCAIDS

For information address St. Martin's Press, 175 Fifth Avenue, New York, NY 10010.

ISBN: 978-1-250-18156-5

Our books may be purchased in bulk for promotional, educational, or business use. Please contact your local bookseller or the Macmillan Corporate and Premium Sales Department at 1-800-221-7945, ext. 5442, or by e-mail at MacmillanSpecialMarkets@macmillan.com.

Printed in the United States of America

G.P. Putnam's Sons edition published 1977
Berkley Medallion edition / July 1977
St. Martin's Paperbacks edition / May 1999

St. Martin's Paperbacks are published by St. Martin's Press, 175 Fifth Avenue, New York, NY 10010.

10 9 8 7 6 5 4 3 2 1

TO BETTIANE

The Unwavering One

On the Plains, history was telescoped. White men still breathe who began as buffalo hunters, turned cowboy when the bison vanished, plowed and reaped on farms with the first settlers, freighted goods to the new towns and made fortunes as frontier merchants, drilled oil-wells, dug mines, built factories as industrialists, and ended as financiers sitting behind mahogany desks in skyscrapers.

—Stanley Vestal

The Kincaids

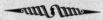

BOOK ONE

―✦―

KANSAS

1871–1884

PROLOGUE

Clouds of orange and white butterflies floated lazily on a gentle breeze, and the fragrance of chokecherry blossoms filled the air. The plainsman scrambled out of an arroyo, where he'd left his horse tied, and cautiously worked his way up a grassy knoll. Crawling, the last few feet on his hands and knees, he stretched out flat, hugging the earth, and slowly eased his head over the crest of the hill. He lay motionless, scanning the distant prairie as a wisp of wind brought with it the pungent buffalo smell. He filled his lungs with it, savoring that moist gaminess, full of fresh droppings and sweaty fur. But he waited, as a great cat would wait, unhurried and calm, absorbing everything about him before he began the stalk.

As he always did, he felt himself the intruder here, looking upon something no mortal was meant to see. About these still, windswept plains there was an awesome quality, almost as though some wild and brutally magnificent force had taken earth and solitude and fashioned it into something visible, yet beyond the ken of man. A vast expanse of emptiness, raging with dust devils and blizzards, where man must forever walk as an alien. A hostile land that mocked his passage, waiting with eternal patience to claim the bones of those who violated its harsh serenity.

And however long he roamed these plains, he was still the intruder, an outsider with no sense of kinship for the forces which mocked him. As though—should he wander here forever—he would merely come full circle. Alone, a creature in a land of creatures, yet somehow apart. Which left nothing but the moment, and the predatory instinct that had brought him here. The kill.

Before him the plains were spotted with small, scattered herds of buffalo. At a distance it appeared to be a shaggy carpet of muddy brown stretching to the horizon. But up close the herds took form, and from the hilltop, individual buffalo assumed shape, even character. A hundred yards beyond the hill, two ponderous bulls were holding a staring contest. Their bloodshot eyes rolled furiously as they tossed great chunks of earth over their backs, and their guttural roar signaled the onset of a bloody duel. Suddenly their heads lowered and they thundered toward one another, narrow flanks heaving, legs churning. The impact as they butted heads shook the earth and drove both antagonists to their knees. Stunned, yet all the more enraged, they lunged erect in an instant, locking horns as their massive shoulders bunched with power. The muscles on their flanks swelled like veined ropes; sharp hooves strained and dug for footing; froth hung from their mouths in long glutinous strings; and their tongues lolled out as the brutal struggle sapped their lungs. Then, with a savage heave, one bull flung his adversary aside and ripped a bloody gash across his shoulder. The gored bull gave ground, retreating slowly at first, then broke into headlong flight as his opponent speared him in the rump.

The victor pawed the dusty earth, bellowing a triumphant roar, and like some stately lord on parade, struck a grand pose for the cows. He had fought and won, and while he might fight dozens of such battles during the rutting season, for the moment he stood unchallenged.

The plainsman eased over the top of the knoll while the herd was still distracted by the struggle. Slithering down the forward slope on his belly, he took cover behind a soapweed as the vanquished bull disappeared across the prairie. The bush made a perfect blind; after unstrapping his shell pouch, he set a ramrod and a canteen on the ground close at hand. Then he set up the shooting sticks and laid his Sharps over the fork. He was ready.

Alert, but in no great hurry, he began a painstaking search for the leader. Every herd had a leader, generally an old cow. Shrewder than the bulls—perhaps more suspicious—they made the best sentries. What he sought was a cow that seemed unusually watchful, on guard, testing the wind for signs of danger. Until a man dropped the leader, his chances of getting a stand were practically nil. After a long, careful scrutiny, he finally spotted her. And what a cunning old bitch! Hidden back in the middle of the herd, holding herself still and vigilant, and peering straight at him, trying to raise a scent.

Grunting softly, he eared back the hammer and laid the sights behind her shoulder, centered on the lungs. The Sharps roared and a steamy gout of blood spurted from the cow's nose. She wobbled unsteadily under the wallop of the big fifty slug, then lurched backward and keeled over. A nearby cow spooked, sniffing the fallen leader, and bawled nervously as she wheeled away. Cursing, he yanked the trigger guard down, clawed out the spent shell, and rammed in a fresh load. As he snapped the lever shut, the cow was gathering speed, ready to break into a terrified run. Thumbing the hammer back, he swung the barrel in a smooth arc, leading her with the sights. When the rifle cracked the cow simply collapsed in mid-stride, plowing a deep furrow in the earth with her nose. Alarmed now, several cows gathered around, and their calves began to bawl. The old bull wandered over, snorting at the scent of blood, and started pawing the ground.

But the herd didn't run. Bewildered, hooking at one another with their horns, they simply milled around in confusion for a while. Some of them pawed the dirt and butted the warm carcasses, trying to goad the dead cows onto their feet, yet slowly, without apparent concern, the others went back to chewing their cuds or cropping grass.

He had his stand.

Loading and firing in a steady rhythm, working smoothly now, he began killing the skittish ones. Carcasses dotted the feeding ground, as each new report of the Sharps brought another crashing thud on the prairie below. Still the herd didn't stampede—looking on with the detached calm of spectators at a shooting match—seemingly undisturbed by the thrashing bodies and the sickly-sweet stench of blood. It was a drama of pathos and tragedy he had seen unfold a hundred times over in the last three years. Insensible to the slaughter around them, the dim-witted beasts had concern for nothing save the patch of graze directly under their noses. Eerie as it seemed, the instinct for survival had been blunted by the more immediate need deep within their bellies.

After every fifth shot he sloshed water down the rifle barrel to keep it from overheating. Then he swabbed it out, hurriedly reloaded, and returned to the killing. Yet he was steady and deliberate, somehow methodical, placing every shot with precise care. This was something he did well—took pride in—managed swiftly and cleanly, without waste or undue suffering. A craftsman no less than a predator, but skilled at his trade.

A master of death and dying, and staying alive.

ONE

There is a point of no return in each man's life. An instant, seldom detected at the time, which will alter all his
days on earth. Yet pragmatic men mock such things. Nothing sacred intrudes. Nor does the superstition of lesser men
haunt their resolve. They halt before a river, beckoned onward
by the moment, heedless of what lies beyond. It is merely a
ribbon of water, symbolic of nothing, to be negotiated and
then forgotten.

Jacob Kincaid was such a man. Astride a buckskin gelding, squinting against the sun, he stared out across the Smoky
Hill. The river was appraised at a glance and quickly shunted
aside, an obstacle of small consequence. Rolling grasslands,
sweeping gently onto the limitless plains, were similarly dismissed. After three years stalking the great shaggy herds west
of Fort Hays, one stretch of prairie looked much like another.
A buffalo man, wherever he roamed, saw only the creatures
he killed. Earth and sky and water were simply there. Constant, unchanging, with a deadly sameness that came to be
taken for granted.

Yet he had ridden a hundred miles to see this spot for himself. Where the river made a slow dogleg south beneath limestone bluffs, and a lonesome stand of timber stood defiant on
the far shore. Where a man named McCoy had built a town
called Abilene.

It was this crude collection of buildings, surrounded by

milling herds of cattle, which held Jake Kincaid's attention. Beyond Fort Hays, in a land of solitude and solitary men, there was much talk of this place. The plains grapevine pegged it as the first of its kind. One of a kind. A cowtown. Something on the order of the boomtown mining camps, except that the lodestone was not gold or silver but cattle. Texas longhorns driven north to a windswept Kansas railhead where fortunes were made and lost overnight.

Kincaid understood the lure of such talk. Perhaps better than most men. For it was this very thing that had brought him west, across the swift-flowing Missouri to the distant buffalo grounds. A siren's call. That ancient temptress wielding her goad of high stakes and fast play in a land where the faintheart's puny rules hadn't yet taken hold. Where a man could reach out and grab—claim whatever he was big enough to hold—unencumbered by strictures other than those he might impose upon himself.

But understanding this, there was a greater essential Jake Kincaid failed to grasp. As he kneed the buckskin down the bluffs and into the water, time and circumstance frivolously embraced. That he was here, fording the Smoky Hill on a blistering summer day in 1871, seemed neither uncommon nor extraordinary. No less a nomad than the buffalo he hunted, it seemed quite natural, this urge to look on the place called Abilene. A delicate balance of instinct and curiosity had brought him this far, and like a wolf prowling new ground, he saw no reason to question the impulse. He simply followed his nose.

Afterward though, from the vantage point of hindsight, he would at last comprehend. The Smoky Hill had, after all, proved symbolic. A spectral passage of time—the point of no return—come and gone as his horse splashed through the stream. Unwittingly he had crossed over to the other side, and never again would his life be the same.

Late afternoon shadows splayed across the timbered bottomland as Kincaid brought the gelding up the far bank and rode into Abilene. Ahead lay the Kansas & Pacific tracks, roughly bordering the river, and beyond that Texas street, the town's main thoroughfare. Somehow, taken at first glance, it was less than he had expected. Not at all the grand city conjured up in his mind at Fort Hays. A huddle of some fifty ramshackle buildings constituted the entire town. With the exception of what appeared to be a hotel, the business establishments had high false fronts and an unmistakable look of impermanence, as if they had been slapped together with spit and poster glue. Yet the street was crowded with people, more than he'd seen assembled in one spot for better than three years. Unaccountably, his sagging spirits took a sudden turn for the better.

It wasn't a metropolis risen from the plains. That much was clear. But it was there, ugly and squalid and bursting with some galvanic energy all its own. And in that moment of assessment Jake Kincaid was struck by one of those queer hunches on which a gambling man gladly stakes his life. Grungy as it was, the town had the smell of money. A feel of shifting fortune. Which unraveled interesting speculation for a man whose luck was running strong.

Aside from money, there was also an enervating smell of cow dung. The prairie encircling Abilene was a vast bawling sea of longhorns awaiting shipment to eastern slaughterhouses, and a barnyard scent assailed the nostrils. Yet, oddly enough, it was an odor he found not unpleasant. One he might easily come to relish. It had about it the pungency of gold on the hoof, and in that there was much to recommend it.

Somewhat satisfied with his estimate of things, confident that Abilene would shortly disprove the alchemy of silk purse and sow's ear, he reined the gelding across Texas Street and dismounted in front of a livery stable. Curiously, though the sun was fast disappearing in the west, he had a gut-certain impression that things had never looked brighter.

• • •

An overhead lamp cast a soft, fuzzy glow across the poker table. The spill of light, not unlike diffused cider, flecked through Kincaid's sandy hair, gave his weathered features the burnt-mahogany look of old saddle leather. Three years on the plains had turned him bark-dark as a Kiowa, and the curing effects of the sun had aged him beyond his time. Though he was scarcely twenty-four, his appearance and manner were those of a man ten years older. That he had killed several thousand buffalo, along with a small clutch of hostiles, lent him an air of gravity well suited to his brushy mustache and somber expression.

Just at the moment, though, the men gathered around the table were less concerned with his appearance than with his uncanny skill at cards. Whatever his age, he played poker with the boldness and craft of a Mexican bandit, and most of their money was now heaped in a golden mound at his elbow. They were disgusted with themselves, in the way of all hard losers, and thoroughly astounded by the unchecked winning streak of this greasy, foul-smelling plainsman who had wandered into their midst.

Kincaid was no less baffled himself. Perhaps his best bluff of the evening was in the deadpan performance of someone who knew precisely what he was doing and how to go about it. Quite the contrary, it was fortune who called the turn. He played the cards dealt him, inwardly thunderstruck by his phenomenal luck, and pretended to a skill which was more guile than expertise. He won steadily, slowly busting the other players, and by midnight the outcome was a foregone conclusion.

Already, a local merchant, along with an eastern cattle buyer and a whiskey drummer, had quit the game. When Kincaid sandbagged the next pot, checking on three queens and raising the bet, the Texas cattleman seated beside him slammed out of his chair and stalked from the saloon. That left only one player, Quincy Blackburn, a nattily attired fat man given to blubbery chuckles and glib chatter. By no mere coincidence, he also owned the Lady Gay, the saloon in which they were seated. Like most of his breed, Blackburn operated the dive strictly as a front. He was an accomplished gambler, having plied his trade on the riverboats for several years, and men who thrived on high-stakes poker beat a constant path to the Lady Gay.

Now, gambler and buffalo hunter stared at one another through a haze of stale smoke and dim light. Unspoken, yet shared, was a faint, amusement at this ironic twist, for never had two men been more dissimilar. One, squat and larded with the good life, impeccable in manner and dress. The other, whipcord lean, whiskery stubble marking his jawline, decked out in rancid buckskins that smelled of sweat and tallow and uncured hides. That it was now a two-man game, they never doubted for an instant. Blackburn had a fat man's passion for money, and Kincaid was soaring high on a lethal mixture of euphoria and popskull whiskey. It somehow made sense that they would join hands and butt heads in a final test having less to do with poker than with an atavistic risk of character.

Blackburn's bright little eyes settled at last on the golden mound across from him. Idly, he gestured with a pudgy hand, the mechanical smile of a pitchman touching his mouth.

"How much would you say you've won? Just offhand."

Kincaid shrugged, unable to suppress a grin. "Eight thousand. Mebbe nine."

"Anymore in your kick? Or is that it?"

"Depends. What'd you have in mind?"

"Something—sweeter." Blackburn smiled. "That is, if you're still feeling lucky."

"Try me and see."

"A sporting man! I like that." The gambler paused, darting a glance at the nearby tables, then lowered his voice. "Just between us, your run pretty well tapped the bank. Now, if you

could sweeten what's on the table—say, another thousand—
I'm willing to cover it with a half-interest in the Lady Gay.
All things being equal, I'd say it's a fair bet."

Kincaid's face betrayed nothing. He studied the fat man a
moment, certain now that he had been gaffed in some shifty
dodge as yet unrevealed. Then his gaze shifted and roved
over the saloon in a deliberate, unhurried inspection. It was
the first dive he'd hit after leaving the livery stable, and by
no means a palace. But it drew a good crowd, kept two bartenders and a covey of girls busy, and had all the appearances
of a steady money-maker. While he'd never entertained the
notion of becoming a saloonkeeper, there were lots worse
ways to make a living. Hunting buffalo and fighting Indians,
just for openers. Whatever had brought him to Abilene, this
winning streak was a sign. Unmistakably a sign that he was on
the scent of bigger game, and maybe right here was the place
to start. The Lady Gay.

As for the money in front of him—what the hell? Easy
come, easy go. If he lost there was always the buffalo and
another season on the killing grounds. But somehow he didn't
believe it would happen. Luck had grabbed hold of his shirt-
tail, and a man had to play out his string.

Get a hunch, bet a bunch.

Leaning forward, he pulled a money belt from underneath
his shirt and dumped it on the table. Then, with a peculiar
glint in his eye, he looked across at the gambler. "Let's play
whole hog or nothin'. There's better'n ten thousand in that
belt." He scooped up a handful of double eagles from the pile
on the table and let them slowly trickle through his fingers.
"This and the belt against the Lady Gay."

Blackburn's tongue flicked out, wetting his lips, like a
bullfrog catching flies. The gaff had sunk deeper than he suspected, and he could scarcely contain himself. Frowning,
never one to rush a sucker, he gave it a moment's judicious
thought. At last, jowls flushed, he heaved a sigh and nodded.

"Agreed. Winner take all." Quite casually, he collected the

cards and began shuffling, his stubby fingers moving with the effortless grace of tiny birds. "Stud all right with you?"

Kincaid's thorny paw stretched out, took the deck from his hand, and placed it in the center of the table. Then he nailed the gambler with an icy scowl and very carefully gave the cards a whorehouse cut.

"You oughtn't to use strippers in a friendly game. Course, I'm of a forgivin' nature, so I'll overlook it. Unless you've got some objection, we'll just cut for high card. And like you said—winner take all."

Blackburn blinked, started to speak, then thought better of it. Silently, he watched as Kincaid cut the deck and turned up the king of diamonds. Shifting forward, his hand covered the balance of the pack while his fingers began an imperceptible caress of the cards.

Then he stopped. The metallic whirr of a pistol hammer suddenly stayed his hand and he found himself staring down the bore of a Colt Dragoon. Wooden-faced, without a trace of emotion, Kincaid rapped him across the knuckles with the tip of the barrel.

"Fat man, you draw an ace and I'll tack it to your headstone."

The gambler swallowed hard, eyes riveted on the pistol, and slowly turned over the nine of spades. Kincaid eased back, lowering the hammer on the Colt, and laid it on the table. Several moments passed, then the cold look faded and his lips curled back in a wolfish grin.

"Drinks are on the house. Right after we get it in writin'."

Not long after sunrise, Jake Kincaid took a leisurely stroll through Abilene. He was an early riser, a habit common to those accustomed to a bed of buffalo robes on hard ground. Despite the late night, devoted for the most part to settling his affairs with Blackburn, he saw no reason to waste the morning. At this hour, with the sporting crowd hardly more than asleep, he pretty much had the town to himself. The streets were virtually deserted (even the dogs seemed to be night owls in Abilene) and that fitted nicely with his own plans.

Having adopted Abilene as his new stamping grounds, he felt obliged to inspect the place. Nose around a bit, get acquainted, find out exactly what a cowtown was. Not that he expected it to be all that different from other towns, but it never hurt to scout unfamiliar ground. Get the lay of the land, a feel for the pulse of things. As the town's newest saloon-keeper, sort of an overnight magi-presto businessman, it wouldn't hurt to sniff out the big augurs. Take their measure. Let them know that he'd come to stay—and play—not for chalkies but for all the marbles.

This was the thing that had come clear overnight. Kincaid sensed some irresistible force booting him in the butt. Nudging him first in the direction of Abilene, then toward the Lady Gay, and finally into a showdown that had sealed the pact. Nor was it mere coincidence. Whatever the force, it had brought him here for a reason. In three years he hadn't once attempted to sink roots. Since coming west from Kentucky, turning his back on a worn-out farm and a graveyard overcrowded with family, he had roamed without purpose or direction. And now, finally, he had come to roost. Call it instinct or fate or whatever name suited, he felt it in his bones. The twists and turns were finished, his wanderlust sated at last. Today was a whole new deal, a fresh shuffle, and Abilene was where it started.

Except that he was shod in clunky mule-eared boots, he might have leaped sky high and clicked his heels. The world was green and bright, the sun golden warm, and a gentle westerly breeze brought with it the sweet ambrosia of cow-dung. A day to crow and stretch and drink deeply from the horn. Hallelujah Day.

But if his vision soared, drunk with the glory of himself,

there was nothing erratic about Kincaid's eyesight. Abilene in a bright morning sun was, if anything, more unsightly than it had been the evening before. Undistracted by glimmering lights, crowds, and whooping trailhands, he saw a cowtown at last for what it was. Texas Street stretched north from the railroad tracks for two blocks. Cedar Street crossed east and west, intersecting Texas, for a distance of another two blocks. And that was it. A well-chucked rock would have hit the town limits in any direction.

Perhaps of greater consequence was the glaring disparity among business establishments. Kincaid prowled the streets in dismay, his rosy vision of the future become instead a gushing nosebleed. By rough count, Abilene had thirty-two commercial enterprises, discounting the jail and a slapdash affair proclaiming itself a church. There was a bank, two hotels, a couple of stores, and perhaps a half-dozen other legitimate businesses. The remainder, practically shoulder to shoulder along both sides of all four blocks, were some mongrel combination of saloon, gambling den, or whorehouse. And all of them, the economic cornerstone of fabled Abilene, were direct competitors with his own watering hole. All of a sudden, the Lady Gay didn't look so gay anymore. She had assumed the heft, not to mention the peculiar odor, of a pig in the poke.

After breakfast in the local greasy spoon, Kincaid came away with a case of heartburn that wasn't altogether traceable to the food. Still, gloomy as things looked, it could have been worse. He might have won a cathouse, and according to the counterman in the café, several new brothels were even then being constructed at the east end of Cedar. Some of them with as many as forty rooms! Already this monument to horny Texans had been dubbed with a fitting sobriquet—The Devil's Half-Acre.

Walking back to Texas and Cedar, he stopped and built himself a smoke. The town was slowly coming to life, but he gave the shopkeepers and ribbon clerks scant notice. His eyes were fastened on the Lady Gay, catty-corner across the street. Lost in thought, puffing smoke like a dizzy dragon, he muddled it through again. While he was up to his armpits in competition for the Texan trade, there was an advantage he had overlooked. The Lady Gay occupied a strategic location, the southwest corner of Texas and Cedar, squarely in the center of town. Abilene's one and only intersection. And it stood to reason that anybody fresh off the trail would have to pass this corner whatever direction he was headed. Which gave the Lady Gay an edge on every dive in town. Allowing, naturally, for the joints that occupied the other three corners.

But a damn fine edge, all the same. If a man did something different—made the Lady Gay stand out from the others—then he might just give himself an even bigger edge. Whittle the competition down a notch or two by—by doing what?

Kincaid stood there scratching his head, suddenly at a loss. He had no answer for his own riddle. How to stalk a buffalo herd, where to get the best price for hides, those were the things he knew. About the saloon business, though, he didn't know beans from buckshot. And it slowly dawned on him that he was in over his head. Full of big ideas but short on savvy. All wind and no whistle.

Unless.

The germ of an idea fitted past, taunting him but dancing away before he could grasp it. Maybe something to do with whiskey and girls? He shook his head, discarding that out of hand. Every dive in town served liquor, and women weren't exactly scarce. So that was an itch already being scratched. The same went for elegant trimmings. He'd seen enough this morning to bet that somebody had already rigged out a place with fancy mirrors and all that plush stuff from back east. Not that it would hurt to get the Lady Gay gussied up some. But that alone wouldn't turn the trick.

Something was missing though. A piece of the puzzle he'd overlooked. Sifting through again, he ticked off the enticements that separated men from their money. Whiskey and women and fancy digs. And—why, hell yes, it was staring him right in the face. Gambling.

But that wouldn't hold water either. Half the joints in town had gaming layouts. Which made the Lady Gay just another frog in a mighty big pond.

Unless.

The germ suddenly blossomed, and Kincaid blinked, nerves jangling with excitement. He took a long pull on the cigarette, inhaling deeply, and steadied his hand. Slow and easy, he told himself, that's the ticket. Look it over careful.

Just supposing a gambling den offered something unheard of—*honest games*. Holy Jumpin' Jesus! A man would have to turn 'em away from the door. Everybody just naturally assumed that the dives rigged their games. Walked in knowing they'd be flim-flammed before they could get back out the door. Crooked games were common as dirt. Not one man in a hundred expected to get a fair shake. If they could, though—at the Lady Gay. Why, hell's fire, it'd take two men and a small pony to cart the money over to the bank.

Except for one little drawback. Jake Kincaid glumly admitted that he didn't know his ass from his elbow about operating a gaming den. Which was near certain to get him skinned and hung out to dry. All the same, there was someone who knew the tricks of the trade. A fellow that had just recently come upon hard times.

And for the price, even Quincy Blackburn might get religion.

Jake Kincaid spent the remainder of the day roaring around Abilene like a whirling dervish. When Abe Karatofsky opened his store that morning Kincaid was standing at the door. Placing himself in Karatofsky's hands, he asked to be outfitted in the fanciest duds available. Then he sparked what

was to become a lifelong friendship by informing Karatofsky that he would take three of everything. And damn the
price!

The wizened, eagle-beaked little merchant scurried about
the store like a demented leprechaun. In short order he had
Kincaid decked out from head to toe, selecting with care to
complement the plainsman's lithe build and rugged features.
Slouch hats, with a flat brim and the high crown blocked in
a distinctive, triangular mound. (This was to become Kincaid's trademark, imitated in boomtown railheads for the next
quarter-century.) Tight, finely crafted top boots of the soft-
est calf leather. Broadcloth frock coats, nankeen trousers, and
linen shirts. All topped off with elaborately brocaded vests,
silk cravats in subdued shades, and an enormous pocket
watch the size of a sugar bowl.

Last, and with some difficulty, he persuaded Kincaid to
part with his Colt Dragoon. "Trust my word," Karatofsky observed, squinting over his spectacles, "it is not a gentleman's
weapon." Kincaid acceded at last, and added to the pile of
clothing was a slim Colt Navy of .36 caliber. In the way of
gentlemanly things, it killed a man no less dead but dispatched him with a minimum of gore.

Karatofsky then escorted the plainsman across the street
to Price's Tonsorial Parlor and had Price personally super-
vise the finishing touches. Haircut and shave, with a stylish
mustache trim, followed by a scalding bath that parboiled a
year's accumulation of sweat and grime. When Kincaid
emerged onto Texas Street an hour later the transformation
was startling. Gone was the shaggy, unkempt, rank-smelling
hide hunter. Instead, reeking of lilac water and rosewood
soap, he marched off looking for all the world like an aristo-
cratic pilgrim come to see the circus called Abilene.

His next stop was the office of Joseph McCoy, the town's
mayor and founding father. Slender and congenitally nervous,
with a weak chin and a stringy goatee, McCoy gave the
impression of a myopic ferret. But his appearance was de-

ceptive, an advantage on which he traded with uncommon skill. Back in '67 he had bought a stretch of raw prairie for four-bits an acre and promptly conned the Kansas & Pacific into laying track to his then imagined town site. Scarcely four years later Abilene was a thriving community, if something of an eyesore; before the summer was out, nearly a quarter-million longhorns would be herded north to the stockyards owned by the town's leading citizen.

McCoy was astute, tenacious as a starved rat, and fanatic in the way of all zealots. And Kincaid himself was far too shrewd to underestimate this frail builder of towns. He introduced himself, informed McCoy that he was the new owner of the Lady Gay, and stated that henceforth the games would be run honest and aboveboard. The mayor and his friends, particularly eastern cattle buyers, were welcome day or night, and could be assured of a fair deal. McCoy commented dryly that the news would come as a severe disappointment to Marshal Hickok, whose income was supplemented by weekly— contributions—from the gaming dens. On that note, they parted. McCoy was agreeably impressed, if somewhat skeptical, and Kincaid appreciated the warning. He was familiar with Bill Hickok's reputation, as well as his methods, having witnessed the town tamer in action back at Fort Hays.

Sometime later, Kincaid found Quincy Blackburn drowning his sorrow at the Alamo Saloon. Straightaway he propositioned the gambler with his revolutionary idea, offering one-third the profits for overseeing the operation. Blackburn was in turn dumbfounded, mawkishly grateful, and rather apprehensive that the sporting crowd would take a dim view of his break with tradition. But he accepted.

Kincaid advised the gambler to let him worry about the sporting crowd. Then in a quiet, businesslike voice, he laid down the law. If cheating was ever again detected in the Lady Gay, Blackburn's gonads would replace the little round ball used in the roulette wheels. The fat man broke out in a cold sweat, appalled by the vision of his balls clattering in search

of a number. Like a reformed drunk declaring eternal abstinence, he agreed. They shook hands and the deal was
clinched.

With the gambler in tow, Kincaid then made his first
official appearance at the Lady Gay. After bolting the doors,
he assembled the help and laid it out for them in blunt,
ungarnished terms. The bartenders would serve no more watered whiskey. The girls were to cease picking pockets and
rolling drunks; propositioning customers for outside engage-
ments wasn't forbidden, but neither was it encouraged. The
dealers were to run straight games, relying strictly on the
odds, and forget their nimble-fingered artistry of the past.
Mechanical devices, formerly used to boost the odds at faro,
chuck-a-luck, and roulette, would be removed.

A tone of crisp finality in his voice, he looked around the
room. "Those are the rules. Anybody that can't live with 'em,
draw your time. Whoever stays, just remember you've been
warned. Play square and I'll see that you profit by it. Cross
me and you'll wish you hadn't."

He let them digest that for a minute, then jerked his thumb
toward the front of the saloon. "Doors open at six tonight.
Let's make sure everything comes off without a hitch. Anyone wants to quit, see me in the office."

A bartender and three dealers separated from the others
and headed toward a backroom cubbyhole that served as an
office. Kincaid strode along after them, nodding to the girls
and men who remained, inwardly surprised that he hadn't
scared off the whole bunch. He'd been hard on them, perhaps
more so than called for. But he didn't want any misunder-
standing. Or miscues. Starting tonight the Lady Gay was
just that. A lady.

As he passed the end of the bar a girl standing apart from
the others smiled and clucked her tongue. He stopped, oddly
aware that she was taller than most but round as an apple in
all the right places. Not a stunner but nothing to sneeze at
either.

"You speakin' to me?"

"No, but I was thinking awfully loud." Her smile widened, faintly mocking yet somehow pleasant. "Do you always bully the help that way?"

He liked that. Spunk was a good trait in a woman. "What's your name?"

"Sadie." She held his gaze, still smiling. "Sadie Timmons."

"Tell you what, Sadie. You order supper for us up in my room and I'll let you answer the question for yourself."

"Is that one of the rules you forgot to mention?"

Kincaid smiled. "I make 'em up as I go along."

He left it at that and walked off, anxious to have the quitters paid and out of the Lady Gay. But in the back of his mind a vagrant thought surfaced, and with it a question. He wondered what she'd order for supper. Besides herself.

Kincaid was rarely given to compromise. He had implicit trust in his own assessment of men and events, and more often than not, he arranged things pretty much to suit himself. But he had made one concession to the sporting life. A small accommodation demanded by the rigors of late hours and a fast pace.

After two months in Abilene, he allowed himself the luxury of lolling about in bed long past sunrise. As impresario of the town's most widely discussed gaming den (a title bestowed on him by the editor of the Abilene *Chronicle*) he felt this minor self-indulgence was in keeping with the scheme of things. He had earned it, and with luck still clutching his coattails, he could now afford it.

Yet, while he stayed in bed longer these days, he seldom slept past dawn. Some internal source kept him charged with energy, and unlike most men, he needed only a few hours' sleep to restore himself. Early morning, then, had become a time of scrutiny and reflection. Awake, languid but restless, he lay back while his mind dissected whatever amused or interested him. Like a surgeon poking about in a maze of entrails, he took things apart, examined them closely, and satisfied with his appraisal, put them back together again. Most mornings his thoughts centered on the Lady Gay and his plans for the future, or perhaps the quirky politics of Abilene's even quirkier politicians. But on this particular day, a bright summer morning in late July, he allowed himself a respite from business. As a diversion, not so much interest as clinical curiosity, he was performing a thoughtful examination of the woman who slept beside him.

Streamers of sunlight spilled through cracks in the drawn windowshade, bathing her face in a silty glow. Her head nestled against his shoulder, one arm thrown over his chest, and her hair, falling loose in thick, shimmering waves of amber, was draped over the pillow. She had slept this way from that first night, snuggling close, like a child clutching in the dark at some warm and faithful toy. At first, unaccustomed to sharing his bed, Kincaid felt smothered by her nearness, overcome with the musk of her perfume and the cloyed scent of her body. But within a few nights that had changed. Oddly, he came to like it, found the closeness of her pleasant, and the smell of her a heady opiate which made his sleep full and restful.

Thinking back on it now, aware of her soft, velvety breath on his chest, he regarded it a wonder that she was here at all. Certainly, he hadn't meant for it to become a regular arrangement. Not that first night, nor any of the nights that followed. Entanglements held a man back, slowed both his stride and his style, and were to be avoided assiduously. Yet, quite without knowing when or how, or through whose design, Sadie Timmons had become his woman. His confidante, even. Someone who shared his thoughts, through some witchery he hadn't yet fathomed, as well as his bed.

It surpassed understanding. And left him vaguely disquieted.

Women were playthings to Jake, something to be used and discarded as a feckless boy would swap marbles or butterfly wings. While he had never pondered its deeper implications, he was a creature of swift-felt insights and cold honesty within the core of his own intolerance. As a child, fascinated by all things grisly, he had seen his mother devour his father piecemeal, in the way a female spider eats her mate. Discontent with her world and herself, his mother had feasted on a man too compassionate to fight back. The contest was protracted, if unequal, until finally there remained only the husk of a man. Then, with the husk buried and nothing left to gorge upon, his mother devoured herself and came to rest beside the one she had loved neither wisely nor well.

Later, grown to manhood himself, Jake saw nothing in the buffalo camps and far-flung railheads to alter his view of the hungry spider. He remained fascinated by the duplicity of women, enigmatic creatures who were at once naive and cunning. Who functioned on a perverse logic alien to that of man, and consequently were not to be trusted. Their bodies were both bait and weapon, beguiling instruments, yielding them an incredible power over men. And in that there was an even greater imponderable. Women were known blackmailers, born to the craft negotiating all emotional business with their bodies. Yet men gladly sacrificed their freedom—lied, cheated, spent a lifetime playing silly games, ever baffled by the scatterbrained gibberish that passed for intuitive wisdom—all this and more they gave in tribute for an occasional palliation of their goatlike lust.

It seemed a monstrous price to pay and Jake had never once come close. He frequented whorehouses and dancehalls, taking a moment's pleasure for cash exchanged, and kept clear of the ensnarling web. As he saw it, women were necessary but expendable, and since reaching manhood he had left them where he found them. Until he came to Abilene. And the Lady Gay.

Sadie Timmons, like those who had preceded her, was

meant as nothing more than an evening's entertainment. A quick romp, with no one the loser, and back to business as usual. But something had gone awry. What, exactly, Jake still hadn't determined. The whole affair seemed to defy logic, as if his brains hung between his legs, and rational thought was now the victim of that goatlike lust he mocked in other men. Granted, there was a dimension to Sadie he hadn't found in other women. Or so he had convinced himself, at any rate. As yet, though, he had been unable to define it, much less nail it down as a reasonable excuse for his witless behavior. Just for openers, she was no beauty. Tall and stately, perhaps, but hardly what a man would call dainty. Her face was broad, with high cheekbones, and her mouth too wide. Although admittedly humorous when she smiled, and at certain times sensuous, it was still a lot of mouth. Then there was her body. A dazzler, awesome when first seen. Almost too much of a good thing, which somehow distracted a man. Long sculptured legs, flat-bellied and melon-bottomed; high full breasts tipped with coral, and skin like alabaster glimpsed in the rosy flicker of candlelight. Perhaps her best feature, though, was her eyes. Blue as larkspur, round and expressive, with a certain bawdy wisdom. Yet touched with something apart—a look of vulnerability—which contradicted everything about her. Scarcely what a man expected to find in a saloon girl.

Worse luck, behind that playful teasing manner, the damnable girl was smart. Bright as a brass button. She had the mental presence of a faro dealer, alert and crafty (although among men she pretended otherwise), and that somehow made him uncomfortable, like watching a vixen toy with fieldmice. All in all, he couldn't figure why he had kept her around this long. Why he hadn't given her the fast shuffle and a swat on the rump and called it quits after that first night. Perhaps this, more than anything else, was what bothered him. She had him stumped. He didn't understand her or her attraction. Nor did he understand himself, and that grated. A

hard admission for a man who found life's riddles uncomplicated, susceptible in the way of a rusty clasp to a locksmith's
probe.

He jumped, abruptly jarred from his ruminations. Her
fingers trickled through the hair on his chest, light and
tingling, the caress of a snowflake on matted curls. Twisting
around, he found himself swallowed whole in those large
china-blue eyes, and it crossed his mind that she had been
watching him for some time. No doubt practicing her furtive
witchery, reading his thoughts. Then her fingers swept lower,
snowflakes atop a throbbing shaft of stone, and all else ceased
to matter.

They came together in a violent, wordless clash. Brute
need slaked in molten fire. Their mouths joined hungrily, nib-
bling and probing, one consuming the other. She clung to
him, moaning softly, legs spidered around his thighs. They
rolled and heaved, caught in the furious beat of his stroke,
and she took him in a ravening haze of explosive, agonized
thrusts.

Afterward, breathing huskily, they separated and lay back
in the bed. Spent, words meaningless, they said nothing.
Whatever they sought had been found, and for the moment,
it was enough. A fair exchange, each taking from that brutal
thrash of arms and legs what was needed most. Their bodies
touched, her hand resting gently on his arm, but no sign of
endearment passed between them. They were together yet
apart. Drifting lightly on a quenched flame.

Some time later, with the sun climbing high, he stretched,
yawned widely, and rolled out of bed. Sadie lounged back
against the pillows, feeling soft and kittenish, watching him
pad about the room. His morning ritual seldom varied, and
by this time, she could anticipate his every move. A quick
splash in the washbasin, a short but vigorous scrubbing of
teeth, and a few haphazard strokes at the sandy thatch of hair.
Then, at last, the major decision of the day—selecting a

snappy outfit from his wardrobe. This required considerable study, and some mornings he wasted a quarter-hour or more pawing through coats and pants and vests. That he was vain as any woman delighted her, and that he was wholly unconscious of it pleased her even more. Later, after a bath and shave at the tonsorial, and a leisurely breakfast, he would take his morning jaunt around town. "Makin' the rounds," he called it, which was merely a pretext for keeping his fingers on the pulse of things. And she encouraged these daily strolls, wanting him to be seen and remarked upon. That she was the green-eyed envy of every girl in town—*Jake Kincaid's woman*—gave her a warm shudder similar to what she imagined cats must experience from catnip. Disgustingly shameful, perhaps even gloating, but sweet as honey.

This morning, though, she was thinking of none of these things. Her eyes saw his movements but her mind was fastened upon the man himself. In a scrutiny so calculated it would have given Jake Kincaid the shivers had he sensed her mood.

In the way of certain women, Sadie Timmons was perhaps a bit more nimble than the man with whom she slept. Possessed of an acuity and guile that had nothing to do with years and everything to do with life. Her road to Abilene had been rocky, strewn with memories best forgotten, and along the way she had known many men. Some she had slept with, others she had not, for while she had bartered much, never had she sold herself. Yet, of all the men in her life, she had known none so intimately as Jake Kincaid.

He was arrogant and selfish, an ambitious man, obsessed with himself, as all ambitious men are. Strong and tough and resourceful, lacking either mercy or pity for those weaker than himself. Never skulking or treacherous, but an opportunist nonetheless. Someone who saw the world as a place inhabited by dupes and rogues, and perceived expediency as the cardinal law of nature. A man of monumental calm, capable of violence and cruelty and godlike rage. An eagle soaring high, alone in its lordly pursuit of lesser creatures. Needing nothing. Nor anyone.

But Sadie Timmons observed these things only in passing. What concerned her most was not his contempt for man, but rather his massive indifference to women. While he had much to learn in bed, she liked what she saw on the outside—squared jaw and chiseled features, eyes like flaked chips of quartz. The mark of a determined man who would climb high and fast. And alone, unless she broke through that outer shell. Somehow touched a nerve and led him to invent a reason for taking her along. That she meant to go with him, out of the dungheap and into the clouds, Sadie never questioned for a moment. What remained was the matter of how she would arrange it. Or more precisely, how Jake Kincaid could be inveigled into arranging it for her.

As he started out the door, brushed and scrubbed and his mind racing, she sat up in bed. The sheet fell away, exposing her breasts, and her china-blue eyes lit up in a wicked smile.

"Don't forget our matinée, sugar."

He turned, one bushy eyebrow cocked in a quizzical frown. Then he grinned, understanding both the meaning and the promise. Very slowly, he gave her a broad, exaggerated wink.

"Sis, you just keep it warm. I'll see you directly."

The door closed and Sadie fell back in bed, delighted with herself. Men were such peacocks. And none quite so much as the strong ones. Tweak their vanity—dare to question so much as their virility—and they began pawing the carpet like a bull in rut.

Keep it warm indeed.

Smooth as he was, Mister Jacob Kincaid had much to learn. The weary warrior fell first. None faster than the one who had spent himself on a lover's couch. And among other things he might soon discover, she could outlast him till hell froze over.

She giggled a bawdy giggle, hugging herself with the

cleverness of it all. Then she lay back in the pillows, stretching like a great amber cat, and began devising the next step.

The Lady Gay was a carnival gone wild.

Dealers and stickmen chanted their litanies in the quick, slick cadences of a tentshow barker. A tinny brass band, never quite in tempo with the rinky-dink piano, blended discordantly with the drunken laughter of trailhands and muleskinners and spiffy eastern drummers. And while they drank, a bevy of girls circulated the floor, breasts jiggling, their rouged lips fixed in plaster smiles, appearing somehow magically at the elbow of any man whose glass ran dry.

Like exotic spices churning round in a battered grinder, the hubbub was deafening. Full of squalls and squeaks, shouts and shrieks, convoluting faster and faster in an orgy of sweat-soaked men and painted ladies. A moment of frenzied jubilee, brief and spastic, to be recalled with wonder when the icy blast of winter brought men huddled to the fires of sanity restored.

But at the Lady Gay it was just another night, like any other. An event staged with clockwork precision. Orchestrated in a manner no less tantalizing than a gypsy organ-grinder and his dancing bear.

Under Jake Kincaid's persuasive hand the Lady Gay had become the premier honky-tonk in Abilene. He had a sure feel for the appetites of rough-mannered men, whatever their calling. He reasoned, and rightly so, that the vices of cowhands, bull-whackers, and tobacco-spitting teamsters were every bit as outrageous as those of buffalo hunters. With that as his gauge, he had brought several innovations to the town's night life. After consulting Sadie, whose experience quickly proved invaluable, he hired more girls, had their dresses shortened at the bottom and lowered at the top, and soon had them traipsing around the place in hardly enough clothing to pad a crutch. This created a sensation, and no dearth of talk, for he was still lenient with the girls about their after-hours trade. Next, he introduced Abilene to the game of Monte (a card layout of Mexican origin much favored by Texans and other hot-blooded creatures). Last, to the everlasting grief of Marshal Hickok and his overworked deputies, he made the specialty of the house a toxic libation known as Taos Lemonade (concocted of grain alcohol, red peppers, tobacco juice and a dash of gunpowder, it was savored greatly by men of pugnacious disposition and cast-iron stomachs). All the curly-wolves and self-styled *macho hombres* battled for a place at the bar, and Jake shortly had a monopoly on the Texan trade.

Then he went a step further. A long-held conviction, that the uppercrust takes perverse delight in rubbing elbows with the sweaty masses, was put to the test. Essential to the success of this experiment (and Sadie again endorsed his sentiments) was a garish tone of elegance. He plastered the walls with French mirrors and fake Renaissance nudes; stocked the back bar with a gaudy clutch of fine wines, liqueurs and aged whiskey; and hired a noted pugilist (decked out in a swallowtail coat and ruffled shirt) to serve as bouncer. As sort of a cowtown *pièce de résistance*, he then imported a brass band from Kansas City and installed them on a specially built balcony at the front of the saloon. Added to a fiddler and an ebony-skinned ivory tickler (relics of less sophisticated days) it made for an unholy syncopation that could be heard south of the Smoky Hill. But it also proved his point. Texas herd owners, eastern cattle buyers, even the town's merchant princes and starchy tradesmen, flocked to the Lady Gay nightly, staking out choice seats where they could watch the action and imbibe civilized liquor.

Yet, of all his innovations, perhaps none held Abilene so spellbound as Jake's adherence to honest games. The townspeople applauded this hallmark to progress, and the Texans lustily bucked the Tiger, confident that with a fair shake they could thwart the laws of mathematical probability. Jake left the gaming tables to Quincy Blackburn, and while the odds allowed for an occasional winner, the Tiger relentlessly devoured a whole generation of Texans.

As Blackburn had predicted, the sporting crowd was appalled by this break with tradition. But they merely bided their time and watched. Jake's most ominous threat, shrewdly anticipated by Mayor McCoy, was instead Wild Bill Hickok. The marshal exacted heavy tribute from the gambling dives, and he took it as a personal affront that anyone would undermine his sandcastle. Less than a week after the Lady Gay reopened Hickok and the new owner had clashed. Hickok stormed into the office one morning, blustering and cold-eyed, his shoulder-length locks fairly curled with outrage.

"Kincaid, you and me have got a problem. And I think it's about time we had ourselves a little powwow."

"I'm all ears, Marshal. What's on your mind?"

"Don't gimme none of your sass, sonny!" Hickok leaned across the desk and glowered in his face. "You know gawddamn good and well what I'm talkin' about. Folks are sayin' you don't aim to pony up like the rest of the boys 'cause you figger you're runnin' honest games and that gets you a free ride. Well, lemme tell you something, sport—there ain't no free rides in Abilene. If you want to play, then you got to pay." The lawman straightened, twirling one end of his mustache. "And I'm the gent that does the collectin'."

"Marshal, I've never been one to tell a man his business, but it looks to me like you've got things a little cross-wise. See, it's you that's got the problem, not me."

"And I suppose you got it all figgered out how we're gonna solve it?"

"Matter of fact, I have. You don't tell on me and I won't tell on you."

"Tell what? Whyn't you just quit slingin' all that bullshit, and say whatever the hell you're tryin' to say?"

"Fair enough. You don't tell anybody I'm not payin' you off—which I'm not—and I won't tell the town council that you're gettin' your palms greased by every pimp in Abilene. That way we both come out ahead."

"Sonny, you got a big mouth." Hickok worked up a menacing scowl, and caressed one of the Colts stuck in a red sash around his waist. "You keep talkin' that way and I might just have to put a leak in your ticker."

Jake smiled a slow, glacial smile. "You could try."

Hickok blustered and threatened, and wasted a good deal of energy pounding on Jake's desk, but five minutes later he marched out with his tail between his legs. And a bargain that was to remain a secret despite the inquisitive probing of Abilene's finest.

In his jaunts around town Jake had turned up an interesting piece of information. Hickok was also collecting payoffs from Abilene's whoremongers, Rowdy Joe Lowe and the Earp Brothers being the most scurrilous of the lot. Gambling was one thing, but money from the flesh game was tainted. Had the town fathers been apprised of this unsavory alliance Hickok would have been out on his ear, hat in hand. Never above a good horsetrade, not to mention a little blackmail, Jake swapped the hawk-nosed lawman tit for tat.

The Lady Gay operated its games without further harassment from Hickok. And the frontier's most fearsome killer of men went on collecting graft from cowtown pimps. *Quid pro quo.* While Jake would learn the meaning of this ancient custom only in later years, it was a device he would employ with polish and flair for the rest of his life.

Although details of the incident were sparse, townspeople and Texans alike began eyeing this johnny-come-lately with a whole new outlook. Apparently he was no flash in the pan, another of those slick-talking promoters out to fleece the public with some new variation of the shell game. His tables actually were honest, a point grudgingly conceded even by the sporting crowd themselves. And anyone who could make Hickok haul water wasn't to be taken lightly. Not by a damnsight!

Aside from the publicity value, Jake had been amused by the whole affair. He considered Hickok a flamboyant charlatan, trading on an undeserved reputation. Back at Fort Hays the lawman had gunned down two drunks (hungrily billed as gunfights by distant newspapers) and was later run out of town after killing a Seventh Cavalry trooper in a saloon brawl. Hardly the grim reaper of law and order. More to the point, Jake simply wasn't afraid of Hickok. Life on the plains, hunting buffalo and being hunted in turn by hostiles, had blunted his fear of death. He suspected he'd killed more men than Abilene's hawk-nosed marshal, and if it came to a showdown, he had a sneaking hunch who would back off first. Of course there was no discounting the possibility that Hickok might bushwhack him some dark night. But that's what life was all about. A man paid his money and took his chances.

As for his honest games, Jake could scarcely keep a straight face. Everybody was praising his integrity when all the time it was strictly a come-on. From what he'd seen at Fort Hays, and here again at Abilene, ethics and business were seldom compatible. A man outmaneuvered his competition, while distracting the rubes with some flashy sleight-of-hand, and the foxiest of the bunch wound up with all the marbles. It was just that elemental.

All the same, once committed, a man had to hold the line. In late June, Quincy Blackburn had caught a dealer marking cards with a needle ring. Presumably, though it was never proved, the man was skimming off excess winnings before settling accounts each night. Jake acted immediately, and with a ruthlessness that chilled the blood of onlookers. While the crowd watched, he beat the dealer into an unrecognizable pulp, then dragged him to the door and dumped him outside. Dusting his hands, he strolled back inside and ordered drinks for the house.

There was nothing personal about it. Jake held no hard feelings toward the dealer and he had administered the beating with stony detachment. It was strictly business. An object lesson for the other dealers, and a graphic, if somewhat gory, testimonial to the Lady Gay's policy of honest games.

And now, in late August, with the cattle season in full swing, Jake Kincaid's standing in the community was unassailable. The sporting crowd, headed by Ben Thompson and Phil Coe (who already had their own troubles with Bill Hickok), adopted an attitude of live and let live. Privately they had concluded that while he was a heretic to the gambler's code, this brash youngster would make a better ally than enemy. Abilene's legitimate businessmen, impressed with his forthright character and shrewd thinking, were beguiled from the very outset. They accepted him as one of their own, and became rabid supporters of his struggle to remove the onus from gambling.

Among the first to welcome him was T. C. Henry, founder of the Grangers' Association. Politically, both Dickinson County and Abilene were split down the middle. The reform movement, comprised mainly of farmers, was led by Henry, which made him Joseph McCoy's arch-rival. The McCoy faction, a shaky alliance between less prominent businessmen and the sporting crowd, advocated a wide-open town catering to the Texas cattle trade. Ted Henry, perhaps the more astute judge of men and events, saw in Kincaid's "square deal policy" a break within the opposition's ranks. Always quick to exploit an opening, he courted the younger man at every opportunity, advising him to join the reformers and make a place for himself in the coming new order.

Jake exhibited mild interest, playing for time while he pumped the reform leader on a broader issue. Henry possessed a vision, that the future of Kansas lay not in cattle but in farming. Boldly he had bought up seventy thousand acres of land, planted five thousand acres in wheat, and used his own success as bait to lure settlers into Dickinson County. What he made harvesting wheat was a pittance compared to the profits he gleaned from land speculation. Fascinated with the concept, Jake spent hours extracting details from Henry, while Henry in turn attempted to drag him aboard the reformers' bandwagon.

Ultimately, Jake was converted, though not in the manner Ted Henry intended. Visionary in a more practical way, the young saloonkeeper saw an enormous windfall for the man who amplified Henry's idea on a vaster scale. At the same time, other factors were at work, slowly crystallizing his thoughts about the future.

Late in July, the Santa Fe had laid tracks to Newton, some sixty miles due south of the Smoky Hill. This, along with the reform movement, was certain to sound the death knell on Abilene as a cowtown. Joseph McCoy was busily flitting around the countryside preaching otherwise, but Jake sensed a change in the wind. Over the summer, after ferreting out the facts and weighing all alternatives, he arrived at a firm conviction. It was look ahead or get left behind. And he'd never been one to eat the next fellow's dust.

Now as he strolled through the Lady Gay on this sweltering August night, he had hatched several schemes but as yet no workable plan. Whatever move he made must be engineered with the utmost care, and executed before anyone could sniff out what he had in mind. Play it close to the vest, calculate every step, and then expose his hole card. The rudiments of any gamble worth the risk. In the meantime, the Lady Gay was coining a small fortune and he could afford to ruminate a while longer.

Amid the uproar of a packed house, as he moved slowly through the crowd, men stopped him time and again to shake his hand or slap him on the back. There was a curious magnetism, some force of character, which drew other men to him. Part of it was respect, perhaps fear, for they had witnessed the ferocity he unleashed when crossed. But there was something more, an aura of sorts. Aloof and inscrutable, quietly arrogant, he emanated a sense of raw vitality that couldn't be suppressed. Like some urbane and curiously civil wolf who allows himself to be petted and stroked, but only so long as no one crowds him too closely. Whatever his attraction, men sought him out, and quite without knowing why, went away feeling invigorated by the experience.

He paused midway down the bar, exchanging a few words with Print Olive and several cronies. They were all wealthy herd owners, addicted poker players, and had been here before. After a moment Jake gestured toward a private backroom, where he ran a table stakes game for high rollers, and the cattlemen, all smiles now, drifted off in that direction. Trailing them, he stopped at the end of the bar for a word with Sadie. She had become his stout right arm, sort of a voluptuous top sergeant in peek-a-boo gown, and he relied on her to keep the operation functioning smoothly when he was off the floor.

"Any problems I ought to know about?"

"Not a one, sugar. Just perking along as usual."

It never ceased to amaze him. How that musky scent of hers, jasmine or some such, came to him even in the stink of a sweaty crowd. Damned queer.

"I'll likely be in the private room most of the night."

She gave him a pouting smile. "What a shame. I had something extra special planned for later."

He knew the look. "Yeah, what's that?"

"Well, sugar, it's not something a girl could talk about." Her eyes went smoky and mischievous. "Maybe if I'm still awake when you get through plucking your pigeons I'll show you."

"Maybe I'll just wake you up and find out for myself."

She sighed and the peek-a-boo gown slipped a notch lower. "That's all I get these days. Promises, promises."

Laughing, he entered the private game room and softly closed the door behind him. The Texans were gathered around a baize-covered table, stacks of double eagles before them, loaded for bear. Jake took a chair, let them wait while he fired up a thin black cheroot. Then he broke open a fresh deck of cards, loosened his collar, and glanced around the table.

"Gents, the name of the game is stud. Ante a hundred."

A cold blue dusk settled over Abilene as the train groaned to a halt before the depot. Steam hissed from the engine in a great swirling cloud, congealed instantly by an arctic chill that swept down out of the north. Toward the rear, behind the tender and the express car, the coaches jarred together, shuddering with the impact, and settled motionless on the tracks.

Jake Kincaid swung down off the last car and strode to the end of the platform. Only three passengers followed him off the train and they quickly vanished into the deepening night. He stood for a moment staring out at the town, curiously unmoved. It was what he'd expected to find, and in that, there was nothing to mourn. Then he shivered, stamping his feet, suddenly aware of the brittle cold. It knifed through a man, congealing the very marrow in his bones, which made it pretty damned dumb to stand around gawking at a dead horse. And Abilene was just that. Hefting his warbag, he stepped from the platform and took off at a brisk walk toward Texas Street.

The town was deserted, saloons and dancehalls boarded up, only a few scattered lights winking forlornly in the darkness. As he trudged along, bucking his way through snowdrifts, it came to him that Kansas was a land of queer moods. When he'd departed, early in October, the last herds of the cattle season were still fording the Smoky Hill. Now, scarcely a month later, the streets were knee deep in snow and Abilene itself had become a frosty ghost town.

Three winters he had hunted buffalo west of Fort Hays, and he'd weathered some bad storms. But none like this. And none so early, striking with an unseasonal ferocity that took even the wild things by surprise. Old-timers called it a freak, a blue norther gone haywire, busted loose before winter opened the gate. By whatever description, freak or otherwise, it was a killer.

Rolling in just before dawn, the blizzard had swept down over the plains with gale force. The temperature plummeted, dropping the mercury to thirty below, suddenly locking the earth in an icy embrace. Howling snow flurries raged unabated for days running, and when at last the storm exhausted itself, the plains lay blanketed in a frozen sea of white. As far as the eye could reach, nothing moved, and an eerie stillness hung over the land like a crystal shroud.

Luckier than many travelers, some not found until spring thaw, Jake sat out the storm in Newton. Huddled beside a potbellied stove in the lobby of a fleabag hotel, he listened much and talked little, collecting scraps of information that would prove vital in the days ahead. After the blizzard slacked off, he caught the first Santa Fe train bound for Topeka. There he switched to the K & P Flyer, headed for points west along the Smoky Hill. And everywhere he looked, it was the same. Devastation.

Still, one man's loss was another man's gain. That was a thought much on his mind as he rattled across the frozen landscape. The caprice of life touched all men, yet some less than others. Whether luck or fate, flaw or strength, he wasn't sure. But he knew that while some men went under, bleating a dirge to ill fortune, others climbed steadily upward and onward. He suspected that being in the right place at the right time was a matter of no small consequence—and yet. If a man lacked the grit and savvy and bulldog determination, then all the luck in Kingdom Come wouldn't make him a winner. Hocus-pocus and abracadabra had never yet turned a turd into a honeysuckle vine.

Though it wasn't apparent to him as yet, Jake's trip south had matured him greatly. The blizzard had wiped out scores of cattlemen, further clearing the way for settlers migrating west. Newton was about to replace Abilene as the prairie cow capital, but only briefly, like a shooting star. That much and more he had nosed out in a little burg called Wichita, down on the Arkansas. Never before had the ebb and flow—the caprice of life—been so clear to him. The world was in a constant state of flux, ever shifting and changing and nourishing itself upon the bones of the weak. The man who understood this could rule caprice—shape events to suit himself. Stand and fight, take what he wanted, build on the very ground where others were swallowed whole. That one thing, universal in its truth, was what he had discovered in the midst of a howling norther. And never had he seen anything more clearly in his life.

When he entered the Lady Gay it was as dismal and dreary-looking as the rest of the town. A single bartender, with no customers, stood idly polishing glasses, and a lone faro dealer dealt himself endless hands of solitaire. The place was still as a crypt, haunted no less by the ghosts of dancing girls, trailhands, and slick-haired gamblers.

Before the barkeep could react Jake waved him quiet and bounded up the stairs. He flung the door open and stalked into the room, filthy, disheveled, half-frozen, and grinning from ear to ear. Sadie was swathed in a woolly shawl, hunched in a chair beside the stove, and for a moment she gaped at him in bug-eyed disbelief. Then she shrieked, rocketing out of the chair, and flew across the room. He caught her on the last hop, swinging her high, and brought her down in a bear-hug that nearly collapsed her lungs. Gasping, her face radiant, she threw her arms around his neck and their mouths came together in a long, hungry kiss. At last, breathing heavily, they broke apart, and his grin burst out again.

"By Christ, that's what I call a homecomin'."

Her lips curved in a smile, but suddenly her face clouded over and she shoved him back with a stiff clout in the chest. "Jake Kincaid, you're a lousy, rotten, good-for-nothing—" She sputtered to a halt, eyes blazing. "Where in the name of God have you been? And why didn't you write me, or at least telegraph? It's been a month. A whole damn month! Didn't you know I'd be scared to death with you out in that storm and me wondering what—"

"Hell's bells, simmer down, will you? I'm full growed and I've been out in snow before. Never got lost either."

She glared back at him, still boiling. "That's no answer at all. You leave me holding the bag and disappear in a puff of smoke. I want to know where you've been, Jake. Right now!"

"I told you where I was headed. Newton"—the grin reappeared—"and thereabouts."

"And thereabouts! You're incredible. Just incredible." She jerked away, started off, then whirled on him. "Have you got any idea of what's happened while you were out gallivanting God knows where? This whole town has gone to hell in a hatbox."

She advanced on him, ticking it off on her fingers. "First, Hickok killed Phil Coe and the town council canned him—"

"Is that a fact?"

"—then Henry and his reformers posted notices in all the newspapers banning Texans from Abilene—"

"Yeah, I know."

"—and now they've tied a can to McCoy's tail, and without him and the Texans there won't be enough trade in Abilene to—"

"I know, Sadie. Goddamnit, if you'd listen, that's what I'm tryin' to tell you. I know."

She faltered, darting him a puzzled look. "You know?"

"Course I know. Newton's not the end of the earth. Hell, they're dancin' in the streets down there. Henry and his reformers handed them the cow trade on a silver platter."

"I don't understand." She moved back to the chair and sat down, visibly distracted. "Abilene is finished, the Lady Gay is busted, and you're grinning. I must have missed the joke."

"The joke's on them. I saw it comin' way back."

"Holy smokes, folks. Jake Kincaid the wizard."

"That I am, smartpants. That I am."

Squatting down, he pulled maps from his coat pocket and unfolded them on her lap. Stabbing here and there with his finger, talking in a husky, gleeful tone, he explained what he'd been up to for the past month. And why.

The railroads were steadily expanding south and west across Kansas. Which meant the cattle trade would shift with the railheads, hop-skipping from town to town as newly laid track shortened the distance Texans must trail their longhorns. But that was small potatoes. The future was in land—settlers. Ted Henry and his reformers had already proved that. Civilization was advancing, gobbling up land and towns and railheads, and eventually it would write an end to the cattle trade.

It was move with the tide or get run over. So he put on his thinking cap and asked himself a real skullduster. What comes next after Newton? That was how he ended up in a little back-woods mudhole called Wichita. And guess what? He was so goddamned smart he couldn't hardly stand himself. Worked out just the way he'd figured. Only better.

Strictly on the hush-hush, the Santa Fe was promoting an outfit called the Wichita & Southwestern. Oddly enough, their charter proposed tracks to be laid between Wichita and—Newton! All of which meant that by the end of next summer Newton would be dead as a doornail—as a cowtown. But then, just like Abilene, it would draw settlers by the carload.

Naturally, after the smoke cleared, Wichita would come up smelling like roses. Probably the biggest boomtown ever to hit Kansas. First, the cattle trade, which he judged would last three years at the outside, and then the cycle would repeat itself. Railheads expanding west, the Texan trade shifting, and settlers pouring into Wichita. And just the right spot for a fellow with itchy pants and big ideas. So he took the plunge.

After prowling around some, looking things over, he'd bought four town lots in Wichita and ten thousand acres of prairie land along the Santa Fe right of way outside Newton. Got it dirt cheap, too. When the time was ripe, of course, he would parcel the Newton land off and sell it to settlers. Meanwhile, he'd already contracted with an outfit in Topeka to build the biggest, plushest gambling dive anybody had ever seen. Smack dab in the center of Wichita.

What it boiled down to was a sure-fire cinch. He'd get them coming and going. And wind up rich as Midas. Hell, richer! Filthy, stinking rich.

Sadie didn't say anything for a long while. She sat staring at the maps, dumbfounded by the audacious plan he'd outlined. At last, still a bit unnerved, she looked up.

"Jake, I've never told you this before, and I know it sounds coarse and unladylike, but honest to God, you've got more balls than a billygoat."

He laughed, a deep, rumbling bellylaugh, and his pale eyes softened. "Like you said, I'm just a natural-born wizard."

"I'm convinced. Judas Priest, am I ever convinced." But with her conviction came an oppressive sense of apprehension. While she had seen a grand scheme unfolded, she'd heard nothing of the only future that counted. Their future. The one she had contrived with stealth and lavender-scented fishhooks, and from the look of things—too little bait.

"You know, I've been doing a lot of thinkin' while I was gone." He stood, holding his hands to the warmth of the stove, his light mood turned sober. "I'm not gettin' any younger, and if things work out the way I figure, why, it seems like I ought to have some sons to leave all that money to."

The words seemed to stick in his throat; but he coughed and snorted and finally managed to spit it out. "What I'm beatin' around the bush tryin' to say is that maybe we ought to get married. If you're of the same mind, naturally."

Sadie wanted to laugh and cry all at once. It was so like him. Only Jake Kincaid could make a proposal of marriage sound like a business transaction between a couple of strangers. But then, perhaps that's what it was. If he loved her he'd certainly never said it—or shown it—and probably never would. That was his way. Unemotional, cold and calculating, ruthless. Yet he had never attempted to hide it, or deceive her. He was what he was, no excuses offered, no bones about it. And whatever he was, whatever he might become, she had decided long ago that Jake Kincaid was what she wanted. Whether on his terms or hers hardly seemed to matter anymore. Perhaps it never had.

Her eyes went dark and moist, then she smiled and carefully folded the maps. "Sugar, it's a good thing I'm partial to a gambling man. The kind of stakes you play for, I'd almost have to be."

Kincaid turned, satisfied with the answer, and his gaze drifted off in a faraway look. Almost as if he was staring toward something dimly visible in the distance. "The stakes'll get bigger. And so will we. Someday there'll be lots of folks waitin' in line to say howdy to the Kincaids. Bankers and Baptist deacons included. You can mark it down in the promise book."

They were married next morning by the only preacher in town. A rheumy-eyed old scoundrel with buttered hair and a hammer-tail coat and a passable acquaintance with the Scriptures. Three days later, with the Lady Gay stripped clean, they boarded a train headed east. Their tickets were punched Wichita, and they never once looked back.

TWO

The house stood on a slight knoll north of town. It was large and roomy, with a wide veranda in front and a towering elm screening it on hot summer days. Looking west from the veranda, it offered a sweeping view of the cottonwood-fringed Arkansas and the emerald prairie beyond. Set back off by itself, by far the biggest house in Wichita, it was considered the local showpiece. Painted a dazzling white, perched atop the gentle rise, it could be seen for miles, silhouetted against the soft blue muslin of open sky. The townspeople pointed to it with pride as the Kincaid House, and in that simple statement there was an unspoken mark of distinction. One reserved exclusively for the small clique which had made Wichita the foremost boomtown on the western plains.

On sweltering afternoons, with the sun at its zenith, Sadie came often to sit beneath the elm tree. There the vapid southerly breeze was always cooler, and these tranquil interludes had become her favorite part of the day. Gazing out over the river bottoms and the bustling town, she felt at peace with the world, content as a pampered tabby cat. Jake spoiled her shamelessly, insisting on a housekeeper, though she could have easily handled the chores herself, and made a perfect pest of himself about rest and daily naps and plenty of milk. According to him, milk made strong babies, and he was determined that his firstborn son would be a lusty specimen. How he knew it would be a boy was a mystery never explained. He just knew, and any nonsense to the contrary was beneath discussion.

Sadie was amused, yet she understood this need for a son, a boy child to carry on the name. It was an urge as old as man himself, enduring and deep-rooted, and in truth, she herself hoped for a boy. A young Jake, with that same strength of character and a rage to live. But with something of her, perhaps. Gentleness and compassion to temper the steely toughness. Just a trace of tolerance for the flaws and frailties of lesser creatures. If she could do that, create within her womb a tiny miracle of strength and forbearance, she would feel truly fulfilled. Graced in a way she could never have imagined before coming to Wichita.

Yet, in many ways, she was already graced more than most women dared hope for. Seated beneath the elm, watching a herd of longhorns being driven across the toll bridge, she still found it hard to believe. So much had happened, and while she accepted it joyously, it was sometimes difficult to separate reality from illusion. Like the stargazings of a small girl, filled with dashing knights and valiant deeds, she expected to blink her eyes one day and see it vanish in a wisp of smoke. After having had so little from life, she wasn't yet able to cope with fairy tales come true. And for Sadie Timmons, born to the wrong side of the tracks, it was just that. A fairy tale touched by the finger of God.

Only in this case it was her own personal god, the one she had married. Hardly a man to welsh on his word, Jake Kincaid had delivered a hundredfold on the promises made that night in Abilene. That they were made as much to himself as to Sadie diminished her joy none at all. Everything had happened exactly as he said it would, and for her, it was enough that she had shared in bringing the dream to life.

Upon departing Abilene last winter, Sadie had simply assumed that things would continue in normal fashion. She would handle the girls in the new gambling place and Quincy

Blackburn (who had agreed to meet them in Wichita) would oversee the gaming operation. Jake quickly dispelled that notion. His wife had not only retired from the business, she was to become a lady. They spent several days in Topeka and it was there the transformation began. He outfitted her with a complete wardrobe of gowns and bustles, hats and shoes, all in the latest styles. His choice varied between conservative and severe (Sadie declared it more on the order of matronly) and he would brook no interference in the selection. After the shopping spree she had a trunkload of fashionable gowns which she considered both uncomfortable and unsightly. But she *looked* like a lady, and Jake observed that they had made a good start. The rest would come to her naturally. All she needed, he noted confidently, was a little time and the right setting. The statement was prophetic, as she would discover some weeks later.

They arrived in Wichita shortly after New Year's. Their buggy, drawn by a matched set of blood-red bays, was trailed by four freight wagons loaded to the gunnels with gambling paraphernalia, furniture, and household goods. It was then that Jake sprang his surprise—and the shock of Sadie's life.

Of the four lots he had purchased, three were in the commercial district. On one, a corner lot in the heart of town, the new Lady Gay was rising fast in a whirlwind of mortar and lumber. The other commercial lots were also located on Douglas Avenue, Wichita's main thoroughfare, and crews of workmen were busily erecting a hotel and a mercantile. The store was already rented to Abe Karatofsky, who planned to close out his operation in Abilene in late winter.

But it was the fourth lot which left Sadie speechless. Situated on a gentle knoll north of town, overlooking the vast panorama of Arkansas River valley, it was breathtakingly beautiful, something out of a dream. And taking shape under a lone gigantic elm was the house. Spacious and rambling, with eight rooms (her very own kitchen!), hardwood floors, and stone fireplaces, it was grand beyond her wildest expectations.

The end of the rainbow. She broke down and cried, the first time Jake had ever seen her shed a tear. He considered that a very ladylike gesture, and promptly took her on a tour of the house. It was the genteel setting he had promised back in Topeka, and here she would take her place as lady of the manor.

The next few months were sheer pandemonium, and though Jake positively gloated over her pregnancy, she saw less and less of him with each passing day. As he had predicted, the Wichita & Southwestern was already laying track and would reach Newton no later than May. Seemingly overnight, the little village of Wichita erupted into a boomtown. Newton's bubble was about to burst, and as the southernmost railhead, Wichita would become the cow capital of the Kansas plains.

Buildings sprouted along Douglas Avenue and Main Street like weeds in a berry patch. Another gaming parlor, the Keno House, went up catty-corner to the Lady Gay. Karatofsky got a competitor gloriously proclaiming itself the New York Store. A second hotel and a newspaper and a variety theater— even a new city hall—were slapped together well before the spring rains had run their course. Joseph McCoy, acknowledged expert in the cattle trade, was hired to build the stockyards east of town, and everybody braced themselves for an onslaught of Texans.

That the longhorns would come, nobody doubted for an instant. But the Texans and their gold proved a lodestone for the sporting crowd as well, and the town fathers quickly awakened to the realities of the cattle trade. Trailhands weren't just partial to vice, they demanded it. After three months on the Chisholm Trail, eating dust and beans and wet-nursing cantankerous cows, they wanted their pleasures kept raw and uncomplicated. Whiskey, women, and gambling, in just about that order. And the wilder the women the better, for of all God's creatures none were more rambunctious than horny Texans.

Word spread fast, and even as Wichita built apace, the

exodus from distant points began. The flotsam of humanity—whores, thimbleriggers, bunco artists, and an army of tinhorns—descended on the town bag and baggage. Rowdy Joe Lowe and the Earp Brothers were among the first to arrive, followed shortly by Chalk Wheeler, reputed to have been the kingpin whoremonger in now defunct Newton. Bawdy houses, clip joints, and unsavory gaming dens began to appear on Water Street, which bordered the river along the east bank. Before anyone quite realized the problem, Wichita had itself a sleazy eyesore, not to mention a potential troublespot which could affect the life of every decent citizen in town.

Mayor John Meagher, after consulting with City Marshal Sam Atwood, called the town council into emergency session. While they were Wichita's original settlers, having incorporated soon after the Osage tribe was dispossessed by treaty back in '68, they knew absolutely nothing about governing a cowtown. Now, like goldfish dumped in a tank of sharks, they faced a sinister peril. Unless they acted fast Wichita was about to become a hellhole, dominated by rowdy Texans and the sporting crowd, the same as other cowtowns. But just as Abilene and Newton had failed to contain the violence (and the wide-open policy at its root) the town council now had to admit that they were stumped for a solution.

Late that night, after hours of fruitless debate, someone suddenly remembered the newcomer, Jake Kincaid. It was common knowledge that he had outfoxed the sporting crowd in Abilene, deftly forcing them to accept honest games and fair treatment. Moreover, he had invested heavily in Wichita, and legitimate businesses at that. He had as much to lose as the next man, and might well be persuaded to lend a hand in this common crisis. They put it to a vote and Sam Atwood scurried off toward the house north of town.

That was the night Jake Kincaid began manipulating strings—and politicians. After hearing them out, he asked a few questions, allowed them to subtly twist his arm, and finally agreed to help. Over the next week he arranged a series of meetings with Chalk Wheeler, who had appointed himself czar of the sporting crowd. They negotiated a settlement that was both fair and reasonable, and since Wheeler had the muscle to make it stick, the agreement was honored to the letter. The town council passed an ordinance creating West Wichita on the other side of the river (someone dubbed it with the name Delano and everyone else promptly forgot why) and the bawdy houses were banished forever from the town proper. Chalk Wheeler got his own little kingdom, which he proceeded to run with an iron fist, and Wichita got a reprieve that was to prove shortlived.

After that, it all came together and the Kincaid fortunes began to snowball. The longhorn herds started fording the Arkansas in late May, cattle buyers swarmed in on the new railroad (which the Santa Fe acquired in a nifty bit of legerdemain), and it was Abilene all over again. The Lady Gay, plusher than ever and twice as big, became an instant money machine. Settlers began trickling into Newton, where they were met by an oily promoter representing the Kincaid Land Company. And every nickel of profit gleaned from the Kincaid enterprises was plowed back into raw prairie along the Santa Fe right-of-way. Quietly, operating through lawyers in Wichita and Newton, Jake embarked on a program of land speculation that was little short of staggering in concept.

Bursting with vitality, working night and day, he still somehow managed time for dabbling in politics. With a group of investors (several of them town councilmen acting as silent partners) he obtained a charter and constructed a toll bridge spanning the Arkansas. The Texans fumed and cursed and ground their teeth, but it was safer than fording the treacherous river, and they paid through the nose to get their cattle safely across. At the same time, he maintained a casual alliance with Chalk Wheeler, acting as a middleman between the Delano faction and the town council. This facilitated the extraction of license fees from bawdy houses and hooch joints, and greatly endeared him to John Meagher, who as mayor tussled constantly with the budgetary needs of a mushrooming town. One hand washed the other, though, and Jake tactfully called the debt in early July. After declining a position on the town council, begging off with the press of business, he suggested instead an introduction into the State House. Meagher obliged, and following a trip to Topeka, the way was greased for the next step in Jake's plan.

In fact, though there were never enough hours in the day, Jake seemed to have time for everything but Sadie. Yet, despite the lingering hurt, she seldom complained. If he failed to see her need, and her love, it lessened none at all her fascination with his vitality. On warm afternoons like today, when she came to sit beneath the elm, she pretended she could see Jake on the streets below. Hammering and sawing, wheeling and dealing, kicking up spurts of dust as he raced to and fro building his town. It was a comforting thought, and only by degree an illusion. For as she had known from the beginning, he fully intended to own Wichita.

Suddenly she winced, distracted from the scene below by a lusty kick in the stomach. There was a moment of angry pummeling and punching, then quiet. She smiled, gently caressing her swollen belly, struck by the vagrant thought that Jake had been right all along.

Like his father, little Jake was a scrapper. Still in the womb, he had already begun the fight. Anxious to stretch and test himself, eager to get on with the business of living.

Jake had the door open, his face set in a dark scowl, as Horace Quillman mounted the veranda steps. The physician was a portly little man, heavily larded around the beltline, and he was perspiring freely. Huffing and wheezing, he took the last step and hurried across the porch. He was much too old and much too fat to be climbing hills in a scorching August sun. But a summons from the Kincaid house was hardly to be ignored. Night or day.

"You took your own sweet time gettin' here, Doc."

"Jake, I came as fast as I could. There are lots of sick people, and I'm just one man."

"Mister, as of right now you've only got one patient. And she's waitin' for you in the bedroom. That plain enough, or you want me to spell it out?"

Horace Quillman wasn't accustomed to taking orders. He blanched at the curt tone and began a retort, then he saw the look in Jake's eye. After a moment he shrugged and dropped his hat on a vestibule table.

"Suppose we forget other matters and just concentrate on Mrs. Kincaid. Is she in labor?"

The scowl dissolved, and in its place came a quick grimace of concern. "I don't know what you'd call it, but she's hurtin' something fierce. The housekeeper told me to get you up here pronto."

"Your housekeeper is with her now?"

Jake nodded.

"Has her water broken?"

"Jesus Christ, Doc, how the hell would I know a thing like that? What d'you think I sent after you for?"

Quillman smiled and patted him on the shoulder. "You're right, of course. Why don't you fix yourself a drink while I examine her? And try to relax. I'm sure there's nothing to worry about."

The physician turned and walked off toward the back of the house. Jake stared after him for a long while, then wandered into the parlor. Distracted, his mind elsewhere, he moved several steps in the direction of a decanter and glasses on top of a sideboard. Then he stopped. Whiskey somehow seemed uninviting. It had never solved his problems in the past and he hardly needed a crutch to prop him up today. What he needed was a clear head and his wits about him. Something wasn't right back in that bedroom, and despite the pudgy sawbones' confident manner, he had a bad feeling down in the pit of his gut.

Jake was restlessly pacing the floor, unable to still his misgiving, when Quillman entered the parlor some minutes later. Their eyes locked and his sense of dread leaped higher. Whatever the doctor had seen in the bedroom wasn't good, and it showed in his face. Finally Quillman hawked, clearing his throat, and strode forward with his hands in his pockets.

"I'm afraid my optimism was a bit premature. We seem to have some complications."

"Complications?" Jake's chin came up, and his mouth set in a hard line. "What kind of complications?"

"Nothing to alarm yourself about. Your wife is fine and I'm confident she'll come through nicely. It's just that the birth will be a bit more—involved—than we anticipated."

"Doc, I never could stand for a man to pussyfoot around when I'm askin' him questions. Now, why don't you quit treatin' me like a dimdot and just spit it out?"

"Very well." Quillman's jowls bunched in a loose fold above his collar as he selected the words with care. "What it amounts to is that Mrs. Kincaid is built wrong for having children. Normally this is a problem we experience with women of a somewhat more delicate constitution. Without going into detail, let us say that your wife's—uh—female organs are not as they should be. Just an oversight of nature. Not uncommon at all. I suggest you take my word for it and let the matter rest there."

"Boiled down, you're tellin' me she's in for trouble."

"Yes and no. Truthfully, it could go either way. I won't try to deceive you, Jake. She's going to have a rough time. But I have every reason to believe she'll pull through in fine shape."

"And what about the baby?"

Quillman sighed heavily and his gaze drifted away. "I regret to say that medicine is an inexact science. There's so much we don't know." His head came up and he managed a rueful smile. "Jake, I can't promise you a thing. Except that I'll do my damnedest. Small consolation, I know, but it's all I have to offer."

They stared at one another a long while, both aware of what the physician had very discreetly left unsaid. At last, the younger man nodded, accepting it for what it was. A cast of the dice. With stakes neither of them had the nerve to articulate.

"Can I see her?"

"By all means. She still has a ways to go and a word from you would be an excellent tonic."

Quillman blinked, thoroughly bemused for an instant, then watched spellbound as a transformation occurred before his eyes. Jake Kincaid straightened, appeared somehow to grow taller. A great calm settled over his features, not unlike the quietude of a monk fingering beads. Then, shoulders squared, his qualms submerged beneath a mask of composure, he marched from the parlor.

At the bedroom door he halted, waiting a moment. Bess Murphy, the housekeeper, was sponging Sadie's face with a damp cloth, murmuring all the while in a soft, lilting brogue. Widowed, and her own children grown, she suddenly seemed a godsend to Jake, and he reminded himself to give her a substantial raise in wages. Entering, he caught Mrs. Murphy's eye and she stepped back, moving with obvious reluctance toward the door. After she passed by, darting him a worried glance, he silently approached the bed.

Sadie's eyes were glazed with pain, and her face glistened beneath a beaded film of sweat. Suddenly her eyes snapped shut as a contraction swept her body, and hard little knots formed at the back of her jaw as she gritted her teeth. But she didn't whimper or cry out. She fought the pain, steeling herself against it, holding on tight till the contraction subsided. Standing there, watching her in utter helplessness, he had never felt so proud in his life. She was one of a kind. With enough spirit for half a hundred women.

He took her hand, squeezing gently, and her eyes rolled open. Slowly, as if the effort drained her of strength, she focused on his face, and a wan smile touched the corners of her mouth.

"Jake. I missed you."

"Well, I'm back now, so rest easy." He brushed a damp wisp of hair from her forehead. "Had a talk with the doc and he said you're comin' along fine. Everything's right on schedule."

A little spark flickered in her eye and she laughed softly. "Oh, Jake, you're such a terrible liar. I'm botching it all to hell." She gave his hand a desperate squeeze. "But I'm trying. Honestly, I'm trying real hard."

"Damn right you're tryin'. And you'll get the job done, too. Doc says you've got more gumption than any woman he ever tended."

"Oh, I hope so, sugar. I hope so." Her eyelids fluttered, suddenly heavy, and her words came in a whisper. "I so want to see young Jake."

Something thick and pasty hung in his throat, and he swallowed hard. He searched his mind for some word of reassurance, anything he could say that would help her. But even as he collected himself, smothering that single coal of emotion, he heard a fearsome pounding on the front door. Whoever it was persisted, and he cursed the witless fool in a burst of outrage. Moments later Mrs. Murphy appeared at the door, motioning frantically, and he eased away from the bed.

"Lord deliver us, Mr. Kincaid. There's a wild man out there. Crazy as a loon, he is. Says you must come now and talk with him."

"You stay with Mrs. Kincaid. If she wakes up, tell her I'll be right back."

Jake hurried toward the front of the house, ready to thrash the living bejesus out of someone. But as he stormed into the vestibule his anger evaporated, and it struck him that this whole day was slowly turning into a nightmare. The man standing just inside the door was Tom Hardesty, and the look on his face was explanation enough. There was trouble in town. Likely big trouble. Otherwise the committee would never have sent for him.

Hardesty confirmed his suspicions in a few terse sentences, stressing the urgency of the situation. Jake listened attentively, asking only one question, and Hardesty's reply left his face clouded with a grim expression. Turning back, he took his gunbelt from a wall peg and strapped it around his hips. Horace Quillman was standing in the doorway of the parlor and they exchanged an uneasy glance.

"Doc, how long before my wife hits the bad part?"

"That's hard to say. Perhaps an hour. Perhaps more."

"I have to go out for a while. You just make sure she's all right when I get back."

Quillman ignored the veiled threat. "Vigilante business, I presume."

"You presume right."

"It's a dirty undertaking, Jake. Dirty and uncivilized. Not many would agree with me, I suppose, but men shouldn't set themselves up to play God."

Jake jammed a hat on his head, then paused, glowering back at the physician. "Bill Martin and his gang murdered a man not an hour ago. In broad daylight on Douglas Avenue. He was a black man—hod carrier that whipped one of Martin's boys a few days back. I guess lots of people would say one nigger more or less doesn't mean much. Trouble is, a thing like that's catchy. Tomorrow it might be Jew storekeepers. And the next day anybody that's cross-eyed. Before long they might even work around to potbellied sawbones."

His mouth creased in a thin, tight smile. "You think about it, Doc. Might give you a whole new outlook on things."

A moment later the door closed behind Hardesty and Jake. Quillman stood, brow furrowed in thought, mulling over what he'd just heard. Against his better judgment, he had to concede a certain logic to Kincaid's argument.

Sam Atwood was the salt of the earth, and before the

boom had policed Wichita with good-natured tolerance. But as marshal of a cowtown he had proved an unmitigated disaster. The trailhands ran roughshod over Atwood and his deputies, and the town was in a constant state of turmoil. With such feeble law enforcement, Delano in particular soon became a haven for gunslingers, toughnuts, and garden-variety badmen. Hurricane Bill Martin and his gang, renegade Texans suspected of cattle rustling and horse stealing, had a virtual hammerlock on the town. Chalk Wheeler himself had complained of their destructive sprees, but Sam Atwood seemed incapable of halting the rowdiness. He was an easygoing softy in a job that called for backbone and a hard fist.

Toward the end of July, several leading citizens got their heads together and formed a Vigilance Committee. It was an extreme measure, but Wichita was virtually under siege, and the people were demanding action. Lem Tucker, a fiery young lawyer, was selected to lead the vigilantes. This gave the committee a quasi-legal character, and Tucker's name looked good on the warning posters tacked up around town. But it fooled hardly anyone. Jake Kincaid was the moving force behind the vigilantes; that it was he who called the shots remained the worst kept secret in Wichita. Yet, until today, the Vigilance Committee's threat of summary punishment had put the quietus on Delano's rougher element. This morning's killing was apparently meant as a slap in the face. Bill Martin and his gang had called the vigilantes' bluff, and the outcome would determine who ruled Wichita.

Horace Quillman abhorred violence in any form. Especially mob violence. Still, however grudgingly, he had to admit that the only alternative to law was anarchy. And perhaps vigilante law, repugnant as it seemed, was better than no law at all. Certainly it was man's oldest law. Enduring as the rocks. An eye for an eye.

All of which brought the little physician to an even greater enigma—Jake Kincaid. Everyone in town knew that he was deeply immersed in politics. Yet he refused public office; remained a shadowy, behind-the-scenes figure. Wichita's burgeoning kingmaker, perhaps? Only time would tell. Meanwhile, scorning all vestments of power, he raced off at the head of the vigilantes on a day his wife lay in the throes of childbirth. It fairly boggled the mind.

"Doctor!"

Bess Murphy's terrified shriek jarred Quillman out of his funk. On its heels came a pitiful animallike moan that curdled his blood. Slinging off his coat, fat buttocks pumping, he rushed toward the bedroom. But as he waddled down the hall, Quillman was struck by a vast irony. Time accommodated no man, commoner or otherwise. Not even Jake Kincaid could make the clock stand still. Nor could his wife await his return. Her time was now.

Some hours later Jake entered the house as Dr. Quillman emerged from the kitchen with a sandwich and a glass of milk. The little physician gave him a wry smile and hoisted his glass in salute.

"Congratulations, Jake. You're a father."

Jake marked the event with a wooden look. Then, emotions clamped tight in that inner vise, he asked the question. "How's Sadie?"

Quillman stopped smiling. "She pulled through, but that's about all. My professional opinion is that she shouldn't have any more children. The next one might kill her." He paused, not so somber now. "If you don't mind my saying so, Jake, that's a hell of a woman you've got."

Jake just nodded and walked off toward the bedroom. Quillman started to take a bite of his sandwich, then caught himself and hurried forward.

"Hey, you didn't ask if it was a girl or boy."

"No need. I already knew."

"Is that a fact?" The obvious question seemed in order, but

his mind suddenly leapfrogged. "By the way, what happened with Bill Martin?"

"We hung him."

Quillman halted, sloshing milk over the floor. Again he was struck by the curious intercourse of irony and enigma. Hung a man on the day of his son's birth and had yet to bat an eye. Perhaps, in his own way, Kincaid had made the clock stand still after all. Just for an instant. Long enough for two souls, the dead and the newborn, to pass swiftly in an ancient exchange.

Had Quillman known it, he could have inscribed yet another mark on the enigma. At that moment Jake Kincaid stood beside the bed, staring down at Sadie and his son. There was a strange buzzing in his ears, and his vision was somehow blurred. Unmoved on the outside, stoic as roughly chiseled granite, the man inside wept openly, and thanked a god he himself denied.

Standing in front of the vestibule mirror, Sadie critically inspected the woman who stared back at her. It was a long, appraising scrutiny, as if she were examining a rival for some hidden flaw or slight imperfection.

Her hair was worn back, with a single cluster of curls at the front, and radiated a soft auburn sheen. She had darkened her eyelids with kohl, accenting the blue of her eyes, and lightly rouged her cheeks. This feminine artifice was something she never wore in public anymore. Genteel ladies pinched their cheeks and bit their lips; only loose women stooped to painting their faces. But Jake's tastes in such things were still somewhat philistine, and at home, she fixed herself to suit him.

The dress she wore was gossamer satin, done in a delicate Pensee shade of purple, with fluted piping around the bustle and the overskirt. The bodice was scooped low, with sheer muslin tufted around the edges, all of which allowed a rewarding view of her breasts. Styles in Wichita still clung to Victorian severity, but Jake liked what he liked, and on their last trip to Kansas City he had insisted she change to this latest rage of fashion-conscious women.

Twisting this way and that, Sadie patted her stomach (secretly delighted that she had regained her figure so quickly) and gave the image in the mirror an approving smile. There was no denying what her eyes confirmed. She presented a fetching appearance. In fact, modesty aside, she was absolutely ravishing.

Which left but one problem. There was no one to ravish her.

Disgusted, she gave the mirror a haughty sniff and marched into the parlor. There she halted and stood for a moment glaring at the Christmas tree. Somehow the very sight of it seemed to mock her. Every limb was festooned with gay ornaments, while a cherubic angel floated gracefully at the crown and piles of brightly ribboned presents lay heaped at the base. She blinked, craned her neck around for a better look, and her jaw clicked shut in a pique of annoyance.

Even the angel seemed to mock her!

She whirled away from the tree, muttering salty little invectives left over from her saloon days. However much a lady she had become (though she sometimes felt like a stage actress caught up in a world of make-believe), she still knew how to curse. And perhaps more to the point—she knew who deserved the cursing. It wasn't the angel that mocked her. Or the glittering tree. Or the ravishing creature gussied up to look like a lady. It was Jake Kincaid—damn his black heart. Who had left her alone, unwanted and unravished, on tonight of all nights.

The thought goaded her anger to a higher pitch. Everybody celebrated Christmas Eve. Even scoundrels and confirmed drunks came home to their families on this one night of the year. But not Jake Kincaid. He was off politicking or slinging together another deal or—somewhere. These days God himself couldn't keep track of Wichita's ringmaster and ace whip-cracker.

Sadie walked to a chair in front of the fireplace and plopped down with an aggrieved sigh. The flames licked merrily up the chimney, scarcely in harmony with her mood, and the crackling warmth offered little in the way of solace. There was a certain fascination nonetheless about the fiery, golden plumes, and as she stared into the flames, her anger slowly drained away. Distracted for the moment, perhaps mesmerized by the flickering mating dance of wood and coals, her thoughts turned inward, drifting listlessly in time and space.

Somehow she felt out of place, and just a little lost, in this big house. Lady of the manor was a role she brought off with difficulty, if at all, and Wichita's social whirl left her lukewarm. Not that the town was overrun with cultural activities. Quite the contrary, she found the whole thing a bit ridiculous, and riddled with hypocrisy. Starchy women with starchy ways, pretending that tea parties and the literary guild and the Ladies Temperance League made them the sacred cows of Wichita society. Yet most of them, just like everyone else, had starved and scrimped and lived in squalor when they first came west. And not a few of them (if the truth ever came out) were retired whores and dancehall girls. Only now that their husbands had made some money, or gone into politics, they were suddenly respectable and riding a highhorse that set them above common folks. She detested their stuffiness and their pretense, and since the baby was born, she had employed every flimsy excuse imaginable to avoid their company.

Her only true happiness these days was young Owen. They had named him after Jake's father, but never had a child looked more like his own sire. Hardly four months old and already he possessed that square jaw and a patch of sandy hair, and that same squalling determination to have things exactly his own way. Jake called him a "dead ringer," and was inordinately proud that he had fathered a husky likeness of himself. At first, it had delighted Sadie, and she felt sure that this awakening of Jake's deeper feelings would draw them closer together. But oddly enough, it hadn't.

That greater fulfillment she had expected with the baby's birth simply never materialized. Jake was gone from home more than ever before, and when he returned, his time was devoted first to Owen, then to the litter of papers on his desk, and finally, if he wasn't too exhausted, a few moments for her. She felt like a faithful little dog being thrown scraps of affection, and never had she been so discontent.

Alone much of the time, and miserable, she sensed that the gulf which had always separated them was steadily widening. Jake seemingly had what he wanted from the marriage—a son—and was apparently content to let things rock along on a hit-or-miss basis. Sadie in turn felt misled somehow, cheated of that greater fulfillment she had envisioned. As days turned into months, and nothing changed, she sensed a withdrawing inside herself. An erosion of emotion which was slowly transforming itself into a protective shell. And what she felt for Jake was now being lavished on the baby, as if in desperation she must love something that could love her back.

The horrible part was that she loved Jake. She even liked him, which was altogether different yet somehow a measure of the man. He was intelligent, witty in a sardonic fashion, and an omnivorous student of human nature, though she thought his contempt for other men was sometimes too cynical. He had an innate flair for style, kept himself nattily dressed, and was generous to excess if the mood seized him. Whenever he went to Topeka or Kansas City on business, he usually took her along, and there they dined in fine restaurants, saw the latest theatricals, and invariably ended up in a shopping spree that left her draped with jewelry and expensive gowns.

Nor could she fault him in bed. Beneath that stony composure he was a passionate man, who demanded love nightly (whenever he was home), and she remained exhilarated by his lean hard body and the need that surged out of him in those final moments. It wasn't as good for him now as it had been before the baby, but he never complained. On Dr. Quillman's orders he used the latest precaution—a moistened covering of finely scraped membrane from lamb's intestine, to safeguard against pregnancy—and unlike many men, he hadn't taken this as an excuse to visit the houses in Delano. Of that, if nothing else, she was reasonably certain. His urgency in bed was simply too great, and her own instincts too finely attuned, for it to be otherwise.

Still, though the thought itself appalled her, there were times when she almost wished he would take a mistress. Another woman would have been merely a temptation of the flesh, and she could have waged battle on even ground. Instead she faced a mistress of infinitely more cunning, one which claimed a man's mind and proved invulnerable however often the battle lines were drawn.

Jake had never been an easy man to live with. His waking hours were governed by ambition, leaving time for little else. From the outset, though, she had accepted this, resigned herself to it, felt she could be content with sharing those odd moments of his life left over from business.

But the baby had changed that. In a way she could never have anticipated. Jake now had a son—an heir to whatever kingdom he built—and he drove himself like a man possessed. His thirst for wealth and power and above all, land, seemed insatiable. He was in perpetual motion—Newton today, Topeka tomorrow, Wichita occasionally—never pausing to rest or catch his breath. His days, and nights, were filled with deals and deals and more deals. Operating businesses, ramming through political compromises, obligating others to him with favors, and always, however hectic his schedule, acquiring more land. Yet this acquisition of land was forever conducted in secret, cloaked behind a growing army of frontmen, and his ultimate purpose was something he shared with no one, including his wife.

Perhaps this troubled her as much as his casual indifference to her own needs. In the past he had always discussed his deals with her, actively sought her counsel, generously acknowledged the value of her judgment. Now he kept his own counsel, endlessly reflecting on some deeper scheme locked tightly within himself.

The change was apparent in other ways as well. Though he was civic-minded and exhibited an intense interest in public affairs, privately he had lost whatever small fondness he once held for the human race. If she had admired his arrogance and fierce combativeness—traits common to all ambitious men—she found it increasingly difficult to admire what he had become. Larded with scorn for the chinks he saw in others, he had slowly versed himself in the manipulation of men and events, using people as pawns to achieve his own ends. Where before he had been open and aboveboard, whatever his tactics, he was now smoother, almost sinister somehow, masking his ruthlessness with the quiet diplomacy of a hungry spider.

Whenever she broached matters of business, or attempted to discuss his deepening cynicism, he gave her that indulgent hairy-male look and patted her on the head like a precocious brat. Somehow she always emerged from these sessions feeling humiliated and slightly embarrassed, like a child rebuked for believing in the tooth-fairy. Afterward he went on about his business and the chasm between them had been widened another notch.

Yet, despite everything, she still loved him. Still liked him, although she found it ever harder to admire him. It was just that she could no longer talk with him. Or perhaps, though she refused to admit it, he had simply lost the urge to talk with her. As if, in the rush and bustle of his ceaseless maneuvering, he could no longer spare the time.

Staring into the fire, she wondered where it would all end.

It was a question she often asked herself these days. With no satisfactory answer, or even a palpable explanation, as yet.

Then, in a moment of deeper insight, she was struck by a profound thought. Perhaps, for men like Jake, there was no end. The man and the obsession were one. Fused together in some unearthly caldron, afflicted with an unquenchable thirst, they went on and on and on—forever. Incapable of surfeit. Enough never being enough.

"Merrrrrrrry Christmas!"

Sadie bolted from her chair as the roar reverberated through the house. Standing in the hallway entrance was the wanderer returned, crocked to the gills and listing dangerously to port. Never more astonished in her life, she saw that he was decked out in a red stocking cap and a cottony beard, with a sprig of mistletoe dangling across one ear. Draped over his shoulder was a huge gunnysack, knotted at the top with a candy-striped ribbon.

Laughing and crying, tripping on the hem of her skirt, she raced across the room and threw her arms around his neck. The impact almost knocked him flat, but he managed to keep his feet and even gave her a slobbering, glassy-eyed kiss. She hugged him fiercely, tears of joy and love and frustration sluicing down her cheeks. But somehow, what she felt stuck in her throat, and the best she could manage was a small, cheerless "Merry Christmas."

Winter that year was mild but long. One dreary month faded slowly into another, hobbling along like some crippled animal, and at times it seemed the dismal skies would last forever. But spring finally awakened from its chilled slumber, and as if to make amends, the prairie blossomed overnight in a garish rainbow of wildflowers and luxuriant shortgrass. Then the floodwaters passed, and across the latticework of rivers to the south appeared an endless column of bawling longhorns and dusty, cursing cowhands. Late in coming, the summer of '73 suddenly burst alive along the banks of the Arkansas, and Wichita waited with open arms to embrace the good times ahead.

But good times, like the weather, seemed elusive and unpredictable that year. The cattle market was sluggish, with wildly fluctuating prices, and somehow the expected boom never quite materialized. As summer skittered along, with an estimated half-million longhorns plodding toward Wichita, ominous tremors rippled through the financial world back east. Most men just scratched their heads, uneasy but confident that all would right itself before long, and went on about their business. Others, who saw the distant rumbling for what it was, moved fast to hedge their bets. Good times had gone by the boards. Unless the sign was more deceptive than it appeared, hard times were about to overtake anyone who failed to look ahead.

On a sweltering afternoon in late July, Jake sat at his desk, hands locked behind his head, staring out the window. Visible below was the bustling town, doubled in size in a single year and overrun with trailhands eager to make it the most prosperous railhead on the western plains. Yet the sights and sounds of Wichita flickered erratically, distortions that seemed somehow far removed. What he saw instead was in his mind's eye, sharp and shiny bright—an onrushing collision with economic chaos.

Back east the Wall Street moguls were slugging it out with brass knuckles. Vanderbilt against Gould. Pierpont Morgan against Cooke. And several lesser luminaries snapping at the heels of everyone like a pack of jackals. While Jake had much to learn about high finance, he had already grasped a truth which as yet eluded most of Wichita's businessmen. The west, for all its cattle and mines and virgin land, was still dependent on the east—susceptible to the slightest quiver in the economic structure of a distant money market. As he saw it, a gathering storm loomed just over the horizon. When it broke a tidal wave of economic ruin would be set in motion, gaining momentum as it swept westward across the plains.

That it would come, he had no doubt whatever. America's financial giants were locked in mortal combat—fighting for control of railroads, banks, and hundreds of millions in stock—and it was the unwary smallfry who would get crushed underfoot. Which was all very well as far as it went. But there was a missing link, and that's what had him stumped.

How to avoid the short end of the stick?

This knotty question seemed to defy answer. Two days now he had wrestled with it, discarding dozens of ideas that were either impractical or unworkable. With the problem isolated, logic seemingly deserted him. The harder he thought, the more frustrated he became, yet he doggedly refused to back off. There had to be a way. Something he'd overlooked. A key to that missing link, and through it, a clue to yet a larger riddle.

Abruptly his concentration was broken. He heard the rustle of skirts, and without turning knew that Sadie had come again to badger him. Over the past two days she had repeatedly invaded the parlor—dusting, moving furniture, cleaning lamps—despite his request that all household chores be set aside until he indicated otherwise. Housework was Mrs. Murphy's bailiwick anyway, so it was obvious that her sudden preoccupation with cleanliness was merely a pretext. She was in a snit, annoyed by his preoccupation, and apparently meant to distract him in every conceivable way. And she had succeeded admirably.

Sometimes Jake felt an almost irresistible urge to turn her across his knee and blister her rump good. Since Owen was born she had become a constant source of irritation. Seemingly, nothing he did could please her, and like a spoiled child, she was forever pestering him with selfish demands. That she had a house and a maid, fine gowns and her own buggy, wasn't enough. Apparently their social position in town, and the fact that it had made her into a lady, wasn't enough either. According to her, she had everything and nothing. Translated, that meant she wanted a ribbon clerk for a husband. Someone who was home every night, cooing like a turtle dove, so stuck on her he couldn't keep his pants buttoned.

And he found all this a little queer. From the outset Sadie had shared his dreams for the future, and before the baby was born she'd never once pitched a temper tantrum. But things had changed drastically since then. She was touchy as a scalded cat, always in a way that made him feel he'd done something wrong when all the time he knew he hadn't. It was damned confusing. Almost as if she'd married a man for what he was and then set out to turn him into what he wasn't. Which chafed him in all the wrong places, especially when she showed no signs of backing off.

Jake had given the matter considerable thought, and it seemed to him that women never quite got the hang of how a man looked at things. In his mind, a man's feelings were like the shafts of an old mine. The depth of those feelings existed on several levels, some darker than others; and at the very core, there were certain things that never saw the light of day.

Business came first of course, at least in Jake's scheme of things. A man spent most of his life and the greater part of his energy building something substantial. Not exactly a monument to himself, but something that would mark his passage more than a fancy headstone. Probably his son came next, for it was only right that a man invest of himself in the one who would carry on the line. Then, at another level came his wife, who deserved, and rightfully so, a good home, security, and a certain amount of affection. But there a man had to watch his step; women who demanded an overdose of affection had ruined many a poor soul before he ever rightly got started.

At the very core of what a man was (Jake tended to think of this as his soft spot) came something hard to define. Tenderness, warmth, compassion—he'd never quite been able to tag it with just the right word. But he knew that it had to be suppressed and kept buried; allowed to corrode until a thick shell insulated it against emotional blunders. Exposed to outside forces (especially females trying to plumb the soft spot), it could cause a man a world of grief. Long ago, he'd seen it happen to his daddy just that way, and he'd vowed then that it would never happen to him.

Not that he thought Sadie was the spiteful type, but it didn't pay to take chances. Better to keep the soft spot under tight rein; hold affection strictly to the physical. That way things rocked along on an even keel and nobody got their feelings hurt. The trouble was, Sadie had let her thinking get out of kilter somewhere along the line. Near as he could tell, it dovetailed pretty neatly with Owen being born. Which led him to believe that it might be a phenomenon peculiar to women with young babies. If so, it would pass, and he took a certain comfort in the belief that it was a temporary condition. All he had to do was let her sulk, and keep her happy in bed, and before long she would come to her senses again. Anyhow she'd better, and damned soon, too. It wore a man out, playing little games just to keep peace under his own roof.

If Jake was nettled by someone bustling around the parlor, Sadie was absolutely livid with curiosity, not to mention a mounting indignation. She slowly worked her way across the room with a featherduster (though she had dusted the place spotless only yesterday), determined that this time she would have it out with him. He had been brooding around the house for two days now—sour-tempered, withdrawn, ruminating within himself. Something had him deeply disturbed, but characteristically, he kept it bottled up inside. She knew it was bad, for he had completely ignored his business ventures, and that was astonishingly uncharacteristic of Jake Kincaid. She felt shut out, at a loss to explain his strange behavior. By whatever ruse, she meant to rattle his sphinxlike composure and get to the bottom of it right now.

She flicked the featherduster at nothing in particular, and moved a step closer. "Sugar, the house is on fire."

That struck him as absurdly childish, and suddenly, he refused to play. Half turning, he gave her a vacant nod. "Fine. Call me when it's done."

Sadie froze, speechless for just an instant. Then her temper flared, and her body seemed to quiver in a small paroxysm of rage. Tearing across the parlor, she halted beside the desk and shook her featherduster in his face.

"Damn you, Jake Kincaid, you didn't hear a word I said!"

"Like hell I didn't." He fixed her with a murderous glare. "And get that goddamned thing out of my face."

"You did hear me?"

"Course I heard you. I'm not deaf."

She brandished the featherduster like a shillelagh. "That does it! After everything else and now you treat me like the village idiot."

One eye on the featherduster, he studied her with an owlish frown. "What's that supposed to mean—everything else?"

"You haven't said *boo* to me in two days."

"I've been thinkin'. Got a lot on my mind."

"You haven't even looked at me."

"That's not so, and you know it."

"Oh, it's not, is it?" Her bludgeon descended in a feathery swish. "Then why do you roll over and play dead every night in bed?" Tears scalded her cheeks and she stamped her foot. "And don't you dare tell me you're thinking."

Jake wavered. Tears weren't included in Sadie's bag of tricks; she cried only as a last resort. But more than that, he had committed what he himself considered the cardinal sin. He had ignored her in bed, deprived her of the affection that was every wife's due.

"C'mere, spitfire." He took the featherduster from her

hand, tossed it aside, and pulled her into his lap. "You're right. I'm thoughtless and inconsiderate, and damn shy on excuses."

She snuffled something, choking back the tears, and buried her face against his shoulder. "Don't sweet-talk me, Jake. There's something wrong, and I want to know what it is."

"Just business, that's all. Nothin' to worry yourself about."

She pushed away, looking him straight in the eye. "Fiddlesticks. If it's just business, why aren't you out tending to it?"

"Honest to Christ, you're the most suspicious female I ever run across. I'm tellin' you, it's just business. Doesn't have a thing to do with us."

She straightened and jerked a handkerchief from her sleeve, dabbing at her eyes. "That's the cruelest thing you've ever said to me, Jake Kincaid. Since when did your troubles cease to be my troubles?" She scooted around, planting herself more firmly in his lap. "I intend to sit right here until you tell me. And I mean it too. I won't budge."

He managed a lopsided smile, convinced now that he couldn't weasel out of it. She was stubborn enough to sit there all day, and some lame story wasn't about to put her off. It had to be the real goods.

"Well, don't say you didn't ask for it." He took a deep breath, then let it out in a rush. "The big moneymen back east are scrappin' amongst themselves, and if I'm right, they're gonna pull the whole country down with them. Hard times are about to come knockin'."

Sadie's hand went out to him. "And you're afraid this will destroy everything you've built."

"Why, hell, no! Where'd you get an idea like that? The only thing I'm worried about is how to beat 'em to the punch."

"Beat them? You mean take advantage of it somehow?"

"Sadie, the time to get fat is when the other fellow's eatin' lean. A man that's got money in hard times can pretty well write his own ticket." He paused to rub his chin abstractedly. "Trouble is, the ideas I've come up with so far are kid's play.

Chickenfeed. Christ, do you realize I mightn't never get a chance like this again?"

Her expression was one of mild shock. "That wouldn't bother you—taking advantage of another man's hard luck? I suppose there's nothing illegal about it, but don't you think it's just a little—well, a little slippery?"

The thought apparently had never occurred to him. He chuckled softly. "Honey, a long time ago folks thought the earth was flat. Then some wiseacre convinced 'em it was round. But people finally wised up and figured out it's just plain crooked. Anybody that thinks different, and tries to act like the Good Samaritan, is a damn fool."

"So that makes it right, to tinker around with other men's lives?"

"God A'mighty, what's *right* got to do with anything? Men are the cheapest thing on earth. You buy 'em like soda crackers—by the pound or by the keg. That's the real truth of the matter, and nothin's changed it yet. All that stuff about 'your brother's keeper' is pure hogwash."

She gave him a tart glance. "The gospel according to Saint Jacob."

He grunted, and let out a gusty breath. "There's another old sayin'. If reason offends you, become a preacher. The world operates on certain rules, Sadie, and right has got nothin' to do with it. You monkey with the rules and you get spiked to a cross. The man from Galilee proved that the hard way."

Sadie looked away, silent a moment. She agreed that the world was that way. But she found it bitter as wormwood that her own husband fancied himself high priest of cynics. At last, she sighed and turned back.

"I don't know much about it, but maybe there's a way to help somebody else while you're feathering your own nest."

Jake eyed her skeptically, somewhat underwhelmed by this radical line of thought. "Yeah, how's that?"

"Well, if money and mortgages and things like that get tight, won't the farmers back east be hit hardest of all?"

"Sure they would. Fact is, it'll get them first."

Sadie brightened. "Then that's your answer. All you have to do is work out a way to sell them some of your land and give them a fresh start."

Time was arrested, almost as if Jake had gone into a trance. After a long while his words came in a hoarse mutter. "Goddamn if I don't think you've put your thumb right on it."

"Really, sugar?" Sadie clapped her hands and jiggled around on his lap. "Do you really think it will work?"

"Not just the way you meant, but it sure gave me the clue I've been lookin' for. Now if a certain fellow in Topeka thinks the same way, we'll be up to our ears in clover."

She pouted. "That means you'll be going out of town."

He stood, lifting her in his arms. "Train won't leave till after supper. That give you any ideas?"

Her lashes fluttered in kittenish guile. "You're a naughty man, Jake Kincaid. And the answer is yes."

Bess Murphy was a bit startled to see the mister carry his lady into the bedroom—in broad daylight. But she was too old to blush and long past being shocked by the goatlike ways of men. She retreated to the kitchen, curiously short of breath, and tried not to think about it.

The bubble burst in late September. Jay Cooke & Company, most prestigious financial institution in the country, closed its doors at a quarter past noon as torrents of rain pelted Wall Street. That afternoon thirty-seven banks and brokerage houses went under. An hour later, the board of governors suspended trade on the New York Stock Exchange. And before the debacle ran its course, five thousand businesses would be forced into bankruptcy.

The Panic of '73 was at last under way.

Perhaps of greater consequence to Jake Kincaid was the devastating effect on the nation's railroads. Investment capital simply withered overnight, and construction on the western lines slammed to a halt. This was essential to the plan he had devised back in July. Other than himself and his connection at the State House (who would provide the necessary political clout), the scheme remained a closely guarded secret. Now, on a gloomy October morning, as he emerged from his hotel in Topeka, he was gripped by a sense of exhilaration. He felt alive, galvanized with strength, invincible in what he was about to undertake. Attired in a conservative frock coat and matching vest, glowing with the ruddy vitality of a man on the rise, he set out at a brisk pace toward the corporate offices of the Santa Fe Railroad.

All things considered, Jake had reason to congratulate himself that morning. The economic collapse had come about just as he predicted, although it had taken somewhat longer than he anticipated. Still, he had curbed his impatience, no small feat in itself, and spent the time adding polish to his plan. When the nation's financial institutions crumbled in ruin he moved swiftly, driving ruthless bargains with those who had been caught short.

Banks in Wichita and other Kansas communities found themselves in perilous straits. Those that managed to stay afloat were forced to call in all outstanding loans, and quickly suspended activity on new loans. At the same time, the cattle market hit bottom, hovered there a couple of days, and then simply sank out of sight. Cattlemen were caught in a particularly vicious squeeze. Whenever the fall market dipped they were accustomed to taking loans on their herds, wintering the longhorns south of Wichita, and then selling when prices peaked in the spring. But this year the banks had no money to lend, and the Texans were faced with a disaster of monumental proportions.

With close to a quarter-million longhorns stranded in Kansas, a man could virtually name his own price. Which was exactly what Jake did. The Texans were willing to accept any offer, reasonable or otherwise, and his take-it-or-leave-it price was ten cents on the dollar. Before the first week of the panic ended, he had himself twenty thousand cows and a small army of grateful cowhands to herd them through the winter. It was speculation involving high risk, but just as he had foreseen the collapse, he felt equally confident that the cattle market would recover before another summer passed.

His next foray was among landowners, who were hit almost as hard as the Texans. Working through his lawyers, he snapped up vast blocks of acreage outside Wichita, Newton, and Great Bend. Again, at his own price, ten cents on the dollar. When it was finished he had something more than $100,000—every penny he possessed—riding on the line. Even for a gambling man, it was the ultimate gamble, and it all rested on the turn of the last card.

This fortnight of wheeling and dealing served yet another useful purpose. Caught up in laying the groundwork, Jake was restrained from playing his hole card until the timing was exactly right. With the panic in full swing, and venture capital nonexistent, the railroads were trapped in an acute financial bind. He had done his homework well over the past few months, subjecting the highly devious art of railroad building to close scrutiny, and his conviction remained strong that he had come at last to the right spot at the right time.

Railroading in America, as practiced in the decade following the Civil War, was a classic study in chicanery, graft, and political skulduggery. Stocks were universally manipulated for the enrichment of a small inner circle; the taint of corruption touched Senators and Congressmen by the score; at least one Vice President; and ultimately a man who was later elected to the highest office in the land. It was an era of boldness and daring, and unparalleled access to the public coffers. What amounted, in a very real sense, to a license to steal.

As an inducement to build west, the railroads were awarded government land grants which in a few short years encompassed millions upon millions of acres of public domain. These grants were in the form of alternate sections (640 acres) along the railroad-right-of-way, stretching from ten to fifty miles in depth depending on how well the promoters had greased their political cronies. Congress and various state legislatures were corrupted with stock, campaign contributions, and outright payoffs; they became, in effect, the tool of the robber barons, affably passing legislation favorable to their benefactors. The railroads were the first great lobby in American politics, and in their day and time, it became an incontestable fact of life that they wielded the power of ducal lords.

Yet these audacious builders of empires had a common flaw—they were hardheaded individualists who fought savagely among themselves—and it was this congenital weakness that Jake Kincaid meant to exploit. Over the years internecine warfare had flared sporadically as one robber baron raided the holdings of another. Jay Gould and Jim Fisk had given Commodore Vanderbilt one of the few shellackings of his life. Edward Harriman and James Hill had battered one another bloody with dynamite, legal shenanigans, and pickax handles. Pierpont Morgan had annihilated Jay Cooke through subterfuge and yellow journalism, inadvertently triggering the Panic of '73.

And from the carnage of this financial holocaust, like a phoenix rising from the ashes, emerged a bearded, squint-eyed little genius who threatened to devour all the rest. With railroad stocks paper-cheap, and investors fleeing for cover, Jay Gould promptly gobbled up the Union Pacific, the Kansas Pacific, the Denver Pacific, the Missouri Pacific, the Central Pacific, and the Texas & Pacific. He stood on the threshold of becoming czar of all the railroads, and only one major line remained free of his tentacles—the Atchison, Topeka & Santa Fe.

The Santa Fe was the brainchild of Cecil Hollister, something of a buccaneer in his own right. He had organized the line, whip-sawed counties into voting bond issues for working capital, and finagled nearly three million acres in land grants from the territorial legislature. Along the way, he was instrumental in making Topeka the capital city, and by no mere happenstance, became the single most influential man in Kansas while it was still a fledgling territory. And it was this man, a rough-and-tumble fighter of the old school, whom Jake Kincaid meant to beard in his own den.

Since late September, watching events unfold as the panic widened, Jake had at last found the key he sought. A thumb-screw of sorts, which he meant to apply to Cecil Hollister with finesse yet with whatever force the situation demanded.

The Santa Fe was stripped of cash. Construction had halted west of Dodge City and there was barely enough operating capital to keep the line running from Topeka to the end of track. Station agents and conductors were working without pay so that engineers and firemen, without whom there would be no railroad, could draw their regular wages. It was a grim predicament, brightened none at all by the ever-present shadow of Jay Gould, who was eyeing the Santa Fe as his next victim. Cecil Hollister recognized the danger, as did his major stockholders, and it was only by the skin of their teeth that they had held on so far.

Which was precisely the wedge Jake Kincaid meant to employ. He was betting everything he possessed on a single turn of the card, and in truth, it was nothing more than a monumental bluff. But Cecil Hollister had far more to lose; the stakes he wagered were millions of dollars and an entire railroad. And given those odds, Jake never doubted for a moment that he could have suckered God himself.

When he was ushered into Hollister's office shortly after ten, exuding confidence and good cheer, he had the look of a man sitting on a lead-pipe cinch. Striding forward, he smiled and stuck out his hand.

"Mr. Hollister, I'm Jake Kincaid. I believe our mutual friend at the State House mentioned you could expect me this morning."

The surprises came hard and fast after that. Hollister was big as a bear, which he hadn't expected, and came near crushing his hand. But if the sheer girth of the man was intimidating, his manner was imperious as that of a king. With a patronizing nod he waved Jake to a chair, and resumed his seat behind a desk only slightly smaller than a Santa Fe boxcar.

"Kincaid, I'm not a man to mince words. You pulled some strings and our—mutual friend—insisted I see you. That entitles you to about five minutes." He took a diamond-studded pocket watch from his vest, snapped open the case, and laid it on the desk. "In the railroad business everything runs on schedule, and that includes me. We're on your time, so start talking."

This was hardly the way Jake had envisioned the meeting, and there was a moment of strained silence as he appraised the man across from him. Hollister had the look of a molting owl with a severe case of constipation. He was bald, with a white fringe over his ears and snowy muttonchop sideburns connected to a bushy mustache. His broad face was open, though scarcely amiable, and his restless eyes mirrored a quick, searching mind. Judged on past performances, he had all the social instincts of a cobra, and it was said he would spit in the Devil's eye to make the Santa Fe the dominant line on the western plains.

Staring into that remote gaze, listening to the watch tick away the seconds, Jake could believe it. Just for an instant he felt like a harelip kid trying to recite poetry. Which was a bit unsettling to a fellow who seldom blinked in a staring contest. Then, quite suddenly, he recalled the tenet that had served him well in Abilene and Wichita. Perhaps the governing tenet in gaining the upper hand in any showdown. What made a man powerful was not his real strength, but rather his strength in the eyes of others. Hollister was using the same tactic—on him! And yet it was he who held all the aces in this game.

Collecting himself, he settled back in his chair and pulled out a long black cigar. He flicked a sulfurhead to life on his thumbnail, took his time about lighting the cigar, and at last blew a roiling cloud of smoke across the desk. Back deep in that remote gaze he saw a tiny shadow of uncertainty spring to life, and he smiled, once more himself. Not cocky but supremely confident, and inwardly amused by a stray thought. Hollister didn't know it just yet, but this was the morning he had bit off more than he could chew.

"Mr. Hollister, a little bird tells me the Santa Fe has its back to the wall. What would you say to that?"

Hollister arched one eyebrow and looked down his nose. "I'd say your little bird has been sniffing goofer dust."

"Well now, that's funny. The same little bird tells me Jay Gould is breathing down your neck sort of hot and heavy."

Hollister's expression betrayed nothing.

Several moments elapsed; then Jake smiled and examined the coal on the tip of his cigar. "Suppose I showed you a way the Santa Fe could bail out financially and get the jump on your competition. Think you could spare more than five minutes?"

Hollister studied him a second, then closed the cover on the watch and tucked it back in his vest. His manner was still condescending, but he now seemed curiously attentive. "By all means, Mr. Kincaid—enlighten me."

Jake deliberated an instant longer, aware that his entire plan hinged on the questions he was about to ask. At last, after a leisurely puff on his cigar, he looked up. "The Santa Fe's land-poor, isn't that so?"

"As are all railroads. That's common knowledge."

"And you don't know how to unload it, correct?"

"I wouldn't say that"—however reluctant, the words were a tacit admission—"we have several proposals under consideration."

"I would've been surprised if you didn't, Mr. Hollister." Leaning forward, Jake flicked ashes into a cuspidor. "You know, it's a queer thing. I own some land, too. About five hundred thousand acres. Most of it along Santa Fe right-of-way." He paused, allowing Hollister to digest that, and settled back in his chair. "What I'm suggesting is that we join forces. You give me an ironclad contract as Santa Fe land agent and I'll show you how to lure immigrants out here by the carload."

"Did I understand you to say immigrants?"

"That's right, Mr. Hollister—foreigners."

"Just for the sake of argument, we'll suppose you could do that. What would you expect in return?"

"Ten percent of everything I sell for the Santa Fe and the right to sell my own land at the same time. Since the Homestead Act limits settlers to a hundred sixty acres, we'd go after the people who want big farms. Naturally, seeing as we own the big blocks of land between us, we'd fix the price and hold to it firm."

Hollister began a quick reappraisal of the younger man. He looked to be in his late twenties, maybe younger, but there was a hardness about him that had little to do with age and everything to do with experience. And what he'd just proposed was a damned shrewd idea. Simple and tinged with larceny, as good ideas generally were. Whether it would work remained to be seen.

"Let's just say I'm interested. Tell me more."

"Glad to. It gets a little tricky in spots, so you just jump in if I go too fast."

Haltingly at first, he began outlining the details of his plan. But as he warmed to the subject, he dumped his cigar in the cuspidor and started pounding one meaty fist into the other to emphasize the step-by-step machinations he had engineered so carefully. The scheme was simple in design, yet complex in its execution, involving a regiment of land agents, heavy promotion expenditures, and a bit of hocus-pocus that would have dazzled a medicine show pitchman. Several minutes passed, the timbre of his voice mounting with excitement, and not once did Hollister interrupt. When he at last concluded, the railroad baron was up on the edge of his chair, eyes bright and his face slightly flushed.

After what seemed a long while, Hollister smiled. "Mr. Kincaid, I underestimated you. That's the slickest piece of thinking I've heard in years. Suppose we call my aides in and you repeat it for them just the way you told it to me. I'd like to get their opinion before I give you a firm answer either way."

Jake regarded him with an inscrutable look. "No—I'd just as soon we keep it to ourselves till after I get your answer."

"I presume you have a reason, if you don't mind my asking."

"Let's say there are a couple of reasons. If you accept, then we'll shake hands and we're off to the races. But if you turn me down and then use the plan, I'll know who crossed me."

"That sounds like a threat."

"It is."

Hollister cocked his head in mild disbelief. "You'd actually kill me?"

Jake riveted him with a cold glare. "Deader'n a doornail."

A turgid silence settled over the room. Hollister met and held his gaze, fully aware at last of how badly he had underestimated the younger man. He had been warned that Kincaid played rough, but he hardly expected this. The insolent bastard actually would kill him! Then, in a sudden flash of introspection, Hollister perceived that he and Kincaid were two of a kind. What they were discussing was honor, and neither of them was a man to be troubled by meaningless abstractions. After a moment's sardonic reflection, he was forced to admit Kincaid had a point. A man who relied on trust rather than muscle and hardheaded pragmatism would soon find himself jiggling a beggar's cup.

"Kincaid, anybody with that much brass is a man after my own heart." He rose, smiling widely, and lumbered around the desk. "You have yourself a deal. My hand on it."

Jake shook hands and gave him a tight grin. "Long as it's a deal, I don't suppose you'd be insulted if we got it on paper. Nice and legal like—just so there won't be any loose ends."

Hollister smote him across the back and let go a woofing roar of laughter. And as quickly as that an unspoken accord passed between them. Partners they would become, perhaps even friends. But just as they trusted no man, never would they trust one another. Given the nature of the game, and the stakes for which they played, it was a most sensible arrangement. Perhaps the only arrangement for birds of a feather.

THREE

That winter Jake seldom paused to catch his breath. He worked eighteen-hour days, seven days a week, existing on coffee, a meal snatched here and there, and quick naps that passed for sleep. But he thrived on this spartan regimen. His energy was boundless, and he seemed to be everywhere at once—which was yet another illusion he had learned to employ in the management of men and things. Faced with ever-growing demands from his diverse interests, Jake grudgingly conceded he could no longer juggle the work load by himself. Time had become a relentless adversary, and however reluctantly, he was forced to delegate authority in certain critical areas.

Quincy Blackburn was promoted to overseer of all Wichita enterprises. This included the Lady Gay, several stores leased to merchants, and the Occidental Hotel. The moon-faced gambler had proved himself a capable businessman, if somewhat fond of unorthodox methods, and Jake allowed him a degree of freedom in day-by-day operations. That the trust was not misplaced soon became evident. Blackburn reveled in his position of importance, and displayed a flair for boosting profits.

Another vital post was filled by Jigger Musgrave, a Texan trailboss stranded in Kansas by the Panic of '73. Musgrave was tough as whang leather, known for his prodigious consumption of snakehead whiskey and an absolute genius at demolishing saloons. But he had forgotten more about long-horns than most men ever knew, and as a ramrod, had the knack of molding fiddle-footed cowhands into a reliable, hard-working crew. Jake made him foreman of the entire cattle operation, with the authority to do as he saw fit in bringing the steers through safely to spring market. Musgrave hired himself a crew, split the cows into twenty small herds, and scattered them across the watered grasslands down near the Nations. Then he spent the winter patrolling far-flung line camps as if the longhorns were a family legacy. Again, Jake's judgment of men proved unerring; under Musgrave the cattle operation functioned smoothly and without mishap as a blustery winter settled over the plains.

With Blackburn and Musgrave to shoulder much of the load, Jake brought his full energies to bear on the land scheme. Cecil Hollister had been as good as his word (and the contract which required some three days of haggling). Jake was appointed sole land agent of the Santa Fe, with what amounted to autonomous power, and the board of directors appropriated $50,000 for promotion expenditures. Turned loose, money in hand and his imagination spinning, Jake set in motion a program which was to revolutionize the railroads' slipshod methods of converting land grants into ready cash.

Quickly, he hired men who were to form the nucleus of his organization. With the Panic in full bloom, bunco men, grifters, and thimbleriggers were a dime a dozen, and these swift-thinking slick-talkers were precisely what the job demanded. That they had got in on the ground floor of a legitimate undertaking—which had all the overtones of a sophisticated con game—tickled their fancy and seemed to make them work all the harder. So far as they could see, it was simply a refined version of bait the sucker and sink the gaff, only in this case they had nothing whatever to fear from the law.

At the same time, Jake hired a Chicago journalist to write an elaborate, profusely illustrated guidebook of some fifty pages extolling a Garden of Eden known by the more prosaic name of Kansas. This guidebook, along with circulars and a series of advertisements, depicted windswept prairie as farm soil rich beyond belief. Then he imported a professor of languages from the east and had all of the literature translated into German, Dutch, Swedish, French, Danish, and Russian. Afterward, a Topeka printer worked his presses night and day printing bales of material, first in English and then in the foreign versions.

Once he was set, Jake opened the campaign with a salvo that reverberated across the Atlantic and beyond. Advertisements appeared in newspapers throughout heavily populated rural areas of eastern America and Europe; a blizzard of circulars materialized overnight on fenceposts and trees across two continents. Hard on the heels of this opening broadside came a small army of articulate, highly persuasive lecturers. Their lectures were free and open to the public, whether they spoke in Cedar Rapids or Düsseldorf; more often than not they appeared under the auspices of the Emigrant Aid Society. And the message they preached was a heady one indeed.

Vast blocks of farmland, ripe with thick black topsoil, never touched by a plow. Available to anyone on terms of a modest down payment and eleven years to pay off the balance (at an equally modest interest rate). Special trains at special prices to transport them west, including the new "Zulu" boxcar specially engineered to hold their furniture, farm implements, and livestock. A new start in a bountiful land, where opportunity beckoned and the rich earth yielded abundance beyond man's comprehension. The stuff of dreams—heady, seductive, all but irresistible. And it brought them west in one of the world's great displacements of humanity. A migration of peoples and Old World cultures unlike any in recorded history.

Perhaps no one was more astounded than Jake Kincaid himself. He had expected a solid response, envisioning a gradual but steadily growing influx of immigrants, but this westward flood of settlers caught him completely off guard. Though he was at a loss to explain it (unless the world was in sadder shape than even he suspected), he kept his own counsel and allowed Cecil Hollister to believe it was part and parcel of the master plan. Hollister went further, though, labeling it a stroke of genius, and it shortly became apparent that the competition agreed wholeheartedly.

By early spring every railroad west of the Missouri had duplicated Jake's program virtually to the last detail. While he had the jump on them by several months, and was swamped with a mounting avalanche of inquiries, the contest for more affluent immigrants grew keener every day. Shady tactics surfaced; some of his best men were bribed to switch sides; every line in the west scrambled to build an organization of glib, honey-tongued hucksters to peddle their dusty bonanza. And as this fledgling boom steamrollered into the summer of '74, the competition went from tricky to just plain dirty.

After several immigrant parties were shanghaied by rival lines—spirited from dockside to waiting trains—Jake kept a stream of his own agents shuttling back and forth between Topeka and New York. They met every boat at the pier, took the prospective land purchasers in hand, and wet-nursed them through the long ride to Santa Fe territory. There they were greeted warmly (with the Professor delivering a welcoming speech in the proper language), fed a hearty meal, and immediately hustled off for a look at the Garden of Eden. The endless prairie, flat as a billiard table, never failed to impress them, for it was virgin farmland of immense potential. But whatever their reaction, their signatures were soon affixed to the dotted line. Jake ran a fast, slick operation, allowing them one day to locate a chunk of land which appealed to their particular needs. Then the soft soap disappeared, and through various pressures (some less subtle than others), they were induced to sign the contract which separated them from their horde of gold. The Santa Fe agent then wished them luck, hurried back to Topeka, and began his pitch with a fresh collection of pioneers. It worked marvelously well, and money poured in by the tubfuls.

With some justification, Jake's conviction grew stronger than ever that he was possessed of the magic touch. His commissions on Santa Fe land, added to sales of his own land, would soon rank him among the wealthiest men in Kansas. The various Wichita enterprises continued to coin a small mint, for even in hard times people gambled and caroused, perhaps with greater abandon than when they were flush. And as Jake had predicted, beef-hungry easterners created a meat shortage that winter, and slaughterhouses sent the cattle market spiraling to record heights. In early May, he sold his steers at the peak, and after expenses, cleared a tidy $186,000. All in all, he could be excused for occasionally gloating over his own good fortune.

The only irritant he faced was constant bedevilment by competing railroads, but even that was not without its lighter moments. Late in May, he had personally escorted a train-load of Germans to inspect land west of Newton. They were among the more affluent immigrants to arrive that spring, and he felt that with a bit of coaxing they could be persuaded to buy a huge tract outside the town of Great Bend. But however much they seemed to like the land (and he had shown them several choice parcels throughout the day), he'd been unable to force a decision. Toward sundown, perplexed and thoroughly irate, he at last detected a rat. A man dressed in immigrant clothes had been circulating among the Germans all day, constantly whispering in their ears. Upon closer observation, Jake decided there was something peculiar about the fellow. Just a hunch, but at that point he was grasping at straws.

He attempted to engage the man in conversation, but was met with smiles and shrugs and some gibberish about not speaking English. Then he noticed the Germans had sidled off—oddly reluctant to help their comrade—and that clinched it. All smiles and bonhomie, he took the fellow's arm and marched him around to the other side of the engine. There the smile faded, and he stuck the muzzle of a Colt .44 in the man's bellybutton.

"Mister, if you don't sprecken the English by the time I count three, you're gonna spring a mighty bad leak."

Not only did the man speak flawless English, it soon came clear that he was in the employ of the Kansas & Pacific. He had infiltrated the German party back in Topeka, and had them all but sold on a stretch of land along the Smoky Hill. Jake liked his style, though, and hired him on the spot. Then, with an assist from his new associate, he settled the Germans on ten thousand acres just east of Great Bend. Never a man to overlook a good idea, Jake later used the same trick on several of his competitors.

And in a fearsome sort of way, everyone shafted everyone else on into the summer.

But Jake's organization had the other lines outclassed, and it was the Sante Fe that invariably landed the big fish. Early in June he was approached by a British syndicate calling itself the Western Land & Cattle Company. Englishmen had recently become enamored with the American west, and London investment capital was suddenly plentiful. Still, this particular group was composed of British aristocracy, including members of Queen Victoria's family, and represented a prize catch. Jake knew that these men had been feted royally by several railroads, but he sensed something about them that his competitors had missed. They were practical, hardheaded businessmen, with an inbred immunity to the colonial red-carpet treatment. And he had an inkling that they were just the least bit pinch-penny.

After three days of looking at land he brought them back to Cecil Hollister's office. They were suitably impressed with a tract northeast of Wichita encompassing some seventy square miles. But they haggled like fishwives over price, confirming his earlier suspicion—a stiff bargain was more important to them than the site itself. Kansas or Wyoming made little difference; dollars were the point at issue. Cigars and whiskey were served, and after some perfunctory small-talk, everyone settled back for what they knew would be the final round of dickering.

"Gentlemen, I think you've made a wise choice." Jake cocked his head and nodded, as if thinking out loud. "Good graze, plenty of water—and near a railhead. That's a hard combination to beat."

The three Englishmen just stared at him, unmoved by this favorable commentary on their wisdom. Some moments passed before their spokesman, a stuffy earl with watery eyes, finally fashioned a riposte.

"My dear Kincaid, I dislike redundancy, but you seem frightfully determined to avoid the issue. Your price is simply too high. Frankly, we are inclined toward a most generous proposal from the Union Pacific."

Jake pursed his lips. "I suppose they told you about the winters they have up that way—awful hard on cows. Course, down here our weather's milder, and cows just naturally do better."

"Yes, but at the risk of repeating myself, I must again mention a disparity in price of twenty-five thousand dollars. I daresay that would compensate us handsomely for those harsh winters. Now, you're jolly good fellows and all that—and we do like your land—but I'm afraid some adjustment is necessary if we're to do business."

"You know, there might be a way at that." Jake gave the ceiling a moment of heavy contemplation. "I'm thinking of a reduction in freight rates." Out of the corner of his eye he saw Hollister stiffen, and he rushed on. "Let's say that over the next five years the Santa Fe will rebate twenty-five thousand dollars of the usual charge for cattle shipments. Seems to me that's a fair compromise."

Hollister groaned softly, and the earl fixed him with a stuffed-owl look. "I say, isn't that sort of thing considered—somewhat irregular?"

Jake smiled his lopsided, faintly sardonic smile. "Not if we don't tell anybody about it, it's not."

And that's how they worked it out. A gentlemen's agreement between British aristocrats and western buccaneers. Later, after contracts were signed and the Englishmen had departed, Jake could scarcely contain himself. But Hollister was glum and thoughtful, forehead wrinkled in a scowl, clearly disturbed.

"Not to mention being risky, you're suddenly very liberal with the Santa Fe's money."

"Cecil, there's all kind of ways to skin a cat. Today we separated those birds from a hundred and fifty thousand dollars. Tomorrow you can raise your freight rates. Then next year you raise 'em a little higher. And when it's all said and done, Earl what's-his-name will have paid you a bundle he thought he'd saved. Which just goes to prove the grifter's old proverb—the easiest man to outslick is the one with larceny in his heart."

Jake helped himself to another drink, and a trace of mockery crept into his voice. "Hell, if you were a sportin' man you'd give me a commission on that freight raise I just put through for the Santa Fe."

Hollister wasn't amused. Nor could he bring himself to meet the younger man's brazen look. All of a sudden he felt like an aging larcenist who had himself been outslicked. And it occurred to him that it likely wasn't the first time. Or the last, unless he somehow put a leash on this hungry carnivore he'd turned loose on Kansas.

Jake Kincaid savored life like a drunken god. What he wanted, he took, and all he sought had been found. Had he been a philosophical man he might have pondered the deeper significance of his meteoric success; explored the root causes and dared to probe the phantom tides with affect each man's race with time. But he remained the eternal pragmatist, a creature of expediency and determination who gloried in his own godlike vitality.

That he was gifted with uncanny foresight, and the iron will to flaunt all odds, few men doubted any longer. Within the span of nine months he had brought the Santa Fe from the brink of bankruptcy to the top of the heap. Working tirelessly, and sometimes ruthlessly, he had created the funds to stave off Jay Gould, and provided the wherewithal for the Santa Fe to accelerate expansion toward the distant Rockies. At the same time, while much of the nation wallowed in economic chaos, he had brought prosperity to southern Kansas. The settlers were an infusion of new blood and new money, both of which were needed desperately by communities struggling for their very existence.

And in Wichita, where cattle was still king, his presence had been no less instrumental in shaking off the doldrums. He counseled town leaders and businessmen to hold firm, expressing confidence that beef prices would rise, and that, come spring, the Texas herds would return. His optimism was contagious, and just as he predicted, it all came true. Though America had been a nation of pork eaters before the Civil War, its masses had developed a fondness for rich, red beef in the years since. Supply and demand exerted its inexorable leverage on the marketplace, and eastern slaughterhouses sent up an urgent clamor for more cows. The first herd appeared in late May, and in the month since, the Chisholm Trail had been choked with a dusty, bawling sea of longhorns. Wichita had weathered the storm, come through the panic bruised but unbroken, and prosperity returned once more with the golden-hooved horde.

As for Jake personally, he had made a fortune in this period of hard times. Oddly enough, though, the people of southern Kansas displayed neither envy nor loathing for the man who had grown wealthy on the misfortune of others. Instead, they held him in even higher esteem, fascinated by his wily maneuvers, and credited him with driving the wolf from their doors. Businessmen now sought him out, asking advice; the town council was more than ever an instrument of his will; and his political influence in Topeka was slowly spreading throughout every level of state government. In two years he had come far, higher than most men dared dream, his reach exceeded only by his grasp.

Yet, with all he had, Jake wanted more. Not money particularly, or even more land. Nor was it the esteem of others, for he had a low opinion of his fellow citizens, and considerably less tolerance for mankind in general. What goaded him onward was some obsessive urge that revealed itself to him in fits and starts. In rare moments of introspection (for he was not a man given to self-scrutiny) Jake supposed the lodestone was most likely power. Having acquired a modicum of wealth, and with it, the secret of how one tapped the horn of plenty, it seemed only natural that he would attempt to scale some greater obstacle. But there his thinking became a bit murky, and that greater obstacle somehow ill-defined. Power to what end? Power over people or things—or both? Or perhaps merely power for power's sake? He wasn't sure, and no ready answer presented itself. Like all of life's riddles, most of which he had solved to his own satisfaction, it wasn't something to be rushed. Take it apart and put it back together again. Toy with it. Slowly reduce it to its fundamentals. And one day, in a sudden little twitch, it would all come clear.

Then he would not only know the nature of the power he sought, but more important, what to do with it. That in itself was perhaps the first fundamental, for in Jake's mind a thing without purpose had no value. The end must justify the means, yet there was still a higher level, where both the end and the means must justify the effort.

On a Sunday, late in June, he sat at his desk, idly toying with this new puzzle. Before him were stacks of paper work— payment vouchers, contracts, miscellaneous correspondence— all demanding his attention. But it was a warm, lazy morning, where the blast of the sun had not yet seared the earth, and he found it damnably difficult to concentrate. Gazing out across the river, his mood listless and dawdling, he amused himself with his new plaything. It was a diversion of sorts, a momentary respite from his crushing work load, but deadly serious all the same. Just as he never wasted effort in his work, so was his playtime meant to pay dividends. Not today perhaps, or even tomorrow, but soon. When he at last discovered the character and purpose of this thing so loosely defined as power.

Jake suddenly sensed he wasn't alone. Out of the corner of his eye he saw his son crouched low, sneaking ever so carefully, a step at a time, across the parlor. It was a game they played. Owen was the Indian, naturally, and Jake's topknot the prize. But to claim the trophy Owen must approach stealthily, quiet as a skulking Comanche, and spring unobserved on his father's back. Jake usually let him win, surrendering his scalp in a ritual of mock terror that never failed to delight the boy.

Intent on the game, eyes glistening with excitement, Owen skirted the divan and crept closer. He was big for a boy going on three, built like his father, already thick through the shoulders and his chubby features beginning to assume the square jaw and ridged brow of a Kincaid. An unruly cowlick leaped out from sandy curls and there was that same look of quiet determination about him. Bess Murphy called him a "spitting image of the mister," and in that she was right. He was a miniature Jake Kincaid, childlike but sprouting fast.

And in a last silent rush, he leaped as high as he could, pouncing on his father's shoulder. Jake obligingly rolled out of the chair, moaning pitifully as the boy swarmed over him. Owen screeched wildly, clutching at the treasured scalplock with his tiny fists, and Jake thrashed about frantically, finally scrambling to his hands and knees. This, too, was part of the ritual, and in an instant the boy hopped aboard his back, transformed magically from Indian to Texas cowhand. Jake, just as magically, became the horse. Owen spurred him hard, whooping a childish imitation of the Rebel yells he'd heard downtown, and Jake went bucking across the parlor in great froglike leaps.

Abruptly, horse and rider slammed to a halt. Before them was a voluminous patch of mauve satin, and higher still, an even more insurmountable obstacle—the young cowhand's disapproving mother. Sadie gave them a look of tart annoyance, arms folded primly at her waist.

"Jake, I talk till I'm blue in the face and you don't hear a word I've said. He's just a baby, and you play too rough. What if he fell off, or hit his head on something? How would you feel then?"

Uncoiling from the floor, Jake swung Owen over his shoulders and tossed him high in the air. The boy screamed in terrified glee and Jake caught him up in a growling bear hug. After a moment of nuzzling the youngster's neck with his bristly mustache, Jake lowered him to the floor, spun him about, and gave him a playful swat on the rump. The boy started back for more but Sadie caught his arm. She was pregnant again, some five months along, and had difficulty stooping over. But she held him till he quieted down, smoothing back his cowlick, and then kissed him on the cheek.

"Now, sweetheart, I want you to run along and play with your train. Get all the cars lined up just exactly right, and when you're ready, I'll come help. Go ahead, now, like a good boy."

Owen cast a beseeching look up at his father, but Jake winked and jerked his chin—a man-to-man signal that they'd best play along. The boy hung his head a moment, then brightened in the mercurial way of small boys, and scooted off toward the far side of the parlor. Roughhousing with his father was the best fun of all, but the train wasn't a bad idea. It had been a gift from Cecil Hollister, an exact replica of a Santa Fe passenger train, and he spent hours each day chugging it around the house. And sometimes, when he chugged it through the kitchen, he came away with cookies and all kinds of special treats.

Sadie watched after him a moment, waiting till he was out of earshot, then flashed Jake a stormy look. "Honestly, you're turning him into a little ruffian. And don't you dare tell me boys are supposed to be tough. There is time enough for that when he gets bigger."

Jake grinned and turned away. "You've got your dander up 'cause I won't let you make a mama's boy out of him." He seated himself at the desk and began shuffling papers. "Sadie, he's all Kincaid, which means he's about half barbarian, so you might as well quit frettin' about it and just let nature take its course."

"And I suppose you mean to sit there and work all day?" She rushed over to the desk, not yet ungainly but large enough that swift movements had become awkward. "Well, I just won't have it, Jake Kincaid. I simply won't stand for it."

He knew morning sickness left her in a foul mood, but generally he was out and gone before she awakened. Today looked to be his day in the sticker patch, though. Setting the papers aside, he twisted around in his chair.

"There's a week's work jammed up here, and it's got to be on the mornin' train to Topeka. But I'm willin' to make allowances as best I can. Now, what did you have in mind?"

His sudden turnabout took her by surprise. She was spoiling for a fight, and his conciliatory manner left her momentarily nonplussed. She shifted from foot to foot, undecided, and her temper slowly fizzled away.

"Well, I guess your work does have to be done." She faltered, then just as quickly collected herself. "But that's no reason to ruin a whole Sunday. Mrs. Murphy has a ham baking, and after dinner I think a buggy ride in the country would be nice. Owen would enjoy it, and I could certainly use some fresh air myself."

"You've got yourself a deal. I'll work till dinnertime, then we'll go strut our stuff and do a little rubbernecking." He started back to his papers, then caught himself and threw her a searching glance. "Say, what about your condition?

You sure a buggy ride won't—uh—well, you know, jostle things up?"

She scoffed at the idea. "I've never felt better in my life. Dr. Quillman says I'm healthy as a horse. Although I'm not sure I appreciate the comparison."

Jake's features darkened in a scowl. "The less I hear about that quack, the better. Him and his goddamn lamb skins. I still think I should've stretched one over his head and dumped him in the river."

Quillman had explained that the lamb skins were a new product, still unperfected, but as yet the best safety device available. Sadie accepted his explanation, but Jake had yet to simmer down. The fact remained that one of the devices had failed at a most unfortunate moment, and Sadie was pregnant. And Jake deeply regretted that he hadn't strangled the little sawbones the very night it happened.

"Sugar, it was an accident," Sadie chided softly. "Things like that happen, and there's absolutely nothing to worry about. You just wait and see if I'm not right." She gave him a vixenish smile. "Besides, I wanted another child, and so far as I'm concerned, the Good Lord just settled it in his own way. So if you want to yell at someone, take it up with him instead of scolding Dr. Quillman."

Unaccountably, a chill settled over Jake. It passed quickly enough, but it left behind a residue of uneasiness. When he answered there was a defensive gruffness about his words that he couldn't disguise.

"Maybe so, but the Good Lord should've had better sense. Him and Quillman between 'em managed to get us in a pretty pickle."

"Horsefeathers! You're just a born worrywart and that's all there is to it." She leaned over and gave him a naughty kiss. "Now finish up with your silly papers. You have about thirty minutes before Mrs. Murphy serves dinner, and that, Mr. Kincaid, is the end of your work day."

She flounced off with a swish of her hips, quite pleased

with the way she had delivered the ultimatum. Joining Owen across the room, she gingerly lowered herself to the floor and began helping him connect a string of coach cars to the engine. But once the train was assembled, and the boy had lost himself in a make-believe world of fiery cinders and chuffing smoke, her gaze drifted back to the desk.

Jake was staring out the window, his paper work again forgotten. At times like this, when he was absorbed in one of his inner ruminations, she thought he had the look of a chicken hawk zeroing in on a plump hen. Fierce and determined and so very intent. As if life itself was at stake, and he couldn't be bothered by the trivial distractions that decoyed less fearsome hunters.

Then she smiled to herself. That was only partially true, and she knew it very well. Jake had changed in the last few months, quite gradually but in ways she had been quick to notice. He was still riddled with ambition, obsessed more than ever with business and politics. That hadn't changed in the slightest. But now he talked with her, seemed more open somehow, willing to share his thoughts and plans. Quite often (and this had become particularly apparent when his land promotion seemingly mushroomed overnight) he sounded her out for a reaction to some scheme he was contemplating. Moreover, he listened, evidencing respect for her opinion, and on occasion had even revamped his plans after one of their discussions. Which was all very gratifying, yet at the same time something of a quandary.

She could trace the change in Jake, almost day by day, back to the time they became certain she was pregnant. And that led her to speculate that he had not so much changed as merely reverted back to what he was when they were married. The quandary came when speculation led to greater speculation. Had he become more attentive simply because she was pregnant? Or was he suffering some form of guilt, blaming himself for her condition? There was an even deeper imponderable. Could she (with Owen's help) have at last broken through the shell and touched the real Jake Kincaid? She wasn't sure, and perhaps she could never be wholly certain. However much he revealed himself, there was always something inscrutable about Jake. A deeper part of himself, buried and well hidden, something he seemed incapable of exposing to anyone.

Still, whatever the reason—whether he had changed or reverted or finally come to trust her—she had never felt so loved in all her life. Not in words, for that wasn't Jake's way. But his actions spoke with an eloquence which surpassed anything he might have said. That greater fulfillment she craved and needed so desperately had at last become hers. She had a home and a loving man and a darling imp of a son.

And soon—just maybe—a daughter.

The day was bright as brass, without a cloud in the sky. A gentle breeze, ripe with the smell of cowdung, drifted in from the south, and huge white butterflies floated lazily on warm updrafts of air. High overhead a hawk hung suspended in the sky, a speck of feathers caught against the blaze of a noonday sun. And Wichita sweltered in the still, fierce heat of a Kansas scorcher.

A crowd of some forty men, all freshly barbered and decked out in their Sunday best, had gathered at the depot east of town. With the exception of the Lady Gay band, the group was comprised of Santa Fe land agents and a gaggle of fast-spiel promoters used on the lecture circuit. A small crowd of townspeople and cowhands, curious onlookers to an even more curious assemblage, were being held at a distance by the city marshals.

While everyone else slowly fried to a crisp, Cecil Hollister paced back and forth on the shaded depot platform. He was attired in a hammertail coat and a top hat, and his features were knotted in a scowl of boiling frustration. Sweat trickled down his face in salty rivulets, and as he paced, growing huffier by the moment, he somehow resembled a mad bull hooking at cobwebs.

Deeper in the shade, near the station house door, Jake stood talking quietly with Mayor John Meagher. They were discussing matters of local importance, business and politics, but their eyes trailed Hollister as he marched back and forth in mounting anger. Wichita seldom had such a distinguished visitor, or ceremonies of such magnitude, and the mayor was clearly troubled by Hollister's glowering displeasure. Jake seemed more amused than concerned. He thought Hollister was making a fool of himself.

Abruptly, Hollister veered off course and stalked toward them. His face was red as ox blood, glistening with a florid sheen, and his once-starchy shirt collar sagged limp and wilted. Quite plainly, he had worked himself into a seething rage. Ignoring Meagher completely, he halted before Jake, biting down hard on an urge to shout. His jowls quivered, splattering beads of sweat down his coat front, and his words came with the brusque rumble of distant thunder.

"Don't say I didn't warn you, Jake. All along I said this harebrained scheme wouldn't work. And I was right." He flipped out his watch and checked the time. "The train is now thirty-seven minutes overdue. Which hardly gets us off to an auspicious start."

"Cecil, I'm beginning to think you're superstitious."

"What's that supposed to mean?"

"Why, you're carryin' on like this train being late is a bad omen of some kind. Hell, it's just business as usual for everybody else. So far as I know, the Santa Fe hasn't run on time since this depot was built."

Hollister grunted sharply. "Be that as it may, I'm still of the opinion that we have bought ourselves a peck of trouble. Good God, man, do you realize that if this thing goes badly they'll roast us alive in every newspaper in the country?"

Jake hardly needed to be told. A fiasco here today would have a disastrous effect on Santa Fe land sales. And slam the lid on his own profits as well. Still, it was a risk that had to be taken. A calculated risk, to be sure, but one that might yet blow up in their faces.

In a moment of inspiration he had invited reporters from fifty newspapers in the east and midwest to come inspect Kansas for themselves. All expenses paid and no strings attached. At the time it had seemed a brilliant ploy, just the stroke needed to offset partisan editorials labeling Kansas as "The Great American Desert." Editorials which, all too unfortunately, bore an element of truth.

Some three weeks past, Kansas had been hit with a grasshopper plague that virtually brought the state to its knees. Great clouds of the foul little beasts appeared out of nowhere, swarming so thick in places that they blotted out the sun. Voracious as tigers, some as big as a man's thumb, the grasshoppers moved eastward across the plains, devouring everything in their path with the steady hum of millions of tiny jaws. The stench of their greasy bodies, and the whirring roar as they took flight, drove livestock mad and sent farmers scurrying to their root cellars to escape the onslaught. Crops were completely wiped out in a score of counties; when the horde finally passed a swath of devastation some ten miles in width stretched from one end of the state to the other. Hundreds of settlers merely salvaged what they could, admitting defeat, and began the long trek eastward. Those who remained behind faced a bleak winter, empty bellies and more hard times.

Newspapers in the east proclaimed it just another disaster in a land where natural calamity was a way of life. If it wasn't grasshoppers, their editorials crowed, then it was drought or blizzards or prairie fires, and the poor farmer suffered the brunt of each new nightmare. This highly provincial journalism produced the desired affect. Settlers contemplating a move westward were scared off, and overnight land sales plummeted to an all-time low.

But Jake sensed an opportunity in disaster. Southern Kansas had suffered little from the grasshopper plague. The insects had skirted west of Dodge City, then swung northeast across the state, roughly paralleling the Kansas Pacific tracks. If he could somehow turn this to advantage—make settlers aware that the Garden of Eden remained unblemished—then the Santa Fe would profit handsomely. After a savage argument with Cecil Hollister, he had set the telegraph wires humming with messages to every major newspaper in the country.

And now, facing Hollister's wrath for the second time in a fortnight, his conviction remained firm that he could pull it off. With a bit of luck, aided by western hospitality and some sleight of hand, it should work out exactly as he had planned. Under the right circumstances, which he'd already organized with painstaking care, he had every confidence that journalists would prove as gullible as the rawest hayseed.

Smiling, he met Hollister's bulldog scowl. "Cecil, do you know what day this is?"

"Of course I know what day it is. It's July Fourth."

A barrage of gunfire and firecrackers from Delano seemed to emphasize the point, and Jake's smile widened into a grin. "Seems to me we would be mighty poor hosts to ask all these upstanding gentlemen of the press to work on the day our country is celebrating its independence. Doesn't it strike you the same way, Cecil?"

Hollister crooked one eyebrow. "Jake, I'll say this for you—you're about the sneakiest bastard I've ever done business with. Now suppose you stop holding out on me, and tell me exactly what you have in mind."

John Meagher suddenly decided he had business elsewhere. Fascinating as the conversation was, he had no intention of getting caught in the middle of a rhubarb between this pair. Excusing himself, he stepped into the depot and made a beeline for the water barrel.

Jake waited until he was through the door, then glanced back at Hollister. "I guess sneaky is as good a word as any.

You see, Cecil, what I've got in mind is a little trick card-sharps call *flash*. That's when you make a fellow see things as you want 'em to appear, instead of the way they are. Now, before we send these reporters off on their excursion, I thought we'd treat them to a western-style Fourth of July." He paused and cocked his head toward the land agents gathered at the end of the platform. "Every one of those boys has got his pockets stuffed with cash. Their job is to entertain our guests. Let 'em see how Texans hoorah a cowtown. Take 'em to the gambling dives and cat-houses, and in general show 'em a good time. But their most important job is to get our little bunch of pilgrims blind, stinkin' drunk. That way they'll wake up in the morning with the goddamnedest hangover anybody ever heard tell of."

Hollister started to interrupt, but Jake held him off with an upraised hand. "No, let me finish. Now, bright and early tomorrow, we'll rout 'em out of bed and pour 'em on a train, then we'll take a run out to Great Bend and show 'em all those prosperous Germans tilling that rich Kansas soil. They won't see any grasshoppers or drought or anything else. They'll just see what we want them to see, and their heads will be hurting so bad that's all they'll remember. And the point I'm tryin' to make, Cecil, is that when they get back home, that's all they'll write about. Good times and a land of plenty—so long as a man buys his farm from the Santa Fe."

A long while passed as they stared at one another, and at last Hollister sighed wearily. "Jake, you're one of a kind. And that comes from a man who thought he'd seen them all." A quizzical look crossed his face. "The thing that baffles me is why you waited until today to tell me all this. You know, it is *my* railroad. Or at least it was. Sometimes I'm not so sure anymore."

An ironic smile touched the corners of Jake's mouth. "That's exactly why I waited, Cecil. You are the head of the Santa Fe, and the top man shouldn't be mixed up in shenanigans like this. That way your hands are clean, and if it doesn't work you can feed me to the board of directors like fish bait."

"Except for the fact that you've got a contract Jesus Christ himself couldn't wiggle out of."

"Well, there is that. But don't get yourself in a lather before we pop the cork. I've got an idea things'll work out just about the way I planned."

Hollister threw up his hands in resignation. "Spare me any more, Jake. I'm sold. Whatever kind of snake oil you're selling, I've bought the limit. Just tell me why I'm standing here, and what, if anything, I have to do with your—what did you call it—your flash?"

"Why, hell, Cecil, I've already told you. You're Mr. Santa Fe himself, and you're here to greet our guests with a welcoming speech. A real Fourth of July humdinger."

A train whistle sounded in the distance, and they saw a puff of smoke far down the tracks. Hollister and Jake stepped to the edge of the platform, joined again by Mayor Meagher, and the Lady Gay band broke out in a sprightly tune. The three men stood and waited, saying nothing. In the way of things with Jake Kincaid, it had all been said.

As dusk fell early the next evening, an eastbound train groaned to a halt before the Wichita depot. The three passenger cars were curiously silent; the absence of sound or movement might have led a casual observer to deduce that the coaches were empty. But inside the dimly lighted cars was a scene reminiscent of hospital trains evacuating wounded from a distant battlefield. Sprawled about in their seats, still as dead men, were some fifty reporters and almost as many Santa Fe land agents. Their faces were pallid and sickly, heavy with exhaustion, and even in sleep they appeared to be suffering some virulent affliction. Occasionally there was a pitiful moan, or the hoarse retching of someone struck by the dry heaves, but mostly it was fetid silence broken only by drunken snores. To a man, they were disheveled puddles of sweat, dozing fitfully in a numbed coma.

The rear door of the last coach opened and Jake Kincaid stepped onto the depot platform. Cecil Hollister followed him out, bleary-eyed and haggard, his fine swallowtail coat rumpled and caked with grime. Both men sucked in deep drafts of air, clearing their heads of whiskey fumes and the stench of vomit, and the color slowly returned to their faces. After filling their lungs several times, they appeared almost normal. As if, given adequate care and sufficient rest, they might one day recover from their ordeal.

Collecting himself, Hollister managed a weak smile. "Jake, if it's all the same to you, next time count me out. I'm not sure I could live through another one of your excursions."

"Yeah, I know what you mean." He cast a rueful glance at the coaches. "Hope none of them die on you before you get back to Topeka. Christ, they're some bunch of swizzle-guts, aren't they?"

"I'd say that's something of an understatement. But it worked, my boy—worked like a charm. You're to be congratulated. Once they sober up I have a feeling the Santa Fe will be the subject of some very favorable editorials."

"Hell, it better be. After what they put us through, we earned it."

"Amen to that," Hollister sighed wearily. He slapped Jake on the shoulder and turned back to the coach. "Well, I'll be on my way. And remember, next time you make your own speeches. I'm getting too old for this nonsense."

Jake nodded dully, then suddenly came alert. "Say, Cecil, before you take off, I just thought of something I forgot to mention. There's a World Trade Exposition in Philadelphia next month and I've already reserved space for the Santa Fe. We'll set up a sales booth and take along some of those Germans to exhibit their farm produce. Should get us some good publicity and help boost sales back up where they're supposed to be."

Hollister groaned and rolled his eyes heavenward. "God save us. Now don't beat around the bush, Jake. How much is this little venture going to cost me?"

"Hardly nothing. Five thousand. Maybe less."

"And I suppose you expect me to ram it through the board of directors?"

Jake grinned. "Well, it is your railroad."

"I wonder. Sometimes I really wonder."

Hollister grunted something unintelligible and stepped through the car door. Moments later the train lumbered into motion and pulled out of the station. Jake stood watching until the rear coach disappeared in the twilight, then turned and trudged off toward town. He'd never been so bushed in his life. Or so pleased with himself.

Cecil Hollister hadn't seen anything yet. Just a sampling. The tip of the iceberg.

Santa Fe land sales climbed to record heights in July. While other lines, most notably the Kansas Pacific and the Union Pacific, limped along on marginal profits, the Santa Fe flourished as never before. Cecil Hollister graciously credited Jake Kincaid with this phenomenal showing (a fact which was common knowledge anyway), and the board of directors promptly voted their chief land agent an unexpected, and most impressive, bonus. This windfall Jake shrewdly split among his own men, and shortly afterward his largesse brought about a handsome dividend from an unusual quarter—Russia.

Along with the normal press of affairs, Jake was busily engaged in preparation for the World Exposition, and he had little time for long-shot schemes. But he knew a good idea when he heard it, and long shot or not, he had learned to encourage men who displayed imagination and boldness. Carl Johnson, one of his land agents, had all that and more, and Jake turned him loose on a most unlikely project.

Johnson had stumbled across a German settler, Otto Schmidt, who was of the Mennonite faith. That in itself made Schmidt something of an oddity, for most Germans were avowed Lutherans. But the greater wonder was that Schmidt had undertaken a one-man campaign to sell distant relatives on the utopia called Kansas. Schmidt had begun writing letters almost from the day he settled outside Great Bend, and just *how distant* his relatives were provided Carl Johnson with the strangest surprise of all.

Mennonites were an ancient sect, founded originally in the south of Holland. Medieval intolerance, and persecution by the church, ultimately drove them into Germany, where they fared little better. Their gentle ways were both peculiar and offensive to a warlike race, and while their cause drew many converts, they again found themselves oppressed by church and state.

Catherine the Great, Empress of Russia, at last offered them sanctuary. Their exodus was gradual, and while many chose to remain in Germany, the majority established religious colonies in the Crimea. And there, for almost a century, they lived a frugal life of brotherhood and peace.

But in 1870 a new czar, Alexander II, abolished the royal edict, and the Mennonites again sought refuge from tyranny and persecution. This time their eyes turned toward America, where German Mennonites had already settled in Pennsylvania, Illinois, and Kansas. And it was then, during the winter of 1874, that the letters of a lone zealot in Kansas began reaching distant relatives whose ancestors had emigrated to Russia nearly a hundred years before.

Carl Johnson encouraged Otto Schmidt in his solitary campaign, and late that spring the letters bore fruit. Some two thousand Mennonites from Sevastopol had decided on America as their new home, and they were favorably impressed with Schmidt's description of Kansas. A hasty exchange of letters followed, and the Mennonites agreed to meet with Santa Fe representatives upon arrival in New York.

This last letter reached Schmidt even as the pilgrimage was under way, and he hurried immediately to Wichita in search of Carl Johnson. After reading it, Johnson took a few minutes to catch his breath and congratulate Schmidt, and then raced off toward the Kincaid House. There he and Jake hoisted a few to mark the occasion—for it had indeed been a long shot—and quickly set about formulating their plans. Jake was scheduled to depart for Philadelphia, and the World Exposition, in less than a week, and the Mennonites were due to arrive in New York a fortnight later. But secrecy was imperative, for if the other lines got wind of the deal they would fight like starved dogs for a shot at the Russians.

At length, after discarding several clandestine stratagems, Jake decided on an open approach. Johnson and Schmidt would accompany him to Philadelphia, where Schmidt would serve ostensibly as one of the German settlers exhibiting Kansas farm produce. Then, at the appointed time, they would sneak out of Philadelphia, meet the Mennonites at dockside, and whisk them back to Kansas. It required precise timing, several trains standing by ready to roll, and above all, utter secrecy. Cautioning Johnson to put a muzzle on Schmidt, he shook the land agent's hand vigorously and sent him hurrying back to town before the German had a chance to spill the beans.

A short while later Sadie entered the parlor and found Jake staring spellbound at the letter. His expression was one of bemused astonishment; like a small boy gawking at his first Christmas tree, and involuntarily her heart skipped a beat. She had never seen such a look on his face, not once in all their time together. "Jake?" He didn't move, nor did he seem to hear her. Anxiously, concerned now, she came closer. "Sugar, is there something wrong?" Her touch broke the spell, and his head swiveled around.

"Sorry, guess I was stargazing. You say something?"

"Yes, I asked you what was wrong."

"Wrong? What gave you the idea anything's wrong?"

"Well, you look funny. You're all flushed and"—she put her hand to his forehead—"why, you are warm. Jake, I think you have a fever."

He gave her a dopey smile. "Damn right I've got a fever. But it's not the kind you're thinkin' about." Almost lovingly, he held the letter up.

"See that?"

She glanced at the scrawled, dirt-smudged page. "Yes."

"Bet you think it's a letter, don't you?"

"Isn't it?"

"Not on your tintype, it isn't." The dopey smile widened into a dopey grin, and he rattled the letter. "This here is one hundred thousand dollars—maybe more! Negotiable at any and all railroads west of the Missouri."

Sadie blinked uncertainly. "I don't understand."

"Course you don't. I wouldn't have believed it myself till Carl Johnson waltzed in here and laid it in front of me."

None of it made any sense, and she started to lose patience. "Believe what?" Suddenly she stopped and wrinkled her nose in a rabbity sniff. "Jake, have you been drinking?"

"Hell, yes. You might even take a snort yourself after you hear what's in this letter."

Briefly he described the letter's contents, elaborating on Otto Schmidt and the Mennonites and the sheer outhouse luck of the whole affair. But it wasn't the number of settlers involved that had him dazed. Or even the happenstance which guided them at this very moment toward Kansas. It was the amount of money—stated very plainly in the letter—that they were packing with them to the new land. Nearly $2 million in gold.

As he spoke the figure, almost with a touch of reverence, it dazzled him all over again, and he shook his head in mild disbelief. "Don't you see what that means, Sadie? At rock bottom, I'll come out with a hundred thousand. And hell, who knows, if I can steer 'em onto land I own outright, we might even double that. Jesus—two hundred thousand simoleons. Wouldn't that be something!"

Sadie eyed the letter skeptically. "Sugar, I'm not trying to throw cold water on it, but you talk like you already have the money in your pocket. And all you really have is a scrap of paper with some funny scribbling on it. Good Lord, what if their ship sinks? Or a hundred other things that could go wrong. It just worries me to see you get yourself all built up when it might come to nothing."

That stung. The thought that their ship might sink had never entered his head. "Yeah, I guess you're right. Hell, we could even lose 'em to one of the other lines unless we play it awful close to the vest." Suddenly his face clouded over, and he took a swipe at his mustache. "Course there's one little hitch I forgot to mention. Might queer the whole deal before it even gets started."

"Hitch?" Sadie echoed faintly.

"Yeah, and it's a lulu, too. Seems like these Mennonites have got some odd ways, and the oddest of the bunch is that they don't hold with fightin'." He tapped the letter with his forefinger. "They say we've got to promise they'll never be called up for military duty or else it's no soap."

Sadie just stared at him, appalled. "But, Jake, that's impossible. How could you ever promise a thing like that?"

He pulled at his ear reflectively, puzzling over it, and finally shrugged. "Why, I suppose I'll have to put the bee in somebody's ear up at Topeka."

"You mean Cecil Hollister."

"Him, among others. There's lots of folks up there that owe me favors. Looks like it's time to call the debts."

"Call the debts, or pull the strings?"

He glanced at her stiffly. "That's what politics are all about. Hell, what good are lawmakers if they can't fix the laws to suit the people?"

"Sugar, don't try to gaff me. You're not talking about

the people. You're talking about fixing the laws to suit Jake Kincaid."

"Well, in a way it all amounts to the same thing. Kansas gets itself a bunch of new settlers. Businessmen get theirselves a lot of trade they didn't have before. And the Santa Fe gets the money to keep on operatin' a railroad that helps everybody."

She smiled wickedly, and tweaked one end of his mustache. "And Jake Kincaid gets himself two hundred thousand simoleons. Isn't that what it's really all about, sugar?"

He grunted, and pulled her down in his lap. "Did I ever tell you you're a regular witch? Goddamn if it's not spooky sometimes, livin' with a woman that's always walkin' around in a man's mind."

Then he rubbed her swollen belly and nuzzled the soft nerve of her neck. "I'll be in a helluva fix if that's a girl. Only thing worse than one witch is two witches. 'Specially if she was little and cuddly and looked like her mama."

Thinking on it later, after he'd caught the evening train for Topeka, Sadie discovered something about herself. She had been genuinely swayed by his words, despite her aversion to his business methods. Within his rationale there was something profound, something of greater essence than perhaps Jake himself realized. She saw it now for the first time, with startling clarity.

There were no rules for men like Jake. Or Cecil Hollister. Or any of the breed who explored and built cities and railroads, and brought civilization to wilderness frontiers. They risked themselves, and all they possessed, to give people homes and jobs and a comfortable life, to transform land that had lain fallow for hundreds of centuries into a productive instrument for future generations. They were hard and cynical, lacking in scruples, ruthless men who used cunning and power as a stonemason used mortar. But at the same time, they were the visionaries—men who dreamed infinite dreams, and dared greatly, while others played it safe—and without them the earth might have lain fallow for another hundred centuries. That made them a breed apart. Not sacrosanct, or immune to the codes of lesser men, but above the frail strictures which governed the petty, mundane lives of those around them. And while this failed to excuse their methods, it was justification for the ultimate good born of their vision.

Sadie thought about that for a long time, and quite slowly, somewhere within herself, she found a sense of inner peace. At last she had reconciled all lingering doubts about the man she loved. He was callous, sometimes brutal in his dealings with others, but above all else, he was a builder. A visionary who would have scoffed at the label, yet a man whose dreams become the reality of all. And in that there was vindication for both her love and her belief, her ever-constant hope for a brighter tomorrow.

On a hazy afternoon in early September Jake Kincaid returned from New York like a conquering Caesar. Stretched out behind him were four trains bearing almost two thousand Mennonites fresh off the boat from Russia. As he had feared, the secret of their emigration leaked out, and several competing lines, chiefly the Union Pacific, had attempted to pirate them straight off the dock. But Jake fought fire with fire, countering every offer with rock-solid promises of his own. At the very outset he had Otto Schmidt make a welcoming speech, which gave the Santa Fe an immediate edge. Then he himself spoke of 100,000 acres west of Newton, and when questioned (though he knew absolutely nothing about the subject) assured his listeners that it was the finest wheatland on the continent. While the price of the land was high, he offset this with an offer to haul building materials, livestock, and farm implements without charge for an entire year. And then, in a final grandstand play, he simply wiped the slate clean of competition. Holding a parchment scroll overhead, he informed the onlookers that here was a law recently enacted by the Kansas legislature—exempting them from military service for all time!

The Mennonites praised God, and struck their bargain with Jake Kincaid.

They were a queer-looking bunch, though. The men heavily bearded, dressed in black coats and tight trousers, and wide stiff-brimmed hats. Their women clad in poke bonnets and drab high-necked dresses with wide skirts. And among the entire party not a musical instrument or a rug or an easy chair, not even the simple luxury of a mirror. They were a frugal people, Jake was to learn, who believed in the simple life and disdained all things material. They had come to America not for wealth or possessions or freedom from toil. They had come to farm, and to live as one with their God.

And Otto Schmidt, in a stirring speech at the depot, performed a benediction that was only slightly apocryphal. Like Moses before him, the fiery-eyed zealot proclaimed, Jake Kincaid had brought an end to their nomadic wanderings. Led the people home, at last. To the Promised Land. Not Canaan but Kansas.

Jake thought it a fitting tribute, and too, a very fine joke. As with most suckers, Otto Schmidt had worked for free. Like Moses before him.

The bedroom was toasty warm, but outside a dismal autumn wind rattled the windowpanes with its low, keening moan. Shadows flickered across the walls, fluted distortions of the pale glow from lamps at either side of the bed, and the room seemed swathed in a spectral gathering of grotesque, misshapen images. A small potbellied stove, installed after the weather turned unseasonably brisk, crackled cherry-red in one corner, and a pan of water on the top burner oozed vaporous tendrils of steam. The room was quiet, yet somehow suffused with sound, locked in stillness but strangely alive with fluttered, pulsating motion.

Jake sat hunched forward in a chair beside the bed, holding Sadie's hand. Her eyes were closed, and though he wasn't certain, he thought she was dozing. Off and on for the past hour she had drifted in a gentle netherworld of consciousness and fitful sleep. The doctor had given her a small preparatory dose of laudanum, enough to lessen the pain yet short of the amount needed to put her under completely. She was lucid, if somewhat tranquil, and occasionally floated back to wakefulness with a dreamy smile. These moments were all too brief, but she clearly took strength from Jake's presence, and he hadn't moved from her side since early afternoon.

The room was close, languid with warmth from the stove, but the drowsy quiet dulled his senses none whatever. His mind was alert, keenly aware of the slightest sound. Somewhere in his chest there was a hammering thud, every heartbeat seemingly stronger than the last, and his stomach churned as if he had swallowed a jar of butterflies in some witless moment of lunacy. Though he hid it well, his face set in a stony mask, he understood the signs, knew them for what they were. Not anxiety or concern or even heightened apprehension. None of those. It was fear, raw and suppurating, perhaps the only true fear Jake Kincaid had ever known, and it gnawed on his guts like some slobbering beast come to rip and shred and eat its fill.

Watching Sadie, acutely sensitive to the rise and fall of her breathing, he felt awestruck by the courage she displayed. He wondered if all women, confronted with such an ordeal, would have reacted as well, and he thought not. They would have wept or come unstrung, or at the very least gone pale with fright. But Sadie had done none of these things. After Quillman had completed his examination she listened intently, poised and comprehending, calmly accepting what must be done. She knew the danger involved, yet not for a moment did she allow it to unnerve her. Nor by word or action did she evidence the slightest trace of resignation. Instead, she expressed utter faith in Quillman, which seemed to be more than the physician had in himself. And when Jake began snorting fire, demanding alternatives that no longer existed, she serenely assured him that the operation was hardly more than having a tooth pulled. In the face of her remarkable composure, he could only agree, and hope somehow to function with the same grace she had shown.

But after hustling Quillman into the parlor for a blunt, and none too courteous, interrogation, he came away shaken and grimfaced, the marrow in his bones suddenly gone cold. As Quillman readily admitted, a Caesarean section was the last resort, a surgical procedure to be attempted only in the direst extremity. While the operation was ancient even in biblical times, physicians still knew little of its complications, and the mortality rate was to be mentioned only in whispers. Generally, the child was sacrificed to save the mother, and even then, fully three-quarters of the women who went under the scalpel failed to survive the operation. Given an option, however unorthodox, any physician would avoid the risk of a Caesarean. Unfortunately, in Sadie's case, there were no options. Unlike her last pregnancy, any attempt at normal delivery meant almost certain death. A Caesarean, dreadful as it was, represented the lesser of two evils, and the risk must be taken.

To make matters worse, Quillman had no choice but to perform the operation in the bedroom. There were no hospitals in Wichita, and his dingy office was hardly the place for such delicate surgery. Mrs. Murphy would assist him, for the nearest professional help was a doctor in Newton (reputedly a butcher with a scalpel), and every precaution humanly possible would be taken to safeguard Sadie's life. Further than that, Quillman could make no promises. Nor could he offer much in the way of encouragement, except to advise prayer and tender the hope that the odds would favor a most gracious lady.

While the doctor and Bess Murphy began their preparations, Jake returned to the bedroom to be with Sadie. And now, as darkness claimed the land, the fear within him tore at his vitals with quickening intensity. Soon Quillman would come, scalpel honed and freshly sterilized, banishing him to the parlor, and the thought curdled his blood. That steely dispassion, after serving him so well through the years, had deserted him now, and he wasn't sure he could manage it—simply walk from the room and leave her to some cowtown quack's thirsty knife.

Slowly, still a bit fluttery, her eyes opened. The opiate had worn thin, and her gaze focused on him with sharp clarity. Just for a moment he was held speechless, caught up in those pools of larkspur blue, even now as deep and startling as that first night he'd met her in the Lady Gay. Then her hand moved, tightening in his with surprising strength, and a tiny smile touched the corners of her mouth.

"That's nice. I was just dreaming about you, and here you are."

"Course I'm here." It came out gruffer than he intended, somehow defensive. "Where else would I be?"

"No sucker trains today"—the words were soft, without condemnation, spoken in a teasing lilt—"or business meetings?"

"Nothin' that can't wait till later."

"Later what?" she prompted.

"Why, you know, till after you're fixed up." He appeared flustered, almost sheepish, as if the fact that he was sitting there, troubled and concerned, made him uncomfortable. A moment passed and he dismissed it with an idle gesture. "You said you were dreamin' about me. Anything good?"

"Ummm. Scrumptious." She saw a flicker in his eye, and laughed softly. "No, silly, not that! I dreamt you were sitting in front of the fireplace holding Laura, and she was sleeping like an angel."

His heart thudded faster, and for an instant he couldn't believe she was serious. Then he saw it in her face, that inner unshakable serenity. He swallowed hard, and through sheer force of will managed a waxen grin.

"You sound mighty sure of yourself. What makes you think it'll be a girl?"

She gave him a smug look. "The same thing that made you think Owen would be a boy."

"And you've already got a name picked out. Don't I even get consulted?"

"No, you don't. Laura was my mother's name and it's already decided. I just forgot to mention it, that's all."

"Suppose it's a boy? You could be wrong, you know."

"Oh, pshaw! If it's a boy, you can name him anything you please. I'm right, though. You just wait and see."

He faltered, groping for some bright comeback. But his wits failed him. There was a sense of the unreal about this conversation. As if Quillman and his knife didn't exist, and somehow, magically, she would deliver a baby girl with perfect ease. She wasn't delirious, nor was she still giddy with laudanum. Of that, he felt quite certain. Her eyes were clear and her cheeks glowed with a healthy apricot tint. She spoke as she always spoke, natural and slightly impudent, without a trace of incoherence. Yet, unaccountably, it was as if she were discussing someone other than herself. As though fairy tales really did come true, and people lived happily ever after. An icy dread settled over him, and an imperceptible shiver went down his backbone. Suddenly, for the first time in his life, he was rattled, and his massive self-control took an abrupt nosedive.

His voice quavered, and he almost strangled on the words. "Sadie, are you sure you understand what this operation is all about?"

She patted his hand, as if comforting a small boy in the

dark of night. "I'm sure. And there is nothing to worry about. Everything will be all right. You'll see."

He shook his head, thoroughly at a loss. "Christ, I don't get it." Then he looked up, a quick, searching look, and a sickening comprehension spread over his features. "Oh, Jesus, I am some kind of dummy. You're tryin' to make it easier on me. That's it, isn't it?"

She gave him that old vixenish smile. "Why, Jake Kincaid, I do believe you've lost your poker face." She raised one eyebrow, studying him, then lowered it in an exaggerated wink. "Don't worry, though. I won't tell anyone. Cross my heart."

His mouth opened, then clicked shut, as though words and reason and reality itself had escaped him. When he didn't say anything Sadie wrinkled her nose, mocking him with a small, wistful pout.

"Now, sugar, don't scowl so. I want Laura to see her father smiling. And regardless of what you say, it will be a girl." She tilted her head and smiled impishly. "Wanna bet a little something on it, mister?"

He bit down hard, forced himself to play the game. "Lady, you got yourself a bet."

"Seal it with a kiss?"

He leaned over the bed and took her in his arms. Her lips parted, moist and soft, covering his in a long kiss that was somehow fire and nectar, incredible sweet warmth. When they parted her hand lingered on his face, tracing the outline of his cheekbone and jaw and lips. There was a look of infinite tranquillity in her eyes, as if she had seen his soul and committed it to some inner place of quietude and unalterable peace. She started to speak, his name formed on the gentle curve of her mouth, then she blanched, shuddering with pain, and uttered a small, stifled cry.

"Oh, sugar, I think you'd better fetch the doctor."

The urgency in her voice was unmistakable. Gently, he eased her back on the pillow, then whirled and headed for the door. But halfway across the room her voice pulled him around.

"Jake."

He turned, took a step toward the bed, and stopped. She was smiling, her eyes fixed on him with a serenity that seemed to swallow him whole.

"I love you, Jake."

He knew then. Understood at last the meaning she had given to these precious moments. And the words came easily to his lips, as though they had been there forever, just waiting.

"I love you, too. I always have."

An instant slipped past, a fragmented hearbeat frozen in time, and between them passed a communion of all they were, and of all they had become to one another. It was quickly done, without words of mawkish sentiment. But it was enough, a silent exchange of souls, the culmination of all that had gone before. And in that final moment, they knew it could never be taken from them.

Jake spun away, calling the doctor's name, and hurried blindly through the door.

They buried Sadie Timmons Kincaid on the crest of the knoll, beneath the great elm where she loved to sit on warm afternoons and gaze out over the river. All of Wichita, great and small, came to stand at her graveside. Cecil Hollister and the governor and a phalanx of politicians were there, gathered in a brisk November wind to pay their last respects. And Jake Kincaid, with Owen clutching his hand, looked on with tight-lipped stoicism as her coffin was lowered into the chilled earth.

Offers of a formal service, extended by every church in town, had been brushed aside. But at the urging of friends Jake had agreed that a local minister might perform the rites of burial. It meant nothing to him, yet in her own way Sadie had been a God-fearing woman, and he allowed it simply because she would have felt it proper. The preacher was nervous and ill at ease, having never met the deceased, and the wind scattered his words like flurries of dead leaves. Still, based on what he'd been told, he delivered a stirring eulogy, praising her as a wife and mother, a gracious lady, and a woman of Christian charity. That she had been struck down so suddenly, not yet twenty-six and in the flower of life, the preacher could only attribute to the mysterious workings of the Lord God Jehovah. The mourners bowed their heads solemnly, while the bereaved husband bored holes through God's middleman, and flustered by that pale, flinty stare, the preacher hastily concluded with the Twenty-third Psalm.

Afterward, with Owen now entrusted to Mrs. Murphy, Jake moved through the crowd, speaking to no one, acknowledging whispered condolences with a stiff nod of his head. Once inside the house, he walked straight to a room near the end of the hall, entered, and stood staring down at the tiny form in a bassinet. Somehow it seemed so unfair, a travesty of all that was reasonable and just. The mother consigned to a cold grave and her offspring swathed in warm blankets. That wasn't how it was to have been. The odds favored a different outcome, and it should have worked out the other way round. Yet, unreconciled as he was to this harsher reality, it lay there before him, alive and healthy and blissfully unaware that it had killed.

The baby stirred, gurgling softly, and thrust a chubby arm from beneath its blankets. Jake stared at it, his throat clogged with a brackish filth. Even in death her wish hadn't come true. Instead of the girl she wanted, a delicate cameo he might have cherished in her place, it was a boy child that had clawed his way from her womb. Which somehow made it all the more loathsome.

Staggered with remorse, damning himself for the thought, he backed away from the crib. He couldn't shut it out, though. The thought persisted, feeding on itself, and within him burned the wish that it was not Sadie but his helpless infant who lay beneath the ground. God, he would have made the trade in an instant! Without a twitch of conscience.

A queer hollowness came over him. Suddenly he was revolted by himself, appalled by the bittersweet taste of his own malice. There for a moment he had almost lost control, like some brutish animal, unreasoning in its fury, striking out instinctively at the thing which had hurt it most. Disgusted and confused, filled now with self-loathing, he stalked from the room in a blurred haze of desolation.

But moments later, decanter in one hand and a glass in the other, slumped in a chair before the fireplace, he faced it for what it was. That most ancient of truths. It is not the dead who haunt our lives but the living. The survivors.

And the wish was still there.

FOUR

As a commercial enterprise, the Santa Fe land program became something of a legend in a decade marked by westward expansion and growth. While its land grants were not as large as those of the Union Pacific and other lines, the Santa Fe operation was efficient, well organized, and remarkably aggressive. By early summer of 1880 thousands of immigrants had been persuaded to settle in southern Kansas, and well over two million acres of virgin prairie had been sold. This represented nearly three-quarters of the Santa Fe's original grant, and the program was considered all the more extraordinary in light of the Panic of 1873 and the severe economic depression of 1877. Although many railroads were hard hit, the Santa Fe emerged stronger than ever, and entered the new decade with an ambitious program of expansion into distant markets.

The immigrants themselves were not so fortunate. Life on the plains was hardly the utopia depicted in railroad brochures. Winters were harsh and unrelenting, a time of blizzards and howling winds; summers were blistering hot, with never enough rain, and often as not crops simply withered and died as the parched earth turned its bowels to the sky. Some settlers, those accustomed to deprivation and sacrifice, did well. Of them all, the Mennonites were perhaps the hardiest and most industrious of the lot. They brought with them red Turkey wheat, which flourished marvelously well on the arid plains, and being tree-loving people, they planted vast groves of mulberry, wild olive, and apricot. Their communal villages dotted the prairie, surrounded by orchards and great fields of wheat, and for them, Kansas was indeed the Promised Land.

But many settlers lacked that indomitable spirit so essential to survival on the plains. They watched their crops shrivel into dust, never fully comprehending the land or its rejection of certain forms of plant life; they perished from malnutrition, overwork, and broken hearts; and every winter hundreds of families subsisted on a starvation level. Their dreams were shattered on the flinty soil, and Armageddon for them was a sod house on some sun-baked stretch of prairie. They failed, as they had failed elsewhere and would fail again, and upon returning east offered the feeble excuse that "Kansas was fine for men, but hell on horses and women."

Though hardly benevolent, the Santa Fe possessed a corporate conscience of sorts, and provided them free passage to any destination of their choice. Over the years, particularly when drought and economic depression struck simultaneous blows, settlers in great numbers took the easy way out. But those who remained behind, that hardier breed of grit and tenacity, battled the land on its own terms, and in time transformed an ocean of buffalo grass into a shimmering sea of bright, golden wheat.

And through it all, few men prospered so greatly as Jake Kincaid. When settlers failed, agents of the Kincaid Land Company were Johnny-on-the-spot, with the balm of ready cash in exchange for a quitclaim deed. This land, acquired for a pittance from men hollow-eyed with defeat, was in turn sold to eager émigrés fresh off the boat, who hungered for the soil.

Along with his land sales for the Santa Fe, this yearly turnover of settlers brought Jake a constant, and seemingly self-rejuvenating, source of profit. That he grew rich on the misfortune of others bothered him not at all. More than ever he saw the world as a place of dupes and rogues, and it was in the nature of things that those who took seldom got taken. He made it a cardinal rule never to give the other fellow an even break, and while he was above outright chicanery, he had become a master of guile and subterfuge.

The years had treated Jake well, if the measure of a man is to be found in wealth and power. His holdings in Wichita had increased manyfold (it was rumored he owned half the downtown business district), and at any given moment his land company held title to upwards of a quarter-million acres. He had slowly but gradually invested enormous sums in cattle, and each spring, when the market peaked, he rarely sold less than thirty thousand head. Never one to overlook newer and greener pasture, he had also branched out into other fields. With railroad stocks at an all-time low during the depression of '77, he had quietly purchased sizable blocks of stock in both the Santa Fe and the Missouri, Kansas & Texas (a young, brazenly aggressive line more commonly known as the Katy). What with cattle and land, various stocks and considerable town property, he conservatively estimated his worth at something over $2 million. And while this scarcely placed him in the league of tycoons such as Cecil Hollister and Jay Gould, it was nothing to sneeze at for a man of thirty-two. Those who knew his background, buffalo hunter turned gambling impresario, often remarked that he had come far in a short time.

Yet they could only surmise the extent of his wealth, for Jake had become a secretive man, one who confided in others only when necessary, and even then, with grudging disclosure of what little he revealed. Since his wife's death, not quite six years past, those most closely associated with him had noted other changes as well. While he had always been somber and somewhat phlegmatic, he was now aloof and taciturn, almost astringent, as if fools and their follies were an intolerable demand on his time. Seldom, if ever, was he seen to smile, and on those rare occasions when he employed wit, it was with a barbed sting that was more ridicule than humor. His face had become a stone wall—hard, uncompromising, revealing nothing—only in his eyes was there life and animation. But here again, the change left men uncomfortable in his presence. They saw nothing cordial in those eyes, no charity or forbearance, but instead a pale, frosty glint that was at once detached and deadly. The eyes of some sleek carnivorous cat, alert and waiting, ready to pounce on the instant. Though he was civil, seldom known to raise his voice, men found it difficult to fathom what lay beneath his words, and none but an imbecile would have ventured a guess as to his thoughts.

Nor would they presume to surmise the extent of his political power, or to what ends he might use that power if provoked. Newspapers hinted at his influence within the capitol, and there was speculation that aside from Cecil Hollister and Ted Henry (who had become president of the Kansas Grangers' Association) he was the most powerful individual in the state. If the rumor mill was to be believed, he had handpicked at least a dozen legislators from various counties in southern Kansas; it was an indisputable fact that in those counties settled by the foreign element, especially the Mennonites and the Germans, the name Jake Kincaid ranked second only to that of Jesus Horatio Christ.

Still, there was nothing overt about Jake's political machinations. Just as he controlled the Wichita city council from behind the scenes, so he remained a shadowy figure in the corridors of the State House. Except for a small group of men in Topeka, each as close-mouthed and secretive as Jake himself, the extent of his power remained a matter of conjecture and idle gossip. But what people suspect is often more intimidating than what they know, and men took care that their own schemes were never at cross-purposes with those of Jake Kincaid.

That Jake fostered this enigmatic guise, and in truth, derived sardonic pleasure from the wariness of others, was something else he kept to himself. With the passing of time he had become more urbane in his dealings with men, cultivating a manner that relied less on bare-knuckled force than on a quiet, understated sense of menace. Always observant, he had come to the conclusion that men of power, those who shape the course of events with godlike impunity, operate in just this fashion. They manipulate and maneuver, sometimes employing brutal methods, but with a suave, unctuous under-handedness rarely recognized for what it was. While he had no wish to ape the bland affectations of eastern power bro-kers, he was quite willing to borrow those devices which could serve his own ends. Gradually, chipping away at the rough edges, buffing and smoothing, he had acquired a polished, almost lordly manner. The attitude of one who dispenses favors or retribution—as the situation demands—simply by lifting a hand. It was very effective, sinister some-how, and more persuasive than a cocked pistol.

With some calculation, then, Jake had become an assidu-ous student of power, and the powerful. The past six years had been spent watching and listening and learning, and though his formal education was scant, he slowly evolved a philosophy which would serve as a template throughout the rest of his life. Rudimentary as it seemed, he found that the source of power was not money alone. Given adequate funds, a man could corrupt and bribe, mortgage the loyalty of others, perhaps even purchase some lofty station for himself. But there was yet a higher level of power, one where money was merely a tool. To reach it, a man must possess a true instinct for the jugular, never squeamish or contrite, unhindered by any code except that which served the moment.

Curiously, his ruminations on power had led him back to his days as a buffalo hunter. Quite by accident, his mind dredged up a scrap of trivia long forgotten and seemingly meaningless. But upon deeper reflection it proved the very key he sought. A fundamental staggering in concept.

Among Indians it was commonly accepted that nothing could gain a hold over a man's spirit if he mastered pain. All of the plains tribes had elaborate rituals for conquering this fear of pain, some more barbaric than others. And within this very barbarism lay the key.

The conquering of fear.

Whether the white man's soul or the Indian's spirit, fear was the common denominator. The hoodoo which haunted all men. And while it might be impossible to rule a man's soul completely, it could be broken—through fear—just as the spirit of a horse or any other animal could be broken. Discover where a man was vulnerable. Drive the wedge deep enough to get a hold on that inner quivering he himself had never mastered. And he was yours.

And that was power.

The real power. Unlike that of a tyrant, it sought not to rule but merely to be obeyed. The man subjugated was still free, perhaps to profit even as he served, yet the lash became unnecessary, for fear alone was weapon enough. And if one man could be broken, then it seemed reasonable to assume that many men could be broken, until the will of a single individual became the will of all within the sphere of his influence.

Afterward, certain that he had at last stumbled upon the fountainhead of all power, Jake was forced to a sobering conclusion. Others also knew the secret. Employed it daily. Had spent years perfecting their skill in the use of fear. Beside them he was a rank amateur, a sparrow among hawks, and it would be foolhardy to test his wings among such company. So he kept his discovery to himself, awaiting a better time. Slowly, he began honing his own skills, learning through trial and error, practicing on the people he knew best—his nimble-witted, sticky-fingered political cronies in Wichita. And on a warm evening in early May, he got the chance to practice in a way wholly unexpected, and hardly to his liking.

Dave Flatt, leader of the local reform movement, was assassinated as he returned home from a Temperance League rally. Elections for county and city posts were upcoming, and it was generally believed that Flatt's murder was a warning to the vociferous reformers. The street where the shooting took place was dark, and the only witness was a barfly sleeping off his load in a nearby alley. But the county attorney, who in the past had steadfastly refused Jake's support, saw the killing as political dynamite. Based on the drunk's fuzzy recollection of having seen three men, the county attorney gleefully issued warrants against Mayor John Meagher, City Marshal Sam Atwood, and Delano's vice boss, Chalk Wheeler. In one stroke, even if they never came to trial, he had created the illusion that Wichita's city government was aligned with the sporting element. That the illusion was, in fact, a reality simply made the affair more embarrassing for everyone involved.

The accused men were released on bond after a preliminary hearing, and late the next night Jake summoned them to his home. He felt reasonably certain that none of them had personally pulled the trigger, but he had no doubt whatever that one or all of them had ordered the killing. The murder itself, however, was inconsequential. What mattered was that his political support had kept Meagher and Atwood in office for four consecutive terms, and through his influence Wheeler had been allowed to operate Delano without interference from the law. Now, they had acted on their own, appropriating power that was his alone. Worse yet, their blundering had come near linking the Kincaid name with a messy, and wholly uncalled for, political scandal. He meant to convince them that it shouldn't happen again—ever.

After they were seated Jake took a chair opposite them. Meagher had grown paunchy with good living, his cheeks puffy and his eyes bloodshot. Sweating profusely, he couldn't meet Jake's gaze. Nor could Atwood, who sat fidgeting with his hat, slouch-shouldered and thoroughly abashed. Only Chalk Wheeler returned the stare, cool as ice. Time had changed him little, either in manner or appearance. He was still trim and hard-eyed, never to be underestimated, a dangerous man versed in the use of violence.

Jake had assumed an air of elaborate ease, though it

scarcely masked his contempt. After several moments he steepled his fingers, letting the silence mount, then eyed each man in turn.

"I won't ask who did it. But I will tell you that he's one stupid son of a bitch. Anybody with brains enough to fill a thimble would have known that killing Flatt could only add fuel to the fire. Yesterday the reformers were no particular threat, but they are now. You've given them a martyr—the very thing they needed most!"

Meagher spread his hand in a bland gesture. "Jake, for Christ's sake, let's take first things first. They've got us up on a charge of murder."

"So they have, John. A circumstantial case from what I hear, but with the mood of the town what it is, they might just stretch your neck anyway."

The mayor blanched and darted a nervous glance around at his fellow conspirators. Atwood squirmed and silently twisted his hat into knots, but Wheeler stiffened, eyes squinted in narrow slits.

"You wouldn't be thinkin' of throwin' us to the wolves, would you?"

Jake's jaws clenched so tight his lips barely moved. "Chalk, I allow a man only one mistake. You've had yours, and if there is a next time, you won't have to worry about courts or juries." However discreetly couched, the judgment was final, unalterable. "I'll see that the charges against you boys are quashed. But if you step out of line again, I don't even know your names."

He rose, ending the discussion. "That's all I called you here to say. I suggest you take the message to heart."

They did, to a man. Not even Chalk Wheeler, who had never backed off from a threat in his life, cared to dispute the issue. They were shaken, something deep in their vitals touched by an enervating fear, and as they went out the door, none of them doubted what they had heard. It was neither pardon nor commutation, but rather a stay of execution. So long as they behaved themselves.

Early the next morning Jake called on Robert Kelly, the county attorney. He laid out a dossier cataloging Kelly's indiscretions at various whorehouses in Kansas City and St. Louis, and also proof that certain campaign contributions had been used to defray the mortgage on Kelly's home. That afternoon the charges against Meagher, Atwood, and Wheeler were dropped, and in an interview with the *Beacon* Kelly apologized most abjectly for having besmirched the names of three such honorable men. At the same time, he announced that for reasons of ill health he was withdrawing from the election, and would support the candidate of the opposition ticket, an old and esteemed colleague who could better serve the needs of Sedgwick County.

All in all, Jake thought it had worked out quite well.

Not long after sunset the wind dropped off sharply, and the washed blue of the plains sky grew smoky as dusk settled over the land. Later, when nightfall deepened and stars sprinkled the inky darkness, the wind would again rise, slipping across the prairie like some warm-fingered wraith come to caress the slumbering earth. But in this brief interval, while dusk softly gave way to night, the plains lay shrouded in stillness, a place of solitude and peace and eternal quiet.

In those sanguine days long past, when his only worries were killing buffalo and dodging hostiles, this fleeting moment of calm had been Jake's favorite time. Gathered around the campfire with his skinners, their bellies filled with hump meat, lazily swapping windy tales, it had been the best of all worlds. Lacking nothing. Something a man remembered with crisp, savory goodness all the days of his life. But times changed, a man's hungers grew sharper, and with it he lost the youthful gusto for small and simple pleasures.

Now, approaching the town of Caldwell at dusk, Jake had little thought for the solitude around him, and within the corners of his mind there was neither quiet nor peace. The steady hoofbeats of his team, and the constant jolt as the buggy slithered along a rutted trail, were something apart, unfelt and unseen. He handled the reins mechanically, allowing the bays to set their own pace, aware only that the dusty ribbon before him was there and would lead eventually to his destination. Since departing Wichita at the crack of dawn, it was as if all things external had been suspended, shunted somehow from consciousness and sight. His mind had turned inward upon itself, as happened often these days, rummaging through an assorted heap of problems. And it was a very large heap, one that for all of his labors and hectic rushing about seemed never to grow smaller. Like some organism which breeds from within, it split and sprouted and mounted ever higher, an endless cycle that left him lagging far behind in a constant race against time.

Today he had spent the fifty-mile ride, nearly twelve solid hours, in a detailed examination of the cattle trade. Before the night was out he would meet with some thirty ranchers, a meeting called at his own request, and what he told them could have far-reaching implications. Perhaps more significantly, if the Kincaid Cattle Company was to emerge the chief beneficiary, which he fully intended it would, then he must hammer out an accord among men who were muleheaded and pugnacious, and acutely suspicious of one another. That was a tall order, fairly seething with pitfalls, demanding ready answers and a persuasive argument. Which was precisely the reason he had devoted his day to the quirks and complexities of a highly muddled situation.

The problem was essentially one of bureaucratic despotism within the Department of Interior. This was the agency charged with supervision of all Indian reservations, and in Jake's view it was operated with godlike arrogance. Always skeptical of politicians, particularly those at the federal level, he was convinced that Washington bureaucracy had created the problem, and in the long run would somehow manage to compound it with their highhanded tomfoolery.

Jigger Musgrave, foreman of Jake's cattle operation, had unearthed the problem strictly by happenstance. Sometime in the fall of '75 he had ridden south into the Nations, scouting for winter grazing land. Southern Kansas had become overcrowded with settlers and small ranchers, and what he hoped to find was a stretch of grassland adequate to support the rather sizable Kincaid herds. Almost by fluke, he stumbled across the Cherokee Outlet.

Of all the bizarre creations spawned by federal bureaucracy, the Cherokee Outlet was perhaps the greatest anomaly. Earlier in the century, when the Five Civilized Tribes were removed from their ancestral lands and settled in Indian Territory, the Cherokees were granted seven million acres bordering southern Kansas. As a further concession, they were granted a long corridor extending west, which provided hunting parties with an unimpeded gateway to the distant buffalo ranges. Some one hundred and fifty miles in length and sixty miles in width, comprising more than six million acres, it was designated by treaty as the Cherokee Outlet. The legal status of this strip, however, was an exquisite bit of bureaucratic convolution.

The Cherokees held title to the Outlet, but they were forbidden by the Department of the Interior to dispose of it in any manner, whether by lease or by sale. Since their lands to the east were sufficient for the entire tribe, the Cherokees rarely ventured into their western grant. As a result, this huge land mass had remained unoccupied and forgotten for nearly a half-century, mired in the obfuscation of federal balderdash.

But if the Cherokees had no use for the Outlet, there were others who did. The Chisholm Trail blazed straight through Indian Territory, and Texas cattlemen were quick to discover this lush stretch of graze. Rolling plains and fertile valleys, watered by the Canadian and the Cimarron, made it a perfect holding ground for trail-weary longhorns. Each summer during the early 1870s, the Texans halted their herds for a week or longer in the Outlet, allowing the cows time to fatten out before the final drive to a Kansas railhead. And it was this grassy paradise which beckoned Jigger Musgrave southward in the fall of 1875.

Upon hearing Musgrave's report, Jake moved decisively, ignoring both Washington and the Cherokee Nation. The Kincaid herds were trailed into the Outlet, and there they stayed. Permanent line camps were established, and for all intents and purposes, Jigger Musgrave's crew became squatters on land owned by the red man. All went well for nearly four years. The Cherokees passively overlooked this intrusion, perhaps fearful of outright confrontation with white men, and the Kincaid Cattle Company flourished as never before. But Jake's boldness scarcely went unnoticed in other quarters. By late spring of 1880 some thirty ranchers had staked out similar claims, and the strip had become a kingdom within a kingdom, swarming with cattle.

That was simply more than the Cherokees could tolerate, and they reacted in a most businesslike fashion. Accompanied by a squad of Light Horse Police, Major D. W. Lipe, treasurer of the Cherokee Nation, rode into the Outlet in early May. With perfect aplomb, he levied taxes of forty cents a head on grown cattle and twenty-five cents a head on yearlings. When he returned to Tahlequah, the Cherokee capital, he had collected more than $8,000—and a good deal of ill will from his white tenants.

Yet the real threat, as Jake was quick to perceive, lay not in Tahlequah but in Washington. The bureaucrats had been bypassed in a most cavalier manner. Should they become alerted to the situation, and decide to vent their indignation, it could spoil a very nice arrangement for everyone concerned. Better to strike an accommodation with the Cherokees, strictly on the hush-hush, and keep the Department of the Interior in the dark as long as possible. Then, should the deal ever attract official censure, it would be something of a *fait accompli*, and might easily convince the bureaucrats to leave well enough alone. Particularly if the Cherokees became unruly about the loss of revenue from an idle chunk of land that had at last proved itself of value.

As if one fly in the butter wasn't enough, affairs in Kansas made the situation all the more critical. Settlers had homesteaded most of the land south of Wichita, and there was a great clamor for a quarantine law barring longhorns from the eastern part of the state. Should the legislature pass an embargo act during the fall session, not only would Wichita be finished as a cowtown, but the longhorn herd owners would be banned from whatever grazing lands remained in eastern Kansas. Which made the Cherokee Outlet a vital force in Jake's future plans. And not coincidentally, the town of Caldwell itself, where he was preparing another little surprise for Cecil Hollister.

This meeting tonight, then, was of the utmost gravity. Unless he could organize the ranchers into a cohesive faction, however rudimentary its structure, there was every likelihood they would all be out of the cattle business before first snow. That the other outfits were smaller than his own, operating on a shoestring and a prayer from season to season, struck him as a distinct advantage. While he could afford the loss if necessary, they were in hock to their eyeballs and stood to lose everything they owned. Which meant little to him one way or the other. But it might well make them more manageable, willing to listen to reason.

And boiled down to its essence, that's what this meeting was all about. Cold, hard logic. United we stand and divided we fall, that would be his message. But in the end, if all went according to plan, there would be only one big winner. And while some might quibble over his motives, he felt it an exceedingly fair arrangement. Damn near munificent.

Shortly after dark he brought the buggy to a halt in front of a saloon in Caldwell. So far it wasn't much of a town—

couple of stores, a blacksmith shop, and the saloon—but with a bit of luck he'd soon have the place humming. Last week his agents had purchased the saloon, and by now he might own half the county. Which was all part and parcel of what he had simmering on the back burner.

Inside the saloon he found that his orders had been followed to the letter. Tonight the place was closed except to invited guests—cattlemen from the Outlet—and it came as no great surprise that they had heeded his summons. Like a flock of turkey buzzards, wondering whose bones were to be picked, they had gathered on neutral ground. From the hush that fell over the room as he came through the door, Jake felt reasonably certain that they considered him the greatest turkey buzzard of all.

Something else he knew. These men wouldn't be fooled by a genial manner, nor could they be persuaded with a glib line of chatter. They were tough and resourceful, hard men accustomed to hard knocks, and the only thing they would understand, or accept, was straight talk. Nodding to Jigger Musgrave, who had stationed himself near the door, Jake strode directly to the bar and turned to face the cattlemen. His bearing was brusque and businesslike, and while the saloon reeked of suspicion, he sensed that this was the only approach they would respect.

"Gents, I appreciate your showin' up here tonight. I can promise you nobody will go away thinkin' he's wasted his time." They stared back at him, attentive but unconvinced, reserving judgment till they had heard more. "When Jigger asked you to this meeting he couldn't tell you what it was about because I hadn't told him. Now, I don't suppose any of you trust me, and just to be blunt about it, I haven't got any particular reason to trust you. But I figured that in order for us to work together, we'd have to meet here like this—face to face—and thrash out some damn thorny problems we've all got down in the Outlet."

"Kincaid, I got a question for you." A man seated at a table across the room climbed to his feet. Like most of the ranchers he was a transplanted Texan, and had little use for Yankees, a broad category which included foreigners in general and Jake Kincaid most especially. "Where'd you get the notion we'd wanna work together? 'Pears to me we've got along pretty well with ever'body workin' on his own hook."

Several of the men muttered agreement, but Jake had come prepared for hostility, and he countered quickly. "Mister, when you get to know me, you'll find out I don't yell *wolf* just to hear myself talkin'. Now suppose you give me about five minutes, and when I get through, anybody thinks he's sittin' in the wrong pew can just go on about his business. Fair enough?"

The Texan sat down and everyone else waited. They would hear him out, their curiosity whetted all the more by his abrasive manner. As it happened, Jake talked for considerably longer than five minutes, but none of them objected. Nor was he interrupted. He talked their language, plain and unvarnished, brutally frank.

He spoke first of the rustlers preying on their herds. The Outlet was a land without law or courts, and the cattle thieves were growing bolder. Unless they joined forces to stamp out this common threat, their losses would mount ever higher. That drew a murmur of grudging assent. Then he spoke of the need for joint roundups, to be held on fixed dates, and some method of arbitrating disputes over strays and unbranded stock. That also made sense, for it was a common enough practice in Texas, and again, there were nods of approval.

With the stage set, he then broached the greater problem—their shaky truce with the Cherokee Nation. Step by step, he led them through a sobering evaluation of the obstacles that lay ahead. Repeatedly stressing certain points, he hammered away at the common danger. The Department of the Interior. Governmental restrictions on the Outlet. Petty bureaucrats, with an inflated sense of self-importance, and a very real power to banish all cattlemen from Indian lands. The truth, harsh as it seemed, was that they could not deal with the government. They must deal directly with the Indians. Which meant forming an organization of cattlemen and levying heavy taxes upon themselves. In effect, paying the Cherokees enough so that it made it worth their while to defy Washington. Otherwise, every cattleman in the Outlet would shortly be out of business. Bluntly stated, unless they formed a coalition of sorts with the Cherokees, they hadn't the chance of a snowball in hell against an aroused bureaucracy.

When he finally stopped talking, they just sat there. Nobody walked out, and for a while, nobody said anything. Then the outspoken Texan again rose to his feet. "If I get your drift, you're sayin' we've got to cozy up to them gut-eaters?"

"That's right. Sweeten the pot enough so that the Cherokees won't stand still for Washington messin' around in their sandbox."

"Suppose some of us don't cotton to that idea?"

"The man who holds out on the Cherokees becomes a risk to everyone operating in the Outlet." A look came over his face, cold and hard, that none of them would ever forget. "I'm not huntin' trouble. But there's too much at stake to let some peckerhead spoil things for the rest of us. When it comes down to cases, anybody that's not with me is against me." He paused, and a saturnine smile tugged at the corners of his mouth. "I guess it's no secret that I make a better friend than I do an enemy."

The Texan snorted. "And I reckon you had yourself picked out to ramrod this organization we're talkin' about?"

"That's up to you gents. I've got the political connections, and I know where to use money so it'll do the most good. But we'll leave it to a vote."

After a bit of squabbling, that was the way it worked out. Stubborn proud as they were, the ranchers knew when they had been euchred. Their fledgling organization was called the Cherokee Cattlemen's Association, and with only one dissenting vote, Jake Kincaid was elected president. That they had been bullied, slick-talked, and outmaneuvered would forever remain a sore spot. But they weren't men to bellyache over lost causes. They respected power, if little else, and however reluctantly, they had aligned themselves with the man who wielded the biggest stick.

Later, when the cattlemen had gone, Jigger Musgrave joined Jake at the bar. Musgrave was waspish and short-tempered, with the lean flanks of a horseman and skin the color of charred leather. The bearded stubble on his face looked as if it had been sprinkled with salt and pepper, and flecks of gray had cropped up along his hairline. Yet his years in the saddle had done nothing to dull his wits, and he had a keen instinct for the shifty ways of all "Gawd's critters," four-legged or otherwise. Elbows hooked over the bar, he slewed a sidewise glance in Jake's direction.

"Think they'll stick by you if push comes to shove?"

"Hard to say. I expect most of them will, though."

"And them that don't?"

Jake shrugged, unconcerned. "Then we'll just have to tie a knot in their tail."

Jigger Musgrave chuckled a soft, vinegary chuckle. That's what he liked about working for Kincaid. None of them fancy rules about keeping it clean. The bastard fought to win, and if it got dirty in the clinches, then everybody just took their licks the best way they could. Which, in a manner of speaking, was what separated the shit from the shovel.

There was them that flung, and there was them that got flung.

The Kincaid Land Company occupied a building at the east end of Douglas Avenue, near the train depot. It was one of the few brick structures in Wichita, and like a bank, meant to convey an impression that the firm housed within was reliable, trustworthy, and substantial as a rock. All of which was true. The company's cash flow was enormous, particularly during the summer months, and its credit line at the

Merchant's National was greater than that of any other business in town. The fact that Jake was a stockholder in the bank, sitting on a very respectable one-third of the outstanding shares, lent his firm an added note of substance.

The inside of the building was as impressive as the outside. The waiting room was filled with sturdy but expensive chairs and settees (quite unlike anything the settlers themselves would ever possess), and beyond this was a maze of some twenty cubicles, each appointed with roll-topped desks, leather-backed chairs, and walls ablaze with surveyor maps. Here the land agents brought their clients, talking expansively of Kansas and the richness of its soil, and in a most solicitous manner arranged a deal beneficial to all concerned. That the land agents were mostly reformed grifters and bunco artists was seldom apparent to the settlers. Mortgage in hand, quickly arranged through the Merchant's National, they walked from the building wide-eyed with wonder at their own good fortune.

Though they knew he existed, the new landowners rarely caught a glimpse of the man who made it all go round. The back of the building was devoted exclusively to Jake's office, and it was an inner sanctum which few entered. The room was large and tastefully furnished, somewhat reminiscent of Cecil Hollister's office, with a massive walnut desk and overstuffed leather chairs. It had a private entrance, opening onto an alleyway, and the land agents themselves sometimes went for days without seeing Jake. By now he had a manager and a couple of aides to handle the details, and while he kept himself abreast of events, he was no longer involved in day-to-day operations.

Trainloads of settlers were still pouring west, but Jake devoted little time or attention to what now seemed a mundane business. On any given day the front office was a real barnburner, jammed with immigrants and displaced Americans who fancied themselves pioneers, yet he simply couldn't be bothered. The challenge had gone out of it, for at this point the land operation functioned like a well-oiled machine, and just the thought of it made him yawn. Procedure and routine had never been his strong suit, and when an element of rote reared its head, he soon became bored to distraction. Like the town properties, which Quincy Blackburn managed, and the cattle operation, which was Jigger Musgrave's responsibility, the land company was left to his underlings out front. He stayed in his office and concentrated on what it was he did best—hatching new and more intricate schemes.

There were days, though, when nothing seemed to arouse that old spark. Odd moments, random but with a certain regularity, when he lost the urge to do battle with the world, and not even the challenge of outwitting Cecil Hollister could bring him around. Then his mind drifted off in a gray funk, leaving him glum and listless, and at such moments he felt some deep-rooted need to snatch comfort from the jaws of turmoil. This was one of those days, come again in its methodical cycle of gloom, like the waning of the moon. And while he had long ago tagged the mood for what it was, he still found it strange and nonetheless unsettling.

Time had become a silent hourglass, passing unnoticed, buried beneath the press of greater urgencies. But as the fabled healer, possessed of uncommon curative powers, time had failed him miserably. There lingered within him, smoldering corrosively, an aching wound that flared and dimmed but never really passed. At its best it seemed a vast hollow emptiness, as if some part of his vitals had been carved out, leaving behind a raw and mangled void. Then there were the bad days, like today. When the ache took hold, fanned alive into white-hot coals, bringing with it remembrances of things dead and gone. That throaty laugh, a flickering image of her face, and perhaps worst of all, those times when they had touched, come together, linked in a way that not even the passage of years could erase. It seared and blinded and numbed, and when it was upon him, there was nothing else. Just the memory, and the ache.

At first, when she died, he had sought refuge in the bottle. But he had no real taste for liquor, and oddly enough, the ghost of her was easier summoned back drunk than sober. While he was not a man to break or shatter, he slowly came to realize that he lacked the strength to bury her. Put her from his mind. Lay the dead to rest. His love for her was too great, and his need greater still. Yet only in the black pit of grief had he seen that for the truth it was, and known, at last, that he would never escape what she had meant to him.

After a short but spectacular binge, he had crawled out of the bottle and turned to a more ancient opiate—work. He drove himself like a madman, delving into every niche and cranny of his far-flung business empire. There was no detail so small as to elude his attention, and his disposition gradually went from amiable gruffness to churlish wrath. Kincaid employees, barkeeps and cowhands and land agents alike, began to dread the sight of him, for in his race to outdistance sorrow he had become a man of spleen and bitterness. Nearly a year passed before he made any distinction between night and day; he threw himself on a bed for a few hours' fitful sleep only when he was exhausted to point of collapse. Even then he couldn't stop the dreams—lovely, torturously exquisite nightmares of a time gone forever—he would awaken, throat clogged with puke and bathed in sweat. Sickened by his defenselessness in sleep, he knew only one antidote—a greater work load and an even faster pace.

Jake grew enormously wealthy in that year, for he kept every division of the Kincaid enterprises operating at a fever pitch. But in the process he drove his entire organization to the point of mutiny, and came very near losing his own sanity. At last, physically and emotionally drained, with some dim awareness that he had been victimized by his own sorrow, he pulled back and took a hard look at himself.

What he saw revolted him, for it was a performance better suited to some fainthearted pisswillie than to Jake Kincaid. But even in his disgust, the knowledge that he had wallowed shamelessly in self-pity, there emerged a bitter truth. He could never forget Sadie, exorcise himself of their years together. However great his work load, whatever super-human demands he made of himself, he could not outrun the memory, or the pain. It would never really be gone, but merely ebb and flow, worse at certain times than at others. And before he turned himself into a raving lunatic, he must somehow learn to live with it.

His pragmatism, reasserting itself in gradual stages, had been his salvation. The memory dimmed none at all, nor did the ache diminish in intensity. But as a hophead might learn to control his addiction, and face life with some degree of normality, so Jake reconciled himself to the barrenness of his existence. He survived, never fully suppressing the canker-ous ache within, and by Spartan self-discipline mastered the urges which had nearly destroyed him.

Yet he was never again the same man. Always ruthless and calculating, he was now cold and pitiless and detached, as free of sentiment as an assassin. Except for those bad days, like today, when for a few brief, excruciating hours he lived again in the past. Then there was neither escape nor salva-tion, but simply the dull throb of something lost, the numbed paralysis of an enervating need which could never be as-suaged.

Seated at his desk, gripped by a terrible loneliness, he stared sightlessly out the window. The commotion in the outer office was an irritant, further chafing an already grisly mood, and the muscle at the back of his jaw ticced in a hard, pulsating knot. Suddenly the prospect of spending the after-noon at his desk, listening to the pandemonium outside, was more than he could take. Uncoiling from the chair, he jammed a hat on his head and slammed out the door. Behind he could still hear the racketing din of land agents pitching the rubes, and it occurred to him that the day would probably be unconscionably profitable. The thought gave him little solace.

Unwittingly almost, Jake ended up at home less than an hour later. It wasn't where he'd meant to come, and hardly suited to his present frame of mind, for the memories were sharper here than anywhere else. Sadie's haunt still walked these floors, as if some ethereal part of her lingered behind, and at times it was all he could do to spend a night in that back bedroom. But after stopping off for a drink at the Lady Gay, and a bit of desultory conversation with Quincy Blackburn, he simply couldn't stomach the noise or the crowd, nor the fawning cheeriness of those he met on the street. Like an old and crippled dog, mindlessly seeking familiar ground, he was drawn inevitably to the house on the knoll.

If anything, it was worse. Standing at the window, eyes fastened on the headstone beneath the great elm, he knew he shouldn't have come here. Not today. A man was a fool to confront the furies where they dwelt the strongest, and here, as nowhere else, the black mood savaged him with witless abandon. He should have found a poker game. Or gone to Delano. Maybe assaulted a whorehouse, lost himself in sweat and cheap perfume and a night of rutting. Anything but this. A ghoul, throat parched and hollow-gutted, staring mutely at a grave.

As he turned from the window a shrieking wail erupted in the kitchen, and in the next instant Brad tore through the dining room and into the parlor. His shirt was ripped, tears and dirt smudged his cheeks, and one striped stocking was pulled loose from his kneepants, bunched around his ankle. The boy slid to a halt, startled, when he saw Jake, and almost fell. Then he righted himself, face gone purple with childish rage, and cried all the louder.

Jake had never quite come to grips with how much the boy

resembled Sadie. He had her coloring, the dark hair, her mercurial temperament, and the slim, coltish build. Though Brad was five now, bright and full of devilment, Jake still felt uneasy stirrings in his presence. However little, the youngster was Sadie Kincaid incarnated, a constant reminder of a bleak day and ugly thoughts, some of them best forgotten.

Mrs. Murphy appeared in the doorway, holding Owen by the scruff of the neck, and the abashed look on his face told the tale. Despite the difference in their ages (Owen was almost eight, with his father's sturdy build and rough manner) Brad thought nothing of tangling with his older brother. They got along well enough, for all their dissimilarity in character, but the younger boy seemed forever bent on causing mischief. Owen would stand it for just so long, then he would explode and whale the daylights out of his little brother. Later he was always ashamed, a minor curiosity which Jake never fully understood. If Brad hadn't tormented him, then there would have been no trouble. And invariably, it was Brad who brought the licking on himself.

Jake had troubles enough of his own just at the moment, but he gathered himself and fixed the younger boy with a stern look. "Stop that bawling. Right now!"

Snuffling, choking back quick little gasps Brad ducked his head. A few vagrant tears spilled over cheeks, puddling at the base of his nose with a trickle of snot, but he was no longer crying. He knew what it meant when his father used that tone of voice, and he wasn't about to chance two whippings in the same afternoon.

"All right," Jake said wearily, glancing from one to the other, "suppose somebody tell me what happened."

Brad's head came up, and he pointed an accusing finger at Owen. "He hit me! Knocked me down and tore my shirt and I didn't do nuthin'! Not nuthin'."

"That's a dirty rotten lie!" Owen bristled and started forward, but Mrs. Murphy had him firmly by the neck. "He's a little sneak, Pa. I was out playin' with the fellas and he wouldn't take no for an answer. Just kept buttin' in even after we told him a hundred times to buzz off."

"Liar!" Brad squawled. "Big fat liar! I didn't do no such thing."

"Don't you call me liar, you little ninny!" Owen's face mottled with fury, and he cast an imploring look at his father. "Pa, you go ask the fellas. Just ask any of 'em. They'll tell you who's fibbin'. It was him pokin' in where he's not wanted that caused it. Just ask 'em."

"Wasn't either me." Tears of frustration welled up in Brad's eyes, and his lower lip quivered. "They would've let me play. It was him that started it."

"That's enough! Both of you settle down."

Jake's sharp command had the desired effect. The boys fell silent and stood eyeing daggers at one another. After a moment he frowned, and let go a gusty breath, clearly exasperated. "Owen, you get on back outside. And next time don't be so damn rough." He gestured at the smaller boy. "Just so you'll know I mean it, that shirt of his comes out of your allowance. Now scat!"

Owen smiled brashly, cocksure now that he'd won his point. He darted his little brother a scathing look of triumph, then turned and marched straight as a tin soldier toward the kitchen door. Jake could barely restrain a smile—*the little bastard had enough brass for a three-legged bulldog*—but when Owen passed from the room his expression changed. Hands locked behind his back, he regarded Brad with a dour, brittle gaze.

"Young man, if you're determined to make a pest of yourself, then you'll have to learn to take your licks. Seems to me it would be more fun playin' with boys your own size, anyway. How is it you always have to tag after Owen?"

"I dunno." Brad shrugged, and wiped his nose with a grimy hand. "Just do."

"That isn't much of a reason. Suppose you give it some

thought and see if it wouldn't be better to rustle up a gang of your own."

Brad sulked a minute, and then, quite abruptly, his eyes glistened with tears. "I didn't wanna play with that bunch of crumbs, anyhow."

Wheeling away, he ran from the parlor and banged out the front door. Jake grunted an oath, almost tempted to go after him. Then he glanced up and caught the housekeeper studying him with a caustic scowl. Her lips were pinched tight, and for some reason, she appeared to be staring down her nose.

"Something on your mind, Mrs. Murphy?"

The years had turned Bess Murphy into a lumpy woman, with huge slack breasts and pudgy work-reddened hands. She had lived under this roof nearly a decade, performing her duties without complaint, caring for the Kincaids as if they were her own family. Never once in all that time had she voiced an opinion on what she'd seen or overheard, or found reprehensible. But suddenly, perhaps because she more than anyone else had raised the boys, she could no longer hold her peace.

"I've never questioned your ways, mister. Sure'n you know that to be a fact. But someone's to tell you before it's too late, and if it's not me, then who's to do it?"

"Tell me what?"

"Maybe it's not my business, mister, but it's God's own truth. You favor the older one, and forever take his side. I've been watchin' it since the day the little one was born, and whatever your reason, it's there to see. He knows it too, and don't think he doesn't. That's your answer why he torments Owen so much. And if you don't want it worse, then you'd best be doing something about yourself. There now, I've had me say and I feel better for it."

Jake regarded her with a great calmness. "You're right, Mrs. Murphy. It's none of your business." Walking past her, he moved through the vestibule toward the door. "I won't be home for supper."

The door closed behind him, leaving Bess Murphy in a

bemused daze. Several moments elapsed as she mulled it over, unable to believe that he knew what he was doing. Or knowing, cared so little. Her breasts lifted in an enormous sigh, and a shudder swept over her. He knew well enough, and little she could do but light a candle for the souls of the damned. Him most especially.

Slowly, almost ponderously, she trudged back to the kitchen.

Chalk Wheeler's office was strictly utilitarian. Located in the back of his gambling dive, it contained a battered desk, some rickety chairs, and several much-abused spittoons. As the kingfish of Delano, it served his needs well. Here his squad of hooligans met weekly to deliver collections from the bawdy houses, dance halls, and hooch joints west of the river, and on occasion a reluctant contributor was brought in for a private chat with the big man himself. This was seldom necessary, though, for everyone knew what happened to troublemakers. Those who listened to reason showed up with bruises and loose teeth and broken bones. The others simply vanished. Unreasonable men, Wheeler called them, and let it be known that they had departed Delano for reasons of health.

The message was lost on no one. While it had never been proved, it was suspected that these troublemakers had departed by way of the swift-flowing Arkansas, along with other deadwood. And those who preserved their health, the madams and tinhorns and busthead operators, did so with a weekly contribution to Wheeler's protection plan. It had become a way of life in Delano, and hardly anyone would have changed it if they could. Which they couldn't.

As for his grubby office, Wheeler felt no great urge to impress anyone. Those who resided in his little kingdom were already suitably impressed; fancy trappings would have been a needless waste of money. Something of an austere man, he followed the same rule in his personal attire. Whatever the occasion, he wore black broadcloth suits, with a black vest and a white shirt and a black four-in-hand. Though somber, and displaying small flair for a man of his means, it created an image which served his purposes. Somewhat funereal, and deadly serious.

And that he was a serious man, rarely given to jest, had been evident from his earliest days in Wichita. He was tall and swarthy, with muddy eyes and sleek, glistening hair, and his mouth looked as if it had been fashioned with a single, and very precise, slit of a well-stropped razor. Because of his dark skin and high cheekbones, some people thought he was a breed, but it was an opinion they kept to themselves. For there was a sinister aspect to Wheeler, an undeniable air of quietly contained malevolence. When he smiled, which was seldom, his lips skinned back like a snake baring its fangs, and those graced by this mirthless visage went away with the uncomfortable feeling that they had just swapped grins with a leering death's head. It was a thought not far removed from the truth.

Visitors were a novelty in Wheeler's office. His henchmen came there only when summoned, and everyone else in Delano shared an absolute passion to stay clear of the place. An invitation carried with it menacing undertones, for Wheeler was something less than a convivial host. Like a warlord of ancient times, he made alliances, not friends, and seemed perfectly content with the scheme of things. By nature he was a loner, and that others were uneasy in his presence bothered him none at all. He played a solitary hand, confiding in no one, and quite in character, remained distrustful even of those who helped enforce his will in the vice district.

On both sides of the river there was but one man who commanded Wheeler's respect, and that was Jake Kincaid. In many ways they were much alike, and while their methods differed markedly, there were no illusions between them. Wheeler acknowledged the fact that Jake was ruthless, perhaps even vindictive under the right circumstances, and possessed the power to destroy all he had built in Delano.

Being a realist, he accepted things as they were, content to hold what he'd won so long as he was left to his own devices. At times, when he indulged himself in a small pipedream, he even felt something akin to friendship for the other man. But that lasted only until the opium had worn off. Then he knew better.

Never having experimented with such exotic pastimes, Jake gave no thought whatever to friendship. To him, Wheeler was but a cog in the machine, albeit an important cog. He admired the way Wheeler dominated Delano, and often wondered if the vice lord's method of eliminating rivals wasn't superior to his own. Still, he always felt a bit slimy doing business with Wheeler, and while the thought of killing in itself wasn't repugnant, he believed he had graduated to more sophisticated forms of mayhem. He didn't like Wheeler, nor did he dislike him. He merely needed him, and the votes he controlled in the vice district.

There alone was where they met on common ground—a mutual need for the electorate. Jake needed Wheeler's votes to control the political apparatus of the county, and Wheeler needed Jake's influence to keep Delano free of restrictive ordinances and meddlesome lawmen. That Wheeler's need was greater gave Jake a decided edge in their arrangement, for if necessary, he could have managed without the Delano vote. It would require some nifty footwork, but he had become an old hand at walking the fence, and thus far, he had yet to lose his balance.

On the other side of that fence lay a reform coalition comprised of Grangers, prohibitionists and shorthorn cattlemen. As yet they were not a dominant force in Sedgwick County, but Jake had seen the shape of things to come. With every election the reform movement gained strength in the state legislature, and in time they would dictate the course of future events in Kansas. That was a foregone conclusion, and pragmatic as ever, Jake intended to come out on the winning side. To that end he worked both sides of the fence, playing one faction off against the other as the transition occurred, and he now courted the reformers as ardently as he had once courted the old order. His varied interests, encompassing railroads and settlers, cattlemen and the sporting crowd, made the tightwire act possible if sometimes slippery.

So it was, late in May, Chalk Wheeler evidenced little surprise when Jake entered his office one evening. Unaccustomed as he was to visitors, particularly those who showed up unannounced, he had been expecting the call for more than a week. Delano's kingfish was scarcely a novice in the political arena, and while elections were still some months off, the candidates had already begun campaigning. Which in the most devious of all games made a great deal of sense. Wichita's leading citizen was out collecting old debts.

Jake declined a drink but accepted a cigar, and once he had it fired up, he tilted back in his chair, surveying the office. Curiously, he had always felt comfortable around Wheeler, perhaps because they understood one another and had no need of artifice. With just a hint of mockery, he smiled and gestured about the dingy room with his cigar.

"Christ, you ought to spruce this place up, Chalk. Man in your position needs to toot his own horn a little. Let folks know you're somebody."

Wheeler barked a sharp, short laugh. "Why feed oats to a dead mule? Them that had any doubts about who runs Delano aren't around anymore."

"Yeah, I suppose you're right." Jake studied the coal on his cigar a moment. "Leastways Dave Flatt wouldn't have any doubts, would he? If he was still around, I mean."

That was something Wheeler had always liked about Kincaid. Never tried to soft-soap a man. Just stuck the knife in and shoved till he hit a nerve. He pursed his lips, seeming to deliberate.

"Damnedest thing, Jake. I don't ever recall sayin' I killed Flatt. You know yourself, I've always been partial to them upstandin' Christian types."

"Well, it's water under the bridge now, isn't it? I guess folks forgot all about it once the charges were dropped."

Wheeler grunted. "You're dealin'. Any need for me to ask the ante?"

"Let's just say we'll swap favors. Your part is seeing to it that Delano votes a straight party ticket."

"What about the reformers? Does that guarantee you'll keep them off my back?"

"Chalk, that doesn't guarantee you a goddamned thing. Except my goodwill." Jake smiled without warmth. "But you let me worry about the reformers. Turns out they owe me some favors, too."

"I'll just bet they do. Seems like you're playin' patty-cake in both camps these days."

"You got some objection I ought to hear about?"

Wheeler shrugged, aware that he'd almost overstepped the line. "No, guess not. Just makin' an observation."

"Good. Glad to see you've got your ear to the ground. Wouldn't want there to be any secrets between us." He took a long pull on the cigar and slowly exhaled. "You know, that's a damn good smoke. Better than what I get across the river."

"Glad you like it. I'll send over a box."

"Much obliged. Maybe I can do something for you one of these days." Jake rose and walked to the door. Almost as an afterthought he looked back. "See you at the polls."

Wheeler sat puffing on his cigar for a long time after the door closed. The visit hadn't bothered him. It was expected, and he would deliver as promised. But he was troubled all the same. He suddenly got the feeling Kincaid was loaded with secrets. Lots of them. And the sorry bastard was keeping them all to himself.

After crossing the bridge, Jake avoided the central part of town, keeping to back streets. It grated on him, skulking around in the dark like this, but the alternative was even more disturbing. As Zalia had commented on occasion, if he wouldn't consider marriage, then he could damn well observe the proprieties. And in that he was forced to concur. If the bluenoses ever got wind of their little arrangement, her reputation in Wichita would be mud.

Hugging the shadows, feeling just the least bit ridiculous, he came some minutes later to Chambers Street. It was a quiet, residential street, with modest homes and barking dogs and nosy people. That irritated him as well, for he never came here but what his hackles went bristly stiff as a wire brush. He always had the creepy sensation that some titillated old prune was watching him from behind lace curtains. Which was very likely the truth. Goddamn busybodies!

Near the end of the street he approached a well-kept frame house, much like the neighboring houses except that it somehow looked more prosperous. The yard was dotted with flowerbeds, and out front was a whitewashed picket fence. He slipped through the gate, thankful that Zalia kept the hinges oiled, and quickly crossed the yard to the front porch. As he yanked the pull bell, he noted with wry amusement that the drapes were drawn and the vestibule lamp had been extinguished. Zalia was a caution, no doubt about it. Under different circumstances she would have made somebody a damn good spy.

The door opened almost instantly and he stepped through, aware of the faint scent of jasmine and rustling skirts. Then the door closed with a soft click as the lock turned, and he felt her hand on his arm.

"Good evening, Jake." She came up on tiptoe and kissed him lightly on the cheek. "I'm so glad you could make it."

"Evenin'." He sounded a little disgruntled. "Would've been here sooner but I had an errand to look after."

"Let me take your coat. It is frightfully warm in here, I'm afraid. Can I fix you a drink?"

Zalia Blair hung his coat in the hall and led the way into the parlor, chattering all the while. She was a small, compact woman, always cheerful, with a saucy disposition and a kind of bustling vitality. Though quite short, she was neither delicate nor plump. Her gown fitted snugly over fruity breasts and tightly rounded buttocks, and she dressed to accentuate her youthful figure. Her oval features were framed by hair dark as obsidian, and something of the imp lurked behind eyes as wide and bright as buttons. But for all her puckish ways, she was keenly perceptive and possessed a sharp, inquisitive mind. That was the thing Jake liked about her most. While she was not yet thirty, and still turned the head of anything in pants, he found himself attracted more to this rare mixture of spontaneous wit and mental acuity than to her good looks.

"Isn't this heat simply dreadful?" She handed Jake a drink and took a place beside him on the settee. "I shudder to think about the summer ahead."

He suppressed a grin and sipped at the whiskey. She looked cool and poised, although the room was uncomfortably warm; sometimes he suspected she didn't sweat like normal human beings. This nonsense about the heat was merely her way of helping him to unwind, and he was reminded again that she was a remarkable woman. Nothing prissy about her, either. Cigars and whiskey and feet up on the table. Whatever made a man comfortable.

"Well, I guess it's like that general said—Sheridan I think it was. If he owned Kansas and hell, he'd rent out Kansas and move in with the Devil."

"Did he really say that?" She rushed on, the question left dangling. "What a boorish thing to say. The man should be court-martialed, or something. That's simply scandalous. Now, tell me about the boys. What rascals they are!" Her eyes twinkled, and she smiled guilelessly. "Would you believe it, everyone in town says they are just like their father."

She had a disconcerting genius for the non sequitur, nimbly leaping from topic to topic with hardly a pause for breath. While it amused him, these sudden shifts sometimes took a moment to untangle. "The boys? Why, they're fine. Just fine. Mean as sin, of course, but I guess that's all part of growin' up."

"That's what I meant. Mischievous. Just like their father."

He smiled suggestively. "You think I'm mischievous, do you?"

"Not often enough." She gave him a brazen look, and laughed softly. "Oh, Jake Kincaid, you should see the glint in your eye. But time enough for that. Have your drink and tell me what's been happening. And don't leave anything out. I want to hear all the juicy little tidbits." She paused, deliberating a moment. "Let's see, you can start by telling me who you hornswoggled today."

She was an absolute delight. Vivacious and animated, and forever fascinated by his business dealings. Which pleased him immensely. At times, he thought himself a fool for not marrying her, but the thought seldom persisted. They had been keeping company for four years now, and though she made no effort to conceal her own feelings, he gave little in return.

Oddly enough, it was business that had brought them together. Edward Blair, owner of the local hardware store, had been struck down by pleurisy the winter of '76. Zalia suddenly found herself alone, without family or anyone she trusted implicitly, and there were decisions to be made about the store as well as various parcels of land her husband had bought on speculation. After a brief period of mourning, she appeared in Jake's office one afternoon, outlining her predicament with candor and openly seeking advice. She seemed to have no fear that he would take advantage of her, and in that, she was right. Jake quickly found a manager for the hardware store, providing her with a reliable source of income, and agreed to sell her land holdings on a commission basis.

At first, although he was attracted to her from the start, he was nothing more than an advisor. Morality was never the issue, for he was a virile man and shortly after Sadie's death had become a frequent customer in some of Delano's more elegant houses. Of all sexual aberrations, abstinence had always seemed to him the strangest. But he wanted no permanent attachments, nothing to encumber him or rekindle emotions he had ruthlessly suppressed. Quite without realizing it, however, he soon found himself in Zalia's bed, and afterward, he always suspicioned that it was he who had been seduced.

Still, despite her beguiling ways, their arrangement was on his terms from the beginning. As a widow with a tidy nest egg, she could have married any one of a dozen men, but she quietly discouraged all suitors. She made no demands on him, and aside from jests about his skittish attitude toward marriage, she was careful that he never felt trapped or threatened by their relationship. Apparently content with what he was willing to give, she never pressed for more, and it was on the basis of this understanding that they remained lovers.

Whenever he called, generally two or three nights a week, their routine seldom varied. She fussed over him, attentive to his creature comforts, sometimes fixing a late supper, and then they talked. She had a way of drawing him out, encouraging him to speak of things he discussed with no one else. Like an exuberant child, eyes shiny bright, she listened raptly, on occasion interjecting a pertinent question, and more than an audience, she had proved a highly perceptive sounding board for the ideas and plans forever churning around in his brain. He found her a remarkable woman. Indeed, a rare combination of beauty and understanding and horse sense. But he still had no intention of marrying her.

Tonight was little different than other nights. As Jake talked, Zalia slowly closed the gap between them on the settee. When he finally ran dry of words she was somehow snuggled close in the crook of his arm. Almost as if some ritual were being acted out, he kissed her and began fondling her breasts. Her response was shamelessly passionate, love and need brought quickly to a white-hot incandescence. And when it became unbearable she rose, dimming the parlor lamp, and led him toward the bedroom. As he had so many times in the past, Jake went along willingly, short of breath himself and scarcely needing to be coaxed, but there was always the thought that he wasn't quite in command of the situation. That he had been buttered and basted, tenderly roasted to a slow turn, and then seduced again. It was the damnedest feeling. Somehow strange. But pleasant. Very pleasant.

Cecil Hollister chomped down on his cigar and glowered like an old bull. It was the last day of May, sweltering hot, and the temperature in his office had risen by leaps and bounds in the past few minutes. Seated across from him, slouched down in a chair and looking insufferably smug, Jake puffed his own cigar and casually flicked a widening rosette of smoke rings toward the ceiling.

"If it's not too much trouble," Hollister demanded, "I'd like to know where you got that notion."

"Cecil, what can I say?" Jake spread his hands in a helpless gesture. "You know a gentleman never reveals his source of information."

"Gentlemen be damned!" Hollister thundered. "We're not playing parlor games. I want to know where you got the idea that I'd even consider laying track to Caldwell."

"Well, you did buy out the charter." Jake smiled lazily. "Didn't you?"

This was common knowledge. Last year the Santa Fe had acquired the Cowley, Summer & Ft. Smith, a fleaflicker railroad with only one asset—a charter granting it the right to lay rails between Wichita and Caldwell. As yet, the Santa Fe had done nothing with its paper railroad, and so far as the public knew, probably never would.

Hollister jerked the cigar from his mouth. "So what? That still doesn't answer my question."

"Let's just say my boys in the legislature told me the same thing your boys told you."

"And what might that be?"

"That the reformers will pull it off this time. Come the fall session, they'll pass a quarantine law, and when they do, Wichita goes down the chute as a cowtown."

Hollister grunted, and his eyes narrowed in a sly look. "So you think I'm going to lay track to Caldwell to save you and your buddies? And don't put on that innocent act. I got word you'd hoodwinked the Cherokees before the ink was dry."

"Wouldn't exactly call it a secret, Cecil." Jake was still smiling, but it was a cold, hard smile. "Seems like you held out on me, though, doesn't it?"

"For Christ's sake, will you stop spinning riddles? You act like there's some Borgia plot afoot. What, precisely, am I supposed to have held out on you?"

"The last week in April—that's over a month back, Cecil—the Santa Fe board of directors voted to lay track to Caldwell. You knew then that Wichita had only one season left, and you had your plans laid to jump into Caldwell with both feet. But you never said *boo* to me. That's what I call holding out."

"Well, I'll be goddamned." Hollister was clearly thunderstruck. "How the hell did you learn about that?"

"It's those little birds. They keep tellin' me things."

"Jake, I never cease to be amazed by your talent for subterfuge. And despite the fact that you obviously have a spy on my staff, I mean that as a compliment."

"Thank you, Cecil. I appreciate the kind words."

"Be that as it may, however, I'm still somewhat at a loss. Other than running cattle in the Outlet, what interest do you have in Caldwell?"

"Why, I'm always interested in makin' money, Cecil. If

you had given me the inside word I could have done it the easy way. Since you didn't, I had to do it the hard way, and that'll wind up costin' you more."

Hollister suddenly became very alert. "I don't follow you."

Jake blew a couple of smoke rings, deliberating. "Suppose we take it step by step. The quarantine law will stop longhorns from entering eastern Kansas. So in order to get by that the Santa Fe has got to lay track south and build stockyards right on the border. That way the cows are actually loaded in Indian Territory and never set foot on Kansas soil. Is that right so far, or did I leave something out?"

"That's close enough." Hollister eyed him skeptically. "But I still don't see what it has to do with you."

"Cecil, I hate to be the bearer of bad tidings, but I own a strip of border land that stretches to hell and back. Way things shape up, if the Santa Fe wants to put stockyards right on the line, you'll have to buy from me."

Hollister bit through his cigar, and the stub toppled to the floor. "Kincaid, has anyone ever told you that you're a conniving, underhanded son of a bitch?"

"Lots of people. But comin' from an old graverobber like you, I'll take that as mighty high praise."

"You're out to skin me, then?"

"You shouldn't have held out on me, Cecil. Not after all I've done for you and the Santa Fe."

Hollister spat shreds of tobacco from his mouth and sighed heavily. "I suspect a pound of flesh will soothe your feelings. Come on, let's hear it. How much?"

Jake chuckled softly and pulled a slip of paper from his vest pocket. He tossed it across the desk, then eased back and resumed blowing smoke rings. The first lazy circle barely made it to the ceiling before Cecil Hollister exploded in a paroxysm of rage. Then he balled the scrap of paper in his fist and swore a melodic string of obscenities known only to railroad barons and mule-skinners.

FIVE

The winter of '82 had been raw and stormy. Blizzards swept the plains with icy ferocity, and in January a great freeze-up had buried the land beneath a crystal shroud. Wichita became little more than a shivering island in a vast sea of white; at times even the railroads ground to a halt, as snowdrifts higher than a locomotive blocked miles upon miles of track. But in late March the wind shifted and temperatures soared. A warm breeze scudded in from the south, and within the week the prairie was transformed into a quagmire of soft, squishy mud. Travel was out of the question, impossible by wagon and hazardous at best by horse. Trains were the only thing moving, and unless a man had business that couldn't wait, he simply stayed home, content to let the land rally back from winter at its own pace.

By early April the Arkansas was in flood, a roaring turbulence filled with uprooted trees and dead animals and debris sloughed off by nature in its spring rampage. Every street in Wichita was a bog of greased, axle-deep dough, with suction like that of quicksand. A walk to town might cost a man his boots, mired forever in the earth's slippery bowels, and while life went on, the tempo of things slowed to a sticky, heavy-footed hobble.

On a crisp moonlit night, after an evening with Zalia Blair, Jake slogged back across town, doggedly plowing his way through the muddy clutch of near-impossible streets. It struck him as preposterous that a man would venture out on a night like this. Especially for a brief, and none too fulfilling, romp in the hay; he felt somehow mocked by his own rutting instinct. Yet there was more to it than that, and in the same thought he knew that nothing was ever quite so elemental. Zalia ministered to something over and above mere physical needs, and without that he likely wouldn't have bothered. Certainly he wouldn't have trudged to Delano and back tonight, however horny he was. A whore might well have sapped his juices with greater artistry, but lust was only part of it. And in a sudden insight, he saw that it was perhaps the smallest part of what he shared with Zalia.

The thought gave him a boost. Rutting was, after all, a bodily function, like a healthy crap, and its mockery of a moment ago had been turned back upon itself. The mind functioned on a higher level, with greater needs, and in that there was an acceptable rationale to tonight's mud-caked excursion. Pleased that he'd worked it out so neatly, he churned on up the hill and into the house.

Mrs. Murphy had banked the fire for the night, but he stirred the coals back to life, added kindling and logs, and quickly had the fireplace crackling with a cheery blaze. The nights were still nippy, and after sloshing around in the cold mud his feet felt brittle as icicles. He jerked off his boots and got himself a tumbler of brandy (one of the smaller refinements Zalia had introduced into his life), then pulled a chair close to the fire and held his stockinged feet to the flames. The warmth spread through him, a volatile mix of brandy and snapping logs, and he was soon scrunched down in the chair like a dreamy cinnamon bear.

But years of habit were not to be neutralized by the mellow glow of fancy liquor and a toasty fire. Even in repose Jake's mind clicked and calculated, clinking along like some perpetual-motion machine that could rest only as it worked. With time, he had come to realize that life could only be understood backward, and he often spent odd moments reflecting on the foibles and follies of the past. It was a game he played with himself. By isolating weaknesses and flaws, harshly evaluating his own performance, he girded himself for tests yet to be faced. Like the reformers. His allies one day and his nemesis the next, but by whatever definition, an albatross which seemed to shadow past, present, and future.

Last year, despite the arguments of saner men, they had voted Kansas dry. At times, he still couldn't quite come to grips with it. The sale of all alcoholic beverages now a violation of the law. It surpassed belief. Yet they had steamrollered the bill through, and it was very much a fact of life.

Still, irrational as the law was, things weren't as bad as they might have been. A last-minute compromise had left enforcement of prohibition to the duly elected county authorities, and in Wichita, a tenuous compromise had been effected. The town proper was dry as a bone—the Lady Gay had been converted into a mercantile emporium—but Delano was allowed to operate much as it had in the past. This patchwork arrangement had been negotiated by Jake shortly after the dry law was enacted. Meeting with George Martin, leader of the local Temperance League, he had laid it on the line.

"You can't legislate morals. Not yet, and especially not overnight. There are people in this country who still like their sin, and one way or another, they'll have it."

A crusader of sorts, Martin had bristled at that. "If necessary, we can call on the governor to enforce the law. Like it or not, people must change their heathen ways. The days of Sodom and Gomorrah are past."

"George, there's such a thing as winnin' the battle and losin' the war. You know, Wichita isn't as advanced as Topeka and some of these other towns. If you bring the state in now, things will just go underground. So long as whores and gamblin' aren't policed, people will figure out a way to sell whiskey. Take my advice. Let it lay a year or so, then crack down. Give folks a chance to get used to the idea."

As a gesture of good faith, Jake had moved the Lady Gay

to Caldwell, and ordered the sheriff to close down every dive on the Wichita side of the river. His compromise plan had worked, and it was still working. Although how long he could manage to hold the lid on was anybody's guess. The Prohibitionists weren't exactly the most rational bunch he'd ever dealt with.

But for all of their fanaticism, they were as pragmatic as the most corrupt of politicians. Banded together under a loose confederation called the Reform Movement, three major factions traded favor for favor, each supporting the cause of the other. Although their goals were but dimly related, the end result was what counted, and prohibitionists gladly supported the shorthorn breeders in order to vote Kansas dry. That they deplored this very pragmatism in those they fought—the sporting crowd and the railroad lobby and the longhorn cattlemen—seemed in no way to contradict the righteousness of their cause. It never occurred to the reformers to think of themselves as hypocrites. They fought for the good of all men. And if by chance they benefited in the bargain, it was merely God's blessing being showered upon the children of good works and holy deeds.

That their alliance worked marvelously well was all too apparent. Since the fall season of 1880 they had held the state legislature in a virtual hammerlock. They had pushed through the quarantine law that year, barring longhorns from the eastern half of the state, thereby placating the shorthorn breeders. Then the next year they had rammed the dry law down everyone's throat, which squared accounts with the Prohibitionists. And now they were working on an embargo act, which would ban longhorns from all of Kansas, as well as measures to curtail the power of railroads. Presumably the latter was to satisfy the Grangers, although no one as yet had presented a logical premise for their wrath against the very organizations who had brought them west. It seemed explanation enough that power in itself was to be abhorred. Unless of course it rested in the hands of God's children.

Jake chuckled sourly to himself. What a joke—God's children! They were worse than the robber barons or the grubbiest political hack. When such people twisted the law to suit their own ends they at least saw it for the great farce it really was. The reformers mouthed scripture and holier-than-thou platitudes in the name of a cause that would have curled Christ's hair. More than a farce, it was a travesty. The worst kind.

All the same, he had no choice but to deal with them. What he'd foreseen a couple of years back was slowly coming to pass. The frontier was inexorably being pushed westward, forced to give ground before the juggernaut of civilized men and their churches and their petty strictures. The Reform Movement was gaining momentum, bracing itself for the final onslaught, and when the dust cleared, Kansas would dance to a new master. As George Martin had observed, "Like it or not, people must change their heathen ways." And while it gave him a queasy feeling down in the pit of his stomach, Jake knew that the dictum included him. If he was to come out on the winning side, hold what he had, and consolidate power for the future, then he must change with the times.

Not that change wasn't profitable. It was, far more so than he had envisioned. Wichita's demise as a cowtown had made his land, and the land of the Santa Fe, all the more desirable to settlers. Sales had never been better, and in the last two years his personal worth had grown accordingly. (Estimated by the newspapers to be in excess of $5 million—which Jake neither confirmed nor denied.) Ironically, the fall of Wichita and the rise of Caldwell had made him yet another fortune. Cecil Hollister had gnashed his teeth like a bee-stung bear, but he knew when he'd been snookered. Jake owned the land, and the Santa Fe had paid handsomely for the privilege of erecting their stockyards on that intangible line separating Kansas and Indian Territory. Caldwell itself had become another of those instant boomtowns (by now a phenomenon linked with the Kincaid name and the Santa Fe's prestige), and hardly to anyone's surprise, it turned out that Jake had bought most of the commercial property sites while the town was still a wide spot on the prairie. As usual, the latecomers paid an exorbitant price for the honor of doing business in Caldwell.

Yet, oddly enough, Cecil Hollister and everyone else acted as though Jake had hung the moon. They might moan and groan, cursing him for a bandit, but they respected a man who was always one step ahead of the pack. Wherever Kincaid took a hand there was money to be made, plenty for everybody, and in some queer way they felt almost obligated to him. And the way things worked out, perhaps it was preordained that those who would respect him the most were the men of the Cherokee Cattlemen's Association.

The Association now maintained an office in Caldwell, and its members jumped through whatever hoop Jake cared to hold up. Being realists, they knew that he worked for himself rather than the common good. But whatever benefited Jake Kincaid also benefited the Association, and as men will, they sacrificed rugged individualism for the sake of greater profits. The Cherokee Nation, under Jake's brand of diplomacy and persuasion, proved a tolerant landlord; the only time they saw an Indian was when the Cherokee treasurer came to collect the annual lease payment. And because of Jake's foresight, Association members hadn't lost one nickel owing to the quarantine law. In fact, things were better than ever. The railroad had come to them!

But for all their good fortune, there were problems nonetheless. Cattlemen in eastern Texas still used the Chisholm Trail, driving their herds to Caldwell, and they thought nothing of encroaching on Association graze. Their beeves needed to be fattened, the land was there, and they simply ignored the lease arrangement with the Cherokees. Last year Jake had suggested that they use the Creek Nation, south of the Outlet, as a holding ground. Affronted, the Texans had rejected his proposal out of hand. The Creeks demanded payment, and as they always had, the Texans intended to graze in the Outlet for free. The season had ended with hard feelings between the Association members (former Texans themselves) and the Texas cattlemen.

After stewing on it through the winter, Jake decided that sterner measures were needed. Association members agreed, and by early spring their crews were busy fencing off the entire Outlet. A corridor would be left open for the Texans to drive their herds to railhead, but they would not be allowed grazing rights within the Outlet itself. The plan would also eliminate costly roundups, as well as disputes over unbranded strays, and bring about greater profits for everyone. But the more immediate goal was to put the quietus on the Texans and their trail-starved herds.

Still, however justified he felt in fencing the Outlet, Jake had few illusions about the possible consequences. Texans considered *fence* a dirty word, and the mere mention of barbed wire had been known to set them off in a frothing rage. It was a calculated risk, as were most of his moves, but one which might well provoke a shooting war between Association members and Texas drovers. There was no backing off, though. A man held what was his, by whatever means necessary, or someone eventually took it away from him. Life was like that. Lots of little dogs always trying to divvy up the big dog's bone.

Trouble. Trouble. Toil and trouble. Sipping his brandy, Jake ruminated on the truth of that little profundity. Nothing was ever easy. Whatever a man built in life was inevitably laid on a cornerstone of adversity. But if it was easy, perhaps it wouldn't have been any fun. Adversity put a man on his mettle, made him think, kept his reflexes sharp and attuned to the world about him. And if he was a farsighted man, a bit cagier than his fellows, he soon discovered that adversity paid handsome dividends. Especially for the big dog.

Staring spellbound into the fiery-orange flames, he suddenly found himself wishing Sadie were here. After all these years she was still with him, somehow still alive, a blithe haunt that dwelled near the core of what he was. And he would have given all he owned to have her here, this very moment, to see for herself that all his visions had come true. How she would have gloried in the sheer witchery of his hard-won reality.

A vagrant twinge tugged at his conscience. Perhaps he was being unfair to Zalia. Leaping from her bed only to summon back the ghost of Sadie. All the same, he'd never deceived her. They were both full grown and she had accepted his terms right from the start. That she was a good woman, comforting and selfless and understanding, he never doubted for a moment. But then, the world was full of good women.

There was only one Sadie.

Caldwell was dirty and dusty, a small blemish on an emerald prairie. But it had a vulgar lustiness that cattlemen found irresistible. All that was sordid and depraved and iniquitous about former cowtowns had been imported to this last outpost of rampant vice. Whores and gamblers, thimbleriggers and grifters, gathered like jackals drawn by a freshening wind to tainted meat. Killings were so commonplace that the undertaker worked nights, and a man's best chance for survival rested squarely on his hip. The town marshal was a retired outlaw from New Mexico, the mayor a vagabond flesh merchant come recently to politics, and the city council a collection of rogues who made larceny something of a sport.

There had never been another cowtown like it. None so low or vile, and certainly none so deadly. Vice was its only industry, trailhands and cattlemen its only clientele, and those who called it home positively reveled in its infamy.

As the noon train shuddered to a halt on a blistering June day, gunshots erupted along Chisholm Street like a string of firecrackers. The season was in full swing, and cowhands out to hoorah the town, blasting holes in the sky with their six-guns, staggered drunkenly from one dive to the next. The enticements were many and varied, some more exotic than others. Outside every saloon and dancehall stood doll-faced women, with painted cheeks and low-cut gowns and the fluttering Jezebel wink of a hussy practicing her trade. In one form or another, every business establishment in town was out to fleece the Texans; except for a clapboard hotel, a couple of cafés, and a smithy, all of Caldwell was devoted to man's raunchier pursuits. Hitchracks were jammed with horses, the street seethed with trail crews out to See the Elephant, and through the doors of every dive blared the raucous clamor of squealing women and laughing men. It was circus time in Caldwell.

At the train depot Jake stepped from the last passenger coach and stood gazing south along Chisholm Street. Owen and Brad scrambled down behind him, instinctively sticking close to his coattails. Just for a moment they were absolutely motionless, like saplings taken root, gawking in slack-jawed wonder at the riotous antheap before them. Caldwell was hardly the place for small boys, especially a pair decked out in short suit jackets, kneepants, and button shoes. But Jake had brought them along as part and parcel of their education. The part that wasn't taught in schools.

Dodge City and Caldwell were the last of the great Kansas cowtowns. Before long, as the railroads probed ever deeper toward Texas, these last remnants of a rowdy, tumultuous era would fade into obscurity. Like Abilene and Newton and Wichita, other trail towns which had sparkled briefly in the glory days, they would survive in the only way left to them. Sodbusters would come with their plows, gouging neat furrows across the grassy plains, and even as they seeded the earth an era would have ended.

But while it lasted, Jake meant for the boys to see life at its rawest. When they were grown, he wanted them to look back and remember. To recall the excesses of men, their witless lust for rot-gut whiskey and four-bit whores and

blood-splattered brawls. To reflect not on the storybook nobility taught in schools, but rather on the realities of life. That
men at their best were creatures of thought and cunning, restrained on a leash of social taboo stretching back across un-
told centuries. And at their worst, brutish throwbacks with a
visceral instinct for the jugular, one step removed from walking on their knuckles. Today, in perhaps the most fundamental link of their education, Owen and Brad were to see men
at their worst.

The boys were all eyes as they followed their father down
the street. Wichita had been tamed by the time they were old
enough to understand the tomfoolery of grown-ups, and while
they had sneaked across the river into Delano a couple of
times, they had never seen anything like this. Owen, at the
advanced age of ten, understood more than his little brother,
although he was still a bit fuzzy about the reasons. But he
had Jake's knack for scrutinizing things closely, watching and
listening with the intense calm of one who is curious yet un-
involved. Nothing surprised him, or if it did, he seldom betrayed himself with any outward expression, and he squirreled
away everything he saw or heard, to be dusted off and examined at some later time. He was no less eager than other
youngsters, he simply didn't show it.

Quite the opposite, Brad was a small bundle of dynamite
whose fuse glowed red hot around the clock. His eyes were
glittering, diamond-bright, darting here and there, almost as
if he gulped the sights down with the swift, greedy thirst of
one who savors every drop. Guileless and mercurial, his face
mirrored everything he felt, awe and fright, bewilderment
and glee, shifting quickly through a gamut of sensations that
left his nerves humming and his head dizzy with exhilaration. He was caught up in the excitement of swaggering cowhands and brazen women, a carnival atmosphere that
promised lions and tigers and great snorty dragons, and in
childlike innocence he questioned nothing, accepting all.

Their first stop was the Lady Gay, where Jake paused for

a word with Quincy Blackburn. Fatter than ever, bloated by time and self-indulgence, Blackburn looked like a bright pig, with small beady eyes and wide nostrils and quivering jowls that undershot his jaw. These days he split his time between Wichita and Caldwell, managing the Kincaid properties, and for all his blubbery good cheer, he had proved himself an astute businessman.

"Couldn't be better." He preened, flashing his gold tooth, in answer to Jake's question. "Not exactly the swank crowd we used to get in Wichita"—his look took in the swirling madhouse around them—"but what they don't spend over the bar they lose at the tables. No sir, can't fault 'em on that score. They're better'n a gold mine."

Jake nodded, surveying the crowd. These calls were by now a mere formality. He trusted the fat man implicitly, for Blackburn feared him no less than he feared the wrath of God, and the monthly profit statements bore testament to his scrupulous honesty. At least in his dealings with Jake Kincaid.

"Well, I won't hold you, Quince. Just thought I'd drop by while I was here." He glanced down at the boys, who flanked him on either side, sticking close as mustard plaster. "Brought the sprouts along to give 'em a look at a real, live cowtown."

Blackburn chuckled, regarding the youngsters with the jolly benevolence of a man who finds children one of life's greater abstractions. "Boys, you're in for a treat, take my word for it. Caldwell's about as wild and woolly as they come. And believe you me, there's nobody better suited to show you the sights than your Pa. Yessir, you're in good company."

All smiles, the fat man walked them to the door and shook Jake's hand with the gusto of a Bible salesman. They left him there and turned south along the boardwalk, slowly threading their way through the boisterous cowhands who jammed the street. The boys' eyes grew wider and brighter, scarcely able to absorb the shouts and drunken laughter and gunshots, as if it were some whimsical fantasy come to life. A few doors down the street they came to a false-fronted building with dusty, fly-specked windows, and an overhead sign emblazoned with the words *Cherokee Cattlemen's Association*. Jake steered the boys through the entranceway and stepped inside.

Will Rutledge, office manager for the Association, was seated at the only desk in the room. A middle-aged man, with beefy shoulders and evasive eyes, Rutledge was also mayor of Caldwell. One of Jake's axioms was that business flourished best in a convivial political climate, and Rutledge, along with the town council, were all handpicked men. Beaming an oily grin, Rutledge bounded from his chair and strode forward.

"Well, Mr. Kincaid. Good to see you. Didn't expect you till later in the month."

Jake gave his hand a perfunctory shake and let go. "Will, say hello to my boys. Brought 'em down to see what a rip-snortin' cowtown looks like. Boys, this is Mr. Rutledge. He's sort of the ringmaster of that circus outside."

Owen caught a tinge of mockery in his father's voice. Over the past year he had begun noticing such things, and it had slowly dawned on him that men feared his father. Before he'd simply thought that men liked his father, and went out of their way to be nice to him, but the truth had gradually become apparent. He saw the fear in Rutledge's fawning manner, just as he had seen it in Blackburn and other men, and it no longer seemed strange to him. Instead, for reasons not yet clear, he sensed that these men were wise to fear his father. And the thought was somehow enthralling, as if he'd discovered a secret which grown-ups pretended didn't exist.

"They're a fine-lookin' pair, Mr. Kincaid." Rutledge grinned wider, inspecting the boys with an appreciative eye. "Say, come to think of it, you couldn't've picked a better day. Liable to be lots of fireworks. Ol' Spotted Horse is on the warpath. Got himself likkered up and took a knife to Ed Beal this mornin'. The marshal's out huntin' for him right now."

Spotted Horse was something of a town character, a Pawnee who had quit the reservation to follow the white man's road. Everyone spoke of him as "Caldwell's tame Injun," and he generally behaved himself. But once he'd cadged a few drinks too many, he sometimes proved less tame than people believed. Apparently this was one of his off days.

Jake appeared mildly indifferent to the high jinks of Spotted Horse. The only Indians that interested him were Cherokees. "Anything happening I ought to know about? Business or otherwise?"

"Naw, it's pretty quiet. The Texans ain't too happy with us stringin' fence, but there's nothin' they can do about it. Lots of bellyachin' and such, but hot air never hurt nobody." Rutledge suddenly hesitated, pursing his lips. "There was one thing, though. Sorta queer in a way. Some of the boys sent word that the Cherokee agent showed up. Been nosin' around askin' questions about our fences. But he didn't get huffy or nothin', acted real polite. That's what I mean about it soundin' queer. Close as I recollect, that's the first time he ever set foot in the Outlet."

A moment passed as Jake considered it. Then he shrugged. "Probably just curious. We'll wait till the monthly meeting and I'll get it firsthand from the ones that talked with him. No need jumpin' at shadows." He turned and started out. "I'll be around if you need me. We're taking the evening train back to Wichita."

Rutledge trailed along behind them, still smiling his oily smile and assuring Jake that everything was under control. But as they reached the door Jigger Musgrave galloped past on a lathered horse, happened to glance in their direction, and slid his mount to a dust-smothered halt. Reining about sharply, he rode back to the office and flung himself from the saddle. Urgency was stamped across his face, and he hurried forward, sweat-soaked and breathing hard from the long ride.

"Gawd a'mighty, ain't you a sight for sore eyes. I was just on my way to the depot to telegraph you. All hell's busted loose. We got ourselves a regular war brewin' out there. Mebbe already started for all I know."

Jake stopped him with an upraised hand. "Take it easy, Jigger. The world's not comin' to an end. Just slow down and get yourself a deep breath. Then you can tell me what you're talkin' about."

"Boss, I am tellin' you! Them gawddamn stupid Texans tried to break through our fence. Said they was gonna graze their cows and we could like it or lump it. So we stampeded their herd to hell and gone, and peppered their ass with some gunpowder while they was hightailin' it."

He paused to catch his breath, and his mouth creased in a hard line. "Course that ain't the end of it, not by a damnsight. They'll be back, more'n likely with a bunch of cousins and such, you savvy what I mean? So I figgered I better get you on the telegraph and find out what the hell's to be done."

"You're sure they'll come lookin' for a fight?"

"Sure as I'm standin' here. It's ol' Simp Dixon's outfit, and they're meaner'n a barrelful of snakes."

Jake frowned, mulling it over, for some reason acutely conscious that Owen and Brad were watching him with round-eyed intensity. After a long deliberation he looked back at Musgrave, his manner cold and decisive. "If we let one bunch through there'll be no stoppin' the rest of them. Contact the other ranchers and get as many men as you need. Tell them any man that holds out will answer to me personally." A curious glaze came over his eyes, like polished stone. "Whatever you have to do, Jigger, I want it stopped right here. If the Texans want a fight, you give it to them in spades. Understand?"

Musgrave bobbed his head, grim as death itself. "That's the way she'll be. You gonna hang around in case I need you?"

Jake smiled. "You won't need me, Jigger. Handle it your own way and let me know how it comes out."

The foreman shot him a vinegary grin. "Why, hell, boss, it'll come out the way it always does. With us on top."

The boys were curiously silent after Musgrave had ridden off. Even Brad, not yet eight, understood that his father had just ordered men killed. And for nothing more than crossing a fence! He couldn't imagine what was so important about a fence, nor could Owen. But if they were tempted to ask the question, Spotted Horse robbed them of the chance.

Marshal Henry Brown caught up with the not so tame Pawnee in front of the Longhorn Café, directly across the street. Staggering drunk, Spotted Horse responded to the marshal's command to come along peaceable by pulling his knife. His first step forward was his last. Without a flicker of emotion, Brown calmly shot him in the chest four times. The impact of the heavy slugs drove Spotted Horse backward in a nerveless dance; then his knees buckled and he rolled off the boardwalk into the street. Brown shucked out the empty shells and reloaded, oblivious to the stares of the crowd, then holstered his pistol and walked off. A swarm of flies buzzed around, looking interested, and settled over the blood-splattered corpse. Everyone else went on about their business, mere spectators to an event now concluded and no longer worth their bother.

The rest of the afternoon was all downhill. Jake tried to entertain the boys with a tour of Caldwell's dives, and an inspection of the stockyards, but he knew their minds were on Spotted Horse. And the casual ferocity which had snuffed out a human life. Oddly enough, he couldn't understand why he regretted their having witnessed the killing. It was why he had brought them here. To see men at their worst. To show them the nature of the beast, and how low it could sink. Yet, while he had meant well, perhaps the lesson had been a bit gory for a couple of youngsters. They still looked a little green around the gills, and even though the killing hadn't affected him one way or the other, he had to admit that men at their worst were pretty strong stuff.

Later that evening, on the train, Brad seemed to perk up and began squirming around in his seat. At last, unable to smother his curiosity, he looked across at his father. He knew he was prying, which was strictly forbidden in the Kincaid household, but he desperately needed an answer.

"Pa, what kind of fence was it you were talkin' to that man about?"

"Just a stock fence. What the devil made you ask that?"

"Oh, nothin'." The boy fidgeted, looking out the window. Several moments passed, but try as he might he couldn't resist the impulse. "If it's just a stock fence, then how come you're gonna kill them Texans if they cross it?"

Jake darted a hurried glance around the coach, then leaned across and grabbed the boy's arm. "Little man, if you don't want your ears boxed then you'd better close your mouth and keep it closed. You understand me?"

Brad burst into tears. Wrenching away, he scooted farther into the corner, and buried his face in his hands. Baffled, Jake eased back in his seat, wondering why it was always the young one who aroused his anger. He had no ready explanation, but it was a fact nonetheless. Slowly he became aware that Owen was staring at him, and he found it difficult to decipher the boy's look.

"Something botherin' you, son?"

Owen shrugged, dropping his gaze. "Guess we was both wonderin' the same thing. Brad just didn't think it'd hurt to ask, that's all."

"About the fence?"

The boy nodded, eyes still downcast.

Jake waited for the anger to come, as it had a moment ago. But instead he felt gripped by a need to justify his actions. As if, in some way he failed to comprehend, Owen was due an explanation. "Son, let me ask you something. Do you think the marshal was right in killin' that Indian when he came at him with a knife?"

Owen looked up, clearly surprised. "Why, sure he was, Pa. Cripes, he didn't have no choice."

"That's right, son, he didn't. He was protecting himself, and that's something you ought to think about. Every man has to look after what's his. Whether it's his life or his home or his land. That's why I couldn't let those men cross my fence. Because if I did, they'd be taking something that belongs to me—my land. And if I let them take my land, then what's to stop them from taking my life?"

Owen's face lit up. "Sure, Pa. You're just doing what the marshal did. Protectin' yourself."

"That's what it boils down to, son. Plain and simple."

The irony of it left a bitter taste in Jake's mouth. Henry Brown had ridden with Billy the Kid. He was a common killer hired to do the dirtiest job imaginable. Yet as a lawman, his quickness to kill could be twisted around to win a boy's approval. Sanction by process of distortion, and with it, a father's right to kill.

Sometimes it was a strange goddamn world. Strange and odious.

As Jigger Musgrave had so accurately observed, all hell broke loose. But it had less to do with Texans than with bureaucrats.

Never one to disregard an order, the foreman had followed Jake's instructions to the letter. Before nightfall he had commandeered a band of some fifty cowhands from ranchers in the Outlet. Though the cattlemen displayed a certain reluctance to fight fellow Texans, their native loyalty proved no great obstacle. Musgrave delivered Jake Kincaid's ultimatum—retaliation against those who failed to support the Association—and everyone quickly fell into line. At dawn the next morning, the hastily organized defenders waited at the fence line separating the Outlet from the Creek Nation.

Had Musgrave been less feisty, some peaceful settlement might have been arranged. But the Texans were spoiling for a fight, and he gladly accommodated them. Led by Simp Dixon, whose herd had been stampeded the day before, nearly forty drovers rode toward the fence. When Musgrave ordered them to halt someone fired a shot, and the battle commenced. Afterward, both sides blamed the other for firing first, but in light of the outcome, it seemed a moot point. The fighting raged for more than an hour, and when it was done, five men had been killed and some twenty others seriously wounded. The Texans withdrew, and the fence still stood, yet it soon became apparent that there were no winners that day.

Later, Jake Kincaid would look back on his decision to fight as one of the greatest mistakes of his life. What happened next would probably have happened anyway, but it was a question he never fully resolved in his own mind. That the Texans were the catalyst, however, precipitating what followed, was never in doubt. Newspapers across the country bannered it the CHEROKEE OUTLET MASSACRE, and in Washington the bureaucratic pot boiled over.

Suddenly everyone was looking for a scapegoat. The Secretary of the Interior passed the buck to the Commissioner of Indian Affairs, who in turn passed it along to the Indian Agent for the Five Civilized Tribes at Fort Gibson. But if one had been negligent, thundered the newspapers, then all had been negligent. There was an undeniable logic in that, and in a neat turnabout, the bureaucrats quickly closed ranks. Instead of flailing one another, they determined a wiser course of casting the onus elsewhere. Although late in coming, their public announcement purported to identify the real villain in this tragic affair—the Cherokee Cattlemen's Association.

There was a certain regimented lunacy to the dizzying events which unfolded over the next month. The Department of the Interior issued a broadside of statements denying all culpability in what had occurred. By law the Cherokees were forbidden to live in the Outlet, much less lease it to white men. While grazing permits might have been overlooked as a minor infraction, there was no defensible excuse for allowing the erection of permanent buildings and more than a thousand miles of fence—all of which had led to the infamous bloodbath with Texas drovers. Clearly, the Cherokee Nation had been hoodwinked by the Cattlemen's Association, and the entire scurrilous transaction had been kept secret from authorized government agencies. With the culprit firmly fixed in the public eye, the bureaucrats then went to work in earnest.

The Secretary of the Interior issued an order demanding that the Cattlemen's Association remove its bunkhouses and line camps, and its fences, within twenty days. Should more punitive measures become necessary, he further requested that the War Department furnish troops to destroy all improvements erected in the Cherokee Outlet. Everyone in the Department of the Interior thought it a masterstroke, brilliantly executed, and sat back to await results.

But there developed a slight hitch. The boys at the War Department didn't think much of the idea. So far as they could see, it was the same old story—they were being asked to pull Interior's fat out of the fire. As had happened countless times in the past quarter-century, the Bureau of Indian Affairs had bollixed itself into another mess, and it was the Army who would be called upon to do the fighting. Their disenchantment was further compounded by the disturbing news that the Cattlemen's Association exhibited no rush whatever to comply with Interior's order. Word drifted back to Washington that some hothead named Kincaid was all but daring the government to try moving him out. And ever conscious of their image, the generals cringed at the thought of headlines announcing that the Army had taken the field against white men. It was simply too much.

The Secretary of War bounced the problem back to Interior. In a carefully worded communiqué, larded with convoluted jargon, he requested that the War Department be shown provisions of law which would protect the Army from legal redress should it destroy private property within the Outlet. As an instrument of bureaucratic evasion it was without equal. All of Washington burst out in a whopping bellylaugh when the communiqué became public.

All, that is, except the thunderstruck officials back at

Interior. There were no such laws, as the Army well knew, and the Bureau of Indian Affairs found itself juggling a hot potato that had all the earmarks of a political bombshell. Without Army troops Interior had no way of enforcing its order, which left it in a position that was both untenable and embarrassing. The Secretary of the Interior quickly issued a new directive, suspending his old order, and instructed the Indian Agent at Fort Gibson to conduct a more exhaustive investigation of affairs in the Cherokee Outlet. It was rumored in certain Washington circles that the Indian Agent had also been instructed to take his time. Out of sight, out of mind seemed to be the best solution for all concerned, particularly if it could be kept out of the newspapers.

While the furor raged in Washington, Jake had put on a bold front, stating publicly, and loudly, that nothing less than a full-scale campaign by the Army could evict the Association from its leased grazing lands. It was all show, a monumental bluff, for his political connections stopped at Topeka; his one hope was that the bureaucrats would muddy the water so badly that the main issue would become obscured. Which, in their own way, they had done very nicely.

But when the matter was once more dumped on the Indian Agent, Jake saw at last the chance for constructive measures. Although it was difficult to deal with the vast labyrinth of departments and bureaus in Washington, it might well be possible to deal with one man. Especially a man at the bottom of the heap, who was poorly paid and unappreciated, and made to play the goat for his superiors.

A realist, never one to delude himself, Jake knew that he had won little more than a breathing spell. Of all politicians, none were more vindictive than petty bureaucrats made to appear the fool. The Secretary of the Interior and the Commissioner of Indian Affairs wouldn't forget. Nor would they forgive. They would bide their time, awaiting an opportune moment, receptive to any skulduggery that might oust the Association from Cherokee lands. And if the Indian Agent's report was unfavorable, providing them with fresh ammunition, the game might yet be lost.

On the other hand, it might just as easily be won. There were ways and there were ways. Some less scrupulous than others, but all highly persuasive. Confident that one of them could be made to work, Jake mounted his horse on a bright, steamy morning in late July and rode toward Fort Gibson.

Sticking generally to the banks of the Arkansas, he set a leisurely southeastward course into the Nations. It was new land, somewhat more hilly than the Outlet, with wooded river bottoms and wide expanses of timber, and he allowed himself time to look it over thoroughly. The one constant in life was change, and while he had no designs on the Cherokee Nation itself, it never hurt for a man to know his way around. Just in case something interesting cropped up down the line.

The trip consumed five days, a distance of some hundred and fifty miles, and Jake found it a most enjoyable hiatus from the pressures back in Wichita. Late on the afternoon of the fifth day he rode into Fort Gibson, and fixed in his mind was a plan he thought might well turn the trick. It was a simple plan, as most good plans are, and relied not so much on cunning as on sheer greed.

The Indian Agent for the Five Civilized Tribes proved to be a most gracious host. Tall and somewhat cadaverous in appearance, he had been stuck with the unlikely name of Hiram Short. He greeted Jake warmly, almost as if he had been expecting the visit, and invited him to spend the night. They dined on a meal of unusual elegance, with fine crystal and expensive china, and by the second bottle of wine, Jake had a hunch he'd picked a surefire cinch. After supper, Short led him into the study, poured snifters of brandy, and gestured him to a wing-backed leather chair.

"Well, Mr. Short, I'll have to admit I'm surprised." Jake grinned and shook his head. "Not that I ever gave it much thought, but it never occurred to me that Indian Agents lived this well. I always figured they were off in the sticks somewhere tryin' to make do with a log cabin and a couple of pots."

Short smiled, studying the amber swirls in his brandy. "I suppose it's a common belief. Of course the way I live is nothing compared to men of wealth in the Tribes. Now there, Mr. Kincaid, is what a man might truly call opulence."

"Is that a fact?" Jake filed the thought away for future reference. "Maybe I'll visit the Cherokees one of these days. Might be interesting to see how they're spendin' all that money the Association pays them."

"The Association." Short let the words roll off his tongue, lending them a curious emphasis. "Would I be correct in assuming that the Association's recent—problem—in Washington is what prompted your visit, Mr. Kincaid?"

"You know, Hiram—is it all right if I call you Hiram?—good. Never could stand formality. Anyway, what I started to say, I always liked a man who didn't beat around the bush. And to answer your question, it's the Association that brought me here."

"I see. May I inquire as to what purpose?"

"Well, I heard sometime back that you'd been over in the Outlet inspectin' our operation. Now the word's around that you've been pegged to write a report on how we're treatin' the Cherokees."

"Yes, that's true." Short let a moment of silence drag out; then he smiled. "Does my report interest you?"

"Depends on what it says." Jake silently congratulated himself. He smelled the strong aroma of larceny in the air. "If it was favorable to the Association, it could interest me a lot."

"You're a businessman, Jake, so I'm sure you know how reports can vary. Under the right circumstances a report can be most favorable. Under other circumstances, let's say it can be—not so favorable."

"Now that's a coincidence, Hiram. Damned if it's not. I was just sitting here thinking that under the right circumstances your report might even be favorable to you."

"How so?"

Jake had felt the nibble too often to mistake it now. "Suppose we say five thousand in whatever bank you name?"

Short took a sip of his brandy, waiting, as if savoring the moment. "Suppose we say ten thousand. In cash."

"Hiram, you've got yourself a deal." Jake raised his snifter in salute. "Guess you wouldn't be offended if we made it half down and half when you finish that report."

"Why, Jake, I think that would be most satisfactory. Very businesslike, in fact."

Very businesslike. Cold and impersonal. Precisely the way Jake liked to handle such matters. Yet, oddly enough, he felt a keen sense of disappointment. It had been too easy. Almost as if Hiram Short's avarice had, after all, proved unequal to the contest. Like bribing a child with candy, it produced the desired result but very little satisfaction.

A queer sting of self-mockery came over him, and he felt a sudden urge to laugh. Why should he have expected more of Hiram Short than of any other leech? Bureaucracy was organized not to protect the rights of the people, but to consolidate the power of politicians. And to serve the vested interests. Bankers and railroad barons and steelmakers—and Jake Kincaid. It was an elemental flaw in the system, always had been. Power corrupts the weak, and gives the strong a hammerlock on the source of wealth. Which was what made the wheels go round. Dupes and rogues. An ancient struggle, forever unequal. But then, even the apes knew that.

"Hiram, here's to you." Jake lifted his brandy glass a bit higher, and smiled disarmingly. "I like a man with style. Always have."

There were times when Jake felt like a one-man fire brigade. Worse luck, it seemed that he had but one bucket, and was forever called upon to battle several fires simultaneously. No sooner was one blaze doused than sparks ignited another and still another, as if some diabolic prankster had been turned loose with a box of sulfurheads. Harried, scurrying back and forth between fires, Jake could almost believe that it was him against the world. However much he filled his bucket, he simply couldn't be everywhere at once. And in the way of things, fire somehow seemed more plentiful than water.

By late fall he had stalemated the Department of the Interior. Hiram Short's investigation and his subsequent report were most favorable to the Association. Dwelling at length on the cattle industry, and its importance to the nation, he concluded that the Outlet ranchers were gainfully utilizing land that nobody wanted, and further, that they had fairly compensated the Cherokees for leased grazing rights. Stymied by the report, the Secretary of the Interior let the whole affair fizzle out as unobtrusively as possible. Around Washington it was whispered that he considered the report a political godsend, and that Hiram Short had been commended highly for his zeal and his unflagging devotion to the Cherokee Nation.

But if the report caused Interior to breathe a sigh of relief, it created a whirlwind of agitation in the border towns of southern Kansas. The dying spark of the Outlet controversy was fanned alive within a broader issue, and a ragtag horde known as the Boomers raised a new battle cry. Hiram Short's investigation merely affirmed what they had contended all along—that the Indians had far more land than they needed. Land which could be made productive, beneficial to a hungry nation, if opened to white settlement.

While Jake had been the moving force in luring settlers to Kansas, he violently opposed the opening of Indian Territory. Cattlemen had a good thing for themselves below the line, and as president of the Association, his was the voice raised loudest against the Boomers. Let the sodbusters gain a toehold, he argued, and within a few years they would drive the cattlemen out. It had happened in Kansas, just as it had happened in Nebraska, and unless nipped in the bud right at the outset, it would happen in the Nations.

Jake was busily engaged battling this latest threat when he received a telegraph message, shortly after New Year's, from Cecil Hollister. The wire was cryptic and terse, without a hint as to purpose, asking him to come at once to Topeka. His many business ventures, along with an ever-widening political involvement, demanded constant attention, and with time at a premium, he resented Hollister's imperious summons. All the more so since most of the Santa Fe land now had been sold, and what remained hardly merited a special trip to Topeka. But he went, just the same. Hollister rarely did anything without a reason, however murky, and it generally had to do with money or politics. Or both. Which sufficiently aroused Jake's curiosity that he boarded the evening train.

Early next morning he appeared, unannounced, at Hollister's office, and was ushered in immediately. Age had begun to thicken the old buccaneer's figure, but he still moved and spoke with vigor. Nor had his manner of conducting business altered with the years. As always, his character was like spring steel, tough and resilient, unsparing of himself or others. He greeted Jake with a broad smile and a crushing handshake, and waved him to a chair. After they had fired up cigars, and sparred around a few minutes with meaningless smalltalk, Hollister came at last to the purpose of the meeting. While his words were brusque and demanding, he was foxy as ever, and chose to make his approach by a circuitous route.

"Jake, how much money you reckon you've made off the Santa Fe?"

"Why, Cecil, I imagine you've got that calculated to the penny. Course, it's not near as much as I made *for* the Santa Fe."

Hollister's eyes narrowed, and a tiny smile appeared at the corners of his mouth. "Then I suppose the way you figure, you don't owe me any favors?"

"None I can think of just offhand."

"Thought not. Never hurts to ask, though."

They sat smoking their cigars in silence. Jake sensed that he was being stalked, but as yet he couldn't fathom the reason. It was his practice to listen a lot and talk very little when someone else was dealing. Invariably it placed the burden of pressure on the other man, and forced him to expose his hand quicker than he'd planned. Some time passed, and it was Hollister who blinked first.

"Just out of curiosity, wouldn't you say it's a wise man who adapts to circumstances?"

Jake shrugged. "Guess it depends on whose ox gets gored."

The observation was as cryptic as the question, and Hollister found himself enjoying the game. Of all his associates, only Kincaid had the audacity to try matching wits. "Would you agree that we should never trust men to know their own best interests?"

"Can't really say I ever gave the other fellow's interest much thought. I'm too busy tendin' to my own berry patch."

"Well, let me be a little more specific. Would you consider it even a remote possibility that I might have your best interests at heart? That in a—certain situation—I might consider your welfare on an equal with my own?"

"Why, sure, Cecil, it's a possibility. Like you say, it's remote, but if the only way to help yourself was to help me, why I suppose you could muster up some charity."

"Then you agree—so long as our interests are served equally?"

"I've heard it said that only cream and bastards rise to the top. Always thought there was a pearl of wisdom in that." Jake slowly flicked the ash from his cigar, and waited for it to splatter in the cuspidor. "Just to be frank about it, Cecil, I don't think either of us got where we are by wipin' the other fellow's nose."

"Precisely my point!" Hollister could scarcely contain

himself. "Where mutual need exists then there's a basis for trust."

"All depends." Jake smiled sardonically. "How much do you need me?"

"You're a cynical bastard, aren't you?" Hollister chuckled, shaking his head. "The answer to your question is, I need you a lot. The last time I didn't take you in on a deal it ended up costing me a lot of money. This time I want you on my side."

"Unless the beeswax is thicker'n usual, I get the idea you've already got me figured for the other side."

"You are opposed to Captain Payne and his Boomers, aren't you?"

"I haven't exactly made a secret of it."

"Then that puts you on the other side. Against me and the Santa Fe and some pretty powerful factions."

Wiping his mustache, Jake scrutinized the older man carefully, like a gamecock sizing up an adversary. The purpose of this meeting was now out in the open—Hollister meant to sway him away from the cattlemen—and the defiant jut of his jaw made Jake's stand unmistakable clear. Just as speeches and newspaper interviews had already demonstrated his antagonism toward the Boomers and anyone else who coveted Indian lands. These days, as he had been quick to discover, that included just about everybody.

At root was the scarcity of good farmland. The flood of settlers pouring west had already claimed the choice homestead lands; the clamor to open Indian Territory to settlement had swelled to a public outcry as the westward migration intensified. The primary goal of this land-hungry horde was known as the Unassigned Lands. Embracing some two million acres of well watered, fertile plains, it was land which had been ceded by the Creeks and Seminoles—as a home for tribes yet to be resettled. But the government eventually announced that it had no intention of locating Indians on these lands. The howls of white settlers then rose to a fever pitch, and their demands now included the Cherokee Outlet, which abutted the northern border of the Unassigned Lands.

The settlers were backed by several influential factions, all of whom had a vested interest in the western expansion. Already the Katy railroad had crossed the eastern corner of Indian Territory, and competing lines had no intention of being left behind. Pressure mounted in Washington for a solution, equitable or otherwise, to the problem.

Opposed to settlement was a diverse group comprised of cattlemen, the Five Civilized Tribes, and assorted religious organizations. The churches and missionary societies asserted that government dealings with Indians formed a chain of broken pledges and unfulfilled treaties. In that, the Five Civilized Tribes agreed vehemently. They had ceded the western part of their domain for the purpose of providing other tribes with a home—not for the enrichment of white farmers and greedy politicians.

At the forefront of this struggle was Captain David Payne. A drifter and ne'er-do-well, Payne had served briefly in the territorial legislature and the Kansas militia. Yet he was a zealot of sorts, and in the settlement of Indian lands he at last found his cause. Advertising widely, he made fiery speeches exhorting the people to action, and gradually organized a colony of settlers. Every six months or so he led his scruffy band of fanatics into the Unassigned Lands, and just as regularly, the Army ejected them. After several such invasions, each of which was spectacularly unsuccessful, Payne's followers became known as the Boomers, since they were said to be *booming* the settlement of Indian Territory. Lately, Payne had trained his guns on the most apparent, and perhaps the most vulnerable, obstacle blocking his path—the Association. Lambasting politicians in Washington, he declared that refusing settlers entry into lands already occupied by cattlemen constituted a gross injustice.

And while saner men deplored his tactics, Payne wasn't alone in his fight. Railroads and politicians and merchant princes, all with their own axes to grind, had rallied to the cause. That they were using the Boomers to their own ends defied exaggeration. But Payne and his rabble scarcely seemed to care. At this point, frustrated martyrs in a holy quest, they would have joined hands with the Devil himself to break the deadlock.

Now, another deadlock of sorts existed, between Jake and Cecil Hollister. But it was Hollister who sought compromise, and Jake again waited him out, merely returning his stare without expression. There was something here as yet unrevealed, and until all the cards were dealt, Jake was content to listen a while longer. Several minutes passed before Hollister finally grunted and leaned forward with an earnest look of concern.

"Jake, what if I told you that the Santa Fe has begun a lobbying campaign for a charter to lay track straight through the middle of the Nations. Would that change your thinking?"

The disclosure shook him, but Jake remained pokerfaced. "Sounds like you're pretty damn sure of yourself."

"I'm not sure, Jake—I'm certain. Congress will open Indian Territory to settlement, that's a foregone conclusion." Hollister puffed his cigar, deliberating as he wrestled over the best approach. "Now, if you're bullheaded enough to fight it down the line, you'll probably wind up with nothing. But if you throw in with me, you'll come out smelling like a rose."

"How so?"

"Because I want you to scout out the Santa Fe route through the Nations. Pick the best town sites and lay out a line through the choice farmlands. When the boom comes, both you and the Santa Fe will make a killing."

"Why me, Cecil? You keep skirtin' around that."

"Let's just say I'm getting soft-hearted in my old age. Hell, call it superstition if you want to. The truth is, I don't want to fight you, Jake. Since we hooked up I've drawn nothing but aces, and I want to keep it that way. Might spoil my streak if I had to haul your ashes."

"Then you don't figure I've got much chance to whip the Boomers?"

"One in a million. Christ, man, look what's lined up against you! Not Payne and his hardscrabble riffraff, but Congress and the railroads and the business community. Big money, Jake, and men willing to spend it liberally in Washington. And who do you have on your side? A bunch of mealy-mouthed preachers, and some noble red men who haven't beat the government in a hundred years. Hell, it's no contest."

Jake's flinty gaze came level. "But if I don't fight I'll lose everything I've built in the Outlet. Seems to me the options are pretty limited."

"That's where you're wrong. Your organization is the only one that has any clout in Washington. Without the Association behind them, the tribes won't have a leg to stand on." Hollister paused, and fixed him with a steady, penetrating look. "You'll have to take my word for it, but it was the boys in Washington who asked me to have this little talk with you. They don't want any trouble, and they especially don't want the newspapers stirring up a hornet's nest. Now, if you'll play along, and quit making a stink, I can assure you that only Unassigned Lands will be opened to settlement. The Cherokee Outlet won't be touched. At least for another five years, or so. Guaranteed."

Hollister hesitated, then smiled. "Take an old horse trader's advice. Half a loaf is better than none."

The younger man's laugh was scratchy, abrasive, like a match being struck. "Goddamn my soul, Cecil, that's what it is. You're offerin' me a deal. All that stuff about friendship and us workin' together was just a crock of horseshit. You were talkin' horse trade all along, weren't you?"

"What if I was?" Hollister's tone was gruffly defensive. "You're such a hardheaded son of a bitch a man can't come at you straight on."

"Well, hell's bells, why didn't you just say so?" Jake lolled back in his chair and grinned. "Looks like we got ourselves a deal, partner. You can tell the big augurs I won't even open my mouth to belch from now on."

This sudden turnabout startled Hollister into speechlessness, but only for a moment. Then he cursed himself for forgetting at the outset what he'd just seen demonstrated so vividly. Seated across from him was a pragmatist who dealt in harsh realities, seemingly impervious to the simplest emotion. His decision here today merely stressed the fact. He would play along to get along—but only so long as it served his purpose. Very realistic and very pragmatic. And shortly to become very disillusioning to those who believed that every man was his brother's keeper.

Late in April, some four months after their meeting, Jake returned from the Nations with a Santa Fe surveying crew. He laid before Cecil Hollister a map detailing two prime townsites and a meandering course over which track would one day be laid. He spoke of the enormousness of the empty land, the abundance of game and water and timber. He talked at length of the ripe, virgin soil and lush grasslands, far more hospitable than the parched prairies of Kansas, and in the way of all visionaries caught up in a dream, he spoke of towns and farms and great ranches. A wilderness forgotten by time that men might conquer and tame and shape to their own ends.

But it was his final insight, keen and incisive, which made Cecil Hollister's mouth water for a glimpse of this great land. He observed that irony was forever the goad between red man and white. Somehow the land the government gave the Indians always turned out to be the horn of plenty. The Promised Land in yet another transmigration.

While it was true that politics sometimes bred strange bedfellows, Jake Kincaid was of the opinion that business and friendship were mutually incompatible. He trusted Cecil Hollister only slightly more than he would have trusted a man-eating shark, and if that earned him a reputation as a cynic, then he accepted it as the highest accolade in a world of dubious honors. Other men might snooker him in a business deal from time to time, but they would never do so because of misguided trust. Nor could he be fooled by offers of conciliation, or honey-tongued flattery. A man survived, and attained his goals, because he never accepted the other fellow's motives at face value—not even those of Cecil Hollister.

Upon returning from Indian Territory, Jake set in motion a plan which would cover his backside. Simple in design, if somewhat complex in execution, the plan was meant to counter any future threat from Washington bureaucrats. And the Boomers. And the shadowy coalition of businessmen and politicians who had selected Cecil Hollister as their front man.

At the monthly meeting in Caldwell, Jake presented documents which would charter the Association as a full-fledged corporation. The members were stunned, but they were forced to agree with his reasoning. As of now, they were merely an alliance of individuals with no legal standing. On the other hand, a corporation could negotiate contracts with the Cherokees, and only in a lengthy and time-consuming court battle could the government overturn those agreements. In the meantime, while corporate lawyers delayed and hedged, their cattle would still be grazing in the Outlet.

The ranchers knew nothing of Jake's deal with Cecil Hollister, and he meant to keep it that way. What they didn't know couldn't create dissension, and in the scheme of things, he was protecting their interests as much as his own. Better that they be kept in the dark, happy and dumb. But for all their ignorance of his backroom maneuvering, the ranchers understood plain-spoken common sense when they heard it.

The motion passed unanimously. And the Cherokee

Cattlemen's Association was issued articles of incorporation three days later in Topeka.

As president of the corporation, Jake quickly took the next step in his plan. With a battery of lawyers working night and day, he drafted a proposal to the Cherokee Nation requesting a five-year grazing lease on the Outlet. The proposal was airtight, and while it left the leasing fee open to negotiation, it was an instrument of incontrovertible legality once signed. Before the week was out, Jake sent this hastily constructed masterpiece on its way by courier to Tahlequah.

If Association members had been dazzled by Jake's footwork, absolute pandemonium broke out among the Cherokees when the proposal was delivered. Dennis Bushyhead, principal chief of the tribe, huddled with his advisers and attempted, somewhat skeptically, to divine the usual white-man chicanery beneath this extraordinary document. Oddly enough, the harder they looked, the more enticing it became. Despite its intricacies, it was nothing more or less than it purported to be—a remarkable offer. The Association had, in effect, handed the Cherokee Nation a bank draft and told them to write their own ticket.

After considerable ear tugging and head scratching, the chief and his advisers concluded that the proposal was above suspicion. In and of itself, an incredible feat for white men. But it represented a long-term commitment, with far-reaching implications, and astute politicians that they were, Bushyhead and his cabinet weren't about to act recklessly. A courier was dispatched to Caldwell with a most favorable response. Chief Bushyhead would give the proposal his personal stamp of approval; however, any final decision would be left to the Cherokee tribal council. A special session of the council would be convened within the week.

The message was encouraging, but Jake regarded it with mixed feelings. While he knew little or nothing about Cherokee customs, he knew a great deal about politics. Red man or white, bargains were easier struck with a single leader than with a bunch of connivers fascinated by the sound of their own voices. Left to the vagaries of governmental process, be it a state legislature or a tribal council, the best laid plans were often, and most times unceremoniously, still-born. The morning after receiving Chief Bushyhead's dispatch, Jake mounted his swiftest horse and rode south into the Cherokee Nation.

Whatever tales he might have heard about the Five Civilized Tribes, Jake was dumbstruck by what he found in Tahlequah. Though he knew that the Cherokees had been slave owners before the war, and reportedly operated plantations as large as any in the south, he was unprepared for the extent of their cultural progress. He expected to find run-of-the-mill Indians, like the Comanches and the Kiowas, savages who had turned to farming after being whipped into submission by the government. Instead, he was greeted by a proud, dignified people who had taken the best from both worlds, and somehow made it work.

The Cherokee Nation was, for all practical purposes, an independent republic. White men were not allowed to own property within the Nation, except through intermarriage, and Washington exerted minimal influence on the conduct of Cherokee affairs. Unlike western Plains Tribes, and Jake was quick to note the distinction, the Cherokees accepted no handouts from the federal government. They had made the best deal they could, upon being dispossessed of their ancestral lands in the south, and they retained their independence by being wholly self-sufficient.

They cultivated the soil with something approaching reverence, and while many Cherokees owned sprawling plantations, most were simple farmers. Yet, large or small, they all lived well, though it was obvious that the rich lived on a grand scale befitting their position. Approaching Tahlequah, Jake had passed magnificent baronial homes, with wide colonnaded porches anchored by towering Grecian columns, all quite reminiscent of antebellum plantation houses of the Old South. While log cabins and unpretentious frame houses outnumbered the lavish estates a hundred to one, he saw nothing inequitable in that. It all seemed very democratic.

Quite shortly, and much to his disgust, he was to discover just how democratic the Cherokees were. With slight variations, their form of government was patterned on that of the white man. A tribal chief acted as head of state, although with far less autonomy than a president, and his tenure in office depended solely on last week's performance. If he violated the people's trust, or delivered less than promised, he quickly found himself back on the farm jockeying a plow. The legislative body, called the tribal council, was comprised of two houses, similar in structure and function to the white man's Congress. Except that the Cherokees, if anything, were more rabidly political than their counterparts in Washington. Issues were closely drawn in this miniature republic, and the two political parties, the Union and the National, were bitterly hostile toward one another. They agreed on very little, and then only after the pressure of events had forced a compromise.

Somewhat ruefully, Jake had to admit that there would be no under-the-table deals with the head man. The fate of any long-term lease on the Outlet would be decided within the Cherokee council. And according to the chief, it promised to be a bruising fight from start to finish.

Dennis Bushyhead had received Jake graciously, and like the Cherokee Nation, its chief proved to be somewhat more than expected. He was an educated man, trained in the law and affairs of state, and possessed a flair for diplomacy that seemed better suited to a European court. Acting the role of host, he insisted that Jake be his guest while in Tahlequah, and in the two days remaining before the council convened, he undertook to enlighten his bemused visitor about Cherokee ways. That Jake was bemused, not to say astounded, was apparent from the very outset.

A man of tact and discrimination, Bushyhead at first made no mention of Jake's mission in Tahlequah. Not that he wasn't curious, for he had heard much of Jake Kincaid—and his methods. Major Lipe, the Cherokee treasurer, had subtly collected a storehouse of knowledge about the man who ruled the Association, and over the years they had put together a comprehensive portfolio on Kincaid and his associates. Just as they kept similar portfolios on other white men with whom they did business. But the reason for Jake's sudden appearance seemed patently obvious, and Bushyhead concluded that statesmanship would better serve the moment. In good time they would come to business, and until then, it would do Kincaid no harm at all to learn more of his landlords.

A direct approach would have been more to Jake's liking, but he was content to play the waiting game. These Cherokees were clearly a different breed of redskin, and he sensed that it would be a mistake to rush heedlessly into a discussion of the Outlet question. The first night he dined with Bushyhead and his wife, who was charming and witty, and dressed in a pensée gown that would have been the talk of Wichita. Afterward, over coffee and cigars, the chief gave him a detailed sketch of Cherokee politics, and the problems in dealing with an unruly council. It was then that Jake got some inkling of the fight to come, yet Bushyhead neatly skirted the Outlet issue and kept his comments to the fractional divisions within the Nation.

The next day Jake was turned over to an aide and given the grand tour. Their first stop was the capitol building, which housed all governmental offices as well as the council chambers. It was a large, two-story brick structure, with a sweeping Corinthian portico in front, and dominated the town square. Jake was suitably impressed, as were most visitors. There was an air of bustling efficiency about the place, and it occurred to him that the bureaucrats in Washington might well take a lesson from their wards in Tahlequah. Nor did it escape him that the building itself was only slightly less stately than the capitol in Topeka. Despite a long-held scorn for the noble savage—an opinion universal among frontiersmen—he couldn't slough off a growing sense of respect. These people wore swallowtail coats and top hats, spoke flawless English, and conducted themselves with the aplomb of diplomats. And from all appearances, they were as prosperous and industrious as the most advanced white community back in Kansas. Quite plainly, the Cherokees were most uncommon Indians.

After a pleasant luncheon with Major David Lipe (who never once mentioned the Outlet or lease payments), Jake underwent yet another shock. His guide escorted him through various business establishments on the square, and then took him on a tour of the seminaries. To his complete amazement, these academies of learning surpassed the finest white school in Kansas. Here, Cherokee children received a thorough education, in both their mother tongue and in English, with a separate institution for boys and another for girls. The most promising students were later sent to Carlisle University in Pennsylvania, where they were groomed for positions of responsibility and leadership. In effect, the Cherokee Nation was looking to the future, building from within, training the best of each generation in business and law and medicine. And doing it on their own, without guidance or financial charity from the Great White Father.

Thinking about it later, Jake concluded that it would be a great mistake to underestimate the Cherokees. They moved softly and spoke in tones of moderation, but there was something inexorable about them. Like a quiet but unrelenting stream, which slowly erodes earth and stone to widen its channel. And it came to him in the same thought that perhaps this was the message, the purpose of the tour and the delay. Arranged by a sly old Cherokee chief who understood that a lesson was best learned through a man's own eyes.

The hunch became a certainty that evening. After another lavish, candlelit supper, Dennis Bushyhead at last got down to business. Seated across from Jake in the library, tactful to the end, he broached the subject in an oblique manner.

"Well, Mr. Kincaid, I gather from our dinner conversation that you don't feel your day was wasted. Do you approve of the way we manage things here in the backwoods?"

Jake couldn't resist a chuckle. "Chief, I'll have to admit it's been a real eye-opener. Not exactly the reason I rode down here, but I think you'll understand if I say that it was worth the trip."

Bushyhead smiled, nodding. "I understand perfectly. My people will be gratified that a man of your standing found our efforts—instructive." He paused, lending subtle emphasis to the last word. Then he steepled his fingers, reflecting a moment, and his face grew sober. "Now, as to the purpose of your visit. Tomorrow the council will meet to debate the question of a longterm lease on the Outlet. I presume this is your major concern?"

"No, sir, it's my only concern. I genuinely believe that a longterm arrangement is the best safeguard against those meddlers in Washington. Both for the Cherokees and the Association."

"I agree most emphatically." Bushyhead frowned, peering over his fingers. "Are you aware that a group of Texans has made an offer on the Outlet? An offer doubling what your Association now pays."

Jake stared back at him woodenly. He had no reason to disbelieve the old man, but there was something fishy about the deal. As if, at the last moment, a trap had suddenly been sprung. "Chief, I'm sorry to say that's the first I've heard of it. Am I to understand you think it might jeopardize the Association's proposal?"

"Definitely. There is a faction within the council who opposes any long commitment to white men. They prefer to deal with the Texans because their offer is on a year-by-year basis. And involves more money, of course." Bushyhead spread his hands in a bland gesture. "What can I say, Mr. Kincaid?

Personally I support the Association, but without a substantial counteroffer I fear it will be a bitter fight."

The odor of fish got stronger, but Jake merely smiled. However discreetly stated, he now knew the rules. "I appreciate your position, and without imposing, perhaps I could ask your advice. If the Association were to make an offer, what would you consider substantial?"

Bushyhead fell pensive, considering it at some length. Finally he grunted and looked up. "Nothing is absolute, Mr. Kincaid, but I believe you might well carry the vote with an offer of a hundred thousand dollars."

"For a five-year lease, no restrictions?"

"Only one change, Mr. Kincaid. All improvements on the land would become the sole property of the Cherokee Nation at the expiration of the lease."

Jake cocked his head, nodding, and grinned. "You fill in the round figures and I'll sign it."

"One other thing, Mr. Kincaid."

"Name it."

"We would prefer the money in gold. Delivered here in Tahlequah."

"Consider it done. I've got a bunch of cowhands that could ride shotgun on the U.S. mint."

Bushyhead smiled benignly. "Yes, I seem to recall the incident. Although our own newspaper hardly thought it qualified as a massacre. But then, that is what makes horse races, isn't it, Mr. Kincaid?"

Shortly before noon the next day, Jake rode out of Tahlequah with the contract in his pocket. The Cherokees, one in particular, thought they had outfoxed the white man with consummate skill. But Jake knew different, and the knowledge left him smug as a street-corner grifter. Had Bushyhead asked it, he would have paid half again as much. Double the amount. Damn near anything.

As of today the Outlet was his. Locked in tighter than a drum for five solid years. A small kingdom inviolate to the dictates of anyone except Jake Kincaid. And not even Jesus Christ himself could weasel out of the contract.

The farther Jake rode, the smugger he became, and after a while he got so cocky he could hardly stand himself. But somehow he managed, for in a manner of speaking, he'd never been in better company.

SIX

The quiet seemed odd, somehow unreal. He caught himself listening for the whoop of drunken laughter and Rebel yells and that peculiar bawling moan of longhorn cows. But there was nothing, just stillness. The deep, tranquil silence of a town come of age. All grown-up and citified, its bawdy youth a dim, fleeting image glimpsed through the haze of time. Reflecting on it, he thought that pretty well summed up Wichita these days. Citified. And dead as a graveyard.

Seated at his desk in the land office, Jake explored the thought a bit further. Funny it had never come to him just that way before—a graveyard. But that's what it was. At least in his mind's eye that's what he saw. A boneyard haunted with spooks and misty glimmerings of the past. Texas cowhands and their stringy cattle clattering across the toll bridge. Gamblers and whores and dance-hall girls, all decked out in getups of spectacular vulgarity. Immigrants pouring off the trains in their baggy clothes and queer little hats, staring goggle-eyed at the great rolling plains. The strident, hammering wail of brass bands and honky-tonk pianos, flooding the street with a gaudy, circuslike vitality. And Sadie. Always there, eyes bright as nuggets, her face radiant with the sheer wonder of it all. Eager and curious and joyously alert, forever clapping her hands at the rowdy spectacle of life kicking up its heels. Just the way she'd looked that first day he brought her to Wichita. When it was a wild and woolly cowtown, with its glory days ahead, filled with the sweet, ripe scent of money and cowdung and sweaty men. The smell of boomtimes burst to life in a noisy raucous whirlwind of ripsawed lumber and mortared stone.

Yet gone now. All gone. Except for the spooks and the lingering refrain of their bawdy laughter. And the memories. As if a cold winter wind had swept the earth bare of all that was warm and golden and shimmering bright.

Jake shook himself and jerked upright in his chair, suddenly disgusted with his own maudlin sentimentality. It wasn't like him to look back, to dwell on things dead and gone. Nor was there any reason to mourn the past, to regret the loss of some tinseled moment in time. Life changed, and a man changed with it. Or else he climbed off the carousel and watched it pass him by. Things were just that elemental, and glumming around in the debris of what had been bought a man nothing but gassy bowels and a splitting headache.

His momentary lapse was all the more aggravating because he had so little to regret. And so much to savor. Of course Wichita had become nothing but a big hick farming town—but so what? He'd made a fortune on the immigrants, and he was still turning a pretty penny every time some sodbuster with itchy feet called it quits and sold out. And what if the reformers were about to take over Kansas for good? Hell, anybody with half a brain knew that '84 was their year. Besides, it was no skin off his nose anyhow. Let them embargo longhorns and enforce the dry laws and shoo off the sporting crowd. Let 'em do any damn thing they pleased. He'd made his peace with the party leaders and found them as susceptible to corruption as anyone else. Christ, between him and Cecil Hollister, they had dished out enough campaign money to buy every candidate in the state, whatever his politics.

Kansas was a vast grain belt now, a land of farmers and churches and stiff-necked morality. Even Dodge City was about to fold as a cowtown, the last of a breed. But again, so what? He'd brought the settlers here, shown them the land of milk and honey, and taken their money. If he didn't like their hidebound ways, and the dull drudgery they'd imposed on the once wide-open cowtowns, then he had no one to blame but himself. All along he'd known what he was doing, pushing the frontier ever westward, and he'd been well paid for it. The only alternative was to blaze out again, lead the Santa Fe and the Boomers into Indian Territory, and the thought tempted him more than he cared to admit.

That would be the last frontier, what many were already calling Oklahoma Territory, the last fling for men who abhorred codes and strictures and petty little laws. A year had passed since his trip to the Unassigned Lands, and almost a year since he'd slickered a contract out of the Cherokees. And in all that time, as he watched the reformers take a stranglehold on Kansas, not a day passed that he wasn't tempted by the siren's call. The lure to chuck it all, strike out fresh, ride the wild, high updrafts one last time. But at the core, he remained a confirmed pragmatist, and only a fool traded a bagful of marbles for a shot in the dark.

Aside from the tedium of life in Kansas, he had a hell of a lot to say grace over. His name was respected across the state, feared by high people in high places who had mortgaged their souls. He had wealth and position, influence and power, and however rough his business practices, his word alone was bond enough for any man. On the other side of town a vibrant, loving woman awaited the sound of his footstep, always there and anxious to please, never demanding more than he was willing to share. And he had two fine sons, boys any man could be proud of, although at times the younger one seemed hell-bent on making a nuisance of himself. But all in all, for a man not yet forty, the ledger sheet balanced out pretty well. The sum and substance was that Jake Kincaid had made his mark in Kansas. Boldly, on his own, and without obligation to God or man.

There was only one problem. Having won all the marbles,

he was bored shitless. Which was exactly why he was sitting around lamenting the good old days instead of concentrating on the ax job yet to be done tonight.

A knock at the door jarred him out of his reverie. Somehow he welcomed it, felt a surge of relief that the waiting was over. However distasteful, it was an act of necessity, and being necessary, it was best done. Squaring himself, he swiveled around in his chair.

"C'mon in, Chalk. The door's open."

Chalk Wheeler entered the office with an elaborate air of confidence, like a trader come to the marketplace with some rare and precious commodity. The years had scarcely touched him. He was still lean and tough, eyes lusterless as stones, his face stamped with the telltale ashen pallor of a gambling man. The door swung shut behind him, and he walked forward. As if no invitation were needed, he casually took a chair and tossed his hat on the desk.

"How's tricks, Jake? Haven't seen much of you lately."

"Well, you know how it is, Chalk. Seems like there's always more irons in the fire than I can rightly tend."

"Yeah, I get that feelin' myself sometimes." His words seemed guarded, somehow wary, as if, having come face to face, he wasn't quite sure of an opening move. "Glad you could spare me the time. Thought maybe we ought to get our heads together and hash out a few things."

Jake waved his hand in an expansive gesture. "Never too busy for old friends. What did you have in mind?"

"Same thing as everybody else in Delano. The elections." Wheeler faltered, clearly struggling with some inner conflict and fighting a losing battle. "Jake, I figure we go back too far to pull punches, so I'm gonna say it straight out. I've been hearin' some disturbing rumors. About you and the reformers. I came over here tonight to ask you point-blank—is there any truth to it?"

"Truth to what? I haven't heard anything yet."

Wheeler fixed him with a piercing stare. "They say you're gonna throw me to the wolves."

"Chalk, I don't know as I like your choice of words."

"Goddamnit, they're not my words!" Wheeler flared back. "It's what everybody in town is sayin'."

"Then you've been listenin' to the wrong people," Jake answered stiffly. "I've never knifed anybody in my life. And the man who says different better make damn sure I don't hear his name."

"Jake, I didn't come here to bandy words. Just give me a straight answer. Are you dumpin' me or not?"

"Yes and no. Now, hold your horses and let me explain. Yes, I am going to support the reform ticket. But that's just good politics, and anyone with sense enough to spit knows it for a fact." Wheeler started to interrupt but Jake stopped him with an upraised hand. "Let me finish, for Christ's sake. The other part is that I'm not throwin' you to the wolves. If you hadn't sent word you wanted a meetin' I would've called you over anyway. Delano may be finished but you're not. There's a whole raft of legitimate businesses you can sink your money in—and I'll show you how to do it. So you see, Chalk, despite what all the scissorbills are sayin', I don't forget an old friend."

"In a pig's ass!" Wheeler snarled. "Who do you think gave you the clout around here all these years—your uptown pals? Hell, no! It was me throwin' the Delano vote whichever way you wanted it. Seems like you forget mighty damn fast when the wind starts shiftin'."

"Chalk, you just put your thumb on it." Jake leaned forward, his chiseled features very earnest. "Don't you see, the old days are gone—washed out. These straitlaced monkeys own Kansas now. Fellows like you and me have only got two choices. We can climb aboard the bandwagon and show 'em what makes politics really tick. Or we can fold our tents and go find someplace that's not civilized yet. Hell's fire, any gambler worth his salt doesn't bet into a pat hand. You think about it a minute."

"I don't have to think about it. We can fight 'em! And that's what I intend to do. So long as we control the county, we can run it any damn way that suits us. Now, you paste that in your hat and see if I'm not right."

"You're dead wrong. Once they control the legislature and the governor's office—and believe me, Chalk, after the elections they will—Delano won't stand a prayer. I know these people. They're fanatics. And if they have to, they'll send in the militia to close you down."

Wheeler raked him with a contemptuous scowl. "You know what, Jake, I think you've lost your taste for a fight. All that money has turned you soft."

"That would be the biggest mistake you ever made." Jake's eyes hooded in a cold glare, and his voice went gritty. "Let's have it understood. If you fight, it won't be just the reformers you're up against. You'll be fighting me."

There was an ominous finality to the words, and for an instant they glowered across the desk at one another. Then Wheeler kicked back his chair and stood, lips compressed in a murderous slit. "You called the turn. And if I was you, Mr. Kincaid, I'd stay out of Delano. Folks over there have got their own way of dealin' with a Judas."

"Chalk, I'll give you some free advice. You mess with me and you'll get squashed. Take it as gospel."

"And I'll give you some advice, big shot! Sit this one out. It's gonna get dirty in the clinches, and I don't think you've got the stomach for it anymore."

Wheeler stalked out of the office, rattling windowpanes as the door slammed shut behind him. Curiously, Jake felt little anger. Nor was he troubled about the outcome of the election. Instead, much to his amazement, he felt a twinge of what bordered on pity. Some people just couldn't face reality. Couldn't admit that an era had ended, and that in the scheme of things, there was no longer a place for the sporting crowd. Sadder still, somebody would have to kick them in the teeth before they saw the light.

Suddenly he chuckled, mocking himself with sardonic bitterness. Christ, maybe Wheeler was right after all. Maybe he had gone soft. There was a time, not too far back, when kicking men in the teeth had been his specialty. Relished it, by God! The more the merrier. Unwittingly, his grin widened, and in a moment of wry speculation, he laughed out loud.

Hell, maybe things in Kansas hadn't gotten so dull after all.

She wiggled closer, urging the warm curves of her body snug against his. They had fallen asleep like this, with his arm around her, and she felt herself being pressed closer still as his arm tightened in response. Time lost both measure and meaning for Zalia in these moments, as if the world somehow stopped in a brief, intoxicating interlude while she lay enfolded in his arms. At times, in his eagerness, he was rough and brutish when they made love. But if he rushed things too quickly, and caused her pain, it was made bearable by the pleasure she gave him. And later, when she gentled him, there was a greater pleasure that she herself sensed beyond the pain. A deep shuddering release of frustration, clinging naked to his hard-muscled frame while he carried her past the threshold of her most wicked fantasies.

Then, their ardor spent, they slept, and he held her with a tenderness that was perhaps more fulfilling than the passion itself. Lying in his arms now, sated with love and the musky man-smell of his body, she wondered if his wife had treasured these moments in the same way. It was a thought she had considered often in these past six years. She knew that Sadie was still part of his life, grasped it through some sensory perception that had nothing to do with words, for he had never once spoken of her or their marriage. Zalia could only speculate, but this same intuitive certainty told her that Sadie had also failed to penetrate the wall separating his emotions from his outward self. A woman's nature made her want to probe the innermost depths of her man's mind and soul, and in that they had both been defeated. There was a part of Jake that he shared with no one, and a woman simply made herself miserable unless she stopped short of the limits he himself had proscribed.

Thinking about it, snuggled close against the matted curls on his chest, Zalia felt a tingling shiver of exhilaration. Perhaps after all, she had succeeded where Sadie failed. Tonight he had needed her! Truly and unashamedly needed her. And that this need was born of anger and bafflement and personal defeat bothered her not at all. He had turned to her, seeking solace and comfort in a dark hour. Almost like a small boy bringing his hurt to have it kissed and made well. Of and in itself, that was enough, fulfillment unlike any she had known. At last, after all this time, he needed her. And where there was need there was something more. Something that could be nurtured and brought to light, and with care, urged to grow.

Her soft lips traced a path up his chest, pausing to nuzzle his neck, and then arching herself higher, she playfully nibbled his earlobe. He stirred, fully awake now, and aroused, and the arm which encircled her began to squeeze tighter. Another moment, another nibble, then his mouth would find hers and she would be pulled beneath him, locked again in that fierce, demanding embrace. Sleek as quicksilver, laughing blithely, she squirmed from his grasp and slipped out of bed. A spill of light from the doorway silhouetted her in an amber glow, flecking her raven hair with sparkles of russet and gold. She smiled, glancing over her shoulder as she donned a peignoir of sheer ocher cambric. Her rounded hip and firm, ripened breast stood out in bold relief against the soft light, and in her eye was a naughty little twinkle, as if she had posed there, purposely teasing, allowing him to look but not touch.

"Would you like a brandy, handsome?"

There was a throaty innocence in her voice, at once beguiling and sultry and filled with promise. Her smile was smoky and warm, like an autumn sunset, and her mercurial elusiveness only made him want her more. Which was how she meant it to be, as they both understood, a small game to kindle his anticipation and make his mouth lust for the taste of her. But knowing what she was about diminished his need not in the least. His mouth felt thick and pasty, and while he ridiculed himself for the thought, her lush figure somehow seemed more tempting framed against the lamplight than it had a moment ago in bed.

Lounging back in the pillows, he eyed her with a faint, indulgent smile. "Brandy sounds good. But I ought to warn you, it'll stoke the boiler hotter than it already is."

"Why, of course it will. Don't you know that fallen women always have a method to their madness?"

"Just so you know what you're lettin' yourself in for."

She flung her hair back with a devilish laugh, and whisked out of the room. The moment she was gone he closed his eyes and sank deeper in the downy mattress, wondering how long she would make him wait. However heated these games they played, he never fully lost a sense of cold objectivity about her. She was sensual as a brood mare, and here in this house, he was aware of her in the way of a man seated beside a bonfire. But he often caught himself studying her, as if she were something he had bought on a whim and couldn't quite decide what he'd got in the bargain. That he kept coming back, and had no desire for other women, said a great deal. Although precisely what it meant was something he'd never been able to formulate into words. Perhaps only that she was a stunner and hot-blooded and knew how to jitterate his juices. And perhaps that was enough. All a man needed from a woman.

Yet there was more than that between them, and had been for some time. She filled a void in his life, brought gaiety and wit and gentleness where none existed. Aside from the boys, she was the only bright spot in days that all too often seemed drab and lonely. Though the discovery had come late, he knew now that certain aspects of a man's life could be enriched only by a woman. His dealings with men were, in the main, antagonistic (even those in his employ respected him rather than liked him), which was precisely the way he wanted it. A lone wolf by choice, he derived satisfaction not from friendship but from strife; winning was what counted, and the fact that other men resented him, or better yet, even hated him, merely added spice to the victory. Still, however large his collection of scalps, there was always a certain emptiness which remained after every fight. As if, in the winning, there came some atavistic gratification but very little personal fulfillment. And while it disturbed him in reflective moments, he had to admit that it was Zalia who filled the void. Almost as if by osmosis, slowly and ever so cautiously, she had wormed her way into that part of his life where he needed her most. But only that part! He drew the line there, and in a very real sense, it stopped at her front door.

She appeared in the doorway again, carrying a small tray on which rested two glasses of cognac, and his determination went soft as mush. The sight of her, revealed so fetchingly beneath the sheer dressing gown, brought the pasty taste back to his mouth. Later, striding across town, the night air would clear his head of her jasmine-scented witchery, and it was then he would curse himself for allowing his brains to dangle between his legs. But here, in her bed, his resolve invariably weakened, and like some debauched hedonist, he gave himself over to the enticement of her body—and her utterly captivating genius for making him forget.

"Here we are," she said gaily, "nectar for my impatient satyr."

He mumbled something unintelligible, not quite sure what he'd been called, and took a brandy glass from the extended tray. The room was dimly lighted, but as she set the tray on a nightstand and scooted into bed, she caught the look on his face. Curiously withdrawn, it was a look of brooding, as if his thoughts were torn between the moment and something outside her ken. And it was a startling change in mood from what he had displayed only minutes before. Quite naturally, Zalia assumed that it had nothing to do with her, and everything to do with his latest drubbing by the bureaucrats.

"Mercy sakes alive, I can't leave you alone for a minute, can I?" She cupped his jaw in her tiny hand and squeezed gently. "You big ninny, drink your brandy and forget it. We agreed it was over and done with, and besides you haven't really lost anything. Now, be honest, have you?"

Jake slewed an odd sidewise glance in her direction. "That wasn't what I was thinkin' about. But since you brought it up, you're damn right I lost something. Six million acres, just to be exact."

"Oooh, pshaw!" she admonished, wrinkling her nose in a little sniff. "How can a man lose something he doesn't own?"

"Easy as pie, that's how. All you've got to do is let your guard down just once, and them vultures in Washington will give it to you below the belt. Quicker'n you can say scat."

"But, Jake, sweetheart, you're avoiding the facts. You told me yourself that the Cherokees actually own it. And even I know that a lease is scarcely the same thing as a title. So that makes the question inescapable—how can you lose what you never had?"

"Lemme tell you something, smart britches. Titles don't mean a hill of beans. A man owns what he can hold onto." He held up a thorny hand and knotted it into a fist. "I had it in my grasp. Hell, I could feel it, damn near taste it. And you talk about ownin' it? Why, Christ A'mighty, there was more of my sweat in that land than the whole Cherokee Nation put together."

"Yes, but it's not the end of the world. Now really, be truthful. As catastrophes go, it's not all that great a tragedy, is it? I mean, there's scads of land, and you can always work but another deal somewhere else."

"Not like that, I can't. You just don't find six million acres layin' around loose every day of the week. Hell's bells, some of them European kings don't claim that much land. Don't you see, it would've been like ownin' my own country." He paused, staring absently at his brandy glass. "Makes me sick to my stomach just thinkin' about it."

"Jake Kincaid, I do believe you're a bigger scoundrel than I imagined." She examined his face in the fuzzy light. "You never meant for the Association to own that land. You had some sneaky trick all worked out to get it for yourself, didn't you?"

"Of course." Baldly stated, such an outrageous truth seemed somehow absurd, and he couldn't help grinning. "Might have taken a few years, but I could've eased them out one at a time. Before long I would've had myself a regular little kingdom down there."

A peculiar light flickered in her eyes, like a tongue of flame behind dusky onyx. She was silent a long while, then at last, shaking her head, she smiled. "You say it's the land, but I think it's your pride. Someone finally beat you at your own game, and you're fit to be tied. Honestly, I don't mean to snicker, but you'll have to admit it's funny. Women are supposed to be the vainest creatures on earth, and really, it's the other way round. You men are such peacocks." She leaned closer, and soothed his cheek. "Oh, Jake, don't carry on so. They only plucked one tailfeather. You have lots more left."

Though made in jest, the remark struck a nerve. Jake had received the bad news only that afternoon, in a telegraph message from his Washington lobbyist. Nearly six months of conniving, not to mention thousands of dollars in bribes, shot down by an official announcement from the Interior Department. He was sore as a boil, and he had come here tonight for solace and pampering, not flippant little witticisms. As Zalia had so aptly perceived, his pride had been tweaked, and he wasn't a man to take a licking in stride. Quite the contrary, it was the first time in his life he had ever been whipped, and he was proving a remarkably poor loser.

A scheme to purchase the Cherokee Outlet had taken root in his mind shortly after last summer's visit to Tahlequah. The gestation period was hurried along by the threat of Boomers on the one hand and reformers on the other, and in no small degree, by a congressional investigation into the bribery of Indian Agents. Jake had every confidence that the investigation was the handiwork of the railroad lobby, and he developed a sudden appreciation for Hiram Short's insistence that the payoff be made in cash. Nothing could be traced back to him, but he didn't wait around to see what might be unearthed by the inquiry. Before anyone could catch his breath, he had the Association committed to a bizarre intrigue that reached into the very heart of Washington bureaucracy.

The first step was simplicity itself. The Association offered the Cherokee Nation three dollars an acre for title to the Outlet. Association members were flabbergasted by the total price—$18 million—yet Jake's reasoning was beyond reproach. Now was the time to move, while they had the leverage of a five-year lease, and before Indian lands were opened to white settlement. Once ownership was in private hands, the Outlet would be immune to the caprice of petty bureaucrats, however much the settlers clamored to be given something for nothing. And the price had to be right, so generous that the government couldn't fall back on the old excuse of white men trying to hoodwink the noble savage.

If the cattlemen were unnerved by the amount of money involved, Dennis Bushyhead and his Cherokees were staggered. They found it difficult to conjure up an image of such a sum, much less translate it into the realities of their agrarian economy. But the shock affected their judgment none at all, and the tribal council moved with alacrity. Chief Bushy-head informed the Association that the offer was acceptable. Pending approval by the Interior Department, of course.

With the Cherokees in his pocket, Jake moved on Washington. He hired a lobbyist, and over the summer and early fall, they shelled out money by the trunkloads. Congressmen and Senators, cabinet members and bureaucrats, were wined and dined and bribed in lavish style. At times, it seemed that half of Washington was on the payroll, but for all his crafty overtures, the lobbyist failed to land the biggest fish. The Secretary of the Interior and the Commissioner of Indian Affairs proved to be that rarest of all species, honest politicians. They resisted pressure from the White House and the Congress, and even from within the labyrinth of their own bureaucracy. And in the end, determined that no Kansas hayseed would usurp federal prerogatives, they put the quietus on Jake's grandest scheme.

Just that morning, a brisk September day which promised better things, the Secretary of the Interior had announced that the Cherokee Nation lacked power of transfer to the Outlet lands. He then informed the public at large that over some suitable period of time the government itself would purchase the Outlet—at the munificent price of $1.25 an acre. That the Cherokees had little choice in the matter was clear to everyone, and the noble red men in Tahlequah heaved a collective sigh of disgust. But the Secretary of the Interior awarded them a consolation prize of sorts by affirming their right to lease the Outlet. So long as it remained a part of the Cherokee Nation.

This afterthought spurred Jake to action. Angry as he was at that decision, and even more furious that he had lost his first major engagement in Washington, he could still think straight. How long the Cherokees would continue to own the Outlet was anybody's guess, but a legally executed contract was a binding instrument. Exempt from all acts of piracy, including those perpetrated by the federal government. He dispatched a messenger to Tahlequah, requesting a five-year extention on the present lease—with annual lease payments of $200,000. All things considered, he felt reasonably confident that Dennis Bushyhead and the Cherokee council would move with something more than deliberate speed.

Afterward, nursing his wounds in private, Jake concluded that his brash assault on Washington had been somewhat premature. This time he had been able to salvage bits and pieces from a messy situation, but next time he might not be so lucky. Clearly, the acquisition of clout along the banks of the Potomac required planning and organization, and a gradual cultivation of the power brokers. Determined that any future skirmish would yield tangible results, he had composed a lengthy letter to his lobbyist in Washington, enclosing a bank draft for a substantial sum.

And now, lying in bed with Zalia, he seemed stumped for a snappy comeback. She was a clever woman, no denying that. Pride was his touchy spot, always had been, and apparently his motives were as obvious to her as they had been to—! The thought struck him with such force that it was as if his ears had suddenly come unplugged. Zalia was wise to him in the same way that Sadie had seen through his wiles and dodges. And the similarity didn't end there. Except for looks and size, they might have been a matched pair. The same impudent manner and saucy outlook on life, and that great well of intuition which laid bare a man's secrets. It went beyond mere coincidence, defied probability and the element of chance. Thunderstruck, he found himself staring incredulously at the woman beside him, aware for the first time of why he had chosen her. And why he stayed with her. She was Sadie Timmons incarnated. A gay and charming cameo of his own personal ghost.

The silence deepened between them, and Zalia had the queer sensation that he was looking through her. Somewhere beyond her. Alarmed by his glazed stare, her own eyes turned darkly intense. "Jake, is something wrong?" She waited, but he didn't answer. "I was only joshing, honey. You know that, don't you? I wouldn't hurt your feelings for the world."

Something in her voice broke the spell, and he blinked several times, as if clearing his vision. Then he downed the cognac in a single gulp, and waited as the molten slug hit the pit of his stomach. Himself again, composure restored, he slid his arm around her waist and pulled her close. "Nothin' wrong that a little lovin' won't cure. Unless you're tuckered out, or lost the urge."

"Foolish man." She smiled engagingly and batted her lashes. "I thought you would never ask."

She took the glass from his hand, slipped from bed, and placed it with her own on the nightstand. Then, very slowly, with luxuriant feline movements that were somehow exotic and tantalizing, she let the peignoir fall to the floor. She knew it excited him, her standing there revealed in the murky amber glow, and she allowed him to look an instant longer. But she was a sorceress with passions of her own, and in the next moment she flung herself into bed and his arms.

The three men trooped into his office muffled in greatcoats and woolly scarves and heavy gloves. The weather was unseasonably brisk for October, and a blast of chill air swept through the door. Stamping their feet, the men removed their outer garments, commenting that it looked to be an early winter, and in the solemn unison of three wise owls, shook Jake's hand. At his invitation, they took chairs arranged on a line in front of the desk, and sat waiting with a kind of bovine patience. He offered them neither cigars nor whiskey, though they were aware that he indulged himself in both. Uncharitable men at heart, they nonetheless chose to overlook these worldly vices, for they represented the Redform Election Committee, and in the way of things political, they had made their peace with Jake Kincaid.

Whatever their own self-inflicted virtues, Jake never allowed it to inhibit his personal habits. Selecting a cigar from the desk humidor, he clipped the ends with a pocket knife and took his time lighting it. The flare of the match dissolved in a wreath of smoke, and as he studied them through the haze, his mind quickly sifted the mental catalog he had compiled on this somber threesome. Oscar Belden: grocer, deacon of the Methodist Church, and president of the Temperance League. Ben Eckhardt: farmer, country preacher, and head of the local Grangers' Association. Cleve Suggs: rancher, general gadfly and nuisance, and president of the Shorthorn Breeders Association. Alike in mood and conviction, they were glacial, humorless men, with the oddly marled stare common to all zealots. As politicians they had much to learn, but despite their rigid moralism, they were surprisingly eager pupils. Already they had absorbed the basic tenet of compromise, and with it, the fact that they would never carry the election without his own support and that of the Santa Fe. It was a good start, and the rest would come with time.

Just now, though, they appeared abnormally sober. Added to their usual pinch-lipped expression, this gave them the look of tyro gravediggers at an undertakers' convention. In the face of this sepulchral delegation it was difficult to muster a smile, but Jake pulled copiously on his cigar and gave it a game try.

"Gents, I'm glad you could drop by. Never hurts to get our heads together, 'specially with time growin' short. Now, what can I do for you?"

Oscar Belden, who generally acted as spokesman for the group, cleared his throat. "Well, Mr. Kincaid, it seems we've got ourselves—uh—well, what you might call a problem."

"That a fact?" Jake replied amiably. "Funny, I was under the impression everything was hummin' along according to plan."

"No, sir, I'm afraid it's not." Belden grinned weakly and darted a nervous glance at his cohorts. "That's why we asked for this meetin'. Thought we'd better get some things ironed out before the rally tonight."

"Fire away, Oscar. That's what I'm here for, to lend a hand wherever needed."

Belden appeared flustered by this chipper diffidence. He hawked again and shifted uncomfortably in his chair. "Doggone it, Mr. Kincaid, I feel lower'n a polecat comin' to you like this. But me and the boys talked it over, and we figured this thing's gotta be stopped 'fore it spreads any further."

"What thing? You've still got me in the dark, Oscar."

"Well, sir, I don't know how to say it except straight from the shoulder. Word's all over town that for years you was the—awww, tarnation—what'd they call it?" His face screwed up in a perplexed frown. "Cleve, gimme some help. What was that word they used?"

Suggs jumped as if he'd been goosed with a hot poker. "The bagman," he blurted, "must've heard it fifty times if I heard it once."

"That's it, the bagman. And he's right, Mr. Kincaid. Ever'-body in town's talkin' about it. They're sayin' you were the bagman between the Delano crowd and the City Hall, and the boys at the courthouse, too."

"Meaning I collected the payoff money and distributed it among the crooked politicians?"

"Yessir, that's exactly what they mean. Folks are sayin' Delano could never've held out long as it has if you hadn't fixed it with the right parties."

"And I suppose this talk, as you call it, just got started this morning?"

"Matter of fact, it did. But there's more to it, Mr. Kincaid. They're sayin' you only quit playin' footsy with the sporting crowd when it come clear that the reform movement couldn't be stopped. Across the river they're callin' you a Judas."

A silence fell over the room—a silence of deliberate waiting, weighing, measuring. The committeemen were somewhat in awe of him, for he had ruled Sedgwick County with an iron fist over the past decade. And they had seen strange things happen to men who heedlessly opposed his will. Business failures and besmirched reputations had become commonplace afflictions among those who challenged Jake Kincaid. Belden and his friends sometimes felt as though they had joined hands with Satan himself, but they were nothing if not practical. They needed this man's influence to win, and in sheer desperation, they had come here today seeking guidance from their political mentor.

For his part, Jake was simply a better bluffer. He needed them as badly as they needed him. The battle lines had been drawn for some months now, with the river as the dividing point. The reformers in Wichita against the sporting crowd in Delano. Jake and his uptown cronies controlled the swing vote, and with it, the reformers could carry the election. But it made for an uneasy alliance, and Jake himself had misgivings about the political status quo once these Bible-thumpers tasted victory. Watching them now, it came to him that they were weak sisters, always jumping at shadows. Politics in Kansas would probably never again be any fun. Not like the old days, that was for damn sure.

"Gentlemen, I suspect we have Chalk Wheeler to thank for all this gossip. Elections aren't far off, and he's starting to run scared. No doubt he figured that with the big rally planned for tonight it was a good time to begin a smear campaign. Spread some half-truths and innuendo hoping the voters would be gullible enough to swallow it. Oldest trick in the book."

Benjamin Eckhardt, a stone-cold fundamentalist with messianic dreams, spoke for the first time. "Mr. Kincaid, you talk of half-truths. Are we to understand that this gossip isn't entirely false? That it bears some element of truth?"

"Ben, the first rule of politics is to act like a dummy when one of your partners gets smeared with mud. I'm glad to see you've taken the lesson to heart." Jake's voice was larded with sarcasm, and for what seemed a lifetime, he sat boring holes through the farmer. Then his mouth curled in a sardonic smile. "You boys knew what I was and how I ran this county long before we made our deal. So let's don't hear any belly-achin' just because Wheeler has started playin' dirty pool. Sometimes politics gets downright raunchy, and my only advice is that if you can't stand the heat, then get out of the kitchen."

He gave them a moment to digest that, and then dismissed it with an idle gesture. "Don't give yourself a case of the fidgets. That's just what Wheeler wants. Go ahead with your rally and by this time tomorrow the whole thing will have blown over."

The three men exchanged furtive glances, and Oscar Belden's store-bought teeth clacked together like a mouthful of dice. He looked absolutely petrified, but from somewhere he drummed up the courage to say what as yet had been left unsaid. "Mr. Kincaid, I wish you was right, but I'm sorry to tell you I don't think it'll blow over. Not tomorrow, or anytime else."

"Oscar, whatever you're hintin' at, why don't you just spit it out?"

"Yessir, I guess that's the best way." The grocer's Adam's apple bobbed convulsively, and again, he had to dredge up the gumption to speak. "I know it's loose talk, Mr. Kincaid— and mind you, I'm just repeatin' what they're saying—but the word's out that you got your start operatin' a bawdy house in Abilene."

"A bawdy house!" Jake echoed incredulously. "They're saying I ran a whorehouse?"

"That's not the worst of it, Mr. Kincaid, not by half."

"All right, let's hear the rest of it. Evidently there's nothing Chalk Wheeler won't stoop to."

"Yessir, I'm afraid so." Belden couldn't look at him now. "I'd sooner cut off my arm than tell you this, Mr. Kincaid, but they're saying"—he swallowed around a hard knot in his throat—"they're saying that your wife was a fancy woman. That she worked in that house."

A tomblike silence descended over the room. Jake's eyes went pale and cold, hard as steel. Without realizing it, he rose from his chair and stood towering over them, like a god about to smite the earth with sizzling thunderbolts. The look on his face was murderous, a look of rage and hate and savage menace. Several minutes passed before he could speak, and his voice was raspy, low and grating and ominously restrained.

"I'm going to break a rule. Pass the word that I'll speak at the rally tonight. And make sure they hear about it in Delano. I don't care how you do it, but just be damned certain that word gets across the river."

He turned from them and stared out the window, and they saw then that his fists were clenched so tight his knuckles looked like polished stone. Quietly they gathered their greatcoats and scarves, and eased out the door with a vast feeling of deliverance. Behind them, he gazed sightlessly through the window, and a tendril of smoke escaped one fist as he crushed the cigar to shreds. His face was wooden now, a mask revealing nothing.

Politicking on the plains of Kansas was no simple matter. The farm vote alone couldn't carry an election, and conversely, neither could the town vote assure victory at the polls. A candidate seeking county office faced a particularly thorny problem. To guarantee a plurality he must somehow garner sufficient votes from both factions. Which placed him in the position of being all things to all people. Not an easy task, even for those adept at walking fences.

Worse luck, the man with his eye on a county post was forced to travel vast distances in order to contact the farm vote, which meant making several speeches a day. Whatever spare moments he had left over were spent courting the town voters. It was a sunrise to sundown race against time, always running and pumping hands and spreading the gospel in an effort to squeeze the most from each day.

Candidates for town office moved at a somewhat more leisurely pace. Their constituents were readily accessible, and in general tended to be less obstinate than the sodbusters. Better yet, the political machine of Wichita was controlled solely by Jake Kincaid, and those candidates endorsed by the party were virtually assured of being elected. The reform movement, which was backed almost universally by the farmers, had eroded Kincaid's influence with outlying voters. But within the province of Wichita itself, his power remained uncontested. And like a delicately balanced fulcrum, it gave him all the leverage he needed. Without his support the reformers could win only moderately in the county elections, which would result in a stalemate of sorts. But with him they could carry the day, and they were content to leave the town in his hands so long as there was some equitable arrangement in the courthouse and the state legislature.

And it was to consolidate these diverse elements that the Reform Committee had called for a mass rally. Heavily publicized in advance, the rally was to be held some two weeks before the elections, early on a Saturday evening. Just as farmers went to church on Sunday, so it was that they flocked to town on Saturday, and their presence was essential to the committee's plan. Like prize bulls, the candidates would be put on public display, and at last, all doubt would be removed. The townspeople and the farmers would see with their own eyes that the Kincaid forces had severed all ties with the Delano crowd—that once and for all, they had climbed aboard the reform bandwagon. On election day, with the alliance firmly established, everyone could then vote the coalition ticket in good conscience. Timed perfectly, billed as an extravaganza of sorts, the rally would serve as a clincher, presenting the old order and the new in a united front.

A speaker's platform had been erected on Douglas Avenue, with symbolic torches lighting the area and bunting gaily draped across the street. But there was nothing festive about the spectators as they began gathering shortly after dusk. Slanderous rumors had been circulating around town since early morning, and if true, there would be no coalition here tonight. Now an even more chilling note had been added. Word was out that Jake Kincaid himself would address the rally. Always a power behind the scenes, never before had he spoken out in public, and this sudden turnabout, provoked by accusations no man could overlook, lent an ominous quality to the evening's events.

By nightfall the street was jammed with people, spilling back over the boardwalks and stretching fully a half block in either direction. Oscar Belden spoke first, setting a tone of cooperation and brotherhood, asking everyone to pull together in the days ahead. Then the mayor, acting as spokesman for the old order, followed with a rousing speech which promised peace and prosperity, and an end to the iniquitous hellhole across the river. One after another the candidates for town and county offices were then paraded across the platform. They were allowed to harangue the crowd briefly, each spouting some cornball polemics of his own design, and afterward trotted off to a smattering of polite applause. But the onlookers heard little of what they said, and there was a constant buzz of conversation which grew louder as the evening wore on. What had begun as a political rally had become a spectacle awaiting the arrival of its star attraction. Townspeople and farmers, their wives and children, had had enough folksy speechifying by the candidates. They wanted to hear what Jake Kincaid had to say for himself. And they were growing impatient to hear him say it.

At last, they got their wish. The rally simply ground to a halt with the final speech, and out of nowhere, Jake Kincaid strode to the front of the platform. The flickering torchlight gave his hair a burnished look, and deep within his eyes there was a fiery glow not unlike that of smoldering coals. His face was composed and without rancor, almost detached. But even those spectators at the back of the crowd could see what the effort had cost him. He looked for all the world like a hangman, cold and implacable, come to do a dirty job which was necessary if distasteful. Without introduction or preamble he began to speak, his voice hard and brusque, and somehow malevolent.

"You people know me, and you know what I stand for. So I won't bore you with a bunch of fancy phrases and four-bit words. I'm here for some plain talk. It'll be short but it won't be sweet." Pausing, he let his gaze rove out across the women in the crowd. "I suggest you ladies either plug up your ears or else take the kids for a walk. What I've got to say can only be said one way."

Nobody moved. They stood, hushed and expectant, waiting to hear it. Jake watched them in silence, hesitating a moment longer, then resumed.

"First off, let's have it understood that I believe in the right to free speech. Any man that wants to call me a crook, that's his privilege. But I've got the right to call him a goddamned liar—and I'll say it to his face!"

"You ran crooked games in Abilene!" someone shouted.

"How many farmers have you cheated out of their land?" demanded another voice.

"You're a stooge for the railroad, Kincaid. Admit it!" yelled still a third man.

The accusations came fast and furious, from different quarters of the crowd. Jake had expected hecklers, certain that Chalk Wheeler would have men planted among the onlookers. Acknowledging the catcalls with a slight cant of his head, he forced himself to smile.

"Glad to see you boys could make it over from Delano. Gives me a chance to tell you face to face that you're a bunch of cheap, penny-ante, four-flushers. And since your boss doesn't have the guts to do his own dirty work, you can tell him I said he's the biggest goddamn liar this side of Texas."

That drew hoots of laughter from the farmers. They cared even less for Texans than they did the sporting element in Delano. Jake waited for the cackling to subside, and then lashed out again.

"A man has also got the right to say that I ran a whorehouse. But if he does I'll kick his ass up between his shoulders so he has to take off his shirt to crap. That's my right!"

Everyone laughed now, even the women, for it was a justifiable threat, graphically stated, and they believed he could do it. But after several moments of rib-poking and good-natured chuckling they fell silent. Somehow, in the flare of the torches, the speaker's face had changed. He again had the look of an executioner.

"I've told you what the freedom of speech gives a man the right to say. Now I'll tell you where that right ends." He hesitated, just a mere fraction of a second, and his flinty gaze swept the crowd. "It ends where he defames the dead. And I'm announcing publicly that the next man who slanders my wife's name won't live to get out of town."

He flicked back the skirt of his coat to reveal a pistol holstered at his side. "Since the law doesn't cover such things, I'll just officiate with the powers vested in me by Judge Colt. Anybody that thinks I'm foolin', just step up and try me."

The challenge was starkly dramatic, and the crowd stared back at him in speechless wonder. This was the kind of talk they understood. Blunt and straight to the point, delivered by a man with the grit to back up his word. A man who had been wronged, whose wife had been unjustly slandered, and who had every right to defend the name of the dead. What any of them there wanted to believe they would have done had the roles been reversed.

They waited. A hushed silence hung over the street as Chalk Wheeler's men were given time to take up the challenge. But no voice was raised. Not a sound broke the stillness. Quite clearly, none of the hecklers thought Jake Kincaid was fooling.

A minute passed, then another, and finally the tall figure on the platform tugged his coat back in place. "That's all I came to say. I hope it answers any questions you folks might have had in your minds. Now I'll leave you with a little fodder to munch on. The best answer you can give that pack of rats across the river is at the polls. And I say, give 'em both barrels!"

The crowd broke out in cheers, roaring its approval. Farmers and townspeople slapped one another on the backs, men shook hands and women exchanged hugs, and Oscar Belden looked so happy he almost burst into tears. Without a backward glance, Jake Kincaid turned and walked from the platform. An imperceptible smile ticced the corner of his mouth; then he was down the steps and lost to sight.

The elections were held in an atmosphere of homespun burlesque. Deadly serious as the issues were, the voices came to the polls in a festive mood. After the rally, and Jake Kincaid's brash performance, the outcome had never seriously been in doubt. The attempt to split the coalition (engineered, as everyone knew, by Chalk Wheeler) had been a last-ditch gamble. One which failed miserably. And in an earthy sort of way, the people of Sedgwick County took droll amusement from the plight of the sporting crowd.

Farmers and townmen, united in purpose as never before, flocked to the polls. When the ballots were tallied late that evening, the reform ticket had won a landslide victory. Jubilant, and a bit heady with their show of power, the voters staged an impromptu parade up and down Douglas Avenue. But across the river, the losers held something more on the order of a wake. Demon rum flowed like water, and they drowned their sorrow in a night-long orgy of illicit booze. All of which would shortly vanish forever, along with gambling and whorehouses and sundry forms of vice. Delano had fallen upon hard times, and the sporting crowd understood only too well for whom the bells tolled.

Sin was finished along the banks of the Arkansas. And of all those who celebrated the passing of the old order, perhaps the sense of relief was greatest in the Kincaid household. At breakfast the next morning Jake felt as if an enormous burden had been lifted from his shoulders. While he still had misgivings about the reformers, and the straitlaced future they envisioned for Kansas, it was a comfort to have done with the bitter campaign at last. All the more so since he had emerged on the winning side, with his power intact. Politics might never again be the same, yet the price of change was one he had weighed and, however reluctantly, accepted. He demanded of no enterprise that it be either interesting or enjoyable, but only that it enable him to win. The Reform Movement had done that, and for all its dull, hidebound conformity, he was satisfied with his choice.

But if Jake's sense of relief was profound, what the boys felt was no less remarkable. Both Owen and Brad had shouldered a burden of their own over the last week, an outgrowth of the vile rumors which had circulated through town. Children, oddly enough, made cruel sport out of gossip which merely titillated their elders, and the boys had been razzed unmercifully by their schoolmates. The teasing stopped only after Owen had administered beatings to several of their tormentors, and while neither he nor Brad understood the deeper implications, they somehow felt vindicated by yesterday's elections. As if the vote had been a test of their father's honor and their mother's virtue rather than a factional dogfight between politicians.

Throughout the entire ordeal Jake had never once made mention of it to the boys. He'd thrown out a public challenge at the rally, and he believed that to be answer enough for anyone, his own sons included. Nonetheless, he knew what was happening at school, and he was proud of Owen's skinned knuckles and puffed lips. He would have been prouder still if Brad had bloodied himself, instead of moping about with a sullen look of indignation. But, then, it was little more than he had expected of the boy. Unlike his older brother, Brad was not a scrapper. Whatever his own feelings, though, Jake didn't interfere. Nor did he comment. A man stood toe to toe and slugged it out with life's furies, or else he buckled and allowed circumstances to push him around. Either way, it was a lesson the boys had to learn for themselves.

Still, watching them this morning, Jake had to admit that their appetites had improved enormously overnight. Seated on either side of him at the table, they ate like famished wolf cubs, devouring great stacks of pancakes, pork chops, and calf's brains scrambled with eggs. When he finished with his own plate, and lit a cigar, they were in a dead heat for the last pork chop, and it was all he could do to suppress a chuckle.

"You boys are eatin' like the house is on fire. What's your rush?"

Owen's fork stopped in midair, and Brad looked up with his mouth stuffed so full he could barely work his jaws. They exchanged a quick glance, and Jake saw the older boy shake his head with an almost imperceptible movement. Brad chewed a little faster, swallowing in loud gulps, but he made no attempt to answer. Finally, toying with a soggy scrap of pancake, Owen gave his father a look of bemused innocence.

"Nothin', Pa. Just hungry, that's all."

The remark seemed guileless enough, but Jake wasn't fooled. He was scanning their faces, and as usual, it was Brad who gave it away. The boy had never been able to hide what he felt, and right now, he looked guilty as hell. Taken in tandem with Owen's feigned unconcern, it suddenly aroused Jake's curiosity.

He smiled, puffing on his cigar. "Well, that's good. You being hungry, I mean. Thought for a minute you were in a hurry to get out of here for some reason."

"Not us, Pa." Owen's disclaimer came a bit too quickly,

somehow overdrawn. "We just like pancakes and stuff, and Mrs. Murphy cooks it awful good. I'll betcha there's not anybody in town that cooks as good as she does."

"You agree with that, Brad?"

The younger boy swallowed the last of his mouthful, and nodded vigorously. "Sure, Pa. Nobody's better'n her."

"No, I'm not talkin' about Mrs. Murphy's vittles. I mean, do you agree with your brother that there's no reason to hurry?"

Brad would shortly turn ten, and each day he grew more like his mother. Both in looks and temperament. He had that same ingenuous quality about him, and it constantly betrayed his innermost thoughts. Just now he appeared flustered, and squirmed uneasily under his father's steady gaze.

"Yessir, we was just hungry." He flicked a sidewise glance at Owen, and his ears reddened. A sure sign that he was skirting the truth. "Heck, we're not in any rush to get to school, are we?"

The slip was no sooner out than the youngster bit his tongue, and Owen shot him a dark look. Jake caught the byplay, and abruptly it dawned on him what they were about. But he gave no indication, still smiling and drawing leisurely on his cigar.

"Well, I'm glad to hear it. My feelings were beginning to get hurt, the way you two acted. Why, I'll bet between the both of you, nobody's said a dozen words to me since we sat down to breakfast."

The boys again exchanged glances, a signal of some sort. From the looks of it, Brad had been warned to keep his mouth shut. Not by virtue of age alone was Owen the leader here. Of the two, he was the cooler, the more deliberate, and invariably, it was he who stood up to his father when trouble arose. Now, almost brazenly sure of himself, he speared the last pork chop with his fork and smiled that same infectious smile.

"Cripes, Pa, we didn't mean nothin'." He crammed a hunk

of pork in his mouth as if to demonstrate the point. "Guess we was just too busy eatin' to talk."

Brad's hangdog look belied the words, but Jake let it pass for the moment. "I can see that," he observed dryly. "Course you might've said something about the election. Or maybe you don't care that your old man's side won the whole shootin' match. Likely that's it, huh?"

Owen stopped chewing and darted another warning at his little brother. "Aw, Pa, that's not so. Honest Injun! You just ask Mrs. Murphy. Before you came in for breakfast we was tellin' her how you'd whipped the stuffin' out of that ol' Wheeler fellow and his bunch. Criminy, everybody'll be talkin' about it! You wait and see if they're not."

"I suspect they will. Guess that's why you're in such a rush to get to school, isn't it?"

There was an instant of absolute silence, and Owen slowly resumed chewing, not nearly so puzzled as he appeared. "I don't get you, Pa."

"Don't you? I suppose you'll be tellin' me next that you weren't plannin' to rub their noses in it?"

"Who, Pa?" The boy's face was blandly quizzical. "What're you talkin' about?"

"I'm talkin' about the kids at school. The ones you've been bustin' upside the head for the last week or so."

Watching them as they stared at one another, Brad had the queer feeling that he was an outsider here. Young as he was, he sensed that this conversation had nothing to do with him. It was between his father and his brother. A special thing, which he'd never been a part of, or shared, yet had come to recognize whenever they looked at each other just this way. And today, in that funny, roundabout manner his father used, Owen was being praised for whipping the school smart alecks. While he was being ignored (which was worse than being punished) because he'd turned a deaf ear to their smutty talk. Still, it was little different than it had always been. As far as he remembered, he'd never felt he measured up in his father's eyes. Not the way Owen did. It bothered him a lot, and he often wondered why things had to be that way. But at his age, hurt came quicker than reason, so he contented himself with living in his older brother's shadow. There, hidden in the shade, it was safer, and people didn't shout so much.

Owen was seldom at a loss for words, but his father had surprised him this time. The pork chop lay forgotten, and it was a while before he could collect his wits. Then he smiled sheepishly. "Guess I oughtn't to've kept it a secret from you— huh, Pa?"

"There's not much I don't hear about, sooner or later." Jake took a pull on his cigar, and his words came out in little spurts of smoke. "Course seein' as they asked for it, I think you ought to finish the job."

"What job? I don't understand, Pa."

"The hell you don't, and quit tryin' to bandy words with me. Go on and get it done, just the way you intended. Rub their noses in it till they yell *uncle*. Maybe it'll teach 'em a lesson."

The youngster grinned, eyes brightening with excitement, and darted his brother a look of savage jubilation. Then, as if he now had time to spare, he took the pork chop in his hands and gnawed juicy sweet meat from the curve of the bone. Brad stared straight ahead, desperately hoping that his father would offer him similar words of encouragement. Just this once. But nothing happened. The only sound in the room was the grating of teeth on bone, and it seemed to go on forever.

An hour or so later, walking down Main, Jake had to pause every few steps to accept the congratulations of those he met. Passersby stopped to pump his hand, and people came out of stores to engage him in conversation. At one point a small crowd ganged around, jostling to get close to him, and their lighthearted shouts could be heard all along the street.

"Tied a can to their tail, didn't we, Mr. Kincaid?"

"Great days ahead, Mr. Kincaid. Yessir, hallelujah!"

Jake smiled and waved, tolerating their pawing hands and banal platitudes. And finally, with a good deal of effort, he managed to extricate himself. Before it could turn into a full-scale rally, he sped on toward the center of town, wishing now that he had stuck to backstreets. But the thought prompted some inner voice, more sardonic than testy, and he rushed along chortling to himself. Hell, everybody loved a winner. Especially one who was a reformed sinner! That it rhymed somehow made it funnier, an even better joke, and he almost laughed out loud.

Hurrying now, he turned the corner onto Douglas Avenue, and headed toward the land office. Somehow, though, it seemed to be his day for getting waylaid. People began popping out of the woodwork at an alarming rate, and within moments his brisk pace had slowed to a crawl. Another crowd commenced forming, and more than ever, he cursed his witless promenade through the heart of town. He should have known better. Then, quite suddenly, a jarring shout racketed over the clamor, somehow out of tune with the other voices, and it took a moment for the words to penetrate.

"Kincaid! You whoremongerin' son of a bitch. Show yourself!"

The yammering and good-natured banter abruptly ceased and everyone began looking over their shoulder. A moment passed, and then, as if cleaved in half, the crowd parted. Standing in the street, a pistol held loosely at his side, was Chalk Wheeler. His clothes were rumpled, muddy eyes bloodshot, and he reeked of stale whiskey. Clearly he'd been up all night, and it took only a glance to see that he was crazy drunk and spoiling for a fight.

"Time to pay the piper, Kincaid!" His voice was shrill, gibberty, the spooky cry of a loon in darkened woods. "I've come collectin', you goddamn Judas!"

One eye on the gun, Jake stepped off the boardwalk and

moved toward him. "Chalk, it's all over. Your side lost fair and square, and there's no sense makin' trouble." Slowly, with great care, he spread the skirts of his coat, still moving forward. "Besides, I'm not armed. See, don't even have a hideout gun. You wouldn't want to shoot an unarmed man, now would you, Chalk?"

"Like hell, I wouldn't. But you're gonna talk first, you rotten son of a bitch." He waved the pistol around, and the crowd broke, scrambling for the protection of doorways. "You're gonna tell 'em what a lousy double-crosser you are, Kincaid. Right out in front of God and everybody. You're gonna tell 'em, and then I'm gonna give you a case of lead poisoning."

"You're drunk, Chalk." Jake kept coming, never once breaking stride. "Why don't we talk about it when you're sober?"

Bleary-eyed and disheveled, Wheeler stuck the pistol out and waggled it like an accusing finger. "High and mighty, aren't you? Jesus Christ Kincaid himself. Well, lemme tell you, Mister, it looks kind of funny on a man that married himself a whore!"

Jake took the last step, within arm's reach, and the pistol suddenly exploded in a hollow roar. A sliver of fire knifed through his side, jerking him sideways, and for an instant his knees went rubbery. Then some dark corner of his mind came unhinged, blotting out everything but the rage, and his fist struck with the impact of a thunderbolt. The blow caught Wheeler flush on the jaw and his legs crumpled beneath him. As he fell Jake lashed out with another sledgehammer punch, and the gnarled fist connected with his chin. Wheeler rocketed backward, landing spread-eagled in the dust, and the pistol slipped from his fingers. But while he was down, he was merely stunned and far from out of the fight. He shook his head groggily, trying to focus through a dizzy swirl of lights, and as his vision cleared, he came up on one elbow.

Just for a moment, Jake couldn't believe it was happening. In all the years he'd been busting heads—whorehouse slugfests and countless saloon brawls—nobody had ever taken those punches and come back for more. Still, his wonderment was a fleeting thing. Holding off now was out of the question. Wheeler was dangerous so long as he could move, and Jake's cardinal rule was that once a man went down, he stayed down. Whatever it took to keep him there. In a fight there were no second-place winners, and only a damnfool called it quits before he'd finished the job.

Wheeler reached for the gun and that decided it.

Jake booted him in the ribs, and there was a splintering crunch as bone and cartilage buckled under the impact. The gambler's mouth popped open with a gasp, like some wide-eyed goldfish spitting bubbles, and he retched a gurgled cry for air. But if Chalk Wheeler was a brute for punishment, he was also a man crazed with hate. Rolling away, sucking great drafts of air into his starved lungs, he scrambled to his hands and knees and flung himself in a headlong lunge for the pistol.

There was no mercy in Jake now, nor any vestige of emotion. Cold and detached, operating on a certain nerveless instinct, he kicked Wheeler in the face. The blow nearly tore the gambler's jaw off, and his nose burst in a crimsoned blotch of blood and gore. Yet through sheer force of will, Wheeler somehow hung on, and with agonizing slowness, his hand inched toward the gun. Jake shifted, setting his weight behind the movement, and in an instant of methodical savagery, kicked the fallen man along the ridge of his jawbone.

Wheeler's head wrenched around in a peculiar curve, and there was an audible crack, like a branch being broken, as his neck snapped. Then his body jerked in a spastic shudder and his eyes went white as glazed stones. Like a doll with its stuffing torn loose, his head crooked down over his shoulder at a grotesque angle and he slumped lifeless in the street.

Jake stood for a moment, staring blindly at the corpse.

Somehow it enraged him all the more that it was over so fast. That the bastard had gone down so quickly, died with so little suffering. He wanted to prolong it, feel the crunch of his fist on bone and meat, exact a heavier toll from the filth sprawled out before him. As if mocking him, the sightless eyeballs stared back, and ever so slowly he gained a measure of sanity. His labored breathing eased off and the rage melted away, and in the sallow face at his feet he saw at last the answer. There was no heavier toll. However inadequate, he had exacted the highest price of all.

Then, as if his awakened senses had rebelled, he felt a lazy kind of dizziness come over him. His vision blurred and he swayed drunkenly, unable to focus any longer on the dead man. He felt something warm and sticky running down his side, and quite unexpectedly, his legs gave way. He floated to earth, settling upright on his rump in the street, and he was struck by a crazy urge to laugh. It all seemed so ridiculous, even embarrassing. A grown man acting like a schoolgirl with the vapors. Absurd, that's what it was.

Somewhere in the distance he heard voices and the pounding of feet, but it was all faintly muted, and he couldn't see them. A fuzzy numbness spread over him, and softly came the darkness, until all that remained was a slender thread of light. A spark.

Early one afternoon, with light snow powdering the land, Cecil Hollister appeared at the house. Somewhat reluctantly, Mrs. Murphy ushered him into the parlor, and there he found Jake seated before the fireplace. Zalia was at his side, as she had been for the past month. Since the day of the shooting. And she rose like a ruined saint, reputation in ashes, heedless of gossip and stares and defamation. Heedless of all except the need to preserve the man, and his life.

She crossed the room swiftly, blocking Hollister's path at the door. "Good afternoon, Mr. Hollister. I'm Zalia Blair."

"Of course you are, and it's a privilege to meet you." Hollister was all charm and smiles. "I've been getting regular reports about how you nursed Jake through the worst of it. He's a lucky man, if you'll permit me to say so."

"Thank you." Zalia glanced over his shoulder at Mrs. Murphy and nodded. The old woman sniffed, eyeing Hollister suspiciously, then lumbered off in the direction of the kitchen. Zalia smiled. "You'll have to forgive Mrs. Murphy. She's of the opinion that Jake isn't up to receiving visitors, and I'm afraid she's right."

Hollister's gaze shot past her into the parlor, and his voice dropped to a near whisper. "I got word he was doing all right. You mean to say he's still in some sort of danger?"

"Oh, no. The doctor says he is mending very nicely. But this is only his second day out of bed, and he's quite weak. It was a nasty wound, Mr. Hollister, and he's been through a trying ordeal."

Hollister knew more of that than she suspected. After the shooting, the local Santa Fe agent had kept him advised with a constant stream of wires. The bullet had nicked Jake's kidney and lodged perilously close to his spine. Horace Quillman had operated within the hour, and by the narrowest of margins, his patient had survived the scalpel. At first it had been touch and go, but the crisis passed on the third night, and according to reports, Jake's recovery had been little short of miraculous. Horace Quillman attributed it not so much to divine intervention as to Jake's iron constitution, and round-the-clock nursing by Zalia Blair.

"Well, I wonder if I could see him for just a few minutes"—Hollister was still talking in a whisper—"I've come all the way from Topeka, and believe me, it's of the utmost importance."

"Zalia, for God's sake, let the old buzzard in!" Jake's voice sounded as peppery as ever. "Anybody would think I was on my deathbed the way you tippy-toe around."

She stepped aside, shrugging helplessly, and followed

Hollister into the parlor. Jake wore a heavy robe over his nightshirt, and a blanket was thrown over his legs. His face was pale and drawn, and he appeared a good twenty pounds lighter, but his eyes crackled with that old intensity. He looked very much like a man who had shaken hands with Death, and returned to tell the story.

Hollister halted in front of the fireplace, shedding his greatcoat and hat, and smiled heartily. "By golly, Jake, they said you were back on your mettle, but I wouldn't have believed it. You look spry as a goat."

"Cecil, you're a worse liar than ever. Take a load off your feet." He gestured toward a chair, then turned to Zalia, who was standing at his side, and gently squeezed her hand. "Why don't you give us a few minutes alone? Whatever he's got to say, it's likely not fit for a woman to hear."

She patted his hand, and smiled. "You're a much worse liar than he is, Jake Kincaid. I'll allow you ten minutes, and that's all. Then Mr. Hollister gets shooed out of here."

Utterly in command of things, she marched from the parlor in a rustling swish of skirts. They waited until she was through the door; then Hollister let go to a gusty breath between his teeth.

"Whew! That's quite a handful you've got yourself there, Jake."

"Glad you like her. Course, females always get bossy when they think they got a man flat on his back, so don't pay any mind to her sass."

"Sounds like you ought to take your own advice. Next thing you know, we'll hear wedding bells and find out she's got you up in front of a preacher."

His observation was amiable enough, but a little too off-hand, somehow suspect. Jake fixed him with an owlish frown. "I get the feelin' I've been asked a question. You writin' a book, Cecil, or have you just developed some sudden interest in my private life?"

"Well, in a manner of speaking, I suppose you could say

that." Hollister regarded him evenly, not so jovial now. "Fact is, it might have a bearing on why I came to see you."

Jake gave him a blank stare, eyes flat and guarded. "Care to spell that out?"

"By all means. That's what I'm here for." Hollister came up on the edge of his chair and leaned forward, as if to stress the gravity of his words. "Jake, whether you know it or not, you're a celebrity now. The newspapers come out with a fresh story every day, even if it's a rehash of what they wrote yesterday. And everybody in Kansas is talking about the man who defended his dead wife's honor. Hell, they can't get enough of it." He scribed a headline in the air with his forefinger. "Wounded Widower Kills Gunman with Bare Fists. They're smitten with you, Jake. Absolutely smitten."

"Yeah, I'm just a prince of a fellow. Now c'mon, Cecil, what's your point? Quit beatin' around the bush."

"Well, in a way, that is the point. You've captured the imagination of the people, which is no small thing." He pursed his lips, gathering himself, then edged closer. "Jake, I'm here as spokesman for the boys in Topeka. I'm talking about the reform leaders and what's left of the old crowd. We've been kicking it around for close to a week, and we're all of the same opinion. Come next election, we want to run you for governor."

Never so astounded in his life, Jake looked at him as if he were something that had fallen out of a tree. "You're crazy."

"Crazy as a fox. Listen to me, Jake. You're a natural. A once-in-a-lifetime phenomenon. The people of Kansas think you're a cross between the Avenging Angel and Abe Lincoln. You couldn't miss. Take my word for it."

"You really mean it, don't you?"

Hollister nodded solemnly. "You can chisel it in stone."

"I'll be go to hell." Clearly dumbfounded, Jake knuckled his whiskery jaw, mulling it over. At last he looked up, and the cynical gleam had returned to his eye. "No dice, Cecil. I use politicians, but I don't crawl in bed with them. Besides, I wouldn't work out as governor anyway. You and your boys want a puppet, and I never was much at dancin' to the other fellow's tune. We've butted heads often enough, so you ought to know what I'm talkin' about."

Hollister wasn't to be dissuaded so easily. "Jake, I know you're tired and you've been through hell this past month, so let me make a suggestion. Don't turn it down out of hand. Put your thinking cap on, and give it some deep consideration. And while you're thinking, remember this." He ticked off the points on his fingers. "First, there are no strings attached. You're not a puppet and we know it. But you are a reasonable man, and we believe we can depend on that. Second, you would be the most powerful man in the State of Kansas. I don't have to spell out what that would mean to you, and to the men who back you. Now, will you do that for me? Just think it over. Give it a week or so to gel, and then decide."

Jake grunted skeptically. "I guess there's no harm in thinkin' on it. But that's not to say I'll change my mind."

"Fair enough. I've got an idea you'll see the light, though, once you've studied it out." Hollister rose, collected his hat and coat, then turned back, frowning thoughtfully. "One other thing, you would have to be somewhat like Caesar's wife. Above reproach. That would mean either getting married or else severing the relationship. With the reformers running things, those are the only alternatives these days. But I'm sure you'll make the right choice. You always do."

Jake scowled and waved him off. "Cecil, don't let the door hit you in the ass on your way out."

Hollister laughed and strode ponderously from the room, quite satisfied with his day's work. The seed had been planted, and for the moment, that was enough.

No sooner had Hollister departed than Zalia reappeared. Jake thought for a moment she might have overheard that last exchange—the part about Caesar's wife—but she fussed over him, chattering pleasantly, never once mentioning Hollister or the purpose of his visit. All the same, Jake knew she was dying of curiosity, just as he knew she would bite her tongue off before prying into his affairs. Oddly enough, that made him want to tell her all the more. And upon further reflection, it came to him that she was the one person on earth who had earned his confidence. The one with whom all his secrets were safe.

After stewing on it a while, he finally told her. As near as he could, he repeated word for word the arguments Hollister had presented. Not to detract from the offer, he even explained the interworkings of power politics, and how, with no strings attached, a governor could run Kansas pretty much to suit himself. Particularly with the legislature in his hip pocket. The only thing he left out was Hollister's condition, the one involving her. Somehow, considering the alternatives, he couldn't bring himself to speak of it.

Zalia listened attentively throughout, asking few questions, her face sobered with concentration. When he finished she sat back in her chair, slowly sifting what she had heard, watching him all the while with a speculative look. Then, as if the pieces had somehow fallen into place, her expression once again became animated, and a vivacious sparkle danced to life in her eyes.

"Jake, I know very little about politics," she began, "but it seems to me that everything else is incidental until you have answered the first question. Do you want to be governor?"

"I don't know," he admitted honestly. "It tempts me, strictly from a standpoint of power, but at the same time my instinct tells me to run like hell."

"Why?"

The single word, incisive and perceptive, cut straight to the heart of the matter. It demanded an answer. "I guess the thing that bothers me"—he hesitated, struck by the hypocrisy of what he was about to say, then shrugged and went on—"is that I've always detested politicians so much. By and large, they're a scurvy lot, and I'd hate to think of myself rowin' the same boat."

She laughed a soft, mocking laugh. "Oh, for goodness sake, that's because you were able to corrupt them so easily. Do you honestly believe that anyone—Cecil Hollister included—could mortgage part of your soul?"

"No, I suppose they couldn't." He chortled a little at the thought. "Especially Hollister. I do business with him, matter of fact, I even like the old bandit, but I'd never get myself obligated to him." He paused, pulling reflectively at his mustache. "Maybe that's what it all boils down to. I'm my own man now, and I don't answer to anyone. But if I took their offer I'd be obligated to work with them, even though they weren't callin' the shots."

"Can you trust Hollister? Will he stick to his word about no strings attached?"

Jake mulled that over a bit, weighing all he knew of the man. "Yeah, I think he'd hold to it. Once he gives his word you can take it as gospel. It's the other times you have to watch out for."

Zalia regarded him steadily for several moments, then her eyes flashed and she smiled puckishly. "I think you should accept."

He stared back at her, speechless with surprise, yet somehow amused. She held his gaze, waiting him out, and at last he grinned. "Think I should, do you? Well, I'll just toss your question right back to you—why?"

"If I tell you, your head will swell up and burst."

"Try me."

"All right, I will." Her smile softened, and she seemed somehow less impish. "Jake, you have the ability to do great things for this state. You've said yourself that Kansas is entering a new era. That means change, which never comes easily, and the people will need determined leadership. I happen to believe that you have more character and integrity than you give yourself credit for. You may be cynical and conniving but you're not a crook, and that makes the difference. As governor, you could leave your mark in the history books, and you might just find that serving the people is as rewarding as outslicking them."

She wrinkled her nose in zestful mockery. "There, I've had my say and I'm not sorry. Even if your head does look a couple of sizes larger."

"You said a mouthful, that's for damn sure." He scrutinized her frankly, almost squinting, then his square face suddenly became very earnest. "You know it would change things for us. Might even make it more difficult than it is now."

She gave him a bright little nod. In the vestibule she had overheard Hollister's remark about Caesar's wife, and while she knew that Jake would never marry her—or anyone—she also knew that he would never give her up. They would simply have to be more discreet in the future. Very cautious and very sly. But she mentioned none of this. She merely smiled and patted his hand.

"We'll find a way. We always have."

"By God, you're right! Where there's a will there's a way. And once you get me fattened up again, I'm gonna have lots of will. Might just cripple you for life."

She lowered an eyelid in a lewd wink. "You're a naughty man, but I'll love every minute of it."

That evening, while Zalia and Mrs. Murphy cleared the supper table, he returned to his chair and sat staring into the fire. Her words came to him again, and it crossed his mind that she had hit the mark dead center. He had wealth and position, and along the banks of the Arkansas, enough power for any man. Perhaps there was something to be said for serving the people after all. Not that he couldn't serve himself at the same time. The thought of ruling Topeka with an iron fist, turning an entire legislature into an instrument of his will, appealed to him greatly. But in the years of transition ahead, bridging the old with the new, he might well make the passage smoother for all people, both great and small. And maybe that in itself was a higher form of power, one he had yet to tap. Transforming the common good into a crusade that left him holding all the strings. A man of the people, whose voice was the voice of all, not to be denied.

The thought stirred something dim and forgotten, like poking about in the cold ashes. Sitting straight and still, eyes glazed by the crackling flames and the warmth of the fire, his mind settled backward. For an instant he was suspended in a void of dead years and unexpired emotions, and his thoughts were a kaleidoscope of the past. Then, bit by bit, ever so slowly, it came to him. A wintry night in Abilene and blustery, much like tonight. Sadie was with him, upstairs in their rooms at the Lady Gay. He had just returned from scouting Wichita, and in some clumsy excuse for a proposal, he had asked her to marry him. And then he'd made her a promise. Grand and eloquent it was, peacock proud, and he could still hear the words.

Someday there'll be lots of folks waitin' in line to say howdy to the Kincaids. You can mark it down in the promise book.

So long ago. A lifetime. And yet, in a way he hadn't imagined, it had all come true. Sadie hadn't lived to see it, but there were still the boys. Through them the promise would be fulfilled, and their mother would have liked it that way. As much hers as his own, perhaps never to have been managed without her, it would become in time their legacy.

The Kincaids of Kansas.

BOOK TWO

OKLAHOMA
TERRITORY

1889–1906

SEVEN

The morning was bright and sunny, with a nip in the air, and along the river the trees were faintly speckled by an overnight frost. Yesterday had been a holiday in Wichita— voting day—and the townspeople were slowly recovering from the aftermath of their celebration. Although the results weren't yet official, everyone simply took it for granted that the hometown candidate had won. This time, so they told one another with smug assurance, there was no way on earth for Jake Kincaid to lose. Not with the amount of money the Santa Fe, to say nothing of the candidate himself, had liberally strewn along the campaign trail. And so, on this brisk autumn morning, the people of Wichita suffered their hangovers in good spirits, and confidently if somewhat sluggishly returned to business as usual.

Cecil Hollister had come down on the evening train the night before. Under normal circumstances the candidate would have traveled to Topeka—where the statewide gubernatorial ballots were to be counted—and awaited results at party headquarters. But the circumstances were hardly normal, and however much it defied tradition, Jake had refused to be separated from Zalia since the scandal broke. Hollister felt the decision was ill-timed, merely feeding fuel to the fire as it were, yet his arguments had no effect whatever. Jake spent the last week of the election in Wichita, brusquely turning reporters away from the door, and hadn't emerged from the house for any reason. Least of all Hollister's urgent demands that he issue a statement repudiating his liaison with the lady in question.

And now, seated in the parlor with Jake, the old robber baron had to admire his loyalty if not his judgment. Looking back, Hollister found it remarkable that any man, particularly one with Jake Kincaid's obsessive ambition, could have endured the humiliation of the last four years. Bad enough that he had been defeated for governor in 1886. Linked to the Cattlemen's Association and the Santa Fe, both of which had become dirty words by then, he had been soundly trounced at the polls that fall. The reformers had joined ranks with the burgeoning Populist movement, and the cry went up "to remove the seat of government of Kansas from the Santa Fe offices back to the State House." Which it was, by a vast plurality.

Undaunted, Jake bided his time, plotting revenge on his enemies, and with Hollister's encouragement had again declared himself a candidate this year. And again, as they had two years before, the Populists indicted him as a tool of the railroads, hurling accusations of ruthlessness and social irresponsibility. Yet neither Jake nor Hollister (who had assumed active leadership of the party) were overly concerned by the charges. Kansas hadn't made any great strides under the reform coalition, and the general mood of the voters appeared quite receptive to change. Jake conducted a whistle-stop campaign around the state, lightly dismissing the charges as "old hat," and as election day drew near, it became apparent that the people agreed. This time out they were less concerned with reform than progress, and for all his ties with the railroad, it seemed that Jake Kincaid was the very man to lead them into a new era of prosperity.

Losing ground fast, and hard pressed to defend the administration's lackluster record, the reformers became desperate during the last week of the campaign. Out of their bag of dirty tricks they gathered yet another albatross and hung it around

Jake's neck. With howls of sanctimonious outrage, Populist newspapers across the state ran an exposé of his backstreet involvement with Zalia Blair. The prose was lurid, filled with titillating details, and in one fell swoop, Jake was served up as adulterer, fornicator, and all-round general heathen. Everyone in Wichita greeted the news with a monumental yawn; the affair had been common knowledge among the townspeople for nearly a decade. But throughout the rest of the state the voters were appalled, and Jake's sleeping arrangements quickly assumed the proportions of a full-blown scandal.

Zalia immediately went into seclusion. While her role in the affair was of secondary importance, she was nonetheless branded a scarlet woman and lambasted from the pulpit of every church in Kansas. Jake never once renounced her, nor did he attempt to absolve himself as the scandal became a critical issue in the election. Instead, he stayed by her side throughout the ordeal, ignoring reporters and voters alike. By his attitude, he made it clear that he considered his private life his own business, and while he was seething with rage, his iron impassivity never cracked. With the dignity of an aloof, unflappable old lion, he simply closed the door and left the people to decide for themselves.

Thinking about it now, Cecil Hollister took small comfort from the fact that Jake's instincts had proved correct. In the closing days of the election there had been only passing mention of the affair. Yet, however, golden the silence, Hollister knew that the vote could still go either way. At this point, it was strictly a toss of the coin. Whatever the outcome, though, he felt an obligation to be with Jake this morning. Between them they had shaped the destiny of Kansas, and for the past four years Jake Kincaid had unstintingly carried the party standard. The bond went back a long way, spanning almost two decades, and he felt not just admiration but a great affinity for the younger man. Perhaps the closest thing to friendship Cecil Hollister had ever felt for any man.

Since breakfast they had exchanged few words. Caught up

in their own thoughts, puffing cigars in silence, they merely sat and waited and pondered the imponderable. Shortly before noon Zalia arrived, sweeping into the parlor with a radiant smile, and both men rose to their feet. She kissed Jake on the cheek, greeted Hollister warmly, and waved them back to their chairs as she took a seat on the sofa. The somber expression on their faces told her a great deal, and as if to lighten the mood, she admonished them with a wag of her head.

"Well! Aren't you two a pair of soberpusses? I take it you haven't received word yet?"

"Not so much as a fare-thee-well!" Jake informed her crossly. "I'm beginning to think somebody cut the wires between here and Topeka."

"You're just jumpy, that's all." Hollister peered across at Zalia through a cloud of smoke and grinned. "It's an occupational hazard common to politicians. Known as the post-election jitters."

Jake snorted. "Listen, you old goat, don't start preachin' nerves to me. Talk about a case of the jitters! You haven't said *boo* all morning. Have you? C'mon, own up to it!"

"Now, now, children, don't fight!" Zalia interjected. "I'm sure we'll hear something any minute now. So try not to say anything you'll feel sorry for later."

"That's a laugh!" Jake gestured at Hollister with his cigar. "You couldn't insult him if you tried. And I ought to know"— one eyebrow lifted in a mock scowl—"believe me, I've tried!"

"You know, it's just amazing what a person can learn reading." Zalia's lips curved in a disarming smile. "One of those old Romans made a very wise observation. He said, 'I have often regretted my speech, but never my silence.'"

"By God, she's got you there!" Hollister roared. "Go on, Jake, admit it. She nailed you dead center. Right between the eyes."

"She's smart, all right. Just a regular fountain of knowledge." Jake jammed the cigar in his mouth, puffing thoughtfully a moment; then he gave her a lewd wink. "Yessir, I'll have to admit it. She's taught me plenty."

"Honestly, Jake, you're just incorrigible! I suppose it's a permanent affliction though"—head averted, she slyly returned his wink—"so I'll forgive you this time."

There was indeed a constancy of character about Jake Kincaid, as both she and Cecil Hollister had learned to their grief. From the very outset Jake had ignored the older man's warnings about his private life. Hollister badgered and threatened and predicted dire consequences, all of which changed nothing. At last he simply resigned himself to the situation, but he never fully understood Jake's obduracy, or his skittish attitude toward marriage. Had their roles been reversed, Hollister would have married Zalia Blair with great relish. And a randy feeling of immense good fortune.

Yet Jake would have no part of it. Nor would he discuss it with anyone, least of all Cecil Hollister. It was a closed subject, and like a magician so adept that he fools even himself, Jake neatly rationalized the whole affair in his own mind. While the ghost of Sadie Kincaid no longer haunted his dreams, he nonetheless bore the scars of a man who had loved and lost and had no desire to lose again. However misguided, he believed that without that final commitment—the ring and the vows and the death-do-us-part—he could never again be driven to the excesses of remorse and hurt and self-pity he had once inflicted upon himself. It was a mixture of fear and raw emotion, hardly befitting a man of his stature, but with it he suppressed completely any foolish notions about marriage.

And Zalia went along not out of sympathy or understanding, or even because she agreed, but because she had no choice. It was take him on his own terms or take him not at all, and she had long ago contented herself with that part of his life he was willing to share. Once he entered politics they simply became more discreet; if the circumstances were sometimes strained, and she occasionally felt like a back-alley whore, she kept her anger and her humiliation to herself. The alternative was to lose him completely, yet she knew her own life would be shallow and empty without him, so it was a risk she had avoided assiduously over the past four years. When the scandal burst across Kansas at last, she all but heaved a sigh of relief. Despite the public outcry of *Jezebel* and *Harlot*, she was glad to have it out in the open, willing to be shamed if it removed the burden of living a lie. And in the last week she had come to love Jake all the more, for in his own way he too had made a choice. Rather than give her up, he was willing to risk all he had worked toward, his dreams and ambitions, the State House itself. Which for Jake Kincaid was no small sacrifice, and perhaps more significantly, a grand gesture of his devotion to Zalia Blair.

By no mere coincidence, almost an omen of sorts, she was basking in the warmth of that very thought when a knock sounded at the door. Jake bounded out of his chair as if galvanized and hurried from the room. She exchanged a glance with Hollister, whose bald pate suddenly glistened with sweat, and they heard Jake talking to someone in the vestibule. The front door closed and a moment later he entered the parlor, holding a telegram as if it were some fragile treasure to be handled gingerly and with great deliberation. While they watched, scarcely daring to breathe, he opened the envelope, removed a slip of paper, and read the scrawled message. There was an instant of prolonged silence; then he looked up and a small, sardonic smile tugged at the corner of his mouth.

"The bastards buried us. No contest."

"That's impossible." Hollister appeared dazed, his cigar gone cold and forgotten. "Last week we had them begging for mercy. I just don't believe it."

"Yeah, go ahead and believe it, Cecil." He tapped the

telegram with his finger. "According to this the count was three to one. Any way you cut it, that's a landslide."

"By God, we'll demand a recount! People just don't change their minds that fast. There's something fishy about this whole deal. It stinks to high heaven! And if it's the last thing I do, I'll get—"

"Forget it, Cecil. Wouldn't do any good, and if you kick up a fuss we're liable to come out smellin' worse than we already do. Let's just chalk it up to one for the forces of virtue, and grin and bear it. Who gives a good goddamn anyhow!"

Savagely he wadded the telegram into a ball and flung it in the fireplace. His composure cracked, and beneath the mask Zalia caught a fleeting glimpse of his rage, the terrible fury of a man whose pride had been gouged to the quick. Yet, curiously enough, she felt no disappointment that he'd lost. There was only a sense of regret that he had been hurt, and an urge to somehow mitigate the torment she saw in his eyes.

"Jake, don't take it so hard, sweetheart. There's always another election, and I wouldn't be at all surprised if this turned out to be a blessing in disguise. Why honestly, after another term with those do-gooders in office, the people will go down on their knees to put you into the State House. Just wait; you'll see! I've never been more certain of anything in my life."

With a great effort he took hold of himself, suppressing the rage just as he suppressed all other emotions. Somehow he even managed to smile at her, and after a moment he returned to his chair. But as he sat down Hollister gave him a queer look, and without words, some deeper sense of irony passed between them. Then, as if Zalia had never spoken, their eyes drifted to the fire and the ashes of the telegram, and presently the old robber baron cleared his throat.

"I suppose it's over." Hollister frowned, reflecting on it at length, and finally shook his head. "Damn shame, though, that it had to end this way."

"Cecil, I don't know about it being a damn shame, but it's sure as hell the end. You can bet on it."

And in his own mind, Jake Kincaid did just that. He bet on himself and tomorrow and to hell with Kansas.

As noon approached a trooper rode slowly to a high point of ground. He carried a bugle, a flag, and a large pocket watch. Below, a thin line of cavalrymen, extending east and west as far as could be seen, held their rifles pointed skyward. Silence enveloped the land, an eerie unnatural silence, broken only by the stamping hooves of horses and the chuffing hiss of locomotives. On the small knoll the trooper stared at his watch, and in the distance, hushed and waiting, some fifty thousand homesteaders stared at the trooper. The Oklahoma Land Rush was about to begin.

Never had there been anything like it. President Benjamin Harrison's proclamation opening the Unassigned Lands to settlement had created a sensation. Newspapers and periodicals across the nation carried stories of the "great run" and what was described as the "Garden Spot of the World." America turned its eye toward Oklahoma Territory, drawn once again by the lodestone of free land. And the scintillating prose of journalists brought them hurrying westward by the tens of thousands.

Unstated in these news stories was the tale of intrigue and political skulduggery which lay behind the opening of Indian lands. The Boomers were commonly thought to be the moving force, but their squalling demands were merely window dressing, loud and impressive if somewhat meaningless. Instead it was the railroads, and their free-spending lobbyists, who brought unremitting pressure to bear on Congress. The first step was to declare the right of eminent domain in Indian Territory, and by 1888 four railroads (including the Santa Fe) had laid track through the Nations. This cleared the way for settlement, and shortly after his inauguration, President

Harrison decreed that the Unassigned Lands would be opened to homesteading at high noon on April 22, 1889. But it would be on a first-come-first-served basis—a race of sorts—with millions of acres of virgin prairie as the prize.

The land-hungry multitudes cared little who was behind the settlement issue, or for whose ultimate benefit it had been organized. America had grown to a nation of nearly 100 million people, with hundreds of thousands of immigrants pouring into the country each year, and they were concerned not so much with the land of the free as with free land. Here was something for nothing, and they flooded westward to share in the spoils. Farmers and merchants, carpenters and blacksmiths, gamblers and saloonkeepers—100,000 strong— they gathered north and south along the borders of the Unassigned Lands. They came in covered wagons and buckboards, on horseback and aboard trains, straining for a glimpse of what would soon become Oklahoma. And of a single mind, they came to stay.

Among them were Jake Kincaid and his sons. Like thousands of others, he had come seeking opportunity, a new life, and in no small sense, a place to start over. The old life was gone, his power and prestige in Kansas withered to nothing, and his gaze had turned toward this last frontier. A land where men of determination and purpose might scatter the ashes of the past, and look instead to the future.

Now, along with Owen and Brad, he waited at the southern boundary of the Cherokee Outlet for the opening gun. They had ridden in last night, though many of the homesteaders had been camped on the line for nearly a week. The boys had grown to strapping youngsters, with Owen somewhat heftier at seventeen, and both were accomplished riders. Jake had mounted them on blooded horses, conditioned and trained for the grueling race ahead. Their immediate goal was the townsite of Guthrie, some twenty miles south, situated along the Santa Fe tracks just below the Cimarron River. Jake had chosen Guthrie over the other major townsite, Oklahoma

City, based on his assessment of the political and economic future of the territory. Before nightfall he meant to have a sizable stake in that future.

Many men shared his intention, and some, known as Sooners, since they crossed the line too soon, couldn't wait. Despite the soldiers' vigilance, they had sneaked over the border under cover of darkness, planning to hide until the run started and then lay claim to choice lands. Cavalry patrols had flushed hundreds of them out of hiding, but word circulated that there were several times that number who had escaped detection. This left the law-abiding homesteaders in an ugly mood, gripped by a pervasive fear that there wouldn't be enough good land to go around. And as noon approached their mood turned to near hysteria. Since early morning the Santa Fe had moved fifteen trains into position, one behind the other, loaded with thousands more land-hungry settlers. Men on horseback had every confidence they could outdistance the trains, but those in wagons and buckboards (by far the greater number) knew they would arrive too late for a chance at the most desirable claims. Tempers flared, fistfights broke out, and as the minutes ticked away fully forty thousand people jostled and shoved and brawled for a better spot along the starting line.

Then the trooper put the bugle to his lips, and as the hands of his watch merged, precisely at high noon, he blew a single piercing blast, waving his flag at the same time. On signal, the cavalrymen discharged their rifles into the air, but the gunfire was smothered beneath a thunderous human roar. Horses reared and whips cracked, men dug savagely with their spurs, and in a sudden dust-choked wedge, a wave of humanity plunged across the starting line. At first it seemed a mad stampede, as the earth trembled and trains gained headway, but within moments the race was decided. Out of the blinding dust cloud emerged the swiftest horses, spurred into a wild-eyed gallop, and behind them, strung out and gaining speed, came the trains. Scattered across the countryside, quickly losing ground, wagons and buckboards, and even one solitary soul on a high-wheeled bicycle, brought up the rear. America's first great land rush was under way at last.

Shortly before two that afternoon, Jake and the boys forded the Cimarron and rode into the Guthrie townsite. The stamina of their mounts had given them a slight lead over other horsemen, but there was little time to waste. Jake's chief concern was a prime town lot, and only when that was staked would they worry about claiming a quarter-section. He led the way over the riverbank and gigged his horse into a final burst of speed.

Before them stretched a rolling plain, bordered in the distance by stunted knolls. The Santa Fe tracks curved off to the southwest, roughly parallelled on the west by Cottonwood Creek. East of the tracks, directly across from a meandering bend in the stream, was a small depot flanked by a section house and a water tank. Several hundred feet east of the depot was an even smaller structure, the federal land office, and the rest was empty land. Three buildings and a water tank constituted the town of Guthrie.

As Jake and the boys skirted the depot, headed on a beeline for the land office, they heard a train whistle in the distance. There were now only minutes to spare, and they urged their horses onward. Reason dictated that the center of town would be located near the land office, and it was here that Jake meant to stake his lot. But even as they rode into sight several men were already erecting a tent catty-cornered from the land office. Out front was a crude sign proclaiming their operation the Choctaw Land & Town Company. That they were quite obviously Sooners bothered Jake not in the least; he was perfectly satisfied to let latecomers argue the matter. Piling from his horse, he paced off twenty steps due north of the land office and an equal distance east of the tent. There he drove his stake, with his initials carved in bold letters at the top. And not a minute too soon.

The landscape all of a sudden sprouted horsemen and trains and a bedlam of humanity. Where moments before there had been a tranquil prairie the earth was now covered with a frenzied swarm of men and women, racing mindlessly to plant their stakes in what seemed the choicest spot. Disputes erupted immediately, as men attempted to claim the same lots, and within minutes a dozen slugfests were in progress. But no one came anywhere near the corner north of the land office. Jake stood beside his stake, pistol in hand, glaring daggers at the milling crowd, and both boys were armed with Winchesters. The message was clear, and however desperate the harum-scarum masses, they heeded it.

An hour later, with some sense of sanity restored to the townsite, Jake admonished the boys not to budge from their tracks, then mounted his horse and rode off. West along the Cimarron some five miles from the railroad bridge, was a stretch of prairie he recalled from the summer of '83, when he had scouted this very land for the Santa Fe. He meant to stake out two homesteads, side by side. One in his own name, and one in the name of Zalia Blair. Although a mere 320 acres, seemingly insignificant at the moment, it was all part and parcel of the grander scheme he had in mind. Something for the future, a hedge of sorts.

By nightfall Guthrie was a city of tents. And once again pandemonium broke out. The Santa Fe station agent quit his post to homestead a claim, and a southbound train collided head-on with a northbound from Oklahoma City; cavalry troopers battled mobs of claim jumpers, who found their dirty work easier done in the dark; saloons conducted a thriving business from planks resting across barrels, and bordello tents began servicing customers who apparently had a highly attuned sense of direction. There were no sanitation facilities and no law enforcement, unfouled drinking water was in short supply, and the stench of a garbage dump slowly settled over the land. But there were better than ten thousand delirious souls squatted on their claims, and they had themselves a town.

Jake took to it like a bear to honey. Land speculation flourished, rising to a fever pitch under the dusky glow of a crescent moon, and the action was fast and furious. Hundreds of men had staked claims for no other purpose than to sell them to the highest bidder; many lots, particularly those centrally located, were bought and resold on the hour. These were the very lots Jake sought out, moving swiftly from location to location, trading and dickering and swapping as he gained a feel for the future shape of the city. Of all the men in Guthrie that night he was perhaps the wealthiest, with a stuffed moneybelt beneath his shirt, and he was rarely outbid at a prime location. Trailed by a gang of hooligans he had imported on the evening train, he left armed men to guard each lot after it was bought. When he finally called it quits around midnight he had acquired thirteen lots, not including the one he had staked out himself. Eleven of these were situated in what he judged to be the heart of downtown, and two were located on high ground to the east, which in his view would become the prominent residential district.

Upon returning to his corner lot, across from the land office, he found Brad bedded down near a small fire and Owen standing watch, rifle cradled in his arms. Still charged with energy, full of plans and bold ventures that needed sorting out, he ordered Owen to his blankets, commending the youngster for the way he'd handled himself. Then Jake walked to the edge of the lot, and stood staring out over the thousands of campfires which dotted the town. Somewhere down around his bellybutton the sight brought a warm glow, and he grunted with a deep inward satisfaction. It had been a good day, and a damn fine start. And suddenly he was in a rush for tomorrow. Relishing what was to come with a gusto too long dormant, too long untasted.

. . .

Guthrie mushroomed overnight. But unlike frontier boom-towns of the past there was nothing haphazard or patchwork about its growth. A Committee of Fifty was formed the morning following the opening, composed of men such as Jake Kincaid, some more forceful than others, yet each one a man of character and substance. After a day or so of chaos the Committee, supported by Army troops, restored order, and thereafter reason prevailed. Those of an unreasonable bent were posted from town, and none too gently persuaded that the state of their health would be improved elsewhere. Although quasi-legal, the Committee's edicts had a certain finality which was seldom ignored.

At the end of the first week a mass meeting was called in a field south of the townsite. Nearly five thousand people attended, and in a very democratic fashion, delegates were selected from each state represented by the citizens of Guthrie. These delegates then met in caucus and formed a town government, appointing a mayor, seven men to serve as the town council, and a chief of police. Afterward streets and alleyways were surveyed, tracts were reserved for parks and schools, and land was set aside for public buildings. Other towns which sprang up in the territory—Oklahoma City, Kingfisher, and Edmond—experienced considerably more difficulty. There, lawlessness and disorder were slower to be quelled, and the Army had its hands full maintaining some semblance of peace. But the infantry company encamped on Cottonwood Creek had little to do in Guthrie. A rational and speedy process, allowing the people a voice in their own government, had opened the way to progress. And the pace quickened in a breathtaking surge of construction.

By the close of the second month a small miracle of sorts had taken place on the once-barren prairie. The tent city had disappeared completely, and out of this humble beginning, Guthrie became a town with the solid look of permanence and bustling industry. Saloons and gambling dens were everywhere in evidence, as well as several sporting houses. The most spectacular of the lot was the Reaves Brothers Casino, where it was advertised a man could find honest games, fine whiskey, and the flossiest women in town. All of which proved to be true. Yet, despite its fascination with the sporting life (which in times past had been the economic mainstay of any boomtown), Guthrie was gearing itself to the day when it would become the center of commerce and trade for the entire territory. Under the sure hands of carpenters and stonemasons some fifty buildings were in various stages of construction. Among them were three banks and a city hall, two opera houses and three hotels, not to mention a post office, five newspapers, and several office buildings. While all of this activity was noteworthy in itself, what distinguished Guthrie from other towns was the caliber of its business leaders and their vision of the future. The structures they erected were being built to last, in many instances constructed of brick and stone, and there seemed little doubt of their determination to make Guthrie the frontrunner in this fledgling territory.

From the outset Jake Kincaid had played a leading role in bringing stability to the town's civic and business affairs. His name was known, as well as his association with the Santa Fe (which was fast gaining in Oklahoma whatever influence it had lost in Kansas), and he was unquestionably the wealthiest man in Guthrie. Rumor had it that he was a millionaire ten times over, perhaps more, and the magnitude of his investments around town had done nothing to discourage the thought. All of this commanded a certain respect, and it seemed natural that men of foresight and ambition would seek out his counsel. He had been instrumental in forming the Committee of Fifty, and from behind the scenes had taken a hand in selecting the men appointed to city offices. Though he had been urged to accept the post of mayor (by a near-unanimous resolution of the delegate caucus), he had declined the honor. After twice being humiliated in Kansas he had no taste for either title or public office. Here, as he had done for so many years in Wichita, he would act as the power broker, working behind closed doors and in secret. Experience had taught him that political influence was far more rewarding than political office, and he meant to remain the unseen man, the one who wielded the big stick.

But if he was a shadowy figure in civic matters, Jake soon became eminently visible in the world of business. As he had surmised that first night, the corner of Oklahoma Avenue and Second Street became the hub of downtown Guthrie. The land office was on the southeast corner, and beside it the post office, and on the southwest corner was a large mercantile emporium. Opposite this the city hall was taking shape, delayed briefly while the owners of the Choctaw Land & Town Company were adjudged Sooners and put to flight. And on his own corner, Jake was building himself a bank.

Never one to scrimp, he intended it to be the most imposing structure in Guthrie. Three stories high, with a massive cupola overlooking the intersection, it was constructed of native stone, with polished granite columns at the entrance, and would ultimately dominate the downtown area. Although he had competitors (one only a block up the street at Oklahoma and First), the Citizen's National was the first bank to open its doors for business. Already the ground floor was completed, and as offices on the second and third floors were finished they would be rented to professional men and business concerns. Aside from the profit factor, and the prestige, Jake had several reasons for becoming a banker. Foremost among them was that it allowed him a near-sacrosanct base from which he could expand into other fields.

Even before the bank opened for business certain aspects of this expansion program had been put into motion. By prior arrangement with the Santa Fe an entire trainload of lumber and building materials was freighted into Guthrie the day after the run. Much to the chagrin of less enterprising businessmen, none of the material was for sale. Along with the building supplies Jake had also imported a regiment of carpenters, bricklayers, stonemasons, and general laborers. Scarcely had his town lots been recorded at the land office than these craftsmen were busily engaged erecting commercial buildings which were rented before the first nail had been driven. One of these was next door to the bank, and it was here that the town's leading newspaper, the Guthrie *Statesman*, came into existence. This seemingly routine business arrangement with Omar Marquand, the newspaper's publisher, was no mere whim on Jake's part. In years to come, it was an alliance which would prove itself a devastating adversary in the political arena.

Another of Jake's notions, which was not without some forethought, was to own a hotel. But it had to be a plush affair, with the latest conveniences, suitable to attract a select clientele. Construction began shortly after the run, one block south of the bank, across from the Reaves Brothers Casino. When it was finished he officially crowned it the Palace Hotel, and everybody in Guthrie agreed that it was certainly palatial. Big and elegant, and with just the right touch of class.

As for his personal accommodations, Jake Kincaid was no less discriminating. He hired Maurice Foucart, a Belgian architect who had somehow found his way west, then turned him loose with a blank check and instructions to design two houses of distinctive mode. Foucart was equal to the task, and spent money with the abandon of a mad Bohemian. The first house, what was to become Jake's mansion, was located on the gentle heights of Noble Avenue. It was of the French Style, currently in vogue, with large windows surrounded by heavy stone and Corinthian columns, and covered with a patterned slate mansard roof. In front, the entrance pavilion formed a tower with a series of grotesque superposed orders, ending at the top in a crown of garlands and cornices and iron spikes. People came from miles around just to stand and stare at it.

Foucart's eclecticism was somewhat more restrained when he came to build the second house. It was situated on Warner Avenue, one block north of Jake's home, and easily accessible through a connecting alley. Here the architect constructed an Italian villa, with a square tower over an arched porch, narrow windows, projecting balconies and canopies, and a series of wide overhanging eaves and gables. Quite unwittingly, his sense of taste and moderation found an appreciative and thoroughly enthralled patron. On a warm afternoon late in June, Zalia Blair took up residence in the Warner Avenue house.

All in all, Jake was quite pleased with the rather tidy nature of things. He still controlled grazing rights in the Cherokee Outlet; he had himself a bank and a hotel and several highly profitable commercial properties, and with only a superficial observance of propriety he was again reunited with Zalia. What he'd left behind in Kansas suddenly seemed small potatoes, and after two hectic, if gratifying, months in Guthrie, he sensed bigger things in the offing.

As was his usual habit, he made the rounds each day, checking the progress on his various projects. This particular day, a lazy morning in early July, he had just finished in the bank and stepped outside, accompanied by Owen. They stood for a moment on the corner, regarding the long lines of people in front of the land office and beside it, the post office. Sometimes the lines stretched all the way down the hill to the railroad tracks, and Jake never ceased to wonder at the enormous waste of man-hours spent shuffling forward one step at a time. But then, as Maurice Foucart was so fond of prattling, Rome hadn't been built in a day. Nor would Guthrie and the territory come of age until land disputes and postal service and a host of problems had been ironed out.

Which, in a circuitous manner, brought him back to a problem of his own. Hawking, he spat, watching the spitball raise a puff of dust in the street, then glanced at Owen. "Where's your brother? Thought he was supposed to meet us here."

The youngster's eyes remained fixed on the crowd. "Beats me, Pa. Keepin' up with him is like trying to catch fireflies."

"Damned if it's not." Jake studied the ground a minute, then shrugged. "Well, go hit all the pool halls and see if you can chase him down. After you get through meet me over at the hotel. I've got some business with the mayor, so it'll probably be awhile."

Owen gave him a brash grin. "Today the day?"

"What day?"

"When you're gonna sell the mayor on that streetcar idea?"

"You got something against progress?"

"Nope. Just wonderin' when you was gonna stick it to him, that's all."

"Bud, let me tell you something. Nobody likes a smart-ass. 'Specially when he's still wet behind the ears." Jake smiled, and playfully rapped him in the belly. "Now get a move on. And tell your brother he better damn sure be there. Between him loafin' around and you all the time lippin' off, I might just tan the both of you."

Owen ducked out of reach, laughing, and headed south along Second. Jake stared after him a moment, noting the cocky walk and the assured manner, reminded of himself twenty years back. Then he chuckled to himself and crossed the street to the city hall. By God, the button was right.

It was a good day to sell some streetcars.

Summer turned to fall, then winter arrived, but Jake hardly noticed the change. He was far too busy for talk of autumn leaves and blizzards, and what other men spoke of as the harshest winter in memory. Each day, whether bone-chilling cold or merely brisk and frosty, was a new challenge, created especially for Jake Kincaid. And he positively thrived on it, galvanized to excesses of energy which left those around him mildly baffled, and sweating heavily.

Over the winter he seemed to be everywhere at once, and more disturbing to the businessmen of Guthrie, he apparently had a finger in every pie around town. They sweated not because of the pace he set—none of them tried to match that—but because he was rapidly organizing a business empire which would compete with almost every commercial enterprise in the territory. Yet they could scarcely complain, much less condemn his drive and resourcefulness, for if progress had come to Guthrie it was undeniably the handiwork of Jake Kincaid.

Town improvements were perhaps the most dramatic, if not the most profitable, ventures to claim his attention. Jake was determined that Guthrie would become the foremost city in Oklahoma (and its capital, when Washington finally enacted territorial recognition), and in quick order, he brought to the community every modern convenience science and industry had to offer. By the waning months of that first summer Guthrie had a waterworks and pumping station south of town, and along with it, a rudimentary sewerage system. In early fall rails were laid and horse-drawn streetcars began servicing the main thoroughfares. October brought a generating plant, providing streetlights at the major intersections, and the wonder of electric illumination in offices and business concerns in the downtown area. And plans were already under way to extend this remarkably efficient and economical service to every home in town.

Wisely, Jake worked through city hall in promoting each of these projects. Bond issues were floated for town improvements and schools, with capable assistance from the Citizen's National, and the politicians were allowed to bask in the admiration of a grateful community. Perhaps wiser still, Jake made no attempt to hog all the action for himself. At his urging various individuals formed companies for each project, including prominent businessmen among their list of investors, and the profits were distributed in what seemed an equitable manner to those who wielded influence in the affairs of Guthrie. But it was hardly a secret that one man had provided both the impetus and the imagination for this extraordinary civic progress, and it was commonly accepted that the name to be reckoned with, whether in politics or business, was that of Jake Kincaid.

On the personal side of the ledger he had been no less energetic. With the Citizen's National as his base, he had branched out into several highly lucrative businesses. At the west end of Cleveland Avenue, near the Santa Fe railyards, he built a warehouse and organized Guthrie's first wholesale grocery company. Directly across the street he established the town's largest lumberyard, buying in trainload lots, and outsold all other competitors combined. After sampling the water at a mineral well south of town, he bought the land, organized a bottling plant, and began selling Mineral Wells Elixir Water throughout the territory. Then, not to let a good thing go to waste, he built a bath house at the corner of Oklahoma and Vine, piped the water in from the well, and charged outrageous prices for people to luxuriate in the warmth of a mineral bath. Nothing with the smell of profit escaped his attention, and if Guthrie laid claim to a resident tycoon, his name headed everyone's list.

But while he was admired and envied, and in some quarters feared, there was never a hint of resentment over his spectacular business success. He brought money into the town, kept it circulating, created supply and demand, and by the very magnitude of his own activities, stimulated an ever-accelerated rate of growth within the community. By the spring of 1890 Guthrie could boast of a flour mill, two creameries, a distillery, a bookbinding factory, five daily newspapers and three weeklies, a wholesale meat company, two brickyards, a gristmill, and a cotton gin. And Pabst had built a brewing plant large enough to service the entire territory.

Nor were the professions and retail establishments found wanting. A city directory listed thirty-nine doctors and eighty-one lawyers (although as yet there was but a single city court), nineteen drugstores, half a dozen mercantiles, forty cafés, and forty-six grocery stores. At city hall, where the directory was prepared, the public servants were nothing if not discreet, and unlisted were eighteen saloons, five gambling dives, and several flourishing whorehouses. As people create markets, attracting business and industry, so must their vices be served, and in its quiet, unobtrusive way, the sporting crowd did quite well in Guthrie.

Still, while the town itself prospered, homesteaders in outlying areas had been considerably less fortunate. Their first crops brought bitter disappointment, for the land yielded grudgingly to the plow, and with winter came hardship and poverty and near starvation. Thousands sustained themselves on cowpeas and turnips, and whatever game they could shoot. Men sought work wherever they could find it, trying to raise cash money, while their women remained on the homesteads, caring for livestock and broods of runny-nosed children in the face of blizzard, sickness, and hunger. If, in that first year, there was victory over a raw wilderness, it could be traced to the heartbreaking sacrifice of pioneer women. But as winter gave way to spring there was little to say grace over, and very few left to say it. Nearly half of those who had homesteaded claims admitted defeat, and departed the territory. The strong and the resolute survived, and of those who had failed, the lucky ones were able to sell their claims for enough to start over again in more hospitable surroundings.

While the homesteaders suffered and shivered, battling the primitive forces of nature, Jake regarded their struggle with spidery patience, and waited for them to fail. He had, in fact, counted on their failure, and seemingly benevolent, had encouraged them to take small loans with the Citizen's National. Yet, though his motives went unquestioned at the time, these loans were curiously limited to homesteaders who held claims west along the Cimarron. Near the claims he himself had filed the day after the Land Rush.

With spring, Mordecai Jones, a flint-hearted New Englander who had been hired as president of Citizen's National, was instructed to foreclose the loans. Scarcely more scrupulous than his employer, Jones quickly discerned what was afoot, and with somber glee evicted some fifty home-steaders. Jake in turn bought the quitclaim deeds from the bank, then sent land agents riding the Cimarron, their saddlebags stuffed with cash, offering an easy out to settlers who had yet to hear of the Citizen's National. By the first week in May he had put together a block of land exceeding ten thousand acres, and had every confidence that with time he could easily double his holdings.

The only hitch in Jake's quietly elaborate scheme was Owen. Shortly after the New Year the youngster had started work at the bank, where he was to be schooled in the intricacies of finance and business. Alert and maturing rapidly, he saw through the subterfuge of the foreclosures within a matter of days. Toward the end of the first week, repulsed by his father's shady tactics, he broached the subject one evening after supper.

Halting at first, groping for words that were both tactful and truthful, Owen expressed a certain sympathy for the settlers and their plight. At length, when he'd made his case, Jake smiled and gave him a look of wry amusement.

"Son, it appears to me you've got things a little bassackwards. See, you're thinkin' like a missionary, not like a businessman. Now charity is fine for them that's heard the callin', but it's got no place in business. The idea is to make money—not give it away—so you operate by a whole different set of rules altogether."

"I didn't exactly say that, Pa." The youngster almost let it drop. Under the Kincaid roof there was little room for dissension, and his father seldom yielded on any point, large or small. But he felt a sudden compulsion to talk back, to defend what seemed to him not a matter of charity but honesty. "All I'm saying is that there's no need to take advantage of people. Instead of just kicking them off their land, why not offer them a fair price? I mean, it's not like we can't afford it, and it'd sure leave folks with a better taste in their mouth."

"Alms for the poor!" Jake chuckled. "Great God A'mighty,

boy, that's what I'm tryin' to teach you. In business you make money by holdin' some kind of leverage over the other fellow. Do it to him before he does it to you! Like it or not, that's the way things work, and all that Christian charity won't get you nothin' but an empty belly and a lot of grief."

"Where's the harm in just making them an offer straight out? You'd still get the land, Pa. And at a fair price, too. So why hoodwink 'em with that mortgage scheme?"

"Hoodwink! Listen here, boy, you better wake up and see what makes this world tick. That's not a Sunday School out there, it's a goddamn jungle. The only choice you've got is to eat or get eaten. Those sodbusters knew what they were doing, so quit wastin' your tears. They paid their money and they took their chances. And so what if they lost? Hell, it's all part of the game. Them that can't afford to lose ought to have better sense than to bet."

"But you could've done it on the up and up, Pa. You didn't have to sucker them into signin' their lives away."

Jake's fist slammed into the table. "That's enough! Nobody held a gun to their heads. They came askin' for those loans. You hear me, beggin' us to loan 'em money. And I'll be goddamned if I'll sit here and listen to you tell me I baited 'em into some kind of mousetrap."

Owen flushed, shaken by the rebuff, but he refused to accept this uncharitable philosophy of dog-eat-dog. There followed a bruising argument, with little give on either side, ending in something of a standoff. Owen still disapproved, stubborn to the last, and Jake was thoroughly exasperated. With time and hard knocks, he advised the boy, perhaps his view of things would become more realistic. Owen declined comment, and that was where they left it.

Jake felt somehow betrayed, stung by the condemnation of his own son, but it altered his plans not in the least. Last summer a commission had been sent to Tahlequah to negotiate federal purchase of the Cherokee Outlet. While the Cherokees had balked, refusing even preliminary discussion, it was clearly a matter of time. By hook or crook, Washington would eventually take possession of the Outlet. The cattlemen would then be kicked out and the land opened to settlement, and it might well happen before the Association's lease expired. Jake meant to fight it down the line, but if worse came to worst, he now had an ace in the hole. Should the Outlet become a lost cause, he would simply shift his cattle operation to the Cimarron. Reduced to fundamentals, it was the very point he had made with Owen—there were lots of dogs but damn few bones. And the squeamish invariably ended up with no bone at all. Which didn't include Jake Kincaid.

As he did on most nights, Jake had cut through the alley to Zalia's house after his argument with Owen. He was hurt and angry, and trying to hide it, but he needed to talk. Brad was worry enough, over the past year having become an irresponsible loafer who exhibited interest in little besides pool halls and saloons. And now Owen had reared up on his high horse acting like some pulpit-pounding moralist. It was hardly what he deserved, not from his own sons at any rate, and seated in Zalia's parlor, rehashing this latest episode, his anger slowly turned to bafflement. She listened closely, prompting him with an occasional question, offering little in the way of advice. However much he revealed to her, and by now there were no secrets between them, she sensed that Jake had to find his own answers. She could coax or suggest, but never beyond a certain point. What he needed most was not a custodian spouting pearls of wisdom, but a good listener, a sympathetic ear.

Zalia never let herself forget that she was as much his confidante as his mistress. And at any given moment, she instinctively played the role dictated by his mood. But she very wisely avoided the pitfall of setting herself up as his conscience. At times his business practices were shady, and regretfully, his problems with the boys were more his fault than theirs, yet she could never change him. Nor could she influence him to any great extent, for he was obstinate and rigidly opinionated, and not easily swayed. Reconciled to that, she had long ago contented herself with what Jake Kincaid was and always would be, and simply left the rest of the world to fend for itself.

This attitude seemed to her most realistic, and if it was moderately cynical, she laid that at the doorstep of intolerant busybodies always anxious to cast the first stone. The scandal in Kansas, and her public flagellation in the newspapers, had caused her months of anguish, and branded her forever with the stigma of a kept woman. But she had lived through it, and all things considered, time had treated her gently. She was a bit plumper now, a vagrant strand of gray here and there, but still breathtakingly attractive. As vivacious as ever, yet somehow more mature, her spontaneity and zest for life had dimmed none at all with the years. Whatever scars she carried were well hidden, and if her love for mankind had diminished perceptibly she compensated for it by idolizing the man who, even at the height of their ordeal, had never once renounced her.

In her eyes, he could do no wrong, for whatever she had sacrificed he had sacrificed double. And as she had so many times in the past, she now let him vent the sting and the hurt, gave him momentary refuge, and upstairs in her bedroom, secure in one another's arms, they locked out the world and all its worries. They loved and slept, and loved again. And as false dawn lighted the sky with a faint purple tinge, Jake hurried through the alleyway back to his own home. Revitalized, the concerns of yesterday forgotten, he was himself again. The iron man.

"Bastards! Conniving double-crossing bastards!"

Jake pounded his fist into the desk, and slammed out of his chair. He strode to the window overlooking Oklahoma Avenue and glared down at the confused hubbub of wagons and buggies and clanging streetcars. The muscles in his jaws knotted, and his lips compressed in a thin, bloodless line as he ground his teeth in fury. His shoulders and backbone went stiff as a post, and there was an air of sulfureous malignance in the room. As if one wrong word might trigger something volcanic in nature, and indiscriminately violent.

Mordecai Jones knew when to keep his mouth shut. He was a gnomish little man, with the wrinkled features of a peach pit and the heart of a slave trader. But he was also a coward, appalled since childhood by physical violence, and he had learned the sagacity of prudence when tempers flared. Now, he kept his eyes lowered, studying his neatly manicured hands, and waited.

They were in Jake's second-floor office, above the bank, on a sweltering afternoon in late August. Jones had seated himself before breaking the bad news, fully anticipating some explosive outburst of anger. By now he could predict with a degree of accuracy the moods of his employer; beneath that stoicism and massive calm lay a smoldering godlike wrath. And once unleashed there was something diabolical in its seemingly random choice of victims. Jones knew there was nothing at all random about it, and he continued to sit very still and very quiet.

Jake glowered out the window, still grinding his molars as he struggled to get hold of himself. Lately these outbursts of temper came with greater frequency, and it irritated him to lose control in front of Mordecai Jones. He detested the little banker, however clever his ways with money and investments; all too often he caught himself wishing that Quincy Blackburn had lived to see Oklahoma. He missed the fat man's blubbery good cheer, and damned him for having debauched himself into an early grave. Things somehow lacked that old verve with this humorless, fish-eyed little skinflint as his frontman. But aside from that he had no room for complaint, and it was merely avoiding the issue at hand to take his anger out on Jones. Drawing a deep breath, he released it in a slow, almost metronomic, cadence. Then, having gained a measure of composure, he turned back to the desk.

"You're sure? It's not just some harebrained rumor?"

"Quite sure," Jones assured him. "The *Statesman* stopped their presses so they could get it in the evening edition. I understand Marquand is writing an editorial that will scorch the entire legislature. Particularly those who switched sides."

"Sons of bitches!" Jake growled. "Somebody must've paid them a pretty penny. We had that vote sewed up six ways to Sunday."

"Nothing critical intended, but it seems that someone unraveled your stitches. For all practical purposes, Guthrie has ceased to be the capital."

"Not by a damnsight it hasn't. Not yet."

Jones eyed him speculatively. "Well, the legislature has the right to locate the capital anywhere it pleases. Even if Oklahoma City is backward and unprogressive. Today's vote would seem to settle the matter."

"Except that there's a joker in the deck"—something changed in the timbre of Jake's voice—"the governor's right to veto."

"Veto?" Jones echoed hollowly.

"Why not? It's all part of the democratic process, isn't it?"

"Certainly, but it would be so obvious. Just out and out partisan politics."

"Hell's bells, man, what do you think today's vote was?"

"Yes, but they'd crucify him. I think you're wrong. The governor wouldn't dare veto."

Jake snorted, and gave him a cryptic look. "Wanna bet?"

That seemed to end the conversation, and Mordecai Jones trailed him downstairs, where they parted on the street. But the banker couldn't put the matter from his mind, and once in his office, he sat puzzling over this latest contradiction. For all the predictability of Kincaid's moods, there was an odd paradox to the code by which he lived. Earlier that spring he had ordered thumbs down on the use of violence to dislodge stubborn homesteaders whose land bordered the Cimarron ranch. Other cattlemen were harassing the nesters, stampeding herds over their crops, even burning them out when all else failed. Yet Kincaid would have no part of it. While on the other hand, he wasn't above slickering the homesteaders, and found nothing unsavory in manipulating politicians to suit his own ends. Jones thought it an interesting study in character, almost apocryphal. Perhaps the difference between a horse trader and a horse thief. Although they were both considered crooks, one conducted his affairs openly and with all the trappings of a legitimate businessman. Which was not so much delusion as illusion. And maybe that was the answer. Kincaid delighted in fooling others but never tried to fool himself.

The little banker's lofty ruminations would have amused Jake. He considered himself something more on the order of a superlative thimblerigger. In his game there really was a pea under the shells, if only the rubes could find it. Which seldom happened, either in business or politics. But his thoughts were on matters of greater consequence just at the moment.

Striding along Oklahoma Avenue, mechanically tipping his hat to the ladies, he turned south on Division Street. The governor's office was in the Herriott Building, located at the corner of Division and Harrison, and Jake had a hunch his visit would come as no great surprise. Not after today's shabby betrayal in the legislature. Sooner than he'd expected, and sooner than he would have preferred, today was the day he started pulling strings.

The fight had been brewing since May. At that time Congress had passed the Organic Act, officially designating Oklahoma as a territory. Included in the Act was No Man's Land (which quickly became known as the Panhandle), and all Indian lands west of the Five Civilized Tribes. It stipulated that these lands would become part of Oklahoma Territory only after being opened to settlement, which was a diplomatic way of telling the Indians they had best get ready to move over. The new Territory was divided into seven counties, with lawmaking powers vested in a legislature to be elected by the people. The office of governor was to be filled by presidential appointment. And there the political broth began to thicken.

Lobbyists for the railroads and cattlemen trotted out their bag of tricks, and opened a glittery campaign among their contacts at the White House. When the hoopla and shouting died out, George W. Steele of Indiana had been selected as the first governor of Oklahoma Territory. Those who were disappointed with the choice wailed a fresh chorus of an old song, declaring Steele a carpetbagger appointee. That Guthrie had been designated the interim territorial capital, and gave the governor a rousing welcome in late May, spoke for itself. Confident of greater days ahead, the city council set aside four square blocks at the east end of Oklahoma Avenue for the future capitol grounds.

Governor Steele issued a proclamation in early July calling an election for the thirty-nine members of the legislature. Oklahoma Territory immediately split into two loudly antagonistic camps—those who favored Guthrie as the capital and another faction beating the drum for Oklahoma City. At issue was not so much the future of the Territory as the future of two cities; the capital would confer both prestige and economic dominance on whichever city won the fight. The newly elected legislators convened in late August, primarily to provide the Territory with a code of laws. But the session wandered far afield from mere lawmaking; the intrigue of deals and counterdeals would have done credit to a Byzantine court. The legislation enacted left everybody, particularly the governor, in a mild state of shock. Norman was awarded the university and the insane asylum (a combination which sparked knee-slapping drollery throughout the Territory). Stillwater got the agricultural and mechanical college. Edmond took the normal school as consolation prize. And Oklahoma City came up with the juiciest bonbon of the lot, the capital.

Guthrie got nothing, not even a polite brush-off. And it made for interesting speculation that of the three towns awarded concessions, two were within spitting distance of Oklahoma City. The losers were quick to note that political skulduggery had played a key role in selection of a capital city.

But while his fellow townsmen raised a disgruntled cry of protest, Jake Kincaid moved to checkmate the legislature. He marched into the Herriott Building unannounced and, despite a waiting room crowded with petitioners, was ushered immediately into the governor's office. There he found George Steele wavering between anger and humiliation, with the latter rapidly gaining ground. One of his first acts as governor had been open support of the Guthrie faction, and today's vote was a direct slap in the face.

Steele was a capable administrator, with a distinguished career of public service behind him. Somewhat patrician in manner, he dressed the part, invariably attired in frock coat, striped trousers, and stiff-winged collar, all properly accented with a black cravat and pearl stickpin. His gray mustache was neatly trimmed and waxed, which added a certain touch to his attitude of decorum and somber probity. This afternoon, though, he appeared distracted, perhaps a little unnerved, and as he motioned Jake to a chair, there was a slight tremor in his hand.

"I regret we meet under such circumstances, Mr. Kincaid. Frankly I had hoped this would be a day of celebration in Guthrie. But now I—"

His voice trailed off, and Jake quickly took the lead. "Governor, out here we've got a sayin'. Don't get mad, get even. They handed us a lickin' today and nobody'll deny that. But if you're game, I think we can still pull the fat out of the fire."

"I don't believe I follow you. Game for what?"

Jake studied his face with an eagle's predatory concentration, watching for any telltale sign. "A veto."

Steele's reaction was instantaneous, and alarmed. "Veto! My God, man, they have just made me the laughingstock of the Territory. If I veto the bill and they override me, I might as well resign and return to Indiana."

"Governor, just to be blunt about it, things aren't a helluva lot better'n that right now. They gave you a black eye, and if you turn the other cheek, they'll give you another one. Either you whip 'em here and now, the first time out, or they'll make you eat dirt till you can't stomach it anymore."

"You're talking about prestige of the office, loss of face."

"Call it what you want, but if they beat you now the Territory will be run by the legislature, and nobody else. You'll be nothing more than a figurehead."

"And how do you propose we stop them from overturning my veto?"

"Suppose you leave that to me. You see, Cecil Hollister named this town after an old crony of his, Judge John Guthrie, and I've got an idea he'll be plenty ticked off when he hears how things worked out. Between the two of us, we'll be able to muster whatever votes you need. How we do it isn't important, and it seems to me you'd be better off not askin'."

"I suspect you have a point." Steele regarded him thoughtfully for a long while, then nodded. "Very well, Mr. Kincaid, we'll fight back. The moment the bill reaches my desk I will exercise the power of veto. And, I might add, hope for the best."

"Set your mind at ease, Governor. It's in the bag, and you made a wise choice." Jake rose and extended his hand.

"Guthrie will make a fine capital, and the people here won't forget you. Take my word for it."

Jake was right on both counts. Guthrie remained the capital, and the townspeople never forgot their first citizen. But George W. Steele was a marked man, and the opposition hounded him relentlessly. Scarcely more than a year later he would resign in disgust, yet his willingness to fight at the right time carried the day. Overnight, Guthrie became the foremost town in Oklahoma Territory. And thereafter, Jake Kincaid saw to it that the issue was never again brought to vote.

The corner of Harrison and Second was the liveliest spot in town. Chambers for the state legislature occupied the upper story of the International Building, which was located on the southeast corner. Across the street was the Palace Hotel, where the politicians made their home away from home when the legislature was in session. The Reaves Brothers Casino, fanciest sporting emporium in the territory, stood three stories high on the northwest corner. And directly opposite that was the Blue Bell Saloon, a most democratic bucket of gore catering to anyone with the price of a drink. On any given night this intersection was a regular beehive of activity, whose businessmen and gamblers, hard-cases and politicians, whores and barflies came together in sweaty pursuit of the fast life.

But while the hotel was elegantly posh, and the casino an orderly temple of vice, the Blue Bell Saloon was a hangout for the town's rougher element. Locally it was known by such jolly aphorisms as the Slaughterhouse and the Butcher Shop, and most nights, liberal doses of blood were spilled on its sawdust-covered floors. Gunplay was frowned on by the management, whose resident bouncer was a bullet-headed gorilla armed with a lead-filled bungstarter. Knives were also outlawed, tending to produce more blood than the sawdust could comfortably accommodate. Rough and tumble, though, with bare knuckles and stomping and eye-gouging, was considered a legitimate sporting event. So long as the contestants didn't wreck the place. Then they had to deal with the gorilla and his bungstarter.

And it was in the Blue Bell that Brad Kincaid had chosen to celebrate his seventeenth birthday. Not that his presence alone marked the occasion, for the Blue Bell was perhaps more his home than the mansion on Noble Avenue. At first he had come here to shoot pool in the backroom billiard parlor, but gradually he had worked his way into the saloon, graduating from beer to whiskey, and in time he had become one of the regulars who lined the bar nightly. That he was still a kid generated small interest among the sporting crowd. Nor were they overly impressed that he was Jake Kincaid's kid. In the Blue Bell it was every man for himself, and anyone who couldn't hold his whiskey or look after himself in a scrap soon hit the street headed in the wrong direction.

Oddly, considering Brad's childhood aversion to violence, he had become something of a brawler. There was no scarcity of men who could lay him out, and many had done just that. But he was pugnacious and determined, and he'd won their respect by always coming back for more. Not as tall as his father, nor as thick through the shoulders, he was fast and lithely built, and made up in speed what he lacked in brawn. Although genial enough when sober, a few drinks under his belt quickly turned him belligerent, and he had acquired a reputation as a troublemaker. The regulars chalked it off to Dutch courage, and unless pushed, talked him out of the notion. Nonetheless, there was always someone around spoiling for a fight, and if the youngster became too obnoxious, he usually found all the trouble he could handle.

As much as they liked Brad, though, the regulars in the Blue Bell never quite understood what made him tick. A rich kid bumming around in a sleazy honky-tonk was peculiar enough to whet their curiosity, but Brad volunteered nothing and they didn't ask. That was another rule of the house—nobody asked questions—and as a result, the kid's rowdy behavior remained something of a mystery. Nor could Brad have explained it himself. When people spoke of kids with all the advantages, that fitted him in a nutshell. He'd had more schooling than most boys his age; his father was the wealthiest man in Guthrie; and he had a good job at the Kincaid Wholesale Company. Yet he spent his days loafing off in the warehouse and most of his nights at the Blue Bell. The mansion on Noble Avenue seemed to him more prison than home; except for bed and board he avoided the place as much as possible. Which was most of the time.

Periodically, his slothful ways earned him a sharp tongue-lashing from the elder Kincaid, but generally his father was too involved with business to notice. Or care. At least that's how it seemed to Brad. In his father's eyes he apparently couldn't do anything right, for if he had, it had never been mentioned. The things which drew attention were his devilment and laziness (his father's favorite words), and the rest of the time it was as if he didn't exist. Some perverse streak gave him immense pleasure in goading his father; as a rule, he went out of his way to invent new and ever more infuriating forms of deviltry. Being lazy, which required no effort whatever, was the easiest part of all.

Sometimes, when he was daydreaming down at the warehouse, Brad had the eerie feeling he really wasn't a Kincaid. That he'd been found on the doorstep in a basket and taken in out of common charity. Certainly he didn't look like a Kincaid. Where Owen was ruddy and sandy-haired (already taller than the old man, and beefier through the shoulders), he was considerably darker, wiry of build, and had brown wavy hair. His father said he favored his mother, and let it go at that. But as Brad had grown older he came to realize that in the case of the Kincaid family, looks were merely the visible barrier. It went deeper.

There was no single incident which stuck in his memory. Nor did he recall a certain time in his childhood when he'd become aware of the barrier. It was simply there, as far back as he could remember. His father resented him, seemed forever annoyed by his actions; at times it was all the elder Kincaid could manage just to be civil. No one had ever told him why his father felt this way, but no one had to tell him it was a fact. That was something he'd learned for himself. The hard way. Through seventeen years of stinging rebukes, and his father's pretense that no barrier existed.

Jake Kincaid had only one son. If not literally correct, it was nonetheless a fact so far as Brad was concerned. Owen could seemingly do no wrong, and that's the way it had been since they were children. Flip the coin, though, and the younger brother was somehow always wrong. Brad had learned that it was never a toss-up; forced to choose between them, his father was unerringly consistent. And while he was jealous of Owen, an embittered and festering kind of jealousy, Brad had never been able to dislike him. That was an emotion he reserved exclusively for his father.

However much he toadied or groveled or tried to ape his brother, it was all wasted effort. His father saw him as a cross to be borne, someone to be tolerated but never accepted, and nothing would ever change that. So they suffered one another whenever necessary, and went their separate ways. But Brad's spite seldom went unslaked. If his old man was the meanest son of a bitch in town, then in that, at least, his son could go him one better.

And tonight Brad was feeling very mean indeed. Not that he really expected anything from his father. After all, his birthday had never before been an occasion for roman candles and fireworks. So what made this time out any different? But the sorry old devil could have made some gesture. Anything. Even a curt word of congratulations would have been better than nothing at all. And Owen. Goody-goody big brother. So damned hoodooed by his big-deal job at the bank that he couldn't think of anybody but himself.

Since quitting time at the warehouse, almost two hours now, Brad had been holding his own celebration in the Blue Bell. But it was a solitary celebration, and somewhat short on merriment. Elbows hooked over the bar, glazed eyes staring back at him in the mirror, he took his whiskey neat, and in copious doses. The bottle in front of him was nearly half empty, and he wasn't so much drunk as ossified. His vision was fuzzy, there was a faint buzzing in his ears, and his lips were skinned back in a youthful scowl. The regulars recognized the signs, and they had shifted away from him along the bar. Another couple of drinks, three at the most, and he'd come out swinging. Whoever got in the way wouldn't be in any great danger, but they liked the kid, and if it could be avoided, nobody wanted to floor a young pup merely because he'd lapped up too much sauce. Better to leave him the hell alone, and hope he wouldn't get too rambunctious for his own good.

But Brad's mood had gone from touchy to surly, and like a tightly wound spring, he was on the verge of busting loose. All he needed was a little nudge off center, and four sports carrying a load of their own gave him what amounted to a shove. Staggering into the joint, pickled to the gills and clutching at one another for support, they made for the only open spot at the bar. Directly alongside Brad. Unmindful of anyone else, just four playful hogs rooting at the same trough, they jostled Brad aside and sloshed his drink over the counter. Lurching backward, Brad grabbed the bar to hold himself upright, and planted his feet in the wide, if none too steady, stance of a barroom pugilist.

"Watch who you're pushin'!" he growled, slurring the words with a slobbery lisp. "That's a good way to get your stalk stunted."

The meaning was a bit garbled, but drunk as they were, the foursome got the gist of the message. The nearest one reared back and looked down his nose, a dopey grin plastered across his face. His chums oozed down the bar and draped themselves over his shoulders.

"Watch yerselves, boys!" he crowed in mock terror. "Them little ones is allus meaner'n tiger spit."

Brad was having a little trouble focusing, and instead of four he saw eight. Ornery as he felt, though, that made the odds just about right. Without warning, he lowered his head and waded in, windmilling the air with a flurry of harmless punches. The drunks split apart, just long enough to get him boxed up against the bar, then swarmed over him in a wild tangle of fists and boots and thrashing arms. Although the glassy-eyed quartet were about as dangerous to themselves as they were to Brad, he was absorbing considerable punishment simply by being in the middle. His lip split under a meaty fist, spurting blood, and a blow to the eye set off a chain of skyrockets inside his head. But he somehow kept his feet, and blindly flailed back at what now seemed a zithering hornet's nest of hard, raw knuckles.

The Blue Bell regulars had never exactly considered themselves the kid's wet nurse, but he was one of the crowd. And these four strangers weren't. All of which was incidental, except that several of the regulars were spoiling for a little action themselves. Several turned out to be the closest five, and within seconds the fight leapfrogged from a one-sided skirmish to a knock-down-drag-out brawl. And for the Blue Bell, that in itself wasn't especially noteworthy. Or disturbing. Until someone miscued and hurled a bottle which converted the back bar mirror into tinkling shards of glass. Then the management got upset, and signaled an end to the festivities.

Owen Kincaid walked through the front door just as the bullet-headed bouncer commenced cracking skulls with his bungstarter. The Blue Bell's resident gorilla did neat work, and the steady thump of wood on flesh began to take its toll. Men slumped and crumpled, out cold even as they collapsed, and before Owen could cross the room the brawl had assumed all the earmarks of a massacre. Luckily, Brad was trapped in the middle of the pack, and the deadly bungstarter hadn't yet reached him. But the bouncer was fast as well as neat, and he was rapidly hacking a path to the center of the action. Owen entered the melee from the opposite side, delivering short, chopping punches as he cleared his own path through the grunting brawlers. Almost as if he and the bouncer were in a race, the tempo of their blows accelerated, and it came down to a dead heat. Owen's arm snaked out, jerking Brad clear just as the bungstarter swished past his head. Ducking and twisting, Owen hurriedly backpedaled away, hauling Brad after him, and they left the bouncer to complete his dirty work. A particularly loud crack of the skullduster quickened their retreat, and as they went through the door the last warrior was laid out stiff as a wedge. The gorilla had won again.

Outside, Owen heard the sharp blast of a whistle and saw police hurrying down Second. Still clutching Brad's arm, he hustled the youngster along Harrison Avenue and darted into an alley halfway down the block. The fight had cleared Brad's head of whiskey fumes, but his face and shirt were splattered with blood, and his left eye looked like a rotten plum. Owen propped him up against a wall, thoroughly disgusted now that they were clear of the fracas, and gave him a slow, astringent once over.

"You're really a prize, aren't you? Beat to a pulp and so drunk you couldn't ride a hobbyhorse. What if the law had tossed your ass in jail, you ever think of that? Look real nice for Pa, wouldn't it? Jake Kincaid's kid in the pokey."

"I don't shive a git," Brad muttered. "Whole bunch of you can go to hell."

"Yeah, sure, just so you have your fun. Well, that's all the old man needs, to get you locked up for boozing and bustin' heads. Then that bunch in the legislature could really rake him over the coals."

"Awww, come off it, will you? He ain't got no room to bitch. Everybody in town knows he's got his own personal whore. And I don't see him tryin' to hide that."

Owen slammed him into the wall and backhanded him across the mouth. "Listen to me real close, Brad. Don't you ever badmouth Pa again. His private life is his own business, and that's the way it stays." He grabbed a fistful of shirt, and lifted the younger boy up on his toes. "You got me, or do I have to spell it out?"

Brad laughed drunkenly. "Regular little tin soldier, ain't

you? Old man beats the drum and you march along to whatever tune he plays. Whyn't you try thinkin' for yourself sometime, big brother? You might like it."

Owen nailed him with a cold look, tempted to slap him again. Several moments passed as they stared at one another, but the insidious smirk never left Brad's face. At last, Owen jerked him around by the scruff of the neck and gave him a rough shove out of the alley.

"Come on, tough guy. You're late for your birthday party."

"Birthday party?" Brad slewed his head around in a skeptical glance. "Who d'you think you're funnin'? Nobody said anything to me about a party."

"Why else would I waste my time hunting you down? That whore you were talkin' about baked you a cake and sent it over on the q.t." Owen pushed him again, harder than before. "Go on, keep moving. You got anything else to say, you can say it to Pa. I've had a bellyful of you for one night."

Brad stumbled off down the street, Owen at his heels nudging him along. He'd made an ass out of himself and he knew it, but despite the hangdog look on his face, he regretted nothing. Somebody should have told him, and that they hadn't was their lookout, not his. Suddenly a thought surfaced in some distant corner of his mind. His brow creased in a frown, straining to remember. It was fuzzy. Something that had happened back in the alley. Something he'd meant to remember. Then he had it, all in a rush, and remembering quirked his mouth in a bitter smile. Owen had sounded exactly like the old man back there. A chip off the old block. Like father, like son.

A son of a bitch. Double-distilled and sour as bear piss.

The birthday party was called off. Jake took one look at Brad and ordered him to bed. Bruised and bleeding, and still none too sober, the youngster hadn't argued. Instead, laughing to himself at some private joke, he reeled upstairs and collapsed across his bed in a drunken sleep. Later Owen undressed him, tending the worst of his cuts, and left him snoozing peacefully. By then Jake had stormed out of the house and cut through the alley to Zalia's. That he had held his temper, merely ordering the boy to his room, was perhaps the most remarkable part of an otherwise dismal evening. But the incident had yet to run its course.

Early next morning, just as the boys were finishing breakfast, Brad was summoned to the study by one of the servants. There he found his father seated before the fireplace, calmly puffing on a cigar. Jake waved him to a chair, seemingly in a tolerant mood, and inquired, with what appeared to be genuine concern, about his injuries. The youngster's bottom lip was split and puffy, and his left eye had turned a peculiar shade of dusky mauve; but he was hardly fooled by his father's solicitous manner. So far as Brad was concerned, sympathy had never been a conspicuous factor in the Kincaid household. And somewhat skeptical of this abrupt turnabout, he answered the questions with a wary, monosyllabic woodenness.

At last, having demonstrated his fatherly concern, Jake felt he could move on to other matters. He wasn't particularly pleased with the boy's attitude, yet it came as no great surprise either. His youngest son had always been something of a puzzle, and while he was at a loss to explain Brad's behavior, it never occurred to him to question his own actions. In his view, one had nothing to do with the other, and he would have been flabbergasted had anyone ventured the opinion that he had only himself to blame. He looked upon his sons as an investment, much in the same way he perceived any enterprise in terms of profit and loss. Thus far Brad had shown a poor return on the dollar, but Jake was confident the situation could be rectified. Logic and a little deft manipulation were called for, and while it might require more time than he could comfortably spare, he was willing to make the effort.

"Boy, let me ask you something."

Brad was acutely conscious that his father never called

him *son*. It was always *boy* or *bub*, or if the old man was in an especially good humor, perhaps by name. By the same token, he was aware that his brother was seldom if ever addressed by name. As far back as he could remember, Owen had been called *son*, while he was called whatever seemed handy at the moment. Still, considering the trouble last night, his father was acting unusually cordial this morning. And it suddenly occurred to him that he might do well to play along. So he did his best to look alert and interested, and accepting that as a favorable sign, Jake waved his cigar in an expansive gesture.

"Now just for a minute suppose you were in my boots. I know that's hard to do, but let your mind go and try to think of yourself as me. Can you manage that?"

"Well, I don't know, Pa. I guess I can try."

"Good! Now just imagine yourself sittin' here smoking this cigar and wearing a fifty-dollar suit and sportin' a stickpin that costs more'n most men earn in a year. You beginning to get the feel of what I mean?"

"Sort of, I guess. It's like one of them plays down at the opera house."

"That's exactly what it is! You've stopped being yourself for a minute, and you're actin' like you're me. Now that you've got the hang of it, let's go a little further. Think about yourself down at the bank and the lumberyard and the warehouse. Kind of get a picture in your head of what it's like bossing all those men around and keepin' everybody on their toes. See what I mean?"

"Sure, Pa, that's easy. I've watched you do that lots of times."

"All right, now this next step might be a little more difficult, but you concentrate real hard. Think about yourself tellin' the mayor and the governor and all the rest of those politicians what's what. Imagine them coming to you for advice and hangin' on every word you say and hardly ever making a move unless they check with you first. Can you feel it, boy! What it's like holdin' up the hoop and everybody jumping through it just to make you happy? Try real hard and tell me, can you feel it?"

"Yeah, Pa, I do. Honest, I mean it!" Brad's eyes got round as saucers, and it was as if the thought had him mesmerized. "It's like the circus. Every time you crack your whip the whole bunch of 'em jumps up and does their tricks."

"Not me, boy. You! Remember that, it's you."

"Yeah, that's right. I'm you, and it's me crackin' the whip."

Jake looked immensely pleased, and he let the youngster dwell on the fantasy for a moment. Then he took a long pull on his cigar and slowly tapped the arm of his chair. "Now that you've got yourself turned into me—and remember, you've got politicians and bankers and half the town lickin' your boots—I want you to imagine yourself sittin' in this chair. Right here, right this minute. And you're sittin' here looking at a wet-nosed squirt who spends most every night making an ass out of himself and a fool out of you. Can you do that, boy? Can you sit here and look at yourself the way I see you?"

Too late, Brad saw the trap. He blinked, and the broad canvas of his fantasy dissolved before his eyes. What he saw was his father—*not himself*—and he suddenly knew that it had never happened. That it was more of the old man's hocus-pocus. That they had never really traded places at all.

"C'mon, bub, don't dummy up on me. You're sittin' over here lookin' at yourself, and what you see is a kid that seems dead set on smearin' mud all over the Kincaid name. Now I want you to *tell* me. In your opinion, what ought to be done with that kid?"

Brad shrugged helplessly. "I dunno."

"You don't, huh? Now be real sure about that, buddy boy. I don't want you to ever say I didn't give you a chance."

The youngster shook his head, staring blindly at the carpet.

"Well, in that case, I guess I'll have to tell you. From where

I sit, there's one of three things I can do with this kid. First, I could just say to hell with it and let him go on making an ass of himself. But that won't work because at the same time he keeps on making a fool of me. Or second, I could ship him off to one of them fancy eastern schools and be rid of him for a while. But I don't want to do that because they'd just send me back a sissified smart aleck with his head crammed full of nonsense. So that brings us down to the last choice, and that's the one I mean to take."

Leaning forward, he suddenly jerked the boy's chin up and stared him full in the eye. "The next time he drags the Kincaid name through the gutter, I'll personally beat the livin' bejesus out of him. And let me tell you something, bub. If I ever have to do it, you'll find out that them saloon brawls you're so fond of aren't nothin' but church socials. Now, do we understand each other, or do you want me to spell it out?"

The boy bobbed his head and Jake roughly let go of his chin. "That's all I've got to say, but you just make real sure I don't hear any bad reports. Now get the hell out of here and go on to work."

Brad rose from his chair and walked straight to the door. But as he stepped into the hall tears stung his eyes, and something hot and brackish clogged his throat. Humbled, bullied into submission, he felt like a whipped dog crawling off to lick his wounds. And yet—there was something more. Something he'd never felt before. Not just rage but raw hatred, inimical and all-consuming. A fiery coal deep down in his gut that demanded revenge. Vindication. Payment in kind for the humiliation he'd just been made to suffer.

Someday!

The word leaped out at him, and through his tears he saw it with the stark clarity of a blood oath. An indelible promise to himself. Someday soon he'd show them all. The old man. The town. The whole goddamned world. Someday! Someday! Someday! Hide and watch and see.

Someday very soon.

EIGHT

It was autumn. Trees along Cottonwood Creek roared and clattered in a bright and nimble wind. The tawny grasslands bordering the stream were littered with drifts of scarlet and gold and brown and umber. Already there was a frosty nip in the air, and thin streamers of ice had begun to form along the banks of the creek. To those who could read the sign, it was a portent of things to come. Howling winds and searing blizzards, and a long bleak winter that would paralyze the land under a hoary carpet of snow.

But the people of Guthrie scanned the autumn skies without qualms or misgiving. Life had treated them exceedingly well, and as they were quick to remind one another, 1893 was their year. In four short and magic years their town had attained the status of a mature city. The population had nearly doubled, and with growth came new businesses and lavish homes, and an array of civic enterprises ranging from a dashingly uniformed fire department to a booster's club dedicated to cultural enlightenment. Perhaps of greater consequence (according to the Ladies Temperance League) the community now had eleven churches and a small but active college. And not to be outdone, a local gadfly by the name of Carry Nation had recently organized the Anti-Saloon League, with a hatchet as her symbol of righteous indignation.

Guthrie was a town of pluck and spirit, founded by men reaching for the mystic promise of the brass ring, and the veneer of wealth was everywhere present. The downtown area was a place of broad and busy streets, with an unmistakable smell of prosperity in the air. Quiet residential sections, east and west of the commercial district, were crowded with elaborate Victorian dwellings, homes designed for gracious living and sophisticated entertaining. And even those who eked out a day-to-day existence had escaped the smothering poverty common to the laboring class. In Guthrie there was no shanty town, and while a child might be born on the wrong side of the tracks, it was scarcely a lifetime affliction. Opportunity was available to all in this thriving, wildly venturesome environment, and a man with the nerve to act on his dreams might still gain a place among the town's burgeoning upper crust. Those who reached for the sun naturally expected to get a few blisters, but the chance was there nonetheless. It required only determination, and the willingness to dare greatly.

Of all the opportunists in Guthrie perhaps none had climbed so high as Jake Kincaid. Seemingly he had the golden touch, whatever the endeavor, be it politics or business. His bank dominated the financial affairs of Oklahoma Territory; his many and varied business ventures lent prominence to his name in the marketplace; and in the territorial legislature, however crucial the issue, his word alone delivered the key vote. Yet, like others whose reach forever exceeds their grasp, he had acquired his share of blisters. And just as his achievements were somehow larger than life, so were his blisters of gargantuan proportions.

On a brisk September day, that fall of 1893, he stood at his office window staring down on the heavily congested street. The people of Guthrie were in a festive mood, and a celebration of sorts was under way, but Jake viewed their exuberance with mixed feelings. Bittersweet was his mood, with perhaps a dash more bitter than he could gracefully accommodate.

At high noon, barely two hours past, the Cherokee Outlet had been opened to settlement.

Not that the event was unexpected. On the contrary, the run itself was something of an anticlimax. Nor had Jake been caught unprepared. His ranch along the Cimarron now encompassed better than twenty thousand acres, and the cattle operation had been headquartered there for nearly two years. But while the fight for the Outlet had been lost the winter of '91, today's land rush rubbed salt into a wound that was still raw and suppurating, and tender as a boil.

Washington had been devouring Indian lands piecemeal for the last three years. The Jerome Commission, originally appointed by President Harrison, had at first been stalemated by the Cherokees. But bureaucratic persistence, like that of mosquitoes, once again proved itself inexorable. Snipping away at the flanks, the Commission secured agreements by which members of the Iowa, Sac and Fox, and Shawnee-Potawatomi tribes were each allotted 160 acres in severalty; the remainder of their lands, something over a million acres, were ceded to the government. These reservations were opened to settlement in the fall of 1891, resulting in a mad scramble by twenty thousand eager homesteaders.

Negotiations had meanwhile resumed with the Cherokees. As a clincher, the President issued a proclamation forbidding further grazing on Outlet lands; by executive decree the Association was ordered to remove its cattle within sixty days. Congress was generally susceptible to persuasion, and in some cases the White House itself could be influenced, but this time the cattlemen were confronted by a political *fait accompli*. They trailed their herds from the Outlet for the last time in early December. Deprived of their lease rights, and all revenue from the Association, the Cherokees were finally forced to the wall. They sold the entire Outlet, almost nine thousand square miles, for $1.40 an acre, nearly $8 million less than originally offered by the cattlemen.

Matt Braun

The following year the Cheyenne-Arapaho reservation was opened to settlement. The Commission again alloted to each tribal member, regardless of age, a sterling 160 acres. Their surplus land, nearly 4,300,000 acres, was then purchased by the government for $1,500,000—a munificent sum of thirty-four cents an acre. That the land hadn't been stolen seemed a mere technicality, one of those ironic twists in which the robber also happened to be the law.

And now the most spectacular run of them all, the Cherokee Strip, had brought another two hundred thousand settlers pouring into the Territory. The Strip included the former Cherokee Outlet as well as parts of the Pawnee and Tonkawa reservations, and encompassed nearly six million acres. By far the largest land rush in the brief history of such events, it resolved a question which from the outset had been but a matter of time.

Oklahoma Territory was white man's land at last.

Politically, this was no trifling matter. In four hectic years the Territory had multiplied in size ten times over; its population had doubled and then doubled again. It had railroads and towns, courts and mayors and police, and a legislative body duly elected by the people. Perhaps of greater significance, what began as a financial windfall for the railroads had now become a juicy political plum. Or a hot potato, depending on which party controlled Congress and the White House.

This very thought was the cause of Jake's ambivalence on that chilly September day. After all this time it still rankled that Washington had rather unceremoniously ejected him from the Outlet. He suffered defeat with small grace, and while the bureaucrats had played with marked cards from the beginning, it lessened none at all his personal sense of failure. However long he had delayed them, the one inescapable fact was that he'd lost. And in his book there was no room for losers. Especially if the name happened to be Kincaid.

But as he gazed out the window, it occurred to him again that the Outlet had been merely a battle. And he might yet win the war. A war in which the stakes had been upped by millions of dollars, and for the first time in his twenty years on the frontier, a chance to consolidate political power on a national level. Not just Congress, but in the halls of the White House itself. As clearly as he saw his own reflection in the window glass, he could forecast the shape of things to come. The future of both Oklahoma Territory and Indian Territory would be played out in the political arena, along the banks of the Potomac. There the issue of statehood would be decided, and long before it was settled, the man who delivered the votes could write his own ticket. Or perhaps better yet, a license to do whatever he pleased wherever it suited him. Whether in the land of the white man or the red.

The more he ruminated on it, the less bitter became the bittersweet. With time, he might look back on this day with no twinge of regret at all. Perhaps, when the last battle had been fought, he would recollect the Cherokee Strip not as a defeat, but as a sacrificial pawn played off the advantage. It could happen just that way. Pragmatism, in fact, dictated no other course, and with his wits about him, victory might well be sweeter than even he had imagined.

Turning from the window, he walked to the desk and lowered himself into his chair. Then he leaned back, hands locked behind his head, and began a detailed examination of Indian Territory. He was still there, eyes dulled with concentration, when the sky darkened and a swift autumn dusk settled over the land.

On a Sunday afternoon in early October Brad Kincaid returned to the house on Noble Avenue. Neighborhood children stopped their play to gawk at him, and faces appeared in the windows of nearby houses as he rode past. Astride a fancy roan gelding, decked out in range clothes and a wide-brimmed Stetson, he made quite a sight. Nor did anyone miss the stag-handled Peacemaker strapped to his hip, and the Winchester stuffed in a saddle boot. Inwardly pleased by their reaction, he decided to give them the full treatment. Ornate Mexican spurs, with rowels like daggered spikes, adorned his bootheels, and he lightly feathered the gelding's ribs. The horse responded with a spirited sideways trot, switching sides every few steps, and as he pranced and snorted, little cottony puffs of vapor spurted from his nostrils. Everything on the block came to a standstill while the neighbors watched the show.

Satisfied with his performance, Brad reined the gelding off the street, ignoring the hitchpost at the curb, and rode to the direct center of the Kincaid lawn. There he halted, and sat for a moment studying the house. Grotesque as ever, unchanged in its foreboding massiveness, the house seemed to stare back at him. Brad found that it still resembled nothing quite so much as a prison, and the thought surprised him none at all. It had always been just that in his mind, the place where his keeper lived.

But if the house was the same, the youngster's appearance had altered sharply with time. Almost twenty now, he was taller and filled out through the shoulders, no longer the beanpole kid who had once haunted the Blue Bell Saloon. His face was burned darker, and he had the perpetual squint of a man who spends his days in the saddle, scanning distant plains under a broiling sun. And yet, despite these outward differences, there was nothing changed about his eyes. That same reckless, devil-may-care glint still lurked just beneath the surface, and those who knew him well were convinced he'd never had a serious thought in his life.

Perhaps, more than anything else, this foolhardy streak had been the cause of Brad's leaving home. Constantly badgered by his father, never able to measure up or shoulder responsibility, he had steadily grown more rebellious. By the summer of '91 he was acknowledged throughout Guthrie as the town's resident hellion. Brawls and drunken benders had become commonplace, something of a joke within the community, but it ceased to be a laughing matter the night he wrecked the Reaves Brothers Casino. Unlike the owners of sleazier dives, the Reaves boys took a dim view of such nonsense, and the fact that the kid's name was Kincaid fazed them not in the least. They had him jailed.

That was the last straw for Jake. He paid the fine, but once he had the boy home the fireworks began in earnest. The louder he shouted, the more it tickled Brad's funnybone, and at last, all else having failed, Jake lost his temper and gave the youngster the thrashing of his life. Which proved to be not just an error in judgment, but the final split between father and son. Brad was gone the next morning.

In the two years since, Brad had been home only once. It was a stormy, acrimonious visit, with Owen acting the part of referee, and ended without reconciliation. An outcast by choice, secretly delighted with the role of black sheep, Brad had become a saddletramp, drifting from ranch to ranch as he learned the tricks of the cattle trade. The summer of '92 he'd signed on with the Slash O outfit, up near the Osage Nation, and was enough of a cowhand by then that they had kept him on permanently. Through his contacts with cattlemen, Jake managed to keep track of the boy, but they had never corresponded. Until last week.

Staring at the house now, Brad felt himself almost a stranger. As if he had been summoned to the home of a distant acquaintance and couldn't quite figure why he'd come. Mainly out of curiosity, he supposed, or maybe a chance to watch the old man faunch and snort fire. Whatever, he expected little to come of it. On the way into town he'd decided that if there was any squirming to be done somebody else would have to take the lead.

Stepping down from the saddle, he left the horse ground reined and walked toward the house. As he went through the door the roan began grazing on the neatly manicured lawn, and a gang of bug-eyed kids gathered at the curb. On Noble Avenue a cowboy sporting a pistol wasn't exactly an everyday event, and they meant to get a gander at whatever came next.

Brad entered the house without knocking and found his father seated before a fireplace in the study, leafing through the Sunday *Statesman*. It was a somber room, heavily paneled, with dark leather furniture, and seemed to fit the elder Kincaid. They stared at one another for a moment, as if some assessment were being made, then Brad gave him a curt nod.

"I got your letter."

"So I see." Jake motioned toward a chair. "Want something to eat? Or maybe you'd prefer a whiskey."

Brad regarded him with a brash, amused impudence. "Nope. Quit drinkin' before the sun goes down." He ambled forward, the jingle-bobs on his spurs chiming musically, and flopped down in the chair. "Where's Owen? 'Fraid he'd get caught in the middle again?"

"No, he's over at the Webbs'. He hung around awhile, but we didn't know if you'd come or not, so he went callin'. Should be back before long, though."

"Still sweet on Julia, is he?"

"He doesn't say much, but I suppose he is. She's a fine girl, and easy on the eyes, too. Make him a good wife."

The youngster's reply was overdrawn, a little too guileless. "Well, I don't reckon that'd get anybody's nose out of joint. Rich as old man Webb is, I guess the Kincaids would end up just about ownin' Guthrie."

"You could take a lesson from your brother on that score."

"Since you're gonna tell me anyway, I might as well ask. What's the big moral this time?"

"Butter wouldn't melt in your mouth, would it?" A moment passed in a leaden drop of silence. "Hell, boy, don't play dumb with me. It's all over town about that squaw you've got yourself up in the Nations. Course you had no idea word'd get back here, did you? Or maybe you just don't give a good goddamn."

Brad pulled out the makings and built himself a smoke. He seemed in no rush, and after lighting it, he glanced up with a lopsided grin. "You're right, Pa. I don't give two hoots 'n a holler what this town thinks. And if you got me down here to lecture on sins of the flesh, you might as well save your breath. I don't need no sermons."

Jake bit down hard, holding himself in check. "All right, we'll skip that part. Wasn't really why I sent for you, anyway." He shifted uncomfortably in his chair, suddenly hesitant, not at all sure he could tolerate the boy's insolence. "Tell you the truth, I thought we might be able to talk things out. We've both had time to think on it some, and—well, what I'm tryin' to say is maybe we could wipe the slate clean. Make a fresh start."

"I'll be dipped." Brad appeared puzzled but somehow amused. "You mean you want me to come home?"

"Yes, I do. Owen and me have talked it over, and he's convinced me that's the way it ought to be. Hell, it's not right, you out punchin' cows for somebody else. Not when we've got a spread of our own. If you want to be a cattleman, then the place to start is on home ground."

Brad took a long, deliberate pull on his cigarette, then smiled and shook his head. "Think I'll pass, Pa."

"If it's not too much trouble, would you mind telling me why?"

"You won't like it." His father waited, silently demanding an answer, and the youngster shrugged. "Reason we don't get along is 'cause you run things like one of them Mexican generals. Anytime you say frog you expect everybody to squat. Hell, Owen don't hardly take a leak 'less he checks with you first. Comes down to cases, I guess I'm just not built right to take orders. That's it, plain and simple."

Jake's eyes went smoky, his lips clamped in a tight line. Brad watched him a moment, suppressing a grin, and flipped his cigarette into the fireplace. "You know, it's the funniest thing, Pa. I got an idea it was your lady friend that put you up to this, not Owen. What d'you think of that?"

"I think I should've started boxin' your ears long before I did."

"Yeah, maybe you should've." Brad stretched lazily, and yawned a wide jaw-cracking yawn. Then he uncoiled from his chair and stood. "Guess I'll head on out. Had myself a hard night, and I got a long ride back."

"Let me ask you a question." Jake fixed him with a waspish look. "You've got something else in your craw, don't you? Something you haven't said."

"Pa, you're really a bear for punishment." Brad grinned and left the question hanging. He walked toward the door, and then, as if he'd suddenly changed his mind, he turned back. "Fact is, though, you're right. You've spent your life makin' deals and slingin' businesses together, and I reckon it always galled me that Kincaid & Sons wasn't what you had in mind. You built it for Owen, and I've known it since I was old enough to spit."

Jake came up out of his chair, fists clenched, his voice harsh and cutting. "That's a goddamn lie! I never once played favorites. Never!"

"Didn't you, Pa?" Brad's mouth twisted in a mocking smirk. "Well, I guess it's like the fly walkin' across the mirror said—it all depends on how you look at it."

"Get your butt outta here! You're an ingrate, and you always were. I don't even know why I bother with you."

"You never did, Pa. That's what I've been talkin' about."

The youngster turned into the hall, jamming his hat on his head. Jake stood, unable to move, listening to the melodious jangle of spurs. And hearing again the cruel indictment of those last words. Then the door slammed, and suddenly he felt very old and very tired. As he lowered himself into his chair, it occurred to him that he also felt hurt, and that disturbed him. The boy was wrong. Dead wrong. He'd always treated them the same. Always. It was hard, but he'd done it. And nobody could tell him different. Nobody.

Brad returned one week later, and this time the neighborhood exploded in a furor of excitement. Beside him, mounted on a chocolate spotted pinto, was an Indian girl. They left their horses on the lawn, and without a backward glance, marched through the front door. The same gang of kids came again to stand at the curb and gape, while their parents sat back and watched, waiting for the roof to blow on the Kincaid house.

Inside, taking their regular Sunday dinner of fried chicken, Jake and Owen were seated in the dining room. It was a large room, baronial in size, with intricate carvings on the paneled walls, baroque tapestries and a tingling incandescent crystal chandelier. The table was a massive affair, appointed with gleaming silver and a centerpiece that vaguely resembled a swan. Owen and his father were seated at opposite ends of the table, concentrating more on the chicken than on conversation. The first indication of anything out of place was Owen's incredulous look of astonishment, and a drumstick frozen halfway to his mouth. Jake stared at him a moment, mildly baffled, then twisted around in his chair. Standing in the doorway were Brad and the girl. Her tawny skin and high cheekbones stamped her unmistakably as Indian.

Brad was obviously drunk, eyes glazed and bloodshot, his hat cocked at a rakish angle. As he walked forward, tugging the girl after him, his step seemed unsteady and his mouth widened in a foolish grin. He halted beside Jake's chair and pulled the girl closer to the table, then swept off his hat with a courtly flourish.

"Pa. Owen. I want'cha to meet my wife." He looked down on her with immense drunken pride, and his words fell like a thunderclap in the stillness of the room. "Mrs. Grace Six-killer Kincaid."

The silence deepened while everyone stared at the girl, who in turn ogled the room with childlike amazement. She stood absolutely motionless, almost spellbound, looking at the tapestries and the chandelier and the furnishings as if it were some sort of museum where she must touch nothing and reverently memorize every last detail.

Grace Sixkiller was tiny. Her head scarcely cleared Brad's shoulder, and she had a dainty, doll-like figure. An Osage, she was not as dark as most Indians, but she had great black eyes, dusky oval features, and hair the jet-black brilliance of a raven's wing. Her expression was intelligent and sprightly, somehow effervescent, but beneath the thick lashes and laughing eyes there was a hint of the steely determination which had once made her tribesmen the most feared warriors on the plains. Underneath a heavy woolen shawl, she wore a plain cotton dress and ornately beaded winter leggings. And until this very moment, standing awed by the baronial splendor of the room, she had thought herself beautiful.

Jake's appraisal of the girl was less than charitable, a mixture of raw disbelief and cold rage. At last, dreading the question, his gaze shifted to Brad. "Did I understand you right? You've actually married her, not just jumped the broom or some such thing?"

"Yep. Got ourselves hitched with a preacher and the whole works. Had a helluva party, too. You should've been there."

"Get out." The words were brittle and dispassionate, like chips of ice. "And don't come back."

Owen started out of his chair. "Wait a minute, Pa!"

"Shut your mouth, Owen." Jake's face was immobile, as if cast in cement. "You heard me, Brad. I don't want to see you again."

"C'mon, Pa, don't be a sore sport." Brad laughed, and gave the girl a bearish hug. "What about all your fancy friends, don't you want 'em to meet your new daughter-in-law? Hell, she'd knock their eyes out."

"Let's not bandy words. You married yourself a heathen and that's that. I wash my hands of you."

Grace Sixkiller shrank back at the fury of his words, but Brad crowed loudly and slapped his leg. "Heathen? Judas Priest, that's rich, Pa. 'Specially comin' from you. Truth is, she's a better Christian than the rest of us Kincaids. Damnsight better."

"Maybe I'm not gettin' through to you, Brad. So far as I'm concerned, you're not a Kincaid anymore. Understand? I just crossed you off the list. Now take your squaw and get the hell out of here."

They stared at one another, and while Brad's gaze never wavered, little knots ticced at the back of his jawbone. Then, as if it were all a monumental joke, he laughed crazily and wheeled away. Grace Sixkiller, terrified even to look back, followed him through the door and into the hallway. Cursing, Jake slammed his fist on the table, and glared sightlessly at some distant point in space.

Owen kicked his chair back, heedless now of his father's anger, and raced out of the dining room. Tearing down the hall, he caught up with Brad and the girl just as they reached the front door. He grabbed his brother's arm and spun him around.

"Brad, you can't leave it like this. Come on back and talk it over. Hell, you just sprung it on him too fast, that's all."

"Why, thank you just the same, big brother, but it 'pears to me everything worked out peachy keen." Brad canted his head to one side, and grinned a smug grin. "You buttin' in that way almost ruined the whole thing. And case you think I'm drunker'n I am, I'll let you in on a little secret. I rode a long way to watch that old bastard squirm, and I got my money's worth. So quit your worryin'."

Owen recoiled as if he'd been slapped. "You planned that on purpose? God A'mighty, you must've known what he'd do."

"Course I did. Contrary to what he thinks, there ain't no

idiots in this family. He's gonna find that out the hard way when he starts explainin' to his ritzy friends how come his son married a squaw. Goddamn, I'd give a bunch to see that. They won't never quit rubbin' his nose in it."

Brad burst out laughing again, and walked off with Grace Sixkiller at his side. Owen stood on the porch as they mounted and rode away, and for what seemed a long time, he could hear the eerie cackle of his brother's laughter. Dazed and bewildered, he couldn't make any sense of it just then. But thinking about it later, he came to the explanation that was both reasonable and frightening. And bitterly sad.

Stripped of meaning, love became a four-letter word spelled hate.

Harlan Green was a squat fat man who did business in the Choctaw Nation by virtue of his marriage to a fullblood Choctaw woman. He had a pocked moonlike face, plump fluttery hands, and few charms except a gift for making the best of a bad situation. Just now the situation was very bad indeed, and his eyes glittered with fright while his pudgy nicotine-stained fingers nervously toyed with a well-munched cigar.

His fidgets were alleviated none at all by the hawklike stare of Jake Kincaid. They were seated in the parlor of Green's house, a short distance outside the village of Poteau. Hardly more than a crossroads, Poteau was located in the southeast corner of Indian Territory, some two hundred miles by rail from Guthrie. The errand which brought Jake to this backwoods hamlet had to do with Green's unsavory past, and a scheme involving coal. He had appeared, unannounced, less than ten minutes ago, and promptly spilled an old, but highly volatile, can of worms in Green's lap. And now, quite clearly rattled, the fat man had at last worked up the nerve to speak frankly.

"How did you find out?"

"What difference does it make? The point is, you either

deal with me or spend the next twenty years in a federal prison. Those are the only options you've got."

"Mr. Kincaid, did it ever occur to you that I might have you killed? It happens all the time in the Nations. Strangers just disappear and they're never heard from again."

Jake laughed. "Green, don't ever try poker as a livelihood. You'd lose your ass." The smile dissolved, and his gaze suddenly went flint hard. "Let's cut the hogwash and get down to facts. First off, you haven't got the guts to kill me. Second, if anything happens to me I've already instructed the Pinkertons to notify the U.S. marshal as to your whereabouts, and they'd have you in irons quicker'n you can say scat." His hands spread in a dismissive gesture. "That's how I got on to you, the Pinkertons. Seems like trackin' a fat man is a snap. So don't get any bright ideas about runnin' again."

Although convincing, the statement was somewhat exaggerated. Jake had hired the Pinkertons well enough, but his requirements presented a tall order. They were to locate a wanted man, hiding out in either the Choctaw or Creek Nations, and one who was married to a fullblood. Moreover, he had to be smart, resourceful, and fairly glib, something of a con man. Since Indian Territory was a sanctuary for lawbreakers, there was no dearth of candidates. Locating one who filled all the qualifications, however, was hardly the snap Jake made it seem. Nonetheless, within a month Pinkerton operatives had traced a fugitive embezzler from Kansas City to the remote village of Poteau. The day after receiving the report Jake had boarded a train for the Choctaw Nation.

Sweating heavily now, Harlan Green realized that he was in a box, and this hard-eyed character sitting across from him had just slammed the lid. By treaty, U.S. marshals were allowed to arrest fugitives hiding out in the Nations; killing Kincaid would only worsen his predicament, and running would merely postpone the inevitable. A realist of sorts, though scarcely a mental wizard, he decided to make the best deal possible under the circumstances.

A shallow smile touched the corners of his mouth, and he shrugged. "You seem to be holding all the trumps, Mr. Kincaid. Exactly what is it you want of me?"

"Green, believe it or not, I'm here to make you a rich man." Jake selected a cigar from his pocket case, lighted it, and motioned around the drab, poorly furnished room. "You do what I tell you and inside of a year you'll be rollin' in clover. That twenty thousand you stole will start lookin' like peanuts—if you play it smart."

Some of the tension left Green's face, and his beady little eyes brightened. "You sure know how to get a man's attention. I'm all ears."

"Thought you might be." Jake admired the tip of his cigar a minute; then his gaze came level, curiously sharp and watchful. "I mean to organize a coal mine near here. You're gonna be my frontman."

"But I don't know anything about operating a coal mine."

"Doesn't matter. Some of my people will actually be runnin' things."

Green began to fidget worse than before. "Jesus, I don't know. I mean, the Choctaws have gotten awful leery in the last couple of years. And besides, we'd have to bring in white men to work the mine. Way the Choctaws figure it, there's already too many whites in the Nations."

"That's why I picked you. Married to a fullblood and all, they won't be as suspicious of you as they would an outsider. I'll supply the money, and you spread it around where it'll do the most good. Human nature being what it is, I suspect we won't have any trouble gettin' a license."

"You're talking about bribing council members."

"Course I am. Red or white, politicians are the same. And take my word for it, money talks the loudest." Jake puffed his cigar, exhaling a cloud of smoke, then resumed with the studied air of a field commander issuing orders. "Now get the beeswax out of your ears and pay attention. I want this done step by step, exactly the way I tell you."

Jake's plan centered on a loophole in the conduct of business within the Nations. The Five Civilized Tribes expressly prohibited a white man from owning land in Indian Territory; the single exception was a white man who had intermarried within a particular tribe. Exempt from the normal restrictions, such an individual could not only purchase land, but found it considerably easier to obtain a tribal license for certain types of businesses, sawmills and coal mines in particular.

As yet unexploited to any great extent, this loophole represented a factor of vast economic significance. While Oklahoma Territory was composed largely of windswept plains, Indian Territory was more hilly, and in certain parts distinctly mountainous. Dense woodlands covered much of the terrain, and in the southeastern quadrant, there were extensive pine forests. The rainfall was also heavier, and as a result, the vegetation was more luxuriant. Perhaps of greater consequence, the Nations possessed almost all of the coal and other mineral wealth to be found in both territories. And for his opening gambit in Indian Territory Jake had zeroed in on the coal industry.

Coal mines had begun operating on tribal lands as early as 1871, when the Katy first laid track across the Nations. The largest of these mines was located in McAlester, in the Choctaw Nation, and for the most part had remained under strict tribal supervision. Their principal customers were the railroads, and for nearly two decades the industry had operated in an orderly fashion. But with the rapid growth of Oklahoma Territory (and the steadily increasing demand for coal as home fuel and in industry) white entrepreneurs turned a greedy eye on the red man's natural wealth. As usual, Jake simply beat them to the punch.

His plan, as outlined to Harlan Green, involved those old reliables of chicanery, duplicity, and corruption. Employing the utmost secrecy, Green was to bribe sufficient members of the Choctaw council to obtain a mining license. Then, with as little fanfare as possible, he was to purchase outright certain lands indicated on a map supplied by Jake. Once these initial steps were accomplished, engineers, mine workers, and mining equipment would be imported. Operations would commence according to a rigid time schedule, and for all practical purposes, the mine would be an island of whites in the red man's ocean. Harlan Green would function as the owner of record, and to whatever extent possible, the Kincaid name would be kept in the background. Profits, according to Jake's financial projections, would be enormous.

Harlan Green had little choice in the matter. Nor did he offer even token resistance. The plan was shrewdly plotted, anticipated every contingency, and was a masterwork of audacious subterfuge. He had every reason to accept Jake Kincaid's assessment of the future. Within a year he would be a rich man. And to all outward appearances, legitimate as a Baptist preacher.

When they clinched the deal with a handshake, Jake had but one final word of advice. "Play it straight and you'll be set up for life. Try anything slippery and you'll wind up at the bottom of a mine shaft. Like you said, I hold all the trumps, and I've got a nasty shaft. Like you said, I hold all the trumps, and I've got a nasty habit of playin' for keeps."

This parting thought left Green a sodden puddle of sweat. The words, not to mention the stony eyes behind them, had made him a true convert. He believed, as zealots believe in Jehovah's manifest omniscience, that Jake Kincaid would strike him dead for any and all transgressions. Double-dealing and sticky fingers heading the list.

Later, on the train back to Guthrie, it occurred to Jake that Harlan Green, like most embezzlers, was a man of limited imagination. This coal mine, along with other schemes he had brewing, were merely chips (albeit blue chips) in a far larger game. One in which power sandbagged the odds, and the ultimate stakes were statehood.

While politics were still chaotic in Oklahoma Territory

(three governors in three years), both parties were united on the issue of statehood. The power brokers agreed that Indian Territory and Oklahoma Territory must be joined as one state. Only in this manner could the natural resources of the Nations be exploited to the fullest. Naturally, disregarding the profits involved, the benefits of this development program would be shared by all peoples in the twin territories. It seemed a matter of small consequence that the populace, both red and white, strongly favored separate statehood. With millions upon millions of dollars in the balance, such naïveté could scarcely be indulged.

Leaders of the Five Civilized Tribes, grown cynical with the white man's altruistic guise, lodged fiery protests against single statehood. They feared the Oklahomans would monopolize government and politics, as well as various state institutions. And with some justification they suspected a conspiracy between white money barons and the federal government. As the Indians of Oklahoma Territory had been dispossessed, one by one, of their tribal lands, it now appeared that similar machinations were to be employed against the peoples of the Five Civilized Tribes.

That their suspicions bore an element of truth soon became apparent. Both the power brokers in Oklahoma Territory and the administration in Washington were in accord—joint statehood would be impossible until all Indian lands had been allotted in severalty and the tribal governments abolished. Congress quickly responded to pressure from various quarters and authorized the President to act. Shortly afterward a commission was appointed, headed by Henry Dawes of Massachusetts, and instructed to enter into negotiations with the Five Civilized Tribes to extinguish tribal title to their lands. A stench, old and odiously familiar, settled over Indian Territory. The last fight was about to be joined.

Rattling along on the train that night, homeward bound, Jake felt as if he had the world on a downhill slide. He had been instrumental in prodding Washington to act, and in league with a small group of men, he wielded the political clout in Oklahoma Territory. Now, while the others twiddled their thumbs, he had gained a foothold in Indian Territory. And before the pack caught up, he meant to skim the cream in several directions, with never a moment's respite. Which, to his way of thinking, was how it ought to be. The man with the biggest thirst should always carry the largest dipper.

Owen paused before the Herriott Building, and stood staring up at the second floor. Now that he was here, about to take the plunge, a momentary feeling of absurdity came over him. Evett Nix might well laugh in his face. Or worse, turn him down and spread the story around Guthrie. Which would give the busybodies another gem to add to their growing collection about the Kincaids. What with the youngest son a squawman, and the elder Kincaid's not so secret back-alley romance, the jokes were already flying thick and fast. One more would likely set the whole town to buzzing, and not so quietly either.

Just for an instant he almost turned and headed back to the bank. Then, determined to take this last step before his resolve wilted, he pulled the door open and hurried up the stairs. The matter was settled in his own mind, and it was way past time to quit hedging. Unless he did it now, while his father was out of town, he might never again work up the gumption. And if he was to live with himself, instead of loathing what he'd become, today was the day. The compulsion was simply too strong to ignore. He had to get out from under his father's thumb, somehow become his own man. Otherwise, he'd wake up one day and find himself a dead ringer for his old man, corrupt and ruthless, without a trace of human feeling. Everything he had come to despise, and yet, perversely, couldn't help but admire in someone like his father. The ones who built things and destroyed people.

Upstairs, he went past the governor's office, the territorial court and the federal court, and halted before a door at the end of the hall. Lettered across the frosted glass inset were the words U.S. MARSHAL, and below that OKLAHOMA TERRITORY. Again he hesitated, but having come this far it was somehow easier to quell his apprehension. He grasped the doorknob, squaring his shoulders, then took a deep breath and shoved. The door swung open with a faint creak, and inside, seated at a lone desk, Evett Nix glanced up from a sheaf of papers.

"Well, Owen!" Nix sounded surprised, but genuinely pleased to see the youngster. "Come on in. Haven't seen you in a month of Sundays."

"Guess it has been awhile, Mr. Nix." Owen closed the door and stepped into the office. "Course you know how it is, they keep me pretty busy over at the bank."

"I'll bet they do. How's your dad?" Nix motioned with his hand. "Pull up a chair and rest yourself a spell."

Nix was a close acquaintance of Jake Kincaid, as was anyone with an interest in politics. A storekeeper by trade, Nix had secured appointment as United States marshal earlier in the year, shortly after a delegation of Jake's cronies had visited the President. To the amazement of opposition critics, Nix had proved himself an excellent administrator, displaying a natural flair for organization. He was also a man of intense loyalty, particularly toward those who had supported his appointment. Just now, watching Owen take a seat, he was wondering what prompted a visit from Jake Kincaid's older son. Whatever it was, he intended to listen a lot, and play it very cagey.

"Pa's just fine," Owen replied, settling into the chair. "Been out of town a few days, but he's due back tonight."

"That's your dad all right. Way he drives himself it'd put ten normal men in their graves."

Nix chuckled amiably, and tilted back in his chair. "Well now, what can I do for you, Owen? If you're anything like Jake I suspect you didn't pop in here just to shoot the breeze."

"No, sir, I didn't." Owen sat up a bit straighter, and he suddenly appeared very earnest. "Truth is, I came to ask you for a job."

"A job? I don't follow you, Owen. What kind of job?"

The youngster faltered, swallowing hard, then spit it out in a husky voice. "I'd like to sign on as a deputy marshal."

Evett Nix was visibly startled. He'd expected many things, mostly of a political nature, but hardly this. It took him a moment to collect his wits, and even then he sounded a bit nonplussed.

"You're a sackful of surprises, I'll say that. Would you mind telling me what brought this on all of a sudden?"

"Nothin' sudden about it, Mr. Nix. I've been thinkin' about it a long time, and I finally decided to get out on my own. Today just happened to be the day I picked, that's all."

"But what about the bank, and the family businesses? Jake must need you more than ever now. What I mean to say— well, you know—with your brother gone and all, I'm sure he's depending on you to take over where he leaves off."

"Mr. Nix, if you know my pa then you know he'll never leave off. Not as long as he can still fog a mirror, anyway. Besides, that hasn't got anything to do with it. I've made up my mind, and if you don't take me on then I'll try Judge Parker over at Fort Smith."

Nix scrutinized the boy more closely. Strangely, though it just now dawned on him, it was as if a younger version of Jake Kincaid were sitting across the desk. Taller certainly, perhaps a hair over six feet, but with those same broad shoulders and large-knuckled hands. And that same stubborn cast along the jawline, a look of grim determination. The resemblance was uncanny, and he suspected it went deeper than met the eye.

"Owen, I don't know what's behind all this, and I won't ask. But I'm curious why you think you want to be a lawman. It's a dirty business. The pay isn't much. And frankly, there's a good chance you'll get yourself killed. Bad as I need deputies, I'd still advise you to pick a different line of work."

"I appreciate the sentiment, Mr. Nix, but I've thought it out pretty careful. There's lots of fellows who can push a pen or tote figures, likely better than I ever will. But the way it looks to me, there's not many that would make a good peace officer. With what I've read in the paper, and talk I've heard, it seems to me that right now the Territory needs lawmen more than it does pen-pushers. Boiled down, I guess that's it. I want to do something important with my life. Something folks will respect."

There was a curious emphasis on the last word, and it gave Nix all the clue he needed. People feared Jake Kincaid, and they admired his shrewdness and nimble cunning. But they respected him in the way a man respects a hungry shark. Owen was talking about another kind of respect altogether.

"So you think you'd make a good lawman, is that it?"

"Yessir, I do. Like I said, I've thought it out careful."

Nix turned his head toward the door of an inner office. "Bill! You and Heck come in here a minute. Want you to meet somebody."

The thud of heavy boots sounded in the next room, and a moment later the door opened. Two men, as alike as peas in a pod, entered the office. They were tall and rangy, on the sundown side of thirty, with cold gunmetal eyes and creased weatherbeaten features. Nix performed the introductions, but it was strictly a formality. Everybody in Guthrie knew these men on sight, and their names were a household word throughout the Territory. Bill Tilghman had served for several years as marshal of Dodge City, and was reputedly the deadliest pistol shot in the west. Heck Thomas, formerly a deputy U.S. marshal out of Fort Smith, preferred the sawed-off shotgun, which made him even deadlier in a gunfight. Nix had signed them on as deputies within days of his appointment, and of all the manhunters in Oklahoma Territory, they were considered the most dangerous of the lot.

"Gents, this young fellow says he wants to be a peace officer." Nix studied their faces briefly, then lowered his chair to the floor. "Bill, I forget, how many men is it you've killed in the line of duty?"

Tilghman knuckled his mustache, considering at length. "Well, near as I recollect, it's eleven. Give or take a couple."

Nix just nodded, deadpan. "Heck, what about yourself?"

"Sixteen," Thomas observed laconically. "Countin' breeds and such."

"Twenty-seven between you. Give or take a couple, of course." Nix's gaze swung back to the youngster, boring holes through him. "What about you, Owen? Think you could pull the trigger on that many men and still live with yourself?"

Owen regarded him evenly. "Mr. Nix, I wouldn't have come here if I was squeamish. The thought of killin' a man don't bother me near as much as the thought of him killin' me."

Heck Thomas chortled appreciatively. "Feisty, ain't he? Tell me, sonny, how old are you anyway?"

"I'm twenty-one, Mr. Thomas. And I'll thank you not to call me sonny." Owen could scarcely believe the words had come out of his mouth, and suddenly he felt about half as brave as he looked. "Nothin' personal, but I quit wearin' didies a long time back, and I reckon I'm too old to start in again."

Now it was Nix who chuckled. "By God, Heck, I think you're right. He's feisty as a bullpup." Cocking his head, he glanced at the deputies. "What's your opinion, gents? Think we could make a lawman out of him?"

Something unspoken passed between the men, then Bill Tilghman flashed a brief, very wry grin. "Depends. If he don't get hisself killed off too quick we might teach him a few tricks."

"That's it, then. Looks like you've got yourself a job, Owen." Nix abruptly paused, frowning, and pursed his lips. "Except for one thing. You make your peace with Jake. I don't want him on my back."

Owen's knees felt rubbery, and he could barely manage

to stand. "Don't worry yourself on that score, Mr. Nix. Pa don't call me sonny neither."

They shook hands all around, and afterward Owen departed walking a bit taller than when he'd entered. Tilghman and Thomas exchanged glances, shrugged, and went back to their office. Evett Nix resumed his paperwork, lost in concentration before the door closed.

On the street again, Owen felt like jumping up in the air, clicking his heels, celebrating in some outlandish fashion. But he did none of these things. The euphoric, giddy sensation came and went in a rush, and just as quickly his sober nature reasserted itself. Since childhood he had accepted responsibility with a gravity beyond his years, and within a block of Nix's office the impact of what he'd done jarred him back to reality. Tomorrow, when he took the oath and pinned on a tin star, he would assume an awesome responsibility. One which invested him with the power of life and death every time he rode into the Nations. A responsibility few men cared to consider, and even fewer dared to undertake.

By the time he turned the corner onto Oklahoma Avenue the full burden of that responsibility had become apparent. He saw again the grim-faced features of Tilghman and Thomas, and his step slowed in concentration. Thoughtful, reflecting back on all he'd read and heard, he found himself appraising the situation with a whole new outlook. Before it had seemed exciting and boldly adventuresome. Now, in somber retrospect, he saw it for the very thing Evett Nix had bluntly stated. A dirty business, conducted under the strangest circumstances ever faced by men sworn to uphold the law.

With the advance of civilization, a new pattern of lawlessness began to emerge on the plains. The era of the lone bandit faded into obscurity; outlaws began to run in packs. Bank holdups and train robberies were planned and executed with the precision of military campaigns, often leaving the scene of the raids a battleground strewn with dead and dying. Local peace officers found themselves unable to cope with the lightning strikes; the war evolved more and more into a grisly contest between the gangs and the federal marshals. But it was a game of hide-and-seek in which the outlaws enjoyed a unique, and sometimes insurmountable, advantage.

Gangs made wild forays into Kansas and Missouri and Oklahoma Territory, terrorizing the settlements, and then retreated into Indian Territory. There they found virtual immunity from the law, and perhaps the oddest sanctuary in the history of crime. Though each tribe had its own sovereign government, with courts and Light Horse Police, their authority extended only to Indian citizens. White men were untouchable, however heinous their offense, exempt from all prosecution except that of a federal court. Yet there were no extradition laws governing the Nations; federal marshals had to pursue and capture the wanted men; and in time the country became infested with hundreds of fugitives from justice. Curiously enough, the problem was compounded by the Indians themselves. They had little use for white man's law, and the marshals were looked upon as intruders in the Nations. All too often the red men connived with the outlaws, offering them asylum, and the chore of ferreting out lawbreakers became a herculean task. Adding yet another obstacle, even the terrain itself favored the outlaws. A man could lose himself in the mountains or along wooded river bottoms, and in some areas there were vast caves where an entire gang could hole up in relative comfort. It was no job for the faint of heart, and upon reflection, Owen was all the more awestruck by men such as Tilghman and Thomas.

Thinking about Heck Thomas, he recalled that the marshal had served under Judge Isaac Parker for several years. Until recently Parker's court in Fort Smith had had sole jurisdiction over Indian Territory. Known as the Hanging Judge, Parker's administration had been punctuated repeatedly by the dull thud of a gallows trap. In eighteen years on the bench he had sentenced one hundred and sixty men to die, and of that number, sixty-seven had been hanged. But in the process sixty-five marshals had lost their lives tracking outlaws across the Nations. All things considered, Evett Nix's statement was hardly an exaggeration. The job was both dirty and dangerous.

Still, as he neared the bank, Owen was reminded that he had yet to face the most formidable threat of all. Tonight he must tell his father. And there, indeed, was no job for the faint of heart. Chasing outlaws suddenly seemed pretty tame stuff. In that he would at least be armed, and able to return their fire on even ground. In an argument with Jake Kincaid it was strictly an uphill battle. Something like playing King of the Mountain, except that this particular game was rigged. The old man owned the high ground.

That evening, upon returning from Poteau, Jake reacted with something less than equanimity. At first dumbfounded, he heard Owen out, hardly able to credit his ears. Then, wholly in character, his face mottled with scorn and he exploded in a fiery outburst of rage.

"A lawman! Are you crazy? Answer me, goddamnit! Where the hell did you get a tomfool notion like that?"

"What's the difference, Pa?" Owen shrugged, bland as butter, but not nearly so composed as he appeared. "My mind's made up and Mr. Nix hired me, so that's the end of it."

"In a pig's ass! Lemme tell you something, boy. You're gonna be a banker. You got that? A *banker*! And if Evett Nix tries swearin' you in as deputy, I'll have him back tending store so fast he won't know what hit him. You know I can do it too, so just mark it down as gospel and let's not hear any more nonsense about the law."

"I'm sorry, Pa, but it won't work. This time my mind's made up, and nothin' you say can change it. If Nix won't hire me, then I'll catch the train to Fort Smith and sign on with Judge Parker. There's no need to try bluffin' about that, either.

You don't carry any weight over there and we both know it. So I reckon the Judge would be willin' enough to give me a badge."

Jake stared at him incredulously for an instant; then his voice lashed out in a loud, hectoring roar. "That's the thanks I get, is it! You'd just walk out on me and the business and everything I've planned. Not a by-your-leave or what's what or a nickel's worth of talk. Just kiss my foot and adios! Is that what you're tellin' me?"

"What I'm trying to get across to you"—Owen told him earnestly—"is that I don't want to be a banker or a businessman or anything else. I want to be a lawman. That's it, plain and simple, so you might as well get used to the idea."

"Not by a damnsight, it's not. I'll write you out of my will like that!" Jake snapped his fingers with the crack of a pistol shot. "You'll wind up with boils on your ass and holes in your pockets. What do you think of that, hotshot? Don't sound like much of a life, does it?"

"I hoped you wouldn't take it like that, Pa, but it doesn't change things. Worse comes to worst, I suppose I can always manage to get in out of the rain."

With a jolt Jake saw that he was on the verge of losing his son. The only son he had left. It was a sobering thought, and of a sudden, he took a grip on his temper. "Look here, maybe I'm too quick to jump. Let's just hold off a minute and back up, before we say something we don't mean. I'm tryin' to understand you, boy, but honest to Christ, I can't see what turned you so pigheaded. I mean, what's so special about being a lawman? Hell, they're a dime a dozen, so just tell me that—why are you so stuck on wearin' a tin star?"

They were seated in the study, and Owen abruptly rose to his feet and paced away. Then he stopped and turned back. "Pa, I guess you'll think it's a bunch of hogwash, but I've got this thing inside me that wants to help people. I don't know, maybe it's like when a fellow gets the call to be a preacher. Not that I'm any Bible-thumper, but down at the bank I never really felt like we were helping anybody but ourselves. I've got an idea being a lawman will change that, so in a way I suppose you could say it's my callin'." He shrugged, at a loss to explain it further, and stuck his hands in his pockets. "That's it."

Jake studied him intently for several seconds, then snorted, shaking his head. "You know what I think? I think you've got something stuck in your gullet and you haven't got guts enough to spit it up."

Owen went stock-still. "Like what?"

"Like the way I run my business. Or the fact that I use people to suit my own ends. Or maybe the way I kicked your brother out of here. Hell, how do I know what's rattling around inside your head? C'mon, you think you've got what it takes to pack a gun. Let's see if you've got what it takes to be a man. Go on, spit it out."

"What if I told you it was all those things, Pa? Would it make a difference?"

"Wouldn't faze me a bit. I don't apologize to anyone. Not even you."

But it did make a difference, and Owen saw the pain in his father's eyes, a look unlike any he'd seen there before. Unwittingly he had let it go too far, and now, knowing it was a futile gesture, he tried to smooth it over with a lie. "Well, I hate to be the one to tell you you're wrong, but it's none of those things. It's just what I told you, Pa. I've heard the callin'."

"Then you're determined to be a lawdog?" When the youngster nodded, Jake grudgingly admitted defeat. "You're a damn fool, but go ahead and get your ass shot off. I won't stand in your way."

The discussion ended on that note, yet for all he'd won, Owen left the house under a pall of shame. However much he detested the old man's business tactics (and blamed him for banishing Brad), he hadn't meant to inflict hurt. As he went through the door, he suddenly felt very selfish, almost penitent, somehow disgusted with himself. Try as he might, he couldn't quite justify what he'd done. Nor could he forget the look in his father's eyes.

Julia Webb was a striking young woman. She had auburn hair, eyes green as clover, and a sumptuous figure. Her face lacked classic beauty—sprinkled with freckles, full lips, and an impudent nose—but it was an attractive face, warm and inviting, somehow unflawed despite its imperfections. She had remarkably even teeth, as if filed level with a fine rasp, and when she smiled there was a great pearly flash not unlike rows of cubed dice. By turn she could be charming and spoiled, affectionate and aloof, and she generally left men less bedazzled than stunned. An evening in her company was an ordeal to some, a vivid experience to others; she was either a bewitching creature or a tart-tongued bitch. And according to those who knew her best, she might well be both.

Tonight she hadn't quite made up her mind. She felt bitchy as a wet cat, but reason told her that the situation called for understanding, larded with affection and gobs of sympathy. Since Owen's twenty-first birthday, nearly six months past, she had waited for him to propose. And she was still waiting, only now a new and wholly unexpected complication had arisen. The big ninny had gone and got himself a badge. Like some feckless, overgrown juvenile chasing fireflies and stardust, and never a thought for tomorrow.

When he'd first blurted it out her freckles turned hot as live coals, and she put both hands to her head as though it would burst if she didn't hold it together. She felt betrayed, stung beyond forbearance, mortified by the insipid looks she would face from her friends. Then, even as a sharp rebuff formed on the tip of her tongue, she heard something in his voice, and she listened closer. He was grievously upset, wracked with doubt and guilt, clearly devastated by the session with his father. As he told it, the meeting had been little more than a collision of wills. But it was apparent that his threat to leave Guthrie was more than the old man could bear. And while Julia absolutely loathed the elder Kincaid, she sensed that his anguish might easily reinforce her own desire in this matter.

A spectator of sorts, listening to a verbal account of the fight, she was perhaps more objective than Owen. Pride was at issue here, pride and the stubborn refusal to back down once a stand was taken. More than blood ties, it involved the kinship of strong men who each saw something of himself mirrored in the other, and the clash had been inevitable. Owen had every reason to make the break (the affair with Brad had been merely a catalyst); if none had presented itself he would eventually have invented one. The curious part was that he had yet to realize his own strength of character, and that this alone had precipitated the fight. Perhaps of equal significance, he had something his father lacked—a conscience. And if handled deftly, she might, in time, work this to her own advantage.

They were seated in the parlor (her parents, equally enamored with the Kincaid name, obligingly left them alone whenever Owen called), side by side on a settee, holding hands. Her intuition told her that now, before Owen's contrition waned, was the time to act boldly. He had fallen silent, apparently talked out, and sat staring blankly at their clasped hands. She looked at him with utter directness, a purposeful look, but kept her voice honeyed with sympathy.

"You mustn't blame yourself, sweetheart. Just remember, time cures all ills. And someday, I'm sure your father will see your side of it." She squeezed his hand reassuringly. "Gracious, he almost has to. I mean, after all, the way things are, you're practically the only son he has left."

Owen flinched, his face beet red with shame. Her subtle barb, delivered with doelike innocence, had struck home, and it took him a moment to collect himself. "You're wrong, Julie. You don't know him like I do. He's hurt, and he thinks I let him down. Course he won't show it, but it'll eat on him till he finally winds up cussin' me the same way he does Brad."

"Oh, for goodness sake. Your father isn't an ogre!" She personally considered Jake Kincaid an insensitive brute, but candor would hardly further her own cause. "You wait and see. After you get over this notion of yours about chasing outlaws he'll welcome you back with open arms. Why, if I'm any judge, the two of you will come out of this closer than ever."

A bemused frown creased his brow. "I guess maybe I gave you the wrong idea. This isn't any notion, as you call it. I aim to be a lawman, and Pa's feelin's won't change that. He told me one time a man has to ride his own furies in life, and I reckon that goes for him, too. I'm sorry, and I wish he hadn't taken it so hard, but that don't change nothin'." He paused, grimly thoughtful, then shook his head. "No, it's done, and that's all there is to it. I'll just have to hope he's a little more tolerant than I give him credit for."

Julia was speechless, taken unaware by the sudden resolve in his manner. Several moments passed before she could trust herself to speak. "Do you mean you're seriously considering this job as—permanent? Your lifetime's occupation?"

"I sure do. It's honest work, and it's work that needs doing. Won't be any tea party, of course, but I've got an idea it's work I'll be good at."

Desperate now, Julia knew that she must take a stand, right this instant. Or else resign herself to the life of a young widow. "Owen, I'm not sure I could go through that. Sitting here, afraid to answer the door. Waiting to hear that you've been killed by some train robber. I mean, really, it's not the kind of life a girl dreams of."

"No, I guess not," Owen announced with surprising bitterness. They stared at one another for what seemed a long time, and as the silence mounted, it became clear she meant to wait him out. At last, wearily, he climbed to his feet. "Maybe we both ought to sleep on it. Seems like tonight just isn't my night."

She was still sitting there, flushed and completely dismayed, when the front door closed. How badly she had miscalculated, and the suddenness of it all, left her on the verge of tears. But she refused to cry. And she refused to be bullied. Sleep on it, indeed! The nerve of that big baboon. The unmitigated gall.

She pulled a hanky from her sleeve and slowly reduced it to a sodden ball.

Across town, in another parlor, a scene no less dismal was being played out. Jake sat slumped in a chair, glum and dispirited, staring vacantly into the fireplace. Tonight, when he was baffled and sorely wounded, his iron impassivity had deserted him. His face appeared slack, somehow older and drained, and his eyes were rimmed with the ugly jaundice of self-pity. He hadn't moved or spoken for nearly a half hour, and the funeral mask covering his features was that of a mourner standing dolefully before an open grave.

Quietly watching, Zalia sat close by in a rocker, her own anxiety heightened by his gloomy, woebegone funk. The misery etched in his face was unlike anything she would have believed of Jake Kincaid, and yet, for some inexplicable reason, she secretly rejoiced that this flint-hearted bear of a man could be brought to his knees. Perhaps, after all, there was hope. However painful this night had been, it might bring to the surface, at last, that spot of tenderness and compassion he'd kept buried all these years.

But she never for a second deceived herself. He could just as easily revert to his impervious, case-hardened stoicism; this display of martyrdom was strange but not all that unexpected. Characteristically, he blamed Owen for the entire affair, blindly absolving himself of any fault whatever. Just as he had castigated Brad, judging him an ingrate, so he condemned Owen as thoughtlessly selfish and immature, without a shred of respect for his father. All the same, as she listened earlier to his version of the argument, Zalia had detected an ill-concealed distinction in what he felt toward his sons. Brad was an embarrassment, the family leper of sorts, and Jake had viewed his departure as good riddance. Owen, on the other hand, represented the future, an heir to perpetuate the Kincaid line and expand the empire that was to be his legacy. Jake had invested heavily of himself in this older son. With every year the commitment had grown, demanding more of his accumulated knowledge and hard-won experience, so that it might be passed on generation to generation in what he envisioned as the vanguard of a family dynasty.

Now, without warning, in defiance of all that was rational and sane, his son had betrayed him. The boy he had sired and raised to manhood, the one infused with his own hardy outlook on life, had turned his back on the family legacy. Chosen instead to become a common lawdog. And worse, had actually browbeat his own father. Threatening to leave home entirely unless his whimsical lunacy was indulged to the fullest. It was blackmail, plain and simple. But it was a form of negotiation Jake understood well, and that a son would use such despicable tactics on his own father had left him grievously hurt, and not a little humiliated.

Zalia saw all this and more. Unwittingly, Jake had always thought of himself as a patriarch, the family godhead whose commands were to be obeyed instantaneously, and without question. Yet, within a matter of months, both of his sons had rebelled, openly defiant, and gone their separate ways. His image of himself, the unsurpassed manipulator of men and events, had suffered a mortal blow. And true to form, he grieved not so much the loss of his sons as the loss of face. Like some lonely, distracted ghost, he now ruled an empty castle.

In all their years together she had never seen him so disconsolate, but while she loved him shamelessly, what she felt now was only remotely akin to pity. Too many times she had seen him bound back from defeat, displaying an almost unearthly resiliency; she sensed that his wallowing gloom here tonight would be short-lived. By tomorrow, or the day after, he would have it all neatly rationalized, divesting himself of any culpability in Owen's unruly disposition. Jake would never write him off as he had Brad; he saw too much of himself in his elder son to sever the cord permanently. Instead, the youngster would be subjected to an unrelenting, and probably none too subtle, campaign to bring him back into the fold. However aggrieved and sorrowful he might be now, Jake was no quitter.

Gently, she set the rocker in motion. "Jake."

A beat in time passed before he roused himself. "Sorry, guess my mind was wandering. You say something?"

"Yes. I was about to suggest that you could use some advice. I've always waited until you asked before I offered an opinion, but I think perhaps tonight is the exception."

"Hell, why not? Everybody else is on their soapbox tonight. You might as well join the club."

Zalia seemed to consider; then she brought the rocker to a halt. "You won't like what I'm going to say. So first, you have to promise me you won't get mad. Rather than have harsh feelings between us, I'll just keep quiet and mind my own affairs."

Despite his hangdog look, Jake couldn't resist a smile. "Gonna iron the kinks out of my tail, are you?"

"Not really. It just seems to me that you need a woman's view of things. You've tried to be mother and father to those boys, and frankly—I think we'll both agree on this—it hasn't worked out very well at all."

She waited, expecting an angry denial, but he merely shrugged, averting his eyes. Satisfied that he would at least listen, she went on. "You're a brilliant businessman, Jake, but the thing you've never realized is that there's a difference between managing a business and raising a boy. God knows, I'm no expert on either one. But it seems clear to me that you expect Owen to follow orders like all your other flunkies. And it simply won't work. Those men are paid to jump every time you crack the whip. Quite candidly, I don't think you have enough money to buy Owen. He's too much like you, and if he weren't, then I suspect you wouldn't give a tinker's damn what happens to him."

She hesitated, watching him steadily, then took a deep breath. "All I'm saying is, let him be his own man. You certainly wouldn't tolerate anyone telling you how to run your life, so don't expect more of him than you do of yourself. If you do, Jake, you might just lose Owen also."

Several moments slipped past before he looked at her. "Think you've got me all figured out, don't you?"

"I hope not, Jake. I truly hope I'm wrong."

His eyes drifted from her back to the fire. "I know you mean well, and I appreciate the advice. I'll keep it in mind."

The words were spoken in a gentle tone, curiously agreeable, but a heavy silence fell between them. Zalia again set the rocker in motion, wishing it weren't so, yet aware that she had merely wasted her breath. That she had been right all along.

The fight for Owen Kincaid's soul had only just begun.

NINE

The years passed swiftly. Months rippled off the calendar like golden leaves in an autumn wind, and with time came immense progress.

Guthrie seemed forever in the midst of change, spreading and building and renovating, caught up in a never-ending cycle of growth. Unlike its rival, Oklahoma City, which remained essentially a cowtown, the territorial capital was a modern, highly aggressive community, with sophisticated tastes and cosmopolitan ambitions. Every home in town had electric lights, and in 1894 the horse-drawn streetcars were replaced with electric trolley cars. Dusty washboard streets gave way to broad thoroughfares paved with brick; added to an already thriving economy were a canning factory and two flour mills, a bicycle plant, and an ice cream producer. And late in the spring of 1896, barely two months past, Alexander Graham Bell's marvel of marvels had set the high wires to humming. Guthrie became the first community in Oklahoma Territory to install a telephone exchange.

The townspeople were justifiably proud of themselves, and if civic boosters tended to beat the drum a bit loudly, nobody thought them crass or uncultivated. They had every reason to brag, and that they did so with romping lusty enthusiasm seemed wholly within the spirit of the times. The territory was still young and squalling, not yet a decade old, and nowhere else could a town boast such enormous strides. Guthrie stood alone, a model of progressive thinking and cultural enlightenment.

But if industrial growth and the wizardry of science had brought the dawn of a new era, certain aspects of territorial advancement failed to keep pace. Despite the efforts of federal marshals and local peace officers, Oklahoma remained a spawning ground for outlaw gangs. Civilization butted heads with these atavistic throwbacks, men who refused to acknowledge either the rights of the people or the might of the law. Across the line, in Indian Territory, the deadly game of hide-and-seek raged unabated, and pitched battles were fought with all the savagery of Stone Age cave dwellers. While the rest of America looked on in morbid titillation, this gruesome, and sometimes unequal, fight to the death seesawed back and forth across the blackjack-studded hills of the Nations. That the lawmen suffered fewer casualties than they inflicted made for bizarre, and wholly misleading, headlines. There were scores of fledgling badmen waiting to fill the boots of every outlaw killed.

At root, the lawlessness stemmed from the rapid settlement of the wilderness, and a vanishing way of life. As farms displaced the great cattle spreads, hundreds of cowhands were thrown out of work, left to idle in saloons and contemplate the menace of railroads and sodbusters and greedy bankers. While most merely grumbled, and eventually went on to other lines of work, many of the cowhands felt society had dealt them a low blow. Misfits in a world that had passed them by, they set about righting this seeming injustice in an occupation which afforded excitement, short working hours, and incomparable wages. They became outlaws.

Several years back the Dalton Brothers had formed the first of the Oklahoma cowboy gangs. With the Nations as their hideout, they staged a spectacular string of raids, until the day they attempted to rob two banks simultaneously in Coffeyville, Kansas. When the gunsmoke settled eight men—

four citizens and four bandits—lay dead in the street. Only one of the outlaws escaped, a blooded killer named Rafe Dolan, but he had learned well riding with the Daltons. Within months of the Coffeyville massacre he had formed a gang of his own, and apparently devoted considerable time and thought to making fools of the lawmen who chased him. Over the next four years Dolan and his band robbed, killed, and pillaged with virtual impunity. In the first six months of 1896 alone they had looted a bank, robbed two trains, one carrying an Army payroll, and killed four men. And in the process none of the outlaws had received so much as a scratch.

There were other gangs raiding out of the Nations, but their leaders displayed little of the boldness and ferretlike cunning which characterized Rafe Dolan's bloody forays. Federal marshals held their own against these lesser gangs, generally killing more than they captured since the outlaws seldom surrendered without a fight. Yet, for all their grit and determination, the lawmen were singularly unsuccessful in running Dolan to earth. Like a will-o'-the-wisp, he struck fast and vanished without a trace; and in nearly five years of raiding he had outfoxed the marshals at every turn.

Aside from his remarkable elusiveness, Rafe Dolan possessed yet another distinction which set him apart from garden-variety bandits. His second-in-command was a wild young hellion by the name of Brad Kincaid. Although there were several versions of how this alliance had come about—and widespread speculation as to why Brad Kincaid had turned outlaw—no one knew precisely where it had all started. But there was no doubt whatever as to the identity of Dolan's lieutenant. Young Kincaid had been seen, gun in hand and smiling pleasantly, at the scene of countless bank robberies and train holdups. And according to wanted dodgers bearing a reasonable facsimile of his face, he had killed no fewer than three men. Probably more.

The people of Oklahoma Territory, particularly those with an ax to grind, found the situation grimly amusing and larded with irony. Always outspoken, Jake Kincaid was perhaps the staunchest advocate of law and order on either side of the political aisle. And his elder son, a deputy federal marshal, was in the unique position of hunting his own brother. As even the Kincaids' enemies were prompt to agree, life sometimes had a grisly sense of humor.

Owen Kincaid scarcely shared their amusement. Nor was he consumed with the irony of brother pitted against brother. He left such profound thoughts to streetcorner loafers and the gossip mongers. Less interested in talk than results, he devoted his energies instead to the business of burying outlaws. And as the Guthrie *Statesman* drolly remarked, it was a very brisk business indeed.

On a brassy summer day in late July, Owen gave the busybodies yet another load of fodder for their gossip mill. Seated in a buckboard, he entered town from the north and drove down Second toward the federal jail. Laid out in the wagonbed, wrapped in blankets, were the bodies of two outlaws, dead as stones and ripening fast under a prairie sun. Bloodstains, dry and crusty, covered the blankets, and a swarm of flies buzzed greedily over the dark splotches. Trailing the buckboard were four deputy marshals, and perhaps the rarest of rare sights these days—a live prisoner. Holloweyed, hands shackled behind his back, he sat slouched in the saddle, staring everywhere but at the blankets.

People along the sidewalks stopped, huddling in little knots, watching quietly as the buckboard rolled past. The prisoner was a novelty, and his mere presence whetted their curiosity. But the dead men hardly rated a second glance. Owen Kincaid hauling corpses into town had become commonplace—almost humdrum—and everyone tended to treat it with a thinly disguised yawn. Not surprisingly, then, today's load generated scant interest. It was what the citizens of Guthrie expected, and the young marshal seldom disappointed them. In slightly less than three years he had killed seven men.

This transformation of a callow youth into a hardened man-hunter had been remarkable in its swiftness. Like a sinner called to spread the gospel, Owen, from the very outset, seemingly possessed a gift for this deadlier profession. A lawman little more than a month, he had killed his first man in a backwoods shootout along the Caney River. Beside him that day were Heck Thomas and Bill Tilghman, masters of the trade indoctrinating a promising beginner. But he was a fast learner, both with a gun and in the tricks of flushing lawbreakers, and he rapidly progressed from raw tyro to skilled hunter. In a game where men seldom got a second chance, he instinctively had a knack for survival, and moreover, the lightning-fast reactions to cover whatever few mistakes he made. By the time he killed his fourth man, he'd been appointed chief deputy marshal, ranked just below Tilghman and Thomas, and given command of a squad of deputies.

Curiously, unlike some marshals, Owen found that killing became no easier as a man's score mounted. Shooting another human, whatever the circumstances, was a repugnant act, and afterward he always felt dirty, somehow unclean. But he never held back once guns were drawn. Nor did he cease firing until the outlaw was down and dead, a threat no longer. Someone had to rid the Territory of lawbreakers, and as Heck Thomas had taught him, a dead marshal in a lonely grave wouldn't get the job done. Owen took the message to heart, and never had he attempted to wound his opponent in a gunfight. He shot to kill.

The deputies who rode with Owen respected him for his cool judgment and nervy quickness in tight situations. Traits which had saved their own lives on more than one occasion. They had all seen their share of hardcases; in the Nations there was no scarcity of the breed. And yet, there was something different about the young man who led them. Never loud or swaggering, but possessed of a strange inner calm, the quiet cocksure certainty more menacing than a bald-faced threat. Almost as if he'd purged himself of fear, and somehow learned to face death with a detachment beyond other men.

Though he was a hard taskmaster, he demanded less of the deputies than he did of himself. His orders were generally in the form of a request, stated in a tone that was at once pleasant and persistently firm, and delivered with never a hint of favoritism. And that he never spoke of his brother was but another of those little mysteries they had come to accept as part of his character. A riddle of sorts, it was something to be dusted off occasionally and inspected as a child would scrutinize an old and treasured toy. But it was a curiosity best kept to oneself, and none of them had ever quite summoned the nerve to mention the Kincaid turned outlaw. A man was entitled to his private thoughts, particularly those dealing with a renegade brother, and that was how they left it.

Still, however impassive Owen appeared outwardly, time and circumstance had exacted a heavy toll. While the sun had bronzed his face, and burned his chestnut hair a lively umber-gold, he now had the steel-gray eyes of a manhunter. Luster-less and inscrutable, it was a gaze which looked at nothing yet somehow conveyed the impression that the man inside saw everything. Over the past three years he had learned a little about life and a great deal about death, and he had few illusions left intact. Instead of twenty-four, he felt forty going on a hundred, someone who saw people not as he wished them to be but simply as they were. These days unusual behavior to him was a sudden attack of constipation; otherwise life held few surprises. And the seven dead men littered along his back trail made the feeling no less intense. For all his good looks and pleasant disposition, he moved with the supple grace, restrained and economical, of a highly skilled killer of men. Which was what he had become. Perhaps the most relentless manhunter, if not the most cold-blooded, in all of Oklahoma Territory.

After depositing the prisoner at the federal jail, and the two dead men at Stroud's Funeral Parlor, Owen dismissed his deputies and went on to Evett Nix's office. Although this latest chase had consumed the better part of a fortnight, his report was held to the bare bones. Four bank robbers tracked to their hideout in the Cherokee Nation, where one was captured, two killed, and the fourth escaped. Nix had come to expect these terse reports, dealing only with essentials; despite their personal oddments, his marshals shared a common quirk. They spoke of their work in monosyllables, and of their killings little was volunteered beyond the names of the deceased. Pleased with news of the prisoner (all too often the marshals left the courts with little to do), Nix kept his single note of surprise to himself. Owen was methodical as a bloodhound on the hunt, and he appeared visibly embarrassed that one of the gang had escaped. Normally he and his deputies brought them all in, and with rare exceptions, the outlaws had less need of a jail cell than an undertaker.

Upon leaving the marshal's office, Owen crossed town to the Kincaid home on Noble Avenue. While he still shared the house with his father, they seldom saw one another. Their paths veered off in opposite directions these days, and Jake's many business interests left him little time for family life. All of which suited Owen perfectly. The old man was like a bulldog in his single-mindedness; on those occasions when they were together he harped incessantly on the virtues of a career in business. After nearly three years, he still refused to accept as final what he termed "this nonsense of wearing a badge." Short of disowning Owen, he had tried every trick in the book to reverse the situation. And far from diminishing, these family skirmishes had intensified with time. Jake fancied himself an irresistible force, and though his son easily qualified as an immovable object, he felt confident of winning out in the long run. Perseverance and constant badgering, to judge by his actions, were capable of pulverizing stone walls. Not to mention recalcitrant young hardheads who ignored the wisdom of their elders.

Julia Webb was just as bad. In what Owen viewed as the

oddest conspiracy ever hatched, she took up where his father left off. Hers was a more subtle campaign, employing feminine wiles, but it was nonetheless dogged. She inveigled, schemed and taunted, and in a coy little speech that by now had become her litany, gave him to understand that she would die an old maid before marrying a lawman. Strangely enough, she made no pretense of hiding her affection, and with all the guile of a temple virgin, she readily used her body as bait. Yet, for all their probing kisses and groping hands, he was allowed only certain liberties. Like a finely adjusted timepiece, she was able to regulate her passion to the exact moment of surrender, and many nights she had left him in such agony that he could scarcely walk.

Several times over the past couple of years they had called it quits, assuring one another that the impasse was beyond resolution. Once Julia had even begun seeing other men, and the Webb household quickly became overrun with freshly barbered suitors bearing waxen smiles and wilted bouquets. But these separations invariably ran their course in a brief while, and through some alchemy neither of them fully comprehended, Julia and Owen were drawn together again no better off than when they had parted.

Owen presumed that their seesaw affair was what the poets called love—if suffering was the criterion, then it qualified on all counts. Yet there were aspects of Julia's nature which gave him pause, if not doubt. So far as he could see, she was never loath to accept the martyr's burden. In some past incarnation she might willingly have flung herself upon the cross, arms outstretched, begging for the spike. Logic rarely fazed her, and like all practicing martyrs, once she had committed herself to a stand it was as if her mind had been cast in concrete and fixed for all time. Her one great and sustaining strength was that she would not retreat. Nor would she compromise. Having taken her stand, however preposterous, she refused to budge.

On deeper reflection, this thought gave rise to still another observation, perhaps more sardonic than the first. He saw in himself many of the same traits he ascribed to her (although hardly so immune to logic). And it occurred to him that they were bound together not so much by love as by a common affliction of the soul. What the preachers dispensed in the guise of brotherhood and eternal salvation. The thing called g-u-i-l-t. It made a man wonder, not just about women and their oddball notions, but about many things.

Early that evening, after soaking away the afternoon in a hot tub, he called on Julia. She made a big fuss over him, which was all part of her repertoire, and following a decent interval of small talk with her parents, he was allowed to lure her out to the porch swing. The darkness was warm and sticky, and the swing creaked like a coffin lid, but they were at one another in an instant. Whenever he returned from a hunt it was always the same; a brief spell in which they declared a truce and attempted to devour each other in a rush of longing. But kissing and fondling quickly aroused lustier instincts, and before long Julia somehow managed to get him at arm's length. Then, according to the rules of the game, a truce was called after which she needled him awhile, and as a final offering he was allowed a good-night sampler.

Tonight she was no less obvious than other nights, merely less subtle. Her hand rested lightly on his arm, and her voice seemed unsteady, vaguely alarmed. "Owen, those men—the ones you brought in today—were they part of Brad's gang?"

He sighed wearily. "No, Julie, they weren't. It was another bunch altogether."

"But they did try to kill you, didn't they?"

"Couldn't we talk about something else? You can read all about it in the papers tomorrow."

She ignored the jab. "And if you ever corner Brad's gang they'll try to kill you—"

"Yes, I suppose they will."

"—your own brother will try to kill you, won't he?"

It was hitting below the belt, but he had to admire her

ingenuity, and that artless note of concern. All else having failed, she would now use his brother, just as she had used the old man. A whip to beat him into submission, only this time she had added thorns to the lash.

He barely heard the rest of it. Back in some inviolable corner of his mind he stood off and watched, almost withdrawn. And as he gazed at the man and woman seated on the swing he wondered why they flagellated one another, and if, after all, they were merely kindred sadists, indulging the other's need to be hurt. Slowly, as if it were some fragile artifact unearthed where least expected, he examined the thought while her voice droned on in a dull and distant buzz.

The phaeton rounded a corner, pulled by a pair of high-stepping bays, and proceeded at a steady clip along Harrison Avenue. Unlike most carriages, it had a driver perched atop a front seat, doors, gilt-spoked wheels, a folding top, and a rear seat for passengers. There wasn't another rig like it in Guthrie, and everyone in town recognized it on sight.

Basking in the sun, Jake luxuriated in the back seat. He was dressed in a somber broadcloth suit, conservative but expensive, with a diamond stickpin in his cravat, a gold-headed cane in his hands, and English boots polished to a luster propped up on the foot rail. A huge black cigar jutted from his mouth, and like some royal personage accustomed to stares, he ignored completely the passersby who stopped on the sidewalk to gawk. He looked prosperous and in good health, which he was, and a trifle smug, if somewhat preoccupied. His thoughts were on the meeting ahead, and had he allowed himself, the faint smile might well have broadened into a smirk. It promised to be a fine day. A milestone, no less, and he meant to savor every moment to the fullest.

Crossing the intersection at Second, the phaeton rolled to a halt in front of the Palace Hotel. Jake alighted from the carriage and stood there a minute surveying the building. He deemed it entirely fitting that the meeting was to be held in *his* hotel. There wasn't a man in the Territory who had been more instrumental in bringing this day about, and however pompous the thought, it was a blunt and irrefutable truth. Cane tucked under his arm, puffing clouds of smoke, he nodded to the doorman and strode briskly into the lobby.

Bypassing the elevator cage, he mounted the steps to the mezzanine and walked directly to a small banquet hall. As he came through the door a silence fell over the room, and he noted with satisfaction that his arrival had been timed perfectly. Already gathered were the leaders of both parties, and politicians to the last, they had split into factional groups along opposite walls. Acknowledging greetings from both sides, Jake moved down the aisle separating them to a speaker's table at the front of the room. He placed his hat and cane on the table, then turned to face them. Clearly, from his manner, the meeting had been called to order, and the men made their way to some dozen chairs which were arranged in rows before the table. He stood quietly, waiting for them to get settled, and at last, when everyone was seated, he favored them with a benign smile.

"Gentlemen, I'm glad to see you could make it. And I appreciate everybody turning out this way. Just goes to show that the spirit of harmony isn't dead after all."

His remark was greeted with awkward silence on one side of the room and cold stares on the other. Whatever their party affiliation, most of the men present were in his debt, either politically or financially. Those who weren't, perhaps four out of the lot, feared him nonetheless. His power was an omnipresent force, and over the years he had ruined bigger and wealthier men than many of those here today.

The smile faded, and he resumed speaking. "I take it everybody read yesterday's newspaper, so I won't waste your time rehashing the details. Let's just say Washington has handed us the whole kit and caboodle on a silver platter, and leave it at that. The reason I called this meetin' was to decide what happens next. Now I know there's no love lost where some of you are concerned, but just to be blunt about it, the time for fightin' among ourselves is long gone. Starting today, even if it sticks in your craw, we've got to join forces and get on with the business of statehood. And in case anyone missed the point, I'm talkin' about joint statehood."

He held up a gnarled finger. "One state, gentlemen! Oklahoma."

A low murmur swept over the seated men, and several muffled cries of dissent could be heard. Finally, Alec Brokaw, leader of the opposition party, cleared his throat and waited a moment for the chatter to subside.

"Kincaid, it seems to me you're sort of whistling in the dark. Everybody in this room favors single statehood. But that doesn't make us bosom buddies. And the fact that Congress finally got off its duff sure as hell doesn't put us on the same side of the fence. Not by a longshot."

Jake regarded him with a tolerant little chuckle. "Frankly, Brokaw, I would've been surprised if you thought otherwise. Trouble is, you've still got your mind in a rut. You're talkin' strictly politics, and I'm talkin' about a big juicy pie waitin' to be split up."

"Horsefeathers! I suppose you're gonna tell us Cassius Barnes won't be appointed governor next year."

"He's a lead-pipe cinch, take my word for it. But you're still talkin' politics."

"Come off it, Kincaid, who do you think you're kidding? You've got your eye on both territories, and there's not a man here that believes different. You can talk till you're blue in the face and it'll still come out the same way—politics."

A spark flashed in Jake's eyes; then his gaze narrowed and the look became veiled. "Brokaw, one of these days you'll put your foot in your mouth and somebody with enough muscle will shove it down your throat. Today might even be the day."

Alec Brokaw started out of his chair, sputtering gruffly, but Jake restrained him with an upraised hand. "Now simmer down and pay attention for a minute. I didn't call you in here to trade insults. And if you're lookin' for trouble, just remember I know where all the skeletons are buried. Especially yours, hotshot."

The room went still as a crypt, and after a moment of indecision, Brokaw eased back in his chair. Jake nodded. "That's better. And just so you'll know I'm playin' it square, I'll admit that this does involve politics. The point I was tryin' to make is that it's not straight-line party politics."

Someone toward the rear spoke up. "Would you mind explaining the distinction?"

"Wouldn't mind at all. What makes this time different is that we're not fightin' among ourselves about who gets to be governor, or which town gets the capital. We're fightin' the tribes, and it's us against them. Statehood's coming whether they like it or not. The only thing left to be decided is who runs the show. Don't forget, their vote will count just as much as ours in a general election. And if we can't get our heads together, then we'll wind up with the capital in Tahlequah and some red monkey sittin' in the governor's chair."

Brokaw grumped something under his breath, and shifted around in his chair. "What about business deals in the Nations? Everybody knows you're already in there with both feet. Are you telling us we're all gonna share and share alike?"

"That's the pie I was talkin' about a minute ago. As for share and share alike, I'd have to turn thumbs down. Everybody will have an equal chance, and a man can bite off whatever he's big enough to chew. But after that it'll come down to which hog roots the hardest."

He paused, eyeing them with a stony expression. "I guess that sort of brings us around to the whole point of this meetin'. There's a hundred fortunes to be made over in the Nations, maybe more. It's richer in timber and coal and just about anything you want to name except grass. But if it's us that gets the goodies instead of them red heathens, then we're all gonna have to start rowin' the same boat. Leastways until we're admitted as a state and got Oklahoma runnin' to suit ourselves."

Every word Jake uttered was the truth, and not a man in the room doubted it. This day had been a long time in coming, but never had the future looked brighter. Politicians and money barons alike were rubbing their hands in anticipation, and all that remained was the mechanics of dividing the spoils. Their friends in Congress had arranged it all quite nicely, and if slow to act, had at last thrown open the doors to Indian Territory.

The Dawes Commission, empaneled by presidential order some three years back, had met with a cold reception from the Five Civilized Tribes. The commission's first task was to convince the red men that their interests would be best served by abolishing tribal government in return for full citizenship within the republic. They were told, with considerable earnestness, that this would afford them equality before the courts, voting rights, freedom of speech and worship, and free schooling. But the Indians had been listening to the white man's specious promises for nearly a century, and based on experience, they had every reason to doubt the faith of the government. Not surprisingly, they were reluctant to exchange independence for the questionable privilege of citizenship. Opposition was particularly bitter among Indian aristocrats who owned large landholdings, but even the lowliest tribesmen preferred the old ways to the white man's road.

Conferences were held time and again with tribal officials, and after each session the Indian leaders met in intertribal councils. Yet the result never varied. Over the period 1893–1895 tribal representatives voted repeatedly not to accept the government's offer. Thoroughly frustrated, the Commission asserted in its annual reports that the situation in Indian Territory was intolerable, and that without a change in the status of the Five Civilized Tribes any hope for progress was permanently blocked. On that note, the negotiations ground to a halt.

Behind the scenes, Jake and his political cohorts had been active in the halls of Congress. At first their efforts to undermine the Indians had been insidious, chipping away at the edges, just as a river at floodtide erodes the shoreline. Within the last year, however, their efforts had become bolder and more insistent. Settlement of Oklahoma Territory, they declared, had left the Nations entirely surrounded by whites, which made joint statehood the only rational choice. Moreover, the number of whites living within the Nations now exceeded Indians by a ratio of three to one, and the inequities they suffered under the red man's domination could be corrected only with the abolition of tribal government. Refusal of the Indians to negotiate, they pointed out, was not only detrimental to the good of the nation, but at odds with the goals of influential parties in Oklahoma Territory. Along with the largesse distributed by certain Washington lobbyists, it proved a telling argument.

Yesterday, shortly before noon, word had flashed over the telegraph, and it was everything Jake and his cronies had worked toward. Congress had enacted legislation directing the Commission to make up rolls of every man, woman, and child in Indian Territory. Ostensibly, this was a preparatory step to the allotment of lands in severalty, but as everyone was quick to recognize, it was also the first step in the dissolution of the Five Civilized Tribes. Flying in the face of both treaties and conscience, Congress had settled the issue in the traditional manner. And the red man bit the dust again.

But in the banquet hall of the Palace Hotel there was no lament for the noble savage. Jake spoke of past difficulties in dealing with tribal councils and the ease with which individual Indians could be manipulated. The men gathered there listened closer as he warmed to the subject and told them how the Nations' resources could be exploited—for the red man's own good, of course! And then the leaders of both parties edged forward on their chairs, solemnly attentive, as he slowly, confident now of their support, began to speak of money.

There was a dusty coolness about the autumn nights, but from sunrise to sunset the earth still trembled in a tawny glare. Although a few leaves had mellowed in color, and the grass was crisper underfoot, today was no different. The glazy afternoon shed splinters of sunlight across the land as Owen dismounted on the slope of a small knoll. He tied the reins to a tree limb, wary of taking the horse any closer, and moved off through a stand of blackjacks. Alert but unhurried, he worked his way downhill to the forward edge of the treeline. Screened by the leafy shadows, he hunkered down on his bootheels, arms crossed over his knees, and began a systematic inch-by-inch examination of the clearing below.

A crude but stoutly built log cabin stood in the center of the clearing, out in the open, where it would be difficult to approach without being spotted. Smoke sifted skyward from the mud chimney, yet there was no sign of activity. Apparently whoever was down there was staying indoors. He scanned the clearing again, searching carefully for any telltale indication of trouble. The corral out back held only one horse, a chocolate-spotted pinto, and so far as he could see, there were no dogs around to sound the warning. A shallow creek skirted the cabin on the west, then curved gently along the front of the clearing. That was a minor obstacle though, almost bone dry this time of year. He could take the stream in a single jump, but crossing the open space beyond would leave him naked for several seconds. Not a pleasant thought.

Still, it was a calculated risk, unavoidable. Just as being here alone, without deputies to back his play, was flirting with the odds. Foolhardy, perhaps. Maybe even useless. But something he could avoid no longer.

Out of habit, he gave himself another minute to study the layout. Everything seemed to jibe, but he mentally ticked off what he'd been told. A lone cabin on Sand Creek. Some ten miles northwest of Pa-hus-ka in the Osage Nation. Where the creek made a slow dogleg to the southeast. As directions went, it wasn't much, not in this tangle of hills and crooked streams and wooded undergrowth. All the same, sketchy as it was, the pieces seemed to fit. And while he didn't exactly relish the idea, there was one surefire way to find out.

He stood, drawing his pistol, and stepped clear of the treeline. Taking his time, one eye glued to the cabin, he moved down the hill and jumped the creek. Waiting, he let his heartbeat settle back to a steady pace and gave his nerves a moment longer to come unjangled. Then, quiet as woodsmoke, he cat-footed across the open ground. A deafening stillness hung over the clearing, and it seemed impossible that he'd gone undetected. But nothing moved, and seconds later, without a whisper of sound, he made it to the corner of the cabin. Listening a moment, puzzled by the eerie silence, he dropped to one knee and leveled his pistol on the doorway.

"Hello, the house! Anybody home?"

Grace Sixkiller Kincaid stepped through the door, and turned to face him. Her expression revealed nothing, but he suddenly felt very foolish and childishly inept.

"You can put your gun away, Owen. Brad isn't here."

A bit flustered, he smiled weakly and jammed the Colt into its holster. "Guess you knew it was me all the time, didn't you?"

She nodded, remote and poised, dark gaze tinged with mockery. "I saw you on the hill. But you did well enough for a *tibo*."

It was the scorn word for white man, delivered with an inflection that stung. "Yeah, I suppose you're right. Must've had all you could do to keep from laughin'."

His remark fell flat. She thawed none at all, merely staring at him impassively. After a moment of chilled silence, he went on lamely.

"Look, I'm sorry I came sneakin' in on you like that. But I had no way of knowin' who was in the house."

"I understand. You thought to surprise your brother and you captured only his woman."

"Grace, I swear to you, that's not the way it was at all. You likely won't believe me, but the reason I'm here is to see you."

She appeared skeptical. "Why would you want to see me?"

"Listen, I feel a little skittish standin' around in the open like this. Could we talk inside?"

Without a word she turned and entered the cabin. Owen trailed after her, pausing just inside the doorway, and examined the single room. It was little better than he'd expected. A battered table and chairs, an open fireplace for cooking, roughhewn shelves for storage, and an ancient brass bed jammed up in the far corner. Still, it was spotlessly clean, smelled of fresh air and strange spices, and had about it a look of cozy warmth. Obviously it suited Brad, and with Grace to fetch and carry, he doubtless lived better than most men on the owlhoot.

Grace waited till he'd finished his inspection, then indicated a chair. He dropped his hat on the table, turning the chair to face the door, and she took a seat across from him. Strained as the circumstances were, he found himself admiring her delicate copper-skinned beauty, and her almost regal composure. She accepted the look, prepared to wait him out, and returned his gaze evenly. They sat there for some time, simply staring at one another, and at last, feeling slightly ridiculous, he looked away. A moment passed as he collected his wits, then he straightened in his chair, himself again.

"Let me ask you something, Grace. Do you think Brad's happy livin' the way he does, always on the run, being hunted?"

"How can a wife answer for her husband? He lives the way he wants to live."

"What about you? Wouldn't you change it if you could?"

"You ask me to judge him, and I will not do that."

Owen grunted, aware that he'd taken the wrong tack. Clearly, she thought Brad had hung the moon; trying to ease around her wouldn't work. He'd just have to say it straight out.

"The law will catch him sooner or later. You know that, don't you? And what do you think will happen then?"

She gave him a quick, intent look. "You are the law, so I will ask you. What would happen?"

"I'll tell you, Grace. Plain and simple. All he's got waitin' for him is a bullet. That or a stiff rope and a short drop."

Her words were soft, almost inaudible, so quiet he had to strain to hear. "Would you kill your own brother?"

"Is that what you think?" His voice was gruff, defensive. "That I'd just walk in here and shoot him down?"

"What would you have me think? You come here with a gun in your hand. It is known that you have killed many men. Would one more trouble you so much?"

His shoulders slumped, and he slowly shook his head. "I guess you've got reason to suspect me. But just think about it a minute. Why would I come here alone? If I meant to kill him I would've brought help."

Her eyes suddenly widened with alarm, and for a mere instant her composure cracked. "How did you find this place?"

"The Light Horse in Pa-hus-ka told me."

"I don't believe you. Osage police would never betray Brad. They know he is my man, and besides, they have no use for white law."

"That's true. But they didn't betray Brad. They know I'm his brother." He leaned forward, curiously earnest, almost as if he were sharing a secret with her. "They also know that the Light Horse of many tribes give me information."

"I still don't believe you." She was visibly startled, but trying desperately to conceal it. "Why would the Light Horse favor you when they hate *tibo* marshals?"

"Because I am the Indian's friend." There was a simple

dignity to his words, somehow beyond dissent. "I look upon all men as the same, red or white. Except for lawbreakers."

"Like your brother!"

Owen met her fiery look, but the admission came hard. "Like my brother."

"Then I am to believe that you come with peace in your heart and a gun in your hand?"

He kneaded the back of his neck, stung by her ridicule, yet determined to hold his temper. "And I ask you again, why else would I come alone?"

Wavering, frightened by her own uncertainty, her voice lashed out. "Do you know why Brad lives the way he does? Why he robs only banks and trains? Do you hear me, Owen, only *banks* and *trains*?"

"Yes, I do know. I've known for some time."

She blinked. "You have?"

"Why should that surprise you? He was my brother long before he became your husband." Frowning, he sighed heavily and knuckled back his mustache. "Brad thinks he's getting back at the old man. Every time he pulls off a holdup he thinks that makes Pa lose face with his banker friends and the railroad crowd. But he's wrong, Grace, dead wrong. Pa doesn't even know he exists. And unless you help me that's how Brad will wind up. Dead."

In a single shock of emotion, she grasped everything the words were meant to tell her. It was understanding and compassion, acknowledgment of a father's cruelty and one brother's love for another. Her eyes went dark and moist, suddenly defenseless.

"You want him to surrender."

"That's right. But more than what I want, it's what he must do." Owen fixed her with a look of stark intensity, cold and hard yet somehow beseeching. "The other gangs are wiped out, Grace. Those that aren't dead are either in prison or on the run. Dolan's bunch is next, and we'll come after him with every man we've got. I don't think I have to tell you what

Brad's chances would be if he's caught with Dolan. You're the only one left who can convince him that he's got to turn himself in. He'll be alive, Grace. And after a while we'll find some way to get him paroled, maybe even pardoned."

The tension seemed to drain out of him, and he slumped back in his chair. "I'm asking you to trust me, and to talk some sense into Brad before it's too late."

She studied him for several moments, torn between an acute sense of loyalty and his unassailable logic. It was like an apparition out of some recurring bad dream, only it was very real, a nightmare she had lived with for nearly three years. Where reason had been displaced by hate, and love was a passionless rutting without meaning or memory. At last, feigning hope where none existed, she spoke.

"I will try, Owen. When he returns I will talk with him, and tell him all you have said."

"When he returns? Does that mean he's off somewhere with Dolan right now?"

"I don't know." Her voice trailed off wistfully. "Brad tells me little of his plans."

"Yeah, that figures. Far back as I remember he's had a case of lockjaw." Owen took his hat from the table and climbed to his feet. "If you have any luck tell him I said to turn himself in to the Light Horse in Pa-hus-ka. They'll get word to me, and I'll come get him. That way nobody will get any fancy ideas about collectin' the bounty money."

"Where life has no value, death has a price."

"How's that?"

"Nothing. Just something Brad said to me after he saw his picture on a wanted poster. He thought it was funny."

"It's funny, all right. 'Bout like a sharp stick in the eye." She looked away, and a moment of uncomfortable silence elapsed before he crammed his hat on his head. "Guess I better make tracks. If you need any help, or—well, anything, just send word. And keep your chin up, we'll work something out."

She nodded weakly, eyes still downcast. Just for an instant she seemed frail and vulnerable, a small doll-like girl struggling against tears, and he had an overpowering urge to reach out and touch her. Instead, smothering the temptation, he wheeled away and walked quickly to the door. He hesitated there for several seconds, listening closely as he inspected the clearing. Then, satisfied nothing had changed, he stepped outside and hurried toward the creek.

"Owen!"

Something in her voice stopped him, a tiny cry of helplessness, and he turned back. She was standing in the doorway, a coppery waif with a brave smile.

"Thank you, Owen."

He waved, words failing, then spun about and headed across the clearing. She was still there, framed in the doorway, as the sun dipped low and he vanished into the trees on the side of the hill.

Rafe Dolan stepped into the alley, guns drawn, and turned to face the street. Tulsa Jack and Dynamite Dick flanked him, taking their assigned positions to cover the gang's withdrawal. Lugging saddlebags stuffed with cash, Red Buck, Little Bill, and Bitter Creek hurried toward the end of the alley where Arkansas Tom held the horses. Brad Kincaid was the last man out of the bank. He slammed the door and took off running as Dolan and his rear guard backed away from the street.

The holdup had taken less than ten minutes, and gone off with clockwork precision. But this was the crucial moment. While robbing banks was simple enough, the getaway was another story altogether. If a job went sour it invariably happened outside, after the bank had been looted, and aroused citizens had a habit of turning the street into a shooting gallery. Like any good tactician, Dolan covered the likely trouble spots with his best men. Which, in this case, meant himself and Brad Kincaid. On all jobs it was a cardinal rule that he would be the first man out the door and young Kincaid would be the last. With front and rear protected, things generally went off without a hitch.

Today was no exception. The afternoon was warm and lazy, and the town of Pineville, just across the line in Missouri, drowsed peacefully under a September sun. Still, while the robbery had gone undetected thus far, there was little time to waste. Within a matter of moments the alarm would be sounded, and a hastily organized posse was almost certain to give pursuit. Nowadays there was the added hazard of telegraph, and between some towns, long-distance telephone. Unlike times past, the gang often found lawmen swarming across the countryside all along its line of escape. Which not only narrowed the margin for error, but made simple bad luck a factor to be reckoned with. Scurrying back to the Nations was no longer kid's play. It had become, instead, a highly refined version of cat and mouse, with the law waiting to pounce in every direction.

Once he had the gang mounted, Dolan led them down a back street at a dust-choked gallop. Swerving through a vacant lot, they hit Main Street at the south end of town and clattered across a wooden bridge spanning a small creek. Behind they heard shouts, and caught a glimpse of an angry mob gathering outside the bank. With luck, they had a half hour headstart before the sheriff restored order and swore in a posse. But the dicey part was behind them—and now it became a matter of fast horses and foxy moves. Dolan led them south for a couple of miles, then they split into pairs and scattered to the four winds. An hour later they assembled some distance to the west, on Elk Creek, and thundered off toward the Cherokee Nation, less than five miles from their rendezvous spot.

The men were laughing and playful now, like small boys who had pulled some monstrous prank and successfully eluded a switching. Dolan still rode out front a ways, and while he understood their need to let off steam, he set a fast pace nonetheless. Wary as an old wolf, constantly flicking glances at their backtrail, he found it impossible to unwind until they had crossed the border. This tireless vigilance, mixed with a healthy respect for lawmen, was the reason he'd lived to be an old wolf. And unlike most outlaws, who viewed their profession with a degree of fatalism, he had no intention of dying with his boots on. That was for suckers and superstitious dimdots, and he meant to live a long while yet. Longer than anyone would have guessed, given the odds.

That he had defied both time and the odds was hardly open to question. The Dalton Brothers had lasted a mere fifteen months before being wiped out in Coffeyville. By comparison, Dolan and his gang had ravaged the border country for almost five years now. And never once had their lives been in serious jeopardy.

Aside from brutish courage and a willingness to kill, the members of Dolan's gang had contributed little to this spectacular record. They were emotionally stunted men, vengeful and reckless, superb haters but not a mental wizard in the bunch. With the exception of Brad Kincaid, they gloried in their nicknames—Red Buck, Tulsa Jack, Dynamite Dick—devoting considerable thought to the selection of a *nom de guerre*. This was their mark in life, a pathetic, if sometimes terrifying, badge of distinction in a world which had branded them outcasts.

It took a strong man, someone with brains and nerve, to hold them in line. Rafe Dolan imposed his will not by force (though he was a deadly enough killer) but rather by cunning and a steel-trap mind. He had started with a band of congenital misfits, converted them into a fierce, tightly knit gang, and never for a moment had he let them forget that it was his savvy which kept them alive. Every job was planned with meticulous detail; the men were drilled until they were letter perfect in their assignments; and in execution, the holdups were staged with a Teutonic sense of orderliness and precision. Anyone who got in the way was dispatched with an impersonal, businesslike efficiency, but Dolan's raids were characterized by the fact that his gang seldom got itself boxed into a gunfight with the law. He was slippery as an eel, elusive as a puff of smoke, and seemingly vanished from the face of the earth after every job. His men looked upon him with a touch of awe, and the law considered him something of a natural phenomenon, like a thunderbolt.

In appearance, there was nothing imposing about Dolan. He was lean and stringy, eyes marled with distrust, his skin seared by years of wind and sun. But he had no concept of morality, which left him with an odd and somewhat unblemished cynicism, like that of a crafty savage. And it served him well. In a world of robber barons and political buccaneers, he had found his niche. He robbed the rich to aid the poor, and since charity started at home, it seemed only fitting that those he aided were himself and his gang.

This self-serving philanthropy, conducted at the point of a gun, was the very thing that had brought Brad Kincaid into the fold. Dolan had the knack for spotting a fellow malcontent; the youngster practically leaped at the chance to join up with Oklahoma Territory's boldest desperado. While the excitement and danger had vast appeal for Brad, the gang leader saw in him an attribute which separated crackerjack outlaws from penny-ante badmen. Young Kincaid hated the rich.

In itself this was hardly an uncommon trait. Nearly everyone in the territory, sodbuster and cowhand and ribbon clerk alike, bore some grudge against the upper crust. But Brad's hate was virulent and obsessive, the hate of a man who has turned on his own kind. It stemmed from the breach with his father, and every time he hit a bank or an express car it was as if he had struck another blow at the old man. The money meant nothing, for in a very real sense, he was waging his own personal vendetta.

Dolan understood such things, and he had a certain genius for channeling the hate of others in a way which benefited him most. At first, Brad was needlessly reckless, almost as if he purposely courted danger. But with time he matured a bit (though he never quite lost that rash, foolhardy streak) and Dolan groomed the youngster to act as his right hand. They worked well together, the caution of one complementing the daring of the other, and Dolan had never had reason to regret the decision. Nor did the rest of the gang begrudge his choice. Of them all, Brad was perhaps the most fatalistic; he could be found in the thick of things, seemingly heedless of the danger to himself, whenever trouble started. This, along with his willingness to use a gun and his remarkable speed, earned him the respect of the other men. They thought him a little squirrelly, if not downright crazy, but they shared a high regard for his deadliness in a fight. Despite his youth, he was considered the wild man of the bunch.

Dolan, who considered himself an astute judge of men and their foibles, found Brad to be an intriguing paradox. The youngster robbed and killed, displaying all the conscience of an aroused scorpion, yet he was almost prudish in his private life. Apart from his drinking bouts with the gang (and in that Brad consistently put the others under the table) he had never taken part in the marathon orgies staged in various whorehouses. After every raid he returned to his squaw in the Osage Nation, and apparently played the role of dutiful husband. Which in itself posed yet a deeper enigma, for he seldom spoke of the girl unless drunk, and his comments then were generally abusive and filled with scorn. Strangely, he seemed bottled up with guilt. As if he were obligated to her for some past wrong, and able to square the account only by remaining faithful.

Upon reflection, Dolan concluded that the youngster had probably used Grace Sixkiller in some way. Perhaps as a weapon against his father. And now, snared in the remnant of whatever morality he once possessed, he felt honor bound to uphold the bargain. All of which seemed a trifle absurd. Dolan preferred stupid romping women of animal gusto and brassy laughter. The kind who made no demands (aside from the wages of sin) and were quickly forgotten once the pole went limber. That young Kincaid had saddled himself with a hair shirt fairly boggled the mind. Still, it made for interesting speculation. And a man never knew about such things. Somewhere down the line it might come in handy.

Shortly before noon, the day after the Pineville holdup, Dolan called a halt along the banks of the Caney River. There the loot was counted, amounting to some sixteen thousand, and Brad took his split. The rest of the men were content to wait until they reached the hideout. Then, rolling in greenbacks and with no thought for tomorrow, the celebration would start. What they didn't squander on women and whiskey Dolan would win from them at poker, until all that remained was a lame pecker and a monumental hangover. But it was easy come, easy go, a fast life and a barrel of laughs. And the sooner they went broke, the sooner the boss would lead them on another raid. So it all evened out in the end.

Dolan walked off a ways with Brad, and briefly outlined what he had in mind for the next job. A plump little bank in Oswego, just across the border in Kansas. As usual, they left it that one of the men would come to fetch Brad a couple of days before the raid. By then the details would be worked out, and they could begin drilling the men in their assignments. Tulsa Jack Blake, who scouted the jobs in advance, likely wouldn't sober up till the end of the month, so Brad could expect word sometime afterward. Probably the first week in October.

When Brad rode off, headed in a beeline toward Pa-hus-ka, Dolan stood for a moment watching him. After stuffing a wad of Climax in his jaw, he grunted to himself, and shook his head with a wry smile. Besides being a damned queer bird, it occurred to him that the kid was about the most unlikely outlaw he'd ever seen. And for all the wrong reasons.

He splattered a rock with a juicy squirt from his quid, and turned back to the men. Almost as an afterthought, he wondered about Kincaid's minx-eyed little squaw. Whatever she had, it was powerful stuff. Had to be! Otherwise the kid would never have got his head screwed on backward.

Early the next afternoon Rafe Dolan forded the creek and rode into the yard. A huge black kettle hung suspended above a fire at the side of the cabin and Grace was bent over a wash-tub scrubbing a shirt. She had seen him on the hill several minutes before, but she hadn't stopped work nor had she given any sign that he was welcome. The few times Dolan had been here in the past she was always civil, and for Brad's sake, went out of her way not to offend the man. Yet she couldn't bring herself to like him, and through some darker instinct, she knew that he was never to be trusted.

Only after Dolan reined his horse to a halt did she straighten from the washtub. She was perspiring freely from hard scrubbing and the heat of the fire; wisps of damp hair hung down over her forehead and the sleeves of her dress were rolled above the elbow. As if unaware of her appearance, there was no pretense of making herself presentable. Tossing the shirt in a rinse tub, she wiped her hands on her apron and walked to the front of the cabin. Dolan was rolling himself a smoke and he glanced up as she stopped a few paces away.

"Howdy, Grace." He smiled, licking the cigarette paper, and deftly sealed it with his fingers. "Brad around?"

"I'm sorry, you just missed him." Her voice was polite but toneless. "He rode into Pa-hus-ka right after dinner."

"Any idea when he'll be back?"

"I don't know. Before supper, maybe sooner."

Dolan struck a match on the saddlehorn and lit his cigarette. "Guess you wouldn't have no objection to me waitin' for him, would you?"

Her expression was neutral, almost indifferent. "I'll heat some coffee. If you're hungry, I have a few leftovers."

"Much obliged. I already ate but the coffee sounds good."

As she turned toward the cabin, Dolan stepped down out of the saddle and left his horse ground reined. Following her inside, it occurred to him that the girl would have made a good poker player. She had no use for him, and he'd known it since the day they met, but never once had she betrayed herself by word or look. Nonetheless, she was afraid of him (that was something she hadn't been able to hide) and as he equated fear with respect, he wasn't affronted by her attitude. So long as she kept her place, the fact that she disliked him was a matter of supreme unimportance. And yet, he wondered.

If all that were so, then why was he here today?

Grace threw fresh wood into the fireplace and set the coffee pot to heat. Dolan took a chair at the table, watching her, and knew she wouldn't speak again unless he spoke first. In that way, he'd always thought the squaws had it over white women. Never pestered a man with a lot of senseless talk or tried to impress him with how bright they were. Just fetched and carried and looked after his needs. And while he couldn't quite admit it to himself, that was part of the reason he'd ridden all the way from Ingalls. Not that he had any special interest in squaws, no more so than he did for women in general. But he was curious about this squaw, and most especially, the hold she had over Brad Kincaid. Oddly enough, and he'd given it considerable thought since yesterday, the idea rankled him. Nothing he couldn't live with but enough that he had trumped up an excuse to make his visit appear legitimate. And found himself puzzling on it all the more as he watched her move around the cabin.

After the coffee boiled, she filled a cup and placed it in front of him. She still hadn't spoken, and unless he stopped her now, he knew she would simply return to her washing and leave him to his own company. Puffing on his cigarette, he inhaled deeply and tilted back in his chair.

"I seem to recollect that you make good coffee."

She shrugged. "It is nothing. The pot does the work."

"All the same, there aren't many Injuns ever get the hang of it. Not the ones I've known, leastways."

She let the remark pass, and he chuckled. "No offense intended. I never seen a white woman that could work deerskin. So I guess it all evens out in the long run." She merely nodded, and after another pull on his cigarette he frowned thoughtfully. "You say Brad went into Pawhuska. Got business in town, does he?"

"Brad often goes to Pa-hus-ka." Her inflection on the word was Osage, subtly heavy, almost a rebuff. "I think today he went for supplies."

"That a fact? Sounds like you're not just exactly sure."

Grace was very sure, and just as determined to keep the actual reason to herself. Brad had gone into Pa-hus-ka to talk with the Light Horse Police. Upon hearing of Owen's visit he had become enraged, damning his brother as a liar, unable to believe that the Light Horse would disclose his hideout to anyone. If it was a trick, some clever attempt on Owen's part to force his surrender, then they would simply find another cabin elsewhere. But if it was true, then they were no longer safe in the Osage Nation. One way or another, he meant to settle the matter today. And Grace never for a moment considered revealing any of this. Since yesterday she had become convinced that Brad had less to fear from his brother than he did from Rafe Dolan. That the gang leader had arrived unexpectedly, acting so strange, somehow different than he had in the past, merely heightened her concern.

Again she shrugged, feigning indifference. "Brad comes and goes as he pleases. I do not question his reasons."

"Maybe you should." Dolan flipped his cigarette into the fireplace and gave her a sly look. "I hear tell there's lots of good-lookin' squaws in Pawhuska."

She smiled, mocking him. "In that case Brad might be later than I thought. Instead of waiting, perhaps you would be better off just to leave a message."

"No, there's no message. Something came up and I need to talk to him about our next job." He studied her a moment, wondering if she was as calm as she appeared, then he grunted. "You don't believe me, do you? What I said about another woman?"

"There is nothing to believe or disbelieve. I know Brad."

"Think you've got him tamed and broke to halter, is that it?"

"Not the way you mean. But I make him happy."

"C'mon, gimme a straight answer. You tryin' to tell me what you've got is so good he wouldn't go lookin' elsewhere?"

"You can answer your own question, Mr. Dolan. Does Brad go to bed with other women in Ingalls?"

"Always wondered about that." Dolan suddenly became aware of the musky scent of her body and the curve of her breasts outlined against her dress. The gingham was damp with perspiration, plastered to her skin, and he could see her nipples protruding through the cloth. "Could be I was wrong. Maybe you've got some stuff that's extra special after all."

"I wouldn't know." She saw the look in his eye and edged away from the table, moving toward the door. "Why don't you ask Brad?"

"To hell with Brad. Let's find out for ourselves!"

His hand clamped around her arm as she tried to slip past him. Grace instinctively jerked away, throwing Dolan off balance, and he toppled over backward in his chair. She lost her footing as he fell, unable to break his viselike grip, and he dragged her down with him as he crashed to the floor. One moment she was standing, the next she was lying across his chest, and before she could react, Dolan's free arm snaked around her waist. He rolled away from the door, pulling her onto her back, and she felt the weight of his body coming over on top of her. All thought ceased, displaced by terror and rage; like some wild creature, trapped and with no place to run, she began to fight back. Twisting her head around, she sank her teeth into the meaty flesh of his forearm, drawing blood through his shirt, and Dolan roared with pain. Unwittingly, his grip relaxed for an instant and she squirmed from beneath him, kicking and scratching, somehow landing on her hands and knees. But as she pushed away, scrambling to her feet, his fist lashed out. The blow drove her forward, and she had some dim awareness of falling, then she hit the floor.

As if in a vague and troubled dream, she felt herself roughly lifted from the floor and sensed that she was being carried. Then someone dumped her on the bed, and the hollow ring in her ears began to fade as her vision cleared. She saw Rafe Dolan straddling her, felt his hands on her thighs and then her buttocks, lifting and shoving as he worked her dress up over her hips. She smelled the fetid odor of sweat and tobacco, and with a shock realized that he had spread her legs. She wore no undergarments, had never felt the need, and his eyes glittered as he stared down at the dark muff between her thighs. He grinned and began unbuttoning his pants.

"Open wide, you little bitch! I'm gonna flush the birds out of that nest."

There was no thought, just a swift instantaneous reflex. A swollen one-eyed monster popped out of Dolan's pants and she slammed her knee into his crotch. Clutching himself, he reeled backward, eyes distended and his organ dangling like a wilted cyclops. Grace rolled off the bed and hurled herself in blind panic toward the door. Somehow the door seemed her deliverance, salvation in the midst of hell. As if she would throw it open and find Brad standing there, come at last to protect her. The illusion was fleeting, however, and even as she ran she knew her mind was playing tricks. There was no one outside. Not Brad or anyone else. She was alone—*alone!* And running for her life. Unless she escaped, somehow made it to the woods and lost him, Dolan would kill her now. That was no illusion. It was a truth, cold and stark and very real, and the thought spurred her to one last leap toward deliverance.

But as her hand closed around the door latch, Dolan grabbed her by the shoulder and flung her sideways. Her dress shredded, torn loose with a violent rending sound as the material came apart in Dolan's fist. She fell sprawled on her back across the table, her breasts exposed and the dress hanging in tatters around her waist. Dolan scuttled toward her, still clutching himself with one hand, nearly bent double in a peculiar crablike limp. His face was contorted, splotched with pain, and his eyes glistened with diabolic rage.

"Goddamned red nigger. You're done for!" he croaked, limping closer. "Take a deep breath, squaw, 'cause it's gonna have to last a long time."

Grace hung there, paralyzed with fear, her knees suddenly gone weak. She clawed at the table for support, and in that instant of terror her hand touched something cold. Cold and sharp. A knife! Her butcher knife. On the table where it belonged, where she always kept it, and now grasped firmly in her hand.

Dolan took the last step separating them and she brought the knife up in a blur of steel. Yet she stopped short—her arm stayed by some inner force stronger than her terror—unable to kill. She wanted to kill him. Knew that even now he might kill her, but she couldn't do it. Desperate and trembling, and afraid for her own life, she found herself incapable of the final act. All she could do was hope, and pray that this *tibo* filth wouldn't see it in her eyes.

She pressed the tip of the knife against his throat and a little spurt of blood trickled down the blade. "I don't want to kill you. But I will! If you force me to, I will."

He blinked, lowering his glance to the knife. After a moment he started to nod, then thought better of it, and the corners of his mouth lifted in a weak smile. "I'm agreeable to a truce if you are."

"No truce!"

She drove him toward the door, forcing him up on his toes as she kept the blade hooked beneath his jawbone. Dolan backpedaled furiously, never once taking his eyes off the knife, and at the door she reached across and pulled the pistol from his holster. With the knife still at his throat, she awkwardly thumbed the hammer back on the Colt and shoved it into his stomach.

"Get out, and don't come back. If you do, I'll shoot you."

"Can I button my pants first? No harm in that, is there?"

"Button them outside. Hurry, *tibo!* Before I change my mind and cut it off."

"Awright, for chrissakes! Just don't get nervous with that pigsticker." Dolan very carefully took his hat from the wall peg and slipped the door latch. But as he stepped outside he turned and looked back. "You aim to tell Brad about this?"

"I don't know. I might."

"Lemme give you some advice. Brad's a hothead, and if you sic him on me, I'll just have to kill him. It wouldn't be no contest at all, and you know it. So if you're smart, you'll keep your trap shut. Savvy?"

At length, searching his face intently, she nodded. "It will be our secret. But I warn you, don't come here again!"

She slammed the door and threw the bolt. Several moments passed before she heard the sound of hoofbeats, yet even then she refused to let herself go. Dolan was right, and those final words of advice had unnerved her far more than his brutality. Brad must never find out. Or even suspect. What took place must be forgotten, wiped away completely. Erased as if it had never happened.

Working calmly but quickly she first set the cabin back in order. Then she collected the remnants of her dress, tore off the rag that still clung to her waist, and after wadding the material into a ball, threw it in the fireplace. At last, standing naked beside the table, she picked up the gun and began looking around the room.

It must be a very safe hiding place. One he would never find.

A noonday sun, filtering through trees gone lurid with autumn, splashed great ripples of orange and gold across the water. Overhead a hawk floated past on smothered wings, veered slowly into the wind, and settled high on a cottonwood beside the stream. The bird sat perfectly still, a feathered sculpture flecked through with burnt amber and bronzed ebony in the hazy sunlight. Then, with the lordly hauteur of taloned killers, it cocked its head in a fierce glare and looked down upon the intruders.

There were nine men, bent low as they crept forward in single file. The creek bank covered their movements, and the rush of water deadened the sound of their footsteps. Some three miles downstream, where the creek emptied into the Cimarron, they had left their houses hidden in a stand of trees. Stealthily, disturbing nothing in their passage, they had spent most of the morning working their way up the rocky stream. Ahead, the bank sloped off sharply, and the water swung eastward in a lazy curve. Beyond this bend, hardly more than a stone's throw away, stood a squalid little collection of buildings. There was a sense of suppressed violence in the air, something unseen but menacing that hung over the ramshackle town. And unaccountably, the hawk held his perch in the tall cottonwood, inspecting these curious-looking hunters with flint-eyed displeasure.

Heck Thomas held up his hand and the men halted, flattening themselves against the creek bank. Except for Thomas, who carried a sawed-off shotgun, every man in the party was armed with a Winchester, and several had an extra pistol tucked in their waistband. Scrambling forward on his hands and knees, Owen Kincaid moved up beside Thomas, and the older man jerked his thumb toward the town. They removed their hats, still hunched over, and slowly eased themselves to eye level at the top of the bank. Quickly, with the gaze of veteran scouts, they subjected the huddled buildings to an intense, door-to-door scrutiny.

Ingalls under a midday sun was little more than a backwoods eyesore. Located some forty miles northeast of Guthrie, it was but a short ride from the southern boundary of the Osage Nation. A single street, rutted and dusty, petered out into a faint wagon road on either side of town. Nearest to the creek was a blacksmith shop, beside that a two-story building which doubled as hotel and bordello, and next door a seedy-looking dive which was clearly the local saloon. Across the street was a general store, flanked by two rickety houses, and beyond that a livery stable. The buildings were crude affairs, constructed of bare ripsawed lumber, and the whole town had about it a flaccid sense of rot and tumbledown decay. A mongrel hound lay stretched out in front of the store; otherwise the street was empty, and the only sound was the steady clang of hammer and anvil from the smithy.

Crouched in the streambed, his forehead creased in a frown, Owen wondered again if they had come all this way on a wild-goose chase. However remote and off the beaten path, Ingalls scarcely had the look of an outlaw hideout. Quite the contrary, it appeared to be just another small burg slowly going broke on the trade of farmers and an occasional traveler. Of course, there was always another side to the coin. Sometimes reality was itself the illusion, especially where Rafe Dolan was concerned. As the girl had pointed out, nobody looked for snakes in their own backyard.

And that map she'd drawn! Tracing over it again in his mind's eye, he had to accept it at face value. The girl had spent time in Ingalls. Of that much, at least, he no longer had any doubts. As to the rest of her story—

Upon returning to Guthrie, Owen had found the marshal's office in a state of bemused pandemonium. The news was both good and bad, and when Evett Nix explained, Owen himself had been rocked back on his heels. The Dolan gang had robbed a bank on the very day he'd spoken with Grace Sixkiller. Which quickly clarified Brad's absence from the cabin. Hardly to anyone's surprise, Dolan and his bunch had then vanished without a trace. Or maybe they hadn't. Incredible as it seemed, the law might at last have struck paydirt.

Rumors of a whore with a story to tell had surfaced among Guthrie's sporting crowd. At the moment she was working in the Reaves Brothers Casino, but it was whispered that she had intimate knowledge of the Dolan gang. While it seemed a longshot, Heck Thomas had arranged to question her. And the story she rattled off, although rambling and undeniably far-fetched, had the ring of truth.

According to the shady lady, Dolan and his boys had been using Ingalls as their hideout for the past three years. While the law scoured the Nations, blindly chasing a phantom, Dolan had been holed up less than a day's ride from the territorial capital. The way she told it, there was an audacious logic to the whole idea. Dolan reasoned that the law wouldn't look for him so close to home, so he'd found himself a town willing to swap silence for the gang's exclusive trade. Which amounted to more money than anyone in Ingalls had ever seen. The bargain was struck, and Dolan's bunch was granted asylum in a spot nobody would have suspected. And still wouldn't if it weren't for a talkative whore.

The girl's motives were as old as the rocks. She was a woman scorned, jilted by Bitter Creek Newcomb in favor of a recent addition to Ingalls' backwoods cathouse. When she raised a fuss Bitter Creek had beaten her insensible, and afterward Ma Pierce, the local madam, sent her packing. Heading for the bright lights, she wound up in Guthrie, and couldn't resist the temptation to brag a bit. Nor was she hesitant about spilling the beans to the law. After all, even a whore had feelings, and whatever Bitter Creek Newcomb got was no less than he deserved.

Unlikely as her story sounded, Evett Nix decided it was worth a closer look. Since Bill Tilghman was hobbling around on a broken ankle, Heck Thomas was tapped to lead the posse. As a formality, Nix offered to exclude Owen in the event he had qualms about hunting his own brother. Owen appreciated the gesture but dismissed it out of hand. He was sworn to enforce the law, whatever the circumstances; moreover, he thought the likelihood of encountering his brother was slim, perhaps non-existent. By then Brad was almost certainly back in the cabin on Sand Creek, not holed up in Ingalls. In fact, everyone but Thomas thought the girl's story was a pipe dream. Rafe Dolan was slick, no doubt about it. But they questioned that even he had the nerve to pick a roost so close to Guthrie.

Stranger things had happened, of course, but thinking about it now, Owen still found it hard to believe. There was a limit to any man's audacity, Dolan included. And besides, from what he could see, Ingalls was far from lively. Not at all the sort outlaws frequented over in the Nations. However much he wanted to believe it, the idea just wouldn't hold water.

Heck Thomas whistled softly between his teeth, and motioned toward the town. Everyone already had their instructions, and as they scrambled over the creek bank, the marshals split into two groups. Owen headed for the store on the far side of the street, tailed by three men, and Thomas led the others on a direct line to the smithy. Taking one building at a time, they were to work both sides of the street simultaneously, each party covering the other with cross fire if they flushed the gang. Unlikely as that seemed, the marshals nonetheless took the job seriously. A distinct metallic snick broke the autumn stillness as one man after another earred back the hammer on his Winchester.

In the life of any man there is a day etched in memory. A fragmented moment of time so brutalizing that the smallest detail remains vivid all the rest of his days. By random chance, and the spite of a jilted whore, this was the day which would touch the lives of every man in the posse. But none quite so much as Owen, for of them all, he alone would carry to his grave a nightmare come true. The stark personal terror of that sunny afternoon in Ingalls.

As the lawmen spread out along the street, Brad Kincaid and Grace Sixkiller rode into town from the opposite direction. They were here seeking refuge, for the secret of their cabin in the Osage Nation was a secret no longer. And despite Grace Sixkiller's agonized plea, Brad had no intention of surrendering. Not to anyone, least of all his brother.

The young outlaw and his wife were approaching the livery stable when he spotted the marshals. His reaction was one of sheer reflex, without thought or regard for the consequences. Calmly, all in a motion, he reined his horse to a standstill and jerked a pistol. His hand blurred, then came level, frozen there a mere instant before the six-gun barked a cottony wad of smoke.

Owen never knew if the shot was meant for him. He saw Brad fire, the bullet tore by so close he could hear it fry the air, but he couldn't move. He could only stand there, paralyzed, watching in mute horror at what came next.

The marshals behind him, and those across the street, shouldered their rifles in unison. The first sharp crack blended into a rolling tattoo, and Brad was flung from his horse as if struck by lightning. Grace Sixkiller leaped from her saddle and ran to where he lay sprawled in the road, but he shoved her aside, rolling to his hands and knees. By some inhuman effort, blood spurting down over his chest, he forced himself to his feet and raised the pistol. The Winchesters exploded in another deafening volley, and Brad was jolted back a step at a time by the impact of the slugs. The last one caught him in the brisket, splattering bone and gore, and like a puppet with his strings gone haywire, he went down in a jarring, head-over-heels somersault.

Suddenly the street came alive with a sizzling hornets' nest of lead. Someone was firing from an upstairs room in the hotel, and the front of the saloon appeared wreathed in a solid wall of flame as men opened fire through the door and windows. The marshal directly behind Owen grunted, clutching at his stomach, and slumped to the ground in a lifeless ball. Slugs thunked into the corner of the store, showering Owen with splinters; his face went stickery, peppered with slivered darts, and the fiery sting at last penetrated his funk. Heedless of the raging battle, he mechanically hefted his rifle and levered four shots into an upper-floor window of the hotel. Glass shattered in razored shards, and an instant later Arkansas Tom Jones toppled over the windowsill, arms dangling as his pistol clattered to the boardwalk below.

Out of the corner of his eye, Owen saw Heck Thomas slip past the hotel and flatten himself along the wall nearest the saloon. It crossed his mind that the saloon had no back door; Thomas had apparently worked into position where his shotgun would do the most damage. Then he became aware that the other officers had concentrated their fire on the saloon, and he swung his rifle in that direction. Another lawman went down, a dark splotch blossomed on his shirt, but the remaining Winchesters hammered out a withering barrage. The saloon windows simply disintegrated in a maelstrom of glass; the whole building seemed to jounce and buckle inward as the heavy slugs shredded the front wall. A third marshal swayed and crumpled to the earth, yet even as he fell the return fire slacked off, then died out altogether. An eerie silence, filled with the acrid stench of gunpowder, settled over the street. The lawmen waited, guarded and watchful, still alert though it seemed impossible that anyone inside could have survived the leaden holocaust.

Tulsa Jack Blake suddenly materialized from the carnage, leaping through a window, and took off running toward the livery stable. Halfway across the street he spun sideways, legs pumping crazily, as Winchester slugs pocked crimson dots over the back of his shirt. Hauled around in a grotesque reeling dance, he collapsed just as Rafe Dolan appeared in the saloon doorway. The gang leader moved quickly but without panic, a pistol in either hand, snapping off measured, well-aimed shots to cover his retreat. And now, at last, Heck Thomas joined the fight.

Stepping clear of the hotel wall, he pulled both triggers and the scattergun vomited a double load of buckshot. Dolan hurtled backward, lifted from his feet by the impact, and slammed to the earth with a dusty thud. A hole the size of a saucer bubbled guts and slime just above his belt buckle, and the ground beneath him puddled foul and bloody as death loosed his bowels. One leg twitched convulsively in a final spasm, then stiffened, and quite suddenly he lay very still.

Heck Thomas broke open the shotgun and calmly reloaded.

Late that afternoon Owen Kincaid brought a wagon to a halt before the hotel. Beside him on the seat, subdued and dry-eyed, was Grace Sixkiller. Wrapped in a blanket, laid out in the back of the wagon, was the body of her husband. Owen appeared haggard, his features pale and drawn, but his hand was steady and whatever grief he felt had been ruthlessly suppressed. After a moment the hotel door opened and Heck Thomas strolled toward the wagon.

"Wondered where you'd got off to. Headed somewheres special, are you?"

Owen nodded stiffly. "I'm taking my brother home."

"Well, that figgers, I guess." Thomas studied the ground, awkward and uncomfortable in the face of the younger man's loss. "I don't know if it'll help any, Owen, but we got 'em all. Ever' last one. There ain't no more Dolan gang."

"Maybe it's finished, then. For good." Owen popped the reins, and clucked at the team. "I'll see you around, Heck."

The wagon rolled away, and Thomas turned back to the hotel. Puzzling over those last words, he had an idea it was finished. At least for one man anyway. Over and done with. Inscribed in stone.

TEN

An ancient contraption of wood and squealing ropes towered high above the flat bottomland. A huge bull wheel groaned, playing out rope thick as a man's wrist, and the crown block at the top of the derrick set up a grinding wail of protest. On the derrick floor a massive beam mounted atop a post bobbed and rose in a teeter-totter motion, and the rope lowered a string of drilling tools deeper into the earth's bowels. Near the bull wheel, a man hovered over a long wooden lever, ready to reverse the rope once the hole was bored another eight feet in depth.

Standing off from the derrick, away from the clattering racket, Jake Kincaid observed the operation with an impassive look of disinterest. The mechanics of it—all those wheels and ropes and screeching pulleys—had never made sense to him. He understood that the drill gouged out chunks of earth, which were then baled to the surface in a large bucket, and depending on sheer outhouse luck, there might be oil at the bottom of the hole. Beyond that it was a mystery, enormously complicated, seemingly incomprehensible to all but a strange breed of men who evidenced small inclination to share the secret.

And this was perfectly acceptable to Jake. He was interested in results, not the method. So long as the rig foreman, Turk McSpadden, brought in a producing well, that was all he needed to know. Oil meant money in the bank, and how

McSpadden coaxed it to the surface seemed almost inconsequential. Jake paid for knowledge and results, and so far he'd got the best of the bargain. That was enough.

Still, he felt it wise to make some pretense of understanding. A little bluff went a long way, and handled properly, it kept the other fellow on his toes. Glancing around at McSpadden, who stood just beside him, Jake cocked one eye at the derrick.

"How deep have you gone?"

"We'll hit a thousand 'fore the day's out."

"A thousand." Jake considered that with a thoughtful frown, trying to frame his questions in the proper lingo. "Any sign of paysand?"

Now Turk McSpadden deliberated. Somewhat shorter than Jake, his barrel-shaped torso was heavily quilted with muscle, and his face had a square, oxlike imperturbability. But the impression was deceiving. He was sharp as a tack, astute and calculating, with an understanding of the oil game few men possessed. And like most drillers, he was a regular miser with words.

"Saw some traces, but we got a ways to go."

"Then you think it'll make a well?"

"Mebbe. Mebbe not. Won't know till we see what's down there."

Without turning, Jake gestured toward another derrick behind them. It was at the north end of the Caney River bridge, perhaps a quarter-mile from the present drilling site, and steadily pumping oil into a huge wooden tank. "Near as I recall, you brought that one in at fourteen hundred—"

"Fourteen hundred and forty-three."

"—and what I'm askin' is, will this one go any deeper?"

McSpadden scratched his armpit. He reeked of sweat and mud and oil, but he was on his own turf here, and not to be hurried merely because the other man paid his wages. After a while, he shrugged. "If we get to fifteen hundred and there's no sign, I'll close 'er down."

"Then what?"

McSpadden looked at him like he was crazy. "Then I'll drill another hole. We're sittin' on a shit pot full of oil here, Mr. Kincaid. You just gotta be patient till I find it."

Jake had spent a few sleepless nights on that very subject. Just as farmers used dowsers to find water, oil men employed doodlebugs to locate drilling sites. Clairvoyance, and other, more sophisticated, forms of witchery were accepted at face value by most drillers. McSpadden employed a doodlebug who claimed to have perfected the only scientific method of divining oil. The man clamped a device in his mouth which had four coiled springs protruding straight out; the springs were plainly marked for silver, gold, iron, or oil. Once on the site he roamed around until the spring marked for oil was pulled by some irresistible force toward the earth. That was the spot. And there Turk McSpadden drilled his wells. So far, Jake couldn't complain. They had drilled three holes and brought in two wells. But it smacked of quackery nonetheless, and his misgivings persisted.

McSpadden suddenly spat on his large-knuckled hands and briskly rubbed them together. "I got an itch that says we're close, mighty close. 'Less you got some objection, I'll get on back to work."

Jake had been dismissed, as he had each time he'd visited the drilling site. Besides practicing his own brand of voodoo, McSpadden was independent as a hog on ice. Which seemed to be characteristic of oil men in general. But the driller got results, and that made his abrupt attitude tolerable if not wholly satisfactory.

"Keep in touch, Turk. I'll expect a wire the minute something pops."

"Count on it, Mr. Kincaid." McSpadden walked off toward the derrick. "You'll be the first to get the word."

Hardly more enlightened than when he'd arrived, Jake crawled in his buggy and headed back to Bartlesville. If he hurried he could still catch the evening southbound out of

Nowata, so perhaps it was just as well McSpadden wasn't a talker. All in all, it would save him a day, providing extra time for the meeting with Harlan Green in Poteau. Which would be time well spent. At this point, the timber deal was no less vital to his plans than another oil well.

Passing through Bartlesville, he allowed himself a moment of gloating pride. Last year the town had been little more than a wide spot in the road, scarcely a village. The single store had done a thriving business in Peruna (a patent medicine much in demand since the sale of whiskey was prohibited in Indian Territory), but commerce as such was virtually unknown. Now it was a bustling community, with houses and small business district, and even a Santa Fe spur line.

That had been the turning point—the spur line. Both for Bartlesville and his flyer in the oil game. Cecil Hollister had passed away some time back, and although Jake still retained a large chunk of Santa Fe stock, it had been touch and go for a while. But the directors had finally seen the light (after a bit of judicious arm twisting) and authorized construction of the spur line. Which gave him tank cars to transport oil and, at last, made the entire project feasible.

Of all the gambles he'd taken, this was perhaps the boldest. Before contacting the Santa Fe, he had leased drilling rights to nearly 100,000 acres in the Cherokee Nation. And with no assurance, assuming he struck oil, that there would be any way of transporting it back east. But it was this very risk which made the lease dirt cheap, and in the end, it had worked to his advantage. Thinking back on it now, he couldn't recall what had prompted him to take the plunge. Instinct, most likely. There was no denying he had a nose for profit, and at the time the oil game had begun to take on the scent of money.

As with all business ventures, Jake had thoroughly investigated the oil industry before making his move. Contrary to popular notion, it was hardly a fledgling enterprise. America's first oil well had been drilled in Pennsylvania, late in the summer of 1859, almost two years before the outbreak of the Civil War. But there was a limited market at the time, which meant marginal profits, and the industry proceeded at a snail's pace. Over the next ten years oil men moved westward through Ohio, Indiana, and Illinois, and in the decade afterward, rich wells were discovered in Kansas. The first well drilled in Indian Territory was outside Muskogee, in the Creek Nation, late in 1884. At eighteen hundred feet it came in a duster and was abandoned. Then, in 1889, a producing well was completed on Spencer Creek in the Cherokee Nation. It was thirty-six feet deep and pumped a half-barrel of oil a day. Scarcely an auspicious start.

All the same, the potential existed, and men continued to sink wells. By the late 1890s there were fewer than twenty gasoline-powered automobiles in the entire country, but the use of *rock oil* for lubrication and illumination had grown into a major industry. When Jake drilled his first well early in 1897 (which came in at a hundred and fifty barrels a day) the single drawback was transportation, getting the oil to market. His arrangement with the Santa Fe solved that problem, and oil men came to stand and marvel at his operation outside Bartlesville. Within months Indian Territory was crawling with promoters, and of greater consequence, the large eastern companies sent their scouts highballing westward. The race was on.

Unlike most oil men, Jake resisted the temptation to put all his eggs in one basket. He held to a hard-and-fast rule of spreading his investments over a wide range of activities, and in the past year, his interest had focused sharply on Indian Territory. Under Harlan Green the coal mine had become an exceedingly prosperous venture. Something over a hundred miners were on the payroll, imported into the Choctaw Nation along with a staff of engineers and management personnel. As Jake had predicted, they became an island of whites in a sea of red men, but their presence provoked little bitterness.

The mine brought an economic boom to Poteau, transforming a tiny crossroads into a bustling community. Stores sprouted, commerce came to the backwoods, and the Choctaws prospered as never before. Yet there were faint rumblings in the Choctaw council, for while few were aware of how the boom got its start, it soon became evident that Jake Kincaid had prospered most of all.

And now, with federal sanction, he prepared to move on a new front.

Earlier in the year Congress had enacted a law abolishing all tribal courts. The legislation also provided that anyone residing in Indian Territory *regardless of race* was subject to federal law, and that all civil and criminal cases would be tried before federal courts. Then, almost as an afterthought, the law decreed that no act of the tribal councils would be considered legal until approved by the President. The meaning was clear. Congress had tightened the noose another notch, and it was now but a matter of time until tribal governments were wiped out altogether.

The Five Civilized Tribes, for all practical purposes, had become wards of the federal government. Faced with the relentless onslaught of Congress, their leaders played for time, fighting a delaying action. Their overriding concern was to salvage the independence of tribal rule, and as a result, it was considered the wiser course to overlook certain irregularities in the administration of Indian Territory. In short, they had enough enemies in Washington, and there was little to be gained by rocking the boat further.

When the Indian Agent in Muskogee was assigned federal control of all timberlands in the Nations, none of the tribal leaders raised a cry of protest. At the time, with broader issues at stake, it seemed a matter of small consequence. And when this same Indian Agent licensed Jake Kincaid to build a sawmill and organize a timber operation in the Choctaw Nation, there was no thought of complaint. That the license had been granted spoke for itself—a white man's *quid pro quo*—but proof of corruption was hard to come by. Moreover, with legal action now restricted to the federal courts, any formal challenge seemed hardly worth the effort. Some men set themselves above the law, and Jake Kincaid was known to have friends in high places. On that note of futility, the whole affair was written off as a lost cause.

Aboard the evening southbound, rattling toward Poteau, Jake allowed himself a pat on the back. Already he had a planing mill under construction in Guthrie, where raw lumber from the Choctaw timberlands would be converted into boxes and crates, doors and flooring, items all much in demand throughout the territory. And Harlan Green, who had served him well in the coal venture, would prove equally valuable in the timber operation. The man was a rascal, never to be trusted, but he had a gift for organization. Like Turk McSpadden and the banker Mordecai Jones, along with others Jake had recruited over the years, Harlan Green got results. And when it was all toted up in the ledgers, that's what counted. Results. Everything else fell into place, followed naturally, if the results were there.

Unaccountably, quite without volition, the thought led Jake to a moment of somber reflection. There was a colossal irony to that aspect of his life, and it amazed him that he'd never seen it before. Here he sat, wealthy as some stinking rajah, a man with the knack of attracting capable men to his cause. Literally surrounded by a retinue of competent and highly industrious flunkies who worked themselves to a frazzle in his behalf. And yet he'd failed miserably in winning over his own sons.

Owen alienated and antagonistic. Unable to forget or forgive. Wasting himself on the ranch when he belonged in Guthrie. Herding cows instead of preparing himself to take over the reins of an expanding business empire. Barely twenty-five, and for all practical purposes a recluse. Withdrawn into his own little world, where he could hide from the ugly truth that life fought dirty in the clinches.

And Brad. In his grave almost a year to the day. Buried in the family plot with little ceremony and a dearth of mourners. His eulogy a wanted poster, and his epitaph a mindless bloodbath in some backwoods hellhole. Notorious in life and more so in death, already sanctified in an outlaw ballad which assured his place in the mythical folklore of a passing breed. Not exactly admirable, but fame of sorts nonetheless, linked forever in verse to the Kincaid name.

Jake felt no sorrow now, just as he had felt none at Brad's graveside. Nor could he countenance the mawkish behavior of his elder son. Instead, staring at his reflection in the train window, he saw mirrored the question that had lately come to haunt his sleep.

At what price had he built this hollow legacy?

The washed blue of the plains sky grew smoky along about dusk. Stillness fell over the land as a stiff breeze dropped off, but there was a lingering nip in the sharp, crisp air. High overhead a vee of ducks, fleet silhouettes against the muslin twilight, winged their way southward. Already there was a brittle smell of approaching frost, and the grasslands along the Cimarron had taken on that tawny look which signals oncoming winter.

Owen dismounted from his horse at the corral gate, and stood for a moment watching the ducks. Of a sudden he felt a curious sense of envy. They were wild and free, beholden to nothing, creatures who heard some ancient call and took wing. Not at all like man, whose freedom was measured merely by the degree of his bondage. A bondage of his own witless folly, perhaps, but one which held him no less certainly than a chained bear. As the ducks disappeared in a dusky wedge he felt some overpowering urge to join them. To answer that call himself, and simply vanish into the darkening sky.

But it was an urge quickly set aside, if not wholly quashed.

A wrangler came to take his horse and he walked off toward the main house. The windows were lighted, blazing a cheery beacon in the gloaming cold, yet the sight did little to dispel his mood. And that bothered him, perhaps more than he cared to admit. Certainly more than he cared to scrutinize, or dwell on at any length.

With fall roundup completed he should have been whistling and frisky, ready to celebrate. This was the best part of the year, when the rigors of gathering and marketing his beeves were behind a man. That lazy interlude when he had time for a spree in town, or might take off hunting deer, or just loaf in front of the fire, toasting his stockinged feet, while he caught up on back issues of the *Police Gazette*. For a cattleman it was the best of all seasons, with the work done and winter still to come, yet Owen's spirits somehow lagged behind. Which came as no particular shock. Nor was he bemused by this listless sense of fatigue. Lately it had become a way of life.

Sometimes he wondered how a man could go wrong so often, and with such baffling consistency. Last year it had all seemed so simple, not just uncomplicated but somehow right. Like a man lost and troubled suddenly come to a fork in the road, and knowing beyond question the way he must take. That was how it had appeared at the time. So obvious and clearly marked, a palliative of sorts at the very moment he needed one most.

Owen had only a hazy recollection of those days following Brad's death. He ate and slept, trailed the hearse to Summit View cemetery, watching numbly as they lowered a rosewood casket into the ground. But he was aware of little about him, absorbed not so much by grief as by an enervating sense of guilt. While he hadn't pulled the trigger, he lived with the knowledge that he had helped to hasten his brother's death. That he had tried to prevent it, offering Brad a way out, gave him no solace at all. That he had killed nine men himself, men who deserved killing no less than Brad, altered nothing of what he felt. By all that was reasonable or just, Brad was to blame for his own funeral, but reason had deserted Owen, and what he felt was not justification. He felt guilty, and in need of absolution. A penitent with no one to hear his confession.

In a week that left Guthrie reeling and the gossips twittering deliriously, Owen administered his own penance. The day after Brad's burial he resigned as U.S. deputy marshal. Three days later he married Julia Webb. And scandalized the town by announcing that Grace Sixkiller, his brother's widow, would share their home as one of the family. Then, in a final act of contrition, he banished himself, along with his bride and his sloe-eyed sister-in-law, to the Kincaid ranch on the Cimarron.

Only once in the midst of this frenetic week did Owen consult with his father. That was to request housing at the ranch and employment as a cowhand till he could learn the business and take over the spread. Jake's opinion was solicited on nothing else, and his argument that Owen belonged in Guthrie, in a position of greater responsibility, fell on deaf ears. At loggerheads, and unwilling to push it further, Jake relented, but insisted that Owen take charge of the ranch immediately upon arrival. It simply wouldn't do for a Kincaid to sign on as a common cowhand, and on that point he was adamant.

The months which followed were a time of trial and revelation for Owen. He gave the foreman, Chuck Bohanon, complete freedom, and set about learning the business from the hurricane deck of a cow pony. His unassuming manner, backed by an inquisitive mind and a demonstrated aptitude with a rope, quickly won the respect of the hands. That he was reputed to be chain lightning with a gun, and tagged by newspapers as one of the great lawmen of Oklahoma, merely reinforced what the crew saw with their own eyes. Chuck Bohanon, in fact, welcomed Owen's assistance. The ranch had grown to some fifty thousand acres, running better than five thousand head, and the foreman took comfort in having a Kincaid around to call the shots. Before spring roundup Owen had assumed active management of the spread, and in the bunkhouse everyone agreed that he was a natural-born cattleman.

But in the main house, a rambling structure of logs and native stone, it was another story altogether. Owen discovered that his wife was a febrile wildcat in bed, but cold as a stone regarding her enforced exile to the Cimarron backcountry. As a practicing martyr she made the most of the situation, and when the honeymoon wore thin, he soon found himself the object of shrewish tirades which inevitably ended in teary self-pity. And Julia, who had presented him with a son late that summer, discovered that marriage and wedded bliss were only remotely akin. Husbands, it seemed, bore small resemblance to the dashing young men met at picnics and church socials. Some ghastly change, cryptic and ominous, came over them once the ceremony had been read. Instead of remaining ardent and gallant, as they were during the courtship, they become boorish tyrants who satisfied their lust with all the finesse of a rooster mounting a hen. Like Owen, who went at it as if he were being clocked against a stopwatch, and even so, with dwindling frequency. It wasn't that Julia disliked it so much—she rather enjoyed being ravaged, left bruised and aching—the problem was one of constancy. She never got enough.

Lately Owen had come to dread the end of his work day, which signaled another evening of acrimony and complaint. For all his irregularity in bed, Julia was pregnant again, and she had greeted the event with waspish annoyance. The thought of being trapped in the house with her all winter, listening to her self-indulgent whining, weighed heavily on his mind tonight. When he came through the door he found her, as usual, sprawled in a chair before the fireplace. One look told the story. She had clearly worked herself into yet another snit, glum and sulky, staring dismally at the crackling flames.

As he hung his hat and coat on wall pegs, she neither moved nor spoke. She merely sat, the aggrieved wife, waiting for some note of sympathy from her husband. But the device was old and worn and overused, and tonight Owen felt decidedly unsympathetic.

He walked to the fireplace and stood warming his hands. She waited, as he knew she would, and several moments passed before he turned, fixing her with a wooden look. "Supper ready?"

"God, Owen, you're so predictable." Her appraisal of him was deliberate, almost insolent, but there was something tense and frazzled behind her words. "Just once I wish my condition would take precedence over your stomach. Or is that too much to ask of a Kincaid?"

He ignored the barb. "I suppose you've left Grace to do all the cookin' again?"

"And what if I have? She has to do something to earn her bed and board."

Owen laughed a short, mirthless laugh. "Yeah, but the question is, what do you do to earn yours?"

"I have babies!" she burst back acidly. "One right after the other. Like a brood sow. Isn't that why you married me?"

"Speaking of babies, who's tendin' to Morg?"

"Oh, for God's sake, your precious son has already been tended to." She gingerly rubbed one breast. "The little brute almost crippled me. I'm sorry to say, he has no more concern for me than you do. Like his father, he thinks only of his stomach."

Morgan wasn't quite a year old, but he was indeed a tiny ruffian. The thought of his greedy rooting and pummeling little fists brought a smile to Owen's mouth. "Well, I guess that makes him a chip off the old block. First things first is the Kincaid motto. Which reminds me—you never did say when supper'd be ready."

She bolted out of her chair, glaring spitefully at him. Then, just as suddenly, her shoulders sagged, and her hand made a fluttering gesture, not unlike a wounded bird. "Go ask your sainted sister-in-law. You seem to prefer her conversation to mine anyway. Or did you think I hadn't noticed?"

Owen's smile vanished. It was as if a shutter had slammed down, and what remained was a dispassionate mask, impersonal and empty. "You ought to take a close look at yourself, Julia. Might be you wouldn't like what you see in the mirror."

She seemed on the verge of falling apart, a tightly strung, barely restrained assortment of nerves. "That's very clever of you, Owen, pushing it off on me. But I haven't heard you deny it. Or are you afraid she'll hear you? Is that it, Owen? Damn you, say something. Is it?"

He regarded her steadily, refusing the goad, and she tossed her head in affirmation of the invidious slur that hung between them. Then, just for an instant, the mask slipped, and his lips curled back in contempt.

"Go to hell."

Julia clamped her hand to her mouth, uttering a small stifled cry, and whirled out of the room. He heard her racing down the hall, sobbing uncontrollably now, and finally a resounding crash as the bedroom door slammed shut. Dazed, slightly shamed by his own cruelty, he stood there trying to sort out the pieces. After what seemed a long time he became aware that he wasn't alone, and glanced around to find Grace watching him from the dining room door.

The sight of her presented a startling contrast to Julia's sullen, woebegone appearance. Since coming to the ranch, Grace Six-killer had undergone a gradual, almost indefinable change. But only in the last few months had Owen become conscious that there was something different about her. Stronger, more poised, possessing a confidence he hadn't seen before. As if, in the aftermath of Brad's death, she had ripened somehow, matured from a childlike girl to a serene, radiantly composed woman. Her face was mobile and curiously alight, with a wide, sensual mouth and lustrous eyes that seemed to lay bare the innermost secrets of those around her.

Quite without realizing when it had happened, Owen discovered that she had become a tantalizing and most unusual woman, with the mental presence of a sorceress and the delicacy of a snowflake. These were thoughts he kept to himself, however, and never by word or action had he displayed anything more than brotherly concern for her welfare. And yet, by some communion he failed to understand, he was almost certain she knew.

Now, painfully aware that she'd overheard the argument, he tried to pass it off. Grinning, he shrugged and shook his head. "Women sure get some queer notions when they're in a family way. Don't let it bother you, though. She'll be herself as soon as she's had time to calm down."

"I'm not bothered, Owen." Her voice had a teasing lilt. "Not if you aren't."

"Yeah, well it's"—his ears turned red, and he appeared momentarily flustered—"you know, she's just upset. It'll blow over."

She gave him a small, enigmatic smile. "I heard you ask about supper."

"Supper? Yeah, that's right, I did. Why, is it ready?"

"Not yet, but soon. You can go ahead and wash up."

"Well, I think I'll catch a breath of fresh air first. Sort of clear the cobwebs. You just give a yell when you're set."

Grace watched him hurry out of the door, and her smile widened as the latch clicked shut. It was the first time she'd ever seen him that way. Awkward and fumbling for words. And so plainly unsettled by the fact that she knew. That she understood what he was thinking.

Sometimes she entertained wicked thoughts about Owen. Wondering how it would feel. Their bodies engaged, his weight pressed upon her. Thrusting, filling her emptiness. But she left it there, a game of sorts. A treasured plaything to be examined late at night when her bed was cold and she ached with loneliness. Perhaps all the more precious because it was the stuff of dreams. And something more, now that she had seen it in his eyes.

Humming softly to herself, she turned and went back to the kitchen.

The New Year had come and gone, but 1898 brought with it small hope of peace on earth and goodwill toward men.

In February, seemingly without provocation, the Spaniards sank the battleship *Maine* in Havana harbor. Inflamed by yellow journalism, which vilified the Spaniards and cheered the Cuban insurrectionists, America's enthusiasm for war at times bordered on lunacy. Strangely, though prominent statesmen smelled something fishy in the sinking of the *Maine*, very few Americans wanted peace. Their own war of independence was but a hundred years past, and they felt strong kinship with the Cuban patriots. The citizens of Oklahoma Territory, like their countrymen, advocated direct intervention, and the drums of war took on a feverish beat.

But closer to home an older struggle raged unabated, and brotherhood suffered still another reversal. Solidarity among the Five Civilized Tribes had at last been demolished. The Dawes Commission, backed by stronger mandates from Congress, convened again in Indian Territory. This time, however, it came not to negotiate but to dictate terms. Like men of all races, some of the tribal delegates were ambitious and vain. Others were merely stupid. And some were as corrupt and venal as their white counterparts. Nearly all had a weakness which could be exploited, and the result was a devastating document known simply as the Atoka Agreement.

The Chickasaw, Choctaw, and Seminole Nations signed the agreement, which specified that all tribal government was to be abolished in 1906. The Creek delegates refused to approve the agreement, and the Cherokees refused even to negotiate. But this was a minor technicality, and of little concern to

Washington. Tribal unity ceased to exist on the spring day in Atoka; it was merely a matter of time until the Creeks and Cherokees fell into line. The Commission, document in hand, proceeded with the allotment of lands as the tribal rolls were completed. In the process town sites were set aside, and coal, oil, and other mineral lands were reserved to be leased or sold for the benefit of each tribe as a whole. Of the nearly twenty million acres in Indian Territory, some four million acres were included in this latter category. By whatever design, this separation of natural resources offered several interesting possibilities to politicians and businessmen alike. A windfall of sorts, it was perhaps more profitable than legal.

Always the highroller, Jake Kincaid saw the broader implications in the Commission's work, and never for a moment lost sight of the ultimate goal. With political connections extending to the White House, he had every confidence that his ventures into coal, timber, and oil would continue to prosper now that the Nations were under federal control. What interested him more, as spring came again to the plains, was an interim report from the Commission. It revealed, according to the staff's best estimate, that barely one hundred thousand people would qualify for inclusion on the tribal rolls. And Jake hardly needed the Commission to tell him that at least twice that number of whites were living in Indian Territory. The arithmetic was simple but the ramifications were far-reaching. Perhaps, after all, the obstacles were not so great as he had imagined.

The campaign for statehood was gathering momentum, and while the Indians would resist to the very last, he had few qualms as to the outcome in Congress. Oklahoma Territory and Indian Territory would enter the Union as a single state. All that remained was the worrisome question of who would control Oklahoma's politics. Until now the actual number of Indians in the Nations had been obscured within the bureaucratic snarl of the Interior Department. But the Commission's report gave Jake a whole new outlook on the shape of things to come. General elections would one day decide the issue, and he found it inconceivable that the whites of Indian Territory would side with their red neighbors. The very idea was repugnant, in his mind tantamount to high treason or desecration of the flag. Simply preposterous.

On a pleasant evening late in April these thoughts and others occupied Jake's mind. Seated in Zalia's parlor, with his boots off and a snifter of brandy close at hand, he rambled on about business and various new projects in the hopper, but always within the framework of the broader issue. Inevitably he returned to the subject of statehood, and politics.

"Talkin' about timber reminds me. You remember last week when I went down to see Harlan Green—"

Zalia sat across from him, listening attentively as she worked on a needlepoint pattern of a large crimson rose. Her appearance was fetching, particularly for a woman who no longer counted birthdays. She wore a dress of flawless navy serge done in Basque style, with her hair gathered in a French roll, and an exquisite strand of pearls looped down over her breast. The pearls had been a gift from Jake, an extravagance he could well afford, and in keeping with the collection of gems and jewelry he had lavished on her over the years. As he paused, sipping at his brandy, she glanced up from the needlepoint and smiled, prompting him with a nod.

"—well anyway, me and Green got to counting and it turns out we got better'n three hundred white men on the payroll down there. Naturally, that includes the coal mine. Course, on the face of it, that don't seem like a whole helluva lot. But when you multiply that by a couple of hundred—roughly sixty thousand give or take—and you figure there's less than half that many Choctaws in the whole tribe, then you've got yourself a horse of a different color. Get it—horse of a different color?"

"Yes, Jake." Zalia humored his pun with a smile. "A white horse."

"Bet your life it's a white horse! And come the day we hold elections them red heathens'll think they've been run over by a whole stampede of pink-eyed albinos."

"Oh, honestly, Jake, why do you insist on calling them heathens? You know very well they're better Christians than most white people."

"Hogwash. Just because an Injun's been baptized don't take the heathen out of him. Way they figure it, Jehovah's pretty powerful stuff, so they just hedged their bet, that's all."

"But they're civilized Indians. I mean, really, they're not like Apaches, or some of those other tribes. Now, be fair, isn't that true?"

"Don't mean a hill of beans," Jake grumbled. "A leopard can't change his spots and neither can a heathen."

Zalia withheld comment on the tangled metaphor. "Well, I hope you don't talk like that when you're in the Nations. It certainly won't win your side any votes on election day. Assuming everybody ends up in the same state, of course."

"It'll come out single statehood, don't you worry your head about that. And what I've been tryin' to tell you is that come election day I won't need any of them heathen votes. We'll roll over 'em like a snowball."

He chortled to himself, pleased with the image. "Yessir. A big white snowball."

"Besides, there's another reason you shouldn't talk that way"—Zalia darted him a mischievous look—"people might just start calling you a hypocrite."

"How's that!" He bristled indignantly. "A hypocrite?"

"Well, it is a case of the pot calling the kettle black, isn't it? Now be honest, Jake. If you ever set foot in a church it might give God a stroke."

He grumped something under his breath, hard pressed for a snappy comeback. "Think you're pretty smart, don't you? But I don't make myself out to be one of the holy-roller crowd, now do I? You'll have to grant me that."

Zalia's reply was cut short by an insistent jingle from the

telephone. They exchanged glances, surprised by a call this time of evening. She set her needlepoint aside and walked to the wall phone. The box jingled again, a loud demanding ring, and she quickly lifted the receiver.

"Hello." There was a short pause; then she nodded. "Why, yes, he's right here. Just a moment."

Turning, she held out the receiver, visibly startled. "It's Owen. He wants you."

Jake crossed the parlor in a rush, and snatched the receiver from her hand. "Owen? What the hell's the idea in callin' me here? You know better—"

He stopped, listening intently, and the color drained from his face. "Aw, for Chrissakes. Son, you're not drunk, are you?"

Another pause, then he sighed wearily. "Well, it's too bad you're not. Maybe I could've got you out of it. Where are you, anyway?"

The crackle of a voice came over the line and he nodded. "All right, you wait there. I'll be over in a couple of minutes."

He placed the receiver back on the hook, and turned from the phone as if in a trance. His eyes appeared glazed, and Zalia saw a muscle jump along the ridge of his jawbone. She put her hand on his arm, suddenly frightened by the look on his face.

"Jake? What is it? What's the matter?"

He stared back at her blankly, almost as if he hadn't heard. Then he blinked and shook his head, hardly able to credit his own words.

"The damn fool has joined the Rough Riders."

The summer of '98 was an eventful time. Spring came early that year, which pleased the farmers, and trade in Guthrie had never been so brisk, which was a source of profound delight to businessmen and bankers. Gold had been discovered in the Yukon, and Congress had the Indians in a hammerlock, topics of enormous interest, if no immediate consequence, to everyone in Oklahoma Territory. And the war against Spain went marvelously well. Which kept the entire nation enthralled.

Americans displayed a curious mania for this odd little war. Hardly anyone could converse intelligently on Cuba (an island thought to be somewhere off the coast of Florida), and the Philippines, a mere dot in the vast unknown of the Pacific, might well have been on the moon. But the nation was flexing its industrial muscles, caught up in a mood of expansionism and world power, and a little war was thought to be not a bad thing. That the Cuban insurrectionists had been fighting for nearly six years, completely ignored by their neighbors to the north, seemed somehow incidental, and best forgotten. America was ready to test itself, and the situation in Cuba happened to be handy. Taking arms against the oppressive rule of Spanish colonial governors was nothing short of a holy quest, and amid outpourings of sympathy for the underdog, America girded itself to fight the good fight.

Owen Kincaid was one of eighty men selected from a mob of eight hundred who volunteered for the Oklahoma Rough Riders. His fame as a marshal, and a leader of fighting men, had dimmed none at all, and the recruiting officers considered him a prize catch. Yet, unlike many of the others, Owen had joined not so much out of patriotism as boredom. After nearly two years on the ranch he had come to the slow realization that he missed the excitement and danger he'd known as a lawman. What he needed was a good scrap—and a long vacation from Julia—and for him, indeed, this crusade against oppression came as a godsend. Consulting no one, least of all his wife, he had volunteered on the very day Congress declared war.

Similar units had been recruited throughout the west, and along with Owen's outfit ultimately reached the embarkation area in Florida. There they got a closer look at Teddy Roosevelt, who even then was something of an *opéra-bouffe* figure, rotund and bulging at the seams, and not above the most bizarre gaucheries in advancing his own cause. Officially designated the First Cavalry Regiment, the volunteers were known from the beginning as Roosevelt's Rough Riders, which was confusing to everyone except Roosevelt. Although second-in-command, Lieutenant Colonel Roosevelt was never one to stand on formality. He considered the regiment his own personal creation, and with the pugnacity of a bull-dog, set about convincing both the troopers and the American public that this was, in fact, the case.

Unlike the public, however, the War Department was not to be swayed by Roosevelt's hyperbole. Long after Commodore George Dewey had annihilated the Spanish fleet in the Philippines, the Army mobilization effort remained mired in red tape and chaos. The Rough Riders loafed in the Florida sun, while Teddy Roosevelt frothed daily communiqués to the press, and the invasion of Cuba took on all the overtones of a shabby, if unamusing, burlesque.

On the home front things proceeded at a somewhat smoother pace. Turk McSpadden brought in several new oil wells; Harlan Green had the timber operation and the coal mine at peak production; and the various enterprises in Guthrie prospered in a boomtime economy. Politically the state of affairs was even more promising, and all in all, Jake felt like a man with the world on a downhill slide. There was only one fly in the butter—his scatterbrained son—and the mere thought of it still infuriated him. He considered Owen's enlistment a feckless and irresponsible act, and he took small pride in the fact that a Kincaid had volunteered to serve his country. Cuba meant absolutely nothing to Jake, nor was he concerned with the colonial tyranny of Spain. But he was deeply concerned for his son and constantly worried that Owen would sacrifice his life in this binge of national altruism. The world, according to Jake's view, orbited around Oklahoma, and the center of the universe was the Kincaid business empire. All else was inconsequential, germane to nothing, and at times, he doubted that he could ever forgive Owen for failing to share in this vision.

Curiously, Jake's displeasure with his son resulted in a tenuous alliance with his daughter-in-law. With Owen gone, he began visiting the ranch on a weekly basis, ostensibly to keep tabs on Chuck Bohanon and the crew. Beneath this charade was the wish to see his grandson; the boy's mother seldom brought him to Guthrie, and Jake had been on the ranch only once since Owen took charge. The time he spent with Morg each week forced him to endure Julia's company, but it was not altogether an unpleasant experience. He found that they had a common interest—Owen's infuriating remoteness— and it was upon this bedrock of mutual aggravation that they slowly joined forces.

Julia's opinion of her father-in-law underwent no remarkable change. She still considered him an old pirate, and never ceased to be appalled that he openly maintained a mistress, flouting all social custom. But she would have aligned herself with Satan incarnate if it offered some hope of luring Owen back to Guthrie, and a career in business. She was aware that her husband, like most men, was a hopeless romanticist, and therefore impractical. Certainly his witless response to this silly little war proved her point. Men loved the heroic, even if it killed them. Essentially they were actors, and it was part of the masculine role that they parade and play at war. Women suffered and gave life, while men struck postures and killed one another. And since Julia was pregnant and close to her term, her conspiracy with Jake ripened all the more quickly because her husband was off tilting at windmills.

They also shared another common aggravation—Grace Sixkiller. Julia was unreasonably jealous of the girl, though she admitted to herself that Owen had no ulterior motives. He had given Grace a home out of some misguided sense of responsibility, and Julia was wise enough never to tamper with his conscience. Jake, on the other hand, failed completely to understand his son's motives. Conscience to him was an affliction of the weak, and Owen was scarcely a weakling, so the girl's presence remained an enduring mystery. He was civil to Grace, but aloof. And suspicious. She evidenced no fear of him whatever, and Jake found it difficult to trust anyone who was unafraid of his power. Privately, he thought her a bit simple, and neatly reconciled the whole matter by writing her off as just another ignorant heathen.

Grace was polite and quietly cheerful, but in turn kept her distance. She looked after the house and Morg (duties Julia gladly relinquished), and made herself as unobtrusive as possible. She had come to the ranch because of Owen, and she remained for the same reason. Whatever secret thing existed between them (and she had felt it since that day he visited her cabin on Sand Creek), she was willing to let him work it out in his own way. It was enough simply to be near him.

As the summer wore on Owen's infrequent letters did little to console Julia. She felt deserted and betrayed, and positively wallowed in self-pity. In late June, when Jake urged that his second grandchild be born in Guthrie, she leaped at the chance to leave the ranch. Grace stayed behind to care for the house, thoroughly content to have the place to herself. Julia and Morg moved in with her parents, the Webbs, and on the last day of June she gave birth to a girl. Secretly delighted that she had denied Owen another son, she named the baby Elizabeth, in honor of her mother. And exhausted, wearied by her ordeal, she then lay back in bed while a battery of servants waited on her hand and foot.

Across the continent, on the very day Julia left the ranch, the Army finally lumbered into action. American forces invaded Cuba in late June, and in swift but torturous advances, fought their way clear of the coastline. The Spanish offered stiff resistance, though somewhat overmatched from the beginning, and the invaders quickly discovered that their main enemies were dysentery, malaria, and the dreaded yellow fever. With its plodding, systematic disorganization, the Army helped none at all by feeding them on hardtack, rancid salt pork, and canned beans swimming in grease.

Still, hindered as they were, the Americans had come to fight. By July 1 they had moved to within striking range of Santiago, the Spanish stronghold. There, confronted with a chain of interlocking fortifications, they engaged the Spaniards in a pivotal battle at San Juan Hill. When Roosevelt's Rough Riders stormed the hill they came under intense fire from a blockhouse, and shortly found themselves pinned down. Acting quickly and decisively, as the situation dictated, Sergeant Owen Kincaid led an assault on the blockhouse. Although wounded in the arm, he kept his feet, rallying his men, and in a savage half hour reduced the blockhouse to a crumbling ruin. The Rough Riders charged, galvanized to blind fury by this valiant act, and within a matter of hours the surrounding fortifications had been overrun.

Some fifteen hundred Americans were killed or wounded at San Juan Hill, and shortly before sundown, as the flies buzzed their hymns to the dead, the critically wounded were evacuated back to the coastline. That night, aboard the hospital ship *Olivette,* Owen Kincaid's left arm was amputated.

Santiago fell within a fortnight, and the Spanish were subjected to the ignominy of unconditional surrender. Cuba was liberated, and when the peace treaty was signed, America came away with Puerto Rico, Guam, and the Philippines.

It had been a dirty little war. But profitable.

A blustery November wind swept over the depot as the train chuffed to a halt. Seated at a window, Owen waited, apparently in no rush, as several passengers crowded into the aisle. For all their bustle and chatter, the other passengers were acutely conscious of his presence, glancing hurriedly at the uniform and the empty sleeve and the medals as they pushed past his seat. By now he was accustomed to stares and clucks of sympathy, and he seemed wholly unaware of their scrutiny. Instead, he peered through the window into a silty, noonday overcast, scanning the depot platform.

People milled about, collecting baggage and greeting friends, but otherwise everything appeared normal. After a moment he grunted, canting his head in an imperceptible nod, satisfied that his father had come alone. He jammed on a campaign hat as the aisle cleared, then stood and moved toward the front of the coach.

His instructions, set down in a letter to his father, had been brutally explicit. There was to be no fanfare or bands, no speeches or crowds or parades. Nothing remotely suggestive of a welcoming-home celebration. Nor were Julia and the children to be at the station. Just his father, and a buggy to take him out to the ranch. Any sign to the contrary and he would simply remain on the train until it reached Oklahoma City. Other than the family, no one was to be told of his arrival, and he had underlined this final condition with bold strokes of his pen.

All of Guthrie was aghast, and not a little miffed, when Jake passed on these demands. The mayor's welcoming committee already had its program planned, including presentation of a key to the city, and now, at the last instant, they were forced to scrap the entire project. Which struck everyone as highly inconsiderate, and just the least bit peculiar. Not every town could boast a Medal of Honor winner, and the civic drum-beaters felt as if they had been slapped in the face by one of their own.

That Guthrie had itself a hero had become a matter of intense personal pride to everybody in town. Owen Kincaid was the only Medal of Honor winner in all of Oklahoma, and the *Statesman* never for a moment let the rest of the territory forget it. A series of articles over the past four months had highlighted every facet of his life. The Battle of San Juan Hill, and his courageous sortie. His exploits as a lawman, and a rehash of the Dolan gang's extermination (with Brad Kincaid's name conveniently omitted). The presentation of the medal at the White House, with Teddy Roosevelt in the background beaming that toothsome grin. And endlessly, in each article, the *Statesman* hammered home the theme that Owen had lost an arm in bringing democracy to backward and oppressed people in far corners of the world.

Yet the conquering warrior, returned home at last, proved a reluctant hero. Whatever his reasons for shunning the spotlight, he kept them to himself. Guthrie fairly hummed with speculation (and a mild case of pique) but the townspeople respected his wishes. When he stepped off the train his father stood alone, a greeting committee of one.

Jake hurried across the platform, making a studied effort to ignore the empty sleeve. It was an uncomfortable moment, but he tried to appear jocular and at ease, merely another father welcoming his son home from the war. He pumped Owen's good arm in a firm handclasp, and forced himself to grin a hearty, jawcracking grin.

"Son, you're a sight for sore eyes. Damned if you're not!"

"Hello, Pa." Owen let go of his hand, flicking a glance around the depot. "You're lookin' pretty fit yourself."

"Aw, hell, you know me"—Jake had the odd sensation he was talking to a stranger—"don't reckon my spring'll ever run down."

"Julia and the kids okay?"

"Never better. Wait till you see little Beth. You've got yourself a charmer there, boy. Pretty as a picture."

"Yeah, Julia hasn't talked about much else in her letters. How's Grace?"

"Grace? Oh, she's fine. Just fine. They're all waitin' for you out at the ranch. Got the place all spruced up and a big feed laid on. Gonna greet you home in real style."

"Sounds good. Why don't we head out?"

"Sure thing. Buggy's right around the corner of the depot. You go ahead and I'll see about collectin' your bags." Almost relieved to get away, Jake rushed off in search of a porter.

Without a backward glance Owen made his way to the end of the platform and started down the steps. Of a sudden he felt very tired, like a man who has journeyed far and seen too much.

After Owen's luggage was stowed in the buggy they drove north from town to the River Road, and turned west along the Cimarron. They rode in strained silence for a long while, both aware of the unspoken tension between them. Jake occupied himself with the reins, eyes trained on the horse's rump, and Owen stared off at the countryside, seemingly content to hold the silence. Never before had their similarity in character been so marked. Stubborn men, proud and assured, possessed of a determination and strength which set them apart. Yet it was this very strength of character, utter certainty in themselves and their judgments, which stood as a barrier between father and son. And never more so than now.

At last, troubled by the lengthening silence, Jake could hold his peace no longer. He had never understood Owen, not the way a father should, and it was time they had a talk, got it out in the open, and being a direct man, he came straight to the point.

"You know, it's a funny thing. I get the feelin' you're not exactly tickled pink about comin' back here. Care to tell me why?"

Owen pursed his lips, deliberating a moment, then shrugged. "Let's just say I'm a coward, Pa. I came back because I didn't have the guts to cut loose."

"Now goddamnit, that's a bunch of nonsense and you know it. They don't give that medal to cowards. Not the way I hear it."

"You think this medal's hot stuff, huh, Pa?"

"Why, hell yes! You tryin' to tell me you don't?"

"Not especially. The only heroes I know come back in a box."

"Son, just to be blunt about it, that's a crock of shit." Jake scowled, and ground his teeth. "Sounds like you're feelin' guilty 'cause you lived to tell the tale. Or maybe you figure losin' an arm wasn't enough?"

"I think you missed the point, Pa." Owen's mouth curled in a thin, sardonic smile. "The way I figure it, losin' this arm was too much. Course I could've been shipped home in a box, so lookin' at it the other way round, maybe I was lucky after all."

Jake looked as if his ears had become unplugged. "That's it, isn't it? You had me call off the celebration 'cause you've got some screwball notion about the war."

"Guess it depends on what you call screwball. I had plenty of time to think while I was laid up in the hospital, and one day it all came clear, sort of sudden like. We thought we were fightin' to free the Cubans, but we weren't. Not if you read the fine print in that peace treaty. We were fightin' because somebody in Washington saw a way to grab off a bunch of islands real cheap. Now we can rattle our sabers and make other countries sit up and take notice, and all it cost us was a few thousand lives. Turned out to be a regular bargain day."

The words had tumbled out, furious and laced with sarcasm, but Jake merely shook his head and chuckled softly. "Well, son, welcome to the human race. I'd just about given up hope there for a while, but you've finally figured it out. What you're sayin' is that you've seen the nature of the beast, and it don't have nothin' to do with Christian charity."

"Charity's the wrong word. What those bastards in Washington did doesn't have a helluva lot to do with being human."

"Why, because they played dirty? Got you all pumped up with brotherhood and justice so you'd win their war for 'em? Lemme tell you something, Owen. There's no morality in the history books. The strong take it away from the weak, and most times, the winners hang the losers. Course, governments change and political systems alter to suit the moment, but in the end the story comes out the same. It's dog eat dog, and the hard truth is that the beast likes his meat raw."

He paused, fixing Owen with a steadfast gaze. "Hell,

you're right. You were lucky. It only cost you an arm to learn that. Most men live out their lives in thimbles 'cause they never do understand it. And they go to their graves no smarter'n when they started."

Owen regarded him woodenly. "You know what the war really taught me, Pa? It taught me that to be a leader you've got to have the capacity to inflict pain. I guess I just don't qualify, so I'll leave that to you and the rest of the politicians."

With an eloquent look, surprised and ruefully impressed, Jake reared back in his seat. "By Christ, it's been a long time comin' but you finally got it out of your craw, didn't you?"

"Yeah, I suppose so. Losin' an arm has a way of clearing a man's vision."

"And now you've got me pegged with those *bastards* you were talkin' about. Or maybe you just finally worked up the guts to say it out loud. I've got a hunch that's what you've had stuck in your gizzard all these years."

Owen felt compelled to get it out in the open, leave nothing unsaid, in the way a hangman feels some grisly compulsion to climb the gallows and have done with a nasty job. "I got suckered into the war, but it taught me that somebody has to stand up and draw the line. Otherwise nothing changes, and it's still a dog-eat-dog world."

He looked his father directly in the eye. "I've decided to fight you on the statehood issue, Pa. I'll stand with the Indians, and I'll work to get them a separate state. That's why I didn't want any brass bands, and that's why I almost didn't come back here. But I've got a family and I need to make a decent living, so I thought if we could set aside politics I'd go back to runnin' the ranch. All the same, I'll be spendin' some time in the Nations. So if you can't swallow that, just tell me, and I'll clear out in the mornin'."

It was a form of honesty, raw and simple, that Jake could appreciate. Several moments passed in silence, broken only by the rhythmic beat of steel-shod hooves on hard winter ground. Then, quite suddenly, he laughed.

"Scratch a begger and find a holy man."

"If that's your answer, you'll have to spell it out."

"Why, it's real simple, son. Anybody that spends half his time tryin' to change human nature spends the other half lookin' for handouts. And when it's all said and done with, he's left standin' on a street corner with a tin cup and a monkey."

"I'm not askin' for handouts. I'll earn my keep."

"Sure you will, and all the time you'll be tryin' to haul my ashes over in the Nations. But, what the hell? Maybe you'll get more of an education than you bargained for." Amused by the absurd irony of a Kincaid pitted against a Kincaid, he chuckled scornfully. "You see, Owen, men like me have an advantage over you dogooders. You're like a lightning bug. His blinker's on his ass, so he knows more about where he's been than where he's headed. Think about it a while and you'll see what I mean."

Jake popped the reins, and the horse responded with a livelier pace. The buggy sped along the road, father and son again fallen silent, but the tension between them had disappeared. They were adversaries now, squared off in an arena of sorts, and in that each of them somehow found a new respect for the other.

Shortly before sunset they pulled into the yard, and brought the buggy to a halt. The front door opened and Julia rushed outside as Owen stepped to the ground. She threw her arms around his neck, uttering a small cry, and hugged him fiercely. Tears, glistening in the sunlight like tiny seeds of spun glass, rolled down her cheeks, and after a moment he put his arm around her waist. Grace came through the door, leading Morgan by the hand and holding the baby nestled in her other arm. She stopped at the edge of the porch, smiling that same enigmatic smile, and watched, saying nothing. But her eyes sparkled bright ebony, and when Owen's gaze met hers, something unspoken, and very private, passed between them. Julia clutched at him tighter, and he accepted her embrace, but his eyes never left the girl.

Still perched in the buggy seat, Jake observed his son's homecoming with a wry, faintly abstracted smile. It was all very touching and, unexpectedly, quite illuminating. As he caught the look in the girl's eyes, and knew instinctively that it was returned in kind, the last piece in the puzzle fell into place. Owen had taken his stand with the Indians, well enough, and it was perhaps more personal than anyone imagined.

Warmed by the prospect, Jake stuck a cigar in his mouth and grinned broadly. There was hope for the boy after all. And he might yet turn out to be human. Especially if some dark-eyed little heathen pulled him down off his high horse.

Down in the muck, where the rest of the pack ran.

ELEVEN

The convention had been called in Muskogee, principal railhead and trade center of the Creek nation. Delegates from the Five Civilized Tribes began arriving on a sultry afternoon in late August, and that evening, while a lightning storm pelted the town with rain, informal meetings were held among the delegation leaders. By morning the sky was clear, and as the sun rose high nearly two hundred delegates gathered in the local meeting hall. There was an air of somber dignity about them, and the grim businesslike attitude of those faced with a herculean task. Brothers in blood if not always allies, these men had come together to draft a constitution, and create the State of Sequoyah.

The occasion was unprecedented, and something of a last-ditch effort to stave off the machinations of Oklahoma Territory and the federal government. Several times over the past seven years the tribal leaders had met in council to discuss the onrushing threat of white domination. But ancient animosities, and the jealousy of vain men, led inevitably to bickering and squabbling, and without fail a breakdown in solidarity. Despite their differences, however, the Indian leaders had drafted resolution after resolution calling for separate statehood.

And Congress disdainfully ignored each new plea.

Now, late in the summer of 1905, time had run out. Less than seven months remained before tribal government, by act of Congress, would be abolished forever. Afterward, as everyone knew, joint statehood would become little more than a formality. If Indian Territory was to retain its independence then it must be done quickly, with some masterstroke of diplomacy. Desperate, grasping at straws, the tribal leaders had taken this germ of an idea and transformed it, full-blown, into the Sequoyah Convention.

That Indian Territory had remained independent this long was sheer happenstance, spawned by the vagaries of politics. Bills had been brought to the floor of Congress time and again, but those who championed Oklahoma statehood had yet to muster sufficient support to carry the vote. It was the considered opinion of both the Senate and the House that the matter might better be resolved after the Indians had been stripped of tribal autonomy. In short, break the horse to halter before hauling out the saddle.

Curiously, the Indians had gained support from an unexpected quarter, and this, too, had delayed action in Congress. A movement had arisen in Oklahoma Territory, shortly after the close of the Spanish-American War, which advocated separate statehood. The leader of this campaign was Owen Kincaid, a newcomer to the political scene, but a war hero whose name alone attracted thousands to his cause. However obscure his motives (there were rumors that he was more Indian lover than white chauvinist), Kincaid advanced logical arguments as he stumped the Territory rallying converts. He urged that Indian Territory had few roads or schools, and that much Indian land would be exempt from taxation. Speaking with some authority, he also asserted that social conditions in Indian Territory were less stable, and therefore prone to unrestrained lawlessness. All of this, he reasoned, would place enormous and unwonted burdens on Oklahoma Territory, which because of its industrial development would bear the brunt of financing the new state. These were highly persuasive arguments, but the opposition (which controlled every major newspaper in Oklahoma) countered with vitriolic editorials and, perhaps more important, a steady sprinkling of funds among Washington lobbyists.

And Congress obligingly twiddled its thumbs.

At first glance, Owen Kincaid seemed an unlikely ally of the Indians. His speeches were a condemnation of both the tribal way of life and the Indian leaders themselves. But several clandestine meetings, always held in some remote part of the Nations, had taken place over the years. From the outset Kincaid revealed his strategy, and talked not of Oklahoma but rather of Indian liberation. In effect, he had set himself up as a stalking-horse for the five Civilized Tribes, devoting his time and energy to driving a wedge of contention between the white factions of Oklahoma Territory. Though the tribal leaders seldom agreed on anything, they were unanimous in their appraisal of Owen Kincaid. However white his skin, he was an Indian patriot to the core.

And on the opening day of the Sequoyah Convention, the name of Owen Kincaid was on everyone's lips. As a gambit to attract national publicity, he had agreed to address the delegates. This was the first hint, publicly or otherwise, that he had any link with the Indian cause and, as such, created a storm of controversy. While there was no inkling of what he would say, journalists from across the country swarmed into Muskogee. Owen Kincaid was news, hot copy, the stuff of headlines. Aside from being a war hero, and one of Oklahoma's legendary lawmen, he was the moving force behind the crusade for state separatism. In that he had become an outspoken critic of Oklahoma's political machine, and by implication, if nothing else, a censor of his own father, who was the single most influential figure in territorial affairs. Hardly anyone thought separate statehood had a ghost of a chance, but Owen Kincaid's presence held the promise of fireworks, and the meeting hall that morning was packed with reporters, some from as far away as New York and Washington.

After convening, the delegates set about electing officers, and within an hour the press had its first sensation. Pleasant

Porter, chief of the Creeks, was elected president of the convention. But of the five vice-presidents elected, two were white men: William Murray, an intermarried citizen of the Chickasaw Nation, and Charles Haskell of the Creeks. Quite obviously, a coalition had been formed between the whites residing in Indian Territory and their red neighbors. The significance of this unsuspected alliance was electrifying, and might well have vast repercussions in the future.

The hall quieted as Pleasant Porter took up his gavel and hammered the delegates into silence. Then, without ceremony, he brought on the keynote speaker, introducing him as a man who needed no introduction. A hushed stillness fell over the room, and men edged forward on their chairs as Owen Kincaid walked to the speaker's podium. Still in his early thirties, he was a striking man. Tall and broad-shouldered, chestnut hair flecked through with premature specks of gray, his bronzed features were very earnest and locked in a square-jawed look of determination. And the empty sleeve went almost unnoticed in an aura of strength and vitality which emanated from his steely eyes and the lithe movements of a man who had all the arms he needed. He stopped beside the podium, staring out over the assemblage a moment, and then lifted his chin in a gesture that was at once proud and humble.

"President Porter and delegates to the convention. You honor me with an invitation to speak before such a distinguished gathering. And I in turn commend you for the noble purpose which has brought you together this day. The Five Civilized Tribes is an old and illustrious confederation, and in the history of man's experiments in government, yours has been an example for all men. *All men*—of whatever race, of whatever color, of whatever creed. If my words here today were merely a testimonial to your heritage, I would recount the indignities you have borne, the injustices you have tolerated, the suffering endured along your trail of tears. But I will speak of none of these things."

He thrust a single finger in the air. "Joint statehood. One state! That is their goal, and ironically they propose to call it Oklahoma—land of the red man. But rather than irony let us deal with the clever arguments they employ to justify joint statehood.

"It is said that one strong and wealthy state would be better than two weak and impoverished states. Translated, this means that your opponents covet what you have, and that it is they who will become wealthier and stronger in the exchange.

"And with the utmost benevolence, it is said that the resources of each territory would supplement the resources of the other, thereby promoting economic stability. Stripped of subterfuge, this means that those who possess no coal, no timber, no mineral wealth will methodically take it from you. At great profit to themselves, and with small return to the red man."

Owen Kincaid spoke for nearly an hour. He talked of money barons, and the audacity with which they were already exploiting the natural resources of the Nations. He disclosed secret plans of white politicians to control the voting and gain unlimited power over the red man's domain. He addressed himself to Congress and the federal bureaucracy, and their conspiracy with white power brokers to hand over the lands and wealth of Indian Territory. And at last, his words crackling with urgency, he flung down what was both a challenge and a warning.

"Lay aside tribal politics and past differences. Rise above the pettiness and deceit and dishonor of your opponents. Draft yourselves a constitution that all of America will applaud, and present it to Congress with the message that brotherhood still lives. And further, that the kinship of all men—red or white—will never perish in the State of Sequoyah."

There was a moment of stunned, breathless silence. Then, to a man, delegates and journalists and spectators rose to their feet in a standing ovation. Owen Kincaid shook hands with

Pleasant Porter and the convention officers, acknowledged the crowd's applause with a final bow, and walked from the speaker's platform.

Newspapers around the country bannered Owen's speech in bold, outraged headlines. His indictment of power brokers and politicians sent shock waves reverberating across the land, and Americans awoke to the national shame that had taken root in Indian Territory. Three weeks later a committee from the Five Civilized Tribes submitted their constitution to Congress, and requested that Indian Territory be admitted to the Union as the State of Sequoyah. All of Washington was amazed by the document, and when it was made public, civic scholars lauded it as the most advanced instrument of democracy in the history of the republic.

A week later Congress tabled the matter for future study.

Oil suddenly became big business in Indian Territory.

The horseless carriage ceased to be a plaything of the rich, and in the process it changed the look of America. Henry Ford's assembly line worked overtime to meet the stiff competition of Oldsmobile, Packard, Winton, and a dozen others. And while there was a paucity of statistics, it was estimated that upwards of twenty thousand automobiles would be sold by the close of the year.

Not to be outdone, westerners took to the automobile with the same enthusiasm as their eastern cousins. Jake Kincaid was among the first in Guthrie to purchase a car, and characteristically, he went about it in style. With a chauffeur up front, he tooled around town in a dazzling peacock-blue Pierce-Arrow. A massive, lumbering affair, scarcely smaller than a hay wagon, it was tricked out with brass fittings, mahogany paneling, and a tonneau lushly upholstered in Morocco leather. The backfire rattled windows, and the mere sight of it was enough to spook wild horses and little old ladies. But Jake thought it was the classiest thing on wheels, and he particularly liked the fact that it guzzled gasoline like a thirsty dinosaur.

These early cars were built with a certain agricultural simplicity, and under full power they wheezed and groaned with a sound not unlike that of a threshing machine. A day spent on the road was nothing short of an adventure, patching and pumping tires, tinkering with engine breakdowns, and finally, if luck prevailed, arriving home under the dim flare of acetylene headlamps. But clunky and crude, and temperamental as they were, the cars came equipped with a common denominator.

They all used gasoline. And lots of it.

Aside from its grand appearance, this astounding consumption of gasoline was one of the reasons Jake had bought the Pierce-Arrow. If he had any reservations about the sudden craze for automobiles, it was the fact that some, like the Ford, drank sparingly of their fuel tanks. He had oil wells scattered across the Cherokee Nation, and the burgeoning automobile industry had transformed his holdings into a gold mine. Black gold, to be sure, but nonetheless immensely profitable, and becoming more so with every car bought by the American public.

Not that his windfall profits were all gravy, or easily come by. There were hazards to the oil game that he had encountered in none of his other ventures, and as the industry expanded the problems multiplied geometrically. Of all his headaches, however, the root-hog-or-die competition was by far the most perplexing. Never before had Jake come up against a breed of men who were as brutal and unscrupulous as himself in a business deal. With corporate empires at stake, and hundreds of millions of dollars in the balance, there were neither ethics nor integrity. Black gold somehow brought out the worst in men, and the industry attracted an aggregation of rogues that made the old railroad barons look absolutely pious.

The major oil companies, mostly eastern concerns, were

almost Machiavellian in their intrigue and double-dealing. They controlled the pipeline franchise in Indian Territory (obtained through bribes at the highest levels in Washington) and, with it, a virtual license to steal. Independent producers found it extremely difficult just to get their oil into the pipelines; even then they were paid roughly one-third the market value of their crude. It was a formidable, sometimes ruinous, competitive weapon, and sanctioned without restraint by the federal government.

Jake fought the majors at first, battling every step of the way, but he quickly discovered that he was outclassed. When oil was discovered in the Osage Nation they simply steamrolled over him, though he was perhaps the wealthiest and most politically active of all the independent producers. Bloodied and battered, shamed that he had been made to back off, the wisdom of his decision was nonetheless timely. Early in the spring of 1905 it became apparent that the majors pulled strings which stretched all the way to the White House.

Unlike other tribes, the Osage were not granted absolute title to their land. At their own request the mineral rights were reserved, and each member of the tribe was entitled to an equal share known as a headright. The Secretary of the Interior was entrusted with authority to lease the mineral rights as he saw fit, and afterward distribute the proceeds among the tribe. It was an awesome responsibility, and hardly immune to pressure from vested-interest groups.

Already it had been demonstrated that vast pools of oil underlay the Osage lands, and as the initial lease period neared expiration, independent producers began offering a bonus per acre which would have meant upward of $15 million (to be split among 2,229 members of the tribe) and several times that amount in future royalties. A small fraction of that sum, however, could accomplish wonders in Washington. And immediately the major oil companies began lobbying for a blanket lease on the Osage lands.

Jake sat that round out, restricting his efforts to the Cherokee Nation. Which was just as well. Though the independents shouted themselves hoarse, and spent a fortune on a lobbying campaign of their own, they never had a chance. It was simply a lost cause.

President Theodore Roosevelt granted the major producers a blanket lease for a period of ten years. The conditions of the lease were curiously favorable to the oil companies, if something less than generous to the Indians. The Osage received no bonus whatsoever, and by rough calculation the tribe lost upward of $30 million. Not an insignificant sum. Quite impressive, in fact, when it appeared in the form of stockholder dividends. And by no small coincidence, many of those very stockholders lived along the Potomac.

Not surprisingly, Jake felt a grudging admiration for the men who had engineered a financial coup of such magnitude. He had little, if any, sympathy for the Osage (although his widowed daughter-in-law held a tribal headright), and his one regret was that he had not shared in the spoils. But in the months to come he found that his strategic withdrawal from the Osage Nation was somewhat like backing off from the schoolyard bully. It merely invited further attack, and on a broader scale.

Shortly before Christmas the ax fell. In a stupefying order the Secretary of the Interior restricted the size of oil leases on Indian lands outside the Osage reservation. Both individuals and companies would be limited to a single lease of 4,800 acres, scarcely enough land to warrant the exorbitant costs of exploration and drilling. The intent was all too clear. With the Osage Nation in their hip pocket, the majors had now eliminated the possibility of an independent producer becoming a serious competitive threat. The squeeze play was on, and anyone who doubted it was quickly treated to an object lesson.

An independent outfit brought in three gushers outside Tulsa, a small village in the Creek Nation. The strike was widely publicized, and every indication pointed to a pool of oil as vast as that in the Osage field. But the wildcatters suddenly discovered that there was no market for their bonanza. They were denied access to the pipelines, curiously ignored by the large refineries, and eventually forced to run their oil into earth storage tanks. Faced with disaster, they swallowed their pride and sold out to a major oil company.

Seated in his office the day before Christmas, Jake was singularly unmoved by the holiday spirit. On the heels of the Interior Department order, this new calamity in Tulsa left him glum and brooding. Oddly enough, he began to understand how the Indians had felt all these years. Outsiders were poaching on his preserve (in his own mind he had always considered Indian Territory as his private hunting grounds), and it galled him to think that these interlopers were beating him at his own game. Yet, unlike many of the independents, he wasn't quite ready to call it quits. Upon closer examination, after dissecting the problem and studying it from every angle, he thought he saw a loophole. It was studded with risk, and offered no immediate solution to the pipeline problem, but he had decided to take the gamble. Allowing these eastern pirates to rob Oklahoma blind, whatever their political connections, simply wasn't to be tolerated. He had his dander up, and he meant to act.

A knock sounded at the door, and a moment later Mordecai Jones stepped into the office. The little banker had grown stooped and wrinkled with time, more gargoyle than gnome as age withered his features. But he was still a wizard of tangled finance, with an undiminished gift for shady deals, and he had served Jake well in expanding the Kincaid empire. Uncannily sensitive to his employer's moods, he now took a chair before the desk and screwed up his face in an expression of solemn attentiveness.

"You sent for me, Mr. Kincaid?"

Jake had his hands locked behind his head, apparently studying some point in space. "Mordecai, you're about as devious as anybody I know, so tell me, what's the best way to outsmart a crook?"

Jones beamed, highly complimented by this candid observation on his character. "Well, just offhand, Mr. Kincaid, the maxim that comes to mind is the one coined by bunco artists. The easiest mark to sucker is the man with larceny in his heart."

"Exactly! You hit the nail right on the head. And that's what we're gonna do to the oil companies."

"You intend to take on the majors again?"

"Damn right, I do. Now pay attention, Mordecai." Jake swiveled around in his chair, eyes glinting. "The Interior Department says a man can lease forty-eight hundred acres so long as he's got forty thousand dollars deposited in a bank as guarantee of good faith. You with me so far?"

Jones steepled his fingers, and nodded thoughtfully. "That was the gist of the order, yes. Although it was stipulated that a man can hold only one lease at any given moment."

"Yeah, but they overlooked something. And that's where we're gonna get 'em by the balls. Now I want you to have our lawyers draw up articles of incorporation for fifty dummy companies."

"Fifty"—Jones seemed to gulp the words—"companies?"

"Take 'em over to Ramsey at the capitol. He'll see that they get approved without anyone gettin' nosy."

"I understand. But you're talking about tying up two million dollars in deposits. Not to mention the cost of the leases."

"That's where the tricky part comes in, Mordecai. But the way you juggle books, it'll be a snap." Jake leaned forward, smug as a cat. "Deposit forty thousand dollars in the accounts of the first five companies. After those companies have negotiated leases, and you've issued affidavits of deposit to the government, then we'll switch the money into the accounts of the next five companies. And on down the line. Before you know it, we'll have ourselves a couple o' hundred thousand acres under lease. You being an upright banker and all, nobody'll suspect a thing."

Jones looked doubtful. "Do you intend to drill on each of the leases?"

"Depends. If we can get most of that land in one big chunk, I've got an idea the majors will hand us a blank check for the drilling rights. Course the tracts that Turk McSpadden thinks look the best, we'll drill 'em ourselves. And if the big boys won't give us access to the pipelines then we won't sell 'em any of our leases. That's what I meant about have 'em by the balls."

"It sounds good, I'll admit." The little banker squinted myopically. "But you're running a risk that they will just wait and freeze you out. The same as they did that bunch in Tulsa."

"I quit playin' for chalkies a long time ago." Jake dismissed him with an abrupt gesture. "Now get a move on. Likely somebody else is workin' on the same idea, and I mean to beat 'em to the punch. While you're at it, get our land agents set for a trip to Bartlesville. We're gonna move fast."

As Mordecai Jones went through the door, Jake again tilted back in his chair. On the street below he heard a Salvation Army band thumping out Christmas carols, and of a sudden, it distracted him from business. He recalled that he was expected at Zalia's tonight, and at the ranch tomorrow for Christmas dinner. All of which struck him as tediously bothersome just at the moment, an unwelcome intrusion. Julia was sure to start her usual harping about moving back to Guthrie (which Jake had written off as another of life's lost causes), and his Indian-lover son would likely just sit there with a mulish look of annoyance. Then they would all stare at one another while the squaw cat-footed around looking like she'd swallowed the canary. The whole situation was nothing short of intolerable, and he'd come to dread these infrequent trips to the ranch.

Except for the kids. Morg was hellion enough to make any grandfather proud. Growing like a weed, too. And Beth. He never ceased to be amazed by the striking resemblance. It was spooky in a way, almost as if Sadie had come back with long yellow curls and eyes green as jade. And that same spunky smile, to boot. Life took some damned queer turns, no doubt about it.

After a moment he put it from his mind, and went back to pondering the vagaries of the oil business. A small smile creased his lips as an image formed, and he caught a glimpse of things to come. How they'd howl when he squeezed their balls. The bastards! Already he could hear the roar, and it had about it the sweet ring of revenge. The melodic bong of great bells being tolled.

He closed his eyes and listened.

Yellow leaves glittered like a sea of a golden coins along Cottonwood Creek. After a long dusty summer there was a nip in the air, a promise of frost, and Guthrie came alive with the zest of brisk sunny days and cool sparkling nights. It was a time of high spirits and jubilant good cheer for the people of Oklahoma Territory, a change of seasons marked by the exhilaration of a dream come true. But for Jake Kincaid the autumn of '06 was a time of recrimination and scorn and dour reassessment.

Statehood wasn't at all what he'd expected.

Since early morning he had stood at the window of his office, waiting and watching. Across the street, at city hall, there was a hubbub of activity as politicians and those with political aspirations scurried from meeting to meeting in smoke-filled rooms on the ground floor. Upstairs, in the city court chambers, delegates to the constitutional convention met in session. They were hammering out a final draft of the Oklahoma State Constitution, which would ultimately be submitted to the voters for ratification. And none of them, white man or red, had come seeking Jake Kincaid's advice.

Still, though by now he knew it was in vain, Jake waited.

A monolithic figure, alone and grim, seemingly hewn from a slab of granite. His face was immobile, crowned by a great thatch of snowy white hair, but the iron-gray eyes smoldered, rimmed with disgust, as he stared at the scene below. By some odd betrayal of his inner thoughts, perhaps in the smoky cast to his eyes, he looked like a man who suddenly found himself standing on a thin sheet of ice, helpless as he watched it buckle and splinter into jagged cracks at his feet. Yet he couldn't move. Some perverse fascination held him there, framed in that window, gazing on as a lifetime of planning and scheming and conniving dissolved before his eyes.

Looking back, he saw now that he had missed the warning signals. His own son taking sides with the opposition, articulating the conscience of those unobtrusive, quietly silent masses. The alignment last year of white men and red at the Sequoyah Convention, and the subsequent rumbles of conciliation throughout Oklahoma Territory. A gradual erosion of his influence in Washington, there for all to see when the oil companies chased him out of the Osage Nation. And that he had outfoxed them in the Cherokee Nation was a moot victory, in retrospect a personal triumph of small consequence in the broader struggle. The oil barons were entrenched in his own backyard, undermining his political machine with their millions, and the seeds of dissension had spread.

When Congress passed the Enabling Act at the beginning of the summer he had again blinded himself to the obvious. The legislation made joint statehood a reality—the very goal he'd worked toward all these years—and he blithely credited himself with having brought it about. Only later did he discover that it was partisan politics, and not Jake Kincaid, which had decided the issue. Jealous of its power, Congress had turned thumbs down on separate statehood for the most elemental of reasons—it would have meant four new Senators instead of the two who would now represent Oklahoma.

The truth, and with it acknowledgment of his waning influence, became apparent to Jake in stages. Under the Enabling Act it was specified that the people of Oklahoma would elect delegates to a constitutional convention. The first blow came in the fine print. Fifty-five delegates were to be chosen from Oklahoma Territory and fifty-seven delegates were to be selected from Indian Territory. Though small, the disparity in numbers came as a shock. And for Jake, it was somewhat like the first explosion in a string of firecrackers.

As the summer wore on he found himself increasingly out of touch. Old political loyalties evaporated overnight, and men who had fearfully accepted his dictates in the past were suddenly unavailable, curiously unafraid. Though he fielded a slate of candidates, it was clear that his best men had hopped aboard another bandwagon, and in the driver's seat sat his chief rival, Owen Kincaid. The campaign for delegates was vicious and hard fought, but the mudslinging tactics that had served Jake so well over the years seemed to have gone out of style. When the votes were tallied, the people of Oklahoma had elected to their convention ninety-nine Democrats, twelve Republicans, and one Independent. It marked the end of an era and the demise of the old order.

But the final shock, and for Jake, the cruelest blow of all, was yet to come. At the opening session, the delegates elected William Murray, of the Chickasaw Nation, as president of the convention. And Charles Haskell, of the Creek Nation, was chosen floor leader of the majority party. These were men who had played leading roles at the Sequoyah Convention, and their appointment in Guthrie left small doubt as to the mood of the delegates. Oklahoma had declared itself, and in a voice that represented all the people, both red and white.

Hindsight held small consolation for Jake. In the end, it was he who had become the lightning bug, with a better view of where he'd been than where he was headed.

He had misjudged the temper of the times, and the conscience of an entire people, blundering along under a cloud of delusion. Worse, he had violated the pragmatist's creed, the one tenet in which he believed wholeheartedly: life's single constant is a capricious and inveterate tendency toward change. These were errors rooted in pride and arrogance, and in politics, particularly for the kingmaker, they were fatal errors. Sober reflection, that damnable hindsight, was, after all, illuminating. He had witlessly miscalculated, compounding it with utter disregard of his own code, and quite simply, it was time to pay the piper.

And now, staring out the window, he suddenly understood why he had waited here these last few days. Owen Kincaid emerged from city hall and crossed the street, striding purposefully toward the bank. Somehow Jake had known he would come. Between them was an account to be settled, a final reckoning. Perhaps, in some small way, vindication of the men they were, if not the barren kinship of father and son.

Jake was seated at his desk when Owen knocked and came through the door. There was no pretense of cordiality. This was a meeting between victor and vanquished, and that they were both Kincaids made it all the more distasteful. Owen walked to a chair and seated himself, nodding curtly. Across the desk, Jake met his gaze, lordly and impervious, seemingly untouched by defeat. A moment passed, and then the old man smiled disdainfully.

"Get your business all done? You and your heathen cronies."

Owen flushed, but let it pass. "I've just come from a majority caucus. I wanted you to hear it from me instead of secondhand."

"Why bother? You don't owe me nothin'."

"I felt an obligation all the same. There's not anything personal in it, and I guess I just wanted you to hear me say that."

"Well, spit it out." Jake's tone was clipped and stiff. "I've got business to tend to. You know, the world don't stop just because a bunch of bleedin' hearts stole the march."

Owen felt neither angered nor surprised by the churlish rebuff. His father was one of a breed, arrant predators evolved throughout the centuries, whose end product had the appearance of a gentleman and the soul of a thug. But there was no changing him. As Owen at last understood, he was immutable as rock, and converting him would have been no less a task than teaching eagles to scratch the earth like chickens. A man could only contend with him, and try not to lose his own humanity in the process.

"We've selected Charles Haskell as our candidate for governor."

"That white Injun!" Jake raked him with a cold glare. "Hell, anybody with a lick of sense knows he couldn't win."

Owen regarded him evenly. "Judging by the delegate vote, he'll take it in a landslide. We've also agreed to a separate referendum calling for statewide prohibition of liquor."

"So why tell me? I don't give a damn if you dictate morals. It's never yet stopped men from drinkin' and whorin'. Won't stop 'em in Oklahoma either."

"That's just the beginning, Pa. Lots of things will change with Haskell in office. The days of corruption and shady deals are finished. I'm tellin' you now so you'll have time to get your own house in order."

Jake had the feeling that he'd lived through all this before, and in his mind's eye he saw again what the reformers had done to Kansas. He gritted his teeth, making knots in his jaws, and stabbed out with a bony finger. "You're puttin' the cart before the horse, aren't you? Christ, you still have to get the constitution approved in Washington before you can even submit it to the voters. Seems to me you and your do-gooders have got a ways to go."

Owen countered with a tight smile. "Maybe you'll recollect I've got a little pull with President Roosevelt. Offhand, we don't expect any delays."

"That crook! Not choosy about the company you keep, are you?" Jake grunted sourly, wondering if he'd struck a nerve. Then, quite suddenly, his eyes brightened, and he riveted Owen with a piercing look. "I must be gettin' addled in my old age. What's your payoff in all this? Lieutenant governor? Senator, maybe?"

"Nope. Sorry to disappoint you, but I guess I won't be able to uphold the Kincaid tradition. Once Haskell gets in office, I'm finished with politics."

"Knowin' you, I suppose it figures. Still beats me though, how I ever raised a son that turned out to be a goddamn' crusader."

"Likely it was that good Christian environment. Just a chip off the ol' block."

Jake grinned in spite of himself. "You always were a smartass. So, what now—back to the ranch? Hide your head in the sand again?"

"It's a better place than most." Owen hitched his chair back, and walked to the door. "Besides, I've got to get my armor shined up for the next crusade."

"Yeah, you do that, King Arthur. And shine it up good. Come election time, me and my boys might just have a few surprises for you."

The door opened and closed, and Owen was gone. Jake's bravado vanished the instant the latch clicked shut, and a look of jaded, bone-weary fatigue crept over his face. Unaccountably, he had the sudden feeling somebody had just run him through a rock crusher. And it hurt like hell.

Harlan Green oozed sweat, rattling on in a reedy, unnerved voice. Something about the Wobblies. Jake caught a word here and there, barely listening, not particularly interested in the fat man's opinion. Nor was he paying any attention to the commotion from downtown. The miners' rally had been under way for nearly an hour, and all of Poteau had turned out to watch, but he couldn't be bothered. Unlike Green, he'd never concerned himself with the loud talk of men fueled on Dutch courage. Hot air was harmless, however much they yelled and beat their chests. The time to start worrying was when they stopped making speeches.

Huddled close to a potbellied stove, he and Green were seated in a watchman's shack near the main gate. Outside the night was cold and inky black, and groups of beefy, hard-faced men stood around open fires warming themselves. Jake had an idea their presence alone, merely a show of force, would put an end to this asinine strike. But if the miners wanted trouble, he'd give them all they could handle, and with the goon squad to back his play there was little doubt as to the outcome. Meantime, while Green droned on in a nervous twitter, his mind was preoccupied with other matters.

The licking he'd taken at the hands of Owen's crowd had affected him a good deal more than anyone suspected. Somehow, in a way he hadn't quite unraveled as yet, it seemed symptomatic of the times. Within the last year his neatly organized life had been thrown into disarray, a muddled shambles which had about it a sense of unreality. Twice he'd been routed completely, first by the oil companies and then by a bunch of political amateurs. Now his coal mine was closed down, threatened by union organizers, and if the strike wasn't quelled hard and fast, he could expect similar troubles at the timber company. It had all happened so quickly, defying reasonable explanation, and for the first time in his life, a sliver of doubt crept into his thoughts.

Was it merely circumstances, one mishap piled upon another in a world gone topsy-turvy with change? Or was he losing his grip? No longer able to cut the mustard against these young upstarts who challenged him at every turn? Until recently the question of age had never entered his mind. Although many of his cronies had retired or died, grown old before their time, he never equated himself with the frailties of other men. He was no withered giant, with his sap gone cold. Some fleshed skeleton bound in leathery skin with his manhood shriveled to a limber twig. When he bedded

Zalia the spark of assurance was still there; he was upon her with the brutish impatience of an aroused stallion. Sometimes his breath grew short, and now and then he nodded off after supper. But these were momentary lapses, conspicuous only by their irregularity. He was still as vigorous as a young stud, galvanized with energy, able by the exercise of sheer will to outwork (and probably outscrew) any man half his age.

Still, for all his undiminished lust, he knew that man was a creature with an infinite capacity for self-delusion. It was easier to believe he was the same as he'd always been—rugged and tough, a young vandal astride the world—much easier to believe that than to accept what he saw in the mirror. In a way it was a mental sleight of hand, an old man's refuge, avoiding the constant reminder of age. Every man activated this defensive mechanism somewhere along the line, trying to shield himself from the advancing years, aware that in the contest with time there could be no standoff. The hourglass was inevitably the victor, and the grains of sand merely a method of keeping score.

But these were new and startling thoughts to Jake. As if it had happened overnight, he awakened one morning to find himself approaching sixty-one, his hair gone white and his step not quite so nimble. The look of age, curiously enough, bothered him not nearly so much as the idea of age. He had always believed that the measure of manhood was a stiff pecker and a hard fist. His performance in Zalia's bed kept him convinced of the one, but his maddening setbacks in politics and business had seeded an uneasy doubt about the other. Perhaps his reflexes had slowed. Or he'd gone mushy between the ears. Maybe he'd lost the knack of rolling with the punch, no longer had the agility and stamina to step in and deliver a counterblow at the decisive moment. For if he was the same as he'd always been, then how had he been whipped so easily, with such humiliating finality?

And yet, caught up in this beckoning spectacle of age, it never occurred to Jake that it was a question of manhood which brought him to Poteau.

Harlan Green was a weak sister when it came to dirty work, and that was the excuse he'd used. All the same, he had a dozen men on his staff who could have handled this job with dispatch and skill. Some of them were outside right now, but they were there to follow orders, not to command. Yesterday, upon receiving Green's telegram, Jake had jumped at the chance to lead this sortie himself. Just the thought of a scrap made him feel twenty years younger, and that it was the Wobblies behind the strike merely added zest to an already tempting dish.

Not that Jake had anything personal against the Wobblies, he detested unions in general. He brooked no interference from anyone in the way he ran his businesses—they were private property no less than his home or his cuff links—and he found something vaguely un-American in a bunch of common laborers monkeying with the free-enterprise system. An outgrowth of this anti-union sentiment was a special grudge against the Wobblies. Known officially as the Industrial Workers of the World, the Wobblies were avowed Marxists, and the most radical of all unions. Their goal was to organize one big union, including unskilled labor, with equality for all. This was at odds with the efforts of the more exclusive craft unions; the American Federation of Labor had already denounced the renegades, condemning them as anarchists overly fond of violence. Yet, for reasons of their own, the Western Federation of Miners had aligned themselves with the Wobblies, thereby providing the movement with a legitimate front. Times were hard for the working man, and for those who labored in mines, life was especially cruel. As a result, employing hooligan tactics and violence, the Wobblies had achieved a reputation as hard-nosed organizers throughout the western mining camps.

Now, suddenly, they had appeared in Indian Territory. Their purpose was to organize not just mines, but business concerns of every nature. And their strategy was to crack the toughest nut first—old Jake Kincaid himself. Having succeeded in that, no one would dare stand against them.

As far as it went, the Wobblies' plan was a good one, but it failed to reckon with the temper of the man. Jake was a firm believer in fighting fire with fire, and just at the moment, he was spoiling for a fight anyway. In a matter of hours he had cleaned out every saloon in Guthrie—offering top wages to an assortment of brawlers and roustabouts—and had his goon squad on a special train heading for Poteau. Coming on the heels of his recent setbacks, he quickly convinced himself that this strike was nothing short of providential. He would use the Wobblies to restore his tattered reputation in Oklahoma. Aside from business considerations, demolishing these Marxist terrorists would also affirm his image as a defender of democracy and free enterprise.

And in the forthcoming elections that would be no small thing.

Apart from this personal rationalization, Jake's reasons for being here suited his mood, and seemed wholly justified in view of the threat to the mine. Seated in the watchman's shack, his thoughts had hardened to resolve, slowly shifting from himself to the task ahead. He wanted this fight in the worst way—something spectacular to grab newspaper headlines—and with any luck the Wobblies could be goaded into breaking the law. All he needed was an excuse, trespassing or destruction of property; then he could turn the goons loose to start busting heads. Afterward, with the Wobblies hightailing it for parts unknown, he might even concede to some of the miners' demands. Throw them a few scraps, just to show there were no hard feelings.

Green's monologue rose in pitch, breaking his concentration, and it occurred to him again that slick talkers seldom had the stomach for dirty work. The fat man was dripping sweat, eyes wide with fear, and the timbre of his voice bordered on hysteria.

"—and the plain fact is that they're not human, Jake. Not like anyone you ever met. They don't give a damn for this country or decency or anything else. They're like jackals— part dog and part wolf—and believe me, they've got the worst habits of both. I tell you, it chilled my blood when the big one—Stroud, I think his name is—walked into the office and told me he was taking the men out on strike. Why, he would just as soon killed me where I sat if I'd opened my mouth. You should have seen the look in his eye. Crazy, Jake. Honest- to-God crazy. And the demands he made—"

A knock at the door spared Jake another rehash of what he'd heard a dozen times over in the last few hours. One of the mine foremen stuck his head inside and grinned, jerking his thumb back toward the main gate.

"They're on their way, Mr. Kincaid. Carryin' torches and singin' like a bunch of drunk Micks."

Jake stood, briskly rubbing his hands together. "Well, what do you say, Harlan, shall we greet our union friends? They've damn sure kept us waitin' long enough."

Green froze, ashen-faced, as if he was screwed to his chair. "Jake, I'm not sure—what I mean to say is—"

"Forget it." Jake shot him a look of mild contempt, then turned toward the door. "I'll call you when the shoutin's over."

Outside, Jake walked directly to the main gate. It was standing wide open, with lanterns hung from the posts at either side. He drew a line in the dirt with the toe of his boot, and then took up a stance just inside the gate. Behind him, close to a hundred strong, the goon squad crowded forward in a tightly packed phalanx. Every man carried a pickax handle, and most were armed with pistols; except for hats and mackinaws, they bore a striking resemblance to some curi- ous gathering of gorillas, grunting and shuffling as they hud- dled together for warmth. Tired of waiting, their whiskey bottles drained dry, the men were glad at last to have the prospects of action. They were cold and bored and irritable, and a skulldusting contest seemed just the thing to ward off the chill night air.

The miners were visible now, strung out in a column along the road from town. At least half of them carried torches, and they all appeared armed with ax handles, logging chains, and lengths of pipe. As they approached the gate it became obvious that they were in an ugly mood, tanked up on rotgut and fired to anger by the rabble-rousing speeches of union organizers. The singing slowly died off, and catcalls began as they closed ranks, advancing in a beefy wedge ringed by torches and little spurts of frost from their taunting chant.

A man in the lead threw up his arm, and the mob halted just outside the gate. He waited, eyes flicking back over Jake and the goon squad, seemingly in no rush. Several moments passed before the miners fell silent, and then he took a step forward, planting an ax handle in the dirt at his feet.

"You must be Kincaid."

Jake cocked his head in a cool look of appraisal, ignoring the statement. The man was tall, spare and angular, with sharp features, pallid skin, and a cold voice. He had the hang-dog expression of someone who could be surprised by nothing but good fortune, yet there was an appearance of solidity and iron will about him. His hands were huge as hams, gnarled from work, and his eyes had that feverish glint peculiar to fanatics. All in all, Jake sized him up as a man who pissed ice water and was afraid of nothing on earth.

"I take it you're the one they call Stroud?"

The Wobbly leader grinned. "Vernon Stroud's the name. And defendin' the working man is my game." He shifted, squaring his shoulders. "Now that you know who you're dealin' with, let's get down to brass tacks."

Jake felt his pulse quicken, but he took a steely hold on himself. "I understand you have some grievances. I'm here to listen."

"You bet your ass you'll listen." Stroud flung a glance back at the miners, then rattled the demands off in a singsong litany. "You're gonna double these men's wages and give 'em better working conditions and a share of the profits and when they're hurt on the job you're gonna keep right on payin' 'em. And lastly, Mr. Boss Kincaid, you're gonna put all that down in a contract with our union and sign your name on the dotted line. That's what we want, and that's what we'll have."

"And if I don't go along?"

Stroud snorted at the absurdity of such a notion. "Why, if you don't go along we'll just march in there and put the torch to all them buildings." He waved a hairy fist off into the darkness. "Then we'll dynamite your equipment and whatever else seems handy, and when we're all done, you won't be in the coal business no more. So what'll it be, bossman? Negotiate or get wiped out?"

"You see that line?" Jake tapped the earth with his boot, and Stroud looked down at the scuff mark. "Anybody that crosses it is dog meat. And, Stroud, that goes most especially for you."

"That's your final answer?"

"Not hardly." Jake's voice went gritty as ground glass. "My final answer is waitin' on this side of the line."

Stroud laughed a wild, braying laugh, and stepped across the line. Jake hit him a whistling sledgehammer punch, flush on the jaw. The union leader buckled at the knees and started down, but the miners surged forward, holding him erect by the sheer press of numbers. A roar went up behind the fence, and the goon squad leaped into the fray as Jake swung and connected with Stroud's nose. Suddenly Stroud disappeared beneath a mass of humanity as the miners and the goon squad collided head on. The fence posts quavered under the impact, and the lanterns cast an eerie flickering glow over the battleground. Like medieval foot soldiers, hurling themselves at one another with witless savagery, the men clawed their way into the center of the action. Within seconds it became a brutish contest of strength, a wild melee of ax handles and lead pipes and swinging chains. Over the grunts and curses came the dull whump of wood on flesh and the mushy crunch of metal shattering bone, and louder still, the hoarse cries of those struck down. One after another men fell, trampled and kicked and crushed underfoot, terrified animals bleating their pain. Yet there was no slackening, nor did either side back off. The fight raged on, thicker and faster as the strong ones waded toward one another, battering and hacking and clubbing in a bestial struggle ripe with the scent of blood.

At the gate, where the action was the hottest, Jake hammered away with savage jubilation. He was in his glory, shifting and dodging, arms lashing out in the blurred flurry, cleaving a hole through the miners as he surged ahead of the goon squad. He had given himself over completely to the fight, operating now on nerve and reflex, exalted every time his fists drove another man to the ground. Slowly the momentum of the battle shifted, and foot by foot the miners were pushed back from the fence. There was a smell of victory in the air, a rout in the making, and his arms flailed faster and ever faster, scattering men before him as if some inhuman juggernaut were leading the attack. He felt alive and godlike in his strength, vitalized by some inner force unlike anything he'd ever known, and he knew then that he could never be stopped. Nothing mortal would ever again stand in his way, and that inner force took him soaring higher and higher as he unleashed yet another thunderbolt and sent a miner plummeting to earth. But it was his last blow, delivered at the very instant victory was within his grasp, yet delivered too late. A lead pipe materialized out of nowhere and struck him squarely between the eyes. His skull burst, blinding him with a crimson spray, and he collapsed as if his legs had been chopped from beneath him.

Distantly he sensed the thrash of bodies and the churn of booted feet, heard the sharp crackle of gunfire, and fainter somehow, the screams of men, the sounds of panic and terror and killing. A dim shape came swimming forward in his mind and he lost track of the sound. He focused on the shape, fascinated by its blurred image, watching it sputter and dance and splash closer. And of a sudden, utterly bewitched, he saw that it was a flame. Not bright or fiery, somehow lessening in intensity, but nonetheless a flame.

Then, gathering itself in one last spark, it flickered and died.

"We therefore commit this man to the ground. Earth to earth, ashes to ashes, dust to dust—"

The preacher sifted moist dirt through his fingers into the open grave. It made a gentle pitter-pat sound as it spattered on the coffin, like lightly falling rain on a shake roof. Lifting his face to the sky, spreading his arms wide, he addressed the heavens in a deep, somber voice.

"—with the certainty that we shall all meet again at the Resurrection, through Jesus Christ our Lord. Amen."

There was a moment of leaden silence, then the preacher moved to the side of the grave where Owen stood with the family. Julia had her arms around the children, staring blankly at a mound of funeral wreaths and flowers. Weeping softly, Zalia dabbed at tears behind her black veil, leaning against Grace for support. The minister offered some whispered condolence to Owen and Julia, studiously ignoring the girl and the older woman, and with a professionally solemn air, drifted off through the crowd. Everybody who was anyone in Guthrie had turned out for the funeral, and like the preacher, they were scandalized by the presence of Jake Kincaid's mistress and his Osage daughter-in-law.

Owen found it all grimly amusing, deriving some perverse gratification from the mewling ripples of shock and outrage. Zalia and Grace were there at his insistence as they had every right to be; the greater blasphemy was in a holy man saying words over the remains of a godless skeptic.

That the townspeople couldn't see the difference merely confirmed their hypocrisy. Still, however canting, their attitude seemed entirely appropriate to the occasion. So far as Owen was concerned, the whole day had been little short of a travesty.

Earlier, at the church services, the governor himself had delivered a stirring eulogy. He spoke eloquently of Jake Kincaid's pioneer spirit; his contribution to the economic well-being of his fellow man; and above all, his noble fight to bring statehood to Oklahoma. That this great and honorable man hadn't lived to see Oklahoma's star added to the flag (the governor's voice quavered dramatically at that point) was no less a tragedy than his untimely demise. But that he had died defending the cause of liberty would live on as a legacy to free men everywhere, throughout the ages. Apparently overcome by his own oratory, the governor then honked his nose into a linen handkerchief and bravely marched back to his seat.

What amazed Owen the most was not the eulogy, but that everyone in the church seemed to share the governor's sentiments. Seated in the pews were businessmen and politicians who had damned Jake Kincaid in life as a ruthless son of a bitch thoroughly lacking in scruples. They knew from bitter experience that his contributions, whether to statehood or the economy, were forever self-serving, meant to benefit no one but himself. Most of them had lived in fear of him since the day he came to the Territory, and more than a few bore scars as testament to his vindictive nature. Yet they sat there with bowed heads, presumably bereft at the passing of this great and noble man.

Outside the church, Owen was again stunned by this public display of sorrow. An enormous crowd jammed the street, watching in awed silence as pallbearers loaded the casket into a hearse. Women were actually crying, and he saw men knotting their jaws to stanch any show of emotion. As he came down the church stairs men he'd never seen before extended their sympathies, and when the funeral cortege was finally formed, it stretched out fully a mile or more along the street. The town's entire police force was there, working desperately to maintain some semblance of order, and nearly a half hour passed before the crowd was moved back and the procession at last got under way.

It was as if the town of Guthrie had come to mourn the passing of a giant. Almost as though death had bestowed upon Jake Kincaid some profound stateliness which had eluded him in life. Watching the faces of those who lined the street, Owen was by turn puzzled and then ruefully amused. His father had joined a very select company. Like all the world's great rogues, he would be remembered not for what he was but for what he had accomplished. A native son, Oklahoma's first homegrown rascal, he had been dipped in whitewash and by the alchemy of inverse veneration, transformed into a plaster saint.

And perhaps the greater proof lay not in any eulogy but in what was left unsaid. Nowhere in the newspapers, or among the throngs of mourners, was there any mention of the thirteen men killed at the Poteau mine. The requiem was for Jake Kincaid alone.

While Owen understood this need for invention (which people found more appealing than the truth), he could hardly accept the sham it represented. His father had been a brazen and unrepentant scoundrel, and somehow, he thought the old man would have preferred to be remembered that way. Nor could Owen condone the sanctimonious snobbery of those attending the funeral. None of them had had the decency to speak some small word of sympathy to Zalia (though everyone knew she had devoted her life to the dead man's happiness), and they had looked through Grace as if she simply didn't exist. All in all, he thought it a vulgar display, petty to the extreme, and he felt even more shamed by the intolerance of those few he considered friends.

After the burial services, he was overcome with a compulsion to have done with this day, to be gone from these people and this place. He gathered Julia and the children, Zalia and Grace, and quickly herded them into a waiting car. As they drove off he glanced back at the grave site, and quite unwittingly, in a sudden rush of something overlooked, he was struck by the most ironic note of all.

Brad and the old man were now laid out side by side. Closer in death than they had ever been in life. In a ghoulish sort of way there was something fitting about it. They had more in common than either of them had ever suspected. One used a gun and the other used his wits, but it was a hairline distinction. Perhaps, if there really was a hereafter, father and son would discover that they were, after all, birds of a feather.

On the drive back to town Owen insisted that Zalia join them for a light supper at the Kincaid house. She looked disconsolate, the only grief-stricken one in the group, and he felt it better that she not spend the evening alone. Julia complained of a splitting headache, and upon arriving at the house, went immediately upstairs to take a nap. Beth and Morg were handed over to the housekeeper, who wisely distracted them from the day's events with a promise of cookies and milk. Owen led the way into the living room, seating Zalia close to the fireplace, and Grace went off to prepare coffee.

Without her veil, Zalia appeared even more haggard. She stared into the fire, eyes glazed, almost as if she were in a trance. Her tears had subsided, but she clearly hadn't regained her composure. As he watched her, it occurred to Owen that she was a remarkable woman. Anyone who could have put up with his father all these years, not to mention the stigma of being his mistress, quite obviously had the forbearance and inner strength of a saint. Hesitant to intrude on her thoughts, he sat quietly for some minutes, but decided at last that it might do her good to talk.

"I don't know as there's any appropriate time to say something like this, but I suppose now is as good a time as any. I just wanted you to know that you'll never have to worry about finances, or anything like that. I'll arrange everything just the way Pa would've wanted."

"Thank you, Owen." Zalia stirred slightly, but her gaze was still abstracted. "There's no need, though. Your father was a very generous man. He provided for me a long time ago."

Owen remembered little of his own mother, but he hoped that she might have had the qualities so apparent in this gracious lady across from him. "All the same, just keep in mind you're part of the family so far as I'm concerned. Anything you need, you just let me know."

Grace entered with a tray and coffee service. She took a seat on a sofa between their chairs, placing the tray on a table, and poured three cups. No one said anything as she served, and afterward the conversation seemed to lapse entirely as they drank in silence. But the warmth of the coffee restored Zalia somewhat, and at last, still looking a bit dazed, she glanced around at Owen.

"What are your plans"—she had difficulty with the words—"now that your father's gone? He never stopped hoping that you would carry on where he left off when the time came."

Owen regarded her thoughtfully for a moment, then nodded. "I suppose I'll take over, but not just the way he had in mind. Fact is, I couldn't work with that bunch he had running things, and they're likely too old to change their stripes anyway. So I guess the first order of business is to retire Green and Jones and the others, and start looking for some men I can trust."

Zalia saw with the sudden vividness of sensory perception what Owen had articulated without actually saying it. The jolt snapped her out of her mental paralysis, and on the instant she took hold of herself. "Pardon an old woman's candor, but I'm glad your father didn't live to hear you say that. It was no secret that you disliked his business methods, but he never for a moment suspected that you were ashamed of him. If you know how much he loved you, then you'll understand why it's best he went to his grave without hearing you pronounce judgment."

Stung by the rebuff, Owen went red as ox blood. "I'm sorry if I offended you, Zalia. Maybe the truth hurts sometimes, but if a man's honest with himself then he has to see it for what it is. That's where Pa and me differed. He could always twist the facts around to where they suited his own view of things."

"I see. And exactly what was the truth?"

"Well, it sure wasn't what we heard today. I don't know who the governor and the rest of 'em were talkin' about, but it wasn't the old man. He would've laughed himself blue in the face if he'd been sittin' in that church. Whatever else he was, Pa wasn't a hypocrite."

"Then you think his eulogy was a lie?"

Owen stalled for time, glancing at Grace as he placed his cup on the table. He hadn't meant it to go this far; somehow he had to smooth over what had become a sticky situation. "Let's just say they embroidered the facts pretty heavy."

Zalia smiled disarmingly. "Are you much of a reader, Owen?"

"Why, I suppose I'm as partial to books as the next man. Anything special you had in mind?"

"Perhaps you are familiar with Montaigne's works. In discussing corruption he wrote that those with influence contribute greed and tyranny, while the weaker sort contribute idleness and futility. The difference has always seemed to me that one builds, whatever his motives might be, while the other merely criticizes. Of course I'm just an old woman who has spent too much time reading about life instead of living it, but since we all corrupt in our own way, you might ask yourself which man ultimately does the most good. The builder or the critic?"

Owen squirmed uncomfortably, amazed by the quiet ferocity of her words. And at some pains to defend himself. "Well, you know, it's funny about things like that. There was an Englishman—I forget his name just offhand—but he said that corruption could exist only so long as good men do nothing. I guess it all depends on how you look at it."

"Poppycock." Zalia fixed him with a look of dark intensity. "Those good men you talk about allow their lives to be eroded by compromise. They survive by virtue of arrangements with their conscience, and their deeds never quite match their convictions. As a result, they seldom accomplish anything."

She leaned forward, gathering strength for one final thrust. "You are a dreamer, Owen. Jake Kincaid was a visionary. Don't ever confuse yourself by thinking they're one and the same. He was hard and unscrupulous, and sometimes cruel, but he was a builder. He made those visions come true, and today people call them Wichita and Guthrie and Oklahoma. Without men like him we would still be living in caves and bartering skins."

Exhausted, her strength spent, she slumped back in the chair. "O God, was he a builder. Just pray that when your time comes you'll have done half as much good as your father accomplished. Quit dreaming, Owen, and get on with the business of living. You're Jake Kincaid's son, and his legacy was the vision. Always remember that."

Her eyes closed, and she sighed. "The vision."

After a moment her breathing lightened, and she fell into a deep, emotionally drained sleep. Owen rose from his chair, and Grace came to stand at his side. They watched her for a long while, and at last, when he spoke, his voice went husky, and something odd happened to his face.

"Do you think she was right, Grace? About the old man?"

The girl smiled her enigmatic smile. "I think you are your father's son."

"You know what I think?" Owen chuckled softly, and put his arm around her shoulders. "If the old man had lived, him and that little lady sittin' there would've whipped the world."

"There's still time, Owen. A whole lifetime."

BOOK THREE

———

OKLAHOMA

1920–1924

TWELVE

The speakeasy was quiet and dimly lighted. A cluster of regulars sat along the bar but most of the booths were empty. This was a workingman's hangout, known locally as The Joint, and the early rush had ended around suppertime. Soon the evening crowd would drift in, men accompanied by their wives or girlfriends, and later, after the last feature at the movie house, the place would remain packed till closing time. Although the bar served nothing but backwoods hooch, and the only music was a rinkydink piano, trade was brisk every night of the week. Since Prohibition The Joint had become something of a neighborhood institution, and the customers gladly provided their own entertainment.

Heads together, talking in low tones, Roscoe Turner and Tub Harris were seated in a back booth with Morg Kincaid. The waiter brought a fresh round of drinks, and the conversation stopped until he moved away with the dirty glasses. Then Turner resumed speaking in the slick, quick cadence of a pitchman, gesturing with short chopping motions of his hand as his voice dropped to a conspiratorial whisper.

"I'm telling you, Morg, it's the chance of a lifetime. You pass on this one and you'll wind up kicking yourself in the butt." He paused, leaning forward with a look of direct earnestness. "You know, it's not every day a man gets in on the ground floor of an investment this big. I'm not talking about nickels and dimes. I'm talking about the three of us coming out of this deal filthy rich. You just think on that a minute, Morg. Filthy, stinking rich!"

Turner and Harris were oil promoters, hometown boys who had earned a slippery reputation as lease hounds. They were several years older than Morg, and while he'd lost track of them during the war, he had no illusions about their honesty. A promoter was by nature a charlatan, relying on guts and blarney and pie in the sky to put across a deal. They might well be sitting on a fortune, as both of them had argued persuasively throughout the afternoon. On the other hand, they might be out to fleece him, simply a fast shuffle to raise a quick stake. Despite their unctuous and repeated assurances, it was strictly a toss of the coin.

"Trouble is, Roscoe, it sounds too good." Morg knocked back his drink in a gulp, and shuddered as a fiery jolt bounced off the pit of his stomach. He was about half swacked, but not so far gone that he couldn't think straight. "If it's everything you say it is, why'd you come here looking for money? Hell, Tulsa's full of wildcatters that would jump in with both feet. 'Specially if you've got something."

"Morg, that's precisely the point." Tub Harris, who was pudgy and moon-faced and squat as a fireplug, edged forward. "If the word got out in Tulsa everybody and his brother would be over there leasing acreage. Then they'd sit back and wait for us to bring in a well, and we wouldn't have a Chinaman's chance of tying up any big blocks ourselves. Secrecy, Morg, that's why we're here. And the only reason you've heard about it is because your name is Kincaid, and we know you've got the wherewithal to back a deal of this size."

That was true. Morg and his sister had inherited the residue of the Webb estate when their mother died while he was in France. He was by no means wealthy, but he could afford what they had in mind. And for the first time since returning from the war, he'd stumbled across something which kindled a spark of interest.

"You said something about equal shares."

"A third each." Roscoe Turner gave him an oily smile. "Now I ask you, is that fair or is that fair?"

Morg pursed his lips and considered. "Fifty-fifty sounds fairer. Seems to me money is harder to come by than a drilling lease."

Turner and Harris exchanged a quick glance, surprised by this sudden and rather outlandish demand. But they were nothing if not flexible. Three drinks later, after considerable dickering, the deal was clinched with handshakes all around. A sixty-forty split with Morg controlling the pursestrings and the two oil men supplying the know-how. Another drink formalized the partnership, and it was agreed they would leave for Anadarko in the morning.

Morg finally slid from the booth, towering over them with a dopey smile. Seated, his appearance was deceiving, and the promoters felt dwarfed by his size. There was an exuberant Norseman quality about him—tall and robust as an ox, with thick coppery hair and pale blue eyes—a quality of vital energy and lithe, corded strength. When he laughed something brutal appeared along the square line of his jawbone and the flare of his nose, and it bothered men that the laugh was never mirrored in his eyes. Sober, he tended to be a loner, minding his own business, and seldom caused trouble. But drunk, he laughed that mirthless laugh, and quickly became belligerent. Every dive in town had barred him at one time or another, and except that he flung money to the winds, they might have blackballed him permanently.

Pumping hands one last time with Turner and Harris, he walked unsteadily toward the door. There, the bouncer threw the bolt, relieved to see him go, and a moment later he was outside on the street. The evening light had quickened, gray and sharp, like the reflection off cold steel. He stood for a moment watching the sky, sobered by some gut feeling rather than the twilight itself. Then it came to him, and the drunken smile slowly dissolved into an ugly grimace. The skies of France had looked like that. At dusk, from the trenches, just before the Krauts started their nightly shelling.

As if to escape the thought, Morg hurried toward his car parked at the curb. Everyone in Guthrie, particularly the police, knew the car on sight. It was a Stutz Bearcat, painted a flaming red except for glossy black fenders. The interior was done in black leather, with a mahogany dash, and the collapsible top was also black. Considered a playboy's raceabout—a toy for the sons of rich men—it could outrun anything in town. Most especially the lumbering Dodge touring cars used by the police. But Morg had bought it with his own money, and while he drove it with what amounted to suicidal abandon, he good-naturedly paid the speeding fines once a month in city court.

Sliding in behind the wheel, he started the motor and let it idle until the engine had warmed. Then he slammed it in low gear, engaged the clutch, and roared off down the street with his foot jammed to the floorboard. Working the gears in a smooth racer's shift; he gained speed and within two blocks had the Stutz hurtling along in a blazing red flash. Corner stop signs were simply ignored, as were the few cars on the street, and moments later he cleared the downtown area like a bullet on wheels.

This blind flight, attempting to outrace his own thoughts, was not a condition peculiar to Morgan Kincaid alone. There was a malaise spreading across the nation, afflicting millions, and it was manifested in a headlong rush to forget—and escape. Americans were weary and confused and disillusioned by the war just ended. The restless, bitter young men discharged from the armed forces brought with them a brutality generated by war, and the belief that they were no longer their brother's keeper. Their hopelessness was expressed by a revulsion against morality and idealism, and an abandonment of Victorian strictures. It was an age of bathtub gin, flaming youth, and to hell with the world.

Like his countrymen, Morg had marched off to war heartened by the belief that he was off to fight the war to end all wars. Yet he quickly discovered that there was nothing chivalrous about the poison gas and machine guns found in the trenches of France. Instead there was something in the killing which suggested humanity's end—and oblivion.

As a Leatherneck, part of the Fifth Marines, Morg first saw action at Château-Thierry and Belleau Wood, where massed German machine guns chopped his comrades down like an invisible scythe. Later, at the battle of Argonne Forest, the carnage was even more terrible, but by then Morg had been brutalized by the sight of death, and he fought with the witless savagery of an animal. Alone, heedless of the risk, he destroyed a pillbox which had stymied the attack in his sector. After the Germans were routed he was awarded the Distinguished Service Cross and the French Croix de Guerre. And the medals meant nothing to him, nor was he thankful to be alive. He was merely tired, and satiated with killing.

But it was not the killing alone which changed him. It was the way those men had died, in a war waged by generals pitilessly committed to the tactic of *attaque à outrance*. A brutal pitting of massed strength against massed strength, in which victory fell to those who demonstrated a superior ability to bleed. To the men of the American Expeditionary Force their crusade became nothing short of an apocalypse, a bloodbath in which the survivors would hobble out of their trenches to exterminate one another with knives and bare teeth.

On the day Armistice was declared something over ten million people had lost their lives. Yet, as quiet fell over the battlefield, there was little rejoicing in the trenches. The stench of death was still too strong, and the men huddled there felt the taint of barbarism deep within their souls.

Upon returning from the Western Front in 1919, the doughboys came away with their faith shaken. In a flush of naïve patriotism they had joined the war against the Kaiser, but never again would they believe in flags or parades. The hell of modern war had become very personal, and their reaction, when it came, was one of massive cynicism and a retreat into apathy. The War to End All Wars became a sham and a delusion, and within a matter of months the hysterical acclaim of cheering crowds turned to callous indifference. The postwar millennium failed to materialize, and indeed, the new dawning became a dirge. The stock market took a nose dive, jobs for veterans were scarce, and farm prices slumped. All of which brought on an economic recession that left millions unemployed.

And America turned its back on the world.

At times, when Morg thought of the war, it was as if he were condemned to carry some putrid and rotting burden throughout all eternity. His memories darkened his vision, making the burden all the more insupportable, and he was like some footsore and weary traveler trudging through a very personal hell. Wandering through this horror of consciousness, he longed for escape, a darkening of memory. Whether emotional or spiritual, he felt the need to accept chaos in a time when order and salvation had lost significance. An age that made truth of lies, and slaughtered millions in some insane perversion of reality and myth. Where human sacrifice was considered the logical instrument of political abstraction.

But there was no escape. And so, like America, he turned his back on the world. Unable to forget, yet unable to accept the bestiality of man, he simply drew a circle around himself, and allowed no one to enter.

A war hero, unmarred by visible wounds, he returned to Guthrie a confirmed cynic at the age of twenty-two. Disdainful of business, financially independent, he became a wastrel, squandering himself and his money in a whirlwind of whiskey, flashy cars, and fast women. Alienated, contemptuous of the established order, he haunted the town's speakeasies, and his name quickly became associated with the rougher element. His recklessness and brawling generated musty comparisons with his outlaw uncle, and though he had never known Brad, he took perverse fascination in being linked with this renegade pariah of the Kincaid family. Yet, for all his hellraising, there was a bitter brownness to the fast life, and while he wasn't unhappy neither was he content. He was suspended in a limbo of sorts, where the chief gratification came from flaunting his contempt before the town.

At first, his father had been tolerant, remembering his own abhorrence of the evils of war. But in the past few months Owen's patience had worn thin, and once voiced, his criticisms led to open conflict. Unimpressed, Morg simply laughed when accused of wasting his inheritance and sullying the family name. The money was his own, and as for the name, he noted dryly, it was hardly without blemish. Soon enough the arguments intensified, and with each new incident, whether a ginmill brawl or another speeding ticket, the schism separating father and son grew wider. Lately, as if by mutual consent, they had begun avoiding one another altogether.

And yet, tonight, as he wheeled into the driveway and screeched to a halt, Morg felt a strange sense of anticipation mingled with his usual apathy. Perhaps he was just bored, gone stale on a steady diet of whiskey and women. Or maybe he was intrigued with succeeding where his father had failed. He hadn't thought it through that far, but the idea could scarcely be discounted. Something about this oil scheme appealed to him, and whatever the reason, he was eager, curiously invigorated, feelings he thought he'd lost in the trenches of France. For the moment, that was enough.

He climbed out of the Stutz, still a bit woozy, and started up the walkway. Then he stopped, struck by a sudden thought, and trained a cockeyed squint on the house. It was a symbol of everything he detested. Power and social position, the quest for prestige. A pile of rocks that had grown even more grotesque with time, one of the sturdier monuments to his grandfather's taste for the bizarre. Out of touch and outdated, a relic from another time, unsightly proof that the evil men do lives on after them. And a testament that good men, like his father, could be corrupted by the very forces they once defied.

Suddenly he couldn't wait to put it behind him. To cut the knot, have done with the past and all its relics. To forget.

To sleep and not to dream.

"Oh, rats! You're such an old stick-in-the-mud, Daddy."

Beth flounced down in a chair, displaying a bit too much leg for her father's comfort. Her short skirt hiked up over her knees, and while her legs were slim and nicely shaped, Owen kept his eyes averted. He hadn't quite become accustomed to having a flapper for a daughter, and he considered it a brazen exhibition.

"Let's not hear any more about it." He unfolded a newspaper and made a great show of scanning the headlines. "So long as you live under this roof you'll behave like a lady. Even if you don't dress like one."

"Merde!" Beth secretly delighted in using the word since her father understood no French. She crossed her legs, and shot him a sulky look. "This is the twentieth century, Daddy. And I'm not a little girl anymore. In case you hadn't noticed, I've grown up."

Owen had noticed, as had every man in town. Which was what bothered him. "Beth, I won't have you chasing around, and that's final. This is a small town, and people talk. Besides, it won't hurt you to stay home a few nights a week." He snapped the paper sharply, as if signaling an end to the discussion. "Sometimes I think it was a mistake to send you back east."

Beth wondered if it might not be the other way around. Perhaps her mistake had been in returning home. Four years at Vassar had prepared her for many things, but the stodgy provincialism of Guthrie society hadn't been included in the curriculum. Nor was she content with her father's protective attitude. However much she loved him, she was a grown woman, with a mind of her own, and she hardly needed protection. Not from Guthrie's rustic, self-styled Lotharios.

She thought about that often, the way men were attracted to her. It was the same here as it had been back east, and she saw nothing wrong with that. Quite candidly, she liked men, and encouraged their attention. Not that she was a tease or a vamp, resorting to the cheap tricks some women used. Nor was she any raving beauty. But she had good features (although her nose was snubbed and her mouth a bit wide), and tawny blond hair combined with green eyes somehow had a curious effect on men. She simply used what she had, and let nature take care of the rest. So far there had been no scarcity of panting young hotbloods willing to teach her the facts of life.

Except that her father now seemed determined to stand guard over her virtue. Which was all rather silly since she'd lost it in Greenwich Village one weekend during her sophomore year. She couldn't tell him that of course, but it made the situation nonetheless ridiculous.

Just for a moment she considered buttering him up, playing Daddy's cuddly little girl. That always melted his reserve, and she knew it would work tonight. Then, upon second thought, she discarded the idea. It was beneath her, juvenile and inane, not to mention demeaning. Instead, she decided on another tack.

"Mr. Harding looks like a shoo-in, don't you think so, Daddy?"

The remark startled Owen, and he was at some pains to hide it. Since the war the world seemed somehow out of kilter, especially the world of women. Short skirts and bobbed hair, and now politics. He had always prided himself on his tolerant outlook, and despite a thatch of gray hair, he was by no means an old stodge. But things were all topsy-turvy these days, and giving women the vote was, in his view, the height of folly.

He slowly lowered his paper. "Warren Harding is a mealy-mouthed hack. But unfortunately, you're right. He'll probably win."

"That's nice." She nodded to herself, somewhat pensive. "Of course, I intended to vote for him all along."

"You intended—!" He caught himself, biting off the words. "I guess I'd forgotten. About women having the vote, I mean."

"That's understandable, Daddy." She gave him a disarming smile. "After all, you forgot I'm over twenty-one, so why shouldn't you forget that women have the same rights as men? Except in Guthrie, of course."

"Now, you listen here, young lady—"

"Owen, don't raise your voice." Grace entered the living room, admonishing him with a gentle look, and settled herself on the sofa. "Goodness, what would the neighbors think if they heard you shouting?"

She already knew what the neighbors thought. After fifteen years in this house (without a marriage license) she had few illusions left intact. That she had retained her figure, and her sloe-eyed beauty, merely added fuel to the fire. Grace Sixkiller Kincaid was a juicy and never-ending source of gossip for the town's busybodies.

"I wasn't shouting," Owen grumbled, "but I'll swear she's enough to try a man's patience." He frowned, glancing at Beth, then rattled his paper again. "Maybe you can talk some sense into her head. Lord knows, I'm not having much luck."

"Why, from the little I overheard, I thought she made perfect sense." Grace turned her head slightly and winked at the girl. "As a matter of fact, I might even vote for Mr. Harding myself."

Owen groaned, not unaware that he was being baited. "Can't a man ever win just one argument in his own house? Now, tell me, is that too much to ask?"

"Well, honestly, what a dreadful thing to say." Grace appeared mortified. "You know very well, Owen Kincaid, that you rule this house like an emperor. Just snap your fingers, and there we are, waiting to serve. Isn't that right, Beth?"

"Don't get her started again. I know when I'm licked." Owen shook his finger as the women exchanged a hidden glance. "There, see what I mean! It's a female conspiracy. You two stick together like mustard plaster."

"Daddy, you know we wouldn't do that to you. Tell him, Grace. We wouldn't, would we?"

"Uh-huh. And fish don't swim either," he snorted. "Don't worry, I've got your number. Women of the world unite. Down with men and up with skirts! Isn't that your motto?"

Beth blushed and laughed all at the same time. Suddenly she was very conscious of her legs. "That's silly. One has nothing at all to do with the other. The hemline is simply an outward manifestation of the liberated woman. The men I know certainly don't think of it as a threat to their manhood. In fact, they find it rather nice."

"You tell him, little sister!"

Startled, they turned and found Morg leaning against the doorjamb into the hallway. He pushed off the wall and walked forward, listing slightly to port. Halting just behind the sofa, he grinned broadly, and a faint sourmash scent drifted across the room.

"Up with skirts! The higher, the better. Right, Sis?"

"Well, not too high or—"

"Sure, why not?" Morg chuckled. "Hoist Old Glory up the flagpole. That's what it's all about."

Beth saw her father frown, and quickly changed the subject. "You're home awfully early, big brother. Don't tell me they've already rolled up the sidewalks?"

"Hey, that's funny! I was 'bout to ask the same thing." His mouth split in a lopsided grin, and he gave her a lewd wink. "What's matter, couldn't the kid get a date tonight?"

Owen cut her off, staring hard at his son. "You're drunk."

"Why, only 'bout half, Pa. Not near as drunk as I'm gonna be."

"No doubt. And is this a special celebration or just a regular celebration? We see you so seldom I'm never sure which is which."

"Say now, I thought you'd never ask!" Morg pulled himself erect, pale eyes glittering, and beamed down on them. "Folks, I wanted you to be the first to know. I'm gonna be an oil tycoon. Just wrapped up the deal tonight."

His statement claimed their attention like a clap of thunder. After months of sullen refusal to discuss business of any sort, this sudden turnabout left them speechless. Still beaming, Morg stuck a cigarette in his mouth and flicked a gold lighter to life. He puffed, inhaling deeply, immensely pleased with himself. Their reaction, one of dumbfounded astonishment, made it a moment to relish. At last, Owen cleared his throat, one eyebrow arched in a quizzical look.

"You mentioned a deal. I take it you've hooked up with some oil men."

"Sure have. Couple of real whizzers. Maybe you know 'em. Roscoe Turner and Tub Harris?"

Owen's face congested, and a knot pulsated at his temple. "Yes, I know them. And unless they've changed, you're talking about drilling on unexplored land."

"That's right! They got a lease down at Anadarko, and we're gonna sink a well on the hush-hush. Before anybody knows what's happening, we'll have leases on the whole country."

"You've been suckered, boy, do you know that?" Owen threw up his hand in disgust. "There's no oil around Anadarko. Never was and never will be. Turner and Harris are sharpers, out-and-out con men. They'll set up a rig, and balloon the drilling costs to high heaven, and skin you out of every nickel you've got. Wake up and get your head out of the bottle. It's the oldest game in the business."

"Well, I wouldn't worry about it, Pa." Morg smiled, inspecting his cigarette as if he'd never seen one before. "Just because you got stung doesn't mean all the Kincaids are snakebit."

An awkward silence fell over the room. Implicit in the tone of their exchange was a sore and oozing animosity. Owen felt slighted and shut out, couldn't understand the youngster's baffling moods, or the reason for his contempt. And Morg, feigning nothing, just didn't give a damn one way or the other.

As the discord between them worsened, Grace had attempted, over a period of several months, to help resolve their differences. She had been more mother to the children than Julia (whose alcoholism was yet another family skeleton), and they both loved her dearly. But try as she might, she had been unable to break through Morg's hard shell of cynicism. The war had maimed him, emotionally if not physically, and finally, in her earthy wisdom, she saw that little could be done. Only time would heal the wounds he'd brought home from France.

But Beth lacked her aunt's keen insights. Nor, in her brash and youthful eagerness, could she hold herself apart from the struggle. Upon returning home from college, she found the men of her family locked in an ugly battle of wills, and it tore at her heart to see them estranged and bitter. Assured, always cheerful and confident, she had set herself up as a buffer between father and son, playing lightning rod to their trenchant exchanges. She had failed abysmally, just as Grace had failed before her, but she refused to be disheartened. And now, watching them stare at one another in strained silence, the urge was as strong as ever. She felt compelled to try again.

"Now before either of you says another word, I want you to listen to me." She looked at her father with utter directness. "Daddy, I think you're being unfair. There is a lot of money in oil, and Morg might very well have come across something worthwhile. The least you could do is let him explain. After all, what's the harm in listening?"

"Honey, I know you mean well, but you don't understand. These men are crooks. Out-and-out thieves. Nobody in the oil business would trust them with a plug nickel. The whole idea is so absurd it's not worth discussing."

Unfazed, she turned to her brother. "Morg, tell us about it. If they are crooks then you ought to welcome advice. I mean, really, what could it hurt? Daddy does know the oil business, and it's just possible he might save you a lot of grief. Doesn't that make sense?"

Morg shrugged elaborately. "Butt out, sis. You're just wasting your breath."

"We'll have none of that talk in this house." Owen's face was a mask of righteous propriety. "Either keep a civil tongue in your head or don't speak at all."

Something dark and immobile came over Morg as he glanced at his father. There was no shame in the expression, nor was there embarrassment. But in the tightening of his mouth there was a cold indifference, naked and revealed.

Unexpectedly, Grace rose from the sofa. "My suggestion is that we all sleep on it. Things always look much brighter in the daylight, and not nearly so complicated."

"I agree." Beth suddenly bounced out of her chair, perky and smiling. "As a matter of fact, that's the best idea I've heard so far."

"I've got a better idea." Morg turned and sauntered toward the hall. "Since it's my last night and all, I think I'll paint the town red. Sort of kiss old Guthrie goodbye in style."

As the front door slammed, Owen stood, and without a word, walked from the room. Beth and Grace looked at one another helplessly, and as if in mute recognition that they had fought a lost cause, a single tear formed in the girl's eye and rolled down her cheek.

Outside there was a screech of tires as the Stutz roared off into the night.

Atlas belched and the world spun on its axis.

At least that's how it seemed to Owen Kincaid. He was just a little above the battle now, fiery at the core, yet aggrieved by what he saw around him. Still full of fight but revolted and withdrawn, in the jejune way of a man who has, at last, seen the folly of others for what it is. And like Atlas, he burped more these days, and sometimes had the queasy urge to have done with the whole affair.

Though he came to his office every day, he never entered the bank. Nor did he concern himself greatly with the other Kincaid holdings. The men who ran these corporations, as well as the Citizen's National, were competent and honest, and except on a policy level, he rarely interfered with their management decisions. His aversion to business had lessened none at all with time, and quite deliberately, he had presided over a gradual decline in the family empire. He felt no regret whatever at having done so, and in the process had come to an even fuller realization that he lacked the guile and mercenary gusto so essential to success in business.

On this particular morning, seated at his desk sifting through the mail, his mood was introspective and somewhat listless. His thoughts centered on business—or more precisely, his business failures—and he wondered if, after all, there might not be some defect in his character. Some trait, hereditary to the Kincaid bloodline, which was absent in his own makeup. The question had occurred to him before, in what seemed a queer blend of spiritual osmosis. The ghost of Jake Kincaid had never fully been exorcised from within these four walls (although Owen had remodeled the office completely); at times it was as if he could hear the old man snorting hellfire whenever the family fortunes suffered another reversal. While it was sheer nonsense, nothing more than mental tomfoolery, his father's caustic presence seemed nonetheless real.

But today the reminder of his business shortcomings was more human than ghostly. Instead of the old man, it was his own son who mocked him. Morg was gone, stubbornly refusing advice, heedless of the risks a wildcatter faced. Still, despite the arrogance of youth, he displayed the determination and boldness that were once the personal trademark of his grandfather. And like the old man, Morg would probably succeed. Not because he was smarter than anyone else, or blessed with some magic touch, but because at heart he was a pragmatist, with that same cold bulldog instinct for the expedient means to an end. It was a trait that had become apparent in Morg only since his return from the war. The very trait Owen himself lacked, by some quirk passed along from grandfather to grandson, like a stone missing a beat as it skims across the water. Looking back, Owen saw it as an erratic trick of nature, and by no means a favor to his son. Yet, as he reflected deeper, the greater question mark centered solely on himself. He wondered what would have happened had the stone not skipped a beat.

Had he been more his father's son, perhaps Owen could have dealt with life on its own terms. But he was essentially a romantic, saddled with a very active conscience, and after Jake's death he never knew a moment's peace. Thrust into the world of business, a world he neither liked nor understood, he discovered to his everlasting grief that nice guys really do finish last.

Zalia Blair's words had come back to haunt him many times. She had spoken of *the vision* as Jake Kincaid's legacy to his son. And however reluctantly, Owen had attempted to carry on in his father's footsteps, but in a way which allowed him to live with his own conscience. Perhaps his first mistake had been in replacing the old man's cronies with honest businessmen; at that point in Oklahoma's development, it was somewhat akin to substituting goldfish for sharks. His second, and most grievous, mistake was in convincing himself that he possessed some shred of his father's vision. He had none at all.

Upon settling the strike at the coal mine, by generously acceding to the miners' demands, he found that enough was never enough. As the union became stronger, ever more strident in its ultimatums, he was forced to the bargaining table with monotonous regularity. Profits dipped as wages and worker benefits spiraled upward, and it took a world crisis to correct the situation. With the outbreak of war in Europe the price of coal skyrocketed, and the mine prospered as never before. But with peace the union presented new demands as coal prices plummeted, and the operation limped along on marginal profits. Caught up in a web of negotiations, Owen had only recently decided to sell the company. It represented an endless headache, a constant source of aggravation and unrest, and while it was a poor time to unload mining stock, he was not to be dissuaded. He merely wanted out.

His timing, not to mention his vision, was equally faulty in the oil business. The large petroleum companies became increasingly ruthless following statehood. Independent producers were harassed, denied access to pipelines, their prices undercut, and in general, squeezed to the limit. Owen found the industry as a whole repugnant, and detested the dog-eat-dog tactics necessary to survival. He sold out, clearing a tidy fortune on the Kincaid wells around Bartlesville, and two years later those same holdings quadrupled in value.

War was declared in Europe, and a demand arose for gasoline and fuel oil such as the world had never known. Prices boomed as America's reserves were drained, and wildcatters opened more than thirty new fields in Oklahoma alone. By the end of hostilities both the oil companies and the independent producers were riding a crest of unimagined prosperity.

Curiously, when Armistice was declared on the Western Front, the demand for oil increased rather than diminished. Throughout the war, the automobile and truck manufacturers had become gigantic concerns; their expansion had a profound effect upon the oil business. By 1920 there were eight million passenger cars on the roads, and Henry Ford's fabled Tin Lizzie placed the automobile within the price range of even the lowliest family. Fears of an oil shortage broke out, and the search for new fields accelerated at an ever quicker pace.

Thoroughly out of it, Owen sat on the sidelines and

watched in a state of numbed bemusement. The war, which he'd failed to anticipate, had provided the impetus for the oil boom, and the automobile industry, which he had also overlooked, ultimately made oil the most profitable business in America. Granted, he was no pauper; the Kincaid fortune now hovered around $20 million. But as a visionary, he felt decidedly myopic, and in dire need of a crystal ball.

Nor was his record in politics anything to boast about. Zalia, whom he came to revere, had encouraged him to remain active politically, and he counted it a blessing of sorts that she hadn't lived to see his utter humiliation. Governor Charles Haskell, the man he had helped to elect, was never accepted by the old guard who controlled Guthrie. The *Statesman* flayed his administration with vitriolic editorials; the townspeople snubbed his family, and the governor himself was considered a social leper. Three years after statehood Haskell vindictively forced a referendum, and the voters chose Oklahoma City as the new capital. The governor had the state seal spirited out of town late at night, and Guthrie was left to wither on the vine. Soon, with its glory days a thing of the past, Guthrie became just another small town, prosperous but no longer the progressive community that had led Oklahoma into the Union.

Owen felt betrayed and, except for the prominence of the Kincaid name, might well have become a social outcast himself. Yet, almost as if he had learned nothing from the Haskell episode, he later embroiled himself in a lost cause that was to have international repercussions. Virtually alone, again misjudging the temper of the people, he publicly declared his support of the League of Nations.

Woodrow Wilson had justified American entry into the war as a crusade "to make the world safe for democracy." Always something of an evangelistic scholar, rather than a hard-nosed politician, he seized on the notion of a League of Nations as the cornerstone of lasting peace. After the Armistice, however, there were irreconcilable differences at home and abroad. The Allies sought territory and revenge; Wilson doggedly clung to some higher vision of peace. What resulted was neither a peace of justice nor a peace that would reconcile ancient European hatreds. The treaty signed in the Hall of Mirrors at Versailles failed on all counts.

Wilson returned from Europe to find that both Congress and the nation had grown bored with his lofty idealism. Despite the efforts of party loyalists, men such as Owen Kincaid, President Wilson insisted that the League of Nations provision be included in the peace accord. And in the end, his noble crusade collapsed in ruin. Congress rejected the Versailles Treaty, which prompted a huge sigh of relief from the people, and America withdrew from the world in a cozy glow of seclusion.

Strangely enough, although he deplored the folly of isolationism, and denounced it as harmful to America's interests, Owen understood the emotion involved. He felt somewhat the same way about Guthrie. Nothing would have pleased him more than to chuck the family business and spend the remainder of his days on the Cimarron ranch. He thought of it as a sanctuary, like a monk who yearns for a cloistered monastery; his fondest recollections were of the times he managed to sneak away, escaping the worries of business, and return to the world of men and horses and cattle. Those were the good days, and all too few.

When Julia was alive those times had been even fewer, for she bitterly resented his attachment to the ranch. Her emotional problems, aggravated at the end by acute alcoholism, had given him little peace. But since her death (during the influenza epidemic of 1918) his business responsibilities, and Guthrie, had become bearable if not wholly satisfying. Secretly, though it sometimes troubled his conscience, Owen felt no sense of grief at her passing. The marriage was hardly a love match, even in the beginning, and those last years had been filled with disgust and unendurable torment.

Still, for all the personal vexations, life was not without

its moments. He had been offered the post of U.S. marshal, although business commitments forced him to decline, and the letter from President Wilson was among his most cherished mementos. As the last of the great frontier lawmen (Heck Thomas was dead and Bill Tilghman had retired) he was now one of a kind. Out of habit, he kept his gunhand in practice, unlimbering the old Colt Peacemaker at least once a week. And because of his extraordinary reputation as a manhunter (along with larger-than-life legends of his skill as a gunfighter) an occasional honor came his way.

Several times he had served in an advisory capacity to the State House, and within the past year, working as a special investigator for the governor, he had exposed the graft-ridden practice of "loaning" convict work gangs to private companies. The newspapers had given it front-page coverage, and aside from being in the limelight again, he found that he still derived immense gratification in the role of a peace officer. Unfortunately, like his trips to the ranch, these moments were all too infrequent. Business came first, and while his managers enjoyed virtual autonomy, his days were seldom his own.

This morning was no different. But as he sorted through the mail a small glimmer of sunshine suddenly punctured his gloomy mood. He pulled a single envelope from the pile, ripped it open, and hurriedly scanned its contents. Then he read it again, carefully noting the figures, and a slow smile spread across his face. Tossing the letter on his desk, he grabbed the telephone, waiting impatiently for the operator.

"Central? Ring Hal Wallace's office for me."

A moment later his attorney came on the line. "Mornin', Hal. This is Owen." He listened briefly, frowning, then interrupted. "Everybody's fine, Hal, thank you. But let's skip the small talk today. I've just had a letter from Consolidated, and they've made us a counteroffer on the coal mine. It's a hundred thousand less than we asked, but I'm going to accept."

There was a sputtering squawk at the other end of the line. Owen brusquely cut in. "Hal . . . damnit, Hal, quit yammering and just pay attention. I appreciate your advice but I said we're going to sell, and that's final. Now get hold of their lawyer and clinch the deal before they change their minds." The line crackled angrily, and he again interrupted. "No, Hal, I don't want to think it over. You just do like I tell you, all right? That's fine. Thank you, Hal. Get back to me when you've talked with them."

After he hung up Owen tilted back in his chair, grinning like a tiger that had just eaten its keeper. With the coal mine gone, he could now concentrate on unloading the timber company. And some of the other businesses. Maybe even the bank. Given time, and a stable economy, he might get out from under the whole mess. Perhaps the ranch wasn't some dizzy daydream, after all. Contrary to what he'd thought this morning, maybe it was just around the corner. A little luck, and a lot of hustle, and he might yet come out free and clear.

Suddenly he couldn't wait to tell Grace. He grabbed the telephone, fairly bursting with excitement, and began jiggling for the operator.

The band was playing "Japanese Sandman." As it was every Saturday night, the country club was jammed with Guthrie's social elite and their offspring. Couples dipped and swayed to the music, gliding around the dance floor, and back behind the swirling lights there was a buzzing hum, like the drone of bees, as people table-hopped and gossiped and caught up on the latest bedroom scandal. An appearance, here, on this one night of the week, had about it the same ritualistic tableau of small-town religion. Just as people attended church not so much to pray as to be seen, so they came to the country club to gawk at their neighbors and titillate themselves on juicy tidbits seldom found in the papers.

The young crowd, by virtue of their lowly spot in the

pecking order, was always seated toward the rear of the room. Beth and her escort, Daniel Woldridge III, shared one of the better tables with three other couples. This favored position, owing in no small part to the elder Woldridge's social standing, left her something less than impressed. Upon reflection, she quite frankly couldn't imagine why she'd accepted a date with Danny Woldridge. She considered him a nurd (an uncharitable, if descriptive, expression she had acquired back east), and to make matters worse, he was a clumsy nurd. While the evening had only begun, her toes already attested to the fact that he was a menace on a dance floor.

At the moment she was oblivious to the lively chatter of her companions. She gazed about her with the leisurely air befitting her role as Guthrie's resident femme fatale. Unlike the warm, affectionate girl her family knew, she had cultivated an image of mystery and experience among others, presenting herself as a woman of the world. It was an easy role to play. While at Vassar she had spent her weekends in Greenwich Village, haunted the swank New York clubs and Broadway theaters, and worked actively in the suffragette movement. With only the slightest effort she was able to project an air of sophistication and witty elegance which left the hometown girls in a snit and the young men in a state of dazed adoration. There was something in her carriage, the way she tilted her head, a poise which made other women seem somehow less refined, almost naïve. Even older women felt uncomfortable in her presence, sensing more quickly than their daughters that it was an uneven contest, and therefore futile.

But if the women of Guthrie were universally jealous, and despised her as a bitchy little snob, the unattached males chased after Beth like clowns in a circus parade. Partly this was because of her languorous gaze and her air of jaded worldliness, and partly it was attributable to the way she dressed. So far, Beth was the only flapper in town.

She wore short skirts, rolled her stockings below the knee,

and kept her hair bobbed in a shingle cut. And in the final break with Victorian morality, she flattened her breasts and hips to effect a boyishly slender figure, smoked cigarettes and openly drank whiskey, and painted her face with an exotic blend of cosmetics. All in all, she presented a startling contrast to the bland, full-bosomed ladies of Guthrie. Without the Kincaid name, her scandalous behavior would have branded her a hussy. Instead, the town matrons expressed shock and outrage, and sternly admonished their daughters not to imitate this brazen display of eastern depravity.

While they heeded the warning, the local girls found the competition undeniably stiff. And it wasn't merely the short skirts or the bee-stung lips. Beth Kincaid exuded a sensuality as palpable as musk. She was sultry and aloof one moment, devilishly beguiling the next, and however wildly uninhibited her behavior, she never lost that bewitching, seductive quality which set her apart. She had a way of speaking as if she were almost out of breath, husky and warm, somehow intimate even when she was risqué. And though she played at being a sophisticate, there was nothing contrived or unnatural about her sensuality. She was simply born to it, a slinky sexy creature who brought men into rut with a mere look; and by the languid ease with which she accomplished it, managed to infuriate every woman in Guthrie.

Just now, though, she was bored to distraction. The band was lethargic, the atmosphere in the country club seemed staid and repressive, and the conversation at her table was apparently limited to banal, sophomoric clichés. Danny Woldridge was bad enough, with his horsy grin and that sterile look common to men who drool within their souls. But at least he made an effort, however callow, to think for himself. The others were intellectual ciphers, hardly more mature than the day she'd graduated with them from Guthrie High. Ungracious as it sounded, she couldn't help but think of them as small-town zombies, affecting a savoir-faire that merely exposed their shallowness and rustic simplicity. She knew the boys were trying to impress her, while the girls would have gladly cut her throat, and the whole affair suddenly seemed inane beyond endurance.

Her chance came as the band went into a slow-tempo arrangement of "Margie." Danny Woldridge leaned closer, and rolled his eyes toward the dance floor. "What about it, Beth? Wanna trip the light fantastic with yours truly?"

"Danny, I was wondering"—she placed her hand over his, and squeezed suggestively—"would you mind if we left?"

"Why, sure thing. Whatever you say." Beads of sweat popped out on his forehead, and his mouth went pasty. "Anyplace special you'd like to go?"

"Oh, I don't know, not really. Let's just see where the wind takes us."

Danny gulped, and darted a quick, sly glance at his pals. "Suits me, kiddo. Wherever it is, I'll get us there."

Mary Lou Hendricks, a corn-fed beauty with huge breasts, gave Beth a fanged smile. "What's the matter, sweety? Our little ol' dance too tame for you?"

The other girls tittered deliciously, and the boys looked pained. Beth rose from her chair, poised and remote as a star. "My, but aren't you the *enfant terrible*, Mary Lou? And such a way with words. Isn't it a shame you never learned the art of syntax?"

Everyone assumed Mary Lou had been insulted, but the subtlety of it left them a bit uncertain. Beth turned, satisfied with their blank stares, and walked away from the table. Daniel Woldridge III jumped to his feet, grinning sheepishly, and hurried along after her. As they crossed the room the droning buzz intensified in pitch, and at every table their early departure became the subject of invidious, and none too delicate, speculation.

Outside in the parking lot, they were no more settled into Danny's car than he was on her with fumbling, goatlike passion. One arm snaked around her shoulders, while his other hand clumsily worked beneath her fur wrap, and he kissed her with a good deal more zest than technique. Apparently he was much influenced by F. Scott Fitzgerald, whose explicit new novel revealed that a sexual revolution was afoot in America; petting, according to the author, had become the younger generation's sole preoccupation, and as the motorcar provided them with a mobile bedroom, they could grapple in relative comfort, freed at last from the surveillance of their elders. Danny had clearly done his homework, taking the message to heart, but it seemed evident he'd skipped some of the more essential passages. He was lousy in the clinches.

Beth suffered his pawing awhile, allowing him to fondle her breast, and even returned his slobbering kisses in a halfhearted fashion. But she had no intention of letting him go all the way; morality aside, she saw nothing to be gained in wasting it on a clod. When his hand slid down to her knee, she gently removed it, admonishing him with a light tap on the cheek, and very expertly disengaged herself from his embrace.

"Honestly, Danny, you could smother a girl that way." She smiled disarmingly, fending him off as she began straightening her clothes. "Now behave yourself and concentrate on driving. After all, you can't expect me to walk into Maxie's looking as if I've just been ravaged."

"Maxie's!" he blurted. "You mean the speakeasy Maxie's?"

"Why, of course, silly. That's why I suggested we leave. Maxie's has the only decent music in town. You do like jazz, don't you?"

"Oh sure, I like it fine." Danny appeared deflated, as if he'd expected something a little hotter than music. "Course that's a rough place. They got raided just last week, you know."

"I know. I was there." Beth giggled at her racy admission. Then her voice went throaty and vibrant, and she touched his arm. "I feel perfectly safe with you, though. Nobody would dare bother us."

Danny's chest expanded a couple of notches, and he flashed a toothy smile. Without a word he started the car, threw it in gear, and roared out of the parking lot. Beth suppressed a small laugh, and began humming softly to herself. The melody she hummed was nondescript, meaningless to anyone but herself, improvised to fit the meter of her favorite poem.

> My candle burns at both ends;
> It will not last the night;
> But ah, my foes, and oh, my friends,
> It gives a lovely light.

Beth sometimes thought the poem had been penned especially for her, as if Edna St. Vincent Millay had captured the essence of what she was in four short lines. But in many ways this bittersweet stanza had become the credo of an entire generation. However isolated, and intellectually impoverished, Beth felt in Oklahoma, the ferment of the Roaring Twenties was sweeping westward, taking root on the plains with no less certainty than it had back east.

To some, the very fabric of America seemed threatened. Bolshevism had the government in a panic, and a witch hunt was under way to eradicate the Red anarchists. The Ku Klux Klan roamed the countryside, lynching niggers and flogging kikes, striking terror with their slogans of white supremacy. And in Congress a movement was gaining support to limit the immigration of those outside the pale of good "Nordic" stock. But the masses wanted escape, not worry. They queued up by the millions each week to watch Douglas Fairbanks and Mary Pickford, Charlie Chaplin and Fatty Arbuckle, and for them the flickering image in a darkened theater was the reality. The world was merely a gargantuan joke, to be jeered and ridiculed and toasted with ribald scorn.

And toast it they did. Although the Volstead Act had gone into effect early that year, no one but fundamentalists and idealistic reformers took it seriously. Tens of thousands of speakeasies sprang up across the land, and the ubiquitous hip flask became a mainstay in American culture. Whiskey flowed as never before, smuggled in by rumrunners, dispensed by bootleggers, and served with unruffled equanimity at the neighborhood speak. Yet, curiously enough, prohibition occasioned little comment in Guthrie. Oklahoma had gone dry on the day of statehood, some fourteen years past, and far from a novelty, the bootlegger had become an institution. In a very real sense, Oklahomans had a headstart on the rest of the country, and with the enactment of national prohibition, speakeasies swapped their former notoriety for a newfound status. Suddenly it was a barrel of laughs, almost respectable, and flaunting the law became one of life's more humorous pastimes.

Still, speakeasies were nothing if not discreet, particularly those who catered to a choice clientele. When Beth and Danny rapped on the door of Maxie's a Judas hole slid open, and they found themselves conversing with a disembodied eye. The eye didn't recognize Danny, and its voice was gruffly suspicious. Then Beth stepped forward, mentioning her name, and magipresto, things began to happen. The Judas hole slammed shut, the door flew open, and an unctuous-looking gorilla, freshly shaved and decked out in a tux, ushered them into Maxie's.

By New York standards, it wasn't much. Formerly a hotel cellar, it rather resembled a dungeon haphazardly redecorated by an out-of-work saloonkeeper. The floors were sprinkled with sawdust, checkered cloths covered the tables, and the bar looked like a holdover from the frontier days. It was crowded and noisy, dense layers of smoke hung suspended in the air, and a dank, fetid smell permeated everything. But Maxie served nothing but the finest, all imported stuff, and as part of the show treated his customers to the liveliest music in town. On a stage toward the front of the room five musicians wailed away at the "St. Louis Blues." They were black, led by a glazy-eyed sax player, and the rhythm they produced was unlike anything whites had ever heard.

The music of the twenties was conspicuously lacking in nostalgia. The ballad disappeared utterly, to be replaced by blues and jazz. Songs were abbreviated, a series of vocal ejaculations, evoking a mood of primitive revelry, or spiritual misery. Jazz in particular was brazenly defiant, music in the nude, rapid and feverish and exciting. A jazz musician's triumph was erratic syncopation, mixed with a bizarre and outré rhythm that seemed an aberration of the mad. And in jazz the saxophone dominated all other instruments. It could imitate a menagerie of wild animals, an asylum filled with maniacal laughter, hoots and honks and howls, every toot and tottle, every blare and blast necessary to the music of the times. Drifting against the tide, blues and jazz had come upriver from New Orleans, spreading across the land, and in an era desperate with the need for escape, this stuttered wailing became the salvation of white America.

With hardly a pause for breath, the band broke out in an earsplitting Charleston just as Beth and Danny reached their table. She grabbed his hand and pulled him onto the dance floor. They were joined by a joyous mob, gone wild with the music, stomping and shouting and hopping about like a gang of well-dressed wrestlers. It was all violently acrobatic, frenzied jazz set to motion, and the floor shook beneath their feet as the tempo quickened. Clumsily, Danny tried to match her flailing arms and thrashing legs, and at last, hopelessly unstrung, he merely bounced along in a sweaty daze. Beth's face was incandescent with excitement, all inhibitions thrown off. Her body abandoned itself to the saxophone, lost in its wail, as if sinking deeper and ever deeper into a lover's arms.

She tossed her head, eyes blazing with green fire, and her fluted laughter melded with a high note. Then, she was alone with the music, at one with herself, immersed in a giddy caress that had no end.

And she danced on.

The sky was like dull pewter, heavy with clouds, and beneath it the earth was cold and still. Trees along a nearby creek swayed in the wind, bare branches crackling like the bones of old skeletons, and a pitted road streaked off through dry grasslands. A flock of crows fluttered against the sky, cawing their litany of death, then wheeled and vanished beyond the treeline.

Morg stopped for a moment, leaning on his shovel, and watched the last sentinel crow disappear. He was caked with mud and grime, sweating freely despite the cold, standing hip-deep in a ditch angling off away from the derrick. Sludge had formed a small dam in the ditch, blocking the drainage of waste and water from the well, and he'd spent most of the morning clearing out a channel. It was a thankless task, backbreaking and boring as hell, but no more tedious than the rest of his chores. Just dirtier. He hawked and spat, tasting grit all the way down his gullet, then went back to shoveling mud.

Six months on an oil derrick had toughened Morg. The whiskey had been boiled out of his system, along with the suet he'd collected loafing around gin mills and pool halls. His arms were corded bands of steel, muscles bulged in his shoulders, and his stomach was as flat and hard as a washboard. Although he was half owner of the outfit, he'd quickly discovered he was low man on the totem pole around the derrick. The driller was bossman here, brooking no interference, and the only way Morg could stay with the rig and keep the peace was to sign on as a roustabout. Nothing more than a common laborer, he washed down the boilers, looked after the steam engine, made repairs on the derrick, and manhandled joints of heavy pipe that went down the hole as the well was drilled. It was hard, grueling work, twelve hours a day and seven days a week, and more than ever, there was an ox-like massiveness to his tall, square-jawed good looks.

But while the life of a roustabout was punishing at best, it was also educational. He'd listened and watched, earning a diploma in the school of hard knocks, and if nothing else, he had gleaned the most important lesson to be learned from the oil fields. Wildcatting was the biggest crap game known to man. And like opium, highly addictive.

A few miles south of Anadarko he and his partners had set up operations. They bought a dilapidated Reo truck, hired a driller and a toolie, and had a derrick erected. Then, over the summer and early fall, they drilled themselves a couple of dusters in bang-bang succession. Turner and Harris spent most of their time down in Texas, buying and selling leases in the Ranger field; they accepted the news of each dry hole with unshaken aplomb. Perhaps they flinched less because it was Morg's money, but their optimism was nonetheless contagious. All evidence to the contrary, he allowed himself to be convinced that it was merely a matter of time. The gusher was there, his partners assured him, and as every gambler knew, third time out was a charm. In late October they spudded a new hole, and Morg hadn't seen them in the seven weeks since. Apparently, with the junior partner to watch over things, Turner and Harris felt their talents could be more gainfully employed elsewhere.

However dismal the picture outside Anadarko, there was much to be said for this line of reasoning. The price of crude was up sharply. Texas was booming. Tulsa had become the oil capital of the world, with several new refineries, and a whole herd of millionaires. Engineers estimated that the Cushing field alone contained a recovery of 455 million barrels, and a discovery well had just been brought in along the western border of Osage County. Even natural gasoline, once considered a nuisance, had become a major industry, clearing Oklahoma producers a neat $31 million since the first of the year. In fact, whenever he had time to reflect on it, Morg figured just about everybody in the oil business was getting filthy rich. Except for the junior partner of Turner, Harris & Kincaid. He was just getting filthy. And slowly going broke. Heady as he found the game, it seemed he had an absolute gift for drawing the busted flush.

That very thought had been on his mind for some days now, and for no particular reason he could identify, it occurred to him that this morning was the time to do something about it. After he'd shoveled out the ditch, he wiped the muck off his hands and walked back to the rig. He caught Wirt Jordan's eye, and the driller nodded as he signaled toward the creek. Although Jordan wasn't much of a talker, it seemed a little conversation was in order. Six months and close to seventy thousand dollars entitled a man to a few answers, and of a sudden, he decided he knew all the right questions to ask.

Up on the derrick floor, Jordan unreeled cable from the bull wheel, set the walking beam in motion, and slammed a string of drilling tools into the hole. He was a methodical man, as well as stingy with words, and believed the job at hand should be finished before proceeding to the next. Clearly he wasn't to be rushed because a young roustabout appeared to have ants in his pants.

Unlike the new breed of drillers, who used a rotary bit to bore out the hole, Jordan was a cable tool man. Standing at the well head, with an inch-thick steel cable strung over the crown block at the top of the derrick, he could tell by the vibration on the line how his tools were doing at the bottom of the well. The bit was a steel bar some five feet in length, shaped like a blunt wedge with rounded sides. It was hung at the end of a string of sockets and stems, altogether weighing a couple of tons, and jerked up and down in the hole by the seesaw motion of the walking beam. This rocking action imparted a jarring impact to the tools, and the wedge-shaped bit pulverized the underground rock formations, literally pounding its way through the earth. It wasn't as efficient as a rotary bit, and it entailed considerably more work. But Jordan had drilled scores of wells with a cable rig, striking paysand more often than he missed, and he wasn't about to change. Besides being methodical and laconic, he was also stubborn.

After drilling another screw (what he judged to be about eight feet), Jordan pulled his tools out of the hole and swung them aside. Then he threw the ropes off the tug wheel, quickly engaged the band wheel, and ran his bailer into the well. When he brought the bailer out of the hole it was full of pulverized cuttings and water. Stooping, he inspected the cuttings, rubbing some between his fingers, smelling it, then climbed to his feet and yelled back toward the engine house.

Slim Higgins, who resembled an articulated scarecrow, stepped outside and ambled forward along the walkway. As the toolie, his main job was to heat the dulled bit over an open forge and hammer it back into shape. Keeping the engine percolating was also his responsibility, and when the steam pressure was back up, he occasionally filled in as driller while Jordan took a break. Clambering onto the derrick floor, he halted, listening silently as Jordan issued instructions. Without comment he turned away, dumping the cuttings into a slush pit, and readied the bailer for another trip down the hole. Jordan moved to the other side of the rig, went down a ladder to the ground, and walked off in the direction of the creek.

Morg fell in alongside him. Neither of them spoke, but he could tell Jordan was in an indulgent mood. The driller's cardinal rule was that cigarettes, cigars, or anything that flamed was forbidden around the rig. Freak explosions were commonplace in the oil fields. Casinghead gas, escaping from the wells, collected in pockets low to the ground, held down by clouds and humid atmosphere. A single spark from an automobile engine could detonate the volatile gas, devastating an entire field, and for this reason old-timers either chewed tobacco or dipped snuff. While there was small danger at the present site (perhaps none, considering they'd drilled only dry holes), Jordan was a man of heavily ingrained habits. Anyone who wanted a smoke had to hike off down to the creek before he struck a match.

The rule applied solely to Morg, for he was the only one in the crew who used cigarettes. And today was the first time Jordan had ever condescended to join him at the creek. It made for interesting speculation.

At the creek they still hadn't spoken, and Morg busied himself lighting a cigarette, not quite certain how to begin. Jordan pulled out a packet of Mail Pouch, and stuffed his mouth with a fresh quid. He was a tall, rangy man, somewhere in his late thirties, but powerfully built from a lifetime of physical labor. His features were grizzled and ruddy, with a hawklike nose and inscrutable, deeply socketed eyes. Unhurried, as if prepared to outwait the younger man, he munched and spit and said nothing. At last, Morg caught on. He was the one who had asked to talk, and it was up to him to set the tone of their conversation.

"Wirt, I'm not just sure where to start." He faltered, puffing in silence a moment. "Hell, I guess the thing to do is just spit it out. What're our chances? Are we going to make a well or not?"

Jordan regarded him with muddy brown eyes, revealing nothing. "Depends. Am I talkin' to a roustabout, or am I talkin' to the feller who's footin' the bill?"

"You're talking to a man who's about broke," Morg countered, "and I'd like some straight answers."

"You know that bailin' I just took?"

"Yeah, what about it?"

"It was limestone. We've hit the cap rock."

Morg understood the lingo by now, and he knew the cap rock was an underground formation generally found just above an oil pocket. A sudden tingle ran down his spine, and his lips felt dry.

"How long before you break through to paysand?"

"Who said anything about paysand?" Jordan squirted a nearby tree with tobacco juice. "Likely there ain't no pay to it."

"Are you saying it's another duster?"

"I hit cap rock at the same depth both times before. My drillin' log reads like somebody copied the pages word for word on all three holes. You draw your own conclusions."

A long silence ensued as they stared at one another. But Morg had caught a hint of something in the driller's voice. An odd inflection, perhaps a note of disgust. He took a drag on his cigarette, studied the fiery tip for a moment, not nearly as calm as he appeared.

"Wirt, level with me. What do you think of Turner and Harris?"

Jordan's gaze narrowed, and he seemed to deliberate. Then he shrugged, as if relieving himself of a burden. "They're promoters. They get another feller to risk his money, and if the well comes in they're on easy street. Meantime, they're off settin' up other deals, and earnin' their bread and butter tradin' leases. Ain't no way they can lose, and the more deals they got workin' the better their odds are."

"What you're saying is that they suckered me?"

"Well, some, I reckon. Leastways on the third hole."

"Why is it you never said anything before?"

"You're full growed. Me, I'm just paid to drill."

"Then how come you spoke up now?"

Jordan flashed a mouthful of brownish teeth. "I ain't paid to steal."

They smoked and chewed in silence awhile longer. Finally Morg flipped his cigarette into the creek, and his pale eyes settled on the driller. "Wirt, let's assume this hole comes in a duster."

"Sounds like a fair to middlin' bet."

"I've got enough left in my kick to drill one more well. Anywhere you say. Now suppose we just forget Turner and Harris. Would you go partners with me?"

"Poor-boy it, you mean?"

"That's exactly what I mean."

Jordan worked his quid and spat, considering it; then he grunted. "If a man ain't a gambler then he oughtn't to be in the oil business. I reckon I'm game if you are."

They shook hands and left it at that. Jordan went back to the rig and resumed drilling. Morg spent the rest of the afternoon chopping wood for the boiler. But his hangdog look had disappeared completely, and in his mind, Anadarko simply ceased to exist.

Two days later they brought in another duster.

A livid moon hung high in a black sky. The bunkhouse windows glowed in the distance, but the earth itself seemed flooded with a spectral light, somehow unreal and drained of life. Out of the north a chill wind swept across the plains, lending an eerie, moaning whisper to the night. Then the moon went behind a cloud, and somewhere far away an owl hooted, distinct and very clear yet mournful in the ghostly silence.

As the moon played hide-and-seek with the clouds Owen listened, standing motionless at the edge of the porch. His eyes scanned the darkness, and he tried to summon back a precise recollection of the old Indian legend. Something about a white owl being the sign of early snow and a harsh winter. After a moment, though, he set the thought aside. The owl had hooted only once, and shown itself not at all. Which made the matter somewhat academic, and left yet another superstition umblemished by facts.

The door opened, and a shaft of light spilled onto the porch. He looked around as Grace stepped outside, closing the door behind her, and walked forward. She had a shawl thrown on over her nightdress, and her hair hung loosely to her waist. It glinted in the moonlight, flecked through with golden shimmering beams, and it occurred to him that she had never been more beautiful. Years melted away in the spectral glow, and it was as if she remained exactly as he had seen her that first time. A tawny little doll, with the soul of a saint and the lynx-eyed zest of a leprechaun.

She snuggled up beside him, and he put his arm around her. But she neither spoke nor looked at him. Nor had he expected it. In all their years together she had never intruded on his thoughts. She knew his moods, perhaps even read his mind; whether he wanted to talk or merely wanted company, she was content just to be with him. They stood that way for some time, wordless and still, communing on a higher level known only to themselves. Then his arm tightened, hugging her closer, and he glanced at the darkened clouds slowly gathering in the sky.

"Looks like snow."

Her eyes lifted, mocking him. "Yes, I heard the owl."

"Backslider," he chuckled softly. "Only the ancient ones believe the owl." He peered again at the sky. "All the same, it still looks like snow."

"Perhaps the owl will come again. Then you can be sure."

They fell silent, listening to the stillness, cloaked in their own warmth. For Owen, these were the best times. Just the two of them, secluded on the ranch, away from the prying busybodies and their wagging tongues. Not that the gossip bothered him. People could believe whatever pleased them most. He no longer concerned himself one way or the other. Guthrie remembered Jake Kincaid and figured he was his father's son and he couldn't have cared less. Evil little minds had no place in the world he and Grace had made for themselves.

She stirred, glancing up at him. "Shall I tell you what the wind whispers to me? It says you are troubled tonight, and stand alone in the cold asking questions."

"No, not troubled. Just thoughtful."

"Is there a difference? I was taught that only a holy man could be thoughtful without worry. But perhaps I was mistaken."

"Matter of fact, maybe you're right at that." Owen's stare seemed fixed on some distant point in the darkness. "I've been standing out here wondering about the kids."

"You're not really worried about Beth, are you?"

"Well, some. Course she's got her head on in the right place, and I suppose she'll get over this wild streak. Or maybe I'm just an old fudd, like she says. Women today sure are different, and that's a fact." He paused, abstracted a moment, then gave her a sidewise look. "I guess I'm not foolin' you, though, am I? Hell, I'm not doing too good a job of foolin' myself. What I was thinking about mostly was Morg. Got to wondering if he means to come home for Christmas."

Grace understood, perhaps better than he suspected. There was a special kinship between a man and his son, and Owen's distress grew increasingly evident with time. Morg was gone, but the feeling hadn't vanished, not for Owen. He worried about his daughter, but he agonized over his son.

Beyond that, she understood something more, and it was perhaps her most astute observation about Owen Kincaid's son. While Morg was hard and pragmatic, at times the very image of his grandfather, he was hardly the cynic he would have the world believe. One of life's simpler truths was that people who constantly harped on the nobler virtues never possessed them. Underneath that tough outer shell, Morg had all the qualities he scorned, attributes he secretly admired but denounced as impractical in a world of rogues. Loyalty and compassion and honesty and love, all these he possessed and more. Yet he kept them buried, hidden away, revealed not even to himself. She sensed that he and his father were forever at odds for this very reason. He saw in Owen Kincaid all those attributes he secretly admired, and he believed himself incapable of being both a good man and a strong man.

As was his father. And though she had never spoken of her feelings to anyone, she understood Morg all the better because she saw him not for what he claimed to be or even as some dim reflection of old Jake Kincaid. She saw him instead for what he would one day become. His father's son.

"He will come back, Owen. When he's worked it out for himself—these things that bother him—he'll come home. Just as you did when you were young."

"Yeah, I suppose so. Trouble was, I came back too late. If I had wised up sooner the old man might be around today. Not that I'm blamin' myself. I guess he would've tackled the union whether I was around or not."

But he did blame himself, and his guilt was never far from the surface. Grace understood that as well; more clearly than he himself realized, she saw that his conscience was all too often his own worst enemy. "You know best, but I always thought you were a wiser man than your father. He lost you because he tried to hold you. Morg will come back because you were wise enough not to make the same mistake."

"Think so, huh?"

"Yes, I think so." She smiled, and turned him back toward the house. "And I think it is time we went inside. A troubled man needs warmth, not cold."

They went through the door, arm in arm, silhouetted for an instant in a streamer of light. Somewhere in the distance, but closer than before, the owl hooted again. Then the night was still and suddenly quite dark, and it began to snow.

THIRTEEN

In the quiet the old grandfather clock sounded like a laboring heart. As Beth came down the stairs the annoying tick-tock seemed ungodly loud, almost as though the pendulum had been implanted inside her skull. She was suffering a massive hangover, and the slightest noise aggravated the pounding throb at her temples. Simply walking, placing one foot in front of the other, brought on a spell of tottering vertigo. Descending the stairs, both hands firmly clasped to the banister, gave her a moment of dizzying angst, and by the time she reached the bottom, beads of sweat covered her forehead.

She stood there for several minutes, collecting herself, fearful she couldn't make it to the dining room. Last night was fuzzy and disoriented; she remembered touring several speakeasies and consuming gin rickeys as if they were water. There was no recollection whatever of her date bringing her home; how she had got undressed and made it into bed was a complete blank. Awakening was real, and her fluttering stomach was real, but all the rest seemed like some vague and disjointed hallucination.

Suddenly the clock struck the hour. She staggered, clutching at the staircase for support, as the ear-splitting bong-bong-bong hammered on without respite. Her head felt like a sore and mushy grape, ready to burst in an ooze of gin-soaked pulp. Then, mercifully, the chimes stopped. Swaying, one hand pressed to the pulsating knot at her temple, she managed a guarded peek at the clock. The hands stood at eleven

She crossed the foyer, entered the living room, and padded unsteadily toward the faint aroma of coffee. Things registered on her in a blur, flickering images that came and went in little swirls of nausea. Through a window she caught a fleeting glimpse of an ice wagon on the street. The iceman cut a block, tonged it onto his back, and carried it up the driveway. Idly, she wondered if an ice pack might cure what ailed her. Then, in a convoluted bit of logic, she decided just as quickly that freezing her entire head wouldn't help.

A bumblebee suddenly zoomed past a screened window at the side of the house, and she witlessly ducked aside. The zithering buzz, in the soft hot silence of spring, sounded frighteningly near. Yet it wasn't, as she realized almost instantly, and she felt a complete fool. Angry with herself, and still a bit unstrung, she tossed her head and marched into the dining room.

The dark, gloomy interior was a relief to her eyes. The walls were paneled in black walnut; a gigantic sideboard and table and china closet were of the same wood; even the mirror and chandelier reflected dark ghostly shadows. After the sun-splashed brilliance of the living room it was as if she had entered a cool and inviting cave.

Grace sat at the far end of the table, polishing silver. She glanced up, appraising the situation at a glance as the girl came through the doorway. Without a word, she rose and hurried toward the kitchen. By the time Beth had negotiated the long room and taken a seat, she was back with a single cup and a steamy pot of coffee. Neither of them spoke, and as if some ritual were being acted out, Grace poured and the girl drank. With three cups down, and a fourth waiting, Beth's shaky look began to fade. A spark of color returned to her cheeks, the dull glaze passed from her eyes, and her hand steadied. As she drained the cup again, the queasy sensation melted away, and her stomach flutters disappeared. She burped delicately, darting a sheepish look at Grace.

"Believe it or not, I think I'm going to live."

"Yes, I imagine you will." Grace was silent a moment. She selected an ornate serving spoon and began polishing. "The way you look, though, I'm wondering if it's worth it?"

Gentle as the rebuke was, it stung. Beth flushed, and averted her eyes. "I've never been this bad before. Not even in college." Her hand went to her mussed hair, then her face, and she suddenly realized she was still wearing last night's makeup. "God, I must have gone off the deep end. I can't even remember coming home."

Grace didn't look up, but her hands paused just an instant. Then she went on polishing. "I had your boyfriend carry you upstairs. He was scared out of his wits—afraid of your father, I suppose—but at least he had the good sense to bring you home."

Beth sat bolt upright, gaping. "Daddy saw me! Like that?"

"No, don't worry. I was careful not to wake him. Once your boyfriend left, I got you undressed and into your nightgown. So far as your father knows, you just came in late. But you can thank your lucky stars his bedroom is at the back of the house. I heard the car pull in and came downstairs right away. Next time you might not get off so easy."

Shaken, Beth stared at the filmy peignoir she wore, ruefully aware that it was near noon and she was still in her bedclothes. A long while passed, and when she finally spoke, her vibrant voice was oddly subdued. "There won't be a next time. I'll never get that stewed again as long as I live."

"But you won't stop drinking?"

"No, I won't stop drinking." Defiantly, she lifted her chin. "Why should I?"

Grace let the question hang, wondering what she could say that would make a difference. Or should she say anything at all? Older and wiser, certainly more objective, she understood better than the girl what lay behind the younger generation's revolt in manners and morals. At root, it was the war which had unsettled Beth, much in the same way it had affected Morg. On the Western Front, two million soldiers had been very far from American morality, and willing mademoiselles were plentiful. Living so intimately with death, the boys acquired a new code which seemed entirely defensible, and a whole generation became infected with the eat-drink-and-be-merry-for-tomorrow-we-die spirit. The war matured them too quickly, and their torn nerves required the emotional stimulants of excitement and whiskey and fast living. Upon returning home, they found it difficult to taper off and settle back into the humdrum routine. Their elders acted as though nothing had changed, as if everyone still lived in a Pollyanna world of rosy ideals, but the younger generation couldn't accept this tattered sentiment. Instead, they rejected it, quite bluntly and at times rather disrespectfully.

American girls came under the influence of these same wartime standards. Their own revolution was accelerated by the suffrage movement and the growing independence of women; no less than their brothers, they rejected the starchy, outdated customs of an older generation. They drank, experimented with sex, and in a mood of disillusionment, explored everything forbidden them by a moral code they could no longer tolerate. The double standard still existed, but it was fast disappearing. Within the past year the flapper had become less of an oddity, and bit by bit Beth became more typical of small-town girls. Like her, they had discovered the joys of burning the candle at both ends.

Grace understood all this quite readily because she herself lived outside the moral dicta of society. Not surprisingly, she felt she had little room to censure Beth. Nor was she a canting hypocrite who could preach one code for others while laying out a different set of rules for herself. But she loved this girl as she would her own daughter, and before it was too late, someone had to say what needed saying.

At length, satisfied that it must be done, she laid the serving spoon aside and folded her hands on the table. "Beth, tell me honestly, are you happy here in Guthrie?"

"My God, no!" the girl burst back. "I hate this damn town."

"You wouldn't be content to marry and settle down, raise a family?"

"Ugh! What a revolting thought. Have you taken a close look at the boys I date? They're dull and boring, and so intellectually stunted I feel like I'm living in a vacuum."

Beth had always detested her mother's affectations, the cloyed sweetness and the love so often exhibited in an alcoholic haze. But her feeling for Grace was genuine, and since childhood she had confided secrets to her aunt that she told no one else. Now, she leaned closer, and although the house was empty, she lowered her voice in a whisper. "I can't even bring myself to sleep with one of them. Really, I mean it. They're enough to turn a girl frigid. Can you imagine me married to someone like that? Why, I'd go stark raving mad before the honeymoon was over."

Grace smiled indulgently, and shook her head. "There's more to marriage than sleeping with a man. But if you feel that way, why stay here? You have money of your own. Why not go back to New York? If the men there are brighter, and you're happier in a big city, why not just leave?"

Beth recoiled at the idea. "You never left. Not even when Mama was alive. And you have money of your own, too, so that wasn't what stopped you."

That was true. Grace's headright in the Osage oil lands had made her a wealthy woman, and she could have gone whenever she chose. But Beth regretted the words the instant she closed her mouth. Although she wasn't positive, she felt sure that Grace and her father slept together. They were utterly discreet, to the point that Grace ran the house without servants, and while Beth merely surmised they were lovers, she had never reproached either of them in her mind. She couldn't, for even in her youthful cynicism, she knew that Grace was somehow different from other people.

Not that she was devout, or in any way paraded her faith, but she possessed a humanity that few mortals ever attained. Her inner eye saw none of the squalor in life, nor did she fault others for their frailties and petty little minds. Instead, tranquil within herself, she saw only that which was infinitely calm and beautiful and without flaw. Yet this inner peace in no way distorted her vision. She was gifted with an earthy wisdom, and had a subtle way—uncanny and disconcerting—of reading another's thoughts as if they had been spoken aloud. And unlike women who create psychic deafness with their constant chatter, she was a woman of few and pungent words. Whenever she spoke people listened, and her remarks were remembered a long time. Particularly by those who had the wits to comprehend what they had heard.

Just now Beth felt obtuse as a brick. She had blurted out the first thing that came into her head, and she was appalled by her own insensitivity. Like the dullards she so often criticized, she had heard the words but missed the message.

Serene, still smiling, Grace responded in a gentle tone. "You do see, don't you, Beth? We both stay for the same reason."

The girl nodded. "Daddy and Morg."

"That's right. No matter what happens in a family, it's the women who hold it together. Without us, it would all fall apart. Sometimes it's painful but we can't think of ourselves. The family comes first. And it only aggravates things if we act irresponsible."

"I know. I'm such a silly little bitch sometimes." Beth's throat swelled around a moist lump, and hot tears stung her cheeks. "I'll try harder to behave. Honestly, I will. I promise."

"Well, my goodness, of course you will. I knew that all along. Now stop your crying and go freshen up. Then we'll have ourselves a nice lunch, and you can tell me all about the boy who brought you home last night. He was scared speechless, but really, honey, he didn't seem like the numskull you made him out."

Grace's smile was infectious. The girl dabbed at her tears and slowly took hold of herself. After a moment she jumped up, hugged the older woman fiercely, and ran from the room. By the time she reached the foyer her head was clear and her eyes shiny bright, and she took the stairs like a butterfly climbing swiftly on a soft warm breeze.

Sniffing a little, Grace jerked out a handkerchief and blew her nose. Then, satisfied with the way of things, she went back to polishing silver.

Wirt Jordan paused at the edge of the creek. Erosion had scooped out a cutback in the bank, and here the water eddied in a shallow pool. Although there was nothing cantankerous in his manner, Jordan never indulged in small talk, nor did he encourage it in others. Now, as he had throughout the morning, he simply ignored Morg, who stood quietly at his shoulder. The driller's concentration was fixed on the swirling pool, and he studied it intently for several moments. A greasy slick floated on the surface of the water, sparkling with tints of gold and green and tar-pitch black. After a while Jordan grunted to himself, apparently all the conversation he felt necessary, and headed upstream though the treeline. Morg gave the pool a last glance, wondering if it meant what he thought it meant, and took off after his partner.

The sun was mild and warm, almost balmy, and a fresh spring wind drifted across the prairie. Overhead sparrows chattered in the trees, and meadowlarks flitted about, lifting and falling on stubby wings. But Jordan saw or heard none of this. Like a bloodhound nosing fresh scent, he plunged on, senses attuned to nothing except the trail ahead. He moved faster now, crashing through brush and saplings, almost as if he knew where the chase ended, and what he would find when he got there.

The creek they followed was located on a farm outside Tonkawa, in the southeast corner of the old Cherokee Strip. Their journey to this spot had been long and arduous, consuming the better part of five months. At times, it had proved bitterly frustrating as well; while they searched, everyone around them seemed to be striking oil. The Osage lands were booming; west of there Ponca City reported new discoveries almost daily; and farther south, the Burbank field was roaring wild. With monotonous regularity, always a day late and a dollar short, they chased an elusive will-o'-the-wisp. And the harder they ran, the farther they fell behind, for it became apparent toward the last that they were running in circles.

Unlike more affluent wildcatters, Morg and Wirt Jordan were operating under a handicap. After drilling the third duster outside Anadarko, they were left with funds enough to sink one more well. But the money would barely stretch, and only then if they cut corners and paid next to nothing for a drilling lease. This eliminated any area near a producing field (where the bonus on an acre ran into thousands of dollars), and effectively confined their search to unexplored land. All of which made it a hit-or-miss proposition, with an element of luck that sandbagged the odds enormously.

Since the first of the year they had practically driven Morg's Stutz Bearcat into the ground. The car limped along, sputtering and backfiring, and there was hardly a section of Oklahoma they hadn't covered at least twice. Yet in all their travels, circling and circling on dusty backcountry roads, they hadn't once turned up a likely-looking prospect. At any given moment, Jordan knew to the dime how much was left in their bankroll, and he wasn't about to risk it on still another dry hole. They repaired the Stutz themselves, lived on sandwiches and soda pop, and kept on circling.

The only high point in the past five months had been a brief stopover in Guthrie. Morg was almost smothered with affection by Beth and Grace, and to himself, he grudgingly admitted that he'd missed them. His father was another kettle of fish. Curiously enough, after some stiff questioning, the old man had taken quite a shine to Wirt Jordan. But the fact that Morg now had an honest partner did little to thaw the chill between them. Owen still thought his son was chasing rainbows, and when they parted, nothing much had changed. Privately, both his sister and Grace assured him they were working on the old man, but so far as he could see, they hadn't made a dent.

Some weeks later Morg and Jordan had stopped for a cold drink at a country store south of Tonkawa. When he chose to employ it, Jordan had a flair for getting other people to talk, and he'd gradually worked the storekeeper around to the subject of oil. The Ponca City fields were less than thirty miles north, and as it turned out, several oil scouts had cruised the area and gone away unimpressed. But the storekeeper ventured the opinion that the bunch of them didn't know beans from buckshot. Jordan bought another round of Cokes, nodding and coaxing him on with a few questions, and by the time they left, he'd told them a most intriguing story about the farm of an old widow woman, Ruthie Mae Tucker.

And now, the day after visiting Widow Tucker, they were trudging along the creek which bisected her farm. She had confirmed the storekeeper's tale (nearly talking their ears off in the process) but she offered them little hope. People had used her medicine springs for generations, and according to her, the only way to turn it into ready cash was to bottle the stuff and sell it. Oil scouts from the big companies had told her the same thing, but Jordan was insistent, and she had agreed readily enough when he asked to have a look for himself.

Although Jordan was a driller by trade, he had accumulated considerable knowledge about the mysteries of oil exploration. Still, like many old-timers, he had no more faith in geologists than he did doodlebugs and clairvoyants. He operated strictly on the principle of creekology, searching for oil where there was plain evidence of its existence: gas seeps, medicine springs, and slicks in low places or along creek banks. Every producing well he'd drilled had been in such spots, and despite the scientific theories being bandied about, he stuck with what worked for him.

Oil companies, on the other hand, had gradually swung away from creekology. They relied instead on geologists, who were just then coming into their own, and by the spring of 1921 seismographs were commonly being used to map sub-surface formations. The current school of thought was that oil migrated through porous underground strata until it reached structural traps. There, the oil accumulated and a pool was formed. The most common structural trap in Oklahoma was an anticline, a formation shaped somewhat like the ridge of a house. Geologists believed that oil, because of its buoyancy, slowly rose to the crest of an anticline, and there became trapped in spongelike sandstone. They also scoffed at creekology, in the way of doctors libeling faith healers, and with great humor, they had left Widow Tucker's medicine spring exactly as they found it.

Undaunted by this academic jargon, wildcatters still depended on a strange mixture of surface observation, superstition, and the occult. Wirt Jordan couldn't quite bring himself to accept the occult, but he was fond of saying, "Only the drill finds the oil." For all their book learning and fancy gizmos, he remained skeptical of geologists. The drill had to be spudded into the earth by someone with the guts to back his judgment with hard cash, and he'd never yet seen a scholar put his money where his mouth was. Confident that the law of averages favored those who kept the faith, he clung to what he knew best, creekology.

And today was the day his faith paid off.

Shortly before noon Jordan and Morg came to the headwater of the creek. They stood there a moment, hot and sweaty, staring quizzically at what they'd found. Instead of the one spring mentioned by Widow Tucker, there were three springs, each somewhat apart from the other but draining together off a low rise to form the creek. The puzzle was quickly solved with an inspection of the springs. The one at the lowest point on the incline, situated somewhat to the east, gave off a strong smell of gas. Heavy mineral deposits were crusted around the bubbling hole, and the water itself appeared slightly different in color from the other springs.

Jordan went down on one knee, with Morg at his side, and pulled a box of matches from his pocket. Almost reverently, like a priest before an altar, he struck a match and tossed it into the hole. A great flaming whoosh exploded in their faces, and an instant later a blue-red blaze leaped skyward. Then the flame extinguished, choked out by the water, and the smell of gas returned.

Morg felt his pulse quicken as Jordan climbed to his feet. The driller's features were creased in a grin, and one eye was cocked askew. "Pardner, if that ain't an oil well I'll kiss your ass and bark like a fox."

"Sonovabitch!" Morg could scarcely get his breath. "You really mean it, don't you? We've found it."

"Gawddamn right we found it. And we're gonna drill it, too. That old widder woman don't know it yet, but we're gonna make her rich as sin."

"What about the lease? You think we can get it cheap?"

"Cheap? Great Crucified Christ! We'll get it for nothin'. And if we keep our wits about us, we can tie up half the county before anybody's the wiser."

"Yeah, but what about the bonus? Our bankroll doesn't have much leeway."

"Bonus, hell! These people think the oil boom passed 'em by. Everybody and his dog'll be beggin' us to drill their land just for royalties. You hide and watch. They'll be huntin' us up in droves."

Jordan whipped out a jackknife, quickly hacked a young sapling in half, and whittled himself a green stake. After studying the lay of the land a moment, he marched off twenty paces and rammed the stake in the ground. Then he turned back, grinning broadly, and gestured at the stake.

"That's where we'll spud in. And sure as I'm standin' here, it'll be the gawddamnest gusher you ever seen."

Morg shook his head and laughed. "Wirt, you're an old phony. What happened to all that talk you've been giving me about doodlebuggers and witch doctors?"

"Why, hell's bells, there ain't nothin' superstitious about that. It's a known fact that a green stake draws the oil. Any fool could've told you that."

Coldly indignant, his grin replaced by an owlish frown, Jordan headed back toward the creek. Morg stared at the stake a moment longer, laughing softly to himself, then wheeled about and trudged after his partner. Of a sudden, quite unwittingly, he had a good feeling about that stake. Hunch or not, he was glad it was green.

The train rattled southward like a scorched centipede. At noonday the fireball lodged high in the sky seared the coach roofs, and inside, the passengers roasted as if trapped in a blast furnace. Seated beside an open window, Owen Kincaid stared wearily at the monotonous landscape rushing past. His eyeballs were gritty and raw, smarting with flecks of engine soot, and his clothes were covered with a layer of powdered grime. The oppressive heat left him drenched in sweat, and his mind felt numbed. Swaying with the motion of the coach, caught up in the mesmerizing clickety-clack of steel wheels on steel rails, he fought against the drowsy lassitude that threatened to suck him under.

And wondered again what the hell he was doing in Mexico.

Then the train slowed as it hit the outskirts of Tehuantepec, and he roused himself, shaking off the logy stupor. The somnolent village was like a hundred others he had seen since crossing the border, and it occurred to him that time had little effect on the casual pace of the natives. Naked taffy-skinned children rolled in the dirt alongside mangy dogs and runty pigs and a motley assortment of bleating goats. Women in sleazy faded dresses tended the dirt-floored adobes while their men lazed in the shade, ever confident that *mañana* would bring about a sharp reversal in their fortunes. Seemingly, these people asked little of life, and expected less. Warm at heart and peace-loving, they wished only to bask in the mellow sun, to be left alone. Not even the Revolution had changed the indolent, unhurried character forged over the centuries. Governments came and went, Zapata and Madero sacrificed themselves to the cause, but the people were forever unchanged. Life was to be lived one day at a time, and there was no rush. Tomorrow always came.

A groaning squeal racketed back over the coaches as the engineer throttled down and set the brakes. Like some soot-encrusted dragon, the engine rolled past the depot and ground to a halt, belching steam smoke and fiery sparks in a final burst of power. The stationhouse was all but deserted at midday (*siesta* time, as Owen had learned over the past week); a grumpy-looking station agent stood in the doorway, yawning listlessly as he watched passengers disgorge from the train. Owen collected his warbag from an overhead rack, waiting until the aisle cleared. Then he walked to the end of the car and scrambled down the steps.

His Spanish was only passable, but he managed to make himself understood, and within minutes the station agent had him pointed in the direction of the local Rurales headquarters. Walking away, he began to appreciate the wisdom of the *siesta*. He felt soaked, limp as a dishrag, and his mouth was a small cavern of salt. Silently, he cursed the heat and Warren Harding and the jaybird named McDonald. But most of all he cursed himself, a damned fool on a damned fool's errand.

Ten days ago, when the call came, he had almost refused the assignment. Then, on the spur of the moment, he'd accepted. Guthrie was pretty dull in the summer, anyway, and like an old war horse, he always had that vague yearning to get back into action. Not that he owed President Harding anything (the man was a hack, and a Republican hack, at that). Nor was he overly concerned about the Santa Fe's profit and loss (although he still held the large block of stock originally purchased by his father). But he'd never seen Mexico, and the idea of a little excitement sounded appealing, so he went along for the ride. Grace hadn't been too pleased, and Beth practically accused him of senility, but he joshed them for a couple of worrywarts, and before he left, things had calmed down a bit.

While he would never have admitted it to the women, he had actually been rather flattered by a call from the White House. And the assignment itself also tweaked his interest. A Santa Fe paymaster had absconded with $18,000, and there was every reason to believe he had hightailed it for Mexico. The railroad requested help from Washington, and at first met with considerable opposition. Relations between the United States and Mexico were still unstable (although the Revolution had supposedly ended last year), and there was reluctance to send a U.S. marshal on what amounted to private business. Still, the Harding administration rarely turned a deaf ear to the requests of large corporations, and the Attorney General finally remembered that Owen had served in an unofficial capacity in the past. The Santa Fe was agreeable, and a few days after the phone call Owen received papers appointing him special representative of the President.

During the journey south, Owen had mapped out a campaign based on what he knew of the fugitive. A creature of habit, McDonald seldom varied from his routine. He had been devoted to his work, lived modestly in a rooming house, and while he was something of a loner, his character was considered above reproach. Apparently, his only known vice was embezzlement. McDonald was no loafer, though, and even with the money, it seemed improbable that he would turn to a life of idleness. Old habits more often than not betrayed a man, particularly someone on the run, and Owen decided that the first place to check was where McDonald would feel most at home.

Upon arriving in Mexico City, he called on the U.S. Embassy for assistance, and that very afternoon gained access to government files of all railroad employees. Before nightfall, his hunch was confirmed. An American, Alan McDougal, had recently been hired as conductor, and was working the line between Tehuantepec and Gutierrez. Quite obviously, Alex McDonald was a man of limited imagination, as well as a victim of old habits. He hadn't even bothered to change his initials. After checking railroad schedules, and verifying the arrival time of the return train from Gutierrez, Owen made plans to intercept the fugitive at the depot in Tehuantepec.

That evening he was granted an audience with Alvaro Obregón in the presidential palace. Obregón proved a genial host, and obligingly signed the necessary extradition papers. Over a glass of brandy, he was at some pains to impress on Owen that Mexico was at last functioning under a stable government. He desperately wanted formal recognition of his regime by the United States, and expressed the hope that Owen would personally convey his message to President Harding. Since most of his predecessors had left office by way of assassination, it was an understandable request. Owen found the man likable and sincere, and left the palace favorably disposed to pass along the gist of their conversation. Perhaps, in some small way, he was also influenced by the fact that Obregón had sacrificed an arm to the *Revolución*.

On the train ride south that night, it occurred to Owen that there was an amusing parallel between Obregón and Harding. Obregón hoped to hold his office through a stable government, and Harding had been elected to office on a promise of a "return to normalcy." Of the two men, it seemed to him that Obregón had perhaps the better chance of success. He considered Warren Harding a hack politico, a practitioner of courthouse intrigue and shady deals, living proof that every mother's son could become President. So far as he could determine, Harding was devoid of intellect, the abstraction of John Doe come to life, an easygoing fat man whose orotund campaign promises lacked both substance and common sense. Of course Obregón seemed to be an honest man, a patriot, and that somewhat weakened the comparison. Warren Harding was nothing more than a backwoods crook.

All the same, Owen respected the office if not the man. While he considered Alex McDonald a lesser thief than the President, he allowed personal feelings no part in the matter. It was a job that needed doing, and he had come a long way to get it done. That was enough.

The Rurales were somewhat startled by the appearance of a *gringo* lawman in Tehuantepec. But the extradition papers signed by Alvaro Obregón quickly dispelled any misgivings. The captain in charge offered to turn out his entire company, announcing that he himself would lead them in the capture of this deadly *bandido*. Owen declined as politely as possible, requesting only two men. Their presence would lend an official note to the arrest, but if possible, he preferred to handle the matter himself. The captain envisioned something more on the scale of a military operation, and it took considerable debate to persuade him otherwise. At last, with a great display of reluctance, he agreed, and Owen departed for the train station trailed by the Rurales.

Toward sundown, when the train arrived from Gutierrez, he stood just inside the depot door. Pinned to his shirt was his old U.S. marshal's badge, and strapped on his hip was the Colt he had carried throughout the Oklahoma outlaw days. Oddly, he felt cool and collected, not the least bit skittish, as if he had reverted by instinct to another time. His heartbeat slowed and his nerves steadied, and he became again the detached, stony-eyed manhunter. Several minutes passed as people poured off the train, and then, just as he'd planned it, his man stepped down from the lead car. McDonald was big and fleshy, with a meaty nose and bright, quick eyes, and a solemn air of deliberation about his movements. Owen motioned for the Rurales to stay back, waiting until McDonald was some ten paces from the depot, and then he stepped through the doorway.

"Alex McDonald, I have a warrant for your arrest. Put your hands over your head and walk toward me."

McDonald halted in his tracks. His eyes narrowed, glinting in an instant of calculation as he took in the badge and the gun and the empty sleeve. What he saw looked to be only half a man, and in that instant of appraisal, the decision was made. His hand darted beneath his coat and came out with a stubby bulldog pistol.

Owen was surprised, expecting the man to come along peaceable, but it hampered his reflexes none at all. His arm moved, the Colt appeared in his hand, and he fired a split second before the stubby pistol came level. A puff of dust spurted off McDonald's coat and a dark crimson stain spread over his chest. He staggered, hurled backward by the impact of the slug, then his knees gave way and he collapsed in the dirt. His eyes rolled back in his head, staring sightlessly, and the little pistol slipped out of his hand.

Walking forward, Owen shucked the empty shell out of his Colt and calmly reloaded. Killing a man, even after all this time, had been as easy as ever. He'd felt nothing when he pulled the trigger, and now, standing over the body, he felt only a vague twinge of regret. But of a sudden he felt something else. Morbid, and perhaps a bit ghoulish, but an honest curiosity nonetheless.

He wondered where the $18,000 was hidden.

The first day they fired the boilers Wirt Jordan had jokingly called it a Coffee Pot Rig. But it was an apt description, and the name stuck. Nailed to a beam on one side of the derrick was a crudely lettered sign.

COFFEE POT #1

Anyone who read the sign naturally assumed the outfit was owned by a confirmed optimist. The numeral implied that this was merely the first in a series of wells to be drilled, and folks from surrounding farms were duly impressed. Oil men, had they bothered to take a look at the operation, would have laughed themselves hoarse. Jordan's wit was unmistakable, at least to anyone in the business, for if ever there had been a poor-boy rig it was the one erected on Widow Tucker's medicine springs.

With timbers from a nearby sawmill, and the help of farmers working for day wages, Jordan and Morg had built the derrick themselves. It bowed in certain spots, and bulged in others, and had the look of a matchstick tower slung together by a bunch of drunks. All of the machinery had been bought secondhand, and had the rusty, worn-out appearance of junk salvaged from a scrapyard. The boilers, which furnished power for the engine and pumps, were ancient and temperamental. Working in tandem, they could generate hardly more than a hundred pounds of pressure, and Jordan was able to drill only minutes at a time before the steam was exhausted. But when the whole affair was thrown wide open, engine and pumps and boilers, it banged and clattered with a deafening racket, and the derrick vibrated from floor to crown block, as if caught in the bone-jarring tremors of an earthquake. Just as Jordan had observed that first day, it sounded and looked, and sometimes acted, like an overheated coffee pot bouncing around on an old wood stove.

On a muggy afternoon in September, however, things at the Coffee Pot #1 were pretty quiet. Morg and Jordan were operating the rig by themselves, as they had for the past three months, and early that morning they had bored through the cap rock. Cautiously, Jordan had drilled a foot, then another foot, and one more foot at a time into the sand, and every load of cuttings he brought up in the bailer had shown streaks of color. But so far there was no flow of oil from the hole, just a lot of gas, and at the moment, his features were set in a dark scowl. The problem was critical, and he had every reason to look worried. A single miscue at this point could obliterate nearly a year of toil and sweat and dreams.

As Jordan knew from hard-won experience, oil was embedded in sand at various depths in the earth. Above or below these beds there were formations of rock and clay, generally impregnated with water. The trick was to tap the oil sand at its upper level, but not to drill so deeply that the hole might extend into water. All day, as Morg watched apprehensively, Jordan had gone down foot by foot, and bailed the hole after each drilling. By relieving the pressure of mud and slush on the oil sand, he hoped to coax the oil to the surface. Yet the oil hadn't budged, and his quandary grew more acute by the minute.

For quite a while now Jordan had been pacing around the wellhead, stopping occasionally to peer down the hole, as if he might somehow will the oil to the surface. But nothing happened; the hole remained silent. At last, unable to stand the suspense, Morg interrupted his pacing.

"What do you think, Wirt? Any chance?"

"How the hell do I know? We're damned if we do and damned if we don't."

"Yeah, but we've got to do something." Morg's bushy eyebrows drew together in a frown, and he stabbed a grimy finger at the hole. "I mean, Jesus Christ, there's oil down there!"

"No shit, Sherlock?" the driller snapped querulously. "Did you get that brainstorm all by yourself?"

"Well, goddamn, don't bite my head off." Morg walked

away, struggling with his temper, then turned and came back. They were both on edge, and he sensed that it was the wrong time to push. "I didn't mean to needle you, Wirt. I'm just a little jumpy, that's all."

"Guess I'm sort o' touchy myself." Jordan sighed wearily, and clapped a thorny paw over the younger man's shoulder. "Forget that wisecrack. I was just lettin' off steam."

By now there was little need for apology between them. After living together for nearly two years, they shared a very close and enduring camaraderie. Along the way they had brawled back-to-back in countless honky-tonks, demolished several whorehouses, and told one another things they had never told anyone else. There were few secrets between them, but because each was willing to let the other remain his own man, they made a good team. Standing there at the wellhead, their anger of a moment ago quickly simmered down, and they lapsed into a thoughtful silence. Neither of them spoke for a long while, but they were of a mind nonetheless. Their thoughts were at the bottom of a hole some two thousand feet below the derrick floor.

At last, Jordan shrugged, and spat a thin jet of tobacco juice into the hole. "What the hell? We'll go another foot and see what she does." He engaged the bull wheel and swung a string of tools over the wellhead. "Just hold your breath and hope we don't roll snake-eyes."

An hour later, after Jordan pulled the tools and ran the bailer, they were right back where they'd started. The cuttings were rich with color, but there wasn't so much as a gurgle from the hole. The tension was oppressive, and they both stared daggers at the wellhead, hardly able to suppress their disgust. Worse yet, a pervasive fear hung between them, the very certain dread that they dared not go another foot. Yet the hole was there, and the oil was there, and something had to be done. Morg finally cleared his throat, wondering how he could tactfully frame the question, but the driller beat him to the punch.

"Don't get your bowels in an uproar," Jordan said quietly. "Gimme a minute to wrassle it around."

The minute slipped past like a phantom, and with what seemed the utmost reluctance, Jordan spoke his thoughts aloud. "Well, one thing's for gawddamn sure. We're done drillin'. Sink 'er another foot and we're liable to wind up bottlin' water."

Morg blinked a couple of times, thoroughly bewildered. "So what do we do?"

"What do we do?" Jordan's words came in a low, muffled growl, like a mastiff. "We shoot the son of a bitch! That's what we do."

Early next morning the shooter rolled in behind the steering wheel of an old Ford truck. His name was Tom Adair, out of Ponca City, and he was reportedly the best nitro man in northern Oklahoma. In the trade, he was addressed simply as Shooter, and it was a tribute of no small distinction. He had blown everything from stubborn holes to storage tank holocausts; not without reason, it was commonly agreed that he had steel cables for nerves and ice water for blood.

On the ground, Shooter Adair presented a rather unprepossessing appearance. He was wide and squat, with scarcely any neck, and his head was fixed directly upon his shoulders. His ears were jugged, he was bald as a billiard ball, and he walked with the rolling gait of a landlocked sailor. He was also taciturn as a rock, and wasted little time on amenities. Jordan had explained on the telephone what the job entailed, and after a brief inspection of the rig, Adair set about earning his pay. Not surprisingly, the owners of Coffee Pot #1 made up a small, but captivated, audience. They were down to their last thousand dollars, most of which now belonged to Shooter Adair, and if he couldn't bring in the well, then they were simply out of business. It was make or break time, the last roll of the dice.

The truck had a rack of heavily padded compartments built onto the back of the cab. In each compartment was a two-gallon can of nitroglycerin, and Adair proceeded to carry the cans, one at a time, to the rig. Morg observed that he walked very slowly, and handled the cans as gingerly as a gigolo caressing a virgin. Next he brought two cylindrical tubes from the truck. They were constructed of rolled tin; about five inches in diameter and ten feet in length; when fully loaded, each would hold twenty-five quarts of nitro. At that point, Adair brusquely waved Morg aside, and asked Jordan to assist with loading the shells.

The driller set the first tube in the wellhead hole, holding it steady, while Adair very carefully poured liquid nitro from the cans. Once the tube was full, they capped it, and lowered it to the bottom of the hole by means of a hook attached to a spool of rope. With the tube resting on the bottom, the hook was jiggled free and the rope withdrawn. Then the process was repeated, and the second tube was lowered into the hole. The idea was to explode the nitro, which would fracture the subsurface formations, thereby freeing the oil from the sand. As the rope was being withdrawn for the second time, Adair expressed the opinion that fifty quarts would get the job done, and based on what he'd seen in the cuttings, Jordan readily agreed.

The three men had just turned away from the wellhead when they heard a strange noise deep in the hole. It was a tinny clattering sound, and as they listened, it grew perceptibly louder. They just stood there, absolutely frozen, like animals paralyzed by the headlamp of an onrushing train. Not even Morg had to be told what was happening. The second tube had squeezed the gas in the well, forming a pressure pocket, and the gas was hurling a cylinder loaded with nitro back up the hole. Staring numbly at Adair and Jordan, he felt tiny worms swarming in his scrotum, and the urge to run was almost overpowering. But he didn't move; like the others, he realized instantly that it would be a futile gesture. When the nitro hit the crown block, everything within shouting distance would be shredded to a pulp.

Without a backward glance, Shooter Adair calmly walked to the wellhead, spread his stubby legs, and listened. He could hear the shell scraping against the casing as it came up, and second by second the clattering swelled in intensity. Then, like a rabbit materializing from a magician's hat, the tube rocketed out of the hole. Adair's thick arms shot out in a blur, encircling the tube at the last instant, and he clasped it to his chest in a bearhug embrace. Petrified, Morg suddenly realized he wasn't breathing, and he let out a great whoosh of air between clenched teeth. A moment of utter silence passed, then Adair's bald head swiveled around, and his mouth split in a lopsided grin.

"Happens every day, boys. Just part of the job."

For all his cheery manner, Morg noticed the shooter's bald dome glistening with sweat. He waited until Jordan swabbed the well, and the shell was again on its way down the hole; then he climbed off the rig and headed toward the creek. His legs were wobbly as rubber, and he could hardly walk straight. He felt dizzy, vaguely aware that his heart was pounding like a jackhammer, and he had a sudden impulse to be as far away as possible from Shooter Adair and his handiwork. Looking back, he saw Jordan scramble off the rig and hurry along after him. Apparently the driller shared the same impulse. His face was ashen, and he was gumming his quid as if he had ballbearings in his jaws.

Adair went on about his business as if nothing had happened. Back at the truck, he selected a somewhat shorter tube, about four feet in length. This one he stuffed with dynamite, whistling softly to himself as he worked, and on the last stick to be inserted into the canister, he added a cap and a long fuse. Next, he filled the tube with dry sand, allowing the fuse to hang out, and crimped the top closed with a pair of pliers. The finished product was a bomb of sorts, perfect to detonate the nitro at the bottom of the hole.

With the tube under his arm, still whistling, Adair returned to the rig. At the wellhead, he struck a match, lit the fuse, and watched it fizzle for a few seconds. Then, satisfied that the fuse was burning properly, he casually dropped the bomb into the hole.

But at that point, Shooter Adair's nonchalance disappeared completely. He jumped to the ground and took off like a peppered duck. Surprisingly fast for a fat man, his short legs churned up a blaze of dust, and he barreled toward the creek in a headlong sprint. Jordan and Morg saw him coming, and quickly dived behind the biggest trees they could find. As Adair flung himself down beside them, a dull whump sent tremors rippling through the earth. Then there was nothing. Absolute silence.

Climbing to their feet, they stepped into the open and cautiously approached the rig. The quiet was deafening, and they went a few steps closer. Still nothing. Suddenly Jordan threw up his hand, and cocked an ear toward the well. They heard it then. A low rumbling, deep within the bowels of the earth. The noise quickened, as if gaining strength; the rig began to jounce and tremble, and the bull wheel ripped loose from its sills. The men halted as the rumble became louder, then louder still, and in the blink of an eye, the well erupted with a wild, volcanic roar that shook the very earth.

Timbers flew and the crown block hurtled skyward as the gusher blew in over the top of the derrick. It climbed higher and higher, blotting out the sun, and at its crest, slowly blossomed into a gigantic black rosebud. An instant later, as if some strange squall had darkened the heavens, the downpour came, and it began to rain oil.

Jordan stood with his arms outstretched, face raised to the sky, splattered from head to foot with thick black crude. Laughing madly, Morg ran through the inky deluge, leaping and whirling and bellowing insane gibberish at the top of his lungs. But his delirious shouting was drowned out, swallowed whole, lost in the savage howl of the gusher. He ran back to

Jordan and threw himself on the driller, then they just stood there, drenched in oil, grinning foolishly and suddenly unable to speak.

Shooter Adair watched them a while, amused by their antics, then turned and trudged off toward his truck. He was pleased, happy to see a customer make the big strike, but he'd seen gushers before. And besides, it was like he'd told them.

It happens every day.

Oil men hit Tonkawa in a wave—wildcatters and company scouts, lease hounds and roughnecks and roustabouts. As news of the discovery well spread, they came in automobiles and trucks, buggies and wagons, and within a month some five thousand people had transformed the tiny village into a riotous boomtown. Main Street looked like a carnival midway, and any semblance of order was lost in the frenetic rush to grab off a piece of land. Everything was done in a hurry, and as the pack thickened and the race became a stampede, there was little time to spare. A stalled car or a flat tire could cost an oil man a lease—and a bonanza.

The rush was so great that scarcely anyone, oil companies or wildcatters, had a chance to assemble blocks of acreage. Kay County was quickly cut up into tiny segments, like a jigsaw puzzle, and a strip of land large enough to hold a derrick was bought and sold and sold again for ever-higher prices. Hardscrabble farmers, who in the past barely eked out a living, now devoted their time to the lease game. And perhaps because they were better at bartering than they were at farming, they flourished as never before. By splitting their land into parcels, the farmers got upward of $3,000 an acre bonus, and even at that price, there wasn't enough land to accommodate the thousands who poured into Tonkawa.

Oil companies were by far the highest bidders. Competition within the industry had always been keen, but since the war it had become increasingly vicious. Several independents had successfully made the transition from small-time concerns to major companies, marketing a wide range of petroleum products from their own refineries. The impact of this turnabout had become apparent only last year, when drilling rights to the western Osage lands had been auctioned off in Pawhuska. Giants such as Standard, Dutch Shell, and Gulf Oil were challenged, and generally outbid, by relative newcomers such as Phillips and Barnsdall, Marland and Sinclair. Twenty 160-acre tracts were put on the block, and each of them brought bonuses exceeding a million dollars. One tract, thought to be the prime quarter-section of the lot, brought a whopping $1,990,000.

Yet, however much the oil companies fought among themselves, it was still within the club, and all rather chummy. By contrast, the tactics they used on independent producers were something more on the order of guerrilla warfare. And while the independent who had made the leap to the big time was tough and uncompromising, he was by far the lesser of two evils. The greater threat came, as it always had, from the majors themselves. They controlled the price of crude, the cost of transportation, and the sources of credit. The very guts and inner workings of the industry. Quietly, without any display of power, pressure would be brought to bear in the right spot at the right time, and with few exceptions, competition from independents was kept to a harmless level.

A wildcatter who opened a new field invariably encountered an old problem. The wholesale market, where he sold his crude, was suddenly glutted with oil from the majors. Prices were artificially depressed, and even at peak production, with adequate transportation, he couldn't market his crude at a profit. It was the old squeeze play, but still effective, and the wildcatter quickly found himself nose to nose with an unenviable choice. Either he organized a refinery of his own (which required heavy financing) and attempted competition with the majors, or he simply sold out for the best price he could get. There were no other options, not the way the majors played the game. Yet, like all dedicated gamblers, the wildcatter preferred a rigged game to no game at all.

Now and then, of course, someone managed to beat the odds. Through cunning or circumstance, or sheer outhouse luck, they stepped from the frying pan onto solid ground, and walked away winners. For Morg Kincaid and Wirt Jordan it was unclear where luck left off and cunning began, but circumstance had proved their ally from the very outset.

As Jordan had predicted, word of their operation at Widow Tucker's medicine spring spread like wildfire. Farmers came to stand and gawk at first, but once they'd spudded the hole, excitement mounted, and people wanted to talk a deal. By the time Coffee Pot #1 blew in they had obtained leases on more than a thousand acres—without paying a cent in bonus. Afterward, when the stampede began, they sold off a few leases to raise cash, and hired two professional drilling crews. Before the boom hardly hit its stride, they brought in Coffee Pot #2 and Coffee Pot #3, and leaked word that they were pumping better than 100,000 barrels of crude a day. Then they sat back and waited.

Oil companies weren't nearly so impressed with the production figures as they were with the thousand acres. The Tonkawa boom was peculiar in that oil men appeared in such numbers, and with such speed, that no one had a chance to tie up large tracts of land. A couple of wildcatters out at Widow Tucker's place held leases on the only big block in the county—and apparently, were in no rush to sell. Circumstances made the old squeeze play obsolete; every company in the business wanted that land, and everyone else knew it. And the rivalry quickened as gushers began spouting with dizzying regularity across all of Kay County.

Then the partnership of Jordan & Kincaid jolted the industry. They announced that the whole ball of wax—leases, wells, and equipment—was for sale to the highest bidder. But there was a joker in the deck. Any company that bid below an *unstated* minimum would be excluded from the second round of negotiations. That put the bee on the companies, forcing them into an auction of sorts, and oil executives began sharpening their pencils.

The idea was Morg's, although it had been based on Jordan's knowledge of how the industry worked. But when wildcatters began dropping around to shake hands and applaud their gall, the driller gave credit where credit was due. He'd found the oil, but if they made any money on the deal, it was his partner who had figured a way to outfox the big operators.

And on a raw day in November they roared into Tonkawa cocky as a couple of bulldog pups. The Unknown Soldier had just been laid to rest at some place called Arlington, and they had downed half a pint in salute. Morg had refused an invitation to lead the Armistice Day parade in Guthrie, which called for a few more. And they were about to meet with representatives of the first oil company in the negotiating stages of their scheme. Which seemed reason enough to finish off the pint.

Morg slid the Stutz to a halt before Tonkawa's new hotel, and switched off the ignition. Then they sat there grinning, and trying hard to look sober. But it was difficult, what with all the things they had to celebrate. At last, Morg got a hold on himself, and glanced over at the driller.

"Now remember what I said, Wirt. Today we're not selling, we're just talking. Nobody gets an answer till everybody's made their offer. You with me?"

Jordan stepped out of the car and bowed, holding the door open. "I ain't with you, Whiz, I'm ahead of you. Let's get at 'em."

Morg scrambled across the seats and nimbly jumped out. Jordan threw an arm over his shoulder, and grinning like jack-o'-lanterns, they strode into the hotel lobby. As they started up the stairs, one chortled and the other laughed, and by the time they hit the landing they could barely walk. Clutching at one another for support, they staggered off down the hall, feeling no pain but lots of confidence. About a pintful.

FOURTEEN

By early spring of 1922 the isolation of rural America had been shattered forever. The automobile, with its range and mobility, was the forerunner in this cultural upheaval. And the movies, which packaged sin and made it glamorous, further accelerated the erosion of small-town values. Yet, for all the disruptive influences of motion pictures and the motorcar, it was the magic of radio which at last toppled an insular and outmoded way of life. A flick of a switch brought instant access to the outside world, and suddenly the planet shrank to the size of a man's living room. The impact on the backlands was wildly euphoric, and rural America was never again the same.

Guthrie, no less than the rest of the nation, was profoundly affected by radio. People clustered around their sets in the evening, already addicted to favorite programs, and sat mesmerized before the talking box. In a way, it was as if they were eavesdropping on the exotic, and sometimes bizarre, secrets of their neighbors. Better, in fact, for the news was pithy and fresh, and generally phrased in such a way as to make it highly repeatable. Moreover, today's news was reported today, and there was an immediacy about the broadcasts which gave them a verve and excitement unlike anything the people had ever before experienced.

But fast as it was on national issues, radio hadn't yet expanded to the local scene. Word of mouth was still the quickest, if not the most accurate, source of information in a small town, and nobody faulted radio on that score. Nor were they anxious to see it change. Gossip, like apple pie, was best served while it was still warm, and no announcer, however dulcet his tones, could give it the flavor of a veteran gadfly. Although Guthrie had grown in the past few years, it remained, at heart, a small town, and hadn't lost its obsession with the affairs of others. The telephone had replaced the back fence but little else had changed; in the clique that ruled Guthrie society, nothing was sacred. A man's bedroom was fair game no less than his bank balance, and in the way of those dedicated to their calling, the town's busybodies generally worked overtime.

Morg Kincaid and Wirt Jordan scarcely hit the city limits before the gossip mill cranked to life. By the next morning all of Guthrie had heard the news, and that evening (without so much as a call to verify the details) the *Statesman* gave it front-page coverage. As the hometown boy who had made good, the story sprinkled kudos over Morg by the handful, and virtually ignored Wirt Jordan. Young Kincaid, so the readers were told, had neatly outmaneuvered the major oil companies, playing one off against the other, and walked away with a cool $4 million. It brought to mind the astute business practices of old Jake Kincaid (no mention was made of Owen's lackluster performance), and several comparisons were drawn between grandfather and grandson. Aside from the money, which was mentioned with a certain enraptured redundancy, the article dwelled at length on Morgan Kincaid's shrewd mastery of the oil game, and his unlimited prospects for the future. All in all, despite some rather glaring omissions, and one monumental inaccuracy, it was the sort of thing that enthralled the mothers of unmarried daughters, and sent the town's civic boosters into renewed fits of drum-thumping.

And Guthrie responded with alacrity. The phone began

ringing that morning, and kept right on ringing throughout the afternoon. Call after call came in from eager well-wishers, many of them dim acquaintances at best; every fraternal organization in town extended an invitation for lunch or dinner, and invariably requested a speech on the mysteries of the oil game. Besieged, with hardly a lull between calls, Morg finally took the phone off the hook.

Beth and Grace were so happy to have Morg home, and so proud of what he'd accomplished, that they would have gladly endured any nuisance. But he seemed annoyed, rather than complimented, by all the attention, and after a look at the *Statesman* his aggravation became even greater. Besides twisting the facts, and exaggerating the loot by nearly $2 million, the story referred to his partner in only the most oblique terms. Almost as if, singlehandedly, he had taken on the Goliaths of the oil industry and brought them crashing to their knees. That infuriated him, for it was a joint venture deserving equal credit, and it was then he quit taking phone calls.

Wryly amused by the whole affair, Wirt Jordan just sat back, sipping bourbon and branch water, and looked on as if he were a spectator at some droll farce. The people of Guthrie meant nothing to him, and their opinion, which appeared to be a matter of sublime indifference, meant even less. He and his young partner each knew what they had contributed to the Tonkawa venture, and the final reckoning for him was the understanding they had between themselves. The hullabaloo created by outsiders, however impartial, bothered him none at all. Still, it warmed him that Morg angrily rushed to his defense. The young cynic he'd taken under wing back in Anadarko had slowly matured into a level-headed man, one whose actions were now the product of deliberation rather than heedless reflex. If somewhat pragmatic, his expediency and intolerance were nonetheless tempered by a sense of fair play, and his anger at the newspaper article merely served to prove the point. Two years ago he would have smiled to himself, and made some sardonic observation about fools and their folly. Today he cared. And for Wirt Jordan, it was just that simple.

By suppertime Morg had cooled down a bit, but the phone was still off the hook. When Owen arrived home from the office, he and Jordan had a good laugh about the hectic turn of events. But at the same time he was flushed with pride, clearly delighted by his son's sudden fame, all the more so since it was at the expense of his old nemesis, the oil cartel. His own phone had been jingling steadily throughout the day, and he was frank to admit to business associates that the youngster had succeeded where he'd failed. Any sense of personal vindication was strictly vicarious; he never for an instant tried to rationalize otherwise. In the oil fields though, some of the tarnish had been removed from the Kincaid name, and it was his son who had done it: While he wasn't a man to gloat, he could scarcely conceal his jubilation, and as a father, he felt immensely proud.

The atmosphere around the dinner table was almost festive, filled with banter and good cheer and easy laughter. However much it irritated him, Morg was still the center of attention, and the others weren't about to let the spirit of the moment be dampened by his testy disposition. Beth was like a young girl smitten with hero worship, bubbly and effervescent, and Grace lavished affection on him no less than a mother reunited with a wayward son. As for Owen and Wirt Jordan, it was strictly a toss-up. Their jocose pride was that of strong men who shared in what a youngster had become. That they felt a kinship in this, without resentment or rivalry, somehow made the bond all the stronger.

Seated at the head of the table, Owen speared a hunk of steak on his fork and then paused, chuckling again at Morg's discomfort. "You haven't seen anything yet, take my word for it. Today was just the tip of the iceberg. Everybody in town is on your trail. Elks. Lions. Rotarians. And the VFW called me so many times they must've been workin' in relays. People just naturally love a winner, so you'd better get used to crowds. I've got an idea they won't take no for an answer."

"Maybe they won't have any choice," Morg remarked glumly. "Everyone acts like I'm some sort of tent-show freak that's willing to perform for his supper. They'll find out different if they wait around long enough."

Jordan cocked one eye in a ribald look. "Your trouble is, you've got no feelin' for human nature. Way I see it, your pa's got the right idea. It's like you was the big winner in a dice game, and everybody wants to touch you for luck." His teeth flashed in a brownish grin. "Just think of yourself as a great big rabbit's foot. Treat folks right and they might even start callin' you Cottontail."

"Think you're funny, don't you?" Morg smiled in spite of himself. "Only trouble is, you've got to catch a rabbit before you can rub his foot. And I don't plan on getting caught."

"You tell 'em, big brother!" Beth gave him a bright little nod, then threw a quick glance at her father. "And, Daddy, you and Wirt stop picking on Morg. Half the girls in this town have got their eye set on him, so you can tell your business friends they haven't a chance. I just imagine his social life won't leave him time for much else."

"She's entirely right," Grace stated affirmatively. "Why from the day we heard about your oil well, girls have been begging Beth for an introduction. Suddenly every marriageable female in town is her oldest and dearest friend."

"Uh-oh. Now you're in real trouble!" Jordan cackled. "Talk about gettin' caught. Once them girls get your number, bud, that's all she wrote."

"You know, Beth might have a point at that." Owen glanced around the table with mock solemnity. "Money does wonders for a man's possibilities. Now you take Morg, here. Ugly as he is, he might still get trampled in the rush."

"That'll be the day!" Morg grunted. "And money's got nothing to do with it. I won't get caught till I'm ready to get caught."

Beth cut her father short. "Honestly, Daddy, you're so crass sometimes. Morg is the best-looking man in this town, and the girls have always been crazy about him. The money is just incidental. I mean, after all, the Kincaids aren't exactly destitute, are we?"

"Save your breath, sis." Morg gave her a broad wink. "He's just trying to needle me. Besides, if it's money those girls are after, they're in for a sad surprise. Half of it belongs to Wirt, and the newspaper doubled the amount we actually got. So I guess that'll weed out the gold diggers."

Owen laughed, and warded them off with an upraised hand. "Wait a minute. I think you've both missed the point. You see, money is just the way people keep score. The thing that actually attracts them is success. It's like Wirt said: They think you've got the magic touch, and everybody wants to get in on the act. Girls included."

"I couldn't agree more." Grace dabbed her mouth with a napkin, and smiled as they turned in her direction. "Just think about it, Morg. Are you any better looking now than you were before? Not a bit. But suddenly all these girls are after you." She paused, watching him, and her eyes twinkled. "Maybe people are like bees. They're more attracted by the scent of nectar than they are the taste of it."

There was a moment of deliberation. Morg had never been overly vain about his looks, but neither was he without pride concerning his conquests. At last, skirting the issue but conceding nothing, he shrugged. "Well, I've always managed to pick and choose my company pretty much, so I don't suppose I'll lose any sleep over it. Course if it gets to be a problem, why Wirt can just get himself a club and help me beat 'em off."

"Hold it right there, Romeo." Jordan trowled butter onto a piece of cornbread and popped it into his mouth. After a couple of munches he swallowed, and smacked his lips. "Wouldn't count on me helpin' out, if I was you. Sort of figured I'd take off for Ohio pretty quick. More'n likely tomorrow, next day at the latest."

"Ohio?" Morg's jaw clicked shut, and he appeared thoroughly dumbfounded. "You never said anything about taking a trip."

"Well, no, guess I didn't. Course you didn't ask, neither."

"C'mon, quit horsing around. What the devil's in Ohio, anyway?"

"Family. At least what's left of 'em." Jordan hesitated, ready to let it drop there. Then he saw the question in Morg's eye, and almost bashfully, he went on. "Just my mother and a couple of aunts. Haven't seen 'em in a spell, and they're gettin' on in years, so I thought—well, you know, now that I've got some money—I thought I might do something for 'em. Nothin' fancy, they wouldn't want that, but I guess I could put 'em on easy street for a change."

"I'll be switched." Morg was more bewildered than before. "I didn't even know you had a mother. I mean, you never said anything, so it just didn't occur to me that she was still living."

"Lots of things you don't know." Jordan began buttering another chunk of cornbread. "Course most of 'em ain't worth knowin'. The things that counted was what I showed you, and the way everything worked out, I'd say you learned pretty good."

Something unspoken passed between them, and the others remained silent, not wanting to intrude. After a while Morg cleared his throat, and gave the driller an uneasy look. "That sounds sort of final. Like maybe you weren't planning on coming back this way."

"Say, where'd you get a tomfool notion like that?" Jordan grinned, but it somehow seemed forced, unconvincing. "Listen here, bud, you've had a good run for your money. But there's more to life than punchin' holes in the ground. Nothin' steady about it at all. Besides, by the time I get back here you might be shanghaied off to church and trottin' around behind some little gal with a ring in your nose."

"Baloney. You know better than that. Or maybe you're trying to tell me you don't like the idea of being partners anymore."

"Nope, I never said that. But it won't hurt you none to ease up and take a look at something besides oil rigs. Might be a real eye-opener. Fact is, I sort of suggested it to your pa, and he agrees. You could do lots worse than settlin' down right here in Guthrie. I know. I've seen 'em all, and it's hard to beat the place you was raised."

Morg flashed his father a dark look. "Thanks just the same, but I can make up my own mind. And Guthrie's not exactly at the head of the list."

"Well, you think about it while I'm gone." Jordan nibbled at the cornbread, averting his gaze. "If you're still of a mind when I get back, we'll have plenty of time to work something out."

The spontaneity and high spirits seemed to disappear. Suddenly there was little talk, and everyone became very intent on his food. Several minutes of stiff silence passed, then, hoping to distract them, Beth plunged into an amusing story about her latest boyfriend. The others laughed in all the right places, and slowly let themselves be drawn back into the conversation. But the mood was gone. They were talking merely to fill the holes, no longer gay or lighthearted. Nor at ease with one another. Like strangers at a party, formal and strained, hurriedly improvising lines that meant nothing. Just talk.

The Duesenberg was long and sleek, somehow phallic in appearance. Unlike a playboy's raceabout, this was a man's car, emanating a sense of strength and power and virility. Perhaps the only car suitable to Morg's status in Guthrie, and certainly the one machine that reflected the inner image of how he saw himself. Which was precisely why he'd bought it.

Hardly by design, but not without forethought, he had become the unchallenged cocksman of Guthrie society. Among the younger set he was considered invincible, and while he kept the score to himself, his conquests were not so much acknowledged as simply taken for granted. He had become a hunter—selecting playmates with all the care of a fastidious tiger—and his instincts were seldom wrong. Any girl who went out with him was assumed to have been seduced, and by whatever standard such things are measured, there was thought to be no immunity to his satanic charm. He dated a different girl each night, bedding them with no more feeling than a robot, and looked on the whole affair as a colossal joke. A diversion of sorts, entertaining and vastly amusing, but like a hobby. Never to be taken seriously.

Tonight he had a date with Margie Gilchrist. Her father had made his fortune in cotton gins, and the family considered themselves genuine bluebloods. Three generations of Gilchrists had been born in Oklahoma, and like the Kincaids, they still occupied a palatial eyesore built by a wealthy, if eccentric, great-uncle. The Gilchrists weren't the wealthiest family in town, but in the upper stratum of Guthrie's elite, they gave ground to no one. By virtue of early marriage and prolific breeding habits, they had lapped the entire social register by one generation. And according to the grapevine, which was virtually infallible in matters of family tradition, Margie was being groomed for a fast sprint to the altar.

The Duesenberg glided to the curb, silent as a phantom in the dusky warmth of a spring evening, and Morg stepped out. The oil field roustabout, caked with grime and sludge, was gone. In his place, sauntering up the walkway of the Gilchrist home, came a dapper young god who might have decorated the pages of a fashion magazine. He wore a smartly tailored linen suit, creamy beige in color, and on his head was a Panama hat, with the brim rolled downward in a rakish curl. Draped from the breast pocket of the suit was a wildly exotic silk handkerchief, which blended nicely with his chocolate necktie, and by contrast, accentuating the outfit, he wore pointed Italian shoes buffed to a mirror polish. The effect was one of casual elegance, suave and debonair and faintly Continental.

Frank Gilchrist met him at the door, shaking his hand effusively, and led him into the living room. There they joined Inez Gilchrist, a nervous, twittering little woman, who was tricked out in a garish hostess gown mildly reminiscent of a Chinese bordello. Apparently they were out to make an impression. A pitcher of gin rickeys was already mixed, and both husband and wife had their mouths set in jocund smiles, as if the expression had been cast in plaster of Paris and slipped in like dentures. By now, Morg knew the drill letter perfect. The parents of every girl he'd dated had staged a similar charade; as Guthrie's most eligible bachelor, and the prize catch of the year, he was treated with the utmost cordiality. The performance seldom varied—fawning affability interspersed with inane questions—and he played out his role with the aplomb of a seasoned trouper. It was all part of the joke.

"Well now, young man!" Frank Gilchrist boomed after drinks were poured and they had seated themselves. "What's new in the oil business? By golly, that was a crackerjack deal you put across. Really first-rate."

"Oh, it was marvelous! Absolutely marvelous." Inez Gilchrist trilled the words like a talking parakeet. "Everywhere you go these days it's the topic of conversation. Why, Morgan, I swear, your ears would just melt if you could hear the nice things people are saying about you."

"Folks make too much of it." Morg gave them his modest smile, guileless and convincing if well rehearsed. "I was just lucky."

Gilchrist hooted. "Lucky, my foot! Say, your grandfather would have been proud of how you pulled that off. You know, I was just starting out when he was still around, and I saw him operate. Take my word for it, you've got the knack, just like old Jake. It's in the blood, and luck doesn't have a gold-urn thing to do with it."

"That is so true," his wife chirped sweetly. "Blood always tells. Why, I wouldn't be surprised if you were to outdo your grandfather ten times over. I mean, really, with what you've already accomplished, you must have some very important plans for the future." She clapped her hands. "See, I can tell by your expression. I'm right, aren't I, Morgan?"

However subtly framed, the question was part and parcel of the drill. And Morg always gave the same answer. "Yes, ma'am, you're absolutely right. Everything is still in the plan-ning stage—hushhush, you understand—but I've got an idea for gas distribution and a chain of service stations that'll revolutionize the industry. With a little luck, I might just give Rockefeller himself a run for his money."

It was a bald-faced lie, but it never failed to draw a look of awed stupefaction. These were the people who had voted a sensible Republican back into office, and they were content to have the "big boys" again running the country. Business was their idol, if not their god, and they had forsworn the Big Stick geopolitics of Teddy Roosevelt and Wilson's silly blath-ering about World Freedom. At the same time, they felt a new kinship with the sophisticates pictured in slick maga-zines at play in New York clubs and on the beaches of the Riviera. Lately they had begun to ape the turgid affectations of Cannes and San Sebastian, and in the way of countrified nouveau riche, the women had adopted the vogue of fashion-able Parisiennes. Lipstick and cosmetics had also become the rage, as ladies began imitating their daughters, and beauty shops had sprung up on every street in a rush to restore the bloom of youth. Yet, while this liberated look was new to the older generation, there was remarkably little change in their attitudes. Business still came first, and a young man with bold ideas played to a captive audience. His elders venerated get-up-and-go, just as they detested idleness and sloth, and an eager beaver with a good name was perhaps the most precious commodity of all.

Morg rather enjoyed this part of the game, when they began an adroit interrogation as to his future business prospects. He had developed a smooth patter, crammed with the most outrageous fabrications, and he led parents through the routine like a ringmaster working trained seals. They gushed and gulped, avidly hanging on every word, and never for a moment suspected they were the central characters in a droll farce. The mockery of it left him with no qualms whatever. He saw it as their show, staged not for his benefit but for their own shabby purposes, and whatever they got was no less than they deserved.

But tonight Margie Gilchrist spared him the full performance. Clearly ready to travel, she entered the living room clutching a beaded bag, completely ignoring her parents, and he cut his monologue short. The Gilchrists followed along as far as the porch, urging him to return soon and finish their chat, and he blandly assured them that wild horses couldn't keep him away. They were still waving, beaming their catatonic grins, when the Duesenberg pulled away from the curb.

Margie Gilchrist proved neither more nor less than Morg had expected. They had been introduced at a dance, and like all the girls he'd met in Guthrie, he found her artificial but eager to please. She was small and trim, attractive if not pretty, and had a good figure. Her dark hair was bobbed in a shingle cut, and she wore what had become the flapper's uniform: cloche hat, short crepe de chine dress with pleated flounces, and stockings rolled below the knees. She was shallow and gay, easy on the eyes, and possessed all the mental acuity of a kumquat. Which suited Morg perfectly. Conversation was the least of his interests, and in bed he'd discovered that a girl with brains was perhaps more inhibited than one without. Not that they weren't as quick to jump in the sack, but they somehow seemed to enjoy it less.

Their first stop of the evening was the Bijou. Rudolf Valentino was appearing in *The Sheik* (Morg rather thought he resembled a gigolo draped in a sheet), but the torrid love scene in the tent did wonders for the girls. At the fadeout, it seemed that a little rape might not be a bad thing. Margie snuggled close, gripping his hand as the tension mounted to a climax, and by the last reel, her breathing had grown noticeably heavier. All in all, Morg figured it was time well spent. Valentino's technique hadn't improved from his other pictures, but it nonetheless set the mood for the rest of the evening.

After the movie, they went to a roadhouse set back off in a grove of trees on the highway to Kingfisher. Unlike regular speakeasies, the roadhouse had inducements other than liquor and music. But most people came there to get zonked and dance themselves into a puddle of sweat, and in that too, they never failed to get their money's worth. The big thing that spring was the music of Jelly Roll Morton, and with it, a frenzied new dance called the Black Bottom. Although the roadhouse was new to her, Margie was clearly no novice at the fast life. She matched Morg drink for drink, and on the dance floor, she shook her pert little bottom with all the abandon of an alleycat in heat.

An hour or so later, when they'd become pretty cozy, Morg suggested an upstairs room. He neglected to mention that he rented it by the month, but he was completely candid in his observation that privacy sometimes added spice to the party. To her credit, Margie acted neither innocent nor coy. But like most girls Morg dated, there was a flaw in her thinking. She genuinely believed he was looking for a wife, and hadn't yet found the right girl. And however misguided her vanity, she believed just as genuinely that after tonight he would look no further. Starry-eyed, giddy with visions of taming this great ox of a man, she could almost hear wedding bells as they left the dance floor.

Upstairs she found out different. The chimes became something more on the order of a temple gong, and while she gasped, her eyes glutted with shock and pain and surprise, the high priest anointed her on a throbbing shaft of stone.

It was a *bon voyage* party, landlocked but afloat on booze. A wild and merry bash to celebrate Mary Lou Hendricks' upcoming tour of Europe. Although her parents had some vague notion that Mary Lou might snare herself a count or a duke, the trip was essentially an exercise in social aggrandizement. Nobody from Guthrie had ever toured the Continent, and this breezy extravagance represented a masterstroke of one-upmanship. By indulging an already spoiled daughter, the entire Hendricks family enhanced their image, and left the country club set livid with envy.

The house was ablaze with light, and the backyard, where most of the older crowd had collected, was festooned with strings of gaily colored Japanese lanterns. Inside, a phonograph blared incessantly, and one end of the living room had been cleared as a dance floor. Couples wiggled and gyrated to the jarring rhythm, while at the other end of the room two bartenders mixed and poured in a dizzying race with the thirsty guests. Nearly everyone inside the house belonged to the younger set, and unlike their elders, the ear-splitting din merely vitalized them to greater excesses of energy. As the evening wore on, they downed their drinks with quickened urgency, their laughter became louder, and the dancers drove themselves ever faster to the fevered beat of the music.

Mary Lou Hendricks was in her glory, surrounded by a steady crush of friends who assured her that it was the wildest party of the summer. *The bee's knees. The cat's pajamas. A blast.* But like most such affairs, their gushing praise was attributable not so much to conviviality as to booze. Despite her father's prominence in the dry movement, it had been a very wet evening.

Lost in the crowd, Beth Kincaid drifted between the bar and the dance floor, avoiding her hostess whenever possible.

Her date was Boyd Dunaway, Mary Lou's cousin twice removed, and it was at his urging they had attended the party. Beth told herself she came simply because she had nothing better to do, and there was some truth to the thought. A smoky speakeasy or a movie were the only alternatives, and it had occurred to her that a late party might postpone the inevitable wrestling match with Boyd. He was pleasant company, not altogether the dull clod she'd encountered in the past, and lately, they had become something of a twosome around town. But while she smooched and petted, and allowed him certain liberties, she had no intention of making it with him. The chemistry just wasn't there, and without it, she found nothing inviting about the back seat of a car. So far Boyd had survived on a diet of heavy petting and cold showers, and she meant to keep it that way.

Her feelings about the rest of the crowd were, if anything, even less charitable. Not that they hadn't changed. These days the girls drank as much as the boys, patterning their behavior on some distorted image of the flapper ideal, and if Morg's reputation was any barometer, sexual promiscuity was rampant in Guthrie. Convention was now old hat, sloughed off by the young set as a snake sheds its skin, and at any gathering, someone invariably began spouting Freud or Jung with all the fervor of a convert. But to Beth it was all pseudo-intellectual garbage, strewn about by people who had read nothing on either psychology or social metaphysics; the dullards who, instead of thinking for themselves, merely parroted clichés they had heard in similar discussions. And however snobbish she sometimes appeared, she knew she was right. Her correspondence with friends back east, which nourished her as nothing else could, indicated that the hometown oracles were as far behind the times as ever.

The climate of the 1920s was one of ballyhoo and whoopee, a time when all traditional codes of social behavior were under assault. Yet there were certain forces, among them science and the arts, which had not fallen victim to this postwar cynicism. Expatriate writers such as Hemingway and Fitzgerald, and the poet Ezra Pound, were particularly influential in shaping the attitudes of the younger generation. But the greater revolution was stimulated not by novels or Leninism or Keynesian economics, but rather by a radical new science emanating from Vienna.

American intellectuals found their new messiah in Sigmund Freud, and to a lesser extent, his disciples Carl Jung and Alfred Adler. A generation of flappers and sheiks began exploring introversion, inferiority complexes, and the libido, and if they sometimes found it difficult to practice what they preached, it was easy enough to anesthetize their inhibitions with a pocket flask of hooch. Theirs became the doctrine of self-expression, which asserted that people were merely animals of a higher form, and that moral strictures were the offspring of ancient superstitions. Horrified mothers heard their daughters declare that sex was the salvation of mankind, and watched, aghast, as they exercised their right to take and discard lovers at will. To be happy and well, according to this liberated gospel, one must obey the libido, and the first prerequisite of emotional bliss was an uninhibited sex life.

This creed of intellectualism, by now more paganistic than Freudian, quickly transformed America into a consumer-oriented paradise of hedonists. People thirsted for new toys, all the better to enjoy their new freedom, and industry churned out cars and radios at an ever faster pace as rich and poor alike indulged themselves beyond all reason. Yet, unlike the sophisticated rhetoric of intellectuals, the cult devoted to materialism all too often slipped into crass vulgarity. One writer hit the best-seller list by stating that Jesus was a hardheaded go-getter who had put together the greatest little sales organization on earth. And an insurance company, in perhaps the most bizarre analogy of the decade, declared that Moses was the greatest real-estate promoter that ever lived.

Everyone laughed, while they poured themselves another slug of gin, and the merry-go-round geared up in a whirl of flashing dreams.

As for Beth, she found herself revolted by this perversion of what had begun as an intellectual renaissance. She had read Freud and his disciples; studied Lenin and the Bolshevist movement; and waded through the uneasy marriage of democracy, free enterprise, and capitalism. She thought of herself as an agnostic, one who believes that inner peace comes through knowledge rather than faith. Although her bedroom contained a small library on philosophy, economics, and politics, she rarely spoke out at public gatherings. Since she couldn't bring herself to say the vapid things expected of women, she simply kept her mouth shut. Those few times she had voiced an opinion it had disturbed her listeners, and further alienated her from the young crowd. Not that she particularly cared one way or the other how they felt. She considered them superficial and boorish, rustic mimes of universality and modern thought. But at bottom, it just wasn't worth the effort. She held herself aloof, and let them grope their own way into the twentieth century.

Later, in a moment of retrospect, it would occur to her that the home of Mary Lou Hendricks was perhaps the most unlikely place on earth to be knocked off her high horse. But that was later. Tonight she had all she could do to cope with the discovery, and the man. His name was Earl Roebuck.

Hot and sticky, tired of dancing, she led Boyd outside for a breath of fresh air. On the patio, several young couples were seated in a cluster around a man whose face seemed vaguely familiar. Then she recognized him from his picture in the paper. Earl Roebuck, magna cum laude of the university law school, recently arrived in Guthrie to join the firm of Brackenridge, Stalder & Barth. Something about the scene, the way the group was gathered before Roebuck, the expression on their faces, reminded her of novitiates seated at the feet of a Buddhist holy man. Amused, she started down the stairs to the backyard when she was suddenly arrested by the tone of their discussion. Tugging Boyd by the hand, she walked back and stopped at the edge of the group.

Vernon Whitehead, a schoolteacher with just enough knowledge to make him dangerous, was speaking. "It's not that I'm disputing your premise, Earl. Actually, I don't think we're all that far apart. But I still contend that economic equality would bring about the ultimate downfall of a democratic society."

Roebuck nodded, smiling. In the glow of the Japanese lanterns, Beth noted that his eyes were uncommonly blue, deceptively tranquil. He wasn't a large man, but he somehow gave the impression of suppressed strength and vitality. He was dark, almost swarthy, which contrasted sharply with his blue eyes and his black wavy hair. Now, his gaze fixed on Vern Whitehead, and his smile was tolerant, venerable beyond his years. When he spoke, there was a sepulchral quality to his words, and with it, a hint of the jester. As if he refused to take either himself, or the discussion, too seriously.

"One of man's nobler virtues is the urge to apply reason and order to a world that's persistently untidy. Goethe and Shakespeare, among others, commented on this peculiar drive. But they also pointed out that man's ambition is all too often in inverse ratio to his endowments. As a result, he sometimes finds it difficult to distinguish between reality and soap bubbles. I suspect that any attempt to equate democracy with laissez-faire capitalism merely serves to prove the point."

Beth smothered a little chuckle, and Vern Whitehead, unaware that he was being chided, doggedly pressed his argument. "C'mon, now, Earl, look at what they've done in Russia. Are you trying to tell us that the Revolution hasn't brought about economic equality?"

"I wouldn't presume to judge the altruism of Mr. Lenin." Roebuck was deadpan, no trace of mockery in his expression. "However, I do question the equality of the proletariat and the bourgeoisie. Whether we're talking about democracy or socialism, it's an inescapable fact that men are born unequal. Some contribute more than others, and ironically, those who contribute the least are usually the ones who consume the most. By reducing everyone to the same level all we really accomplish is to eliminate incentive. Of course there is a certain equality to starvation, but I'm not sure the people would view that as a remedy to social injustice."

One of the girls in the group looked as if she had an acute gas pain. "Maybe I'm dense or something, but I don't understand at all. It sounds like you're saying that some forms of government just stink worse than others. If that's true, then there isn't any cure, is there?"

Roebuck smiled cryptically. "I'd be the first to admit that the crown sits uneasily on the head of the ape. George Bernard Shaw said that all great truths begin as blasphemies. As a matter of fact, he went on to illustrate the point by stating that democracy substitutes election by the incompetent for appointment by the corrupt. Who knows, maybe he's right."

"Merde!"

The word popped involuntarily from Beth's mouth. Heads swiveled in her direction, astonished not so much by the obscenity as the vehemence with which she spat it out. Roebuck looked at her, and for the first time, she felt the full impact of his gaze. It was an actual intrusion, almost as if he were visually undressing her, and she felt the blood rush to her cheeks. But she met the look steadily, defiant rather than intimidated, and after a moment his smile widened.

"Le monde est plein de fous, et qui n'en veut pas voir doit se tenir tout seul, et casser son miroir."

Startled, it took her an instant to collect her wits. Then she tilted her chin a notch higher. "I agree, and since I am surrounded by fools, I see no reason to smash my mirror."

"But you don't agree with Mr. Shaw?"

"I certainly do not. He writes satire, not proverbs."

"Then perhaps you'd prefer Oscar Wilde. He wrote that

democracy is simply the bludgeoning of the people by the people for the people. How does that strike you?"

"Witty but indefensible. In a word, gratuitous."

"Then you don't believe in society as a community of ants? With each little worker sharing the burden as well as the harvest?"

"Of course not. True equality is an unnatural condition."

"Ah, yes, survival of the fittest. Then I take it you lean more toward Richelieu or Machiavelli? Slap a yoke around mankind's neck and keep him happy with an occasional boot in the rump. Revere the brute and roast the saint."

They were like duelists, fencing with words. Thrust and parry, oblivious to the onlookers, locked in a contest of wits. Fascinated, but somehow embarrassed, the couples seated around them broke apart and slowly drifted away. Boyd Dunaway tugged at her elbow a couple of times, and she finally shrugged him off with an impatient gesture, as if swatting at a pesky gnat. He flushed, more stung than angry, and murmured something about needing a drink. Beth knew he'd gone, dimly sensed that she had hurt him, but she made no move to follow. Earl Roebuck watched her from his chair, waiting, his eyes fastened on hers. Neither of them said anything for a long while, but their silence was as intimate as the touch of naked hands on naked flesh. Unspoken, yet very real, something passed between them, and the tension melted away. Not by word or touch or look was it settled. But they both understood. An arrangement, however tenuous, existed.

At last, her voice light and mocking, Beth ended his wait. "What I really believe, Mr. Roebuck, is that you don't believe half of what you've said here tonight. I think you've had yourself an evening's entertainment at the expense of some very silly people who happen to have more money than they do brains."

Roebuck laughed. "The cruelest murder is the killing of a fine theory with a hard fact." She acknowledged the concession with a smile, and he gestured toward a chair. "Have a seat, and perhaps we can explore that further."

She sat down.

The morning was half gone when Morg pulled into the driveway. His suit was rumpled and filthy, bearded stubble marked his jawline, and dried blood had crusted over an ugly split on his bottom lip. But he was stone-cold sober, and grinning. He crawled out of the car, stretching widely to work the kinks out of his shoulders, and filled his lungs with fresh morning air. After a moment, when he was sure the neighbors had an eyeful, he sauntered up the walk, almost flaunting his disheveled appearance, and entered the house.

Inside, he proceeded along the hallway to the kitchen. Grace was seated at the table, shelling peas into a bowl, and she looked up as he came through the door. Her eyes appraised him at a glance, missing nothing, and the corners of her mouth tightened in a small frown. He smiled, doffing his Panama in an eloquent gesture, and strode forward with the panache of a Bible salesman.

"Lady, could you spare a tired and weary feller a cup of java?"

She muttered something to herself, then rose and set the bowl on the drainboard. As he swung a leg over a chair, she moved to the stove, poured a cup of coffee, and brought it back to the table. Unabashed, he reached for the cup, but she took his chin in her hand, tilted his head upward, and studied his face intently. His eyes were puffy from lack of sleep, he reeked of whiskey and stale sweat, and his lip looked as if it had been struck with an ax. She suddenly dropped his chin and whirled away, collecting the bowl as she returned to her chair. Her fingers worked swiftly, squirting peas into the bowl like little green marbles, and a long while passed before she trusted herself to speak.

"Your lip needs tending. That cut is worse than it looks."

Morg woofed a gloating laugh. "You ought to see the other guy. They'll have to stitch him back together with a sewing machine."

"How nice. You and Jack Dempsey seem to have a good deal in common. Of course he gets paid for it, doesn't he?"

"Aw, c'mon, Grace, I didn't start it. The guy was a sore loser. And I never could stand a spoilsport."

She lifted an inquiring eyebrow. "Another poker game?"

"Why not? It's as good a way as any to kill time. Besides, I won close to four hundred bucks. Now that's not bad for a night's work, is it?"

"No, I suppose not. Although I doubt that your father would consider chasing girls and gambling a form of work."

"Let's leave him out of it, okay?" Morg gave her a smile of disarming candor. "Tell you the truth, I've had a bellyful of his lectures on the virtues of shoulder-to-the-wheel and nose-to-the-grindstone. After a while, it's like his needle was stuck."

They sat for a moment, sparring without words, as if fearful of offending one another. At last, Grace sighed. "Your father is very proud of you, Morg. Sometimes I wonder if you really know how much. Words come hard to him, and he's never been a man to express his feelings. But it's there just the same. In a way, you're what his father always wanted him to be, and I suppose he has hopes that you will accomplish what he never could. He doesn't mean to badger you, not really. It's just that he sees something in you that he never had, and he doesn't want you to waste it."

"Yeah, but maybe he's wrong. Did you ever think of that? All this guff about me being another Jake Kincaid really frosts me. I just want to be myself, and I wish everybody would quit pushing so hard. They're in a rut, and if they like it, that's jim-dandy. But it's not for me. I wasn't cut out to be a big-deal businessman, and that's all there is to it."

This constant dialogue about business had become a

blister on his soul. These days he was short of temper, sharp of tongue, and openly scornful of Guthrie's movers and shakers. There was a loneliness and increasing lack of purpose that combined to dull his appetite for life. Yet he felt caught up in the repulsive but beckoning spectacle of small-town society and desperate girls dumped on the auction block by their even more desperate parents. The misgivings he had about the past few months was like a barb that worked deep and festered, poisoning his thoughts. People actually were trapped in lives of quiet desperation, and just as misery loves company, they seemed determined to lure him into their own wretched existence. All that hurry and running and rushing to make a buck and put on a flashy front. And for what? In the end the earth took them back, time pulverized them into dust, and quickly enough they sprouted again as weeds and grass. So the quiet desperation had, after all, accomplished nothing. Everybody wound up as worm fodder, or a moment's browse for some stupid cow. And the man who had played the game by all the silly little rules came out no better off than the one who had gone his own way. Except for one essential difference, and a very satisfying difference at that. Before the worms got him, the loner had emptied the horn. At worst, he went to his grave with a full bladder and a contented cock. Considering the vagaries of life, that was no small thing. In fact, all in all, it seemed a damned fine joke on death.

Grace's voice broke the texture of his thoughts. "What were you cut out to be? If not a businessman, then you must have something in mind."

"Why, sure. I could be any number of things. A gambler or a ladies' man or a good-time Charlie. Maybe a prizefighter." His answer was fragmented, choppy abstractions designed to blunt the directness of her question. "Who knows, maybe I'll just draw one out of a hat and paste it on my forehead. That way everybody will know what I am and they can stop pestering me."

Matt Braun

Her dusky features went coppery bright. "Is that how you think of me, as a pest?"

He glanced aside, abjectly uncomfortable. "Hey, c'mon, you know I didn't mean you. I was talking about people in general. Every time I go to pick up a girl I get the third degree from her folks. Wouldn't surprise me if they all sit around the country club comparing notes."

"And that bothers you, the fact that they're curious?"

"Curious! That's a laugh. They're phony as a three-dollar bill." He pursed his lips, thoughtful a moment, then grunted coarsely. "You know, at first I treated it like a game. Just fed 'em a bunch of nonsense, and sat there laughing to myself. But that got stale real fast. The only thing they're interested in is a son-in-law with a fat bankroll, and after a while it just makes you want to upchuck. Honest to God, I'm not kidding! If Jack the Ripper walked in and showed them a wad, they'd sell their daughter quick as a wink."

"You're awfully harsh on people." Her fingers slowed, and she studied the bowl as if something was revealed in the mound of peas. "Has it ever occurred to you that we're all a little flawed? That it's part of the human condition? Unless you accept that, the world can become a miserable place to live."

He dismissed the idea with brittle indifference. "I don't really care one way or the other. Just so long as they don't mess around in my business. You see, it's not that I blame them for being human, it's that they're so obvious about it. Like a bunch of monkeys picking over one another for fleas."

Baldly stating such an outrageous truth seemed somehow to frame it in absurdity. Yet Grace scarcely reacted. Indeed, her thoughts had turned inward, focused on the young cynic seated across from her. What her inner eye saw, those secret currents and abysses of the mind, was more telling than any jaded utterance. He clearly believed that his expedience and his contempt were his strength. That by holding himself apart, scorning people and their frailties, he was somehow above the pettiness and hypocrisy of the world. He thought himself a realist, scanning the world not through rose-tinted glasses, but in the bare and naked light of truth. Blinded by his own certainty, he failed to see that it was a complete and elemental confession of the futility he felt within himself. What he hadn't yet learned was that real strength lay in taking up the burdens of life. Accepting not just the result of his own actions, but with equal equanimity, the weakness and imperfection of others. This deliberate and conscious disdain was the act of someone who dared not meditate on the contradictions of life. The mark of a man who dared not look too closely at others for fear of confronting himself. Hardly a realist, he was instead an actor, hiding behind a mask of scorn to escape the responsibility of life. Like a fast and nimble water spider, he managed to skitter across the surface of his own self-deception by never being still enough to sink.

All this and more was evident to Grace, yet she saw a deeper truth with the sensory perception of a wise and gifted mystic. However much she wished it so, she couldn't solve Morg's problem for him. That was something he must do on his own. She could nudge him off center, perhaps jar his cynicism and cause him to question, but enlightenment lay within. Until he could face himself, with honest appraisal of what he saw revealed, there would be no resolution. In the meantime, though—hardheaded as he was—she might still rattle his teeth.

"What have you heard of Wirt Jordan?" Abruptly she raised her eyes from the bowl, searching his face. It was a device she used, a sudden question and a penetrating look, to catch an unguarded expression. "You hardly ever talk of him anymore."

Morg averted his gaze, momentarily flustered by her uncanny ability to touch the sore spot. Three months and not so much as a postcard from Jordan. It rankled him, and while he wouldn't admit it, he was stung to the quick. Unaccountably, he felt suspended in limbo, unable to deal with the future until he knew when or if Jordan would return. It weighed heavily on his mind, but he never spoke of it. To him, it was a weakness, this feeling he had for the old driller, and as such, best kept to himself.

At last, perhaps a bit overdrawn, he shrugged. "Well, you know Wirt. He's sort of sparse with words. Written or otherwise. Likely he'll show up on the doorstep some morning, and just wander in like he'd never been gone."

"I suppose you're right. Probably no news is good news." Her inflection was light, almost whimsical, but her allusion to *good news* was something more than humor. She was watching him closely. "Of course it's really neither here nor there, is it? I mean, it's not like you were sitting around waiting for Wirt to pop through the door."

The involuntary rictus of his smile betrayed him. "I'm not exactly holding my breath. Not waitin' on that old graverobber. As soon as I get tired of goofing off, I'll find myself some action. You'd be surprised how many deals come a man's way when people know he's got the long green."

"So it isn't Wirt that's holding you back?"

"Say, listen, my feet aren't stuck in flypaper. If he's not around when I get ready to take off, that's his tough luck."

"Does that mean you're planning to leave Guthrie? The way you said it sounded a little final."

"Well, no, not just exactly." His mouth quirked, and he threw up his hands in a vague gesture. "Tell you the truth, I haven't given it much thought. I'm just sort of marking time till something interesting comes along."

She began shelling peas again, apparently lost in thought, as if his answer was something to be weighed and considered. He took a couple of swigs of coffee, fidgeting uneasily in his chair, then made quite a production of lighting a cigarette. After a few quick puffs, almost as though he wanted to forestall further questions, he lamely switched the conversation onto a safer topic.

"Slipped my mind, but I've been meaning to ask you. How

is Beth's big romance getting along? Every time I ask her, she acts like the cat's got her tongue."

"Why, so far as I know, everything is fine. At least she isn't dating anyone else, so that seems to indicate she's serious."

"She's got stardust in her eyes, that's for sure." Morg took a drag on his cigarette and blew a smoke ring, watching it with a look of profound speculation. "Just between us, what do you think of Roebuck, anyway?"

"I like him. He's well mannered and pleasant. And your father says he's already made quite a name for himself as a lawyer." She darted a sidewise glance out of the corner of her eye. "Now I'll ask you the same question. What do you think of him?"

"Well, he's not what I'd call a regular Joe. But he's smart as a whip, you can tell that just talking to him. From what I hear, he's got some funny ideas about politics and such, but of course Beth's sort of cuckoo that way herself. I like him, though. Strikes me as being—I don't know—sort of steady. Little starchy, maybe, but steady."

Grace deliberated a moment, then her head came up, and she fixed him with a look of utter directness. "Yes, I think that's the right word. Steady. As if he were a man who knows where he's going and how he intends to get there."

Morg felt the words no less than a jolt of electricity. He tried to smile, a puny, flickering attempt that seemed more a grimace. Unsettled, he quickly drained his cup, and stubbed out his cigarette in the dregs. Then he stood, hitching back his chair, all the while avoiding her eyes. Woodenly, with some spatial sense of time and motion having gone still, he turned toward the door.

"Been a long night. Think I'll get some sleep."

Under a full moon and a sky sprinkled with stars, the Packard rolled to a halt in the driveway. Owen refused to be seen in the Duesenberg, even after sundown, so they had taken his car tonight. Like his son, he was attired in a tuxedo, and he seemed in rare good humor. The banquet had been a huge success, with every dignitary in town seated on the dais, and his arm ached from shaking hands. Morg just looked uncomfortable, partly because of the stiff collar and dickey, but to a larger extent because of the ordeal he'd undergone this evening.

At first, he hadn't believed it. Then, to his consternation, it became very real indeed. The Chamber of Commerce had voted him Man of the Year, and as if things weren't bad enough already, he found himself more of a celebrity than before. Perhaps the honor would have been less repugnant if they had simply mailed him a scroll, and let it end there. But the event was one of some magnitude, the highlight of the year; with great fanfare, and considerable civic pride, Guthrie's business community treated it as an extravaganza of sorts. Owen's reaction was practically jubilant, more so than if he'd won the coveted award himself, and Morg hadn't the heart to decline. However reluctantly, he had attended the banquet, accepted an engraved plaque, and made a tactful, if somewhat halting, speech of thanks. Afterward he felt neither honored nor proud. Walking away from the speaker's podium, he merely felt like the world's greatest hypocrite.

His father's jocular mood was somehow a rasp on tender nerves, and the ride home, trapped in the car with all that good cheer, simply added fuel to his simmering discontent. As they entered the house, he was still brooding on his bogus performance, and even more disturbing, he was assessing the distinct possibility that he had become as canting and shortsighted as everyone else in town. Owen, on the other hand, was uncharacteristically animated, lively and talkative (almost juvenile, in Morg's opinion) and seemed loath to end the celebration. It was late, well past midnight, and though the house was silent, he led the way into the living room.

"What do you say to a nightcap?" Briskly, he removed a decanter and glasses from a cabinet, and turned toward the sofa. "Sort of top off the evening, just the two of us."

"You talked me into it." Morg tossed his Man of the Year plaque on the couch, and glumly collapsed into a chair. "Matter of fact, make mine a double."

Owen poured, passing him a glass, and raised his own in salute. "Here's mud in your eye, son. Guess maybe you think I'm belaboring the point, but I'm proud as punch. You really stood 'em on their ear."

"Yeah, I'm hot stuff, all right." Morg knocked back half his drink in a gulp, shuddering as it hit bottom. "Just the hometown ball of fire, that's me."

His father gave him a keen, sidewise scrutiny. "For a man who's got the world by the tail, you've got a funny way of showing it. Why so down in the mouth all of a sudden? Something bothering you?"

Morg uttered a noncommittal grunt. He sloshed the whiskey around in his glass, studying the amber swirls, tight-lipped as a mummy. Quite without warning, for no apparent reason, the mood of the room became oppressively somber. A few seconds slipped past, and when he failed to respond, Owen's look of concern deepened.

"Hey now, what's the problem? You act like the roof just caved in."

"Forget it." Morg's eyes shuttled away, and there was something regretful in his shrug. "Too much excitement, that's all."

"The hell you say!" The older man's voice was suddenly demanding, insistent. "C'mon, out with it. What's got your goat?"

"Leave it alone, Pa." His hand moved in a weary gesture, at once furtive and apologetic. "Now's not the time or the place, so let's just drop it, okay?"

"No, we won't drop it," Owen said curtly. "You've been giving me the runaround ever since they announced the award, and I'm fed up with tryin' to read your mind. Suppose you just talk up, and let's get the air cleared."

"You're sure about that? You really want to hear it?"

"Judas Priest! What'd I just get through sayin'?"

Morg searched his face earnestly, still hesitant, then let it out in a rush. "All right, you asked for it, so I'll tell you what's the honest to God's truth. That banquet tonight? I came within a hair of climbing in my car and heading for the boondocks." His finger stabbed out at the plaque on the couch. "What I really wanted to do was tell 'em to jam that thing crosswise."

A moment elapsed while the two men stared at one another. "What stopped you?"

"What stopped me?" Morg laughed bitterly. "Hell, you're what stopped me, Pa. You wanted a Kincaid's name on that thing so bad your mouth was watering." He ducked his chin at the plaque. "Well, now you got it. Happy dreams."

Owen flushed, but his eyes went hard. "You're right, I wanted it. And I happen to think it's a damn fine honor. What sticks in my craw is that you don't. Now just say it straight out, don't pull your punches. What's wrong with the people of Guthrie honoring one of their own?"

"Why, for Christ's sake, that's simple. What's wrong is the people. They're a bunch of lard-assed hypocrites who haven't got any more spine than a grubworm. The only thing they're after is the almighty dollar, and they'd sell all or any part of themselves for six bits. I ought to know, I've sure as hell been offered enough of their daughters. And you know what, Pa, that's the part that makes you want to puke. The price was always right."

His father frowned, silent a moment, then grunted. "You've sure got a high opinion of yourself, don't you, boy? How's it feel lookin' down on all us commoners? You and the Lord must have a high old time passin' judgment on the greedy little mortals."

"Aw, crud, come off it, Pa!" Morg's face was ocherous. "You feel the same way, and you know it. Until the day

Grandpa died, you stayed clear of business like it was leprosy. You think I don't know why you sold the coal mine and the timber company and all the other stuff? Hell, if you could find somebody with enough money, you'd dump that bank tomorrow and amscray out to the ranch so fast it'd look like a twister passing through." His lips curled back in mockery, and he wagged his head. "Let's not kid each other, okay? You haven't got any more use for this town than I do. And that goes for the people, too. Maybe you won't admit it, but we both know it for a fact."

Owen just sat, knotting his jaws. Everything was strangely out of focus, as if this were happening to someone else, in another lifetime, and he was merely an observer peering through a grimy windowpane. Yet, queerly enough, he was participant as well as spectator, and he saw an ugly, and very personal, truth through that window. One instant like this, a glimmer of revelation brought on by harsh words, and things were never again the same between people. Nor between father and son. The abhorrence of it quenched his anger, and slowly, as if waking from a fitful dream, the tension drained away. He slumped back against the couch, and like a man thinking out loud, he spoke perhaps as much to himself as to Morg.

"A long time ago Grace told me something, but I didn't pay much attention. Maybe I should've. She said if you want a thing very much, then let it go free. If it comes back, it's yours. If it doesn't, then it was never yours to start with. Guess I never really understood what she meant until tonight." He paused, and a look of mild wonderment crept over his face. "You know, it just now occurs to me that men are a little addled about their sons. Whatever common sense they have gets lost in the shuffle somehow. I remember my pa used to say that every man has to ride his own furies in life. Course he was never one to follow his own advice, so he always tried to flimflam me into doing things his way. Didn't work, but that never stopped him from trying. The queer thing is, I've been making the same mistake, and that's pretty damn foolish. So I reckon it's time to quit."

He picked up the plaque and laid it on his knees, tracing over the inscription with his fingertips. "You go ahead and ride your own furies, son. Whatever way it works out, I'll be pullin' for you."

Morg regarded him with a curious expression for a long while, and then, as if there was nothing left to say, he stood and started across the room. "Think I'll take a ride downtown."

When the door closed Owen was still staring at the plaque. Somehow it seemed tarnished, not so bright, perhaps a little blurred. He blinked several times, swallowing around a hard lump in his throat, then took out his handkerchief and began polishing the lustrous brass.

The bouncer swung the door open, and Morg stepped into The Joint. Everything in the place came to an abrupt standstill. The ivory tickler missed a chord, conversation and laughter fell off, and everyone turned to rubberneck the big ox in the monkey suit. Of a sudden, Morg felt like a whore in church, but his embarrassment swiftly passed. These were his kind of people—crude as spit but the salt of the earth—and he wasn't above a little fun at his own expense. Grinning a wide jackanapes grin, he bobbed low in a mock bow to the workingmen and their ladies. Then, accepting the rough good humor of their catcalls and laughter, he strode forward shouting greetings to several old drinking companions. But as he approached the bar a phantasm fleeted past the corner of his eyes. His pulse suddenly triphammered and his head swiveled around; then he stopped dead in his tracks.

Wirt Jordan was seated with a woman in the front booth.

For an instant it seemed to Morg that someone had hemstitched his lips and nailed his shoes to the floor. He couldn't get his mouth open, nor would his feet move; he just stood there, rooted in place, gawking in complete and unutterable astonishment. The trance ended as Jordan grabbed his hand, pulled him into a ferocious bearhug, and smote him across the back. Sputtering questions, his mind reeling dizzily, he allowed himself to be dragged to the booth.

"Holy Jumpin' Jesus!" Jordan boomed. "Don't blow your cork. You're all spiffed up like a gent so act like one." With a courtly sweep of his arm, he gestured to the woman. "This here's Gert. A real little lady with a heart of gold and pure as the driven snow. Gert, this here's my old sidekick and bosom buddy, Whizzer Kincaid."

The woman simpered like a garish kewpie doll. "Pleased to meet'cha, I'm sure."

Jordan stuffed Morg into the opposite side of the booth and seated himself beside the woman. "Gert, you're not gonna believe it, but once upon a time that high-toned dude you're lookin' at was the best gawddamned roustabout in the oil fields."

Gert struggled with the thought. "Why, sugar, any friend of yours is a friend of mine. And such a cute name, too." Her mouth ovaled in a bee-stung pucker, and she tittered a bawdy little laugh. "I'll bet'cha I know why they call you Whizzer."

Jordan roared, and gave her a playful squeeze. "Ain't it the God's own truth? Up beside ole Whiz a rooster looks like he's stuck in molasses."

Morg had finally collected his wits, and he warded them off with upraised hands. "Christ, wait a minute, will you? Let me get a word in edgewise. Where the hell you been, anyway? And don't tell me you were visiting kinfolks all this time. Why didn't you let me hear from you?"

"Lemme see now, where's the best place to start?" Jordan taunted him with a slow smile. "Well, Whiz, it's this way. I spent some time with my folks up in Ohio, like I told you. Then I treated myself to a knock-down-drag-out binge in Chicago. Say, that town's rougher'n a cob, did you know that? I'll tell you about it sometime. But anyway, once I got my head swabbed out, I decided to take a gander at Osage country. Thought there might be some ripe pickin's for a feller of my talents." His face clouded over, and he shook his head. "Lemme tell you, after about a month, I got the hell outta there real quick. I guess you heard they've been killin' 'em off like it was a slaughterhouse?"

His allusion was to the Headright Murders, the latest scandal in the oil fields. A ring of intermarried white men had been killing their Osage relatives in wholesale lots. Afterward, as the legitimate heirs, they entered claim to the oil headrights. The conspiracy involved millions of dollars, and already federal agents had been called in to halt the murders. Only last week, when the newspapers broke the story, Grace had observed how fortunate she was to live in Guthrie. As an Osage without family, worth upward of a half-million, she would have been a prime victim.

"Yeah, sure, I read all about it," Morg replied impatiently. "So where did you go next?"

"Why, right here. Where else?"

"Here! You mean here in Guthrie?"

"Course I do. Got in the first of the week, or thereabouts. Then I run across Gert, and we haven't hardly come up for air since."

"Well, that's a hell of a note. Why didn't you call me, or come out to the house?"

"You know, that's just exactly what I aimed to do. Then I heard the town was all set to make you King of the Hill. So I thought I'd hang around and see if you joined the club." The driller hesitated, training a cockeyed squint on the tuxedo. "From the looks of them fancy duds, I guess I got my answer. Wasn't tonight the big night, when they gave you the key to the clubhouse?"

"By God, that takes the cake!" Morg countered. "You were all set to slip out of town, and nobody the wiser, weren't you?"

"Yep. Matter of fact, I'm leavin' in the mornin'. Looks like you worked your way into tall clover, so I didn't see no need to stir up the ashes. Probably better that way, anyhow. Like I told you before, when a feller's got roots, that's where he rightly ought to stay."

"Got it all figured out, don't you? Well, I hate to break the bad news, partner, but your crystal ball is busted. I didn't join the club."

"You didn't!" Jordan lifted a quizzical eyebrow. "Now ain't that interestin'."

Morg smiled. "I hope you're traveling light. My car won't hold a whole lot."

"It's the only way to go. Light and fast."

"Guess that brings us down to the really important question. Do we get an early start, or do we make a night of it?"

"Say, it's funny you'd mention that." Jordan gave his lady-friend another squeeze. "Gert here just happens to have a roommate. Real knockout too, ain't she, Gert?"

Gert jiggled and squirmed, batting her kewpie doll eyes. "Oh, sugar, a party! Won't that be fun? And Ida Mae will just love Whizzer." Her mouth puckered in a racy little giggle. "Don't tell her I let on, but Ida Mae is sort of fast herself."

As they went through the door, Jordan and Morg were still grinning. Jammed between them, Gert wiggled her fanny in a bouncy roll, and the regulars at the bar nudged one another in the ribs. Then the ivory tickler struck up "There'll Be a Hot Time in the Old Town Tonight" and the crowd roared with laughter. Just before the door closed Gert blink-blinked her buttocks one last time, and like a firefly leading a couple of hungry lions, disappeared into the night.

FIFTEEN

The wind spanked her cheeks and blew her hair in little locks across her brow. High overhead a star fell from the heavens and rocketed earthward. Then the sky settled once more into velvety darkness and the winking stars were like a zillion eyes staring down on them. Earl had put the top down on the car when they left the country club, and the fields along the highway were luxuriant with the scent of wildflowers and lush stands of alfalfa. She was turned in the seat, staring hard at him, willing him to feel her presence. Not just her mind, and the intellectual force they shared, but her physical presence. The musk of her body and her need, and the open invitation in her eyes. It was a game she had practiced on other men, but there was something delicious and risquè about playing it with Earl. All the more so since she knew how it would end if he ever made a serious overture. Unlike those other men, she wasn't trying to vamp him and later send him home to a cold shower. She was deadly serious, and playing for keeps.

If Earl Roebuck felt her stare, it was wholly unapparent in his manner. All through dinner at the club, and now, on this seemingly random drive in the country, he had explored various facets of their running dialogue on the foibles and follies of the world about them. Beth generally took the role of devil's advocate, and whatever the subject, she managed a stalemate more often than not. Although tonight's discussion was by no means a soliloquy, she had been perhaps less responsive than usual. As if unaware of her sultry mood, Earl had carried the brunt of the conversation, and he was still talking.

"Of course, the greater irony is that anyone so innocuous will be judged by history as a supreme scoundrel. I seriously doubt that Harding even knew what his cronies were up to. He simply wasn't that interested, and probably never made a dime out of the deal himself."

President Warren Harding had died recently of a heart attack, and rumbles of the Teapot Dome scandal were already sweeping the country. Beth felt vaguely betrayed by the whole affair, and lacking any great cynicism, she was unable to view it with equanimity. At the moment, her mind was far afield from politics anyway. Yet she was obliged to make some pretense of interest, and with no small effort, she gave her libido a sharp lecture and quickly rejoined the discussion.

"Well, so far as I'm concerned, he deserves whatever epitaph history gives him. My father said all along that he was a venal little hack, and as much as I hate to admit it, the prediction came true. I hope they boil the rest of his flunkies in oil."

Amused by her asperity, Earl held back on a grin. "Actually, there's something healthy in the way fate leaps out to club a hero. Not that there's anything particularly unique about Harding. A man can devote his entire life to worthy causes, but let him slip just once and the great unwashed masses joyously beat the hell out of him. The rest of his life is spent rubbing his jaw and spitting teeth. It's the oldest story in the book."

"I suppose so," Beth agreed, falling thoughtful a moment. "I know my reaction was emotional enough, although I'm not especially proud of it. I mean, if you view it rationally, it's a little unfair, isn't it? Nobody is perfect, and there's something uncharitable about casting the first stone."

"Good Lord, no! That's perhaps the one ultimate hope for

the civilization of the race. Mankind suffers greatly at the hands of its saviors and demigods. There's a kind of poetic justice in the fact that occasionally the herd rises up and guillotines the aristocracy. It's a bit like pruning a rose bush. What you have left is a species of a higher order, not only sturdier but far more cultured."

All the while they talked Beth's expression had been guileless, quietly intent. But now her eyes brightened, and she smiled puckishly. "I'm not denying your premise, counselor, but I detect a few holes in your argument. Now, just for example, take Napoleon or Genghis Khan, or even Caesar. Isn't it true that our villains are often remembered with the same affection we lavish on the good Samaritans? Be honest now, don't you agree?"

"I grant you the paradox." He let her savor the concession a moment, and then, almost as an afterthought, slipped in a riposte. "But my premise still holds. You see, it's in the nature of the beast to gush compassion for villain and savior alike. After he kills them, that is. There's the common thread, he always kills them. Of course, after the heads roll, he mixes a dab of hypocrisy with a dab of self-delusion and very neatly whitewashes reality. His victims always howl bloody murder while they're being guillotined, but later he canonizes them with all sorts of cardboard virtues, and in the end it comes out the fairy tale we call history."

Beth cast him a merrily malicious glance. "Honestly, Earl, you're impossible. The nature of the beast, indeed! You make people sound like one great brotherhood of man-eating tigers. To hear you talk, we haven't learned a thing since we crawled out of our caves."

"That's precisely my point. Think of life as a classroom. If we don't learn our lessons, then we're reincarnated and forced to deal with the same problems over and over again in an unending chain of future lives. Along the way we gain a little nobility, but this paradox—the nature of the beast— merely proves what dullards we are. After thousands upon thousands of years we still dislike virtue in our villains just as we loathe imperfection in our heroes. But only so long as they're alive! Afterward we indiscriminately toss them in the hopper and they come out looking virtually alike. You see, it's not evil or good that fascinates the beast. It's greatness. That's why people are so fond of saying that history repeats itself. They haven't yet learned the meaning of true greatness, so they keep getting themselves reincarnated, and going around and around and around."

"All right, omniscient one, tell me. What is true greatness?"

"How would I know?" he replied straight-faced. "This is my fourth time around."

She stared at him incredulously for an instant. Then his deadpan expression fell apart and a satanic grin spread over his face. She was appalled by her own gullibility, and furious that he had led her into such an outrageous trap. But even as her eyes spat green fire, her sides began heaving, and she collapsed against the door in laughter. Earl kept one eye on the road, chuckling a wry chuckle that was the closest he ever came to outright laughter; they rode some distance like that, one convulsed and the other warmly amused, before Beth was able to collect herself. At last, still choking back little spasms of mirth, she scooted across the seat and snuggled up beside him. Leaning down, he softly nuzzled her hair, and in their happiness, words suddenly seemed unnecessary. As if, in that very precious moment, they wanted nothing to intrude, nothing to disturb the spell.

Beth felt somehow glutted with content, at peace with herself in a way she had never thought possible. This soft-spoken man, with his piercing intellect and thoughtful ways, stimulated her as no man had ever done before. Yet he was never superior, never quite took himself seriously, as though he played the jester on occasion merely to lighten the force of his assured and thoroughly unflappable manner. In light of his background, which she had extracted from him in bits and pieces, it was all the more remarkable. He came from a family of modest means, had worked his way through the university and later the Texas law school, and by sheer determination had risen above the mediocrity life might have imposed on a lesser man. The wealth and position of those born to it neither intimidated nor provoked him, and it was this trait she admired the most. Only a man of character, and monumental inner confidence, could have avoided such pitfalls. Because he esteemed himself, he was comfortable in any company, and despite his humble beginnings, men of influence and power respected him as they would one of their own.

All in all, Beth found him urbane and erudite, gallant and witty, the most fascinating man she had ever met. There was but a single flaw in their relationship, and however much she tried to shunt it aside, it bothered her greatly. Earl Roebuck, for all his worldliness, had proved a reluctant lover.

Not that there was ever any question of physical attraction. She aroused him just as he excited her. From the beginning, they had kissed and petted and fondled, driving one another mad with desire. But to Beth's utter bewilderment, the normal courting ritual had been reversed. Though she was willing, it was always Earl who stopped it from going too far. Offering her a cigarette at the last instant, exerting what seemed an iron-willed control, he never let things get out of hand. It left her frustrated and baffled, and limp as a dishrag. She knew he wanted her, but she could think of no plausible explanation as to why he hadn't taken her. Before, she had always thought it impossible for a man and a woman to have a platonic relationship unless they were married. These days she was no longer so certain. What she had with Earl was by no means a love affair, and yet—

Her reverie ended abruptly as the car veered off the highway onto the river road. Whenever they parked it was always nearer to town, and she remembered wondering earlier about this drive in the country. His suggestion had been casual enough, and she hadn't questioned it then. But now that flickering curiosity suddenly kindled with hope. Scarcely daring to breathe, she edged a bit closer, almost purring as her breast made contact with his arm.

"Earl, why did we turn off here?"

"Something I want to show you. Sort of a surprise."

"A surprise! Way out here in the middle of nowhere?"

He chuckled. "Exactly. Far, far away from everything."

The motion of his arm with the steering wheel caressed her breast, and she felt her nipples growing hard. "Ummm. That sounds like I'm being abducted."

"Maybe you are. We'll find out in a minute."

It was several minutes, but at last they turned off into a rutted trail which ended at a cabin on the riverbank. Quite mysterious now, he evaded her questions completely, and led her from the car to the cabin. Inside, when he flipped the light switch, she had a sudden, overpowering sense of *déjà vu,* as if she had been there before, experienced this exact moment in some past transmigration. Later, she would recall the stories Grace had told her as a child. Stories of a young bride living in a remote cabin in the Osage Nation, a cabin much like this one. But just now her thoughts were jumbled, and her emotions running wild, as though too terrified to question what it meant for fear it might vanish. All she could do was turn to Earl in mute wonder.

Smiling, he took her hands, and looked her directly in the eyes. "However much I wanted to, there's something degrading about the back seat of a car. And sneaking you into a hotel, or my rooming house, was simply too risky. Until I could afford to do it right, I preferred not to do it at all." His gaze went around the cabin, then came back. "Yesterday I bought this for us. Maybe I took too much for granted, but there are some things a man never knows unless he tries. I hope it means as much to you as it does to me."

A tear rolled down her cheek, and she somehow managed to nod. He raised her hand to his lips, and proudly, with simple eloquence, spoke the words. "I love you, Beth."

She came into his arms, her lips moist and inviting, and his mouth covered hers in a probing kiss. A hot yearning flooded her body, and her heart skipped erratically in a fluttered beat. She moved against him with wanton abandon, and for an instant it seemed the universe stopped, that she stood at its core, panting and brazen, unashamed in her hunger. Then a sudden gust of wind rapped a branch against the windowpane, like dusty knuckles on a coffin lid, and she jumped with fright. His embrace tightened, and quite suddenly he scooped her up in his arms and carried her toward the bed.

She felt intoxicated, warmly euphoric, but all her life she would recall what he whispered to her now. "Happiness is a girl called Beth."

The sky was like a dim opal, pale rose and purple, vaguely sad. Rain had fallen throughout the night, and the derrick had much the look of a skeletal giant squatted in a quagmire of mud. Above the overcast there was a dull glimmer of light, as if the sun might yet break through, but an atmosphere of gloom and foreboding hung over the rig. The engines had been shut down and the boilers were cold, and in the pervasive stillness there was a drear and funereal sense of some great behemoth laid to rest. The quiet was deafening.

Standing beside the car, Jordan and Morg stared in glum silence at the silent rig. In a very real sense they were mourners, and while they spoke no words of benediction, their loss was keenly felt. Located some miles south of Breckenridge, latest in a string of Texas boomtowns, this rig was to have been the first step in their comeback trail. A change of luck in what had become a very expensive crapshoot. Now it was simply a hole in the ground, abysmally deep and ruinously dry.

Morg finally turned away, disgust etched across his face, and began scraping mud off his boots on the running-board. After a while he glanced around at Jordan, who was still staring at the rig. "Wishing won't do any good. Christ himself couldn't have brought that one in."

"Hell, I wasn't wishin'," Jordan growled. "I was thinkin' I'd be glad to see the last of the sonovabitch."

"Guess we're both whistling that tune. What scalds my ass is that it started out so good and all of a sudden went bust. Sort of sours your outlook on things."

"Well, my ma was always fond of sayin' that the man who lives on hope will die fasting. Reckon she must've had wildcatters in mind."

"Damned if that's not a fact." Morg twitched his head in the direction of the rig. "Got any bright ideas about what we ought to do with it?"

"Puttin' it to the torch would sure do my heart a world of good. But I guess that ain't very practical. Probably the best thing to do is sell the gear for whatever it'll bring, and then get the hell outta here."

"Out of where? Are you talking about the country or what?"

"I was fixin' to tell you anyway, but I'm glad you asked." Jordan spat, and rolled a marled eye around the bleak countryside. "Here lately, I've got to feelin' like the tomcat humpin' the skunk—he hadn't had all he wanted, just all he could stand. That's the way I'm feelin' about Texas. I've had all the gawd-damned place I can stand."

Morg chuckled, nodding his head vigorously. "By God, I know exactly what you mean. I've been thinking the same thing myself. Matter of fact, the last couple of months I've been wondering why the hell we left Oklahoma in the first place."

"Near as I recollect"—Jordan gave him a slow, deliberate look—"some young peckerhead with a big itch kept sayin' the real action was down in Texas."

"Yeah, that itch took a lot of scratching, didn't it?" Morg studied the ground for a moment; then he grinned sheepishly. "Next time, you've got permission to boot me in the tail."

"Be a pleasure. Specially if you ever mention this hellhole again." Jordan slogged around the car and opened the door. "Time's awastin'. Let's get into town and see if we can peddle this pile of junk. Then by Jesus Christ we'll head for God's country. And none too soon to suit me."

"You've got yourself a deal, partner." Morg was suddenly full of ginger, vitalized by the thought. "We'll point this heap due north and won't even stop to take a leak till we've crossed the Red." He jumped into the Duesenberg and slammed the door. "Look out, everybody, 'cause here we come!"

The motor roared to life and the sleek black roadster took off in a spurting fountain of mud. In contrast to the dismal scene they left behind, Morg burst out in song, his voice clear and chipper, booming the chorus of a popular oil field ballad.

> Say, a driller that never once lied
> Told me how he kept the women satisfied
> Said he invented a giant prick of steel
> And drove it hard with a big bull wheel
> Had balls of brass to spud the hole
> Gears in his ass to grease the pole
> And this thing he'd invented, it run on steam
> Jiggled his tools till they bailed the cream
> So the bull wheel turned and the women groaned
> While that prick of steel just growed, and growed
> And growed and growed and growed

Unlike the driller with the steely phallus, Morg and Jordan had accomplished nothing of legend in the Texas fields. While the rest of the country entertained itself with crazes—dance marathons, six-day bicycle races, and Mah-Jongg tournaments—they went for broke, and came very close to just that. Upon arriving in Texas, Morg's idea had been to multiply themselves, to lay it all on the line by hiring drilling crews and sinking several holes simultaneously. His logic was irresistible, and seemingly flawless. They had scads of money, worlds of know-how, and plenty of guts. The law of averages dictated that one hole in ten came a gusher, so why waste time drilling them one by one? Why not put their money to work and play the odds and break the bank?

Indeed, why not?

Jordan couldn't fault the plan, nor did he try. He was no less a highroller than his young partner, and the idea of one great crapshoot appealed to his sporting blood. So off they went in a cloud of greenbacks, buying leases and hiring crews, erecting derricks and ordering equipment by the carload. By the first of the year they had eleven rigs in operation, and held drilling rights on some twenty locations bordering the Breckenridge field. Regular entrepreneurs at that point, they congratulated themselves on having generated so much activity in such a short period of time. Then they sat back, smugly confident, and waited for the law of averages to do its stuff.

Quite soon, though, the bubble burst, and the harsh light of reality was stark and cold and never more blunt. Somebody had apparently sandbagged the odds. As winter dragged along, and everyone in America began whistling "Yes, We Have No Bananas," they drilled a string of dusters that defied mathematical probability. But like all gambling men, ever the eternal optimists, they quickly took hope from that most ancient of aphorisms. Never quit when losses are heavy. The worm always turns, and the man who sticks is the man who walks away winner. So they stuck, more confident than ever that the worm wouldn't let them down.

Then disaster struck. All at once, and in bunches.

At one well, the driller horsed his engine wide open, trying to fish a broken pipe joint out of the hole, and succeeded in ripping the crown block loose from the top of the derrick. It came down like a bomb, striking him across the skull, and he was killed instantly. At another rig, a roustabout stepped through the bull ropes instead of walking around, which turned out to be his last shortcut. The ropes caught his pants leg and pulled him into the bull wheel. He lived a while, mangled beyond recognition, begging for someone to shoot him. And at still another location, a battery of boilers exploded, converting the toolie into a bucket of mincemeat. With uncanny accuracy, a flue from the boilers splintered the door of a nearby farmhouse. Later, after bits and pieces of the toolie were collected, the farmer was discovered with the flue stuck up his eye. They buried him alongside what was left of the toolie.

Wirt Jordan had always maintained, "There ain't no accidents on a rig, there's only mistakes." However true, it seemed the partnership of Jordan & Kincaid was dogged by misfortune. Throughout early summer they lost no more men, but their record for drilling dusters remained unblemished. Wherever wildcatters gathered, they observed among themselves that the Oklahoma Highrollers had apparently played out their lucky streak. And while speculative, the statement was perhaps more justified than anyone knew. In twelve short months Jordan & Kincaid had dumped better than one million dollars down dry holes.

Although they were hardly broke, the Texas debacle had put a monumental dent in their bankroll. Whether poor judgment or ill fortune, or a combination of both, the verdict of their fellow oil men reduced it to a fundamental truth. They had played out their string in Texas. Like routed generals hastily organizing a retreat, they wanted only to be gone, to withdraw and resume their campaign in that more hospitable land north of the Red River.

Early that afternoon, when they rolled into Breckenridge, Jordan and Morg were in high spirits. As if an omen of changing luck, the sun had broken through the overcast, bathing the earth with shards of light. The streets sizzled with steam, and the air was blistering hot, but the sudden heat wave gave them no discomfort at all. They took it as a good sign. One stop at the oil-supply warehouse, where they could sell off their equipment, and it was good-bye forever to Texas. A couple of frosty beers, and a bottle for the road, and they would then make a streak for Oklahoma.

But their luck hadn't yet changed, and as they hit the outskirts of town, the gods of chance dealt them one last card.

Up ahead, at a railroad siding, the yardmaster climbed onto a tank car. A strange whistling noise had attracted his attention, and more out of curiosity than concern, he unscrewed the domecap and threw it open. An instant later he reeled backward, staggered by a great rush of fumes, and toppled off the car. The gas fumes, expanded by the afternoon heat, flowed out of the domecap and spread over the ground. This unseen but deadly cloud floated past the depot just as a truck driver tromped down on his floorboard starter. The engine turned over and a single spark leaped from the hood, mated in a lethal embrace with the willowy fumes.

The roar was heard twenty miles away. Ignited by the spark, the fumes detonated the tank car, and ten thousand gallons of gasoline went up in a towering ball of fire. The depot and several nearby buildings simply disintegrated in the force of the explosion, and the town's main street was transformed instantly into a tangled mass of bricks and glass and timber. Flames licked through the ruins, leaping from building to building, and within seconds the entire business district was enveloped in a raging holocaust.

Blown backward by the impact, the Duesenberg was hurled into the air and came crashing down on its side, like a child's toy carelessly discarded by some giant hand. Overturned on its passenger side, the car teetered crazily for a moment, then settled motionless in the street. The driver's door was suddenly wrenched open, and Morg, bleeding from a gash in his forehead, jumped to the ground. Unhurt but dazed, Jordan scrambled out and dropped at his side. The concussion of the blast, followed by the jarring crash, had left them both a bit woozy. They lurched away from the car, unsteady on their feet, wandering aimlessly for perhaps a dozen paces.

Then their heads cleared, and in a shock of comprehension, they stood paralyzed by the carnage around them.

What they saw seemed of another world, eerie and spectral, somehow demonic. Both sides of the street, all through town, were a twisted rubble of shattered buildings and crackling flames. The trainyard was totally devastated, a roaring inferno blotting out the sun with huge billowing clouds of smoke. Charred and mangled bodies littered the street, and survivors clawed their way from the wreckage moaning piteous cries of terror. The horror of it was stupefying, like the bowels of hell boiling to earth; the two men looked on as though in a catatonic trance, unable to move. Then a woman stumbled from the ruins of a drugstore, her hair wreathed in flames and blood spurting from the femoral artery in her leg; as suddenly as the men had lost their senses they now came back to life. Jordan threw her to the ground, ignoring her screams as he smothered the flames with his hat, and Morg unhitched his belt, fashioning a crude tourniquet around her thigh. But even as they worked, her screams ceased and her eyes rolled back in her head and her body went slack. She was dead.

Within a single minute forty-eight people were killed that day in Breckenridge, and more than five hundred were injured. Fire engines and ambulances from three counties rushed to the scene, and through the night, thousands of men labored to save the town from destruction. By dawn the fires had been contained, the National Guard had set up a field hospital, and the Red Cross was feeding the survivors. But what had once been a thriving boom-town was now reduced to a smoky ash heap, and on into the morning workers combed the ruins in search of bodies. The stench of death grew stronger as the sun rose high, and in full light, it was as if some diabolic force had scorched the earth, leaving behind a huge black blotch.

Jordan and Morg forgot about selling their equipment.

Late that afternoon they righted the Duesenberg, and after considerable tinkering, managed to get it started. The car wheezed and backfired, limping along like a crippled gazelle, but they pointed it toward the Red and never looked back. A smart man knew when to call it quits, and another night in Texas was more than they cared to risk.

Of a mind, they hobbled north, homeward bound.

The cars sped over a hill past a country cemetery. Against a dingy autumn sky granite slabs stood in solitary silence, and fallen leaves swirled in a gusting breeze. Across the rolling plains the land was stark and empty, broken occasionally by stunted hills, a great sea of grass gone tawny with early frost. It was the fallow time of the year, when the earth turned brown and sterile, held in tomblike stillness until another spring.

The highway was as empty as the land, and the three cars in the little convoy barreled along at top speed. Although the vehicles were unmarked, both the lead car and the one in the rear were packed with state troopers. The center car was a massive four-door Buick, larger than its escorts, and somewhat less crowded. Besides the driver, the only other occupants were Owen Kincaid and the governor. The sun was a hazy globe in the distance, just now cresting the horizon, but they were already some miles east of Oklahoma City. Their destination was Okmulgee, former capital of the Creek Nation, and their mission was a closely guarded secret. Except for the troopers who accompanied them, no one in the state knew where they were or where they were headed. Those had been Owen's instructions, agreed to before he would accept the assignment, and the governor had followed them to the letter.

Staring out the window, Owen saw the graveyard flash past, noted the barren look of the land, yet these were fleeting images, checked off and quickly forgotten. His thoughts were far down the road, centered on Okmulgee, weighing and assessing what lay ahead. The governor had threatened the town with martial law, and the Klan was sure to react. If the grand jury had been called into session, as ordered by the attorney general, there was every likelihood of a demonstration. What happened then was anyone's guess; the variables were simply too numerous to calculate. The mood of the town. How the governor handled himself. The possibility of a hothead in the crowd. And the greater unknown, how hard the Klan was willing to push just at this moment. Like a chess game, an opponent's moves weren't always apparent, or necessarily what they appeared to be. At best, he would have to judge the situation moment by moment, and tailor his actions to insure the governor's safety. Move first and move fast if a threat developed, never allow them to gain the initiative. That was his edge—take them unaware and keep them off balance—quickly, decisively, without an instant's hesitation.

"Something bothering you, Owen?" The governor's words snapped his train of thought. "You're awfully quiet."

"Yessir, I suppose I am." Owen tugged at his ear, grinning. "I've caught a few crooks in my day, but playin' bodyguard is a whole new ball of wax. Takes a little ponderin', that's all."

"I suspect you underrate yourself. People remember you, Owen. And they know your reputation. I'm counting on that to dampen their spirits. Quite frankly, with the climate of things these days, there isn't another man in Oklahoma I'd trust with the job."

The governor's praise, far from being overdrawn, was a simple statement of fact. Curiously, Owen Kincaid's fame was greater now than it had been at the height of his career during the old outlaw days. The new breed of lawmen seemed somehow of lesser caliber, lacking not just the color but the grit and laconic fatalism of the horseback marshals. Already a legend, known to every schoolboy in Oklahoma, the special assignments he'd accepted over the years had transformed him into a figure of mythical proportions. The gunfight in

Mexico, ending in yet another killing, merely added luster to his reputation as a manhunter. He was acknowledged across all of Oklahoma as the one lawman who had never failed. A gunfighter of the old school, who come hell or high water always got his man. In a land that prided itself on such things, it was the highest accolade.

Still, as Owen was known to comment on occasion, there were old lawmen and there were bold lawmen, but there were no old bold lawmen. And now, thinking of the job ahead, he made that very point. "I appreciate the kind words, Governor, but I'm a little skittish all the same. I've come through many a scrape by being prepared for the worst. That way you don't run up on any sudden surprises."

"You're still convinced we'll have trouble?"

"No way to avoid it, not when you show up. Matter of fact, I'd say it's a pretty safe bet the Klan will turn out in force, anyway. Things have gone so far now they can't afford to back off."

"By God, I hope they do!" The governor was scrappy as a bull terrier, and known for his temper. "This terrorism has got to stop, and I mean to convince them I'm serious. All that grand jury needs is a little backbone, and with me there, they'll have to act. Then we'll really see some fireworks!"

A recent Klan flogging (along with a fiery cross on the county attorney's lawn) had brought the situation to a head. Although merely the latest in a rash of atrocities across the state, the one in Okmulgee had been particularly brutal. The governor had finally drawn the line, and declared war on the secret brotherhood. Through the attorney general he had ordered a grand jury empaneled, and was demanding that indictments be handed down against known Klan leaders.

Owen looked skeptical, and made no effort to conceal it. "Like I said before, don't expect too much. Folks are scared, and they're not likely to return an indictment if it means gettin' themselves flogged. I'll cover your backsides, but I've got an idea you won't get much cooperation from anybody in Okmulgee. Or anywhere else, come to think of it."

"You're saying the Klan can bully them into accepting mob rule in place of law. Do you really believe that?"

"Governor, what I'm sayin' is that the Klan has *already* got them bullied. Otherwise you and me wouldn't be takin' this little joy ride."

The statement contained more than a kernel of truth. A mood of isolationism had swept the country after the war, and on its heels came a resurgence of bigotry. Three years past, during the Great Red Scare, some seven thousand *suspected* Bolshevists had been jailed without warrant, and many deported without judicial process. A year later Congress enacted a bill to protect the racial purity of America, limiting severely the immigration of Europeans and banning altogether the immigration of Asians. This hotbed of jingoism provided a fertile climate for the rebirth of the Ku Klux Klan.

The nature of the Klan was rooted in fundamentalism, which in this new era of enlightenment was still hot with bigotry. And the native Puritanism of old (threatened as it was by the moralistic revolt of a younger generation) seldom went begging for champions. Alongside local evangelists there were the more imposing figures of Billy Sunday, and Aimee Semple McPherson, and "the Great Commoner," William Jennings Bryan. Although the Klan perverted the doctrine to suit its own ends, it was nonetheless a perfect outlet for the repressive dogma of fundamentalism. Not surprisingly, the Klan's symbolic method of dealing with transgressors was to strip them naked and flog them—an act of sadism.

And in keeping with the antics of the Roaring Twenties, the KKK ritual was exaggerated to the point of lunacy. Klansmen sang klodes and held klonvocations, led by the Exalted Cyclops and his chief flunky, the Klaliff. The password was *Kotop* and the equally droll countersign was *Potok*. Yet for all its bizarre regalia and its absurd rituals, the movement expanded rapidly, and with it, the atrocities. Within a single year the secret brotherhood was credited with four murders, one castration, forty-one floggings, and a host of tar-and-feathering parties. By 1923 membership was conservatively estimated at five million; the political apparatus of at least seven states was dominated by the Klan. Oklahoma had thus far kept the State House free from entanglement, but the Klansmen controlled many rural areas, particularly those with mushrooming oil towns. There the Klan leaders justified their methods by pointing to the lawless conditions, and with considerable pride, likened themselves to the vigilance committees of frontier days. Okmulgee was merely one among many such towns, but its Klan element was unusually strong; the recent flogging had given the governor the excuse he needed, and he meant to use it as an object lesson for the rest of the state. If the power of the Klan could be broken in Okmulgee, then it could be broken anywhere. That was the message, and by appearing personally, the governor would demonstrate that neither he nor Oklahoma could be intimidated by a gang of hooded thugs.

As for Owen, he saw it in somewhat simpler terms. The Klan was the bastard child of weak law enforcement. Without the collusion of local and county peace officers organizations such as the KKK couldn't exist, much less thrive and grow. In Guthrie, he had been instrumental in nipping the movement at its very roots. Klan organizers were visited by the sheriff, and none too gently persuaded that it would be a mistake to continue recruiting activities in Logan County. Owen had praised the sheriff in a rare newspaper interview, and forcefully advocated extreme measures to stamp out the Klan. The story was picked up by newspapers around the state, and as the most famed lawman in Oklahoma, Owen became an overnight symbol of the anti-Klan forces. Guthrie experienced none of the terrorism that became commonplace elsewhere, and if anything, his already formidable reputation took on an added note of authority.

Had the governor acted sooner, following Logan County's example, perhaps he could have prevented a rebirth of the Klan. But he held back, ever hopeful the movement would run its course, and by doing nothing, merely contributed to its sinister growth. Now, faced with a statewide malignancy and in need of a cure, he had called on Owen Kincaid to help administer the purgative.

A crowd of several hundred people was gathered in front of the courthouse as the caravan rolled to a halt at the curb. When Owen stepped from the Buick a murmur of stunned surprise swept back over the throng. He was known here as he was known throughout the state, and there were many in the old Creek Nation who had reason to remember his deadliness in a fight. One swift look of appraisal was enough to confirm his earlier suspicions. While there were no hoods or white robes in evidence, the faces before him were filled with bitterness and hate, and that peculiar expression of scorn reserved for outsiders. These were Klansmen, and quite obviously, their leaders had ordered them here to intimidate the grand jury. All in all, it was an impressive show of force, but only slightly more than he'd expected.

Then the governor stepped from the car, and almost instantaneously, the men gathered there turned from a crowd to a mob. A dark, muttering growl erupted, and the hate in their faces quickly changed to rage. Before anyone could react, the state troopers formed a wedge, with Owen in the lead and the governor safely tucked in the middle. Owen walked straight ahead, bulling a path through those who failed to step aside, and led the way up the worn marble steps. A moment later the governor's party disappeared into the courthouse, and the Klansmen, not yet recovered from the shock, were left staring at an empty door.

Inside, the building was strangely silent, seemingly deserted, without people or the sound of voices, not even the clack of a typewriter. The troopers' bootheels rang and echoed through the corridors, setting up a ghostly clatter that was as unnerving as the eerie quiet. Still in a wedge, they marched down the hallway and halted before the county attorney's office. The governor motioned for Owen and the troopers to wait, and stepped through the door.

There was perhaps a minute of silence, then a coarse howl of outrage sounded from within the office. The door suddenly burst open and the governor stalked out, his face livid. He stopped in front of Owen, scarcely able to control his voice, and shook a fist back toward the door.

"That bastard has dismissed the grand jury. Tried to weasel out by saying it was in the interest of public safety." The timbre of his voice rose in a derisive hoot. "Public safety! By God, it boggles the mind. I'll have him out of office so fast he won't know what hit him."

"Governor, the real enemy is out there." Owen jerked his chin in the direction of the front entrance. "Until you put the quietus on them, things won't change. They've got fear workin' for 'em, and this whole town jumps every time they crack the whip. You just saw it for yourself."

There was a long, thoughtful pause while they stared at one another. The governor slowly regained his composure, but his jaw set in an angry scowl. "You're right. This town needs to see someone stand up to them, and I'm just the man to do it. I'll give them a tongue-lashing they won't ever forget."

"You could, but what would it accomplish?"

"Accomplish? Owen, let me tell you something that's a"—his expression grew very intent, almost reflective, and after a moment he smiled—"that's a very astute question. The answer is, it would accomplish nothing. Except to salve my pride. That's what you meant, isn't it?"

"More or less," Owen observed. "Course the better reason is that we have to get you out of here in one piece. And if you start making speeches, we might wind up fightin' a war."

"You're right again, even though I'd love to blister them

with a few choice remarks. The important thing is to activate the National Guard and get this town under martial law. After today, I'm convinced that's the only way we'll ever get this mess cleaned up."

"Governor, I couldn't agree more." Owen turned back to the troopers, who had listened bug-eyed throughout the brief exchange. "Boys, we're going out of here the same way we came in. Stick close and take your lead from me. Don't let 'em rattle you, but if anybody starts trouble nail him fast and final." He hesitated, letting that sink in, then nodded. "All right, let's take it slow and easy. Wouldn't do for 'em to think we're in a rush."

Owen led the way, as the troopers again formed their wedge, and they came out the courthouse door in a tight little phalanx. As they emerged from the building they were greeted by a strident chorus of catcalls and jeers. Quickly it became a howling chant, something close to an animal sound, the ugly bloodlust of a mob. The crowd surged forward, and men began jostling and shoving to reach the front rank. Their faces were contorted with rage, and like a great pack of snarling wolves, they bared their teeth, screaming obscenities and thrashing the air with clenched fists.

Alert, but icy calm, Owen crossed the portico in a straight line, directly into the face of the mob, his stride deliberate and without hesitation. The crowd faltered, their gibes momentarily subsiding, again thrown off balance by his lordly air of unconcern; but as he reached the top step a man suddenly lunged out and spat a great stream of tobacco juice into the governor's face. Owen's reaction was automatic, sheer reflex. The old Colt appeared in his hand, and he laid the barrel across the man's skull with a mushy thunk! Blood spurted, the man stiffened like a firelog, then he toppled backward into the arms of the crowd. An angry roar went up, and the mob collected itself, on the verge of rushing him. The Colt came level, hammer eared back to full cock, and his pale eyes stared down over the barrel.

"Stand where you are! I'll shoot the first man that moves."

The mob froze as if turned to marble. Behind Owen, the troopers had drawn their pistols, and while they were outnumbered fifty to one, they appeared as menacing and coldly detached as the man who led them. Absolute silence descended on the crowd, particularly those in the front rank, the ones closest to the guns, and for several moments it was as if the world had stilled in sound and motion. Then, with a certain, quiet arrogance, commanding instant attention, Owen wiggled the barrel of his Colt.

"Clear a path. We're not lookin' for trouble, so keep your heads and nobody'll get hurt."

The Klansmen split apart as if cleaved in half, and Owen led the way down the steps. The silence held and the mob watched spellbound as the troopers followed him to the curb. Quickly, he shoved the governor into the Buick, then waited until the troopers were in their own cars before he eased through the door. When the caravan pulled away, the ugly snout of his Colt was still visible, trained on the mob through an open window.

Early next morning the National Guard placed Okmulgee under martial law. A week later the grand jury was reconvened, and five Klansmen were indicted on charges of conspiracy and felonious assault.

Owen had been unusually quiet all evening, and now, staring into the fire, he seemed to be grappling with some profound and impenetrable abstraction. The flames crackled and hissed, and the hall clock dropped moments into oblivion, but the living room was otherwise still as a crypt. On the sofa, Grace busied herself with her sewing, glancing at him from time to time, hesitant to intrude, yet concerned, and not a little puzzled by his withdrawn manner. Normally, however troublesome the problem, he wouldn't have kept it to himself this long. There was nothing hidden between them, nor was he a secretive man, and this brooding silence, so out of character, merely quickened her anxiety.

Slumped in his chair, Owen was lost in a maze of thoughts that seemed more briar patch than riddle. He wasn't so much baffled as reflective, in the way of a man who has looked into a dark and fetid abyss, and seen revealed there an even darker truth. Perhaps a truth that involved not just men and events, but Owen Kincaid himself, and in the way of such truths, heavily spiked with thistles and thorns. For the first time in his life, he questioned the supremacy of good against evil, and wondered if, after all, it might not be an unequal contest.

Okmulgee had generated the first sliver of doubt, but by no means the last. In September, with Klan tyranny worsening, the governor had placed the entire state under martial law. Early in October he called a special session of the legislature to enact harsh new laws against the secret brotherhood. And it was then with partisan politics at a fever pitch, that Oklahoma learned the true power of the Klan. Instead of laws dealing with terrorism the House drafted articles of impeachment and hastily rushed them to the Senate. Charged with illegal collection of campaign funds, excessive pardons, and general incompetency, the governor delivered a scathing address and afterward walked out of the Senate chamber, refusing to defend himself. The trial began in November, and by an overwhelming majority, the Senate sustained the articles of impeachment. The good of the people had been subverted by the expediency of politics, and only this morning, the lieutenant governor had assumed the highest office in Oklahoma.

Will Rogers had observed not long before that "all politics is applesauce." Oklahomans agreed wholeheartedly, recognizing the comment as a wry euphemism for the more pungent barnyard expression. But Owen found small humor in the jest, and none at all in the actions of the legislature. It seemed to him symptomatic of a condition that dominated not just Oklahoma but all of America. A climate in which apathy bred ever-greater apathy, and the interests of an evil few were allowed priority over the common good.

In Washington the malaise was no less apparent than in Oklahoma City. Calvin Coolidge had assumed the presidency with the utmost reluctance, and he seemed the perfect match for a nation wallowing in apathy. Upon taking office, Silent Cal laconically noted that "the business of America is business," but he was at some pains not to overwork himself—or the bureaucracy. Adopting the philosophy of laissez-faire quite literally, he napped a lot, seldom uttering anything worth remembering, and proceeded to let the nation run itself.

Yet a nation doesn't run itself, nor does a state. However ineptly, the institutions of government are run by men. And that was the thing warting Owen tonight. The process of the by-the-people-for-the-people was forever at the mercy of the corrupt few. Good men, no matter how hard they tried, seemed to have little effect on democracy. The system apparently survived not because of the good men but in spite of them, and in the end, whatever their motives, it was the corrupters who made the wheels go round. Of course, except for the good men it might not have remained a democracy. Perhaps, for all their puny efforts, they contained the evil just enough to halt the spread of something worse. On the personal level, though, that offered him scant comfort, and left him to reflect on perhaps the thorniest truth of all.

Good men were neither victor nor vanquished. They were both.

Grace had watched him silently for the last hour, her nimble fingers stitching a delicate rosette pattern along the sleeve of a dress. She had always made her own clothes (viewing storebought dresses with somewhat the same scorn she felt for storebought bread), and with age, she had become more domestic than ever. These days, except for an occasional trip to the ranch, she seldom went out of the house. Her world revolved around Owen and the children, and from what she read in the newspapers, she was convinced she had the best of the bargain. Although there were times, like his recent trip to Okmulgee, when Owen drove her to distraction. She understood why he did it, and even felt a certain pride that he was still so widely respected, but she couldn't condone such recklessness. Not in a man his age. On the other hand, she had never seriously attempted to stop him. A man who did what he thought was right deserved support, not criticism.

And yet perhaps the time had come. He was fifty-one years old. Hardly a strapping youngster, although he would never admit it. Age might have brought him greater wisdom, but it had done nothing to alter his stubborn streak. In that, he was still a Kincaid. If he was to be persuaded, it must be done slowly and with craft. Something unobtrusive. Sneaky.

"You're certainly pleasant company tonight." She sniffed and gave him a look of mock indignation. "They say it's a sign of old age when a couple stops talking to one another."

"What's that?" With a massive effort Owen jerked himself out of his reverie. "Did you say old? Why, that's plain foolishness. You don't look a day over—"

"Forty-six," she quickly interjected. "And don't try to sweet-talk me, either. A woman knows when the bloom is off the rose."

"C'mon now, be fair. That's not so and you know it."

"Oh, it isn't? Then I suppose there's some other reason you've ignored me all evening? And don't fall back on that old catchall—business."

They both knew that wouldn't work. With time, Owen had sold off most of the Kincaid enterprises; all that remained was the bank and the ranch and several buildings in the commercial district. It had been done gradually, but with unwavering determination, and now, at last, his days were his own. He went to the office only when necessary, and never more than twice a week.

"No, you're right, it's not business." His gaze strayed back to the fire. "I've been thinking about what they did to the governor."

"And you feel the bad guys have won again."

"Something like that, I guess." He was no longer startled that she could read his thoughts. Nor was he unaware that she invented ways to make him talk, to help him unload his troubles. "Here, lately, I've sort of come to think of it like weeds in a berry patch. No matter how hard a man tries to stamp 'em out, they always spring right back. I don't know, maybe it's just the natural order of things."

"So evil triumphs over good after all." She smiled, and shook her head. "That would shock a great many people. Especially if they heard Owen Kincaid say it."

"I'm not sayin' that's the way it ought to be. I'm only sayin' that maybe that's the way it is. Just think about it a minute. Look back at all the work honest men have done to rid this state of scum and give it decent government. But it still hasn't changed a helluva lot from the old days. We've just got a new batch of crooks runnin' things, that's all."

"Perhaps what we need is a new batch of daredevils to fight this new batch of crooks."

The inflection in her voice suggested nothing, but he studied her with a long, speculative look. "Funny, isn't it? I get the feelin' that little zinger was directed at one old daredevil in particular."

"Whatever gave you that idea?" She went right on sewing, seemingly amused by his remark. "Of course, there is a difference between a businessman and a lawman, isn't there? I mean, it just seems that chasing crooks and hitting people over the head with guns is a line of work better suited to young daredevils." She glanced across at him, and smiled disarmingly. "Oh, you know what I mean. The way you were back in the old days."

That struck a nerve. "Are you sayin' I'm too old to cut the mustard?"

"Owen, for goodness sake! Don't you think I know better

than that?" She held him in a steadfast gaze until finally he nodded. "I'm just saying you've given a good part of your life to Oklahoma, and now you deserve a rest. Maybe it's time to give younger men a chance at stamping out those weeds you were talking about."

"I guess you've got a point," he agreed gingerly. "There's only one trouble, though. They don't want the job."

He was thinking specifically of his own son. And to some extent, his daughter. Neither of them wanted to get involved with the world; they were too busy with their own lives to take time out to worry about the other fellow. Beth expressed a certain concern, at least her criticism and high-toned talk sounded like concern. But at root it seemed a passing phase, puppy love, a young girl's infatuation with the mystique of intellectualism. As for Morg, he simply didn't give a damn. He was no less an expatriate than if he had never returned from France.

Owen had never fully understood such attitudes, not even in his own children. Although he had been labeled a romantic, accused of tilting at windmills, he was at heart a moralist, with a very strong sense of right and wrong. Yet it was his own brand of moralism, wholly lacking in religious overtones. Since that day, long ago, when he had pinned on a lawman's badge, he'd always figured that he and God could conduct their dealings in private. Just a couple of hairy males who got together every now and then, without ceremony or ritual, and talked things out among themselves. Which accounted for the seeming contradiction of a peaceful man who could kill so easily. He had his own arrangement with God, and they both understood that principle must sometimes be tempered with compromise. A man was obligated to his fellows, and if he had been gifted with certain strengths, then the obligation was all the greater. He took on the dirty chores in life, the ones other people weren't able to do for themselves.

Of course he was also obliged to things besides the

common good. Like the woman seated across from him. She was as much a part of him as his own soul, and wherever he turned that wakeful inner eye, she was there, not to be discounted. Whatever he had accomplished in life, the kind of man he considered himself to be, she was in no small way responsible, and he owed her. But there was a question still more central to this matter of obligation, and yet it was one he couldn't bring himself to articulate. If he owed her, would she call the debt at the risk of his own self-esteem? In fact, would she call it for any reason other than concern for his welfare? He thought not.

At length, having answered his own question, he twisted around in his chair. There was conviction behind his words, and never had his eyes been more earnest, more filled with love. "There's nothing on this earth I'd deny you. Not if you had your heart set on it. But I want you to understand what we're talkin' about."

Her hands went still, the sewing forgotten, and then he told her. "When I was a little kid—guess it must've been my first week in school—the classroom bully beat the daylights out of me. I came home with a busted nose, feelin' pretty sorry for myself, as I recall, and that night my pa gave me a lecture. He said there's no honor in losing. Told me that no matter how good a man's cause might be, the only thing people remember is that he lost. Before we were through, he drilled it into me that if a man feels obliged to fight, then he's obliged to win. Otherwise he's put a low price on his own honor, and whatever anyone else thinks, he'll never be able to respect himself. The next morning he sent me back to school and told me not to come home till I'd whipped that bully. Cost me a black eye and a split lip, and I had to use a board off a picket fence to get the job done, but I did it."

He paused, never taking his eyes from her face. "More than anyone else, you know there was very little the old man stood for that I agreed with. But he was right on that score, because if a man can't live with himself, then he's not fit to live with the world." A muscle ticced at the back of his jaw, and several moments passed before he could find the right words. "If anybody calls on me for help, I still feel obliged to fight. I know you understand, and what I'm hoping is that you won't worry about it."

Some deep feeling she couldn't define—a premonition, perhaps—welled up in her eyes. She blinked back the tears, forcing herself to smile, and admonished him with a gentle shake of her head. "Honestly, Owen, you can be such a soberpuss sometimes. I'm too old to cry and it hurts too much to laugh, so I'm just going to forget that we had this conversation. Now go back to staring into the fire. I have to finish my sewing."

He stood and moved to the sofa. Then he brushed her lips with a soft kiss, and his voice went husky. "Hang the dress. It's gettin' late and I've got some young ideas."

She laughed after all. A small laugh, but wicked as sin itself.

The road through town was a bog of greased red dough. An early snowfall, which quickly melted off, had left the countryside impassable for nearly a week. Although the drilling site was less than a mile down the road, today was the first day Morg had been able to make it to the store without getting stuck. He had come early, for they were running short of supplies, and there was still a twelve-hour tour ahead of him on the rig.

Huddled beneath the brassy dome of the sky, Cromwell hardly qualified as a town. There were perhaps a dozen houses, one café and a general store, and a blacksmith shop. The café managed to survive by selling white lightning under the counter, and the smithy, who knew more about horseshoes than piston rods, doubled as an auto mechanic. Off the beaten track, located some sixty miles east of Oklahoma City, it was like most farm communities. Everybody scraped by the best way they could, and while no one was getting rich, they ate regular and slept secure in the knowledge that the Lord would provide. Until Jordan & Kincaid hit town scarcely anyone could have envisioned life as being otherwise. Now, they weren't so sure, and every hardscrabble farmer in the county had his fingers crossed. Waiting and wishing, hoping for that one great miracle.

The storekeeper was no less hopeful than the farmers, and he made quite a production of helping Morg load supplies. All the while he kept hinting for news from the well, and Morg finally got rid of him by the simple expedient of starting the car. It was an old Model T, reliable as a plowhorse if not as sleek as the Duesenberg, but a regular circus to get started. He first set the spark and throttle levers beside the steering wheel, then walked to the front of the car and seized the crank in his right hand. With his left hand he pulled a loop of wire that controlled the choke, and quickly spun the crank with a mighty heave. The engine roared to life, which set the chassis to vibrating madly, and he leapt to the runningboard, adjusting the spark and throttle levers. Climbing inside, he hastily engaged the low-speed pedal and made a U-turn in the middle of the street. Then he released the foot pedal, jumping into high gear, and after a couple of thunderous backfires, the Tin Lizzie took off down the road in a cloud of smoke.

As he cleared the edge of town, Morg glanced eastward, grunting softly to himself. A hazy ball of fire had crested the earth's rim, slowly climbing higher as it burned off the chill morning fog. It was a good sign. Clear skies and no more snow, perhaps enough sun to bake the roads hard again. And bring a little warmth to a damned frosty rig. Of a sudden, he was anxious to get back, nudged along by some strange impulse. Whistling between his teeth, he goosed the Model T and clattered on across the countryside.

Unlike times past, the urge which pushed Morg along this morning was somehow less whimsical, not so reckless. Having made a fortune and lost most of it, coupled with the horror of that final day in Texas, had brought about a marked change in his character. He was still hardheaded and arrogant and cocksure, but the traits had been harnessed; instead of the brash, hot-tempered youngster his bearing was now cool and assertive, utterly confident but with the quiet assurance of a man. The trail from Texas to the backwoods village of Cromwell had been long and circuitous, and along the way he had gained in maturity what he lost in rash insolence.

Perhaps this change in attitude was nowhere more evident than in his partnership with Wirt Jordan. The days of the oracle instructing the tyro were gone; after the fiasco in Texas, where they had set some sort of record for dusters, Morg slowly began asserting himself. By now their fortune had dwindled appreciably; the net worth of Jordan & Kincaid hovered around $500,000, and another spate of dusters would have wiped them out. Although Morg still deferred to the driller more often than not, he had come to rely on his own judgment to a greater extent. Not to be dissuaded, he insisted that this time out they simply couldn't afford to sink a dry hole. This had precipitated several violent arguments, particularly during the months they roamed Oklahoma searching for a new location. And in no small part, Morg's refusal to accept blindly was what ultimately brought them to Cromwell.

Jordan still relied on creekology, scorning anything that smacked of geophysics. But Morg had begun reading oil journals, and talking with the new breed of oil men, and he found it difficult to refute hard evidence. The success of the refraction seismograph had proved beyond all expectations. On the Gulf Coast some of the largest fields yet discovered had come as a result of tests made by geologists. Near Houston, the drill had found oil in a salt dome more than 3,300 feet below the earth's surface—at the precise depth recorded by the instruments. Across Oklahoma the story was much the same, and even old-time wildcatters were climbing on the bandwagon. Apparently science had taken the guesswork and superstition out of finding oil, and geologists suddenly became the new messiahs of the industry.

Yet the drilling site outside Cromwell was another fluke, not unlike the medicine springs where Jordan and Morg had made their previous strike. It was located at the base of an elongated hill near Bodark Creek, to all appearances a rather pronounced anticline. Despite the visual indications, however, seismic crews had traversed the Cromwell area countless times without recording any sign of oil. Later it would become clear that the situation along Bodark Creek was unique, a puzzle of sorts, but mystifyingly simple. The land sloped off to the west, and according to current theory, the great pools would be found at these lower elevations. But a remarkable quirk of nature had occurred in the subsurface strata below Cromwell. The oil actually floated through the sand beds—migrating eastward—as it sought the higher elevations. There, near Bodark Creek, it had been trapped by a limestone formation thousands of feet below the earth. By happenstance and the caprice of nature, one of the great fields of modern times would be brought in not by the new messiahs and their expensive toys, but by old-time creekology.

Not even Morg, with his newly acquired admiration of the scientific, could quibble about the location. The hill and the creek and a sulfurous ooze—all the old familiar earmarks—were simply too overwhelming to be disregarded. Jordan took his oath that there was oil down there, and Morg believed him. In early October they had spudded in the hole, and neither of them ever doubted for an instant that they were sitting on an ocean of black gold.

While neither of them would admit to superstition, one other factor convinced them that the Cromwell site was all it appeared to be. If their good luck hadn't yet returned, at least their bad luck seemed to have taken a holiday. Unwilling to waste so much as an hour, they had hired another drilling crew, and for the past two months the rig had operated around the clock. And in all that time there hadn't been a single accident. No falling crown blocks. No boiler explosions. Nothing. So their expectations held strong. Not so much because they were doing things right, but because they apparently weren't doing anything wrong. After Texas, this hairline distinction had become sharply etched in their minds.

And that morning, their faith paid off. When Morg arrived at the rig he couldn't quite credit his own eyes for a moment. Jordan had a control head locked onto the well and was swabbing thick black crude into a dug storage pit. Suddenly Morg believed what he saw, knew what it meant, could almost taste it the sensation was so strong. In a kind of dazed comprehension he regained his wits and bounded from the car. He ran across the clearing, whooping at the top of his lungs, and as he scrambled onto the derrick floor, Jordan threw the brake on the bull wheel.

"'Bout time you got back." The driller's weathered face split in a grin, and he tapped the control head with the toe of his boot. "Thought you was gonna miss the show."

"Goddamn, I knew it. I just knew it! Had a feeling all the way back from town." Morg could barely constrain himself. "Well, don't just stand there grinning like a jackass. Tell me about it. When'd it come in? What happened?"

Jordan warded him off with an upraised hand. "Simmer down and gimme a chance. There ain't a helluva lot to tell anyway." He cocked an ear toward the wellhead, listened a moment, then looked back. "The boys broke through the cap rock right after you left. They woke me up and by the time I got out here the hole had filled to a thousand feet or so. So I started swabbin' and I been swabbin' ever since. That's it."

"That's it! Jesus, Wirt, you've sure got a way with words." Morg glanced around the rig. "Where are the boys anyhow? Why the hell aren't they out here helping you?"

"I figured you'd be back directly, so I sent 'em off to get some shut-eye. Things are liable to get lively around here about noontime, and I got an idea we'll have our hands full. Let 'em get some rest while they can."

"Then she's coming in? We won't have to shoot it?"

"No siree! Not this little lady." Jordan gave the cable an affectionate pat. "I've nursed her up to better'n two thousand, and from the feel of it, there's plenty of gas pressure down there. We'll just keep coaxin' her along and she'll blow in all by herself."

"You're sure then? We've really honest-to-God hit it?"

"Pardner, lemme tell you something." Jordan drawled the words slowly, emphatically, as if to erase any doubt. "The reason I put that control head on there is because I'm absolutely certain she's gonna blow. That way we'll be able to get 'er shut off and hold her until we can get some storage tanks hauled in here. Now if you don't believe me, you just hide and watch."

"Awright, I believe you." Morg suddenly slammed a meaty fist into his palm. "Goddamn, Wirt, we did it again! It's been a long dry spell, but we pulled it off, didn't we? Slick as a whistle."

"Course we did. Like I kept tellin' you, it was just a matter of time." Jordan engaged the bull wheel and made ready to run the swab. "Whyn't you fire the boilers and gimme some steam, and we'll see if we can't sweet-talk this little lady into struttin' her stuff."

Morg laughed and hurried off, muttering to himself, shaking his head and chuckling, as if he might leap in the air and click his heels. Watching after him, Jordan thought he looked like an overgrown ox about to break out in a fit of giggles. And with that thought came another. He felt just the least bit giddy himself. Almost like the first time he'd been with a woman. Which, upon reflection, wasn't all that strange. As he rammed the swab into the hole, it occurred to him that nookie and oil had a lot in common. More than most people might have suspected.

Scarcely an hour later Morg was back on the derrick floor, pacing around the wellhead like an expectant father. He wasn't so talkative now, but the pacing rather quickly got on

Jordan's nerves. Bringing in a well was serious business, and just at the moment he could do without distractions. It took only a few minutes before the driller had had his fill. He was about to invent some chore for Morg, anything to get rid of him, when a mud-splattered Chevrolet pulled into the clearing. The door opened and a man in crisply starched khakis and high-laced boots stepped out of the car. Jordan darted a warning look at Morg, and hurriedly shut down the well. The man walking toward them was Ward McCabe, an oil scout for one of the big companies, and he'd been around before. Like all oil scouts, he was a snooper, paid by the majors to ferret out other people's secrets, particularly if the secret involved an exploration well. That he was here today could mean anything, or nothing. But as Jordan had often remarked, oil scouts were the direct descendants of Judas Iscariot. Higher paid, perhaps, but all in the same line of work.

McCabe passed the storage pit on the way to the rig, and they saw his eyes flick over the crude, widening for just an instant. Jordan and Morg exchanged another glance, each reading the other's thoughts, and quickly clambered down off the derrick. The crude alone was a dead giveaway, but the less McCabe saw the better, and they went to meet him. McCabe was chewing on a matchstick, and as he stopped, he gave them a spare, inquiring grin.

"Mornin', gents. Thought I'd drop by while I was in the neighborhood and say howdy."

Morg cocked one eye skeptically. "You came a long way out of your road for that. Sure there's nothing else we can do for you?"

"Why, nothin' special. Just figured I'd stop by and ask how's tricks. Never hurts to see how the other fellow's makin' out."

"Sorry to disappoint you, McCabe"—Jordan made little effort to disguise his contempt—"but we haven't got any news worth your bother."

"Shucks, Wirt, you wouldn't kid an old kidder, would

you?" McCabe took the matchstick out of his mouth and pointed at the storage pit. "Looks to me like you've got yourself plenty of news. Some folks might even call it good news."

"Not unless they've got sawdust between their ears, they wouldn't. All we've got ourselves here is a stinker. Likely won't make a hundred barrels a day."

It was a good try, but clearly too late. A stinker was a well that had to be teased into production, and rarely pumped enough oil to make the effort worthwhile. McCabe wasn't fooled for a moment, nor did he attempt to conceal it. His Adam's apple bobbed, and he barked a short, gargled laugh. "You call it what you want, Wirt. All I can say is, it's a damn shame you couldn't sew up a big block like you did in Tonkawa. Know what I mean?"

Jordan smiled briefly, but only briefly. He wasn't amused, however much he wanted McCabe to think otherwise. It had become standard practice for major companies to lease drilling rights all over the state—simply another gambit to freeze out the independent producers—and they already controlled much of the land around Cromwell. Moreover, farmers had become smarter about the vagaries of the oil game. These days they preferred to wait and watch, leasing their land in small parcels if at all. Should a new field be discovered nearby the bonus per acre skyrocketed into the thousands; they were quite willing to hold off, and take a chance on hitting a bigger payoff down the line. Unlike times past, baiting the mousetrap hadn't worked on farmers around Cromwell. Jordan and Morg had been able to lease only ten acres, and at that, they paid a stiff price.

McCabe hung around a while longer, but he had what he'd come for, and plainly couldn't wait to be on his way. Before nightfall his company would know that a discovery well had been brought in, and by tomorrow the word would have leaked to every major in the industry. It was a chummy little club, and while the independents wouldn't get the news for a few days, lease hounds for the big companies would be swarming over the county within forty-eight hours. As the Chevrolet spun out of the clearing and roared off down the road, Jordan heaved a huge sigh. Then, in a weary tone of disgust, he observed out loud what they were both thinking to themselves.

"The word wouldn't spread no quicker if that son of a bitch had a stick of dynamite up his ass."

Morg nodded, watching the car disappear, but his mood seemed somehow less gloomy than that of his partner. At last, after a thoughtful silence, he looked around. "Wirt, how many wells do you figure we could sink on ten acres?"

"Don't know, it's hard to say. Depends on how big the pool is."

"Well, let's suppose it's big. Not just sort of big. But *big* big."

"Why, I guess twenty good producers, wouldn't be out of line. Course if it's like Tonkawa we might squeeze in forty, maybe even fifty. Pool that big, there just ain't no limit."

"You know what I'm thinking?" He cuffed the driller across the shoulder. "I'm thinking neither one of us will live to spend all that money. Like to make a side bet?"

"Hell, no!" Jordan burst out in a grumpy chuckle. "You're tryin' to bet a surefire cinch."

"I guess that's my point, partner. We're sitting on one right now."

A moment passed, then they both started laughing. Without another word, they turned and walked back toward the rig. There was work to be done, but as Morg had subtly pointed out, it had really just begun. Whichever number a man chose, whether twenty or forty or fifty, there were plenty of wells yet to be drilled. And from here on out, they were rolling with their own dice, and loaded dice at that.

A winner every time.

SIXTEEN

At night Cromwell was illuminated by the coppery blaze of hundreds of flares. A forest of timbered derricks dotted the town and the countryside, and at each well the volatile casinghead gas had been piped high in the air and set afire. The flares burned night and day, venting the gas skyward, and on a dark moonless night there was something spectral about this man-made phenomenon. Seen from far away it was as if an army of towering giants stood shoulder to shoulder, torches in hand, bathing the earth in an ethereal glow. But the illusion was deceptive, evoking a sense of the unreal only at a distance. Up close Cromwell was very real indeed, ugly and raucous and clearly of this world.

Derricks were everywhere, seemingly scattered at random, some even wedged in between buildings. All across town there was a rhythmic pounding thud, like mechanical heartbeats, as hungry pumps sucked up the black blood of the earth. Hauled to the surface after millions of years, thick with the decayed viscera of extinct and ancient beasts, the oil gave off the primeval stench of something very old and very dead. Yet if the air was saturated with the cloyed smell of death, there was something vital, almost galvanic, about the town itself. In three months it had mushroomed from a sleepy backwoods village into a boomtown of ten thousand riotous fortune seekers. And they were still coming, like worker ants drawn irresistibly to a cache of ripe and pungent offal.

On a brisk spring evening in late March, Morg rolled into town behind the wheel of his new Duesenberg, this one painted a bright canary yellow. Beside him sat Wirt Jordan, freshly scrubbed, with his hair slicked back, decked out in slacks and a striped silk shirt only slightly less resplendent than that of his young partner. Traffic was heavy, and the car inched along, but neither of them seemed concerned by the delay. Practically everyone in town knew them, and the appearance of the yellow roadster had become something of a nightly ritual. As the men who had brought in the Cromwell field they were celebrities, local folk heroes of a sort, and by now they were accustomed to the waves and shouted greetings of complete strangers. But while they basked in the good cheer of fellow wildcatters and oil men, they accepted the heartiness of everyone else with a healthy dose of skepticism. Cromwell was a fast and frisky town, and a man did well to choose his friends with care. Having brought on the boom, and watched it gather momentum, they understood this better than most. Like spectators at some wild and unruly event, they kept pretty much to themselves, and left the sport to those with a taste for the game.

And in Seminole County there was no dearth of players. The Jordan-Kincaid discovery well had set off a stampede that had yet to run its course. Oil scouts and promoters and wildcatters descended on Cromwell in a frantic rush to lease choice locations. Behind them came the trucks, loaded with equipment and men. Derricks went up overnight; drillers and roughnecks and roustabouts poured in by the hundreds; within a month hardly a day went past without reports of another gusher. Quickly it became apparent that the pool was larger than anyone suspected, extending south across the entire county, and the tempo accelerated to an ever faster pace.

On the heels of the oil men came a wave of opportunists, legitimate and otherwise. Tent cities sprang up along the roadways and near the new railroad spur. Within weeks Cromwell blossomed with grocery stores and cafés, laundries and rooming houses and hamburger stands and drugstores. Oil equipment companies erected giant warehouses, and along the outskirts of town there were dozens of machine shops and welding outfits and building contractors. Soon there was a hotel, then doctors and lawyers and a newspaper, and before anyone quite knew how it had happened, they had themselves a rip-roaring boomtown.

Sin also did a brisk trade, for oil men like their pleasures raw and simple, and once the boom started there was money enough to support every vice known to man. Honky-tonks for drinking and dancing sprouted along Main Street. Bawdy houses filled with pajama-clad whores (gay beach pajamas had become the hooker's trademark) took over the entire southwest corner of town. Brigades of bunco artists and con men and thieves and pimps swarmed to the action, and a cluster of gambling dives north of town became their hangouts. These hellholes were crooked as well as dangerous, but they catered to rich and poor alike, and a sport could shoot a dime in a dice game while at the roulette table a highroller dropped a thousand on a single spin of the wheel. It was all lots of fun, and tough in the hard-fisted way oil men thrived on, and somehow the rash of casualties never seemed to dampen anyone's style.

But the real action, as even the gamblers admitted, was in the oil game. Cromwell was a promoter's carnival, and fraud had a bonanza. Lease hounds and catchpenny boomers and blue-sky promoters began gathering within days of the strike. While many legitimate wildcatters had to sell stock to finance their operations, it was open season for the con artists, and in a frenzy of speculation they offered the public a chance to get rich overnight. Their stock in trade was false rumors, and every day brought some new and wilder tale of magi-presto wealth. According to the grapevine, the local garbage man sold his pig pasture for $85,000. Town lots went for $20,000 each, and in some sections an acre of land was reportedly worth $300,000. Of all the rumors circulated perhaps the most bizarre was that of a tract only forty-five feet square jointly owned by four companies—each capitalized at $1 million.

Strike-it-rich incidents, most of which were false, stimulated oil promotion to a fever pitch. An oil magnate needed only to obtain a lease (any block of land would do) and have a blueprint made with a derrick sketched in at the proposed site. Afterward he tacked the blueprint on a board, which exerted some strange spell on unwary passersby, and set the bait on the nearest street corner. He was in business.

To the suckers, who crowded into Cromwell by the trainload, the blueprint was persuasive evidence (backed by obvious geological authenticity) that a well would shortly appear on the spot indicated. And if there was a well in Seminole County, there had to be oil! Waiters and truck drivers, gullible whores and traveling salesmen, and thousands of vagabond entrepreneurs fell for the line. They stopped and listened, taken in by the convincing pitch, and put up their money. After all, it was a sure thing, and if it was paper wealth, that made them nonetheless rich in their day-dreams. A few became rich in fact as well as fancy. The others used their stock certificates as wallpaper, or in a fit of disgust and reproach, for a more utilitarian purpose in the outhouse. And the promoters, always glib and elusive as a puff of smoke, went on to bigger and better hustles.

The gambling dives and the stock swindles held little interest for either Morg or Jordan. Their attention centered on a far richer game, where the stakes were higher, and curiously enough, the risks were virtually nonexistent. Already they had drilled six gushers on their ten acres, and every nickel of profit was being plowed back into the venture. Three new wells had been spudded, and neither of them had any doubt that they would end up with at least twenty producers. Yet, for all their success, they were scarcely reformed. While they avoided gamblers and certain other temptations, they hadn't sworn off the sporting life completely. Jordan still visited the bordellos whenever the urge struck him, which was regularly, and if his young partner no longer accompanied him, it had nothing to do with abstinence. Nor rectitude. Morg's personal habits were as incorrigible as ever, but to the amazement of everyone who knew him (Wirt Jordan hadn't yet recovered from the shock), he'd found himself a regular girl.

At least the arrangement was regular in that Kate Jackson shared her bed with only one man, Morgan Kincaid. Otherwise it was a loose, not to say peculiar, relationship. Despite Morg's repeated efforts, Kitty Jackson (as she was known in the dance-halls) refused to become a kept woman. She worked ten hours nightly in the Palace Ballroom, supporting herself quite nicely, and except for an occasional present, rejected any thought of allowing Morg to set her up in style. This streak of independence both exasperated and intrigued him. As yet, though he'd given it considerable thought, he hadn't figured out why he stuck with this one girl. Aside from her more obvious endowments, he had a vague sense that the attraction was somehow tied to her wild and ungovernable spirit. Like him, she was something of a gypsy, and not to be tamed without a struggle. But he suspected there was more to it than that, and while the deeper reason eluded him, it in no way discouraged him. He kept coming back for more, and he never ceased trying.

That evening, as they did every evening, he and Jordan went straight to the Palace Ballroom after parking the Duesenberg. When they came through the door Kitty Jackson was leaning against the bar, hands on her hips, regarding the scene before her with anticipatory relish. At the back of the room a seven-piece band wailed "Ain't We Got Fun" while several customers shoved their girls around the dance floor with more enthusiasm than technique. This was the liveliest honky-tonk in town with the best-looking girls and the loudest band and a reputation for serving unwatered whiskey. Unlike cheaper joints, the tickets were dollar-a-dance, but the roughnecks and roustabouts never complained. By oil field standards, the

Palace had class. Cuddly girls in peek-a-boo gowns, with soft lights and hot music, made all the difference, and men gladly paid extra for a bit of atmosphere. While it was still early, the place was already jumping, and before long, just as he did every night, the bouncer would be turning them away from the door.

Which was precisely why Morg arrived shortly after dusk each evening. Kitty wouldn't take money from him directly, and she refused to stop working, but he'd quickly found a way around that. Upon entering the Palace every night Morg immediately bought fifty tickets. Since she collected half the proceeds, this not only boosted her earnings but it generally insured that she was his for the evening. The other girls looked upon him as the last of the big spenders, and chided her for not making the arrangement permanent. Kitty just smiled, and kept her thoughts to herself. She knew exactly what she was doing.

Tonight, she evidenced no surprise whatever when Morg greeted her with his usual fistful of tickets. But if she was independent and willful, she wasn't one to hide her feelings. She laughed suddenly, spontaneously, and threw her arms around his neck in sheer delight. Over his shoulder she waved to Wirt Jordan, who shuffled uncomfortably and looked embarrassed by the whole affair. To him, the way Morg flung money to the winds bordered on madness, especially when the flossiest whore in town could be had for five bucks. Like Kitty, however, he kept his thoughts to himself.

Stepping back, she graced them with a dazzling smile. "Well now, aren't you two a fine-looking pair? Silk shirts and hair slicked"—she wrinkled her nose in Jordan's direction— "God, whatever it is, that stuff smells like perfume. What's the occasion? You boys don't get tricked out like a couple of sheiks for nothing."

"Nope, tonight's special." Morg handed her the wad of tickets. "Matter of fact, if this dump serves champagne, I might even order a bottle." He let her hang a second, glancing around at Jordan, but he was too excited to hold out. "We brought in another well. And lady, I'm here to tell you, we've come to celebrate!"

She squealed, and clapped her hands with the greedy savor of a little girl. "I just knew it! I knew all the time you'd do it. Now you're really and truly on the gravy train."

"You bet your sweet life." Morg beamed, and jerked his arm up and down a couple of times, as if blowing the whistle on a locomotive. "*Wrooo! Wroooooo!* Last call for the Gravy Train Flyer. All aboooard!"

Jordan winced and looked away, mortified that she had his partner acting like a ten-year-old. But Kitty had few inhibitions herself, and couldn't have cared less that the crowd was watching them with bemused curiosity. She threw herself on Morg again, kissing him full on the mouth, and then, her body glued to his in a shameless embrace, she uttered a little growl.

"Mmmm! I could just eat you up with a spoon, you big lug. Every last bite!"

Grinning foolishly, Morg felt mesmerized under the impact of her eyes. There was something brazen—bold and nakedly bawdy—in the look. Faintly reminiscent of wild honey, dark brown and flecked with gold, warm and liquid and sensual. As if she were making love to him right there, devouring him with her gaze, heedless of the crowd.

In oil towns across Oklahoma there were legions of men who had fallen victim to that look. It was her stock in trade, and she employed it with devastating effect. Though scarcely twenty-three, Kate Jackson had been around, and she had no illusions about men. They were all after the same thing, and while she had slept with the ones who interested her, the vaster number had never got beyond a free feel on the dance floor. Yet they never became disheartened, and that she dispensed her favors on a pick-and-chose basis merely whetted their rutting instinct. She was tall and slender, strikingly attractive, if not pretty, somehow different from the buxom girls usually found in honky-tonks. Her skin was clear and creamy, with little dimples in her cheeks, and her russet eyes seemed to laugh all the time, as though she were having a joke with herself. Unlike the flappers, she hadn't bobbed her hair. It hung down over her shoulders, sable and glossy, accentuating both her features and her open, minxlike smile. And she seemed forever happy, possessed of a gamy sense of humor, sort of raw and refreshingly naughty. With those warm, smoky eyes, and a smile like an autumn sunset, she could do pretty much as she pleased with men. Generally she left them as she found them, allowing the customers their money's worth on the dance floor but nothing more. Which made Morg Kincaid the envy of everything in pants. So far as anyone could remember, she had never before stuck with one man. She gave oil-rich wildcatters the same fast shuffle used on roustabouts and, until Cromwell, she had always been her own woman.

But all that had changed, and now, grabbing Morg by the hand, she pulled him toward an empty table at the far side of the room. Jordan tagged along, red-eared and a little sheepish, and took a seat across from them. Kitty was still carrying on about the well, and to Jordan's profound disgust, his partner was lapping it up with a look of calf-eyed serenity. He was about halfway convinced that the girl was a witch of some sort. (Although his superstition was generally limited to finding oil, he was willing to make an exception in her case.) Whatever the fascination, which escaped him entirely, it was plain to see she had Morg under a spell. And for all his irascible nature, Jordan felt deeply protective toward the younger man, something very akin to fatherly concern. As yet he hadn't quite deduced what this girl was up to, but in the back of his mind there was a growing conviction that she was just another gold digger. Smarter than any he'd run across in the past, with some mighty sneaky ways about her, but a she-cat on the prowl all the same.

Jordan's ruminations came to an end as a waiter halted before the table. Morg looked up, still grinning that loutish grin, but his gaze happened to stray across the room and he suddenly jumped from his chair. "Hey, Wirt, I just spotted Orville Brown. Order us a bottle of bubbly, will you? And quit frowning. I won't let him talk me into anything."

"Lover, you sure know how to flatter a girl." Kitty put on her best pout, casting him a hurt look. "Just when I get you to myself, you're off like your pants were on fire."

"Aw, don't take on like that, honey. It's business." Morg leaned down and kissed the tip of her nose. "C'mon now, pucker up and look pretty. I'll be back in a jiffy."

She fluttered her lashes and stuck out her bottom lip. "Promise?"

"Honest Injun." Morg crossed his heart, and edged away from the table. "It won't take me a minute. Just hang on and you'll never know I was gone."

Jordan ordered the champagne, and when he glanced around the girl's eyes were trailing Morg as if caught in something sweet and sticky. A moment passed, and then she sighed. "Wirt, who the hell is Orville Brown that he's so important? I ought to sic Lulu on him." Her ever-ready deviltry came to the surface, and she giggled mischievously. "Don't tell anybody, but Lulu's got the clap."

Jordan just nodded, unamused, "Brown's a geologist. He's got some screwball notion nobody'll listen to, leastways till he run across Morg. Now they're thick as thieves." He studied her briefly, without a trace of warmth. "Why, you jealous?"

"No, I'm not"—her smile was one of puzzled ruefulness—"but I think you are."

"Jesus Christ. What'd they wean you on, tiger spit? Lemme tell you something, sis, and you can take it as gospel. I'm too old to swallow that guff, so you can save your tricks for Morg."

"I'll try not to forget." She gave him a look of utter candor. "You don't like me much, do you, Wirt?"

"Tell you the truth, I haven't made up my mind." He cocked one ribald eye at her. "I'm waitin' till you play your hole card before I decide. Bet it's a dilly, too, ain't it?"

The question was clumsy but sly, almost touching in its childlike simplicity. She laughed an indolent, deep-throated laugh. "Wirt Jordan, I ought to tell you to kiss my rusty butt, but I won't. Believe it or not, I think you're pretty swell, and that's not any line of guff." She regarded him with a steadfast gaze, somehow brutally frank. "Don't worry about Morg. I'd cut my tongue and feed it to the crows before I'd hurt him. And you can take that as gospel."

Jordan again merely nodded, digesting the thought. From the little Morg had told him, he knew she'd led a rough life. Youngest in a brood of kids on some dirt-poor farm up near Claremore. Left home when she was sixteen, and knocked around as a waitress till she caught on as a dancehall girl in the oil towns. By no means an angel, but by the same token, a girl who wasn't ashamed of anything she'd done. Which in itself was a form of honesty most people couldn't claim, and maybe the most important thing he'd yet learned about Kate Jackson. But still not enough. He could afford to wait, and watch a while longer, and in the meantime he'd reserve judgment. Let Morg turn over his own rocks for himself.

Before he could frame a reply a shadow loomed over them, and he looked up to see a big rawboned roustabout standing beside the table. As if Jordan wasn't there, the roustabout winked at Kitty and twitched his head toward the dance floor. "How about it, girlie? That music's too good to go to waste, and I'm hot to trot."

A thorny paw settled gently on the man's shoulder, and Morg eased around to his side. "Sorry, friend, the little lady is all fixed for the night. Guess you'd better try somebody else."

The roustabout shook off his hand. "Butt out, Mac, or I'll feed you a knuckle sandwich."

Morg grinned, clearly relishing it. Without a word, he spun

the man off balance and clouted him upside the jaw. The roustabout hurtled backward as if he'd been shot out of a cannon, scattering tables and people as he bulldozed a path across the floor. Then he went down in a great tangled crash of bottles and chairs, and as he hit the sawdust his eyes rolled back in his head like glazed stones. He was out colder than a wedge.

Delighted with himself, Morg turned back to the table, briskly rubbing his hands together. "Say, that fellow wasn't much on manners, was he? But, you know, I think he had a pretty good idea. What do you say, Puss? Let's go cut a rug."

Shaking her head, Kitty took his outstretched hand, uttering a low gloating laugh, and they walked off toward the dance floor. Wirt Jordan hadn't moved throughout the entire fracas; he'd seen the youngster's punch before, so that didn't surprise him. But of a sudden, watching Morg and the girl in one another's arms, something else flitted across his mind. And however grumpy he felt about it personally, he had to admit it for the fact it was. They made a damn fine-looking couple.

The waiter appeared with the champagne, stepping through the wreckage, and Jordan poured himself a waterglass full. Unaccountably, he felt a huge thirst coming on, and he recognized the sign. It looked to be a long and bruising night.

The world was in a state of flux, that summer of 1924, and on both sides of the Atlantic, violence marked the rise of a new breed of thugs. Benito Mussolini and his Fascist party had overthrown the old order in Italy. Stalin had taken over as dictator in Russia, annihilating his opposition in a series of bloody purges. And in Germany an ex-corporal named Adolf Hitler had been jailed after an abortive putsch against the government. All in all, it was a dismal portent of things to come.

Not to be outdone, America had spawned a flamboyant

genus all its own, the underworld mobster. And it was a phenomenon uniquely American, for these homegrown hoodlums were at the same time brilliant capitalists. Ideology counted for nothing while the almighty dollar meant everything; in a remarkable marriage of free enterprise and brass knuckles, violence became just another business expense.

Prohibition had shifted a market worth millions of dollars from legitimate channels to a trade controlled exclusively by the underworld. Before the Volstead Act, crime in America was a small time operation; afterward the rackets ballooned to terrifying proportions. Crime suddenly became big business, but it was a singularly dangerous form of free enterprise. Al Capone would reap profits of some $60 million in 1924, and nearly four hundred gang murders would go unsolved in Chicago. Still, the public wanted its booze, and it was perfectly content to watch the mobsters butcher one another so long as the corner speak never went dry. So the rackets grew and diversified, proliferating amid a climate of violence, cheered on by millions of Americans who simply wanted a drink.

In that respect, Oklahoma was little different from the rest of the nation. Bootleggers and speakeasies operated openly, and except for a handful of federal agents, law-enforcement officials turned a blind eye on the whole affair. Aside from graft, which was no small consideration, the lawmen were merely reflecting public opinion. This accommodation was made easier by the fact that Oklahoma was a wide and thinly scattered market, and had never attracted the attention of organized crime.

Yet mobsters no less than nature abhor a vacuum. While Oklahoma couldn't boast an Al Capone or a Dutch Schultz, it gave rise to a garden-variety gang leader every bit as modern as his eastern counterpart. These backcountry gangsters generally conducted their affairs without the tommy-gun sensationalism of big cities, but there were exceptions. The strife came about when a sudden oil boom generated vast amounts of money and rival gangs moved in to claim the territory. In the past the violence had been bloody but of short duration, and before any great outcry arose, things were back to normal. Then the boom came to Cromwell, and rather quickly, Oklahoma discovered that there were exceptions to the exceptions.

At least nine men had been killed in Cromwell, and there was reason to suspect that the true count was considerably higher. With bootlegging and narcotics, added to protection payoffs from gambling dives and brothels, the revenue from illicit activities in Seminole County was estimated to exceed $5 million a year. Hardly a trifling sum, tempting enough to make murder commonplace, and quite obviously the handiwork of someone who knew his business. Everybody in town knew that various county officials were on the payroll, and while no one spoke of it openly, the identity of Cromwell's underworld boss was scarcely a secret. His name was Virgil Tanner.

Tanner was ostensibly the local hardware dealer, and while there was a good deal of speculation as to his real name and where he'd come from, the townspeople agreed that he looked more like a storekeeper than a gangster. He was a wiry man, of medium build, with a square and earnest face, and a quiet, rocklike simplicity to his manner. Yet he was a man that people never forgot, for there was something of the gargoyle about Virgil Tanner. His features were pocked and coarse; he wore glasses with lenses so thick that his eyes seemed to bulge out of their sockets; and there was a metallic ring to his voice, like a penny in a beggar's cup. In public he was amiable, with a kindly remark for anyone who entered the store, and very much the merchant, apparently eager to serve a customer's needs. But in the backroom, where his real business was conducted, his disposition underwent a startling change. There, his tinny voice became churlish, lashing out in command, and the thugs in his gang had learned never to annoy him when those heavy hoodlike lids came down over his eyes. Although they knew little more of his background than the townspeople, they had a personal acquaintance with the smoldering wrath he unleashed when provoked. On his orders they had killed sixteen men in the past five months, and by following his instructions to the letter, they now controlled every racket in every town of Seminole County.

An innovator, Tanner had recently begun using an airplane to smuggle in narcotic shipments. Cocaine was especially popular in the oil fields, and Tanner's drug peddlers found that it was as easy to make a snowbird of a husky roustabout as it was of a jaded whore. Trade was brisk and the profits were high, and while federal authorities were less tolerant of narcotic smugglers than rumrunners, the risks were considered proportionate to the gain. Where profits are high, however, people get greedy, and this traffic in drugs was rumored to be the cause of perhaps another murder.

There was some question as to details, but there was no doubt whatever that the city marshal of Cromwell had disappeared. Simply vanished without a trace nearly a fortnight past, and hadn't been heard from since. Speculation was rampant, and as the mystery deepened, word surfaced around town that Tanner's henchmen had taken the marshal for a one-way ride. The grapevine had it that he had threatened to expose the cocaine operation to federal agents unless he got a bigger slice of the action. If true, considering the manner in which Tanner had dealt with his rivals, the marshal had virtually signed his own death warrant.

But the fate of the marshal quickly became academic. Whether dead or merely scared off, his disappearance had proved the last straw. A group of reputable businessmen, calling themselves the Cromwell Citizens Committee, sent an urgent appeal for help to the governor. In it, they stated that a mood of fear pervaded Cromwell, and that no honest man could be found who would accept the post of marshal. Nor could they expect assistance from the county; corrupted officials ignored their pleas, labeling it a local problem. All of which presented the governor with a problem of his own. His predecessor had been impeached for calling out the National Guard in a somewhat similar emergency. And to send in state troopers would smack of something even more distasteful, a police state. Faced with a sticky situation, one in which his options were severely limited, he did exactly what several governors before him had done. He called Owen Kincaid.

There was perhaps an instant's hesitation on Owen's part, but no more. He accepted the assignment with a certain unabashed gusto, intrigued by the idea of taming a wild and woolly boomtown. In his long career as a lawman it was the one job he'd never had a chance to try, and as such, it represented a challenge too tempting to resist. Chock-full of confidence, feeling twenty years younger, he strapped on the old Colt, oblivious to the protests at home, and headed for Cromwell. On a steamy July afternoon, when he brought his car to a halt before the marshal's office, he felt like a kid with the keys to a candy store. And as he slid from behind the steering wheel, gazing down Main Street at the gambling dives and whorehouses, his sweet tooth ached so bad he hardly knew where to start. The town was everything he'd hoped for. Worse, in fact. Almost too good to be true, and yet there it was. Just waiting, and all his. Looking at it, he had the odd sensation that his entire life had been little more than a training ground, a drill of sorts, preparing him for this single moment in time. A chance to put right all that had gone wrong, to be himself.

When he entered the office he found two men deep in conversation. One was seated behind the desk, a badge pinned to his shirt, obviously a deputy. The other man was dressed in a suit and tie, which seemed a bit formal for an oil town, particularly in the sweltering heat. As Owen closed the door, they looked around, not exactly startled, but plainly aware of who he was. The men quickly rose from their chairs as he stopped in front of the desk, nodding to the deputy.

"I'm Owen Kincaid. Guess you've been expectin' me?"

"Yessir, Mr. Kincaid. We sure have." The deputy stuck out an arm the size of a firelog. "I'm Dub Watson. Chief deputy." He smiled apologetically as Owen took his hand. "Matter of fact, I'm the only deputy."

Watson was a boozy husk of a man, big as a bear, but seemingly guileless and anxious to make an impression. Alert, if not particularly bright, he seldom thought before he reacted, much like a bullfrog snapping at flies. Yet Owen felt the strength in his grip, sensed a quickness about him, and knew he would be a good man to have around in a fight. Watson suddenly remembered they weren't alone, and let go of his hand as if he had hold of a hot poker.

"Hey, I'm sorry, I plumb forgot. You two don't know one another, do you? Mr. Kincaid, this here's Lon Hill. He's prohibition agent for the district."

Hill regarded him with impassive curiosity. "Pleasure to meet you, Mr. Kincaid. I've heard a lot about you in the last couple of days. Seems like you're something of a legend in these parts."

Owen accepted his hand, but dropped it almost immediately. Hill's palm was moist with sweat, and he detected something of a charlatan in the man, the benign, furtive look of a plaster saint. "Don't believe everything you hear, Mr. Hill." He paused, reflective a moment. "Let's see now— prohibition agent—I reckon that makes you a federal man?"

"Yes, sir, that's a fact. I work out of the Tulsa office."

"Well, from the looks of things, you've got your work cut out for you."

"How's that, Mr. Kincaid? I don't get you."

"Why, all those honky-tonks and gamblin' parlors. I take it they are servin' whiskey, and near as I recall, that is a federal offense. Isn't it?"

Hill seemed to fall asleep with his eyes open. After a while he blinked, and licked his lips. "We do the best we can, Mr. Kincaid. But it's not easy enforcing an unpopular law."

Hill was slouch-shouldered, with bony jaws and rheumy

eyes and a great hook of a nose. His face was locked in a perpetually constipated expression, and just at the moment, it seemed unusually sour and tight-lipped. Watching him, the shadow of a question clouded Owen's gaze, then moved on, set aside but not forgotten. He turned back to Dub Watson.

"What's the word on the marshal? Was he killed, or did he just crawfish?"

"No word a'tall, Mr. Kincaid. He's just gone."

"How about you"—Owen fixed him with a quizzical look—"Tanner couldn't scare you off?"

"Well, you see, I don't scare too easy, Mr. Kincaid. Probably be better off if I did, but I don't."

"Maybe Tanner bought you off, then? I understand the marshal was on his payroll."

Watson stiffened, squaring his great shoulders, and a brutish cast fell over his eyes. "No, sir, nobody bought me off. And I'd be obliged to whip anybody that says so. Even if he's only got one arm."

Owen chuckled, satisfied with the reaction. "Tell you what, Dub. Anybody says that, you come get me and I'll help you whip him." Abruptly, without warning, he switched back to the prohibition agent. "What about you, Mr. Hill?"

"Me?" Hill recoiled, taken unaware. "What about me?"

"Since you're still here, I take it Tanner couldn't scare you off either?"

"Oh, he wouldn't even try. Tanner's too smart to monkey with federal people."

"That a fact?" Owen seemed to deliberate; then he shrugged. "Well, it takes all kinds, I guess. Course you've got my curiosity up, Mr. Hill. What makes you think he's so smart?"

Clearly unsettled, Hill's hand came up, fidgeting with his necktie, and he swallowed nervously, as if groping for words. Owen seemed fully prepared to wait him out, not unlike an interrogator watching his suspect squirm. With a look of profound deliverance, Hill's gaze shuttled across the room as the door opened, and Morg Kincaid walked into the office. Owen twisted around, irritated by the intrusion; then his face suddenly split in a broad grin. He strode forward, hand outstretched, quite obviously delighted.

"Morg! By golly, you're a sight for sore eyes. How are you, son?"

"Hello, Pa." Morg shook hands, but he appeared none too cheerful. "I got your letter, but you could have saved yourself the trouble. Everybody in town knew when you were coming and when you'd get here."

Owen beamed, all the more delighted. "Things never change, do they? Bad news always travels fastest."

"Faster than you think." Morg's tone was clipped, almost abrasive, and he glanced past his father to the other men. "Wonder if you fellows would excuse us? We've got a little family matter to talk over."

Hill was visibly relieved by the request, and with a nod to Owen, headed for the door. Dub Watson tagged along, mumbling something about waiting outside, and a moment later the door closed. Alone, father and son faced one another, measuring quietly, with the wary look of combatants before the beginning of a struggle.

Owen knuckled his mustache, no longer grinning. "I take it you're not exactly happy to see me?"

"Damn right, I'm not!" Morg answered with a flare of anger. "As a matter of fact, I came to ask you what the hell you're doing here?"

"I explained that in my letter. Cromwell needs a marshal, and the governor asked me to take the job. It's just that simple."

"You know something, Pa? I'm beginning to wonder if you're the one that's simple. The old days are gone, or maybe you haven't tumbled to that. Hell, I know you haven't. You act like you're here to catch a bunch of penny-ante cattle rustlers."

Owen regarded him with a level gaze. "I don't need you to tell me my job."

"Well, goddamnit, somebody has to!" Morg blurted hotly. "These are gangsters you're after. Big-time operators. Tanner won't call you out in the street and give you a fair draw. That stuff's gone out of style. He hires people to do his killing, don't you understand that, Pa?"

"Off and on, I've been a lawman for thirty years, and I'm gonna tell you something, Morg. That stuff about old-time outlaws giving a man an even break is nothin' but hogwash. They were out-and-out killers, just like these gangsters you keep talkin' about. Not an iota of difference. But that's beside the point. The fact is, I was sent here to get Tanner. And you can mark it down in your book—just as sure as we're standin' here, I'll get him. One way or another, Tanner and his bunch are finished in Cromwell."

There was calm assurance behind the statement, and while it was delivered in a quiet voice, the very intensity of Owen's words gave it a ring of prophecy. They stared at one another for a moment; then Morg snorted, and his face congealed in derision.

"You still don't get it, do you? Christ, wake up and take a look at yourself, Pa. You pull into town packing a rusty old six-gun and the men you're after probably have a whole arsenal of tommy guns. Doesn't that tell you something? Don't you get the idea you're playing out of your league?"

"Son, I appreciate your concern. And whether you believe it or not, I do understand you're trying to do what's best for me. But that don't change a thing. I took the job, and I'll stick till it's done. Suppose we let it drop there."

"Goddamn, Pa, you need a keeper." Morg seemed genuinely baffled. "You're nutty as a fruitcake, do you know that?"

Owen's look went cold and dour. "You're entitled to your opinion, but I'm your father and that entitles me to a little respect. So just button your lip and keep it to yourself."

"Hell, I'll do better than that. I'll keep out of your way entirely." He wheeled away and stalked off, but at the door he turned back. "When they get you jammed up between a rock and a hard place—and believe me, Pa, they will—don't say I didn't tell you so."

Owen stared at the door for a long time, saddened by the harsh words, but perhaps more thoughtful than hurt. At last, he pulled the old Colt from its holster and inspected it carefully. Then a slow smile creased his face. It was as good as the day he'd bought it. And not a speck of rust. Still a damn fine widow-maker, the best anybody had ever invented. Tommy guns included.

The sun went down behind a fat cloud with fiery edges, and as dusk fell over Cromwell bats began stitching through the darkening air. Striding along Main Street, purposely alone, Owen was letting the town look him over. It was a brag of sorts, but one he felt had to be made. Show them that he was here and meant to stay, that he was willing to accommodate anybody who thought otherwise. The roughnecks and roustabouts made way for him as he moved along the boardwalk, almost as if they were expecting Buffalo Bill or Kit Carson to appear on a white horse and do some fancy tricks. Most of them hadn't even been born when he'd killed his first man, but they knew the stories, and despite his age and the empty sleeve, they found the legend was no less imposing in person. A man with guts was no rarity in the oil fields, yet this was something different, a very special breed, perhaps the last of his kind. They were looking at a mankiller, tough and hard as nails, and they liked what they saw.

Owen regarded them with detached interest, as though he'd happened across a mildly entertaining troop of monkeys. They were merely spectators in this game, and while he'd grown gray and a little heavier around the beltline, understood that these things would be noted and discussed, he wasn't concerned. The thing that counted in the clutch was what a man thought of himself, and on that score he had no doubts. The risk had drawn him to Cromwell as surely as a lodestone. Just as danger had always exerted its pull on him in the past. That he had responded, accepted the challenge of again pitting himself against those darker forces, told him all he needed to know. Times changed and men changed, that was true enough. And nobody was immortal. But some men lived longer than others, and if they had the gift, then as long as they could walk, they could still cut the mustard.

As he approached the hardware store, he saw a man tilted back in a chair outside the front door. It was Virgil Tanner, a dim bulk in the twilight, dusted with glowing fireflies. Owen could barely distinguish the face in the bluish murk of dusk, but he somehow got an impression that the man was ugly as a toad. Then the head moved and the glasses glinted, and behind those thick lenses the eyelids drooped, appraising him in a slow look.

"Good evening, Marshal." Tanner nodded pleasantly. "Out for a stroll?"

"Just markin' out my territory, Mr. Tanner. Always believe in letting the little dogs know the big dog has come to town. You'd be surprised how quick the message gets around."

Tanner merely stared at him as he passed by, declining comment. But a surge of elation swept over Owen, jolting him down to his fingertips. Sooner than he'd expected, the chance had come. And behind those thick glasses he had seen a single blink, an instant of surprise. Virgil Tanner had got the message, and having taken one another's measure, there would be no need for further words. Now they could begin the fight.

"Grace? What's the matter? Are you all right?"

There was no response, and for a moment Beth stood framed in the doorway. Then she hurried across the living room and took a seat beside Grace on the couch. The morning mail was piled on the coffee table, but an opened envelope had fallen to the floor, and Grace held a letter in her hand. She appeared disoriented, her eyes blank and sightless, and Beth's alarm quickened. The girl touched her arm, and as if stung by a live wire, Grace jerked away, falling back against the cushions. Her eyes cleared almost instantly and she sat bolt upright, startled but somehow composed, in control of herself.

"Good Lord, honey, don't sneak up on a person that way."

"I'm sorry, I didn't mean to frighten you. But you looked like you were in a trance when I came in. Is something wrong?"

"Oh, yes," Grace said on an indrawn breath, "something is very wrong." Her eyes went back to the letter, and suddenly she thrust it out. "Here, I think you should read this. It's from your father. He asked me not to show it to you, but I think you should read it anyway."

Beth accepted the letter, and quickly scanned its contents. She bit her lip, obviously shaken, as she came to the end of the last page. Then she read it again, more slowly this time, hesitating on certain paragraphs at length. Finally, her hands fell to her lap, still clutching the letter, and she looked up with an expression of dismay. "I can't believe it. Why would Morg act like that? And this part about some gangster. I don't understand what Daddy means. What does he have to do with gangsters?"

Grace stared at her with a sudden look of candor. "Your father didn't want you to know about that. With the wedding and all, he thought you had enough on your mind, and he didn't want anything to spoil it. We discussed it before he left, and he convinced me it was best not to tell you." She faltered, averting her gaze, and then sighed heavily. "Perhaps he was right, but after reading that letter, I just couldn't keep it to myself. Not any longer."

Beth blinked with surprise, more confused than before. "I still don't understand. I thought Daddy was just there temporarily, until they could find a city marshal. What does that have to do with"—she glanced again at the letter—"gangsters and narcotics? Those are things the sheriff or federal agents are supposed to investigate."

"I know," Grace murmured uneasily. "Evidently the whole county has been corrupted by this man Tanner. The governor asked your father to go in there and clean it up." Quickly she outlined the situation in Cromwell, including the murders and the recent disappearance of the marshal. While she didn't elaborate, neither did she hold anything back. At the end, her hands were balled into fists, and she trembled with anger. "They always call on your father that way, and they have no right. It's just not fair. He's too old for law work, and they've taken enough of his life already."

"If only I had known." Beth appeared stunned, on the verge of tears. "If I hadn't been so wrapped up in my own affairs, maybe I could have stopped him. Together, I'm sure we could have talked him out of it."

"No, nothing would have stopped him. Not this time."

Grace's voice was barely audible, somehow distracted, and her gaze drifted off into space. Until this morning she had endured with something akin to resignation, but now, unaccountably, their last night together flooded back over her. She had argued that Cromwell was too dangerous, not at all like the other assignments he'd accepted, and for the first time in more than twenty-five years, there had been harsh words between them. Yet Owen would not bend, and they spent the evening in bruised silence, stiff monosyllabic questions and brusque answers. The strain was still there the next morning, and as his car pulled away from the house, she couldn't rid herself of a pervasive dread. She felt not just fear but what lay beyond it. Terror. And now, immersed again in that chilling premonition, she became aware that Beth had asked her something. Slowly she gained a measure of composure and, shaking off those darker thoughts, looked around at the girl.

"I'm sorry, honey, my mind must have wandered. What did you say?"

"I asked if you thought Daddy was in any danger." Beth's

eyes were glistening, and she batted her lashes to hold back the tears. "If he is, maybe Morg could still talk him out of it. I'll even go there myself if that would help."

Of a sudden, Grace felt terribly selfish and very weak-spined. She had endured this long, and she could endure a while longer. It had been a mistake to show Beth the letter, to chance spoiling her wedding plans, but it was a mistake that might yet be corrected. She took hold of herself, exerting that steely inner will, and her eyes crinkled with a smile.

"Honey, that's not what I meant," she lied smoothly. "Your father is stubborn as a mule, and he certainly has no business in Cromwell, but he knows how to take care of himself. Don't you worry your head about that. No, it's Morg I'm concerned about, and that's why I showed you the letter. I thought if you wrote Morg a long letter, then perhaps he might patch things up with his father." She tilted her head in a moment of deliberation. "You know, the reason they fight is because they're so much alike. Of course your father is too set in his ways to change. But if you could use some of your psychology on Morg—can it be used in a letter?—well, anyway, you see what I'm talking about. It just breaks my heart that they love each other so much, and yet they're always fighting."

Beth frowned uncertainly, wanting to believe, but not quite sure. "You really aren't worried about Daddy? Honestly and truly?"

"Why, of course I worry about him, but not the way you mean. Child, your father has been chasing badmen since the day I met him, and he's awfully good at it. I've never told him that because I'd prefer he stayed home, but it's the truth. What worries me most of all is the way Morg acts, and I hope you'll write him a good strong letter."

"I will. I'll just scald his ears off." Beth pulled out a handkerchief and dabbed at her eyes. "And I know exactly how to do it, too. If I tell him he's even more hardheaded than Daddy, he'll twist himself inside out to prove I'm wrong. I should have done it years ago."

"Well, it's not too late, so you just lay into him good." The doorbell rang, and Grace quickly retrieved the letter, sliding it under the stack of mail on the coffee table. "Speaking of men, I think yours is here. Where are you going today?"

Beth was off the sofa and rushing toward the foyer. "Oh, we're househunting again. Really, it's turned into an ordeal. All we see are dumps and dumps and more dumps. *Ugh!*"

She dabbed at her eyes again, fixing her face in a jaunty smile, and after opening the door, she kissed Earl briskly on the cheek. Then she grabbed his hand, peppering him with questions, and led him back into the living room. By now Earl Roebuck was considered one of the family, and the formalities had long since been dropped. As they entered the room, he waved to Grace and finally slipped in a greeting when Beth paused for breath.

"Morning. How are you today?"

"Fine, Earl, just fine." Grace liked this man, felt a special rapport with him, and her days were always a little brighter when he came to call. "Beth says you're off to look at houses."

"We are if she doesn't twist my arm out of the socket. What did you feed her for breakfast, molasses and gunpowder?"

Beth sniffed and poked him in the ribs. "Very funny. We'll see if you're still laughing when we come back from the honeymoon and don't have a roof over our heads. Of course you hadn't thought of that, had you? Honestly, men are so impractical."

He just smiled, shaking his head, and turned back to Grace. "You know, before I get in too deep, I've been meaning to ask you something. Does she act like a wildcat all the time, or do I just bring out the worst in her nature?"

Grace quickly fell into a bantering conversation with him, and totally ignoring Beth, they proceeded with a lighthearted discussion of her many quirks and oddities. Earl delighted in joshing her, particularly when they were alone with Grace, and surprisingly, the older woman displayed a rare wit in his company. Standing there, scarcely listening, Beth could only wonder if Grace and her father had found what she shared with this remarkable man. She thought perhaps they had, and hoped it was true, for with Earl she had found not just mental stimulation, but a physical affinity unlike anything she had ever imagined. By easy but breathtaking stages, he never failed to bring her to complete and wondrous fulfillment. A master of her needs as well as his own, he was a gentle lover, considerate and infinitely wise in the ways a man might create pleasure for a woman. Where he'd learned, or by whose wisdom he had gained this experience, never bothered her. She simply felt grateful that he had somehow come into her life. And content, marvelously content. Beyond anything she had ever thought possible.

The fleeting curiosity about Grace and her father returned, and she suddenly wondered if Grace had told her the truth about Cromwell. Or was it a little white lie, an attempt to shelter her from the greater concern? A danger that seemed to leap from between the lines of her father's letter. She wasn't sure, and sensed some deep and foreboding dread of knowing. Unwittingly, the dampness again stung her eyes and a thick moist lump formed in her throat.

By degrees, as if awakening from a drugged sleep, she became aware that Grace and Earl were watching her. Then he lifted her chin, searching her face intently. "Say now, this looks serious. Why the tears? A little razzing shouldn't cause all that."

"Oh, don't be silly." She cocked her head in a funny smile, convincing but somehow disingenuous. "I just started thinking about the wedding and got misty-eyed. That's a girl's privilege."

Earl smiled, brushing a tear away with his thumb, but she

saw Grace flash her a peculiar look and then glance away. She knew they would have to talk, sometime later, just the two of them. But for now it would have to wait. However much the day had been spoiled for her, she wouldn't allow it to be spoiled for Earl. Nor would she allow him to look closer, to see what she had seen. Tucking her arm in his, she spun him about and marched him off toward the foyer.

"I won't be back till late, Grace. Don't wait dinner for me."

"Bye, Grace!" Earl threw a look over his shoulder as she hustled him along. "Pardon the hasty departure, but she's right. We need a place to sleep."

Grace waved and smiled, wishing them luck, but as the door closed her smile faded and her mouth set in a grim line. She took the letter from the table and read it through again. Yet she saw the words not so much as the gnarled hand that had scrawled the letters. A hand that seemed to reach out and touch her, to offer her hope and strength and another day's courage. The words blurred and she clutched the letter to her breast, resigned now, almost stoic, but no longer brave. She was afraid and alone with her fear, and suddenly unable to endure what lay beyond her fear. Those darker thoughts.

After a morning thunder shower the afternoon sky boiled with clouds. The sun blazed down in splintered shafts of fire, and in the summer heat the earth steamed. A vagrant breeze billowed the curtains, and shards of light filtered through the gauzy material, bathing the room in a splash of coral cider. The air was close but not unpleasant, cloyed with the musk of warm flesh and love and a faint scent of jasmine.

Burrowed deep in the hollow of his arm, Kitty lay motionless and languid, watching her breath eddy through the matted curls on his chest. She felt sated and blissfully tranquil, limp with an exquisite kind of exhaustion, perhaps a bit tender from their violent lovemaking. He had knocked on her door, quite unexpectedly, early that afternoon. Surprised and curious, she nonetheless knew the look when it came over him, and they had wasted little time on words. Her need was no less urgent, as demanding and brutally explosive as his own, consuming mind and body in a haze of sweet agony the instant he touched her. Nor had the need diminished, though they took one another in a frenzied burst of craving that first time. The afternoon went past in an incandescent thrash of arms and legs, broken only by brief interludes of languorous quiet. And somewhere in those wilder moments, locked beneath him in a world of swirling lights and shuddering delirium, she had lost count.

Now she lay very still, not daring to wake him. After the last time he had dozed off, and however great her need before, she was hesitant to arouse him again. The tenderness had become a dull throb, not unlike a toothache; it was no laughing matter, but she had the giddy sensation that once more and she might never walk again. Just the thought of dancing gave her a mild case of the stomach flutters. And she had to work tonight. Ten straight hours at the Palace, unless Morg appeared and bought his usual quota of tickets. Which he'd damned sure better! Otherwise he could just keep his pants buttoned till closing time, and forget about matinees.

One thought sparked another, and she was reminded of an earlier question. Why had he come into town this afternoon? Never before had he visited her room during the daytime. Not that she discouraged it. Everyone in the hotel knew that he slept over most nights, and the idea of a matinee certainly wouldn't have embarrassed her. But Morg was a stickler about his work. However little sleep he got, and sometimes they partied all night, he was on the job first thing every morning. And he put in a full day, working as hard as any roustabout on his payroll. All of which made this afternoon not just peculiar, but curiously odd. Out of character.

Kate Jackson had little formal education, but she possessed an inquisitive mind and an uncanny gift for seeing things not as they appeared but as they were. She had been reared in hunger and deprivation, in a home of such poverty that a bag of cornmeal assumed greater significance than love or affection. Later, in the oil towns, she had experienced life at its rawest, and quickly learned that there were worse things than hunger. Yet she emerged not so much a cynic as a seeker, with an incisive philosophy all her own. Which was the very thing that made her irresistible to Morg. Although he hadn't realized it as yet, she was the first woman he'd ever slept with who wanted nothing from him but himself. Not his money or his name or what he might one day become. But just him, as he was, nothing more.

And if she was to ever become anything more than his playmate, then she must help him to see what she already knew about herself. What he was struggling with and had yet to admit. That Kate Jackson, having endured nearly all the evil an evil world can inflict, valued love above all things. Craved it in a way that money or position could never satisfy. In a way that was elemental, apart from material things, the unadorned yet priceless bond between a man and a woman. The day he saw that was the day she would become what she most wanted to be, Morgan Kincaid's wife.

Which was why she took nothing from him. And gave everything. He must see for himself that she was not just a dancehall girl or another conquest or yet another gold digger. She was what he sought, already a part of him, a kindred spirit.

She felt his hand move on her hip, and glanced up to find him watching her. He had only just awakened, but she saw that he looked alert and, worse, refreshed. A slow smile spread over his face. "I must've conked out."

"Well, you had good reason, sugar." She playfully tweaked the hairs on his chest. "Here lies living proof that you've done a full day's work."

"Shucks, ma'am, weren't nothin'." He winked, the smile

became a lewd grin, and his arm tightened. "We're just getting started."

She laughed a deep, throaty laugh, and elusive as quicksilver slipped from his grasp. His arm shot out to grab her, but in a single motion she rolled away and bounded from the bed to the floor. His face screwed up in a frown, at once hurt and disappointed, and it seemed to her that he had the look of a little boy whose ice cream cone had just melted.

"Awww, c'mon, honey, don't be like that. I'm all primed and raring to go."

She wagged her head back and forth, and gave him a vixenish smile. "Sorry, lover. You've had it for today." He came up on his elbow, collecting himself for another lunge, and she backed away. "Now listen, you big lummox, I'm not kidding. That's not exactly a wienie you've got there. One more time and I'll be crippled for life."

He glanced down at the flaccid bulge between his legs. "This little thing? Why, just look at it. You've gone and hurt its feelings." He cut his eyes around at her in a leering smirk. "C'mon, Kitty, don't be a party poop."

She stamped her foot so hard her breasts jiggled. "Don't call me that! How many times do I have to tell you. Kitty works at the Palace"—her arm swept the room—"and Kate lives here. I mean it, Morg, there's a difference."

"Okay! Okay!" He cringed back against the pillows in mock terror. "Pull in your claws, for Christ's sake, I'm convinced." She glared at him a minute, and finally he stretched out his arms. "Come give me a kiss and make up. Then we'll go get something to eat."

She started forward, then caught herself and swerved aside. "Oh, no! None of your tricks, you big bullshooter. Once you got me in that bed, I'd never get out." She whirled away, eyes dancing merrily, and cast him a fetching smile. "If you behave yourself tonight—and buy enough tickets to keep me off my feet—I might just be recuperated by closing time. That's the best deal you'll get, Buster Brown, so don't swell up and pout. Anyway, I've got to get ready for work, so you just lay there and think about it."

She selected a peek-a-boo dress from the closet, gathered up stockings and shoes and underwear, and with a saucy little wiggle, disappeared into the bathroom. All the while Morg had watched her, fascinated as always by her mercurial moods, and especially the way she looked when she was mad. Now, hands locked behind his head, staring at a crack in the ceiling, it occurred to him that Kitty really was the better name. It suited her. She moved with the sleek grace of a cat. Her golden eyes, shiny bright like honeyed bronze, were the eyes of a cat. She had that same air of casual independence, and while she was fond of being stroked, she could manage very well without it. And like a cat, she loved herself best. Or maybe she was more like a prankish kitten. Just so full of her own devilment that she hadn't time to stop and take a look about her. So busy playing with life that she neither saw nor heard what someone was trying to tell her. What he hadn't yet been able to put into words.

And perhaps he never could. However strongly felt, the words somehow got stuck, and instead, he had to show her. Like this afternoon. Not a sudden impulse, but need. Need of her, and what she was. Of a sudden, sitting upright in bed, it came to him that she was right after all. It wasn't Kitty he needed, it was Kate Jackson.

When she came out of the bathroom, cinched into her gown and makeup in place, he was dressed and sitting in a chair, puffing thoughtfully on a cigarette. The glow from the sunlight made soft umber highlights in her hair, like a Flemish portrait, and she somehow looked more ravishing now than she had naked. Without a word, he stubbed out the cigarette and stood. Then he caught her up and kissed her so roughly that she swayed when he set her down. Her hand went to her hair, and it was a moment before she got her breath.

"Sugar, you do have a way with the girls." She moved to the dresser mirror and checked her lipstick, watching his reflection. "Which reminds me. What turned your spring loose this afternoon? I'm not complaining, understand, just curious. You've never come to see me in the daytime before."

He darted her a quick look, then dismissed it with a bland gesture. "Well, we had some lightning this morning, and what with the bad weather and all, I just thought I'd take off."

"You mean, you had to shut down operations?"

"No, it wasn't that bad. We started drilling again as soon as the storm let up."

"So quit hedging and tell me"—she prompted him with a leasing smile—"what brought you into town?"

He wanted to tell her, felt some compulsive need to get it out. But the words again hung in his throat, and instead, he grinned suggestively. "Give you three guesses. And the first two don't count."

That instant of hesitation told her more than he thought. She had no need of guesses, nor was she fooled by his jocose manner. The answer was in his eyes, and she knew what had brought him into town. It was the first crack in that hard outer shell. A beginning, and all the more important because he wasn't fooling himself either. He understood what it meant.

She turned from the dresser and held out her hand, but as he started toward her, a knock sounded at the door. With a regretful little shrug, she moved to the door and opened it. Owen Kincaid stood in the hallway. He had his hat off, and apparently felt as awkward as he looked.

"Sorry to bust in on you, Kate. I was wonderin' if Morg is here?"

Surprised, but clearly pleased, she took his arm and pulled him into the room. They had become fast friends over the last month, and he often met her for an early supper in the café downstairs. What they had in common was his son, but more than that, there was the mutual affinity of two very honest people who each admired what they saw in the other. He knew more about her love life than Morg suspected, and neither the mussed bed nor the drawn curtains caused her the least embarrassment. Closing the door, she smiled, lowering her voice to a gravelly mutter, and jerked her thumb at Morg.

"There he is, Marshal. But watch him, he's a rough customer."

Morg wasn't amused. "How did you know I was here, Pa?"

"Saw your car parked outside and played a hunch." Owen still seemed apologetic, glancing quickly at the girl. "Wouldn't have come up, except I wanted to talk to you in private."

Thoroughly annoyed now, Morg scowled. "This is as private as it'll get. I don't have any secrets from Kate."

"Neither do I. Get her to tell you about it sometime."

"She already has. But that doesn't change anything, so let's quit fencing around. Say what you came to say."

Owen's eyes were sunken with fatigue, and there was a throbbing beat at his temples. But he looked straight at Morg, his face very earnest. "You were right. Tanner's got me between a rock and a hard place. I don't like to admit it, but he's smarter'n I thought."

Morg stared back at him without moving, as if turned to stone. The statement merely vindicated his earlier judgment, and that surprised him not at all. That the old man would admit it, however, left him momentarily nonplussed. They seldom spoke these days, and whenever they happened across one another around town, there was a distant look on their faces. As though they were trying to remember something important and couldn't quite call it back to memory. After exchanging family news, and straining to make smalltalk, they always juggled a promise to get together, but it somehow never worked out. It was scarcely a secret that the marshal was getting nowhere with his investigation, and Morg avoided him as much as possible. Whatever their differences, he had no wish to humble his own father.

At length, groping for some response, he shrugged. "What the hell, Pa? So you got snookered. Nobody can win 'em all."

"Maybe so, maybe not. The game isn't over yet."

"You just lost me. What are we talking about, anyway?"

Owen flushed but went on lamely. "The reason I'm here is to ask for your help. Now, hold your horses and hear me out." There was a moment of calculation, then his son nodded, and he resumed. "I've only got one problem, but it's a doozie. Everybody in this town is too scared to talk to me. What I need is somebody they're not afraid of, somebody they trust. All I want is one solid witness. Vice. Extortion. Dope. Anything that'll nail Tanner to the wall. Don't you see, once somebody starts talkin' they'll all start talkin'. But nobody'll say a word till I get that first witness."

He paused, then his gaze narrowed, became steady and demanding. "Everybody around here trusts you. And you're the only one in this town that I can trust. Which sort of brings us down to cases. I'm asking you to help me get that first witness."

"No."

The word fell like a drop of lead, and there was an outrush of breath from the girl. She had been watching him expectantly, and now she gave him a veiled but searching look. Owen seemed more disappointed than surprised, and after a while he nodded with chill dignity. "Guess it wouldn't do me any good to argue?"

"Not a bit. It's none of my business. Never was."

"Still think you can get a free ride, don't you? Just step off the world anytime you choose."

"Let me ask you something, Pa." Morg's tone was brusque, almost scornful. "What the hell's so important about Cromwell? People get what they deserve, so why do you care what happens?"

"It's my job to care," Owen answered stiffly. "Matter of fact, it's every man's job to care. Someday you'll figure that out for yourself."

Owen jammed his hat on his head and walked to the door, then he turned back. "One more thing. I'll be going home for Beth's wedding. You want to ride with me or take your own car?"

"There's still plenty of time. I'll let you know."

The door opened and closed, and Owen was gone. Morg pulled out a pack of cigarettes, lit one, and inhaled deeply. He appeared abstracted, and took several quick puffs before he became aware of the girl. She was watching him with a peculiar expression, alert and piercing but somehow cryptic.

"Why are you looking at me like that?"

"Because I can't believe what you just did."

"What? That I turned the old man down?" His mouth clamped in a bloodless line. "Jesus Christ, don't you start in on me, too. It's his lookout, not mine."

"That's not so!" she flared suddenly. "He's your father, and he came here asking you to help him. Couldn't you see it? He was almost begging you to help."

"Hell, yes, I saw it." His words were hotly defensive. "What's that got to do with anything? He's got no business in this town. He ought to be home where he belongs."

"You're wrong, Morg." She met his look squarely. "But that's not the point. He's your father and he needs your help. That's the only thing that counts. The only thing."

"Not in my book. He'd just wind up making us both look like fools. Maybe this way he'll get fed up and go on back to Guthrie."

Her eyes dulled, and seemed to turn inward on something too terrible for speech. Her body went rigid, and standing there, with the sunlight streaming through the window, she had the look of some unearthly Valkyrie, blazing with suppressed fury. Afraid to let go for fear of the consequences, something irreversible and ugly. At last, very quietly, she broke the silence between them.

"I'm sorry, Morg. That's just a cheap excuse, and I can't buy it."

"You'd side with the old man against me?"

"Yes, I would. He's your father, and in *my* book, you don't turn your back on someone who loves you and needs you."

He glowered at her a moment, then something cruel ticced

the corner of his mouth. "Well, by God, take him and welcome to him, lady. He's all yours."

Bristling with indignation, filled with some dim sense of betrayal, he stalked from the room. Kate stood transfixed, unable to call out, knowing that she had only to speak to bring him back. Yet something weak and treacherous, a part of herself she couldn't muzzle, ran after him. And she was appalled not so much by the sniveling, piteous thing that trailed him down the hall, but rather by the stark and unyielding creature who so easily remained behind. She felt very empty and very lonely, somehow lost.

Some impressions remain with a man. A wisp of perfume, a few last words, a scent of gunsmoke stand out in vivid detail. Deeply etched, indelible, a part of him for all the rest of his days. Early on a warm summer evening the hand of mortality touched Morgan Kincaid, and left its mark on the man he was to become.

As he came out of the barbershop the earth swam in a bluish dusk, and high in the sky a dark silver cloud blazed like glowing slag from some unearthly cauldron. Trimmed and shaved, reeking of bay rum, he turned uptown and proceeded along the boardwalk. There was something debonair and jaunty about his stride. A lithe, quick springiness uncommon to big men, and he was whistling softly between his teeth. All along the street men greeted him, pausing to exchange a word or slap him on the back, and his smile steadily widened into a broad frisky grin. Never had he felt so alive, on top of the world, intoxicated with himself and the heady stuff of at last taking the plunge.

In his pocket was a ring. And tonight he meant to pop the question.

Nearing the Palace, he saw Wirt Jordan and his father standing in an alleyway which separated the dancehall from a gambling dive. They had their heads together, apparently engrossed in conversation, but his father seemed to be doing all the talking. As he approached, he saw Jordan scowl and shake his head, clearly displeased by whatever he'd just heard. To his knowledge, there had never been a cross word between the two men, and the look on Jordan's face immediately aroused his concern. And his curiosity. Then his father spotted him, and in midsentence, the discussion simply ceased. Their faces suddenly brightened, all smiles and good cheer, and as he stepped off the boardwalk, it struck Morg that they actually appeared sneaky. Like a couple of kids who had just kicked over the neighbor's outhouse.

"By golly, Wirt, get a whiff of that! Smells like a petunia, doesn't he?"

Owen seemed especially jovial, but the best Jordan could manage was a crooked smile. "Yeah, he's sweet all right. And look at the haircut. Damn near got himself scalped."

"You two ever think of trying vaudeville?" Morg scrutinized them closely, one eyebrow cocked in a quizzical frown. "C'mon now, cut the comedy and give me the lowdown. I saw you hatching some kind of plot."

"Plot!" Owen sounded genuinely offended. "Hell, you better get yourself some spectacles, son. We were just chewin' the fat."

"Pa, you always were a damn poor liar. Why don't you just 'fess up and quit giving me the runaround?"

His father muttered something beneath his breath, then turned to Jordan. "What about it, Wirt? Think we ought to let him in on the secret?"

Jordan gummed his quid and spat, no longer smiling. "Why not? I already told you it's about as secret as a whore in church."

Owen grunted skeptically, and his gaze came back to Morg. "Thanks to your partner, I've got myself a little birdie." He grinned, glancing quickly toward the street, and lowered his voice. "Just the kind I've been huntin' for too—a songbird."

"Songbird? Are you talking about a witness against Tanner?"

"That's exactly what I'm talkin' about. Tanner found out one of the madams was holdin' out on him, and he had his collector beat the shellac out of her. Wirt happened to visit the establishment last night and got wind of it. So I hauled her in, and we had ourselves a little talk."

He hesitated, knuckling his mustache, unable to resist building the suspense. Then he laughed, eyes flecked with that old wolflike glitter, and slapped Morg on the shoulder. "Would you believe it, son? She's ready to spill the whole works. Vice payoffs. County officials she entertained for Tanner. Everything I've been lookin' for. And if I get hold of that collector, I've got an idea he'll squeal louder'n her once he sees the jig's up."

Morg studied the ground a moment, visibly unsettled; then he looked up at his partner. "You didn't do him any favors, Wirt. I wish you had checked with me first."

"Hell, I wish I had've, too!" Jordan growled. "What do you think we've been standin' here arguing about? I just naturally figgered he'd get her out of town, but he won't listen to reason. He's got her locked up in that tarpaper jail." He shook his head in raw disbelief. "Christ, ain't that a pretty pickle! Everybody in town must've heard about it by now."

"Especially Tanner." Morg swung back to his father. "Listen to me, Pa. You're playing with dynamite, and it's about to blow up in your face. I'm serious, goddamnit! Quit grinning at me like I was nuts."

"Aw, simmer down, and stop tellin' me how to run my business. I'll get her out of town. But I sure as hell can't take her to the county jail, so the next best place is Tulsa. Say, that reminds me. You know who she says is on Tanner's payroll? Everybody's favorite prohibition agent, Lon Hill himself. Always had a hunch there was something queer about him, and it turns out I was right."

"Holy shit!" Jordan groaned. "It just keeps gettin' worse."

"Wirt, I told you before to stop worryin'." Owen favored him with an indulgent smile. "I'll get her out of town just as soon as I've got that collector on ice. Meantime, she wouldn't be any safer in a bank vault. Dub Watson is standin' guard over her, and nobody'll get past him. Take my word for it."

"Pa, you really are whacko." Morg glared at him, thoroughly exasperated. "We're not worried about some goddamned floozy. We're worried about you. Use your head a minute. If Tanner can't get at her, then what's the best way to make her clam up? Simple. He just rubs you out and that solves the whole problem."

"Me?" Owen appeared flabbergasted by the idea. "That's ridiculous. He wouldn't have the nerve. Anything happens to me and the governor will have troops in here so quick it'd make your head swim."

"Are you willing to bet your life on that? Hell, forget I even asked, just listen to me. That collector you want so bad is probably dead and buried by now. Tanner doesn't leave any witnesses, and if you don't believe me, just remember what happened to the last marshal we had."

Owen started to interrupt but Morg cut him short. "No, goddamnit, you just listen for once. I've tried to tell you before without hurting your feelings but that didn't work, so I'll give it to you straight out. The only reason Tanner has left you alone this long is because you've been running around in circles and everybody in town knew it. It was like a joke, and he had the biggest horselaugh of all. But that's changed. You've got the goods on him, or at least you're damn close to it, so the fun and games are over. It's you or your songbird, and if he can't get to her, then you're elected. And forget about the governor. If he meant to send troops in here he would've done it already. He played you for a patsy, Pa, and as much as I hate to say it, that's the honest-to-God's truth."

His father regarded him calmly, stoic as a rock; and they stared at one another for a long time. At last, Owen nodded, conceding it all with a single gesture. "You've made your point. But the game's not over yet. Not if I get that little birdie to Tulsa and turn her over to the feds. And that's just what I'm gonna do. Tonight."

There was a moment of deliberation, then Morg shrugged and threw up his hands. "We're in so deep now I guess it's the only way. But we'll have to be damn tricky to outfox Tanner. Unless we get her out of town with nobody the wiser, we'll end up fighting our way to Tulsa."

Owen gave him a strange look. "That sounds like you're comin' along?"

"Yeah, hell; you finally sucked me into it." Morg grinned, warding him off as he started to object. "Save your breath. It had to happen sooner or later anyway. I suppose it's something in the blood. A Kincaid just can't stay away from a good fight." He glanced at Jordan, who nodded vigorously, and then back at the old man. "All right, give me a minute to run in and see Kate. You two put your thinking caps on and see if you can come up with a plan. I've got an idea we'll need a lulu to pull this off."

Morg headed toward the street, then stopped, hesitating a moment, and turned back. "Say, Pa, I never mentioned it but I should've. Thanks for talking to Kate. I don't know what you said, but it sure brought her around. I owe you one."

A smile tugged at the corner of Owen's mouth. "Forget it. I just told her the truth. Said the Kincaids were naturally born hard-headed and their women had to be patient with them. Might take awhile, but we always come around in the end." A beat slipped past as he studied his son intently; then he laughed. "By God, the way it worked out, she must've saw it comin' before I did."

"Looks like it. Anyway, I feel like I've been turned inside out."

"Not just you. We've both turned around, don't you see?" He woofed a loud chuckle, and waved Morg on. "Hell, that girl's smarter'n either one of us gave her credit for. Go on and give her a big kiss before somebody beats you to it."

A little thunderstruck, Morg just stood for a moment, then he grinned foolishly and hurried around the front of the dancehall. Watching him, Owen's thoughts of a sudden turned inward. The bare facts, like loose parts of a puzzle, abruptly came together in his head. In an instant of revelation he saw what he had avoided all these years, the thing he'd kept pushing back in memory. Time lays scars on a man, and those scars can cloud his judgment while at the same time giving him wisdom. A contradiction in terms, but one of life's fundamental truths nonetheless. Perhaps no greater proof existed than the fact that he was standing here, this night, in a boomtown controlled not by outlaws on horseback but by a gangster who rode in airplanes. Morg had been right all along. A six-gun against tommy guns. It was absurd. With sudden clarity, he saw that he'd made the mistake common to many pioneers. He had heard the clock strike but he'd counted the strokes wrong. Stubborn pride forever obscured reality, like a nearsighted man who refused to admit he couldn't read the fine print. It was the twentieth century, and yet, somehow, he'd never quite outgrown the horse-and-buggy days. Chiding himself, he turned back to Wirt Jordan as a shadow materialized at the end of the alley.

The roar of the shotgun reverberated like thunder between the two buildings. Inside the dancehall Morg froze, chilled to the very marrow, and in the next instant came the sharp bark of a pistol followed immediately by another blast from the shotgun. Wheeling around, he sprinted for the door, flinging men and tables aside in blind fury. Kate was hard on his heels, and as they burst through the door they saw several passersby cautiously peeking around the corner of the alley. Morg scattered them with a sweep of his arms, and as he jumped off the boardwalk, Dub Watson came running across from the jail. For a split second, that mere instant his feet touched the ground, a numbing paralysis held him locked in a stupor.

His father and Wirt Jordan were down, lying almost on top of one another, their clothes splattered with welling crimson blotches. Jordan was struggling to push himself erect, one arm dangling uselessly, but Owen lay spread-eagled in the dirt, motionless, the pistol still clutched in his hand.

"Somebody get a doctor!" Morg shouted as he rushed forward. Suddenly aware of Watson, who pounded up beside him, he shoved the deputy aside. "I'll look after the old man! You see to Wirt."

Watson caught Jordan just as he keeled over backward, and eased him to the ground. Jerking his handkerchief, he quickly began fashioning a tourniquet around the driller's shattered arm. Morg dropped to one knee beside his father, on the verge of tearing open the blood-soaked shirt. Then his hands fell away, clenched into tightly balled fists. One load of buckshot had caught Owen in the side, along the beltline, and the other was centered on his chest, a gaping hole just above the brisket. In the trenches, during the war, Morg had seen similar wounds, and he knew it was hopeless. A hole that big simply couldn't be plugged. It just pumped and pumped till it was all pumped out.

Kate crumpled to her knees beside him, her features contorted, staring mutely at the horror before them. There was nothing to say, nothing to be done, so obviously nothing that would help. But as they looked on, enervated by the very shock of their helplessness, Owen's eyes slowly rolled open. He blinked, apparently in no pain, yet he made no attempt to move. Then his vision cleared and he saw them, and an eager look of expectancy came over his face.

"Did I get him, son? Did I get the bastard?"

"You got him, Pa"—Morg swallowed hard on the lie—"dead center."

"Thought so. Only got the one shot, but I thought so." His gaze moved to Kate, and the craggy features softened. "That's a fine woman you've got there, boy. You treat her right, you hear me? Take good care of her."

"I will, Pa. Now quit talking and just hang on. The doc'll be here any minute."

Owen coughed and a trickle of blood seeped out of the corner of his mouth. The girl bent forward, wiping it away with the hem of her dress, and he looked at her again. "Funny thing. Katie looks an awful lot like your grandma. Did I ever tell you about your grandma, son? She was a dancehall girl too."

"You told me, Pa. Long time ago."

"Sorta spooky, such a likeness. But nice, real nice."

A wintry smile lighted the old man's eyes and then was gone. Swiftly came a mealy, weblike darkness, and with nothing more than a small sigh, he stopped breathing. The fingers of his hand stiffened and then went limp and the pistol slipped from his grasp.

Morg's face went ashen, drained of color, but his expression was wooden, revealing nothing, coldly implacable. He took the old Colt from his father's hand and climbed to his feet. A hushed stillness fell over the alley, and the crowd gathered on the street edged forward as he turned from the body. His gaze settled on Wirt Jordan, who was propped up against the wall of the gambling dive.

"Wirt, did you get a look at who did it?"

Jordan's arm was cradled across his chest, and his eyes scrunched tight as he bit down against the pain. After a moment he sucked in a deep breath, and nodded. "Saw him when I went down. Him and your dad traded shots, and I caught a glimpse of him in the muzzle flash. It was Lon Hill."

Without comment, he looked around at Watson. "There's only one place he'd feel safe. Have you got the guts to back my play?"

"Hold on a goldurn minute! This here's a job for the law. I'm sorry and all, but we can't start no private feuds."

"Mister, are you going to deputize me"—Morg's voice was gritty, demanding—"or do I go alone? You suit yourself."

Watson cast an uneasy glance at the pistol in his hand. "Can you use that thing? I mean, your paw was slick as grease, but I don't know nothin' about you."

"I took lessons from the Krauts. Now quit stalling and give me an answer. Are you coming or not?"

"Hell, I might as well. I don't know the words, though, so everybody here'll just have to bear witness that I deputized you."

"Let's get at it, then. We've kept Tanner waiting long enough."

He started off but Kate laid her hand on his arm. As if a butterfly had alighted on his sleeve, he stood motionless, waiting for her to speak. "Take care of yourself," she whispered. "And don't give that dirty bastard an even break. Do it fast."

Morg nodded, his jaw set in a grim line. "Look after Wirt. I'll be back."

Dub Watson fell in beside him and they pushed through the crowd. Kate watched after them a moment; then a man carrying a black bag hurried into the alley. Waving him away from the body, she forced back something vile and slimy in her throat, and pulled him toward Wirt Jordan.

A block down Main Street Morg and Watson walked through the door of the hardware store. Virgil Tanner was standing behind the counter, cleaning his fingernails with a penknife. He glanced up as they entered, his gargoyle features clamped in a bland, expressionless mask. Wiping the penknife clean, he snapped it shut, stuck it in his pocket, and greeted them with a slow, unctuous smile.

"Good evening, gentlemen. What can I do for you?"

The store appeared empty, quiet as a church. But Morg quickly scanned the room, ignoring Tanner, and one look was enough to confirm his suspicions. There was an alley door at the end of the counter, and another door toward the rear, obviously leading to a storeroom, or perhaps an office. He had no doubt whatever that Lon Hill was listening on the other side of that door.

Watson advanced a couple of steps farther, and planted

his feet. "We're lookin' for Lon Hill. You'll save yourself lots of trouble, Mr. Tanner, if you'll just hand him over. Where's he at?"

"The prohibition agent? That Lon Hill?" Tanner shrugged guilelessly. "Deputy, I wouldn't have the faintest notion of where to look."

"Cut the double-talk, Tanner." Morg's lip curled back, and he jerked his chin toward the rear of the store. "Who do you have in that backroom?"

"Why, nobody. Nobody at all, I'm the only one in the store."

"Sure you are. And I suppose your gang's not back there waiting to blast anybody that walks through that door?"

"Mr. Kincaid, if I had a gang, which I don't, I assure you they wouldn't be hanging around the store during business hours. You'd better look somewhere else. I'm afraid you're barking up the wrong tree."

"No, I think you just told me what I wanted to know." Morg saw the great owlish eyes widen imperceptibly, and knew he'd euchred Tanner out of the right answer. There was no one back there but Lon Hill. "Suppose we just see for ourselves. Dub, take a look in that backroom."

"I wouldn't do that if I were you." Tanner moved along the counter, halting beside the cash register. "This is private property, and without a search warrant you have no right here."

Morg turned his head just far enough to rivet the gangster with a corrosive stare. "Tanner, I'll only say this once, so pay attention. Stand very still. Don't you even blink."

Then he raised his voice in a loud, hectoring shout. "Deputy Watson! Go on back there and take a look-see. If it's locked kick it in."

The door suddenly wrenched open and Lon Hill darted out with a sawed-off shotgun in his hands. Crouched low, he blindly triggered one barrel, scattering buckshot across the store, and made a dash for the alley door. Dub Watson ducked, then his arm came level, and he planted three shots in Hill's back. The prohibition agent slammed up against the door, hung there a moment, and then toppled backward, upsetting a keg of nails. As he fell, Virgil Tanner's hand snaked beneath the counter and came up with an Army automatic. His gaze flicked to Watson, who was still watching the rear of the store, and quickly shifted back to Morg. He found himself staring down the business end of an old Colt Peacemaker.

Morg grinned, and calmly stitched four slugs up his front, starting at the bellybutton and ending at the breastbone. Tanner was jerked off his feet, twitching convulsively as the impact of the slugs danced him along like a puppet. His blood-gutted eyes were wild and bulging, vivid with shock behind the thick glasses; as the Colt roared for the last time he pitched forward across the counter, dropping the automatic, and then slowly slumped to the floor. A stench drifted across the store as death voided his bowels.

Dub Watson walked back to Morg, shucking the empties out of his pistol, and neither of them spoke while he reloaded. At last, as if he'd got the words framed just the way he wanted, he looked up. "You set him up real smooth. I think the marshal would've been proud of you. Too bad he wasn't here to see it."

"Yeah, it is. This was one fight he wanted all to himself." Morg hefted the old pistol, thoughtful a moment, then chuckled softly to himself. "Course, knowing him, I have an idea he figures he won after all. And in a way, I guess he did."

When they came out of the hardware store, Kate was standing at the front of a crowd bunched up in a knot across the street. Her eyes glinted with that peculiar honey-umber glow, and she began laughing as tears streamed down her cheeks. Suddenly she bolted from the crowd, skirts flying high, and rushed toward him. Morg jammed the Colt in his belt, spreading his arms wide, and caught her on the last bounce.

EPILOGUE

The storm broke at dusk.

The sky went dark and the roar of the wind swelled to a deafening pitch. Then a great bolt of lightning flashed from the clouds, forked in a crackling streaks, seemed to branch out, burn and leap upward, flicking across the prairie, vivid with fire. An instant in time and motion was arrested, and the world froze in a brilliant blue-white opalescence. Suddenly a thunderclap shook the very earth, rumbling and explosive, reverberating endlessly as it clattered off into the distance, dying away by degrees.

A moment of inky calm slipped past, and then the darkness came alive as jagged darts of lightning splintered the heavens. The silvery streaks blinded, searing and inimical, and the boom of thunder stunned the ears, mounting in ferocity as concussions overlapped in a rolling barrage. As though a mere prelude, angry thunderbolts hurled in warning, the skies suddenly burst open and the rain came, tearing and slashing as great torrents of water deluged the earth. A single shaft of lightning slammed through the murky overcast and struck a tree along the river. The jolt rocked the ground, and as the tree burst into flames the wind quickened and the downpour became a raging flood.

Standing at a window, Grace looked on spellbound as nature vented its savagery on the earth. A tiny smile touched her lips, and her expression was one of serenity, deep inner peace. As if he wasn't gone at all, but somehow stood beside her even now, his arm around her shoulders, just as they had so many times in the past. He loved these storms, the lightning and thunder, all the sizzling fireworks nature unleashed when she went on a rampage. Sometimes he'd stood at this window for hours, completely captivated, watching the flash and crackle rend the sky. And how fitting, how terribly pleased he must be that nature gave him such a magnificent sendoff. It was as though all the gods in all the heavens had been summoned. Gathered together by this spectacular display to honor his passing. To mark the day that Owen Kincaid had crossed over at last.

Her smile widened imperceptibly. He was probably laughing at her right now for having such foolish thoughts. He had always teased her unmercifully about her superstitions, the old ways she'd never quite put behind her. Thirty years among the whites, he would chuckle, and she still thought like an Osage. Yet she knew that he was secretly delighted. And perhaps intrigued. If one god was good, then two were better. That had been her argument, and while he joshed her, he had never attempted to dissuade her. Almost as though, in that great gentleness he possessed, he hoped it would work for her.

Once they had even performed the Osage marriage ritual. A quarter-century had passed, but she remembered it as vividly as if it had happened just yesterday. It was the night she refused to marry him the white man's way, perhaps the only time in all their years together that he'd lost his temper. She had married one Kincaid—seen him branded a squawman, humiliated and disgraced, declared an outcast by whites— and she refused to have Guthrie turn its back on Owen. By that twisted morality peculiar to wealthy whites, it was better to live in sin with a squaw than to make an honest woman of her. As a mistress she could be conveniently overlooked, but as a wife she would have been entirely too visible. Owen had finally resigned himself to it, although he hated the pretense, and especially detested separate bedrooms. Yet, curiously enough, he had taken immense comfort from the Osage ceremony. Afterward, whatever the world thought, he had considered her his wife.

Perhaps that was why he'd loved the ranch so much. Here they lived as man and wife, untroubled by neighbors or moral sham. And while they had never talked of death, it was why she had buried him this afternoon on a shady knoll overlooking the river. His favorite spot on the entire ranch, where the Cimarron made a slow dogleg south, and a summer sunset glistening off the water was something wondrous to behold. He would rest easy there, content and happy, perhaps unburdened at last of Brad and old Jake and the guilt he'd never fully outdistanced. And she could take him flowers, sit with him a while each day, tell him all the things he would have delighted to hear. She saw no reason ever again to return to Guthrie. This was her home now, just as it had been the one true home they had known together. All the days that remained, she would spend here. At one with herself, yet tranquil in the knowledge that she was with him. That he waited for her on the knoll, and when the time came, that they would cross over together.

By degrees, reluctant to leave the storm and these very private thoughts of Owen, her mind came back to the room, to the people gathered there. Morg and Kate standing at the fireplace, his arm about her shoulders. Wirt Jordan slouched in an easy chair, on the mend but gingerly carrying his arm in a sling. Beth and Earl seated on the couch, hands clasped, fingers interlaced, drawn closer than ever by the day's ordeal. Her family. Not by blood or merely by name. But by a greater kinship, something of the spirit and the heart. That indefinable bond people called love for want of a better word. And so right, so good for one another. Even the girl, Kate Jackson. A relative stranger, yet clearly a Kincaid. As if she had been born to take the name, to carry on the bloodline, to bear yet another generation of spirited young hellions with chestnut hair and that squared jaw. Now if they would only hurry, get on with it, give Owen his grandchildren. Her grandchildren. By that greater bond, the children of her children. Not of her womb but of her soul.

Watching them now, she was very proud. They bore their grief with dignity, which would have pleased Owen. The time for tears had come and gone, and they honored the man he was by getting on with the business of living. By simply being themselves. Picking up the pieces and carrying on, as he had done in his time of sorrow. Dealing with the here and the now, and all the days ahead. Laughing though it hurt, holding themselves straight and tall, proud of what they were. Kincaids.

Beth was speaking, her voice once again vibrant, imbued with that gay teasing lilt. "You're just an old stick-in-the-mud, Morgan Kincaid. At least you could have a little consideration for Kate. I mean, honestly, how often does this family have a chance for a double wedding? And just think what it would do to Guthrie!" She clapped her hands with delicious spite. "God, the whole town would turn pea-green with envy."

"You missed the point," Morg countered, shaking his head at her antics. "Kate and me have talked it over, and we figure the simpler the better. We'll just find ourselves a preacher somewhere, and let you have the society page all to yourself." His arm went around the girl's waist, and he gave her a playful squeeze. "Isn't that right, Puss?"

Kate smiled, averting her head slightly, and gave Beth a secret little wink. "What he means is, we talked it over and he told me how it's going to be. I'll work on him, honey, but I think it's a lost cause. Your brother has a head like a rock. Solid granite."

"Well, I think it's just dreadful. And shortsighted, too!" Beth cast him a sulky look. "After all, you'll be doing business in Guthrie now, and you have to consider your image. Everybody will think it's awfully gauche that you didn't invite them to your wedding."

"Whoa back, Nellie! You've got your wires crossed somewhere. As soon as we're married, it's *adios* and goodbye."

"That's not—possible." Beth's conviction fell away on the last word. "You have to take over the bank and everything. My God, Morg, you can't just walk away and leave it."

"I don't intend to, but first things come first. The truth is, Wirt and me have a little scheme brewing." His gaze slewed around at the driller; there was a glint in his eye, something devilish and amused. "Ain't that right, old pard?"

Jordan grunted and let out a gusty breath. "Yeah, I suppose so. Might as well tag along and watch you make a fool of yourself." He cocked a marled eye in Beth's direction. "Like Katie said, your brother's thick as a brick. He let some damnfool geologist talk him into the notion that there's oil down around Oklahoma City. Says all we got to do is drill five or six thousand feet and we'll hit the biggest pool this side of creation. You ever heard such nonsense in your life? *Six thousand feet!*" He snorted, grumping something to himself, and shifted his lame arm. "Likely we wind up drillin' all the way to China."

"Morgan Kincaid, you can't do it, do you hear me? You just can't." Beth seemed on the verge of springing at him. "You're the man of the family now, and it's time you faced up to the responsibility. There are people depending on you to take over and run things. The bank and the ranch and everything else. You can't just walk away. And don't look at me like I was loony. You just can't do it!"

An ironic smile tinged the corner of Morg's mouth. "Sis, you're not loony, you're just not listening. Let me ask you something. How would you like to own Oklahoma?"

"Oh, Morg, don't be absurd! I'm talking about everything Daddy and Grandpa worked to build and you're talking about another one of your pipe dreams."

"Yeah, but you know, it's funny about dreams. They have a way of coming true. What would you say if I told you that our little field down at Cromwell—ten measly acres—is worth more than all the Kincaid holdings rolled together?"

Beth stared at him incredulously. "That much?"

Morg nodded. "And in a few years it'll be worth twice that much. But you know something else? This time I don't intend to sell."

"You don't?"

"Not for any amount. That's why I'm so hot to start drilling around Oklahoma City. The future of this state is in oil, and I mean to see to it that the Kincaids have a very large hunk of that future."

Beth glanced at Earl Roebuck, who shrugged; then she looked back at her brother. "I'm not sure I understand. What do the rest of us have to do with your oil wells?"

"Listen, if I've learned anything at all, it's that the fellow who gets the jump on everybody else winds up with the biggest slice of the pie. Before, I always took my money and ran, but not this time. The way I see it we'll never have a better chance, so we're going to shoot the works."

Something in Morg's voice held them spellbound, and a sense of raw vitality seemed to pervade the room. His gaze was curiously distant, as though he stared at some remote point in time visible only to himself, and several moments passed before he spoke again. "I used to tell people in Guthrie about my plans for a chain of service stations. It was nothing but a big joke of course, and I had a lot of laughs at their expense. But it turns out the joke was on me."

The faraway look faded from his eyes, and his gaze settled on Beth. "Once we bring in a discovery well at Oklahoma City, we'll have oil running out of our ears. I intend to build a refinery and a string of service stations and organize our own distribution system. It's the only way to beat the majors at their own game, and I'm convinced we can do it." He paused, staring at her with an intensity as palpable as a command. "I'll need your help, though. We're talking about upward of fifty million dollars, and an investment that size will take everything the whole family—Wirt included—can scrape together. That's what I meant about shooting the works."

Never more astonished in her life, Beth appeared dumbstruck for a moment; then she turned to her fiancé. "Earl, don't just sit there. Help me! Tell this madman brother of mine that he's—God, I don't know, that he's suffering from delusions of grandeur."

"Well, I hesitate to interfere in family matters, but she does have a point, Morg. To fall back on the old cliché, it rather seems you're putting all your eggs in one basket. Which is not to say you're wrong, but only that you might jeopardize the Kincaid holdings. Of course the point becomes academic if you succeed."

"We'll pull it off, don't worry about that." Morg dismissed the thought with an airy gesture. "But I'm glad you spoke up, Earl. Reminds me of something I forgot to mention. You're the same as family now, so you ought to be looking after Beth's interests. And as long as you're at it, I figured you might as well take over running the bank and the ranch and everything else."

Earl Roebuck sat bolt upright. "How's that again?"

"Of course it'll only be for a little while," Morg went on smoothly. "Just till I get the ball rolling down in Oklahoma City. Then we'll set up headquarters in Guthrie, and I can run the whole show out of one office. Naturally we'll need to hire ourselves some good executives, but there's plenty of talent around if the price is right."

"But I'm a lawyer!" Roebuck protested. "I have a practice of my own, and there's even talk of making me a partner."

"Yeah, now that you mention it, I've been having some thoughts on that, too. Seems to me, Earl—and it's just a suggestion—you ought to start thinking about getting into politics. Like you said, we'll have all our eggs in one basket, and I've got an idea a little clout in the right places wouldn't hurt things at all. Might come in real handy, as a matter of fact. Besides, the Kincaids should get back into politics, just on general principles. Looks to me like Oklahoma could use some help, and who knows"—his mouth quirked in a sardonic smile—"we might even figure out a way to help ourselves at the same time."

Roebuck seemed a bit dazed, but before he could collect his wits Jordan cut him off with an irascible chuckle. "Ain't no use to argue. Once he gets a notion in his head, that's all she wrote. Just sit back and enjoy it. Likely he'll figger out a way to make you governor or some such."

"Wirt's right," Kate added with a lynx-eyed smile. "He'll keep after you till he wears you down by bits and pieces." She laughed that bawdy laugh. "If you don't believe it, just ask me."

"Say, look here, Earl, don't let them throw you," Morg assured him earnestly. "That stuff about governor is a long way down the line. We'll have to start out small at first. Maybe county attorney or the legislature. Take it slow and easy, and build a name as we go along."

"Well, if you ask me, I still say it's a pipe dream." Beth sniffed, and fixed her brother with a sultry glare. "Don't misunderstand, I have every confidence in Earl. But honestly, Morg, you're beginning to sound like one of those swami fortune tellers. All this talk of refineries and politics and millions of dollars. Good Lord, you haven't even drilled a hole at Oklahoma City, and already you've got Earl to the governor's chair. Now be truthful, if there was oil that deep, wouldn't someone have found it by now?"

"That's what separates the men from the boys, sis." Morg had that look in his eyes, as if he saw something forever obscured to others. "I'm willing to risk it all when my hunch is strong enough. And you can mark it down, this is only the start. Before we're through, we'll be selling gas on every streetcorner between here and Kingdom Come. That's a promise."

Grace Sixkiller Kincaid walked to the fireplace and

turned, facing them. Her expression was of such verve, so acute and piercing, that a sudden hush fell over the room. Listening to their conversation, a host of disembodied faces had floated across her mind, exaggerated and distorted, as if seen in a dusty mirror. Before her passed the Kincaids and their women. Death and killing and sorrow. Laughter and birth and joy. And however painful, however strong their grief, the love that had sustained them through good times and bad. Yet one face stood out from all the others, and as though the years had melted away, she heard again the words. The prophecy. The very marrow and substance of what it meant to be a Kincaid.

"The day your grandfather died, Zalia Blair described something to your father. She called it the Kincaid legacy, and I've lived to see it come true. Your grandfather built things and your father devoted himself to justice, and neither of them was ever afraid to let the future rule their lives. Now it's your turn, Morg, and yours, too, Beth."

Her eyes kindled, and she spoke the words with reverence, a benediction. "Listen to me, and never forget that this is your legacy. What it means to be a Kincaid, and why no Kincaid will ever truly die.

"A man with a vision lives forever."